GREAT EASTERN HOTEL

Praise for *Great Eastern Hotel*

'Riotously audacious and entertaining – a cinematic, jazzlike humdinger of a novel'

— KAMILA SHAMSIE

'Glorious, brimming with life, *Great Eastern Hotel* contains multitudes. Ruchir Joshi captures crumbling empires and wayward human lives in this headlong, sensory dive into a great city in upheaval. A towering novel – one for our times, and for all time'

— NILANJANA S. ROY

'A film-maker's novel, so vividly immersive it makes mid-forties Calcutta a living being, at once human and epic, a Joycean polyphony of overlapping lives and a granular history of the nation during wartime'

— JEET THAYIL

'The more I pore over the pages of this novel, the more fascinated I am by the narrative style and Ruchir Joshi's fantastic creative ability to evoke the environs and ambience of Calcutta during the Second World War, the roads and hotels swarming with British and American soldiers'

— SUMANTA BANERJEE

'If, like me, you have been waiting for a quarter of a century for what Ruchir would write after his dazzling *The Last Jet-Engine Laugh*, I have some Persian for you: *Der aayad, durast aayad*. Finally, an Indian epic for our times'

— MOHAMMED HANIF

GREAT EASTERN HOTEL

Ruchir Joshi

4th ESTATE • *London*

4th Estate
An imprint of HarperCollins*Publishers*
1 London Bridge Street
London SE1 9GF

www.4thestate.co.uk

HarperCollins*Publishers*
Macken House, 39/40 Mayor Street Upper
Dublin 1, D01 C9W8, Ireland

First published in Great Britain in 2025 by 4th Estate

First published in India in 2025 by 4th Estate

1

A catalogue record for this book is available from the British Library

ISBN 978-0-00-714393-1 (hardback)
ISBN 978-0-00-870147-5 (trade paperback)

Printed and bound in the UK using 100% Renewable Electricity at CPI Group (UK) Ltd

FSC
www.fsc.org
MIX
Paper | Supporting responsible forestry
FSC™ C007454

This book contains FSC™ certified paper and other controlled sources to ensure responsible forest management.

For more information visit: www.harpercollins.co.uk/green

For Zum – Ayan Joshi
missed beyond any words on any page,
beyond all notes of all music

CONTENTS

PROLOGUE

CALCUTTA, 1951

LET'S START IN REVERSE AND make the two of them walk backwards. All the way back from the closed doors of Hangar No. 13, back through the thicket of waiting Dakota airplanes, back out through the gates of the military area, back over the asphalt that is already tremulous under the ten o'clock sun of April, back half a mile to the makeshift bus stop where the old Leyland has come to an unconvincing halt. Let's make the bus driver take his foot off the hot brick of rubber that is his brake, make the bus push its long rear end blindly back to the big road that goes all the way to Jessore if you let it. Make the vehicle undo its right turn towards the aerodrome and go back to the north-eastern edge of Calcutta, to Ultadanga and its morning market with its smells of fish and overripe kumdo, make the rusty rear of the bus push impossibly back through the poke of rickshas and thhelas of Narkeldanga and Belgachia. The cream-coloured grille on its nose dripping steam and diesel vapour, let's pull the old monster back from the tangled lanes at the edge of the city to the centre of town, where the avenues are straight and wide and watched over by the big European buildings. Let's reverse it all the way from Dum Dum aerodrome and squeeze it back between the horse carriages in narrow Waterloo Street on the south side of the big hotel. Let's bring the two of them, mother and child, out of the bus and make them stand again at one end of the huge portico that shades the fancy stores that flank the entrance of the Great Eastern Hotel.

Her name is Nirupama Majumdar. At some point the tall guy tried to get her to answer to 'Nellie' for a couple of weeks, and then 'Pamela' for another five days, until she started twisting his name into Indian and calling him first 'Balaram' and then the more revolutionary 'Bijon' instead of his real name. He didn't like the sound of that 'Ball-o-ram' one little bit, and that 'Bee-John' even less, and so he stopped. Went back to trying to say her name right, as he had at the beginning. In the end, the last thing he called her was what she wanted: 'Niru', the 'r' tripled by his foreigner's tongue, made into a stream jumping over a hollow place, only slightly different from how he said 'Nehru', as in 'that guy Nihrrru needs to get himself a better hat'.

They'd said goodbye a few streets away from here, him touching her on the shoulder, very light, which was more than she allowed him in public, and walked away to the idling jeep. 'So long, Niru,' he'd said. No 'baby', no 'honey', no 'my love', and certainly not the one she liked best of all, 'sugar'. Just 'so long', and then the stress on 'Niru', cutting her name out to keep in the top pocket of his fatigues, like a photograph from a newspaper, leaving all the surrounding columns hanging in strips.

He'd had no name for the boy because, at the time he left, he didn't know the kid was going to come into existence.

The tall guy leaves towards the end of 1944, and we are now sweating in the April of 1951. The boy, born in August 1945, is therefore, already nearly six years old. Niru keeps thinking that he doesn't look at all like his father, that he could pass for an ordinary Bengali kid except he's tall for his age. His hair is straight, his nose sharp, very much hers, his eyes are his – meaning the tall guy's – ever so slightly elongated, which, ironically, makes them more Bengali than anything else. Where she really sees his father sometimes is in the boy's expressions. His wide grin, which topples sacks of tightly packed mischief; his anger, which simmers like Krakatoa before the eruption; his clever look which is not so clever.

Having brought the two of them back to the hotel where the boy was conceived, let's look at them: dwarfed by the huge white building, taking shelter at the very edge of the shade of the portico, away from direct sun, but close enough to make sure the bus doesn't leave without them. Nirupama is in a plain yellow cotton sari with a thin maroon border, a large purse hanging from her left shoulder, her right hand not holding the umbrella she has foolishly forgotten to bring. The boy is wearing half-pants of an indeterminate colour not far from khaki and a clean white shirt that is not at all frayed at the collar. On his feet are leather chappals, what the tall man called 'Indian slippers'. At the moment, one of the slippers is empty because the kid is balancing on one foot and using the nail of his big toe to scratch the back of his other knee. With one hand he holds his mother's shoulder, exactly where she feels the weight of the purse most, and his nose is up in the air sniffing at something like a puppy.

Today, there is a smell of fresh bread wafting over Waterloo Street, and Nirupama can see the boy smelling it, absorbing it for later examination. Leaking out of the hotel's bakery, the bread smell is strong enough to challenge the horse whiff of the carriages and the almost human mix of odours the bus exudes as it stands there and rumbles in the heat. The Markin officer, when he arrives, clipboard in hand, smells of some cologne. When Nirupama looks at him, her eye trips on the tiny spot he has missed out while shaving, a small upside-down terrace of brown stubble just under the jut of his left jaw. Unlike the Britishers, the Markin wastes no time.

'Okay, folks. Let's go,' he says, more warm than brisk. 'I'll take it for clear everybody here understands that...' he looks down at his clipboard to get his points right, 'that this is *not* an auction. This is a sale of US Army Air Force property that the army wishes to... dee-vest. On a first come first serve basis, with no returns allowed. Once you pay for something it's yours forever, and Uncle Sam will *not* take it back, okay? That there is to be *no* fighting or shoving or pushing. Or shouting.' He pauses to pull his goggles down from his forehead and then, to the stare of a black-eyed insect, he adds a grin. 'Once you get to Depot you will see that there will be *no* need for any of this behaviour. As always with the US Armed Forces, there is Plenty for All!'

The Markin pauses to catch his breath. 'Oh. One more thing. Anything you can't carry and fit into this bus to bring back, you will have to arrange to transport within two days. And, folks, please bear in your minds, that's two American working days, not *Calcutta* or *Bengal* working days! So, be careful what you put into your shopping baskets!'

The bakery yeast joins with the Leyland's simmer of diesel and warming leather as they climb in. Normally, when getting into a bus or a tram, Nirupama puts her arm around the boy to protect him from the jostling. Today, she leaves him alone. She can see he is happy with the smell of the whole mysterious adventure, and the dozen or so people around them aren't pushing anyway. They find seats in front of two old Anglo-Indian men who've decided they need to wear suits on an April day in Calcutta, ties and all, and just behind a young couple, also Anglo, the woman in an outrageously thin cotton frock, the man in a bush-shirt and trousers, two people who can barely keep their bodies away from each other on a bus seat. On an April day in Calcutta.

Watching them, something comes back to her about the tall man, his hand flicking away a fly, a smell of sweat, or maybe the lingering taste of whisky from his tongue, and she moves slightly away from the boy to try and reel in the memory better. The boy has his head perched on the window rim and doesn't notice. His puppy nose is still trailing different spoors as they come and go.

Immediately close to the hotel, sparks fly from a tram connector and he gets a nostrilful of burnt electricity; then there is a row of sweet shops, smells he knows well, jilepis, fresh shondesh, milk warming, the sugar world suddenly cut by a sharp tang of onion filluries frying in an open kodhai; a little later, they pass through a factory area and different profitable chemistries briefly fill his nose; then the fresh rot of the bajaar at Narkeldanga, this time the bananas and jackfruit winning out over the fish; the small stretch of open highway brings motor odours: petrol, melting grey-black road, burnt rubber.

On the short road from the bus stop to the aerodrome gates, the whole straggle spreads out behind the Markin officer, the suited-booted men, the young couple, the sharp-looking, racecourse-type characters also in suits but no ties, the fat old man in a dhoti-kurta and a monocle who is the only one who's thought to bring an umbrella. As the asphalt nibbles stickily at his chappals, the boy smells a small pond they pass that reminds him of their village visits, and then a different kind of petrol smell. As they are led through the parked Dakotas, this new petrol is very strong in his nose, and now mixed with the smells of metal and leather cockpit toasting under the pre-noon sun.

Walking under a slanted wing, he asks, 'Ma? What are these?', even though he knows.

'Havai jahaj. Iron birds that fly in the sky,' she replies, knowing that he knows.

'Can we climb on one and fly?' he asks, again with the answer already in his pocket.

'Yes, when you are older,' she replies.

Coming out from under the aircraft, the boy notices there are white marks on the ground: arrows fatter than the spread of his feet that curve or point straight, large English numbers, occasionally a huge capital letter from the English alphabet that he recognizes – an AB, an AC, and then a longer series painted in a slightly smaller size, USAAF SQD 4XB. When he looks up from the signs, he sees they've stopped before a line of huge, green houses made of tin. Houses with no faces and closed doors that are far too big for humans.

The hangar is one in a row of similar big structures, with a large '13' painted on the massive sliding doors. In front of the doors there is a small desk shaded by a large umbrella of the kind Niru has seen in foreign postcards of the seaside. There is a fat sergeant sitting behind the desk, and in his mouth is a fat little stick they can all smell from quite far away. The sergeant gets up when he sees the Markin officer, puts down the stick, and gives the officer a salute that looks as if he's trying to slice off the top of his head with the tips of his fingers. The officer pulls out a packet of cigarettes and lights one. The sergeant picks up his stick and puffs on it as well. The two of them confer, the sergeant sweating under a soft cap, the stub of his cigar held slightly away from the officer, the officer fiddling with his goggles.

Without being told, the group has formed a loose rank about ten feet away from the desk, and none of them can quite make out what the two Markin are saying to each other. The unclear drawl of the soldiers' voices is suddenly drowned out by a loud clattering roar. The sound drops down from above and swirls around them, making one or two people cover their ears with their hands. The two Markin hardly seem to notice it – the officer just looks over to the vast field on his right and glances at his watch.

The boy follows the officer's gaze, and he sees the sound has narrowed into a huge havai jahaj that is falling very fast out of the blank glare of the sky. The plane comes down and, miraculously, begins to roll very quickly on the ground without breaking into pieces. A few seconds later, it goes past, about three hundred yards away, its body flashing against the dark green line of trees at the other end of the aerodrome. As their spinning slows, the boy realizes the bird has four fans, two on each wing, as compared to only two on the ones he has just walked past. Also, the nearby planes are painted a dull grey-green, while this big rakkhosh is all loud and proud silver and white, with big blue letters above the windows and smaller ones on the tail. The boy puts the strange alphabet together in his head: big B, full stop, big O, full stop, big A, full stop, big C, no full stop, because they must have forgotten.

Niru watches the machine disappear behind the line of hangars and only half hears the boy's excitement, 'Four fans, Ma, four fans,' and, 'What is B.O.A.C? What is a boac, Ma?' Someone else says something loudly and knowledgably about this being the flight from Tokyo via Hong Kong and Singapore that will go all the way to London, via Karachi, Cairo and Rome... the names of these strange places meld with the alien machine she has just seen so closely for the first time, as if the plane itself was carrying each unreachable city within its belly. She doesn't imagine she will ever see the inside of an aeroplane – not probable, given the work she has chosen for herself – but she often imagines the boy taking off, older, taller, looking more and more like his father, waving goodbye to her from the top of the stairs before disappearing into the dark hole.

And she has often imagined the tall man leaving, walking on ground such as this, what did he call it? 'Tarmac'. Walking on this tarmac, the huge bag on his shoulders tugging him back. Imagined him climbing up the ladder and into one of these fat, green, metal frogs with his 'buddies', and then she has imagined him getting out at the other end. When her imagination reaches 'home' or 'stateside', she becomes him, the heavy bag suddenly weighing a lot less on her shoulders as she heads towards the exit, a bite of the cold Chicago air he'd described so often coming in through the open door to welcome her. But, but, always, as soon as she reaches the opening, all she can see outside is a wall of white, a wall in which she can make out no snowstorm, no ladder down, and no tarmac.

'I asked, how many do you want, lady?' The sergeant is talking to her, snapping slightly with humid impatience.

'I... beg your...'

'You are allowed five claim tokens to start with,' he repeats slowly. 'I'm asking, how many do you want? How many pieces do you think you will buy? Three? Four? Ten? Do you want to corner the whole stash?' He grins now at his own joke, and the stub of his cigar dances like a stamped cockroach poking out of his teeth.

'I am just looking for one particular thing.'

'Ain't we all, lady, ain't we all?' The fat man snaps out three from a clutch of little cards. 'Here, keep three, just in case you change your mind. It's a big old place in there, long walk back to me. Your purchaser number is 17.' He hands her the tokens and moves on to the next person and the next until everyone has their tokens. Then he leads them to where the hangar doors meet, before turning around and folding his arms as if to say, 'You know what? I don't think I want to let you people through.'

'Okay, folks! Everybody understand the system? You see an item you want, you take the price tag off the item and replace it with one of your tokens, which has your purchaser number. You do this till you finish your tokens. Then you come out to me and the quartermaster here. Then you give me the tags and pay me the cash. Then we walk you back to your chosen items and help you move them aside into your very own little pile. Then you get five more tokens to play with!' He pauses to signal to his men to open the hangar doors. 'Remember! My men are here to help you, but they are also here to stop any hanky-panky behaviour! Any fighting, and you are OUT! Any stealing, and you are IN! In jail!'

The doors slide open with a metallic gurgle as the fat Markin finishes speaking. The '1' of the '13' slides left, while the '3' goes right, like two lovers parting in a puppet opera. A few of the people, the sharp racecourse types, the young couple, are fast off their marks, and they disappear into the darkness before the soldiers have finished rolling open the doors. Nirupama firmly takes the boy's hand in hers and walks across the track lines for the door rollers.

There are bulbs hanging from a grid, but they are no match for the harsh sun outside and it takes a few moments for her eyes to open.

The boy's eyes adjust a touch quicker and he gives off a small yelp of fear. Once Nirupama can focus, she sees why. Standing there, grouped together like that, they are almost human: weird creatures lined up like soldiers, with huge lower bodies and crazily thin necks jutting up into small, curlicued, backward-pointing heads. She takes a beat to recognize them, or it, for she has never seen more than one at a given time, and then she is all right.

'Ma...?'

She holds his hand tighter and takes him over to the stencilled sign hanging off a petrol drum. She squats down to the boy's height and runs her finger over the writing.

'Double?' She points to the first word.

'Dobbol,' repeats the boy.

'Bass,' she says, getting the second word right in the nick of time.

'Baize,' repeats the boy.

'Say it: double bass.'

The boy repeats obediently and then he's on to the next line: 'Q... t... y?'

It takes Nirupama a while to work it out, but she gets it, 'Q-t-y means quantity. Means how many there are. How many double bass.'

'3-5-0, meaning thirty-five!' says the boy triumphantly.

'No... 3-5-0... means many more than that. It means three hundred and fifty.'

'Oh,' says the boy, 'shall we count them, Ma? I can't count that far.'

It takes them a long time to walk past the double bass section. As they go deeper into the cavernous space, Nirupama figures out how the Markin have organized things. The phalanx of double basses forms the left side of a corridor, while the right border of the path is made up of pianos. *Grand Pianos: Qty 100*. Beyond them, catching the light from the windows on the side of the hangar, *Uprights: Qty 175*. Then come *Assorted Xylophones* and *Mini Organs*. Once the bass section ends, they are in a vast terrain of drum sets on both sides of the aisle, *Drums: Qty 1200, incl. Conga Drums and General Percussion Instruments*.

She imagines her fellow bus passengers trying out the instruments, the pluck of the bass and the high chink of the cymbals ganging up to arch her back as she waits for the tall guy to come in with his horn, but no, the cymbals and hi-hats are packed away, stacked next to the large bass drums. She imagines the young couple, the woman perched on a a piano, her thin dress riding slightly high, sneaking above the knee, the crew-cut bush-shirt man's fingers, since they cannot be under the hem of her skirt, probing instead the piano keys, checking the tuning. The woman starts scatting in a low voice, and the man looks up and smiles encouragingly as she goes into some fast riff from a standard, perhaps 'How High the Moon' or, by that time, maybe even 'Miss Brown to You'. Around them, pools of reflections on the tops of the pianos, the pugnacious dolphin noses of the Dakotas outside the long windows turned upside down in the lakes of dark polish, the spoke of their props fanning across the memory of evenings put to sleep on a bed of blues and booze. Suddenly, the thin-skirt Anglo breaks loose from all the scattered tinkering going on around her, takes her voice high and makes it reverberate from the hangar roof... no, stop. Niru forces herself back to the present.

The monocled babu with the umbrella is checking things against a list on his clipboard; the card sharps from the racecourse are diligently removing tags and replacing them with their purchaser numbers, bent, it seems, upon cornering the stash of pianos, if nothing else; the two old men in suits are fingering large saxophones, not putting their mouths to the mouthpieces which have no reeds, examining the state of the levers and keypads before one of them pulls out his wallet to figure out how many pieces they can actually afford.

At the edges of all this are Markin soldiers, balancing their little folding chairs on the back legs, chewing the rubber paan they call chewing gum, busy with their shiny magazines, not looking and yet looking. In and out of this are the flies, lording it over a universe of their own, buzzing back and forth across the hot darkness, across time, across checkposts and heart-borders, not listening to us, not listening to anybody, landing with equal arrogance on Niru's arm and the nose of the private from Alabama flicking through a new copy of *Life* magazine.

Passing the border between percussion and brass, Niru loses both music and child. She realizes the boy is no longer holding her hand. She glances around for him, expecting him to be close by, but he's gone. Nowhere to be seen. She spins a slow circle, searching. Nothing huge, just a small bob of disbelief in her heart – what if she loses him forever in this maze? What if he's sucked up in the slow whirlwind of this departing army and taken back in the mess of tanks and grilling ranges to some distant desert base, with canyons on the horizon and nobody who can speak Bangla within the whole hemisphere? What if he ends up not even in America, but in Germany or Japan?

She spots him, down on all fours between two sets of drums, pushing the foot-lever of the mallet for a bass drum. 'Na–' she stops herself and calls out the shorter version of the kid's name in her most threatening voice: 'Saki! Come back here!' She follows his progress as he comes crawling through the drum sets. A conch-shell-coloured handle passes her, protruding out of a belt, and, at first, she wonders what instrument it is. Once her attention shifts, Niru sees that she's standing not far away from a big officer. The big officer has a junior officer in attendance and he's muttering something to the junior as he looks down into a file. After six years of disuse, her Markin English is not good enough to make out what they are saying, but her eyes alight, greedy as the flies, on the pistol poking out of the big officer's holster. It is what she knows is called an 'automatic', and she has seen one or two before, but none with this pearly-white handle.

She has heard what one of these Markin handpieces can do, much more dangerous than a three-nought-three rifle even, and she finds herself thinking about how she could snatch it. Use the boy as a distraction? Faint on the officer? Set fire to the acres of inflammable wood? She thinks about arriving back in the village, about taking the gun out of her purse and placing it before the others in her cadre; the arguments that would follow, as the men claimed it was too heavy for any of the women to use, as one of the women picked it up and weighed it in her hands, as someone figured out the way to unload and load the big calibre bullets. As he comes out of the jungle of drums, the boy has the sense to get up and curve his path around the big officer, who doesn't even notice him. Niru grabs the kid's wrist and moves on, reminding herself that the days of the gun, effective or not, have gone for now.

As they walk ahead, the kid yanks on her left arm as if he's pulling a chain on a train, sending pain through her elbow.

'Ma? Ma, can we go home now?'

'No. Not yet. We are still looking, remember?'

'Yes, but I want to go now! Home!'

Niru keeps walking without replying, every now and then letting the boy pendulum his whole heavy body on her other arm. The musk of wood varnish changes slowly. Maybe she imagines it, but with the first breath of brass polish the boy eases up on her. Soon the air is heavy with Brasso, a headache of shining gold. Niru finds herself slightly dizzy and more than a bit nauseated. She is the one who now wants to turn back and get away, but the boy is tugging her forward. She gathers herself and turns to her son.

'Eijey, Saki!' she snaps in a mock schoolteacher's command. 'We are looking for a sign that says...?'

'Traaampett!' cries the boy.

'Or *Horn*. Or even *Cornet*,' adds Niru.

'Look, Ma! Here's a T! T for traampet!'

'Yes, but this says... t-u-b-a-s. Tuba is different from trumpet.' Niru is now speaking through a handkerchief held against her nose. 'Look, a baby haathi which is all just nose!'

'Qty... thirty-seven!' says Saki, correctly this time.

They walk through the 37 tubas, 22 trombones, 8 baritone saxophones, 150 tenor, and an equal number of sopranos. The swathe of altos and clarinets is too far away for them to read the quantity. The boy, now drugged by the smell, tries to slip away to the obscured sign. Niru pulls him back.

'No, Nagasaki, look! We've found them. Look! Horns and trumpets!'

'6-0-0...' the boy reads out, 'Ma? Is that six hundreds?'

It is, my beautiful baby, it is. Without warning, her mind slips back to the moment she first laid eyes on her newborn. Six hundred trumpets ring out together, sharp, pumping in perfect unison, rising up and blowing open the sky.

The birth, in the small hospital in Bolpur, was difficult; the baby was too big for her pelvis the doctors said, and she collapsed right after they did the episiotomy and pulled him out. By the time she came to properly, two days had already passed. It was on the evening of that day that she saw the Ingreji newspaper someone had abandoned on the next bed – *The Statesman* from Calcutta, already over a day old, dated 10 August 1945.

Later, when they travelled through villages and small towns performing shadow plays, the sound they used for the bombs had nothing at all to do with trumpets. For the build-up to the first bomb, they had used a single drum and the menacing twang of a khamak; for the actual dropping and explosion, all the drums and cymbals came in with a huge, sustained crash. Then, for the second bomb, the one on Nagasaki, they had taken her idea and the only sound you heard was that of a single, wailing infant.

Niru's own child was older by then, at two, no longer on the breast and no longer always with her, but the name had been given and it had stayed. There had been intense arguments among the comrades while trying to decide: some found the name of a Japanese city too foreign, no matter what the significance, others pointed out that they were remembering the proletariat of Nagasaki who had been as trampled upon by their feudal-imperialist warlords as Bengal's peasantry was, first by the British all these years, and now by the new bourgeois satrapy of the Indian Congress; others yet pointed out that the child was born not only on the day the second atom bomb was dropped but also just two days after Rabindranath Tagore's fourth death anniversary, and perhaps that was important too. Nirupama was adamant about the first name she had thought of, but she also saw the point about Rabindranath. After much discussion, the boy's birth certificate finally read 'Rabi Nagasaki Jones-Majumdar', the patronymic first, followed by the mother's family name, in the Spanish way, in a salute to the Republican comrades of the Spanish Civil War.

Saki and Saki's mother slowly find their way into the trumpet section. The things are stacked in cases, with a sample instrument placed on top of each stack. There are different sizes and makes, and different prices. Saki sees one he likes and points to it. Niru picks it up carefully and shows it to the kid. As Saki watches his face distort in the curve of the bell, Niru fingers the price tag. Thirty-five rupees. It's steep, but she knows it's cheap at the price. Later, when speaking about this moment in an interview, she will point out she had brought a whole fifty rupees for the purpose.

The boy tries to grab the trumpet, to blow on it. Niru lets him have control of it, but without taking her hand off.

Let's start moving away from them as the boy brings his lips to the mouthpiece. We have brought the child to the trumpet and to the beginning of all the frustrations he will go through before he can get a coherent sound out of it. Let's leave him to it, because this is not his story anyway, not really.

The light changes outside, a stray cloud covers the sun for half a minute and then moves, leaving behind a sharper light which bounces off the tarmac and comes through the long windows into the dark hangar. It first catches the trumpets erect as sentinels, and then the forest of saxophones tilted on their stands, before dimming again as it does in April in this part of the world.

As we move back through this warehouse of past and potential sound, we know the Americans are finally leaving after nine years. Though they don't know it, we now know they aren't going very far, that they aren't going to be away for very long, but, again, this is not about the time they return. This is not even about what they leave behind, though, as we move away from the gates of the military area, we do catch the mother and child again, walking in front of two small hills made entirely of glass. Closer inspection reveals that one is a pile of empty beer bottles, the other one of empty Coca-Cola bottles, both about three floors high and together covering half the area of a football field. The sunlight refracts off the bottles into thousands of little prickles which Niru feels as she trudges behind the boy, now carrying the trumpet case which is too big even for her large handbag. The boy is now furiously pushing air into the mouthpiece and getting nothing more than his own saliva spitting back into his face.

Let me take the two of them out of this deep-focus Hollywood set and put them in flat silhouette behind the lit curtain of a shadow play, with night moths and mosquitoes dancing in front. As they walk past cut-outs of palm trees, the boy falls behind, concentrating on his new toy. Niru walks in front, humming a Tagore song: *If no one heeds your call, if no one comes along, then walk alone, walk alone, walk alone, walk alone, my friend, walk alone...*

ONE

Ocean of Peace

7 AUGUST 1941

I

THE POET'S HOUSE

Imogen's first thought is a bomb. A street full of houses wiped out. She turns her head this way and that, looking for accompanying rubble, but the buildings seem intact. Next thought, shoals of fish washed ashore, thousands of little fish smashed out of their water by some infuriated sea. But that doesn't fit either. She needs to turn another doorknob, open another story.

There are binoculars. Being sensible, and having come expecting a distant spectacle, she has brought binoculars. They swing from her neck, knocking gently against her chest, reminding her that they are there to be used. But there is no distance here to pin down, what's there is all around her, and she looks down at the brown case and feels stupid – caught carrying a lacrosse stick on a golf course.

Slippers, she thinks, but not slippers really, what's the word? Chop-something. Choppol. Her teacher is from the north of the country, and he has made many jokes about how the local people cannot pronounce a flat 'a' without turning it into an 'aww'. He would call them 'chuppull', spelt c-h-a-p-p-a-l, not c-h-o-p-p-o-l, but the meaning was the same – those things they walk around in. What they wear on their feet.

She has even tried a on a pair once, when she went to Bentinck Street to one of the Chinese shoe shops. 'Madam, you have large size... I may don't have your size, but if you want, I make you.' She remembers the odd double feeling of constriction and freedom, her big toes trapped by the tight hoops of leather, the rest of her toes naked to the air, her insteps too snug, too intimate with the strap, and her heels sticking out a mile, scraping the cool floor as she walked around the shop, and her mother saying, 'Darling, surely...' her voice stained with panic, trying to stop her wild daughter from jumping out of an aeroplane.

A thick carpet of slippers, chappals, sandals, covering the road everywhere, left ones and right ones all mixed up, as if they had rained down from the sky in a hailstorm of leather. And she feels as though she too has dropped from somewhere, parachuted down, no memory of falling, just landing, and now walking in this alien landscape, on this strange dirty street sprouting thousands of absent feet.

Among the chappals and odd scatterings of flowers, there are a few shoes as well, and she recognizes them – familiar faces in a crowd of foreigners. There's a lone one, black and shiny, a man's shoe, leaning right side up against a wall with its inner sole pulled out like the tongue of a recently slaughtered animal. Even in the vortex of her bewilderment, she feels for it as one does for one's own kin.

She can now see there are layers and layers of them, pulling away from her, turning the corner of the street and catching sunlight, as if a giant with millions of small feet has rushed off to a party. It's not what she has been expecting. She has come because she is taken by an idea of literature, but this is not how she had imagined it before setting off. The death of a poet should have been something gentler, smaller, more within the rhyme and meter of propriety.

As she wades through the small dunes of leather, she notices two urchins picking through the piles, trying to find matching pairs. They play in this vast jigsaw puzzle, their hair caked with dust, their grey-brown rags fluttering around them, both the boy and the girl slapping about in chappals that are far too big for them. Their brown bodies are thin, alive with excitement, and they shout triumphantly to each other even though they are no more than five feet apart. The little girl has found a jute sack and she carefully puts two pairs of chappals into it. The boy hitches up his shorts and moves over to peer into the sack, examining the booty. Then they squat down the way only natives can – she has never seen a European managing to fold himself up like this – and get back to their sifting.

After a while, the boy comes across a small pile of yellow, ball-like flowers, and he picks one up and throws it at the girl. The girl squeals out a laugh. Then he throws another, which she manages to catch and fling back at him. Suddenly, their collection of chappals is forgotten and they are up, tripping and stumbling, showering each other with flowers. The boy throws one hard at the girl, and it misses and flies towards Imogen who tries to catch it. Her hands close too late and the flower explodes on her binocular case, shrapnelling her with petals. The kids petrify into statues, staring at the memshaheb.

The girl is the first to recover, and she whips around, looking for her sack. The boy's legs jerk, about to start sprinting, but his slippers are trapped in the debris. This gives Imogen enough time to smile at them and pull out her binoculars. She puts them to her eyes and cranes her neck forward, pretending to look through them. The children pause, now not sure whether they need to run. Imogen puts away the binoculars and smiles again, desperately trying to remember the phrase for 'it's all right'. But her toddling Hindi has lurched out of reach, so she calls it out in English. Then she pats a hand in the air, trying to indicate both 'sit down' and 'don't worry', acutely aware of how foolish she must look.

The boy understands, and he cups his hands around his eyes, mimicking her, and he tilts his head left and right, a grin shining on his face again. The girl puts down the sack and copies the boy. Imogen mimics them back, tilting her head this way and that, and then they all laugh and it's fine.

Imogen waves goodbye and moves away, leaving them to their business. As she looks around, her eyes now able to stray from the ground, she sees that she is right before the entrance of the famous mansion. The big iron gates are smashed open, one barely hanging on a hinge, the other ripped completely off, lying flat on the ground. She almost reaches for her binoculars, but stops herself. She is already outside of things as it is, there is no need to create further distance. Even though she can't bring herself to go in, she forces herself to look without intervening optics. Beyond the entrance, the trees droop, mourning in the muggy air. The tree-lined drive leads her gaze to the doors and windows of the house which are open, as if the place has just been evacuated before an approaching army. Obviously, there is nothing left to steal. Or, perhaps, even the thieves have gone to the cremation.

BIRTH PLACE

'Ei mmaaaaa! My necklace! My necklace is gone!' The woman's scream cuts through the hubbub of the waiting crowd.

Niru clutches Titir's hand tighter and gets up on her toes, craning her neck, trying to spot the woman.

'Can you see? Where?' Titir pushes up on Niru's hand as if trying to lift her higher. 'What's the point of being so tall if you can't even see anything.'

But all Niru can see is a small eddy of activity in the large, stilled river of people, a tight mess of heads circling around the invisible screaming, men raising their voices and trying to clear a space – impossible in the huge press of bodies. Fronds of sentences breaking off from the shouting. 'Where did you drop it, didi?' 'Arre, talk some sense, how would the lady know where she dropped it!' 'No! Look, she has a small nick on the back of her neck! It didn't fall off, it was taken!' 'Everybody careful! There's a pocket-maar about!' The woman's voice rises again, like a siren during an air-raid drill, 'O mmaaaaaaa! Chor! Chor! Chor!', the wail now picking up rage against the thief-thief-thief.

Niru comes down and feels the grit of the road under her heels again. 'Can't see. Are all your things safe?' She gives Titir's hand a squeeze before relaxing her grip. Titir involuntarily runs her free hand over neck and blouse, even though she's not wearing a necklace. Niru flicks a finger across her face, checking her earrings and nose stud before checking her shoulder bag and adjusting the drape of her sari.

'All my things?' Titir looks at Niru, her eyes wide.

'I know. I just said it like that.'

'I'm carrying four rupees. And someone would have to search really hard to find them.'

'Me, five rupees four annas. Same thing, you'd really have to look.' Titir's hand shakes in Niru's as they both begin to laugh. Like her friend, Niru is carrying her money in a handkerchief stuffed into the top of her blouse. As she laughs, she can feel the coins press against her sternum.

After a moment, heads turn towards them, and they stop laughing. Niru finds it strange to be laughing while the last attack of tears still cruds her eyelashes. As if reading Niru's mind, Titir takes the corner of her sari pallu and makes a point of cloth, wets it in her mouth and wipes around her eyes. Seeing this, Niru herself uses the knuckle of her thumb, using the sweat on the back of her hand to elicit more water out of her eyes, like wetting the nib of a fountain pen to coax out more ink.

The crowds waiting on both sides of Harrison Road begin to swell and spill out on to the tram tracks as more and more people arrive and add themselves at the back. Niru looks up at the old buildings that loom above them, six- or seven-storey blocks of dirty grey and brown frozen in the process of falling on to each other. Covered balconies stretch all the way across the fronts, their lines distorted as if drawn by the shaky hand of an ancient draughtsman, their awnings of faded green woodwork dipping and warping along with the brick, the paint gone from the rusty metal joints. On a normal day, you can see the rows of doors that give on to these balconies, the doors of tiny living spaces, offices, unofficial godowns, and even temples and brothels that push into each other, away from the eyes of the street. Today, the doors are obscured, every balcony is loaded with people, petty businessmen, their women with saris drawn across their faces, clerks, pilgrims staying in the dharamshalas, women with nothing covering their heads, the coolies who toil up and down from the storehouses. Niru knows that, despite appearances, there is a lot of money hiding in these buildings, where extremely rich but parsimonious merchants live cheek by jowl with far poorer people.

'*This* is where modern capitalism was born!' proclaimed Bakul-babu, her professor of history, his voice bouncing off the teak benches. 'You don't have to go to the City of London or the Bourse in Paris! Wall Street comes even much later! This! This Barabajar, this Brabourne Road and Harrison Road, these docks on the Hooghly! This combination of the Shaheb, Seth and Babu, the exploitative colonizer, the exploitative local entrepreneur-collaborator and the exploited yet exploiting ledger-servant! And the working-class they exploit. This unchanging labouring coolie, the unchanging peasant in the fields outside, they are the ones who raised the City of London and sustained the Bourse!' And later, outside class, in the study circle, his voice much softer now, his gaze locking mostly with the boys 'We *see* them as unchanging, or we like to see them as such. But are the masses unchanging? And you lads have to ask yourself – can they remain so?'

THE BEAUTIFUL BOY

Gopal marks the pretty one about three-quarters of an hour before he strikes. He picks him out of the crowd while they are still on Cornwallis Street, a full forty minutes before he gets him.

Then he goes and manages three others, minor, all the while keeping the beautiful boy in the corner of his eye, keeping him as his main prize. He could be wrong, but no. Just something in the way the head is held, something loose and careless about the kurta, and the way the hands swim away from his body, pushing away people, trying to minimize touch but making even more contact because he's trying to avoid other bodies.

Since the news of the death spread across the city, Gopal has been warned that the procession would be big. But this crowd is huge, bigger than anything Gopal has ever seen in his twenty years, washing right up against the walls of buildings on either side of the road. The incredible crush of people is good, perfect beyond dreams, but still, it's not quite right.

What bothers Gopal is the singing. He realizes that day – his last one on the job, though he doesn't know it yet – how much he depends on sound. The clang of the tram stopping, the little argument about standing room, about whose foot is on whose chappal, or maybe the sudden attack of a baby wailing, or some idiot hero striking a match, lighting a cigarette in the middle of a crowd or, sometimes, a big car going paa-paa-paa, trying to shove past the bus, the noise horning into passengers' heads, making them angry and careless. Like the best of them, Gopal works to the kick of sudden noise, uses it as one of his tools, but this singing is not like that, and it feels like it's set up against him.

It is an awful, slow chorusing but people seem more aware of each other because of it, all these wet-eyed fools caught in the web of some soft and stupid grief. The singing is loudest around the lorry carrying the body. Even though the old man is dead, it seems as if these voices are coming out of him. Him, stretched out, wrapped in flowers, like a fish in banana leaves which has suddenly sprouted white hair. Every now and then, someone lobs more flowers on to the bier and some of them roll off in a small landslide of yellow and white, leaving a trailing paste of squashed buds in the procession's long wake.

Gopal looks up at the sky. Near the Jorasanko house there had been a bit of mild sunlight, but here it is overcast and Gopal greedily prays for rain. A bit of water and mud underfoot would help, people slipping a bit as they walk, so many of them barefoot, further distracted by sliding and needing to concentrate on their balance. But there is to be no rain that day and he pushes the thought aside. He doesn't really need it, he tells himself, there's already enough to work with.

Sure enough, in a few minutes Gopal has used the push and pull of the crowd to work himself close to the pretty boy. A little behind him and a little to his left, because Gopal's experience tells him that most people of that class carry it in their left pocket and not the right, the same side as they wear their watch.

With the clunky inevitability of a carriage manoeuvring to hook up with an engine in the Howrah sidings, Gopal now comes up right behind his quarry. Once in position, he stays there, the right side of his body pressed into the left side of his beauteousness, pressed right up against him, building familiarity, normalcy, conveying an apologetic 'What to do, dada? What a crowd, no?' through his partial embrace. 'Never hurry,' his ustad had drilled into him a long time ago, 'the ones who hurry get caught.' And Gopal is now a master at biding his time.

Joined like Siamese twins, Gopal and the pretty boy float with the procession for what seems like a long time. As they move, Gopal notices things: the roofs and balconies of the houses on Grey Street are overflowing with people, all craning their necks to catch sight of the action; he wonders if someone will fall, adding to the death toll of the day like a small drop after a big torrent. On one roof, he sees a man with a cinema machine, a black cloth covering his head and the top of the machine, moving the apparatus left to right on the stand, following the truck; in a second-floor window, he sees a few sadhus, their orange showing out of the shadows, their kartals clanging out a completely different rhythm to the slow song of the crowd, while one of them moves a smoking aaroti in a circle, his lips fluttering out a silent shlok. Overhead, he sees a small aeroplane, banking and circling, flying quite low, obviously some military shahebs wanting the best view; he doesn't need to look at the pretty boy, he needs to feel him properly, and this he does – the bony shoulder, the slim body under the dhoti-kurta, the slight bump of his small buttocks, a pleasurable mound of muscle, pity there is no way to both do the job and get in front of him to feel his – and then, yes, sure enough, on the side of the hip, in the left kurta pocket, the bulge of what can only be a loaded wallet.

While maintaining contact, Gopal is careful not to stay on the wallet too long. He moves his hip away as soon as he confirms its presence; his hands have stayed away from the pocket area throughout – they will only come into play at the last moment and it's crucial not to give the victim any advance notice of their presence.

FIRE OF SEPARATION

Kedar suddenly starts to feel as if he's being carried in the wrong direction by a strong current. He knows why he is here, he is sure of that, he knows how he got here, he even knows his own name, but he no longer knows why he is carrying on.

There are banana fronds tied to the back of the driver's cabin, and he can see them waving gently over the great man's body as the truck inches its way forward. There are people sitting on the truck, and they constantly wave incense sticks in circles, wiping away tears, swiping away flies, and choking as they try to find tributary voices to join the chorus:

There's sorrow, there's death,
the fire of separation burns,
still, there's peace, there's joy,
still the eternal awakes.

As he pushes against the wall of bodies, Kedar can see some people smiling through their tears, one woman with the end of her sari clutched hard against her mouth trying to stifle her sobbing, two small children sitting on their parents' shoulders, flowers in their hands, looking around at the endless spread of heads below them, no tears and no smiles, just pure wonderment on their small, clean faces.

One song ends and another begins: *Aanondo lokey, mongola lokey, beee-raaa-jo... In the blissful land, in the blessed land, may you rule* – it's too much, and the old man was never about too much, there was always a holding back, even in his storms and tempests. Even at his most powerful, he never rained on you. His genius was that he broke open your own monsoon inside you, and this sweaty, crowded death was not right for him. Unavoidable, perhaps. But not right.

Another thought attaches itself to that one, and Kedar realizes it's time for him to get out. But just as he thinks this, a surge in the crowd makes other people push up even harder against him. It's as if other bodies have pasted themselves to his and he can't unglue himself. The harder he tries to move sideways and out of the flow, the more he is caught in its forward-moving crush. The more he tries to breathe in clean air, the more he can smell the body odours, the smoke from the dhoop, the engine fumes from the slow-gearing truck. He tries to calm himself down, and he succeeds at the exact moment the commotion breaks out.

Kedar is not very tall and, at first, he can't see much but he can hear it. Suddenly there is shouting, then a woman screaming over the raised voices, and then a huge current of violent jostling that pulses through the crowd. Kedar feels himself actually being lifted up from the ground and, for a brief moment, he gets a completely clear view of the truck. Two men are wrestling with a thin, dark man who is trying to do something to the dead body. The men grab the thin man's hands and pull them away from the poet's face. Then they try to prise open the man's fingers, trying to get at something clutched in his fist. A policeman leaps on to the truck and, as the man is brought back to the ground, Kedar can see the police baton go up and swing down hard. He can hear the man's cry of pain and then people shouting 'Hair!',

'Hair!', 'He was trying to snatch some of Gurudev's hair!', 'He pulled at the beard!'

By the time a full understanding of the incident sinks in, Kedar finds himself far from the centre of the procession. It's as if someone much bigger has heard him and begun to take him out of the throng, slowly spun him around and sent him bobbing in another direction. For a brief while, he's caught again in a tight knot of people, a stick of sugarcane being squeezed through a juice mill, and then he is out of it, stumbling along a side lane, trying to control his numb legs.

As he moves away, he can hear the next hymn. Someone with a strong voice leads the song Tagore wrote specifically to be sung at this, his own funeral:

The ocean of peace lies in front,
launch the boat, O helmsman...

Kedar shudders, sloughing off the feel of other bodies. As he walks further, his limbs accrue back to him and he begins to enjoy the naked feel of the rough asphalt under his feet.

In a few minutes, he is in another world. A quiet maze of north Calcutta galis, strangely empty. The only sound is that of loitering crows, then a music of kitchen metal, pots and pans being washed in an unseen courtyard, and then, from some other house, the news crawling out of a radio. The newsreader's voice is faint at first, then louder as he passes under the window, then faint again: '... and in the North African theatre, the siege of Tobruk continues as the small number of gallant Anzac troops still defy the might of Rommel's Afrika Korps. In Cairo, the commander of the British forces, General Auchinleck said yesterday that...'

Kedar cuts out what Auchinleck said by starting to hum a song. *Jodi tor daak shuney keu naa aashey tobey ekla cholo re... If no one heeds your call, if no one comes along, then walk alone...*

Walk alone, walk alone, walk alone, my friend, walk alone, walk alone... He's still humming the same tune, his heart now a lot lighter, when he reaches Esplanade and feels the warm metal of the tramline under his feet. He sees his tram leaving the terminus, so he gathers up his dhoti and runs after it, jumping on just as it gathers speed. The conductor shouts at him, irritated at this young fool for trying to get killed on his shift. Kedar smiles, tilts his head in an apology, and reaches into the pocket of his kurta to pull out his wallet.

Walk alone, walk alone, walk alone, my friend, walk alone...

Listening to the tapes, I now realize I have three different versions of the song, each version somehow carrying a different meaning about the business of walking alone, of finding your own path through the thickets of life. Tagore wrote many songs, of course, but this one's among the very few I can bear to listen to. As for the rest, some of them may be great poetry, as people keep reminding me, but the music and singing, please, not my cup of tea. Or, as old Elko once put it far more bluntly, 'That awful noise. Like a cat dying on the rusted barbed wire of Bengali sentimentality.'

Sitting here, though, especially with my apartment windows open in summer, I like to release the odd Rabindra Sangeet into the night air of this deeply racist city. Let some of my more bastardly neighbours get annoyed, the same way they wrinkle their noses when I cook some Indian recipe I've brought back. Fuck them, fuck the heavy, three-note food they are so proud of, fuck their love songs, their own sentimental whinings and the ones they've borrowed wholesale – 'Baby, please don't leave!' – 'I did it my way, I regret nothing' – fuck jazz, fuck the blues and fuck bloody rock and roll.

No, I don't quite mean that. I do like some of their sentimental whinings. And the blues and rock and roll are a part of me, as is jazz. But I hate it when people around here act as if this is the only real music in the world. All this and of course the Classical canon, with a capital C, as if nobody else has any classical music.

I suppose some of Elko's perversity might have rubbed off on me, or I might have stolen some to add to my own barbed wire, but there it is, I'm a bit perverse too. There it is, and here I am, relabelling the cassettes and stacking them, trying to pin down some order and chronology to counter the mess contained in the tapes, as well as what someone could truthfully call the chaos of my own situation.

I like the fact that one can rewind tapes so easily nowadays. I like the very words, 'rewind' and 'fast forward', and the twin arrow symbols these cassette recorders have, indicating express speed in either direction. Much better than the fiddly, pain-in-the-ass spool recorders. I now stick to the cassette player for my usual purposes, because it's good enough to be able to go back roughly to the start of a song, or to stop, more or less, between two movements in a symphony. But yes, there is a problem when one's listening to a recording of someone speaking. Or worse, trying to transcribe two people talking, often talking over each other, sometimes drunk, while interrupting each other.

Listening to them talk – and the time they're talking about – I'm constantly reminded of the fact that normal people had no recorders at that time, no rewind and fast forward at all, unless you count lifting the gramophone needle and putting it back and forth on those spinning 78s.

If I try and put the needle down on the stories one after the other – and at the end of the day it *is* about the stories – I start worrying about novelists' problems, such as introducing too many characters and not being able to render them properly. About not doing each one justice, or trying do justice to them all in the same frame, which you can in a painting or a photograph more easily sometimes than you can in writing. But then, even in a painting you can have the problem of overcrowding, or of placement – a typical amateur's mistake – of making one person too big, and therefore not leaving enough space for one or two of the other figures to be fully rendered.

I do realize there is a fundamental difference between listening to music and reading a novel, but I've always wondered why people get freaked out – sorry, that's too strong – why readers become anxious when a bunch of new characters are introduced in a book. Why doesn't this happen, for instance, when you start listening to a big-band track by Ellington or Basie? There you'll have a whole jungle of instruments coming at you from the first moment, or a lone clarinet joined by a horn, and then perhaps two saxophones, or... why don't people get jittery then?

Why don't they try to immediately place each instrument on some kind of an aural map? You don't start rewinding (though now you can) when a piano riff suddenly breaks in, and try and figure out its provenance. No, people are usually quite happy to let the music wash over them, for the melody to take them where it will. In a book, you'll maniacally start flipping back the pages, like an accountant who's missed an entry, but with your music you just... go with the flow, to coin a phrase.

No, I know. A musical note or phrase is what it is, both complete in itself – reward and satisfaction both attached – yet bearing the promise of more. People are different, they're never complete, or hardly ever, unless it's as a cartoon figure, and you're always unsure of the reward or satisfaction until and unless it's delivered to you – you, who, of course, are a person yourself and not a musical phrase. I know it's different with a story, always a problem, introducing too many characters too quickly.

But maybe you'll bear with me. Even before it balloons up and explodes – even before the things happen to it that happened to it – the Calcutta we're looking at in 1941 is already a city of nearly three million people. And I'm talking about only four or five of these people, so maybe they'll be allowed to take their place in the frame.

In a slight shift from my profession, perhaps you could think of me as an architect-engineer building you a house, or a museum or, yes – beg your pardon – a hotel. Building it room by room, allowing you to enter and occupy each space as it becomes habitable, making sure the wires and pipes are connected, that the window frames fit properly, that the stairs lead where they're supposed to, that landings aren't missing when you step on them. By the end of my assignment, you are in possession of the entire building: rooms and corridors of stories that together make up the whole tale. Let's say you continue living in it, this story-hotel, while I've taken my money and gone. I'd like to guarantee the plumbing won't leak, that the wiring won't short circuit, but this is Calcutta we're talking about, the Calcutta of today, of the 1970s and not the 1940s, and we have to be realistic.

I could also tell you, quite truthfully, that these tapes aren't in a great state of organization. I'm pulling out what I can, culling what I can from my own mess and from the mess those two have left behind. I put away the stack of cassettes I've been listening to. I've put new labels on them, written on them with different coloured markers and they look quite neat. For a moment, I allow myself to feel like I've achieved something, that the project is going well, but all I've done is added to my confusion. Tidying up does not always guarantee clarity.

But then, it has to be said, nor are tidy stories the most interesting or the ones that bring you closest to the truth – all right, no, let's leave all that for now and put the needle back on that day – the 7th of August 1941 – when the body of a great man is just about to be put on the cremation pyre, the novelist inextricable from all the other things he also was, the poet, the essayist, the composer, the painter, the mystic.

And the writer of songs:

Hold up this body of mine,
make it a lamp in your godly home.
May the light's flame burn night and day in song.

2

THE GIRL IN THE MIRROR

This evening, it's not so much the house as her mother's voice that is foreign. The sharp climb of the 'Darling!' and then the next pokey peak at 'crowd' in the 'Darling! You didn't get mixed up with the *crowd*, darling, did you?'

Did you? The didjyu hanging there like an old anxiety, a family heirloom, out of its tissue paper again.

She has noticed it since she was a child – the trick going somewhere new plays on you. This tricky business of going somewhere new and then coming back home. When you leave home, home is home, it's as you know it. Then you go into another world, a strange corner of the city perhaps, north of Euston Station perhaps, or maybe somewhere country. And then, just when you return, then, just as you turn into the street that leads home, or perhaps the crossing that's two corners away from home... suddenly everything feels different because of where you've just been. This strange place where you've just been comes padding back right behind you and infects your house, your whatyouknow, and turns it into a strange place too.

The layout of the house allows Imogen to go to her own rooms without actually passing her mother. She reaches there, flinging a voice up the stairs, 'It's fine, Mummy! I'm fine, it's all right, really!', her own voice now a sketch of her mother's and the sentence a toll she pays as she quickly crosses the hall to her door.

Her shoulders sink as soon as she shuts the door. She switches on the fan and then just stands there, recovering, looking around this strange room she knows so well. Her clothes feel heavier than they have a right to, and it's not just the sweat. You'd think by now they'd be used to people who looked like her, but it seems not. Two hundred years of memsahibs making not a jot of difference, and it often feels as if she's the very first.

Today, as she has walked and wandered, her body has picked up the looks of natives, lookings, starings, like molluscs adhering to a ship, like crows on a cow's back. A hardening of eyes here, a lecherous half smile there, a bunch of women on a passing tram pointing at her and laughing rudely, and then the two old beggar women with their muddy corneas, staring not so much at Imogen as at some half-sensed ghost standing next to her. Today, she has caught all these eyes and carried them with her, been forced to accumulate each gaze like unwanted shopping, each encounter making her more wooden, each contact pushing into her body, the small of her back and the cross of her neck becoming stiffer and stiffer.

Every day is not this bad, though. On some days, in fact, the exchange can be mysterious. Exciting. And, though she dare not say it to people around her, nourishing, yes, nourishing in a strange, guilt-simmered sort of way, secretly helping her keep head above water.

As she tosses her hat on the bed and takes off her binoculars, Imogen suddenly remembers the boy and the girl sifting their shoe treasure. Yes, like those two for instance. Her heart lifting, she steps out of her shoes and curls her toes, testing her calf muscles by moving her ankles up and down. She checks her watch: still two hours before Andrew arrives to take her to the party. She makes sure the thin curtains are drawn and hooks an arm behind her, reaching for the buttons of her dress.

The sticky cotton print peeling off her body exposes her skin to the fan circling above and gives her new energy. She attacks the rest of her garments ruthlessly. Got you, sock! Off! And here's your partner... thumbs in, pull it down, throw. Moe-zaa, singular for sock, moe-zey, plural, jaao mozey, bhaago! Get thee, the pair of you, to a laundry basket! Her brassiere is captured next. It puts up a struggle, but it's wrestled with, unhooked, vanquished, and then sent flying to lie wet and dead on top of the socks. No word in Hindi for that yet, nor for the camiknickers that she unbuttons and wriggles out of, dancing now, trying to snake her waist and hips like the little shoe girl. Nothing saucy about this, no trace of Paris nightclub, just the sheer pleasure of moving freely, of catching the air as it spins down on her hot body. Pick up knickers, start to bring them up to nose for the smell, a habit from back home where there wasn't and will be no dobby woman to wash memsahib's foundationals. Hmm, this not England, very hot weather, no point smelling, best to dispatch – off! Jaao!

She pauses, having run out of hosiery, and catches a glimpse of herself in the long mirror at the other end of the room. The late afternoon light dramatizes her, but she is no Diana, no Aphrodite, no Rodin voluptress.

Freckles. She can see them being cheeky from across the room. And a precise patchwork of dark and light skin, the lines chopping off her upper arms exactly like an old Greek statue, and again in a sharp semicircle around her neck, where the territory of cloth ended and the sun had its full play. The freckles romp across these colour frontiers, ever there, loyal companions that have stayed with her wherever she has travelled – Butlin's, Folies Bergère, Jungfrau, Southampton, Cape Town, Bombay, and now here, in this subtropical hellhole... no... not fair. Honestly, quite a nice hellhole, except for Mummy and Daddy and this monsoon clamminess. Truth to tell, the freckles have rarely been happier.

Her glance traps itself in the mirror again, and this time she can't stop herself. Legs spread wide, hair a frightful brown-blonde shipwreck, naked as the day she was born except, now, much taller than the mother she came out of, perhaps, surely, perhaps she's imagining it, but her downstairs hair now growing quite wild, like an untended, triangular allotment; her eyes a mad, out-of-place blue that she often wishes she could send back to the suppliers in a box marked '*Unsatisfactory for this region. Please replace with a darkish brown*', and now this lunatic smile hopscotching all over her face. She stops trying to stop herself and sends a signal to her knees to squat down like a native. They obey her the best they can, and she suddenly finds herself suspended like a discus thrower, arms stretched out for balance, thighs frozen in protest, her buttocks jutting out, but no closer to the floor than two and a half feet. As she looks at the mirror again, the bothersome laughter welling up in her empty stomach does nothing to alleviate the cramp.

THE TERRACE

Suddenly, Niru realizes her shoulders are trussed up with anxiety. 'Tension', she thinks of the English word, or perhaps it should be 'contradiction', Bakul-babu's favourite usage when lecturing about Marxism. Could shoulders tighten with contradiction?

The news had reached Scottish Church College just after midday and classes had been terminated. When Niru told her professor she was heading to pay her respects, Bakul-babu had laughed. 'Yes, yes, why not? Go and say farewell to your great bourgeois champion. It will help you realize his time is gone, long gone, even before him.' Niru had felt anger rising when she heard this, two kinds of anger, one following the other. First, there was the jerk of dismay that a teacher she respected so much could be so disrespectful and dismissive of a truly great man, and then the anger of a frustrated child who suspects that a grown-up has just said something true, unavoidable and bitter.

Could the great poet ever have imagined that there would be so many waiting for a sight of his passing body? Perhaps. Could he have imagined that there would be street thieves preying on the people waiting? Perhaps, but Niru wasn't sure. Are the masses unchanging? Can they remain so?

Niru feels Titir tugging at her hand.

'Ei, look! Do you see that building?'

'Which one? Dey and Co.?'

'Next to it, Shri Ambe Engineering Equipment.'

'Yes?'

'I think I know someone who lives there. I went in there once, as a child. Shall we see if we can get to the roof?'

'I'm also tired of looking at people's sweaty backs. How long ago did you go there?'

'Ten years, I think. But we can pretend we are looking for those people, even if they're not there.'

They push through, prying open successive human walls, and make their way to the passageway that leads into the old building. Niru begins to miss her chappals the moment the ground changes from the rough pavement to the smoothness of the stairs, which are made from the kind of wood that, rain or not, stays damp through the monsoon and a month after. Under her feet, Niru feels the slimy dirt the city has dragged into the building. She misses the red mud of Birbhum, which is where they should have been to mourn Robi Thakur. Lucky Romola, to be there today and not here, in this meaningless, sweaty push and shove.

The two girls make their way up the dark stairway, all the way to the door leading to the terrace. Coming into the open, they see a row of backs leaning over the parapet. A couple of people turn around and look, but no one pays them any attention, nobody asks them who they are or why they are here – today is not a day for such normal questions. The terrace is matted with liil, the moss in fact covering almost all the exposed surfaces, and Niru can feel both the green smoothness and the black terrace grit underneath. Lucky Romola, to be in Birbhum today, in Santiniketan, where, surely, the poet's spirit went once it left his body. Except that Niru has now understood that there is no spirit, there is just the body, and nothing ever leaves it except bodily materials and breath. It's counter to everything Rabindranath has said, the poet she worships, but now she has a higher loyalty – to empirically provable truths, to the historic inevitability at which those proofs point.

Again, Titir reads her mind and murmurs into her ear. 'Tor toh kono shrodhha nei, tui aajke keno eshchhish?' – You say you have no faith, so why did you come here today?

Niru pretends she hasn't heard the question. The two of them find a narrow space at a corner of the parapet, and Niru leans over to look at Harrison Road through the cat's cradle of electric and tram wires stretching along its length. From above, they can see the crowd shifting and surging aimlessly, the narrow strip of grey road widening and narrowing as the rumours move the bands of people on either side. Around the girls, the people on the roof are knowledgeable. Someone living near Jorasanko, the Tagores' mansion, has used the telephone to call Tulsi-da in the next building, Tulsi-da who also has a telephone. In turn, Tulsi-da has called out the news over the terraces: the divine poet's body had been on a truck initially, but now people had lifted it on to their shoulders. The bier should pass by soon.

Niru looks at the terraces around her. The flat tops of teetering old houses 'as rotted and decrepit as the system that built them, the system that is also about to topple'. The question is, as Bakul-babu had asked them, on whom will this edifice collapse? Bakul-babu had actually used the example of an old temple and answered his own question – obviously on the poor man below! Followed by the next question – and what damage will it cause, what suffering will this disintegration bring to the common man? Answer: whatever the hardship, whatever the human cost on the path to freedom, the process is unavoidable, we have to work towards both the overthrow as well as minimizing the damage to the masses.

The things is, these houses and terraces look as though they have been toppling for a hundred years. Around her, Niru sees a different world, one normally completely cut off from the street below, today connected by the collective downward gaze of people gathered at its edges. Behind the people craning forward, all sorts of things spread themselves out. In this area, the terraces belong either to the poorest in a building – unlucky dependants of the owners, poor relatives or servants, where the worst sordidness of the street seems to have bubbled up through the buildings – or to the very richest people living there, who use the spaces as small, private, open-air palaces.

On a few of the terraces, Niru can see evidence of whole families, small communities living in elevated slums, small rooms that have taken the brunt of the weather, tiny, temporary spaces covered with sheets of tin, lines of faded, frayed washing, clay chulhas still warm from having produced the midday meal, bits of rice scattered on the floor around them, little pools of rainwater gathered where the terrace floors have sunk, children's toys, third-hand, half-broken, an old skeleton of a thakur, the multiple arms barely discernible in the armature of straw and disintegrating clay, a cluster of flowerpots forming a tiny vegetable garden, the plants covered against birds by some sort of a fishing net.

Right next to these are terraces that are spick and span, the well-maintained parapets, railings and floor slabs obviously kept tidy by servants who live elsewhere. Across three or four roofs, she can't be sure, Niru can see a large aviary with brightly plumed birds in a series of shining cages, expensive exotic birds infected by the local excitement, squawking and fluttering from perch to perch. On one terrace across the road, clearly visible because it's a couple of floors lower, she can see a square bamboo shamiana covered with thick, sloping tarpaulin, the thick chicks on the sides rolled up today because it isn't raining too hard. Under the shelter are two plump armchairs in good repair, with a low table in between, an elaborate hookah at one side, and an interrupted chess game on the table, a slab of moneyed comfort inserted between far sadder segments of life.

Why had she come? Well, for one, as her father said, 'this man actually formed the language we bhadra Bengalis now speak'. For another—

Titir taps her arm, jumping up and down with something she's suddenly remembered. 'Ei, Niru! Show me the postcard again, na? I can't help it! Let me read it again?'

Niru shakes her head sharply, 'Not here, not now!' She reaches down into the cloth bag on her shoulder and fingers open the notebook where she's hidden the letter that arrived this morning. She feels for it to make sure it's still there, but she doesn't pull it out – there is no place for private joy amidst this mass sadness, and she doesn't want the letter to be in any way sullied by the chaos.

On the street below, the crowd has thickened. Neither Niru nor Titir notice that the terrace has now filled up with people who've had the same idea as them. There's a noise growing below, down Harrison Road to their left. As she waits for the cortège to pass, Niru feels she is looking down upon a great, churning river.

PROMOTION

The boats tell him the river is good today. Just from the way they nudge each other gently, playing with their mooring ropes like village grandmothers rocking cribs, he can tell it's a good day to go out on the water. Not that he needs to. All he has to do is jump from one tethered boat to another for about seven boats, step on to the rusty barge, cross over the top to the side facing the river, and go down the steps to where the small launch sits at its usual early evening berth.

As Gopal steps off the mud bank on to the first boat, he nods to the two boatmen squatting just outside the curve of its covering. 'Tsaa khaaba na ki?' one of them asks him, fanning the fire in the guts of a small chulha he has lit on the wooden deck. Gopal raises a hand – no time for tea just now – and skips on to the next boat. The launch too has a chulha and there will be tea, tea with much more milk than the boatmen can afford, but it remains to be seen whether he is offered any today. Given the weight of the day's take bulging in his pockets, his best day yet as a pocket-maar, he suspects he may even get something to eat, but life has already taught Gopal never to take anything for granted, and he reminds himself of this as he bounces across the slowly shifting boats.

A sluggish breeze comes off the river, but even that feels cool after the grinding crowd. For several minutes after twisting his way out of the thick snake of people, Gopal felt like a mulch of spices ground by a crazy masalchi. It took him a while to transform himself from a wet mess back into a human being, and then it took all his self-control not to break into a triumphant run. On a nearly empty Strand Road, he pulled himself back, forcing himself into a slow walk until his wits returned to him. Moving south and away from the huge mass of mourners heading to the cremation ghat, he was waylaid by a thought. Stopping to watch some Ingrej soldiers playing football on a club ground at the Maidan, he worked out the idea. The plan led him to a quiet corner of the Victoria Memorial gardens where he spent some time organizing himself. Now he is calm and ready to face his ustad.

Being quietly fond of his own life and the idea of continuing it, Gopal has rehearsed a few times what will happen once he reaches the launch:

'Hm! Gogai! Come here!'

'Ustad.'

'Everything all right? No trouble with the police? People tell me many cockroaches were in plainclothes today.'

'No, Ustad, no problems. Uniform-mamas too busy looking after VIP types. And I kept looking out for plainclothes. Some fool tried to snatch hair from the dead body and the mamas nearly killed him, but otherwise...'

'Hm. Show me.'

From the secret pockets inside his trousers, Gopal will pull out the remaining purses and wallets, the three watches, one heavy golden keychain, everything except the wallet he took off the pretty boy, and lay it all on the floor of the cabin. Ustad will nod approvingly, sifting through the stuff, sorting out paper money, small change, the other bits and pieces people always nest away with their money. Then the old man will contemplate the takings for a while, his eyes journeying elsewhere, as if lost in deep, religious thought. The bigger the booty, the longer, usually, the contemplation. After which he will sort out the share, playing slow chess with the money and the objects.

It was usually during this game that Ustad caught people out. Once, Gopal had seen him suddenly wipe aside another boy's takings with a sweep of his arm and, with the return of the same arm, smash the boy's face, breaking his jaw. Ustad had then turned the whimpering thing over, ripped his pants down and yanked out a sack the poor fucker had tied between his legs, just between his balls and his backhole. What followed with the boy's testicles still turned Gopal cold with fear. On another occasion, Ustad had finished his chess game, looked up at the girl who had brought in the take, and unleashed his teeth in a smile. 'You know Ustad doesn't like to hit girls, don't you, ma? But if you're ripe enough to steal from Ustad, then perhaps you're ripe enough to go to work in Banshibari, yes?' As understanding crept up around her neck, the girl stared back like a madwoman, Banshibari being the worst of the brothels Ustad controlled, the place near the docks where the lowest dirt from the visiting ships took their pleasure.

Others had taken the calculated risk of hiding their loot elsewhere, and they too had paid a price for their mistake. Neither Gopal nor any of the other pocket-maars had yet figured out how Ustad always managed to smell things out from people's heads, but he did.

Gopal is aware of all this, but still, today, for the first time, he is about to try and do what he always advises the others never to even dream about. Maybe the craziness of the crowd has got to him, maybe it's the heady contact with the aroma of real money, maybe just the feel of the pretty boy's body against his own, but today he is going to try and put one over Ustad.

Like a good actor, he throws away the husk of his rehearsals as he climbs on to the barge and works his way through rotting ropes and pylons to the other side. As he's about to jump across the small gap between the barge and the launch, he sees Aurangzeb standing on the deck and he falters. His nerve nearly goes. The launch suddenly feels like a toy boat that a grown-up has decided to take over. One stamp of a foot and the thing will break in two and sink, one wrong elbow and the cabin will go flying into the water, decapitated, one... Aurangzeb brings his huge head up in a stare and Gopal feels his heart rubber-ball up and down. What is the big sisterfucker doing here?

Another body peels out of Aurangzeb as Gaurango steps out from behind the larger man. Both of them here together. Gopal feels his toes lock up and his knees starting to turn him around, every part of his being getting ready to send his body leaping back across the barge and away from these two as fast as he can go. For the second time that day, Gopal stops himself from running. He slows everything down – his legs, his breathing, his eyes. He nods to the two who are now looking at him, jumps across, and moves to go down into the cabin. He even finds the courage to bring his voice in, half grunt, half squeak, nodding at the dark cave of the cabin, 'Ustad bhetorey?' and, somehow, everything holds while Gaurango takes his time before jerking his head in a yes.

'Eijey, Gogai!' The familiar ratchet sound snakes up to the deck. 'Where are you thinking of running to? Don't tell me you're scared of these two!' The voice leaks barely contained mirth, but that does nothing to lessen Gopal's thudding heartbeat. 'Come here, come here, Ustad will protect you from these bad men!' As Gopal ducks in through the low door, the old man is chortling. 'Come here and show me what you've got.'

'Ustad,' says Gopal, nodding his head in salute before starting to reach into his many pockets. As he puts the stuff down in a pile, Ustad grins at him, reaches out a hand and puts it lovingly under Gopal's chin. 'Oh-ho. Looks like you're the king today, Gogaibabu. Was it hard work?'

Before Gopal can reply, Ustad calls out for some tea. Suddenly, everything is back in tune with what Gopal has imagined, the questions about the police-mamas and the plainclothes, the pauses, the looks, almost everything. A difference – when he mentions the man trying to pull hair from the dead body – 'Ah! Now see! Now that poor bokachoda had the right idea. One or two of those hairs might have been worth a hundred times what you've got here!' More guffaws, a cursory flicking through the take piled up before him, and then a subtle shift. A going quiet that Gopal knows all too well.

Gopal realizes the tea is next to his knee on the floor and he reaches for it. Ustad waits until the hot cup is right against Gopal's mouth before asking.

'All this is very good, Gogai. But what did you bury in the Memorial gardens?'

Gopal takes a swig of the tea before replying. He hasn't rehearsed this one, but he is surprised at how little shock he feels at the question. He puts the tea down, controlling the surprise he shows, calibrating its flow like you do water coming out of a tap. Not enough awe at the old man's ownership of the world and he would be suspicious. Too much fear and he would know. But today is Gopal's day for playing everything right, and he handles it perfectly. A slow lowering of the cup, with eyes widening more in admiration than in fear, and then a grin, looking straight back at the man who is the closest thing he has to a father.

'There were too many purses and things, Ustad, I was afraid the bulk was showing even under my shirt, so I got rid of a lot of useless... I can go and get it all back... there's nothing valuable... But, how did you...'

The old man rummages through his beard, trying to stuff his triumphant smile back into his head. 'Eijey, Aurangzeb!' he calls out.

'Shunchhish? Did you hear? Our boy is now old enough to decide what is valuable and what is a horse's egg!'

There is no response from Aurangzeb. Gopal fights the urge to turn around and ward off the sure knife about to plunge into his back. A long horn echoes across the riverside and a wave punches the launch gently as a big boat passes, spreading the water. Gopal absorbs the sideways movement under him. Calm yourself now. No knife. Your hearing is good, and you would have heard anyone coming down into the cabin.

'Don't worry, kono bepaar nahi.' Ustad is now scratching the skin just outside his left eye, a sign that he is thinking how to say something important. 'I already checked what you buried, and you did right, there was nothing valuable there.' Gopal looks down to see a fly nosing around above his teacup and suddenly he is relaxed enough to snap it up. He lets it buzz inside his fist for a moment and then crushes it dead. The old man notices this but leaves it unremarked. He clears his throat.

'Gogai, you know that I don't do all that garbage, about how you've been like a son to me, how I feel like a father to you, and all that time waste.'

This is not anywhere within the furthest spread of Gopal's anticipation. He feels his gut tighten, but he keeps his face blank. 'No, Ustad.'

'I am lucky you are not my son, and you are very lucky I am not your father. Yes?'

Gopal has no idea how to respond to this, so he pays out the smallest nod he can.

'But you could say I brought you up. Made you into a human.'

This is true, and Gopal can now nod a vigorous yes, but his mouth is completely dry.

'Now, listen.' Ustad loses his hesitation. 'If I was a selfish man, I could let you do this pocket-maari business for as long as you like, you're one of the best I have ever taught and – look at today! – you bring in a lot.'

'Yes, Ustad.'

'But if I am to keep bringing you up properly, I have to give you a chance to be something more than just a pocket-maar. Do you understand what I mean?'

Gopal keeps quiet. He knows he is not supposed to understand.

'Pro-mo-shon,' pronounces Ustad, rolling the word in his mouth as if parting with a secret prayer. 'Promoshon. Do you know what that is?'

Gopal shakes his head in a no, a stubborn corner of him still wondering if this is a death sentence.

'Like, when a mama does well, he is moved up from a constable to a havaldar. And then from havaldar to sergeant. Like that. It's called promoshon in English.'

Gopal nods without trying to convey too much understanding.

'So, if the cockroaches can have their promoshon, why not us?' Ustad takes out a cigarette, taps it against the tin and lights it, not expecting any interruption. He takes a long drag and looks hard at Gopal.

'It's different kind of work, but it would mean more money, a lot more. Sometimes easy work, sometimes very hard. And working with Aurangzeb and Gaurango. You have to be ready for that. But I've been watching you and I think... yes, you would be good at it.'

Gopal delivers the nod of gratitude that is expected, still saying nothing, his body now tense in a different kind of way, his earlier fears forgotten, replaced by an excitement that he is unable to name.

Whenever he thinks of this moment in the future, Gopal will find the words gone. The actual substance of what was said will always teeter on the verge of evaporating. Strongest in him will be the memory of smell, the river, the waft of many different kinds of water, the sandpaper whiff of Ustad's cigarette mixing with the smoke from the overworked factories on the other shore, in Howrah, and then the ineradicable tickle of something frying on the chulha outside, onion filluries or fish in batter, he will never be sure, and the smell of fresh kashundi chutney playing hide-and-seek with the monsoon air.

'Anything else, Gogai?'

When Ustad's voice finally pulls up at the expected station, Gopal knows not to jump off. His answer is natural, neutral, one that comes from total belief in what he is saying. At that moment, Gopal has forgotten about the pretty boy's wallet still hidden in his pants. As he replies, he has no reason to doubt that he will be believed. The launch moves under him as his stomach moves under his heart.

'No, Ustad,' says Gopal, suddenly feeling very hungry, 'nothing else.'

A BANANA FROM PANCHPUKUR

If he looks down, he can fool himself that his feet have released a lake of blood. No, not blood, the floor is both too beautiful and too normal for that. A rich, dark red, stretching away, gleaming with forty years of constant footfalls, it's too calm, and the black border too neat. It's too much a part of his sanctuary, his home, to have anything to do with something as crude and as fresh as blood.

The garden doesn't aid thoughts of bleeding cuts and scars either. The grass is now an intense green, a green loaded by rain and, in this coy evening light, made even more gaudy by the white pillars which frame it at regular intervals. Paul Gauguin is the only one he can think of, among them all, who could approach it. And Gauguin did not, strictly speaking, even belong to that particular 'them', but he is the one who would have come closest. Perhaps Van Gogh, too. And after the two of them, Matisse, Picasso, et cetera, but none of the main people. Not Monet, not Pissarro, not even his favourite, Cézanne. From what he knows of it, none of them except Gauguin ever saw this light, none of those stay-at-homes ever experienced what humidity and cloud could do to their normal supply of sun. They had snow, of course, which Kedar has never seen at close hand, and he knows that a European winter puts up a very different kind of obstacle course for the painter, but still, it's very different from a subtropical garden in August. Not that he'd mind a bit of snow under his feet at this moment, though the cool floor feels good as well.

Sitting on the veranda, Kedar stretches his legs as he waits for Raskolnikov to bring him his sandwiches. Though he hasn't shed any blood at all, it does feel as though his energy has leaked out of his battered soles. A loss that needs to be replenished by an immediate infusion of meat, which is why his first demand after coming home has been ham sandwiches.

With clear instructions. Because Raskolnikov, while far from being a dullard, always needs clear instructions. In fact, it is precisely because Rasko is not stupid, precisely in order to stop him from exercising his billiard ball of a brain, that clear instructions always need to be given.

In this case: the good bread from Nahoum & Sons and not foul slices from the bread-walla's morning delivery, the ham from Empire Provisions behind New Market and not the stuff Kaku procures from the Anglo-Indian fellow on Elliot Road and, Rasko, pay attention, proper English mustard, which means not that kashundi stuff you make in the kitchen, mustard, *lightly* spread. And tea. As in proper Darjeeling made from the Benkabari Spring tips. If you bring me any of that Doars sawdust, I will kill you, bujhechho? Yes, Dada-babu, understood.

Kedar is not sure why death makes people hungry, but he has seen it time and time again, the violent gorging people immerse themselves in after the cremations and shraddhos of loved ones. Some do this shamefacedly, but others are not so discreet, quite openly gluttonous in fact, trying to affirm life, scrambling to put up a kind of food wall against the steamroller of mortality. Kedar is sure, though, that his current famishment is not of that ilk. It's just that he has walked barefoot all the way across the city, from Harrison Road and Portuguese Church to Sunny Park in Ballygunge, which is not something he has ever done before. Not that he isn't fit, not that, but playing a few sets of tennis, twice-thrice a week, is quite different from struggling through the massive crowd and then walking – what? maybe four miles? – with his feet getting cut by tiny stones, glass, and all the other unnameable whatnots with which the roads of the city are mined. The whole thing today has demanded the use of different muscles from the ones his body normally deploys, and needed different muscles, he realizes, from his brain as well.

'Different muscles of the brain.' He mulls the phrase over, absently, not really thinking, more just sleepwalking through the events since news of the great man's passing came, just after one this afternoon.

The sense of loss the news brought, of time suddenly carving a different shape out of the fixed sculpture of their lives, is now diminished: something rare – his mother crying openly, bent over the ebony holder shaking in her hand, her cigarette managing to catch some falling tears, the wasp-hiss of the dying tip; his father folding and unfolding his arms behind his back, as if in callisthenics, before finally reaching up into a bookcase for a copy of *Chaar Odhhaay* inscribed for him by Gurudeb himself; then Borun-kaku, his father's younger brother, striding off into the garden as if he had been personally mauled by fate; and last but never least, Raskolnikov, standing behind Ma with the tea tray.

A tall, thin ghost doing aaroti with a tilted tea cosy hatching the bottom of a tea kettle. Garlanded by the steam being emitted, Rasko, eyes afire, suddenly intoning the words of the song he had been taught by Borun-kaku – *Jei raatey mor duaar guli, bhaanglo jhorey...* – getting out the first line in a reverential drone before Ma whirled on him and snatched away the tray, snapping at him through her sniffles to go back into the kitchen at once. Yes... nothing worse than having your servant reciting a love song at the wrong moment.

Kedar remembers Borun-kaku, a few years ago, trying to teach Raskolnikov English, trying to use the song as a platform upon which to build. 'That night, Rasko – dhyan daao! – that night when the storm, storm maaney jhor – pay attention! – that night when the storm broke open my doors!' At the time, the boy had scratched his head, and shaken it in complete fuddlement – what was Kaku-babu saying? But, this morning, Kedar could have sworn he heard him muttering the English words under his breath as he beat a defiant retreat to the kitchen, 'That naaiit. Whuen tha eshtorm. Birokopen. Maii dhores.'

Raskolnikov's name began from Kedar's father calling him 'rascal' when he first arrived to work in the house, a boy carrying some undecipherable age between eleven and fourteen, something like that, but a little older than Kedar, and much, much, taller. A few years later, Borun-kaku, avid reader, changed rascal to Raskolnikov – 'Na, na, o bhishon complex character, o'r onek parts achhey, jemon in Dostoevsky.' The boy's alleged complex character with many parts and facets did not impress Kedar's mother. 'That's all we need,' she said tartly, 'one fine night for him to come up the stairs and murder me.'

'But, Boudi! You are looking at the obvious! Banal! Surface!' Borun-kaku exploded as much as he could with his older brother's wife. 'Do you think Raskolnikov to be a mere murderer of older women?'

The 'older women' was a bad mistake. When recounting the incident to Kedar's father, Borun-kaku amended it to 'older ladies', and he got away with it, at least for that moment. But 'Boudi' being a higher rank in this particular house than 'Kaku', despite Borun-kaku's protests, a typical family compromise was distilled over the next few weeks. The name had stuck, and so it stayed – officially, Raskolnikov – but to appease Kedar's mother it was shortened to 'Rasko', which is what everyone now calls him.

Not once in all of this was Radharomon, from Village Panchpukur, Jila Pingla, District Midnapur, asked what he wanted to be called. And neither did he ever say. But, as he grew up, it became clear that Rasko was the last person in the household who would murder Kedar's mother. Despite her daily insults and snappings, Rasko was completely devoted to Boudi. 'Like a dachshund with legs,' as Borun-kaku put it. Around sixteen, when Kedar was in his detective novel phase, he would work out elaborate plots centred around the murdered corpse of his mother, with the imbecile police inspector always making Rasko the chief suspect, and Holmes or Hercule Poirot or Miss Marple or Inspector Maigret inevitably demonstrating that the murderer was someone else: Kedar's grandmother, Kedar's father, Borun-kaku always a favourite, the meat man, the fish man, the bread man, the maali and, once or twice when the story got away from him, even Kedar himself.

The thought of crime drags Kedar back to his evaporated wallet and the tiny surgeon's slit at the end of his kurta pocket which confirms that he hasn't dropped it. There is still a presence where it used to live, like a limb that's been recently severed. Many times, on the way back from Barabajar, where the conductor – relishing the rare moment of power over an obvious bodolok rich boy – triumphantly ordered him off the tram, Kedar has gone over what he has lost with the wallet. Some money, thirty rupees, not a lot in his mind, though he is aware that four poor families could eat well for a month on that amount, a couple of visiting cards he'd been given at the tennis club, no great loss, a receipt from Salamatally Tailors for his new summer suit, not a problem, they know him well, a couple of other bills and things, again, no great loss, and a tiny reproduction of Cézanne's 'Jug and Peaches' which he'd cut out from a book and put in the photo window. A pity, that one, a painting he really loves, but he'd put it in the wallet to remind him that one day he would reach the Louvre and see the original, so, yes, a loss but not a great one. The main thing is the wallet itself, worth far more than what it contained today. That is Loss.

Bulldog-kaku, his middle uncle, younger than his father by a couple of years, had given it to him on his twenty-first birthday. 'Eijey, young Kedar! This is for you! Finest pigskin from Chalk and Boxall, best leather goods suppliers for gentlemen in London. Quality-ta appreciate korbey! You will not find a better wallet anywhere in the world.' And then, with his fat Lahiri nose frying in the oil of its own humour, 'Also, Kedar, now that you are of age, we expect you not only not to lose it, but also to do some work towards filling it! Hah, hah, hah!' This, accompanied by a breath-destroying slap on Kedar's back from a heavy, artillery major's hand.

Major 'Bulldog' Lahiri is currently serving in North Africa, commanding his Sikh batteries, and there is little chance of his returning soon to question Kedar about his wallet. But – the German not yet being born who can actually kill him – sooner or later, he will be back. And then he is bound to ask, the sound exploding out of his chest, the mouth a mere barrel, 'Kedar! Fellow-me-lad! Show me! How full is that wallet I gave you? And was any honest sweat involved at all?'

War's not going well over there, so maybe he'll become a POW, Kedar thinks, and immediately reprimands himself for such a thought, though in the deepest cellar of his heart, he knows he would much rather Bulldog-kaku gave the Germans a headache than himself or his family. 'Only a major, but thinks he's a field marshal. And we are *jemon*, his foot soldiers,' Borun-kaku likes to say. While on the subject of foot soldiers, Kedar wonders whether there will be any dancing at the party tonight. It seems wrong, somehow, with the whole city in mourning, but that is unlikely to affect the English – their parties will go on, as will their war, regardless of minor events such as the death of the greatest writer India has ever produced.

Kedar catches himself in two minds, three, actually, if the state of his feet is to be taken into account. On the one hand, tonight of all nights, he has no desire to join revelry, especially the kind of desperate thing that passes for jollity nowadays, with all sorts of strange, newly arrived army types, both gora and native, going about as if every drink, every dance and every flirtation is their last, pretending to be heroic-posthumous, many of them well before they have seen any action. On the other hand, he's had his fill of mourning today, a surfeit of damp, romantic gloominess – the juggernaut of tears and quavery song has inexorably pushed his own ability to feel anything into a roadside ditch.

He is, after all, not yet twenty-two, and he reckons he should grasp his golden years, no matter in what tattered shape life was offering them to him. He knows he will mourn Rabindranath's passing and remember it for the rest of his life, but this evening there are enough people across the city doing the expected thing, and he is sure it will make no difference to the great man's spirit whether he goes to a party or not. Then again, he has his feet to think of – the match is set for this Saturday, and he has no wish to give that snooty Cardhu Motherwalla a walkover because he can't walk. And then there was that one thing the girl had said, smiling over her shoulder: 'I hope I shall see you at the party.'

'Dada-babu. Samwhuich.' Rasko stands over him with a tray.

'Hmh,' Kedar grunts, nodding in the direction of the side table. Rasko arranges the tray and gestures to the teapot, asking if he should pour.

'No, leave it. I'll pour it myself.' Kedar lunges forward to grab a sandwich, the upward angle of his crippled feet making him do all the work from his abdomen. Rasko notices Kedar's awkwardness.

'What's happened to your feet, Dada-babu?'

'Feet... hyan... feet,' says Kedar, not paying attention, his eyes wandering over the garden as he bites into the ham and bread. Maybe walking on the lawn would be good for them.

'Mustard,' Rasko assures him, 'I've put mustard like you asked.'

'Mustard, yes, good.' Kedar dismisses him, still not looking up. Rasko turns to leave.

'Oh, Rasko.' Kedar has a thought.

'Hyan, Dada-babu.'

'Listen, bring me a bucket of hot water with lots of salt in it.'

Rasko's look asks the question.

'For my feet, Rasko. Large bucket. Hot water. Salt.' Kedar semaphores the words through a mouthful of sandwich.

'What happened? Where are your chappals?'

'Gone. The crowd ate them.'

'Oh-ho... was there a big crowd, Dada-babu?'

Kedar nods as he chews and then he swallows, which allows him to speak clearly. 'Crowd? Yes, big crowd. Huge. Thousands and thousands of people.'

'Were people crying?' Rasko is now a tall tree curving with curiosity, wanting to know about this great circus he has only heard about. In exchange, he drops small bits of information. 'All the shops are shut. And people crying here all day. Boudi. Kaku-babu. Not joking, even Bodo Babu, for two minutes, even he shed tears. And then—'

'Rasko! Bucket. Hot water. Salt. Go!'

As Rasko hurries off, Kedar's feet communicate something upwards, and he works some of the new muscles in his brain.

'Rasko!'

'Hyan, Dada-babu?' Rasko stops as if he has been yanked by a Meccano hook.

'Come back with the bucket, then I'll tell you all about it. My wallet got pickpocketed.'

Rasko turns around, looking aghast, wanting to engage with this new piece of news, but then he remembers the bucket.

'I'll be right back, Dada-babu. Back at once.' He heads to the kitchen, the white of his bearer's uniform washed mild orange by the setting sun, his bare feet pattering urgently across the veranda floor.

Kedar keeps listening to the sound of the feet long after Rasko has gone. The sound briefly sends him into a poetic detour. Rasko: the first man in the universe walking on the first piece of ground which is, somehow, a long veranda with white pillars and a polished red floor that opens out on to a large garden. A garden that is still being formed by the Cosmic Gardener.

Still the eternal awakes. Behind all its other traffic, Kedar's mind has been trying to understand what came over him at the funeral procession. His friend Rudro, older than Kedar by about four years, keeps insisting that Kedar has a delicate and oversensitive flower at the core of his soul. Kedar knows this to be one of Rudro's jovial insults, but it's one of the more irritating ones precisely because it's so demonstrably untrue. 'Kedu Moshai, the madding crowd is to you what the ocean is to a fine freshwater fish from a small pond! Too big, too open, too salty, and too full of too many nasty creatures. You are as equipped to deal with this vast nastiyota as Red Riding Pomfret is to deal with a pack of wolves!' Rudro said this in the presence of Kedar's other tormentor, Borun-kaku who, for once, jumped to Kedar's defence or, rather, into gleeful attack against Rudro. 'A pomfret, my dear knowledgeable fellow, is first of all a sea fish. And I daresay a pomfret dealing with wolves in mid-ocean might even manage to drown them and survive.' Which then took the duel away from Kedar into the uncharted territory of whether and how far wolves could swim out to sea.

It has been the same since Kedar was a child, Borun-kaku and Rudro ganging up on him, in cricket, or chess, or quoting from the *Encyclopaedia Britannica*. From an early age, Kedar has watched them play things out in their respective styles – Rudro using ten words where three would do, and Borun-kaku the opposite, preferring, at least in matters to do with Kedar and Rudro, to be extremely economical. The ruthless straight drive past the bowler's feet as opposed to Rudro's ornate verbal cuts and deflections. Despite, or perhaps partly because of, this roasting in twin fires, Kedar sees himself as quite a tough character, not easily shaken by the tricks and turns of life. But today, strictly between him and himself, he is forced to invite Rudro's jibe into the analysis.

Absolutely Red Riding Pomfret. Gasping for air in a bit of crowd. Managing to lose his precious wallet to some grizzled old street thief with a rusty razor blade. Bloody idiot. What a moment to get an attack of 'sensitivity', almost swooning, almost like some Victorian memshaheb. Oh, my handkerchief! An utterly clownish panic. Kedar feels a sudden anger welling up at himself, coupled with a mad urge to go back into the crowd, back to the point – though he cannot put his finger on the exact moment – when the pocket-maar struck, and back before that to – should he have stayed the course until Nimtala Ghat? Gone all the way and stood there through the cremation?

No. Out of the question. This is not something he can convince himself about. Just as the anger has risen, a counter-tide of memory, of the sense of freedom once he had torn himself out of the procession, comes surging back to drown the feeling of having been soiled by his own inadequacy. What the devil could one have done? Jaak geye, gelo to gelo, forget about it. Don't let it happen again. He looks up from his cup of Darjeeling and sees that the light in the garden has slid from rich to soft, from a Gauguin extreme to something well within the range of someone like Monet.

Not to say that Monet didn't have range, never, never, never that. In fact, though he doesn't have any of the skill, patience or application, Kedar has often wanted to paint the changing light in the garden the way Monet painted his haystacks. The high English hedge, the square squadrons of dahlias, the unruly, celebratory sprawl of the gulmohar tree, he has watched them all like a hunter watching delicious prey but, somehow, never been able to move in for the kill. His excuse is a flimsy one – that the light changes too quickly – and Borun-kaku's riposte to this is a smash to his weak lob: 'People who are not artists have excuses. Genuine artists have none. They are as if at war. And in a war, you don't talk, you just do!'

The pickpocket had obviously understood this: don't talk, just do. Did that make him an artist as well? An infinitely lesser one than the dead man being carried to his cremation but, unlike Kedar, somehow belonging to the same species as the poet?

The light on the cremation procession has already shifted in his mind, moved now from something he felt bound to attend to something that has damaged him. And, though the going of the wallet hurts, it's not so much the material loss as the cut of realization that it opens. Bengal. Bengalis. Calcutta-Kolkata-Kolikata. *Lok. Jonota.* People. These are words he has taken for granted, as he has the vast districts of meaning they represent but, today, he feels he has made his first real journey into the actual territories, and the trip has jolted him. The thing that began drenched in the hazily innocent sadness of a clean morning is now illuminated by the soiled rays of a sinking sun – the last rays of the last sunset ever to light the earth, now missing Rasko's face as he bends down but washing over the wall behind him.

Kedar looks at the steaming bucket at his feet as if it's a cauldron conjured up by Dante. He looks up at Rasko, who nods encouragement. He puts his feet in and does nothing to stop the scream that escapes from his throat. Rasko links his thick eyebrows, the same two that Borun-kaku has named Ribbentrop and Molotov, and looks both concerned and satisfied at the same time.

'Dada-babu, you had asked for hot, isn't that right?'

His breath now skipping somewhere far out across the lawn, Kedar manages nothing more than a thin gasp. Rasko takes this to be a sound expressing gratitude.

'You ask me for something, Dada-babu, you know I'll do it.' Seeing long-term profit on the horizon, Rasko pushes further. 'The samwhuich was good?'

Rudro's old nonsense slides its way in through the lattice of pain that stretches from Kedar's feet and legs up into his middle. 'Samwhuich? Yes! Capital! Bhery gooood! And also, the samwhuere! But more importantly, Rasko, samhow? And even more crucially, Rasko Ustad, Shomrat of Philosophy, sam*why*?' Rudro's voice slips into Kedar's own ongoing mimicry of Banglish – O Death! Whuere is thaai steeng? Death, thy sting, it is where? It is heaar, at the bhery base of my feets. Or, as in Billy Bunter, the achingness of my blessed feet is, alas, splendidly excruational.

Slowly, his body overcomes the shock, and the palliative properties of heat and salt begin to take effect. Rasko watches with interest as Kedar's grimace relaxes into almost an ecstatic expression, the eyeballs now moving slowly under closed lids. He goes around to the side table, lifts the lid of the teapot to check whether the tea is finished, and takes the tray away.

Kedar hears his footsteps recede and, to his surprise, soon return. He hears Rasko put something down next to him. A plate, perhaps.

'Ki?' he asks, attempting to be testy but not quite managing.

'Niin. Fruit khaan.' Here, have some fruit.

'Fruit?' Kedar opens his eyes and looks down at the table. On it is a white china plate upon which curves a luridly ripe yellow-and-black thing. 'What's this? You know I hate bananas.'

'This is not just any banana. My aunt, Shombhu's Ma, sent a basket all the way from Panchpukur, my village. I've been hiding them from the other servants. In fact, I didn't even tell Boudi and, please, don't you tell her either.'

'Rasko. I hate bananas, whether they are from Panchpukur, Jharbagan or Jamaica. Take it away and eat it yourself. Quietly, if it's so precious!'

'Oh-ho. You are not understanding. These bananas from our village are special. They have many powers. You have had a hard day. This will help bring your strength back.'

'Strength? Special powers? What strength? What's all this nonsense?'

'Not nonsense, Dada-babu, eating one of these keeps a man strong for a day and a night.'

'Night? People sleep at night. Why do I have to be strong at night?'

Rasko hesitates before answering. Ribbentrop and Molotov twitch briefly towards each other. His black eyes shine under them with sincerity as he speaks.

'I'm not saying anything, nothing like that, but these bananas are very good for when, sometimes, you know, for when people don't sleep at night. But also very good after you've had a hard day's labour.'

It takes Kedar a moment or two to understand this, but when he looks back at Rasko he doesn't show any sign of having understood. 'Hm. Thiik achhey. Now go and see that my DJ is ready, and ask Bahadur to ask the driver if there is petrol in my car.'

'Are you going out again?'

'Yes. Why sleep when you've eaten a Panchpukur banana?'

'Dinner here?'

'What's for dinner?'

'Vegetarian only. You know... because of Gurudeb's passing...'

'Hm. Keep a little aside in the pantry. Not a lot. And quietly.'

'Should I tell Boudi when she comes back?'

'Tell nobody anything. If anybody asks, just say Dada-babu went out. And don't say I was wearing a suit.'

Rasko nods and moves away. 'Eat the banana, Dada-babu, don't forget,' he calls over his shoulder before disappearing into the kitchen.

Kedar sits there, thinking. 'For when people don't sleep at night...' Was Rasko reading his mind? Not that he expects life to yield up all its pleasures so soon, not that at all, but perhaps a first step could be... No, do not get carried away, it was just a politeness thrown over her shoulder after quite a formal parting. From whichever angle you examined it, all she had actually said was, 'I hope I shall see you at the party.' A mere nothing, a hollow conversational bone, a mere pleasantry from a mem-girl. This was not a heroine from a Tagore novel but a European, and what was said was exactly what was meant – she hoped she would see him. At the party. However. If Rabindranath Tagore had been his age and in his position, he would have wanted to see her again.

His feet still planted in the bucket, Kedar looks around surreptitiously to make sure none of the gardening staff are looking; for reasons not clear to himself, he doesn't want servants to see him eating an aphrodisiacal banana. Having made sure he is unobserved, Kedar reaches for the champion fruit of Panchpukur, peels it and takes a small bite. He closes his eyes, chews briefly, swallows. Then he takes a bigger bite.

The fridge is dark with food but I'm not hungry. I have everything I need for two or three different kinds of dinner. If I crave other stuff, I can go down and grab whatever I want from the small grocer's or the supermarket just down the street, bananas from the Caribbean, pineapples from Africa, mangoes of strange taste and colour, of dodgy provenance, Chinese food, Italian food and, of course, the huge variety of local stuff, but right now I just don't feel like eating. Some more drink, hopefully not too many cigarettes, and then bed.

Playing back the tapes, I notice that both of them – actually all of them – keep coming back to the day Tagore died. I know that all over Bengal a lot of people didn't eat that day out of a sense of mourning, and many ate sparsely, the kind of food you eat after a close bereavement. On some of the tapes, I ask questions and they answer. I listen to them talk about that day. Others, too, have written or said things – it was as if something was released that day, something evil let loose upon Bengal, as if the old man's going, at the not unripe age of eighty, was an omen for all that was to befall Bengalis, a warning signal, somehow, for what was about to start happening to millions of people, most of whom suffered and died never having read a word written by Rabindranath.

That's bullshit, of course. History isn't like an airliner, it doesn't just start a set of engines on one day or at one moment, the ones on the other wing a moment later, before taxiing and taking off. No, small things constantly shift, like minute brushstrokes building up something in a painting, and sometimes yes, there are bigger marks, bigger slashes, and sudden erasures, or paint spilt on the canvas, or spilt blood, and then the picture changes radically, but always on some already painted ground. Small engines are already whirring deep inside the bigger ones, while nuts and bolts are coming loose in the engines that have been on for a while, if you see what I – no, hell, I'm getting distracted by all these bloody books and comics he's left behind, stuff I had limited access to in my own childhood, all this Biggles nonsense, and these big, hardcover illustrated books, *Aircraft of the Second World War*, *Fighter Planes in History*, *The Observer Book* of these airplanes and those airplanes, and these little, square war comics I haven't seen since I was a kid, *Hawk Squadron*, *Thirst for Glory*, *Outlaw Aces*, all this war hagiogarbage.

No, to get back to what I was saying. Rabindranath Tagore, the great Bengali poet, India's greatest writer and philosopher, is dead. Today is the day of his death. Within a year of Tagore's death, almost exactly to the day, a year after his death, the country – no, never mind what happens a year later, this story is about something else, it starts here and goes somewhere else, or should. Meaning, it will. As in, go elsewhere and go way beyond what happens a year later, a year and a half or two years later. Granted those things were big, huge, in the life of a people or a city, but no one event, or small series of events (yes, yes, a small series of big events, engines within engines) can eclipse or obscure sixty-seventy-eighty years of a history, do you follow?

No, how could you? I'm rambling. Let me try again. Let me get a drink, eject that tape, put a record on the turntable and try again.

What I really know about is architecture, or, I know a little bit about modern architecture because that's my field, roughly speaking. I read somewhere that Louis Kahn had said that you can only really see a building – and the architect's essential intentions – once the building becomes a ruin. His point, I suppose, was that a 'live' structure offers too much confusion, too many curtains of activity, that current reality provides too many obfuscations for one to be able to see the building-ness of a building properly. Now, if one were to take this and apply it to that time, treat that whole period like a derelict building, a structure turned inside out by the tectonic press of passing years, all it's plumbing showing, all the wiring, all the different pipes, the ghosts of its staircases stamped on half-collapsed walls, windows hanging over disappeared floors, doorways talking to other doorways across the abyss, with dunes of rubble at the bottom, then perhaps, just perhaps, one could begin to make sense of things.

So where are we again? Well, as you can see, I'm currently inhabiting the 1970s. To be precise, here I am in this great metropolis of the West, in the late 70s.

If I'm not here, perched inside this squeezed warren of repetitive buildings, then I usually find myself in their house in the countryside, the house they both abandoned – him by dying, her by leaving and never, or not yet, coming back. I sometimes feel she wants me to think of her as being dead as well, a kind of non-wife sati drowning herself after him in the funeral pool of alcohol. As I keep explaining to her, that's not how things work.

Playing back one set of the tapes, I find myself trying to sing from the song sheet of the year 1975, from three years ago, back in their 'country house', surrounded yet again by the shambles the old man had left, his junk almost alive, crawling towards me from all directions, coming to get me like that wood in Macbeth, except neither Old Elko nor me – nor I, excuse me – have blood on our hands, or not that much when you compare him or I – him or me, excuse again – to some of the others. No blood, me, except what he vomited over me as he died, four years ago, and him too, not that much of other people's blood, not on his hands, on his mind certainly, but not on his hands.

What you see spilled on my hands right now, in 1975, where I've gone back to their house a few months after he died, is this clear sticky liquid, stuff that would go cloudy if it was in a glass and one added water to it. But I'm going to wash it off, once I find a working tap attached to this primitive bloody plumbing system. The spill is because the cap on the bottle was loose, but no point blaming Old Elko for such small things. It was the last bottle from which he poured a drink. There was a way he used to look at me, defiant, when pouring yet another hara-kiri, as we used to call it, and he filled half his glass, topped it with water, took down a gulp, brought out a spray of blood in exchange, and that was it. You would think the stuff in the bottle would have evaporated in the many months since then, but the cap was just about screwed on and this weather meant there was still some residual rearguard when I tried to clear it away, like those ancient Japanese soldiers who are still coming out of the jungles in Borneo and the Philippines.

No, I can tell you can tell I'm lying. Sorry.

He'd had to go off the hard liquor and we were drinking that aniseed stuff when he died. And, to tell you the truth, just now I was actually looking for some more to pour into a glass. I'm nowhere as badly gone as those two, but I did need a couple of drinks before starting on this mess. Both of them being who they were, I shouldn't have worried – she, if not he, would have made sure there were enough bottles, and sure enough, after spilling the dregs of the old one, there are two more I've just found. Sealed. The booze in the one I've just cracked open still fresh and pungent.

I knew where to look for them, of course, because she'd shown me. Towards the end, she would try and hide the bottles, hide them, it felt, from both him and herself. 'Darling, this is where I'm stashing them, but do feel free... in fact, you *must* move them again if you see me going loopy.' I'd move them every evening, but she would find them – this being her house, the best hiding places were the ones she'd created. I just found these two survivors in one of her favourite nooks, at the bottom of a cupboard full of women's things in the little passage between the pantry and the back garden, she knew Old Elko would never delve in there, where she kept her old foundation garments and such, cardboard boxes stuffed with ancient brassieres and those large tentlike bottoms she called 'camis'. In this forest of peeling paint, a small alcove of dead organization, the cups of the brassieres like stillborn puppies smeared into each other, the whites bruised, the once pristine knickers encrusted by age, brittle, cloth become almost paper. Two bottles nestling like stowaways next to a black military hat that looks like a small drum, something she'd found in a sale somewhere, a Beau Brummel topi she was inordinately fond of, a whatsit, a kepi.

3

KEPI

Seven in the evening and, so far, it's been a day for laughing. When the sound has come, it has come out odd, scratched slightly with dissonance but, equally, it has come with the inevitability of a full head of steam, some small volcano built up somewhere inside her. Each time, she has not been looking to laugh, and each time it has surprised her, surprised her far more than tears would have. Something in the air, something in the day. Light clouds of absurdity rummaging through the sky above her and all she has to do, it seems, is to breathe. 'Well, at least it's done for the day,' she thinks, as she catches the scrape of Andrew's tyres coming in too fast through the gates. 'Poor driveway,' she thinks, 'poor Mother, who so likes to keep her gravel manicured.'

Niceties have had to muck in with all the other normal things, and Andrew does what he always does when he comes to pick her up – he lets off a couple of clarion-calls on the horn. 'Well, dear, I suppose when in Rome,' Mother has said, placating herself more than anybody else, but Imogen knows the motor horns drive Mummy up the wall. She throws open her curtains and calls down quickly. '*Manners*, Andrew! Do stop! Be right along!' Imogen has no patience with the type of girl who likes to keep a chap waiting, so, purse, then one last look in the mirror – what Daddy calls her 'ammunition check' – then drum down the stairs and out through the door being held open by the bearer. At the door, a turnaround, nearly twisting her ankle on the marble, a duck of her head back through the door, 'Mummy! I'm off, Mummy darling! See you both at breakfast!' And out again, her perfume fighting through the stuffy evening air, trying not to scrape her nice shoes on the gravel, get to the car and there it is again, laugh-sap rising inside her, and she can't help it.

'*Andrew!* What is that... thing?'

'What thing?'

'That thing on your head!'

'Oh, this.' Andrew grins from ear to ear, satisfied with the effect, offering her the open car door but no explanation.

The threat of rain now gone, Andrew has the top down, and Imogen feels her brief crown of mosquitoes falling behind as the old banger accelerates out of the lane. They turn on to the main road and Andrew adjusts the round box on his head to a slightly jauntier angle. Imogen finds a breath between sobs of laughter and asks again.

'Are you going to tell me?'

'It's called a kepi. What the Frogs wear, you know, their officers.'

'Ah. Thought I'd seen it before.'

'Yes, well, Tuggy brought it back from France when his squadron had to scarper. Flew his Hurricane back with this planted on top of his flying helmet. Not much chance of getting a Jerry helmet as a souvenir, of course.'

'No...'

'When he landed, Tuggy's mechanic asked him what he was doing with this and Tuggy apparently replied, "Oh, just in case I was shot down, planned to surrender in the uniform of chaps who are rather good at it!"'

A ricksha-walla yanks his ricksha out in front of the headlights and Andrew brakes hard.

'Oh, blast – sorry, Immy! Prancing about as if he's in broad daylight! Wish they'd at least ban the blighters at night.'

'Hardly prancing, Andrew, he was carrying three people.'

'Count them, did you?'

Imogen brings the subject back to the kepi before the laughing turns into a quarrel.

'So, why on earth are you wearing that... this evening?'

'Oh, thought I'd pretend to be a Mon Capitaine to see if I couldn't worm myself into your affections. Since you like the French so much.'

'Oh, do stop playing the fool Andrew!' The words shoot out of her mouth like an errant piece of traffic and she kicks herself. She usually reserves the refusals for the goodnight moment at her door, always trying, tactfully, to protect the evening's mood. Bad enough the war, bad enough her own, rather negative, standpoint on men at the moment, and worse, a decent fellow like Andrew, so obviously lonely and so obviously sweet on her. Bad enough without having to get into the nitty-gritty of turning him down so early in the outing.

Andrew pretends he hasn't heard her. He begins to mimic, first the noise of the car engine, and then a trumpet solo from some jazz record of his. From time to time, he lets off sharp sounds which could either be gunshots or drumsticks on cymbals, she can't tell which. To her left, she can see the port cranes poking up from behind some buildings, their silhouettes now almost merging into the darkening sky. On the right, a tram tries feebly to race with the car, the dim light from its windows throwing a snake of bumpy, yellow rectangles on the grass by the tracks. Andrew notices her looking at the tram and he accelerates, almost as if to spite her interest, and they leave it behind without effort. Maybe she is imagining it, but there seem to be fewer people on the roads tonight, as if it was a holiday, or as if some large calamity had struck. She thinks about telling Andrew about her outing today, about the sea of slippers and the pair of urchins, but thinks the better of it. Andrew is most decent with the natives he meets, but impatient with her desire to 'get her hands dirty with local things', as he terms it. 'I don't know about the King and Empire, Immy, but we're only passing through, don't you think?'

After a while, they pass the zoo and the car rises on to the small bridge over the canal. Andrew slows down on the bridge and takes both his hands off the wheel to light a cigarette. As he picks up speed on the downward slope, Imogen tries to revive the conversation. Andrew loves to insult the army high command, so that's the route she chooses.

'So, *are* we about to surrender?'

Andrew manages to snort and blow a derisive plume of smoke at the same time, before recapturing his wheel. 'Surrender *where* exactly, dear girl? We are replete with choice at the moment. Egypt, d'you mean? The Atlantic? Then there's always what your Froggos have done in Indo-China—'

'I meant *here*, Andrew! You know, the East.'

'Oh, I shouldn't think so. The Japs are not Jerries, thank heavens. Our duffers should be able to hang on to Singapore, though the Japs may bother us a bit further up the Peninsula.' Andrew brakes lightly and swings the car on to the big road running past the racecourse.

Imogen clutches the door rim, her fingers slightly clammy on the metal despite the breeze. 'What about us here? Daddy won't give me a straight answer when I ask.'

'*Here?* Oh, you mean Calcutta? Don't be silly. Safe as houses. I mean, how would they get here? The little devils would first have to take Singapore. Then Siam. Then they would have to fight through the most frightful jungle in Burma to reach Rangoon. Fat chance.'

'They could come around by sea.'

Andrew jerks forward, nearly losing control of the car. Imogen finds her hands and arms rigid against the dashboard. '*Andrew!* For god's sake—'

'Come... around... by... sea...' Andrew slaps the steering wheel, trying to beat the mirth out of himself. 'Come... come... *around*... she says!'

The fence ringing the racecourse flickers white alongside.

'I say, Immy, that puts me right back in the mood! Can I tell the chaps at the club? We could even have a come-around-by-sea party for your birthday, we could—'

It's Imogen's turn to attack the car. She hits the dashboard hard. Once, twice, thrice, hurting herself. The edge of her hair slashes into her cheek as she whirls on Andrew. Her voice goes into a shout, the words triggered at point-blank range. 'Just you try it! Just you... *bloody well... try it!*' Her eyes widen at her own words and her hand jumps up to cover her mouth. Andrew bites down on his guffawing, shaken now, pretending to concentrate on his driving. Imogen straightens up, flushing red, looking away. 'I'm terribly sorry. I don't know where... that... came from. I'm *so* sorry, Andrew.'

Andrew reaches across to squeeze her hand. 'No, no, my fault entirely, Immy. I'm the one who should apolo—'

'It's tearing everything up, isn't it, this war? I've never used that word before, I don't know where it came from.'

'Don't be too upset, Immy, and besides, I *have* heard you use *bloody* once or twice.'

'No! When?'

'Just the other night, for instance, after the dance. Fort William, when you broke your shoe strap. You were quite merry.'

'No! I didn't, did I? Good heavens.'

'You do mean "Oh bloody hell!" don't you?'

They start laughing again. As he coaxes the steering with his right hand to take them through the club gates, he is still holding Imogen's wrist with his left and, this once, she finds no reason to pull it away.

9-5

'Subhas would never have let this happen!' The young man raises his arm and points it forward and upward like a political leader.

'What? Robi Thakur dying?' His friend pretends to tickle the armpit area exposed by the first man's raised arm. 'Yes, I suppose Subhas could have prevented even that.'

'No, no, you idiot, this is what people were shouting near the gate of Jorasanko, you know, after the first attempt was made to snatch the hair from the old man's beard as they were loading his body on to the lorry. Someone tried to tear out the hair. I told you, there was the stampede, and in the middle of the pushing and shoving I heard several people say this loudly – *If Subhas had been here, this would have never happened!*

'All of them no doubt pushing and shoving themselves!' The second young man claps his hands in delight.

'Of course! For everything they were worth!'

Standing not far from the two students on the small balcony, Niru remembers the crowd pushing past her on the terrace.

'Without Subhas, we Bengalis are a herd of rampaging cattle.'

'With him, we are more disciplined than Hitler's storm troopers.' The first fellow switches to English.

'With him, we *are* Hitler's storm troopers!' The second man also replies in English, and they continue to spar in the Ingreji that Niru finds so irritating sometimes. You can tell from a mile off, just by listening to them, in fact, that these boys are from that factory of superciliousness, Presidency College.

'Yes, when he finally returns to rule over free India, there will be discipline!'

It's the second boy who now raises his arm and points. 'From Multan to Madras!' He grandly swings from the direction of Chowringhee to the Tipu Sultan Mosque. 'From Quetta to Kohima, discipline! Under the iron hand of Netaji!'

'Kohima?' The first boy reverts to Bangla. 'Sheita abar... koi, ma?' Kohima, now where is that, mother?

'O, ho, ho, ooo.' The second boy pretends to flinch at the pun. 'How can you be such a know-nothing! Kohima, in Assam, Naga Hills district, on the border with Burma, one extreme eastern point of British India.'

'But, after Freedom, will they come under Indian India?'

'Who knows? Chiang Kai-shek might want the area. These nationalists are always greedy and aggressive. But those Naga tribals are quite crazy, so who knows? Many Christian converts, so they may not prefer Baldy Bapu's god to Chiang's. My uncle worked in a plantation around there once, that's how I know the name.'

Niru shakes her head and looks down at the postcard again. But it's difficult to get the boys' crudely disrespectful banter out of her ears because here is a related pun in the letter, the words kui maachh, kui fish, where a sentence ends, 'we'll cook two-day-old kui fish if we have to, but we won't starve!' A nonsense dialogue runs through her mind – Kui maachh koi, ma? Kui maachh? Kui maachh, Kohima-tey! – Which she forces herself to translate into Ingreji: The kui fish, where is it, mother? The kui fish? The kui fish, it is in Kohima!

'Speaking of names, how many does he have, now?' The first Presi boy scratches his head theatrically.

'Who?'

'Subhas Bose.'

'Subhas Bose?'

'Yes. Let's count. First, full name, Subhas Chandra Bose, or Boshu if you're saying it in Bangla.'

'Then, Mayor Shaheb. But that was when he was mayor.'

'Yes, they feel far away, the 1920s, almost like the nineteenth century.'

'Then, back to the present, said with altogether too much love and reverence, just Subhas. Shoobhhaash!'

'Then, Netaji, as they say. Netaji will last, even non-Bengalis love this name, *awour liidarr!*'

That is exactly how Niru would pronounce those words and these two Anglofied jokers now infuriate her even more.

'That's one, one-a, two, three, three-a, four, five. So?'

'And how many does Rabindranath have?'

'Well, okay, full, official name, Rabindranath Tagore, in Bangla Robindro-nath Thakur. Then, the internationally famous just Tagore, which some foreigners pronounce as Taa-go-rey—'

'All right, then, in Bangla, just Robindronath, then Robi Thakur, then Robi-babu for those who know him formally, also Kobi-guru, great poet, and then, finally, Gurudeb.'

'Yes. So?'

'So, Robindronath wins 9-5. At nine, he clearly outranks Subhas, at four or five, in the affections of us Bengalis.'

'How so?'

'The more names we have for a public figure, the more we respect him, is it not so?'

'Look, the way the wind is blowing, we Bengalis seem quite ready to forget late-great-poet Rabindranath and replace him with the political peacock Subhas.'

'Right... how long should we wait, do you think?'

'Well, the message was for us to meet at 6.'

One of the boys calls out to Niru, using the respectful address. 'Did you get the same message?'

'Yes, 6. It's only 6.30.' Niru keeps to a short reply, the boys nod and turn back to their chatter.

The meeting is on a first floor, on Dharmatolla Street, in the typing room of a stationery and stamp-making business whose owner is a Party sympathizer. The three of them, student volunteers in the Bengal Provincial Students' Federation, have been summoned there by a man they know only as Akash-babu. The BPSF volunteers are not allowed to call this man by any other suffix but 'babu', and they've been specifically warned never to use the word 'comrade', in case police spies are somewhere within earshot. What usually happens is that Akash-babu comes and gives each of them some sheets of paper, usually handwritten, occasionally typed, the English going to the first boy, the Hindustani to the other one, and the Bangla to Niru. The three of them are not to discuss among each other what they type, though by now they've all figured out it's usually the same matter: announcements of union meetings, statements explaining the Party's policy towards the latest political developments, simply worded open letters asking the city's huge numbers of labourers to join in the struggle for genuine, proletarian freedom. Niru's guess is that, this evening, the Communist Party of India will have no choice but to announce its mourning for the passing of a great, albeit bourgeois, poet.

Niru turns away from the boys and looks across what normally is Calcutta's busiest point, the crossing where Central Avenue and Bentinck Street meet Esplanade, Chowringhee and Dharmatolla Street. Today, as dusk falls on the huge curving criss-cross of tram tracks, there is hardly any traffic or any noise. Even the occasional tram bell sounds mournful and apologetic. The big stores have shut early, and people stand around in clusters, some on the darkened pavements, some on the empty roads, as if unwilling to let go of the day. Across Dharmatolla Street, on a small patch of wall between the shops, someone has blacked out the pasted cinema posters. At the corner where Dharmatolla meets Chowringhee, a beggar stands with a frayed straw basket filled with soiled, bruised marigolds. Even at this distance, his voice is clear: 'Flowers from the cremation ghat! Flowers from Gurudeb's body! Two annas for a dozen! You won't get these again, flowers that have touched Kobi-guru Rabindranath! Not in this lifetime! Two annas for a dozen flowers from Nimtolla!'

So many different ways in which people will not be able to forget Rabindranath in a hurry.

'Not too many names for Baldy, no?'

The boys from Presidency have moved on from Tagore and Bose.

'Well, Gandhi, Mr Gandee, Gandhi*ji*, Bapu, and some are now even using Rabindranath's Mahatma!'

'Naked Fakir.'

'Yes, Naked Fakir, though I think Churchill meant to imply a much more obscene word.'

'Oh, you mean…?'

'Yes, obviously.'

'I hadn't thought of that, but you may be right.'

Niru can't think what the obscene word might be, but she has no intention of asking the boys. For the tenth time today, she pulls out the postcard from her jhola. The excitement it carries clashes with the feeling that her soul has been turned to soot. It's a feeling she remembers from the end of other days of bereavement, when you know the person who's gone is dead and will always, in this life – and now she knows there's no other life – remain so. The light has seeped away from the sky, making it hard to read, but there is a staccato flash of some coloured light that regularly falls on to her corner of the balcony. After a while, she realizes it's from the back of the huge electric advertisement for Lipton's Tea that glares down on Chowringhee around the corner. Clearly, no one has thought to switch it off. As a fourteen-year-old, she loved watching as the white neon kettle tilted and the bright orange tea poured into the white neon cup. Today, when the kettle straightens, she's in shadow, but as the tea pours, she reads.

After a while, she puts away the letter and tries to listen again to the boys. Like Niru, they are students affiliated with the student wing of the Party; and their tone has changed as they have moved back from English to Bangla; it sometimes seems to be the only language in which Communist matters can be properly discussed.

'… they'll have to do something to mollify Josef-jethu. They can't keep the Party under this ban for too much longer.'

'They can use the war to do anything, but hopefully you're right.'

'Well, no, they are sly, the Ingrej, so they will say *yes-yes* to Moscow while dragging their feet, but old Josef-uncle is even more wily.'

'And he is now the Empire's lifeline. What more could the Ingrej have asked for than that the Soviet Union take on the bulk of Hitler's army?'

'Oh, no doubt the Ingrej are hoping that Germany and Russia will now destroy each other.'

'Yes, but they are also now forced to help the comrades. You know, they've begun sending tarpaulin tents from here, from the factories in Howrah, to the Soviets?'

'Yes, yes, and a comrade told me aviator glasses for the pilots also. Therefore, the Party instructions to avoid all industrial action in any factory producing war material for the Soviets.'

'Exactly. So, quid pro quo upon quid pro quo, what will Josef-uncle ask for?'

'Lift the ban on the Party.'

'Lift the ban on the Party, exactly.'

The two pause, while one of them takes out a cigarette and lights it. He takes a puff and hands it to his friend. Niru shudders as she watches both boys taking turns to put their mouths to the same cigarette. Then she tries to remember the meaning of the English phrase the boy has just used. For a while, she is glad just to hear the scattered sounds from the nearly empty streets, even though the air is now fouled with the stink of smouldering tobacco. As the cigarette comes to its end, one of the boys, the English typist, leans over the parapet to check no one's walking past below. The other one, the Hindustani typist, carefully puts out the stub with the sole of his chappal before handing it to his smoking partner who delicately throws the stub on to the road. Suddenly Niru remembers – not Ingreji but Latin, actually. *Quid pro quo: something that is taken or given in return for another.* Both the boys wave their hands about, trying to disperse the smoke. It wouldn't do to be caught smoking by Akash-babu when he finally appears.

'One thing, though, in this whole business with the Soviet Union.'

'Yes?'

'Bose. Where is Bose? Many are saying he's escaped to Russia. If so, what will be his discussions with Josef-uncle, especially now that the Russians and Ingrej are allies?'

'If he went to Russia, he's now probably in some not uncomfortable jail, or maybe, probably, house arrest.'

'Well, he has often claimed to be a socialist. He would try and convince Stalin, surely?'

'Socialist? Did you say socialist?' The voice is a hiss at first. Then it turns into a scratchy roar. 'SHUBASHBOSHU a socialist?'

The boys' voices have climbed louder and louder, carried away by their conversation, and neither Niru nor they have heard the approach up the stairs. Niru finds herself whirled around, looking towards the dimly lit office, her heart pounding, her hand clamped on her mouth, trying to stifle the scream. Akash-babu is using all his strength to hold back the old man, as if to stop him from murdering the pair from Presidency, but the frayed sack of spectacles, bristle and spittle seems to have the force of a big train about to smash into a platform.

'*Socialist!* Never forget, *if* that fat-spectacled monkey Shubhash Boshu ever gains power, we will be the first ones he will attack! But! No one will be fooled by his attempts at buttering Yosefshtalin! You can be sure a cunning old snake like Yosefshtalin is not fooled for a moment!'

The pair from Presidency are rigidly straight now, their bodies turned towards each other, frozen in the process of clutching each other in fright. Their faces are fixed on the old man and Akash-babu, their mouths open and round as cement mixers.

Akash-babu is the first to break out of the tableau. He turns to his companion and begins to drag him away from the three youngsters, whispering hard in an almost inaudible voice. As the pulsating stink of the old man's alcohol-laden breath retreats, Niru can make out segments of sentences, phrases. '... break Party discipline... in front of young volunteers... insulting the great Comrade, calling him a snake... your reactionary Trotskyism will get you into... exactly how much liquor have you... using Tagore's death to do what you increasingly do every day... liver... Party discipline...'

As Akash-babu settles the man into a chair at the far end of the office, Niru and the two boys stand, trapped in the balcony, not knowing what to do or where to look – to turn away would be unimaginably rude, to keep gawking at the scene is equally unacceptable. All three choose to look down at the floor, all three with arms crossed politely and protectively across their midriffs.

After a couple of minutes of whispering to the old man, Akash-babu straightens up and strides towards them as if he's entering the typing office for the first time. He addresses them solemnly.

'Today is, no doubt, a difficult day for all of us. There is no work to be done today, but good that the three of you came at the appointed time. I want you to forget about what you just saw. Your senior was very fond of the Poet and naturally he's upset. Now you should go home without further delay, and I will be in touch with you through the usual channels.'

'Ji.'

'Ji.'

'Ji.'

Akash-babu turns to the boys and puts his hands on their shoulders. 'Niraj, Subroto. Any other day I would have turned your ears red for smoking here. Today, I will just say a few things. One, smoking is a very bad habit, and you should avoid it. Two, there's no point trying to wave away the smoke like lunatic stationmasters if your elders can see you smoking from across the road. Three, never ever again throw a cigarette butt into the street below, it might still be lit, and in any case, it might attract attention. If you must smoke, stub out the cigarette on the floor, put it in your pocket and take it away. Take note that this never happens again, understood?'

'Ji.'

'Ji.'

Akash-babu turns to Niru and smiles warmly. 'Ma, you go home now, it's getting late and your parents will be worried.'

LITTLE PROMISES

The train from Khulna still runs inside him somewhere, coming to the surface only now and then, like a strange creature that can never find its home.

The train is from a time when Gopal wasn't very good at counting the years, though now he has calculated that it was about nine years ago – when he was around twelve. Suddenly, he remembers again the moment he climbed on to the slow-rolling goods bogey, the feeling of a massive, powerful hand enveloping him, moving him and everything around him, as if the engine was pulling the whole world. And then the sticks of sugarcane poking into him, jerking up and down and sideways, always finding the most tender spot on his backside. He remembers the taste of the air as it began to cool with the gathering speed, and the smell of rice and sugarcane filling the bogey and fighting back the wet breeze coming through the open door of the carriage. The other boy, the one he didn't know, who'd climbed in with him, beginning to play balancing games as the train bounced and swayed down the track. Seeing how long he could stand on one leg on the highest of a pile of rice sacks. Seeing how far he could lean out of the doorway without falling out. What it felt like to be upside down as the tracks changed underneath. How to do that without bumping your head.

When the two of them got hungry, god provided. With a little work, their knuckles bleeding a bit, they pulled out a couple of sticks of sugarcane from one of the tightly tied bundles. Their teeth working hard to peel off the tough skin, they bit into the crunchy fibre, tearing out the juice, filling their mouths with sweet movement.

As night dropped, the other boy said, 'Look! Stars still there! Do you think they'll still be there in Kolkata?' and Gopal remembers thinking that the boy was younger than he'd first thought, remembers thinking, 'Doesn't the fool know Kolkata has *everything*?'

It occurs to Gopal that he had been right about the 'everything', it's just that he had no idea, then, of how many kinds of everything there were. As Gaurango throws the motorcycle into a sharp turn, the metal boat of Gopal's sidecar leaps over a hole in the road. The thought bumps into Gopal that, if he knew little, then, about all the different everythings, he now knows that he knows even less.

'Aar beshi kichhu korte hobey na.' You don't have to do anything much, Ustad has said, 'Just listen to what Aurangzeb and Gourangzeb tell you. And keep your eyes and ears open.'

The question had knocked from inside his teeth – what if each tells me to do something different? – but he'd kept it locked in. Among the many things life in the Everything had taught him was that you were allowed to seek only so many answers with your tongue, the rest came from staying wide awake, keeping eyes, ears and brain wide open.

At first, the job had seemed like a joke, yet another one of Ustad's leg-pulls. You will go with these two. They will meet a man who will give them a box. You will carry the box, these two will do everything else that needs to be done. Bas. Aar beshi kichhu korte hobey na. That's it. You won't have to do very much. But the joke feeling had evaporated the moment Gopal saw Aurangzeb and Gourango, or Gourangzeb as Ustad called him, make their preparations.

First, checking the petrol and the tyres on the motorcycle. Then Aurangzeb taking a piece of pipe, about a foot and a half long, and conjuring it away into the folds of the long, Pathan's kurta-like thing he always wore. Gourango then examining the edge on two knives, one long, the other quite small, about the length of Gopal's hand from wrist to fingertip. Just touching the blades to the outside of his left palm, but leaving two parallel lines of perky blood, which he quickly sucked to stop the bleeding. Gourangzeb had caught Gopal looking at him, and he had held the boy's eyes like an owl looking at prey, his teeth on his own hand as if it was Gopal's neck. After a long moment, Gourangzeb had moved his mouth away and used it to speak.

'These are mine. Understand?'

Gopal had nodded.

'Mine, means you don't touch them. No matter what happens.' Gourangzeb had put away the long knife in a leather sheath. Then he had picked up the shorter one and pointed it at Gopal. 'No matter what happens. I drop one, I throw one, I look like I haven't noticed, you... just... don't... touch... it. Understand?' Gopal had nodded again. He had felt a touch. He had looked down to find his thin wrist encased in Aurangzeb's huge fingers. The big man's voice cleaning his ear, 'What he means is, if you touch one, the thing will cut your fingers off. All by itself.' Aurangzeb had held up Gopal's hand for a moment and contemplated it. 'After which, *he* will cut you hand off.'

The train had stopped in the middle of the night. The long, jolting drag of the brakes waking Gopal up. He looked outside and saw nothing. No istashon. Just a slab of black with warm wind coming out of it. Above, the stars had stopped with them. The other boy oblivious, curled on some sacks like a baby, his arms trapped between bent knees, tense little snores pulsing his body. Gopal blinked a few times, trying to get used to the darkness and, at first, he thought his eyes were making the pinpoints of light, as happened when someone punched him on the head. Then he saw that the flashing dots were outside the bogey. Tiny flashes pricking the darkness. Fireflies, he realized. If the other kid had been awake, he would have been shocked – 'What? How come they have fireflies here as well?'

The train grunted, jerked forward, and stopped. And again. Like an old and weary monster trying to wake up. Then it began to roll steadily forward. The wind became cool again, and Gopal turned to try and retrieve the comfortable position he had reached before the stop. Just as his eyes were closing, he saw another pinprick. He opened his eyes again and looked around, and there they were. No mistake, three-four lost fireflies trapped among the sacks. He kept watching as sleep reeled him in, watching them pulsating in the gloom like little promises.

Gourangzeb takes a turn too sharply, forcing Gopal's feet to slide down, and the slabs nearly crush his toes. All through the ride Gopal has kept his chappals propped up against the jute wrapping, but now the chill is beginning to knife out of the double sacking, through his soles and into the balls of his feet.

'Remember,' Ustad has said, 'remember to get the stuff on to ice as soon as you can. And pick up more ice to put around it on the way back. Tell that paan-walla to stay awake and wait for you with ice ready.' Ustad has repeated this about five times. Not his usual way, where you would be lucky to be told something more than once and god help you if you got it wrong.

Gourangzeb stopping in front of the paan shop, Aurangzeb sitting on the pillion, checking his watch several times. At the right time, he has nodded at the paan-walla, and the man has helped Gopal put two slabs into jute sacks and then into the spacious front of the sidecar. Gourangzeb has slammed the motorcycle into speed, anxious not to be late, and Gopal, knees sticking up, feet jammed up against the ice, has suffered.

All sensation gone from his toes, Gopal notices they are now on the road that runs along the lanes and buildings just outside the perimeter wall of the port. The gas lamps throw a faint light on the asphalt from between the dark lorries parked on their right. From each side street they pass comes the much brighter glow of the port's electric lighting. As they go past the turn-off to one dock after another, Gopal wonders how long this is going to take, how long before they reach the meeting point, wherever that is.

They pass a tiny lane, and Aurangzeb grunts softly. Gourangzeb grunts back. He slows down and goes into a wide turn, the old machine swallowing the whole breadth of road before it faces the way they have come. Then he turns into the lane and putters along until they come to a dead end. Slung like a hard curtain between the low houses on either side is a high wall blocking off the road. Someone has built a little shelter of bamboo and tarpaulin against the wall. Gopal can see light from beyond the wall shining on shards of glass cemented into the top and the silhouette of barbed wire playing on top of that.

Gourangzeb switches off the engine as they roll towards the wall. He stops right up against the shelter. Aurangzeb pulls out a torch as he gets off and goes inside the shelter. Gopal hears the sound of something creaking and some bricks being shifted. After a few moments, Aurangzeb pokes his head out from under the tarpaulin and nods. Gourangzeb looks at Gopal, gesturing to the back of the motorcycle.

'Get behind. From here we push,' he says, gripping the handlebars and leaning into them.

DECORUM

'Hickory,' says Wart One.

Kedar's tie is hanging oddly tonight, and he knows it. Both too tight and too loose, same as a dhoti that should fall off but won't. Once he understands what the Warts are saying he doesn't like it, and he doesn't like himself for understanding.

'What? How's that again?' says Wart Two.

'Dickory, old chap, dickory.'

'Oh. Oh yeff.' Swigs at his gin, wonder he isn't chewing up the glass itself. 'Rhyming, are we tonight, Johnny?'

'Hick… hickory,' trips out Wart One.

'Swallowed, I'd say swallowed. Definitely,' says Wart Two.

'Yes, but what? Swallowed, yes, I told you that a minute ago, but what?'

'Dock. The cat swallowed the—'

Wart One leans forward and smashes his glass against the side table in triumph. 'Caaaaat! Good lord, Harry, good heavens, *cat*? I refuse to accept—'

'Well, you can refuse on, but what's wrong with cat? Obvious. Bloody obvious.'

'Fine… all right… cat… Now look, Harry, can I possibly drag you out of the nineteenth centu—'

Kedar is dying to say it. Say it loud. Shout it. But he hides in the covering of his own language. He turns the 'ss' sound to a 'sh' and tries to make up his own rhymes, playing first with 'ghushi' and then 'chushi'.

Wart One shouts. 'Good god man, remember our Yankee cousins!'

'Cousins? Bloody recalcitrant children, you mean. But, but what's that got to do with…'

'What do *they* call it, old boy?'

'Oh! Oh! Got it! I HAVE GOT IT! The—'

Something about the way she turns her head away, trying to bite her lip, that tall girl. Glass shifting from right hand to left, and then back. Huge effort not to break the stem while holding in her sides trying to quell whole mutinies of laughter.

Rudro, older than Kedar biologically by five years, and many more in terms of wisdom, has told him that the memshahebs used to be shocked by this kind of behaviour not two years ago. But now that the war has its hooks into everyone, standards are shifting. Falling one by one like the cities of Europe. 'The days of Great British Rule – numbered,' Rudro has pronounced, 'and the days of Famous British Decorum – gone.' *Shesh. Khotom.* Finished. Therefore, the tall girl barely managing to control herself at all this lewdness.

'Got it, have we, Harry, old son?'

'Yes!'

'Yes? Right. Well, say it then.' Wart One lowers his voice into a hunter's crouch.

Wart Two marries the glass to his mouth and takes it away. He wipes an invisible fleck from the side of his face and tries to begin. He stops, realizing he is facing the wrong way, locates Wart One and turns to him, conducting his finger as if speaking to a child. The people in the vicinity, tall girl included, drop their voices, pretending not to listen, but everyone wants to hear what Wart Two has to say.

'Hickory,' he repeats after a long pause, caning the air with his finger.

'Yes,' says Wart One with dramatically false patience.

'Dickory.' Wart Two gleeful, as he once again fits the second piece into the first.

'Yes.'

'Dock.' Theorem almost in place now.

'Splendid. Do go on.'

'The... the... PUSSY SWALLOWED THE CAT!'

There is a deadly pause before the massed laughter smashes around the sofa and the low table, reverberating off the nearby wall. As the lampshades shake, the men who've seen action almost start to duck, even though they know the noise comes from inside themselves. Above the crash of hilarity, Wart One's voice keeps alternating '*Caaaaaat! Harry! Caaaaaat! Harry!*', wailing out the two words like an air-raid siren. Kedar finds himself doubled forward, the tip of his errant tie now licking the froth from someone's abandoned beer mug. And then his eyes drag up, stretching as far as they will go, searching for the tall girl's eyes. With a shock, he realizes he has found them.

She can't help but look back at him over the wall of the hand she has pressed across her face, even as her body heaves with the effort to bring itself into line. There is a couple just behind her, a captain in Kumaon Regiment uniform, and a woman with short brown hair and short pink sleeves, both bent towards each other, foreheads touching, as if involved in some latest Negro dancing, making no attempt to curb their amusement, shelling huge gusts of hot breath into each other's mouths. Kedar sees this from the corner of some spare eye, his main vision locked up by the pair of blues he's looking into. He forces himself to look away. His glance falls on something shining where it shouldn't be – a tiny shard from Wart One's smashed glass hanging on the curving blade of a leaf of a large lily plant, sharp diamond against bright green, oscillating, held there by some flimsy treaty between gravity and the ceiling fan.

She piggybacks on his look and catches the shard as well. For a moment, this tiny circus of surface tension hypnotizes them both, holding their twinned focus to the exclusion of all that is around them. The ebb and flow of party babble, the clinking of last drinks as people begin to construct their goodnights, the increased shuffle of waiters clearing away, the enveloping net of tobacco smoke and perfume, all get pushed into the wings as they watch the long leaf tremble, as they wait for the broken glass to slide off. Tall Girl still standing where she had been, next to the fireplace, and Kedar still bent forward, moored by his tie to the beer mug.

As he stares at the lily, Kedar feels another gaze nudging his own, and he flicks his eyes back at the girl and straightens up. The tip of his tie leaves a small trail of beer foam on the table, and suddenly they are both looking at it, and then again at each other, and then they are roaring.

The crowd having dispersed, Wart One is now standing a few yards away. The sudden tail of noise jerks his head around. Andrew's girl bent double, laughing. With a local. The little blighter now standing up and doing something with his tie. Cackling like a chimpanzee and doing something obscene with his bloody tie. Actually wringing drink out of it into a beer mug. Enough.

As Kedar works his way around the low table, still looking at the girl, he meets an unexpected obstacle. Wart One standing right up against him, breathing gin down into his face.

'What's so funny, chum?'

'I beg your pardon?' Kedar struggles to understand both the question and the extreme proximity. He tries to look behind him to see if he is blocking the man's path.

'Don't you beg-pardon me, chum. And look at me when I am talking to you.'

Kedar looks up into the man's eyes. He tries to put some space between them before answering, but the man sticks to him as he steps back. Kedar can now feel the edge of the table against the backs of his calves.

'I'm terribly sorry, but—'

Tall Girl has now stopped laughing. He can see her from the corner of his eye, just behind Wart One's shoulder, and it's as if someone has put a different face on her – a mask of indignation and panic. The panic transfers to Kedar as he begins to grasp what is happening. The girl is now standing very close to them and, by some trickery, her arm slides in between Kedar's neck and Wart One's uniform buttons. A long white arm trying to push Wart One back.

'Listen here,' she says, and Wart One looks at her as if wondering what she is still doing there.

'I didn't like the way this fellow was, you know...' Wart One suddenly has a tone of brisk reason, as if talking to a youngster. Something inside the tall girl hardens further, and her arm becomes more determined.

'I'm sorry, but I don't understand what you're objecting to.' Her voice has a challenging edge now. The man yields, moves back a couple of steps. Kedar notices the girl has dark blonde hair but dark eyelashes. And quite a strong arm for a woman – he can feel the print of her elbow on his Adam's apple.

Wart One now turns slightly towards the girl, his body much more controlled, arms clasped behind his back, but his anger now up several notches. His moustache does a little slapstick jig as he bites out his words.

'I'm terribly sorry, Miss – do forgive me, forget your name – but we do have to maintain some form here. Bad enough having to mingle with them. Don't mind putting up with it for the duration. But can't have them rolling about in the presence of ladies, slapping their knees as if they are at one of their own... you know?'

'No, I *don't*, actually!' The girl's shoulders square back and her eyes bore into the man's. 'And I didn't see anyone aside from you rolling about slapping their knees. Given your behaviour, this gentleman and I were amused, and we have every right to be so!'

Wart One steps back as if he has been slapped in the face.

Another uniformed gora bounces up to them, this one wearing a funny topi on his head, and Kedar quickly calculates his chances of escaping. But – even as he concludes that he is now in for it – an anger ripened by full understanding shuts a door inside him. Can't have them rolling about. Put up for the duration. Concernment for personal bodily safety aspects is muchly disappearing with alacritiousness. Koro ja korbey, shala, I'll give you slapping knees. Only one problem now – how to fight back freely without hurting the girl, her with the arm and the eyes. How to fight while keeping her laughter safe?

But the funny-topi gora is different from Wart One. 'Hullo, hullo, hullo! Immy! Johnny! You've met, haven't you?' Smiling, entwining arm with Tall Girl's arm, not something the mem-girl is fully comfortable with, but not fully uncomfortable either, Kedar notes. Funny Topi looks at Kedar and nods. 'Don't believe I've had the pleasure,' he sticks his free hand out, 'Andrew Hillcott, at the moment in the employ of 2 Fusiliers. As major. Extremely daft unit, they also put up with Johnny here!'

Kedar makes himself shake the gora's hand. 'Lahiri. How do you do.'

'Lahiri? Surely there must be more to it?'

'Kedar Nath Lahiri,' Kedar says, and then shortens it to digestible: 'Kedar Lahiri.'

'Kedar. Rhymes exactly with radar, doesn't it?' says Hillcott brightly. Tall Girl cuts in before Kedar can reply.

'I'm Imogen Snell, how do you do,' she says, offering her hand quickly.

Much hesitatiousness, but again, Kedar puts his own hand forward, meets the fingers, careful not to clasp the palm, exactly as Rudro has instructed him, and then kicks himself because he can immediately feel it is the wrong handshake. Feel from her touch that it should have been firm and full, great cities of Europe falling, the meek brushing of fingers not right given the shared laugh and everything afterwards. He wants to shake her hand again, hold it a bit longer, like in the movies, but he knows this is the last time he will have the touch, so he tries to put it out of his mind.

'Well, Andrew, I'll carry on while you make friends here.' Johnny the Wart turns his bulk away, dragging his bristling behind him.

Before anyone else can speak, Kedar gets it out, uncaring whether it's the right thing to say, anything to make up for that stupid, tepid, handshake. 'Miss Snell. Thank you for that... intervention.'

Hillcott turns to the Imogen girl. 'What happened, Immy? Everything all right? I sensed some...'

'Your chap Johnny and his chum were making utter fools of themselves. Everybody present was laughing. Your Johnny didn't approve of Mr... La-hiri and myself laughing in each other's vicinity.'

'What!'

'Yes. A lady of European provenance shouldn't be seen sharing jollity with a... er...' Something in Kedar falters as he sees the tall girl trying to find the correct words, trying, he realizes, not because she cares a jot about how he feels, but because she is at great pains to say the right thing for herself, '... with a native gentleman.'

'That's such utter nonsense!' Andrew takes off his funny topi and turns to Kedar. 'Terribly sorry, old chap, but I do hope you know that not all of us share Johnny's attitude. As far as I'm concerned, you and I can laugh together any time!'

Even though the words are addressed to him, Kedar can feel that it's entirely about the man and the woman, about whatever is going on between them. He knows they will now say goodbye, turn away, and forget him very quickly. His brain lassoes back the truth well before it escapes him – But it's not *you* I want to laugh with. 'Well, that's good to know,' he says instead, and realizes he is smiling as he says it. A full, natural grin, meeting the man's eyes first and then the girl's for a beat longer, erasing, he hopes, all traces of the handshake.

Imogen is caught on the wrong foot by the smile, suddenly slightly flustered, not quite sure why. She turns to Andrew. 'And now, if you'll drive me home, Andrew. Time for this spinster to go to bed.'

It is precisely the wrongest thing she could have said, but it's out now, irretrievably in the middle. Kedar tries to align the word 'spinster' with this bright energy standing in front of him and fails. He looks again for escape, but the other two are blocking his path to the entrance hall and there is no polite way to say goodbye and walk away at the same time. Andrew, his good cheer gone, searches for what not to say, for a bridge to move them all away from this sudden unnecessary intimacy, *home* and *spinster* ringing in his ears like two out-of-tune piano keys. Imogen looks away to the people leaving, hoping desperately that someone will wave to her, give her the excuse she needs to go.

Kedar feels the hand on his elbow just as Andrew finds his voice.

'Can we give you a lift somewhere, old chap?'

The voice that answers for Kedar is soft, but very clear.

'I was hoping, actually, Mr Kedar would drive me back to my hotel.'

Imogen snaps around to look. Dark hair, not black but very dark, tied in a knot at the back. Brown eyes, dark mischief. Small built, beautiful, not Indian. European. Greek? Spanish? No, skin too white, something further north. Deep maroon dress, two years out of fashion, simple pearl necklace, simple but jolly expensive, eyebrows a bit heavy, nose a touch too sharp, older than Imogen, twenty-seven or eight perhaps, but beautiful. As beautiful as the little man, perhaps even more so, and the two as together as toast and marmalade.

'How d'you do,' says Andrew.

'How do you do,' Imogen echoes.

'Hauduyudu,' says the woman.

'Ah, here you are,' says Kedar, knowing it is the right thing to say. Then, with a strange pleasure driving his confidence, he begins, for the first time in his life, to introduce three Europeans to each other. 'This is Miss Attali, and this is Miss... Snell, and Mr Hillcoat.'

He feels the hand leave his jacket sleeve.

'Hillcott,' Andrew corrects as he shakes hands.

'Eva Attali, hullo. Just Eva. Please.'

'Imogen.' Bending forward, shooing away her height. 'Pleasure.'

Kedar notices the two women's fingers link and separate, a tiny ruby ring sparkling, Eva's, no palms involved at all.

Andrew cuts across the women, talking to Kedar, 'So, you're driving, are you?'

'Yes, I've got a car, but very kind of you to offer.'

'Not at all.' Andrew takes Imogen's elbow. 'We'll say goodnight, then.'

'So nice to meet you,' says Imogen firmly, a sensible look taking over her face, no hint of a smile. She lets Andrew's hand steer her away.

The fingers are back on Kedar's elbow, and he likes them there. Eva waits for the other two to go out of earshot before she speaks.

'She is tall, the girl.'

'Very tall. Must be about five feet ten inches or so.'

'Please. I don't understand this feet-inches. How much in centimetres?'

Kedar racks his brain. 'I'm not sure. I can tell you the next time we meet.'

'Then we are still talking about the English girl and her how tall?'

'No... no, I mean... no, definitely not, just that if you wanted to know how to calculate...'

'I was calculate that I don't see you tonight, calcula*ting*, that I *would-not-be-seeing*—'

Something makes Kedar reckless, and he blurts out, 'I wasn't planning to come. I only came because I was hoping to see you.'

'Calculating.' Eva smiles with the small victory over English.

'Yes, calculating.'

They start to move towards the main doors, Kedar oblivious to the looks being shot at them, black man with white woman, Eva very aware, moving even closer to him as they reach the steps.

'I've parked over there.' Kedar is startled at himself, with the ease with which he has said it, no hesitation, no doubts. Despite his earlier admission, he hopes nothing in his manner will tell Eva that he has looked for her all evening and then given up on her with no small despair. He leads the way out of the portico towards the parking area, avoiding the cars slowly growling out to the gates.

They walk past two officers leaning on the bonnet of an army car. One of them is laughing hysterically.

'Good god, man! Did you see the crowds? Some... bloody... *poet!* But you'd think it was their king or pope or something! Some poet writing in *lingo!*'

'*Lingo!*' repeats the second man drunkenly, and Kedar recognizes Wart Two, Johnny's chum from inside, Harry. 'Bloody thousands of them mucking up the place with their howling. Wouldn't have thought that many of them could *read*, you know!'

Kedar stiffens. He thinks about it for a moment and then he does it. Says it in a loud and clear voice.

'Hickory dickory dock. The pussy swallowed the cock.'

'What?' asks Eva, totally at a loss, but before Kedar can say anything, Wart Two jerks up from the bonnet and lurches towards Kedar.

'I *say!* I say, what did you just say?' He nearly falls as he makes his way up to Kedar. 'Dear... fffellow, could you possibly repeat...' He tries to put his hand on Kedar's shoulder, but Kedar keeps himself just out of reach, keeps walking as he repeats the ditty.

'Hickory dickory dock. The pussy swallowed—'

'YESSS! GOT IT, DAMN IT! COCK!' Wart Two turns away, heading for the lights of the club. 'Now where's that blighter Johnny? JOHNNY! WHERE THE HELL ARE YOU? I'VE GOT IT! I'VE *GOT* IT, YOU LITTLE BASTARD!'

Kedar opens the passenger door for Eva and slams it shut after she gets in. He gets in himself and starts the car. Eva leans forward to examine the wide grin on his face.

'This is joke, yes?'

'Yes,' replies Kedar happily, reversing the car.

'Some big joke?'

'Not big... just... satisfying.' Kedar spins the tyres over the gravel and sends the convertible crunching towards the gates.

'And you will explain to me this, yes?'

'Well...'

Eva puts an insistent hand on Kedar's arm. 'You will explain,' she repeats.

'Well, if you promise not to be offended.'

'What is... offen-dead?'

Kedar turns on to the road. There is hardly any traffic, and he presses down on the pedal, releasing power.

'I will explain,' he shouts over the roar of the engine. 'But first, where are we going?'

Eva reaches behind her head and undoes the pins holding her knot. Her hair catches the wind and opens like a pirate ship's mainsail. She looks at Kedar appraisingly.

'We go to my hotel,' she says after a long pause.

'Which hotel?'

Eva sends her arms up above the windshield, her palms cupped for air. For a while, she says nothing. Kedar repeats the question.

'Which hotel? Ah. The best one,' Eva replies, calling out over the noise of the engine.

'And which one is the best one?'

'Actually, the best one is the which one you are staying in that night.'

'And tonight?'

'Tonight? Tonight, Great Eastern Hotel.'

Old Elko could often be genuinely courteous, but in a way that Indians like me – people of my age – find hard to be.

'No offense, dear boy, no offense intended at all, but when you go on and on about your Tagore... you do realize he spent his entire life in his father's hotel, so to speak?'

Hotel, old French word meaning large house or large hospitable mansion, also connected to hospital and hostel. The name Tagore basically anglicized from the north Indian Thakur. So the Tagores, a wealthy and illustrious family of nineteenth-century Calcutta, with vast land holdings in East Bengal and lucrative business interests in Calcutta; into which the future poet, Nobel laureate and giant of the Bengal Renaissance Rabindranath was born in 1861, in the family's large mansion at Jorasanko in north Calcutta.

When someone asks a jobless young Bengali man what he's doing with his life, a common quip is, 'Oh, I'm just staying at my father's hotel.' Now Rabindranath was born in his father's very plush hotel and died there as well. Across his life, it was one of his many houses, and by the time he passed away, it was he who had become the patriarch hotel owner, with dozens of children, nephews, nieces, grandchildren and other walking ancillaries as 'tenants'. Jorasanko, which we could with only miniscule irreverence call Hotel Tagore.

So, Hotel Tagore, or Architecture and its Uses: Elko and Missus are the ones who told me this story from the late nineteenth century, about Tagore's older brother, the oldest of Rabindranath's brothers, Jyotirindranath. After a certain age, Jyoti, apparently, would never leave the sprawling Tagore mansion. During an illness, a doctor came to examine Jyoti and sternly instructed him to get some fresh air. 'You don't have to go for a walk if you don't want to, but at least get into an open ricksha, not in one of your closed horse carriages, and go for a ride! You must do this every day, without fail!' Jyotirindranath, a highly intelligent man – as were most of the Tagores – understood the wisdom of the doctor's instructions, he understood the self-interest involved. Duly, a ricksha-walla was summoned to the mansion and he arrived, pulling his contraption behind him. He was asked how much he would charge to take the Babu for an hour-long spin every evening. Once an agreement was reached, the servants swiftly put ropes around the ricksha and hauled it up to the roof. The ricksha-walla was taken upstairs, where he found his ricksha with Jyotirindranath waiting next to it. 'Babu doesn't want to go for a ride?' asked the mystified man. 'Of course I do, you idiot,' snapped Jyoti, climbing on to the seat, 'why, otherwise, would I go to so much trouble?' As the man gaped, the zamindar babu pointed to the flat terrace stretching for three hundred yards. 'Drive me,' he said. 'Drive me up and down. The doctor says I need fresh air and there is no fresher air in all of Calcutta than on my terrace.'

'No fresher air!' Old Elko's body starts to rack with laughter, and he puts his drink down so as not to spill it. '*That's* the bloody Bengali zamindar class for you! Not that little brother Robi ever wrote about this, mind you!'

'Oh yes, the jomi'dars,' I say, picking up my own drink from where it's nestling in the mess of wires next to the reel-to-reel.

She's in the kitchen, attempting to put together some pretence of a meal. She has the radio on in there, Tom Jones yelling out 'Help Yourself', but she has sharp hearing. The clattering pauses and she totters in, glass swaying in one hand, trying to dance to the song with some quaint old swing movements.

'Another zemeendar story, is it?' She trips but somehow manages to land on the arm of his armchair, drink almost intact. She puts her fingers in his hair and toggles his head like the gear shift of a car. 'And you? Aren't we a bit of a zemeendar ourselves, darling?'

'Don't darling me, darling. Why did you stop making dinner? I'm sure our guest is famished.'

She ignores him and sings along with the radio, her hand now stroking his hair, her voice completely tuneless.

The greatest wealth
in the world,
can never buy
what I can give...

Thinking back, it all blurs in my head, all the colours get mixed up. Sometimes it's she who tells that particular story, sometimes it's the radio that's on, sometimes the music is actually on the record player or the tape recorder, sometimes the tape recorder is that bloody Marantz reel-to-reel he loved so much and sometimes it's the cassette deck I gifted them a few months before the end, I can't be sure. There is the old man, meaning Jyotirindranath, at the end of the nineteenth century, being trundled back and forth by the ricksha-walla across his darkening terrace as Tom Jones frightens the birds from the trees, the rattle of the ricksha, the slap of the ricksha-walla's bare feet bleeding slightly on the terrace grit, sometimes it's the smell of spring flowers from their garden, where does it all come from and where does it eventually go?

About that night, I remember clearly the smell of the food she put on the table. We were, all three of us, completely drunk by then, but the smell still came through and it was not totally bad, especially given she was not one of the world's natural cooks.

'Voila, messieurs. It's not Maxim's at the Great Eastern, it's not... Chef Beauraison, but it should be edible.'

'Bonnemaison, darling, with an N and an M,' he corrects.

'*Tu n'as pas raison et tu n'as pas du maison!*' she slurs into her chair from a standing position. You don't have logic and you don't have a house. The 'even' after the 'don't' is implied, but only because I now know them a bit.

'Your French should... be left... in your pantry cupboard where it serves you best.'

'You, zemeendear, leave my panty cupboard alone!' She's found red wine from somewhere and filled three mismatched glasses. Those I remember: one classic French tulip tumbler, a straight water glass and a proper crystal goblet, naturally for herself.

She attacks our glasses, 'Sante! Chinchin!'

By now the radio's off and he's singing along with some old music on the Marantz.

'I say, do you remember the first time we...'

She takes a swig and speaks out the words, 'Savoy. The home of sweet romance. Savoy, it wins you at a glance.'

He's better at singing, a deep voice that belies the constipatory tendencies of his class and social background.

'Your old form, just like a clinging vine,' he croons, sounding far more Tom Jones than Ella, 'Your lips, so warm and sweet as wine.'

4

SURRENDER

Three distinct smells. She can suddenly smell three different kinds of water, and that trips her up. One: water trapped in foliage, cheeky, fresh, green, wet, *hickory*. Two: damp masonry, drenched bricks and earth, with something slightly metallic – probably car, she's not sure – all mixed, but the smell liquid, *dickory*, trapped heat escaping. Three: the rain tapping a light Morse on skin, not only her skin, but other skin as well, rather nice skin, welcome skin, whisky skin, warm.

'*Diddle*,' she says, quietly, mainly to the third hand she has grown from somewhere. New hand that's managed, somehow, to unbutton the top of her dress. She's trying to tell this new hand, step by step, the whole nursery rhyme she's convinced she can remember. But the hand, not really listening, is managing now to slip her left bra strap up over the hillock of her shoulder and off down her arm without bothering to fiddle with the clasp. Which is cleverly good, because her back is pressed into the corner made by the door and the seat, and difficult to reach. Large new hand, knowing the shortcuts, helping her breast out of its cup and into the open dark where she can feel the rain properly. A drop falls, a small explosion just missing her nipple, and she tenses for the next one, but now there is a cloud of dark hair covering her, right under her chin. And now there is heat, and a wet brush of teeth which makes her push her foot against the floor as if she was stamping on the brakes. Her shoulder blades are hard against the seat and the door, and the mouth works to make her arch her back. One of her original hands is now on the head, and she knows she can push the head away or pull it down further into her, but she can't decide.

There are two different kinds of rain running down her, right down to her ankles, one falling from above, through the branches of the tree, and one from somewhere else, and there's actually not much to decide. Just the question of what she now has to do. To not stop the pleasure.

To honour the whole idea of give and take, of fair is fair. Of goose and... gander.

There's a small current of tongue now, coming out of the mouth, invisible, active and dangerous, and it heads unerringly for its quarry, flicking her nipple, once, thrice, *dish ran away with the spoon*, and her hand is now clawing into his neck, harder than she knows, and she can feel his mouth gasping now, not in pleasure, his nose twisting away from her, 'Can't breathe, darling...' Andrew surfaces from his hair, 'not quite so hard, not quite so... but don't...'

It's difficult to see his face in the faint throw of the lamp post which is far behind them, at the corner of the lane, but she can make out that he's smiling, and that his forehead is sending tears down into his lovely eyebrows and into his eyes and from there down his flushed cheeks into the corners of his mouth. The mouth that's now diving slowly back to her breast.

Imogen stops him at the last possible moment, pushes his head up.

'Andrew?' she whispers, her voice not quite doing its job, 'Let me look at you for a moment.'

He looks at her. *Chehera*. Face. Or... *mukhda*, 'meaning not only *face* but sometimes *facet* also', as her Hindi teacher has said, she can't exactly remember when, not a serious part of the lesson, almost to himself, but now it comes back to her. Andrew. Andrew's face. Hand, Andrew's, in her hand, and she's kissing it, placing it back on herself, then drawing his face down until it becomes hair again, mouse.

Ran up. The clock. But there's no clock now, just a ruck of drenched skirt, and the hand now between her legs, not quite docking, a lone finger playing her open and then working firmly and calmly, trying to reach her spine from the inside.

Her upper left arm is slightly sore, she realizes, from pushing so hard against the car door. It's a wonder the door's still holding, a wonder that they haven't spilled out on to the ground, a wonder the pleasure that she hasn't felt since... Paris, where she thought she'd left it behind, the pleasure, for good, along with the small ivory comb Aunt Amanda – she feels the warm floor of the car through her sock and it's a wonder where her shoe's gone now – the hand now suddenly an old hand at her body, and she leaves it to do what it will and throws her head back over the seat, eyes half closed, a queue of chappals dancing behind an invisible Pied Piper, chappals and shoes, untenanted by feet, dancing-sliding for some reason on a bridge of ice, and she tries to remember the rhyme she was trying to remember and then a pinprick of panic through the pleasure, a sudden wall of thought – that they've left a narrow trail of slippers, like an oil leak. Head still over the seat, she opens her eyes to check the road behind them, opens her eyes just in time to see them coming.

There is a sound that usually precedes, that's missing. The hard tap of their sticks on the ground, and occasionally a call, like a mahout calling an elephant. She is moving even as she realizes why they're being silent – because they've spotted the car in the shadows, dark car with a mess of movement in it, and they know what they want, and they don't want to warn. 'Andrew! Quick! Darwaans!' she hisses, pushing head away with one hand, grabbing his elbow with the other. Andrew takes a moment to react, still rolling in a cocoon of whisky, but then he sits up fast, drawing a small cry of pain from Imogen as his fingers come out too quickly. He looks around, frowns, and then smiles.

'Blighters.' He reaches for his kepi and puts it on, still looking at the pair of guards who are about ten yards away. The two men hear the voice first, a gora voice, and that slows them down. Then they see the hat go on the head and they stop completely, sticks frozen a few inches from the ground. Not only a gora, a miletri gora.

Andrew turns back and reaches out a reassuring hand to Imogen. 'It's all right. I've got the buggers. Take your time.' Imogen doesn't take her time. She is bent double trying to keep herself out of sight, stuffing herself back into her clothes. Damn, why is it more difficult to put breast back in bra without unhooking than it is to take it out, damn! There, done, not comfortable, but all buttoned and done. And now the bloody camis which are half-off, how to...

'I'm just going to leave them,' she says firmly, mostly to herself, having realized that they are not visible under her now corrected skirt. As she is about to straighten, she sees the almost empty bottle of White

Label poking out from under the seat and has a flash of inspiration. She comes up into view, triumphantly holding up the whisky.

'Here it is!' she says brightly to Andrew, 'I knew it hadn't gone walkies!'

Andrew grins as he starts the car and begins to reverse it. He drives straight back, slowly, imperiously, making no allowance for the guards standing in the middle of the lane. The men skip aside and forehead their hands in salute as the car rolls past. Imogen waves the bottle back at them as if it's a trophy. Andrew gives them a brief, hard stare that pulls their heads down, lowering their eyes.

'Bastards,' says Andrew, lighting up as they drive away, 'wanted a wee little look, the dirty bastards.'

Imogen bursts out laughing again. 'Yes, bastards... *filthy* bastards... wanting a look at... another pair of dirty bastards!' With a lewd assurance that surprises her, she pushes herself up against the seat, hikes up her dress and deftly pulls up her knickers. She settles back and smooths the wet fabric over her knees.

Andrew's cigarette dies with a wet hiss, and he flicks it away. 'Oh do come on, Miss Spinstersham... now, don't start telling me I took advantage of you!' He throws his face up to the skies, letting the thick rain smack into his face, briefly letting the car go where it will before looking down and reining it back to the road. A tram passes them, going the other way, silent, lights out, ghosting back to its depot. Imogen glances over at Andrew, his head up again, the rain drumming lightly on the kepi, trying to shake off the whisky. She mulls over the word.

Advantage. As in tennis. Or in quaint introductions. I believe you have the. Of me. No, no undue advantage was taken, sir, in fact, it was exactly as much as I wanted tonight, it was perfect. She realizes she has spoken the last three words out loud and kicks herself, but not too hard.

Andrew grins, deliberately not taking the point. 'Perfect? D'you mean those blighters arriving when they did? Just as we were—'

'No, Andrew, you know exactly what I do mean, so don't you fish for more.'

'I won't, darling, I won't. What I will fish for is another evening not too far into—'

'Yes, well, that. Yes, I might jolly well take that bait, but only if you promise to do away with that ridiculous hat.'

Andrew takes off the kepi and jams it down on Imogen's head. 'There! Done!'

Imogen yanks it off and sends it spinning away into the night. Andrew makes a pretence of trying to catch it before it disappears and then he shakes his head. 'Oh dear, Tuggy boyo won't be pleased with me for that. I'll have to tell him it was for the greatest cause of all.'

'Indeed,' says Imogen happily as she stretches out her arms and presses her palms against the windscreen.

'Not that he'll mind too much, I don't think,' Andrew continues. 'He's got a proper Luftwaffe oberst's one now. Shot him down over Kent, then landed and sprang him from a bunch of local pitchfork merchants. Jerry wasn't half grateful, I'm told.'

'So he gave him *his* funny hat?'

'Exactly, happened to be carrying it with him by some fluke.'

Andrew continues to describe Tuggy's encounter with the German pilot, but Imogen's head is doing odd things again and her mind sways away from his chatter. Suddenly, she feels his touch on her body again but something about it isn't right. Not Andrew's hand running through her hair, different hand. And a different mouth. She shudders without meaning to, and the whisky comes welling up, almost recapturing her tongue.

'Funniest thing was – you know how our boys call them *bandits*? You know, when you're bobbing about in your Spit and you spot German planes you call out "bandits at nine o'clock" or whatever?'

'Yes?' Imogen forces herself to concentrate, anything to move her stomach away from the urge to throw up.

'Well, what d'you imagine the Luftwaffe call the RAF?'

'What? What do they call them, Andrew?'

'Indianer!'

'What?'

'Indians! As in cowboys and Indians! Us being the Indians and those bastards fancying themselves as bloody cowboys! The bloody nerve!'

Not Andrew's hand but a coloured one, brown, smaller, doing things it has no business doing, taking... advantage... yes, no other word for it, unless perhaps it was 'liberties'...

Andrew stops in front of her gate, still mimicking the Germans.

'*Achtung, achtung, achtung!* Indianz at zixoklock, *zwei* Indians at zixoklock, *achtung!* Und *anozzer* vun in ffront ovuzz!'

As the guard runs up to the gates, Andrew discovers his steering wheel has gun-buttons and opens up on the man, '*Rat-a-tat, rat-a-tat, rata-tata-tata-tata-tat!*'

The guard rolls the gates wide, leaps aside and salutes. Then he stands there, stock still and expressionless, watching as the young memsahib opens her door and bends forward to get her face as close to the ground as possible.

BACK STAGE

'So, did you see them take him? Did they go past you?' Niru's father looks down at her from the perch of his chair.

'Arre, in the end we couldn't see anything!' Niru forgets to swallow as she remembers the outrage, and flecks of rice fly out of her full mouth. 'Titir had the clever idea to go up on a chhat. When we went up on top of the building, we could see everything, the road, the crowds on the side, everything!' Niru swallows and pauses before reaching for more food. She is really hungry, but should she eat like a monster on a day like this?

'Eat, ma, eat a bit more. You've obviously not eaten all day.' Her mother quite firmly ladles more potato-rice and dal on to Niru's thaala and adds a bit of pickle.

'We thought we'd found a good place, but just as we sensed they were bringing him, coming up Harrison Road, suddenly a hundred more people appeared on the rooftop and just... pushed us aside! I don't know where they came from! Titir accidentally bit a man's arm as he shoved her, but he didn't even notice! You know, like when your back's to the sea and a wave engulfs you. Like that.'

'A hundred people?' Niru's father folds his legs into the seat of his chair.

'Baba! All right, dozens, dozens of them, thiik achhey? And there were thousands on the streets! Even lakhs!'

'I believe you,' Niru's baba says, using English.

'Arre, what difference does it make whether you believe her or not? She braved the crowds and went. You didn't even go.' Ma turns to Niru. 'I wanted to go, but Baba convinced me it would be a waste of time. So we sat here and he made me read out passages from *Rakta Karabi* instead.'

Niru rearranges her own crossed legs on the floor, leans forwards and eats some more before replying.

'It's all right. Going through all that trouble for a few seconds of a glimpse. In our case, not even that! Baba *was right.*'

'I am often right, if not always right.' Again, in English.

'Chhaado toh, *always right*! He actually wanted to go, you know? Started getting his eyes wet as I was reading...' Ma takes away Niru's empty thaala. 'There's nothing sweet, ma. All the sweet shops were closed, and anyway...'

'Don't want. I only ate because I didn't eat all day, otherwise...' Niru leans forward and starts to clear up bits of food from the floor with the side of her palm.

'Fasting won't bring him back, sadly.' Baba turns to his desk and puts away the copy of *Rakta Karabi*.

'Telling others!' Ma snorts. 'Himself has hardly eaten all day.'

'I last saw Gurudeb for a full ten minutes when he came backstage after a show at Star. That was enough. He appreciated my work, that was enough.'

Both Niru and her mother have heard the story many times, but they both know Baba needs to tell it again tonight. Niru quickly gets up and fetches the jhaadu to finish sweeping the floor. Niru's mother squats at the washing square in the kitchen and rinses the thaala under the tap. Neither needs to prompt Baba, all they need to do is get on with what they are doing. He's well within earshot. Uninterrupted, they know he'll continue.

'What was it, Sumi, eight years ago? No, 1934, so seven. 1934. Jogen-babu's production of *Chitrangada*. At Star Theatre, which was unusual, because they were, even then, always fierce about protecting dates for the commercial plays. We only got it because it was Gurudeb's own *Chitrangada*, and because of Jogen-babu's clout, also because Mallika Debi put no little pressure, she had the main role. In any case, we had tried some new things with the sets and lights and weren't sure how Gurudeb would appreciate them... We were all quite nervous when we heard he was coming for the third evening.'

'I remember you didn't eat much that day either,' Ma calls out from the kitchen.

'I wasn't home all day, we did two whole stage rehearsals again, so how could you know what I ate or didn't eat?'

'You didn't eat all day. I know. I remember. I brought you some jhaalmuri when you were skulking at the back with your notebook, and you put it near your feet and forgot about it.'

Niru moves to the bedroom to make things ready for sleep. She checks that the mosquito net is properly tucked in under the mattress of the big bed before rolling out her own mattress on the floor. 'Ma?' Niru's mother calls out. 'Yes, Ma?' Niru calls back. 'Listen, it's quite cold tonight, so why don't you sleep with us in the big bed?' Niru hesitates, but realizes tonight's not the night to refuse her mother. 'It's not that cold, Ma, but all right.' She rolls up her mattress and pushes it back to its daytime station against the wall.

'Well, the performance went smoothly. And the audience's applause was full, you know, you can sense it when the clapping is sincere, but that didn't mean anything to us that night.

Niru remembers going with her mother to visit Baba after school, tiptoeing into whichever theatre he was rehearsing in on the day. From the hard glare of the street into a mysterious, half-lit cave. Backstage, the whiff of make-up while passing the green rooms, actors' voices chattering, fencing, joking, someone practising an accent, the same phrase over and over again. The odd smell of incense as one leading actress prayed to her deities, the famous face, beatific in worship, seen in a mirror through a door left narrowly ajar. In the theatre, the musty smell of leather from the rows of empty seats sweeping up into darkness, the banks of cream-coloured fans jutting out from the side walls, like large metal insects poking in their heads from the street outside. Through the wings, a black-faced Othello, large as a buffalo, pacing up and down on stage, practising his looking murderously at an empty bed. Above her head, the lights heating up, warming the paint on the set sliders. In the light beams, dust motes hanging in the air like tiny creatures.

It used to upset her that the audience couldn't see her father working, that they hardly knew his name, but she would console herself by thinking that these dust motes were alive, souls of people either dead or yet to be born, and they were her father's real audience. Finding Baba in the shadowed maze was always a game she played silently. During a stage rehearsal, he could be anywhere, crouching in the last row of the balcony seats, leaning against a wall on the side, or perched on a high platform in the wings, his machaan, as he called it, his hunting platform, from where he would signal to the boys handling the dimmers, sometimes with his hands, other times by switching his torch on and off in a sequence.

'After the show, we waited nervously as someone, I think Jogen-babu it must have been, brought Gurudeb backstage. After congratulating Jogen-babu and all the actors, when he came around to me, he asked, "So, Niladri, when are you moving from the stage to the cinema?" At first, I thought he was being sarcastic, though I was pleased he remembered my name. I kept looking down, I couldn't lift my gaze from my feet. And his sandals, poking out from under that long gown. Then I heard that thin, reedy laugh of his. "Why so quiet when you have done such good work? Is the cinema suddenly a bad word in this theatre playhouse? Clearly not so, looking at what Jogen and all of you have done!" I looked up and he was grinning at me with those eyes all crinkled. I was so nervous, I nearly vomited.'

'Einh? E ki? Sometimes you say you answered him calmly. Other times you say he put his arm on your shoulder. Today you are all shy and nervous!'

'Maaa! Baba was shy and nervous, he nearly vomited, but when he saw Gurudeb's smile and felt his arm on his shoulder, he answered calmly.'

Eyes wet, Niru's Baba finds a smile himself. 'See, my daughter knows how to put the story together! I don't know why you have a problem doing the same!'

'Hei bhogoban, Niru, ma, you were a kid at the time, but I remember the whole of the next week! Gurudeb said this, the great man looked at so and so like that but at me he looked like this, and then, as Robi-babu remarked about my set, that – what? – that it reminded him of German Expressionism. BUT! I had also managed to maintain a typical Bangali idiom... whatnot and whatnot and whatnot. It was as if I had married the Greatest Hero of Bengali Backstage!'

'Well, you had!' Niru's Baba gets up from the chair, suddenly lighter in his demeanour, and Niru is relieved. Now it might be easier to break the news to them.

As Niru climbs into her parents' bed in the darkened room, rain starts to patter outside. She takes it as a good omen, forgetting there are no such things. She pulls the net up and tucks it carefully under the mattress, making sure to leave no opening for the mosquitoes. As she slides down under the light cover and settles her head on the pillow, Niru's Ma puts her arm around her chest. Normally, Niru would reciprocate with her own arm, but today she stops herself. She has waited for Baba's story to be over, but she doesn't want its echoes, the happy feeling of it, to be wiped out either by approaching sleep or by some completely different topic.

'Baba? Ma?' Niru doesn't quite want to throw up, but she fights the hard beating of her heart, as she imagines her father must have that night with Robi Thakur. The smell of rain on the trees makes its way through the half-shut window and the mosquito net.

'Yes, ma? What is it?' The softness goes from the arm resting across Niru's chest.

'Do I not know my own daughter?' Baba's voice is alert now. 'Ever since you entered the house this evening, I sensed something was going on. What is it?'

'No, I mean, we were talking, the girls and me...'

'Which girls?'

'Oh, stop being so obtuse, which girls does she talk to now?' Ma's voice is still low, but the snap is sharp.

'... and we were thinking that we would rent a, you know, a small flat, and, you know, live there.'

The rain slapping the leaves outside sounds louder now. There is also someone saying something loudly in the street, though Niru can't make out what's being said. Next to her, she can hear both her parents, each breathing differently.

After a while, Niru fills the silence.

'I mean Roma, Titir and I have been talking about it for a while now.'

Her mother removes her arm from Niru's chest as if it suddenly doesn't belong there.

'And today we got a postcard from Roma.'

'She's still in Santiniketan, Roma?' Baba's voice is quite normal, Niru notes.

'Yes, and she spoke to some relative there, an uncle, who is quite... open-minded, and he has a baari he can rent to us. For only twenty rupees a month. Roma says he wasn't willing to take any money, but we had decided we wouldn't take any obligations from anyone.'

'And where is this baari of yours?' Baba, as ever the practical man.

'Somewhere off Ballygunge Circular Road, I think Dover Road, you know that small road that connects Ballygunge Circular to Hazra Road?'

'I think I know it.' Baba sits up and pulls open the net to reach for the glass of water on the bedside table.

'Ballygunge? Only on the other side of town. You couldn't find anything a bit further? Tollygunge? Or even Canning? Nothing available there?' Ma's voice is still low, but the hurt is loud.

'Ma, now...'

'So when did you get this letter?' Baba settles back into bed.

'Just today, which is why I'm telling you.'

'That Roma never could spell properly in Bangla.' Ma has now moved away from Niru and turned on to an elbow for a proper confrontation.

'Well, part of the postcard was in English. What can you do with someone of Roma's background?' Niru is furious with herself for being drawn into this illogical detour and she doesn't like it that her own voice is also hardening.

'So, barely having given your BA finals, results not even out yet, with a job that earns you barely pocket money, you start living on your own. And so, throwing out all ideas of a master's degree?'

'Ma, I can always do one after a couple of years. First let's see if I pass the BA. In any case, there is this war. And the Movement. There's a lot to be done, you know that.'

'Ballygunge. So the princess will come and grace us with a visit every... what? Six months?'

'Ma. It takes just over one hour by tram when the roads are full. Early morning and late evening time it takes no more than forty minutes. By bus it's even quicker, though you know it costs more. I'll see you every other day, all right?'

'How generous of you to come see your mother every other day! Perhaps you shouldn't put such a strain on yourself.'

'Oh, I'll just come to eat.' Niru finds her mother's cheek in the dark and strokes it tenderly.

'That's the other thing,' her mother ignores Niru's hand but doesn't remove it, 'none of you girls are the greatest cooks in the world. You'll starve. And, here in this house, I'm not cooking for three people every day in the hope my darling princess may make an appearance. It's hard enough going to teach and then cooking. It's hard enough cooking without any help for a man who doesn't know the difference between coming home at seven o'clock and returning at midnight after some rehearsal, it's hard enough r—'

Baba's laughter cuts into Ma's litany. 'Forget cooking! Forget cooking! How will the three of you live in the same house, you with those two *class enemies* of yours?'

'The same way we have been friends since we were fifteen!'

'So, if Roma brings home the next day's Congress pamphlets, you will rush to the Party office and report the contents to Bakul-babu, will you? Or will friendship supersede Party discipline?'

'We have agreed to keep politics out of the house. Or, at least, our official work for our parties.'

'Excellent. I am absolutely delighted.' Baba's low laughter seems unstoppable. 'Communist, Congress-socialist, and devout Hindu confused about Mahasabha all under one roof, all eating, or starving, in the same kitchen! You know what? You should get one more girl, someone who's a worshipper of Subhas Bose. Then your cabal could run the country after Independence!'

'Speaking of worship, what will you and Roma do about Titir's praying and pujo-kirton? Or will she keep Ramakrishna outside the house?' Ma loses her deeper hostility in the shallower pleasure of scoring a point.

'In her room – she will have her own room. Apparently, there is a bigger room that Roma and I will share.'

'Hareyy Krishna, Ramoh, Ramoh!' Even the sigh Baba lets out is loaded with mirth.

'*You* stop laughing so much.' Ma puts back her arm around Niru. 'You know he's actually laughing in relief, don't you? The way you began, I thought you were going to throw the boulder of some boy's name into our quiet pond.'

'What nonsense! Aami ektu o sheita bhaabi ni! I never thought that for a moment! I knew it was something very important.' Baba's voice suddenly loses its fight. 'Launch the boat, O helmsman... oh, so many different meanings to that one line...'

INDIANS

Gopal is the first to hear them coming, though this is something he will only realize later. The other two see the slight movement that Gopal makes, a tiny movement of his head, as if flicking off a fly that's not quite touched him, but it alerts them.

Nothing changes, nothing that Gopal can put his finger on. Aurangzeb continues to feel his beard as if stalking a flea that's hiding in there somewhere. Gourangzeb's nose stays where it is, almost buried in his shawl, his face almost completely asleep and, under the shawl, the arms he has wrapped around himself make a thick, unmoving bandage. Nothing changes, but something shifts. What exactly it is, Gopal will spend a lot of time trying to understand in the coming months. At the moment, though, he becomes even more aware of the space around him.

Behind him, the edge of the jetty, a small gap, and then the iron curve of the dormant ship towering over their heads. Diagonally three paces to his left, further away from the trench of water between jetty and ship, Aurangzeb. To the left of Aurangzeb, a bollard. A few paces away, even further in, Gourangzeb. Behind Gourangzeb, another bollard, and then the other edge of the jetty, below which open water, a hard glare from a spotlight which they can't see, a few lights from other ships, their reflections winking across the dark. To Gopal's right, the jetty stretching back to the main dock and land, dark wood lit by pools of two overhanging lamps – the direction from which the sound comes. Soft at first, then firmer, separating from the night sounds of the port, water lapping, a motor launch puttering across the river, an owl repeating somewhere far off, a smell of oil and rotting plants. Peeling out of all this, footsteps. More than one man, maybe more than two, not more than three. The bouncy wood of the jetty slightly wet but not slippery under Gopal's feet.

No one has told him to stand where he is, it's just where he finds himself. The thought scurries through Gopal's mind yet again, that if something goes wrong they are the ones with their backs to the water, they are the ones silhouetted against the wash of the unseen spotlight, the motorcycle is now far away, landside, and they would have to go through – but as he thinks this, an antidote tiptoes right behind – from what he has seen of his partners, if he's thinking of all this on his first time, they were sure to have thought about it fifty times more.

Something settles in Gopal's stomach just as the men walk into the first pool of light, three of them, one of them carrying a wooden crate – Gopal's job, once they hand it over. Coming under the light, the men slow down just a touch, but it's enough for Gopal to see that there are two goras, both big, and one dark man, quite small, not local, but Indian. As they cross into the shadows, Gopal hears a match being lit and sees Aurangzeb holding it up in front of his face, a couple of beats longer than necessary, just enough to let the men see his face, before he lights his bidi.

The men walk more easily through the second pool of light and come up to them. As they come closer, he can feel their tread making the wood vibrate under his feet. Gourango jerks, as if just waking up. He looks around, slightly befuddled, but Gopal notices that his hands don't move from under the shawl. 'You don't have to do anything much,' Ustad has said, 'a man will give you a box, you will carry it.' A man. One man. But here were three.

'Why three?' says the dark Indian to Aurangzeb, echoing Gopal's thoughts. Some kind of Madrasi, but talking in Hindi.

'Him?' Aurangzeb glances at Gopal contemptuously, 'Oh he's a phaaltu, just the coolie to carry the thing.' Gopal pretends to be deaf and keeps his eyes down, making himself even smaller than he feels.

The Madrasi grunts and gestures to the first gora to put down the crate. The second gora asks something and the Madrasi replies in quick English. The answer makes the man flick a look over Gopal and come forward. He puts himself almost between Gopal and Aurangzeb before taking out a tin from his coat pocket and lighting a cigarette. As he puffs to start it, the smoke billows around his wide shoulders and straight into Gopal's nose. Gopal has never smelt anything so black and foul in his life. A rampant cough starts to build in his throat, but he fights it down, using the smoke to shuffle slightly to his right, so that he is now completely behind the gora.

He is quite unsighted now, only able to see the side of Aurangzeb's head, and more or less blocked off from Gourangzeb and the Madrasi. As for the first gora, he can only sense him beyond the cliff-face of the second one's back. Logic says this is not a good place to be, but his instincts tell him he is doing the right thing by becoming invisible. The handover gets done, the other party goes, he picks up the crate, then the three of them go back to the motorcycle. Get the thing to ice. Simple.

Small, new, insignificant, so no one paying him any attention. Aurangzeb and the Madrasi talk in low voices, so soft that Gopal has to strain to hear. The second gora is wearing a jacket-coat that looks like it's made of some kind of leather. The jacket ends just below his buttocks, which puts the edge of it around Gopal's solar plexus. Out of habit, he tries to calculate the wallet. Baan-haath, lefty, struck the match with his left hand when lighting the cigarette, so good chance on the left somewhere. The extreme height would mean reaching up. It's not an angle he's had to deal with before, but his confidence has never been sharper. He pulls his mind away from such stupid thoughts and notices that a fine drizzle is now tickling the back of his neck.

Aurangzeb and the Madrasi come to some agreement, and Gopal sees Aurangzeb's hand pull out something from his pocket before he steps forward and squats down. There is a click, and Gopal can now see the glow of a hand torch. The first gora hands the Madrasi an iron to jimmy open the crate. After there is some effort, Gopal hears the sound of nails parting from wood, and then something metallic being taken out of the crate.

'Hm. The label is not the same,' Aurangzeb grunts.

'But the thing is the same,' the Madrasi replies. 'Look, that's the maker's name. But below that it says... look, you can read...' The Madrasi speaks out what sound like some letters in English and Aurangzeb repeats them, slowly, not fully convinced.

'Trust me. This is the stuff you wanted,' says the Madrasi.

Aurangzeb's tone hardens a touch. 'So you say. But if my buyers are not happy, I can't come swimming after you.'

The first gora says something sharply to the Madrasi, to which the Madrasi replies quickly. Gopal hears the sound of nails being hammered back. Aurangzeb stands up and steps back, not exactly to where he was earlier but a bit further back.

'And the price,' says the Madrasi.

'Yes?' says Aurangzeb, 'One thousand, as agreed, yes?'

'No, we sent you a message saying fifteen hundred. This took a lot more trouble than we thought.'

'What message?'

The Madrasi's voice goes lower, but it has the same effect as raising it. 'Anyway, if you don't want it, I have people who will take it in Bombay. For two thousand.'

'Bombay?' Aurangzeb's low chortle hits Gopal in the abdomen. 'Bombay? Bombay, your sister's prick. By the time you get this to Bombay, their port police will catch you just by its smell.'

The second gora snaps out something and the Madrasi replies. Gopal can't be sure, but this English sounds different.

'Look, look here.' Aurangzeb is holding out a wad of money. The rain taps thickly on the bunched notes as he pauses, letting them have a good look before continuing. 'Here's the thousand, as agreed. I'm giving it, even though the label is different. We have to go now.'

Gopal is moving before he realizes it. One soft, sideways step to his left, to where he can see. His right foot, following his left, touches the ground just as it starts.

The first surprising thing is that Gourango is much closer to the first gora than Gopal had pictured. The second thing is that everyone has been looking at Aurangzeb's right hand, the one holding the money. No one, least of all the Madrasi, sees the rod in the left hand until it bounces up after smashing his skull. Some dense, metallic object clatters to the ground, and Gopal realizes Gourango has done something small and fast to the first gora. The second gora is even stronger than he had imagined and holding on to his left hand is a problem, except Gopal has grabbed the fingers as they've come around back under the jacket, and he is twisting them as hard as he can. He feels the man's right elbow fly over his head just before the arm hits him. The elbow would have maimed Gopal, but the man has miscalculated the height of his head. The swinging arm hurts enough, though, and Gopal wonders how much blood he has lost, until the gora goes heavy on him and he understands that what he's covered with is not his own blood.

The explosion close to his left ear, he realizes, was Aurangzeb's rod swinging through the second gora's face. Between that, and his own hanging on, Gourango has had enough time to come up and do something to the side of the gora's throat.

'Chhede dey,' Aurangzeb says, leave him, speaking clearly to Gopal for the first time. Gopal turns the heavy, collapsing tower the best he can, and leans him into the gap between the jetty and the ship. Then, his heart smashing up into his jaw, he drops his arms around the man's waist, making sure the positioning is right, of both the gora and himself. He holds on for a moment and then lets go. The body almost touches the ship as it falls, and when it hits the water it sends a scar of sound across the night.

Gopal kneels on the jetty, his back to the other two, and doubles forward, shaking. Aurangzeb calls to him again, 'Chol! Chol!' and he forces himself up, forces his trembling knees into order for the third time that day and looks.

Gourangzeb has finished pulling things out of the dead men's pockets. He puts away the gun dropped by the first gora, stands up and nods to Aurangzeb. Like two practised dancers, they pick up the first gora, take him to the edge and ease him into the water. Then they do the same to the Madrasi. The bodies make no sound as they go in. Aurangzeb moves the cupped torch around, checking the jetty for anything that might tell stories. He straightens up, satisfied, and beckons to Gopal and points at the crate. As Gopal goes to pick up the crate, Aurangzeb stops him.

'Don't touch it. You're covered in blood.' He picks up the crate himself.

'Here take this. Cover yourself.' Gourangzeb shoves his shawl into Gopal's hands.

Gopal wraps the shawl around himself, thankful for the warmth, and stumbles after the men. They make their way to the tiny cabin behind which they've hidden the motorcycle. Aurangzeb takes out the block of ice, pushes the crate in and puts the ice back on top. Gopal helps Gourangzeb push the bike to the wall, Aurangzeb pulls aside the huge tin board showing a map of the port, they push the motorcycle through, and within a few minutes they are on the road.

The paan-walla is waiting when they pull up, and they stuff two bags of crushed ice into the area around the crate. Gopal climbs back in and Gourangzeb puts the motorcycle into gear and twists his wrist to speed it up.

As they turn left between the racecourse and Victoria Memorial, the white fence catches the first smudges of morning light. They are on Red Road when Gourangzeb takes his hand away from the throttle and smacks Gopal on the back of his head.

'Bokachoda!' he snarls. 'If you weren't such a stupid little bastard, we would have had two!'

'What?' Aurangzeb shakes his head, confused.

'Revolvar!' Gourangzeb spits out, looking at Gopal even as he accelerates again. 'The one we got off the gora. If this goatfucker hadn't shit in his pants, if he had just laid the second one down instead of throwing him into the water!'

'Two,' agrees Aurangzeb. 'Maybe we could have had two.'

'Bokachoda! Do you know they are worth more than gold? Especially now that every second bastard's son-in-law has a gun?'

'Yes, but maybe he didn't have one, who knows? Anyway, the boy did all right, for his first time.' Now Aurangzeb smacks Gopal, but not as hard as Gourangzeb. 'And what a first time, hyan, Gogai? Ustad was right. You could learn. Be good at this some day.'

Gopal nods, trying to show both contrition and gratitude. Aurangzeb turns back to Gourangzeb. 'Eijey, what revolvar is it?'

'Only a small one, I don't know, Ustad will tell us, but it's quite small.'

They slow down as they pass Governor House. The warm morning rain is steady on their heads, and the icy water from the crate now sends a constant drip over Gopal's ankles. He doesn't know if the gun he saw Gourango put away is small, but the bulk of the metal pressing against the inside of his leg is certainly bigger, heavier. And the one thing he knows is he is not planning to ask Ustad anything about it.

PARKING

As they reach the end of Red Road, a black Humber slides up behind them. Kedar sees it occupy his rear-view mirror for a while and instinctively eases his foot from the accelerator. Top speed perhaps not as quick as his own car but still pretty fast for something of that size, keeping up with him easily, probably supercharged engine. Which could only mean one thing.

He hasn't had much to do with the authorities, but he has heard too many stories about unmarked police cars jumping out of the dark at people, especially these days and in this official area around Fort William and Governor House house.

'What's matter?' Eva asks, noticing Kedar slowing down.

'Nothing, nothing,' Kedar starts, then he throws her a look and decides to forewarn her. 'Maybe the car behind is police.'

'Ah,' Eva fails to suppress a giggle, 'and they take you jail, *to* jail, because you steal me?'

Kidnap you, Kedar wants to correct her, but he's had just enough drink for the idea to take a light grip. 'Well, you *are* European,' he says, underlining half the problem.

The Humber curves ahead of them as they pass the big gates of Governor House. An arm comes out of the passenger window, waving them to a stop. Kedar takes his foot completely off his accelerator, barely keeping his clutch happy as he eases to a stop by the pavement. The big car breathes up close on their right. The man next to the driver is in a black suit, and so is his voice.

'Wherraarugoing?'

It takes Kedar a few seconds to unravel what he has been asked, but the question obliterates itself as soon as he understands it. The man looking at him is white, impassive, yet the fear the voice brings up in Kedar's mouth is completely different from what he felt when facing Wart One. There are no escape hatches in this face, no extra movement, nothing for Kedar to work with. The accent he recognizes as a Scottish burr comes out of a mask, but not a put-on one, the real mask of a creature completely capable of killing him without a thought.

'Uh... yes...' Kedar tries to hurry out a confident response, but the harder he tries the further it flips away from him. 'Uh... we were...' as his eyes slide away from the policeman's, he feels a clamp come down on his normally free tongue, a cold panic lock around his brain. Eva, on the other hand, has no such problems. She sidles up close to him, as if there is no seat gap or gearstick between them.

'My fiancé was just dropping me home,' she says, her voice smiling behind his ear, arching into vowels that Kedar recognizes as purloined from the couple at the club. At any moment, he expects to hear a bell-like 'I do hope that's all right.' But Eva's genius is that she leaves it hanging in the air, her shoulder and breast jammed up against his arm as if they'd been together for months, daring the policeman to question Romeo and Juliet.

Kedar opens his mouth to shore up Eva's statement, but he can sense from the way the policeman glances at his watch that he has lost interest. The driver leans across and closes the discussion. 'On your way now.' Crisp though his voice is, it sounds a lot more human than his superior's. 'You don't want to be driving so fast.' The Humber pulls away and disappears.

Kedar sits there, caught between the sudden disappearance of terror from his right and the equally abrupt removal of Eva's body from his left side. He realizes that his car has stalled and fiddles around to restart it, his hands shaking slightly. Eva is still and silent, now completely back in her seat. She touches his hand lightly as he engages first gear. Kedar lights a cigarette before letting the clutch out.

'I think this police, he is not so worried about European women kidnap by you. He sees for something different, for something... else. Looks.'

Kedar throws her a nod and moves the car forward. A few yards down the road, he brings it around in a perfect turn to stop before the entrance of the hotel. The doorman rushes up to open Eva's door, saluting and reaching for the handle. Eva stops him with a raised hand. She turns to Kedar.

'You ask him where you park?'

'Park?' asks Kedar, not quite understanding.

'Park car. You ask him? Where? I wait for you here.'

She gets out without meeting his eyes. Kedar looks up at the doorman, working to find the Hindi, but the man is already gesturing and moving down the covered arcade that stretches across the front of the building. 'Haan, saheb! Idhar! Parking! Please follow me.'

Kedar drives slowly, keeping pace, his head suddenly dizzy. The word 'home' sings in his ears, not clear whose voice is saying it, 'hyeuum', my fiancé was just taking me. Home. My fiancé. The doorman gestures him down a narrow street running along the side of the hotel. The other side of the street is lined with horse carriages, and the doorman shouts at the sleeping man in the buggy nearest to the main road. The man grunts awake and clacks his reins, waking his pony. The animal is less acquiescent than his master, and it neighs in protest until a whip cracks on its rump. The jhurrie-gaadi creaks out of the rank, creating a space for Kedar to park. The doorman salutes the young babu and collects his reward for destroying two sets of dreams.

Without the moat of his motorcar around him, Kedar is suddenly even less sure about what to do. Turn and run, snatching the tip back from the doorman before jumping into his car? Run towards Eva and grab her before she disappears, before she can hold out her hand, say 'I was just wanting to saying goodnight like a lady should' and double up in laughter? Nonchalantly light a cigarette and saunter up to where she is standing and offer her his arm? He reaches into his jacket pocket, takes out a cigarette and puts it into his mouth. With the same hand, he brings out his lighter and manages to light up just as he reaches Eva. She raises her eyebrow as he comes close. He senses something is wrong, but it takes him a few moments to understand exactly what it is.

By the time he notices that both his hands are holding lit cigarettes, the doorman has spun away and made himself busy with a detail on the heavy brass-framed door he was about to open. And Eva is, as he has just imagined, holding her stomach and biting her lower lip, trying desperately to stifle loud laughter. After a moment, she gathers herself.

'Thank you so much. I am always leaving in cars these dangerous things,' she says gently, before prying away the cigarette he has lit earlier. Even in his tangle of embarrassment, Kedar realizes that this woman has made sure not to humiliate him here. This brings his confidence back out of hiding. He does exactly the right thing and steps back to allow her to lead them through the door that is now open.

TWO

Ascending and Descending

7 AUGUST 1941 – 6 DECEMBER 1941

CALL ME A SUCKER FOR the old bioscope. Living in this city where I am, how can you not be? It's almost a requirement for getting your staying permit. Call me a film freak or whatever, but I imagine this whole scene in black and white, shot in deep focus by Greg Toland or someone, the whites and light greys ranging themselves in different stages of disrobing, like girls in an old-style cabaret, the blacks, the shadows, caramelized by cleverly cooked emulsion, the highlights judiciously placed to outline the actors, to take our eye towards the action.

The foyer leading to the reception lobby is not too long, but there are high ceilings, and wall-sized mirrors on either side which, in conspiracy with well-placed lamps of warm-looking light, make the whole space seem bigger than it is. The wide carpet the two of them are about to walk on is patterned, dotted regularly with small, grey fleur-de-lis, but its colour is primarily red, which in monochrome shows up as a darker grey. In 1941, this beautiful carpet still has many years to go before it turns into the tattered landing strip for the not-so-rich during the hotel's long decline. The black-and-white chessboard marble floor that will eventually show through the holes is, at the moment, mutely correct and present beyond the edges. Robustly florid tropical plants line the floor, escorting the carpet. The line of extravagant greenery is interrupted by two large spittoons – again, one on either side – which will reflect Eva and Kedar as they come in, stretching them into twisted Dali figures, into slow-moving dark spikes on the surface of the spotless brass.

Since it will be a long time before piped music comes to India, what will surround our couple is the soft non-sound of a classy cage. It is the murmur of deep money you can still find in some places, and it almost invites me to put in my own soundtrack. I'm very tempted to slide in an LP of Ornette Coleman here, but that cactusy alto sax doesn't fit at all. Coleman is from much later, from almost twenty years later, which makes him from another galaxy of time. The sound I veer towards choosing, as the two of them walk in through the door, is from some big-band horn section, from Count Basie or Duke Ellington, most of the smooth brass going one way, one or two deliberately maverick trumpets pulling in the other direction, but that's too obviously dramatic, so, no.

What actually surrounds our couple is this semi-silence of thick wealth, no rhythm section quietly carpeting it, no rim taps matching Eva and Kedar's footsteps as they make their way into the swankiest – all right, *one* of the two swankiest hotels – can't forget that gauche, back-to-front pile on the Bombay seafront – operational between Cairo and Singapore. Although, at this moment, Cairo is being illuminated every night by the syncopated flash of artillery guns and a red-spoked rising sun clock is already ticking down on still-innocent Singapore.

Unlike most other deluxe hotels of the age, the lobby of the Great Eastern Hotel is not directly across the entrance but at the end of this short hallway and a little to the left. The hallway itself leads straight to the grand stairway, with corridors branching out to the right, one leading to the back offices and the other to the restaurants and the night club called Maxim's. Not that a reception manager would pose a problem for her, but the direct route to the stairs will allow Eva to lead Kedar away from the ground floor without any of the usual pleasantries and formalities that accompany the return of a guest to a hotel.

I feel tempted here to conjecture about the various protocols and pitfalls that accompany an unmarried couple entering a ritzy hotel in India at this point in history, about all the possibilities, about what could happen when that couple comprises a white woman and a native man, but the story's refusing to tolerate a pause. The huge doors, all sparkling clean glass and brass, have now been kept open too long by the liveried doorman. As Eva and Kedar step through from the pavement outside, the doorman swings the doors shut behind them, blocking out all the different options, keeping at bay all the different angles of looking back at the moment except this one.

As they enter, we can catch Eva and Kedar from a distance, from as much distance as the hallway will allow; we can even look at their reflection in one of the mirrors to add to that distance, to give our non-existent saxophones, trumpets and trombones a clear shot at a small crescendo, but quickly we must get close again. As they come in, the petite European woman in a deep maroon dress – the one with the dark hair and too sharp a nose, casually hooks her wrist into the elbow of the short, dapperly evening-suited man with the light coffee-coloured skin. With this tenuous rudder she guides him past the high party of four goras stumbling out from the nightclub, three men and a woman renting the carefully strung fabric of silence, already calling for a taxi before they've reached the exit.

Eva nudges Kedar past the long reception counter and the two hotel clerks with their necks craning down, past the lifts and up the stairs, past a porter carrying down heavy suitcases which are not allowed in the lifts – where on earth is someone going at this time of night?

Some deep-rooted man-training in Kedar makes him walk more erect, makes him a fully present party to the pretence that it he who is leading the way – a sahib taking his memsahib up to their room. But inside him, the fear is still potent. What if she suddenly turns and tells him to leave? What if she drops his arm and swings away down a corridor, leaving him lost? He has visited the restaurants here, but never the rooms. He knows from many reports that the Great Eastern's corridors are a frightening maze; what if she reaches her room, says goodnight, and leaves him to find his own way back?

He notes that Eva has decided not to take the lift. Maybe the cargo she's guiding upstairs is also not to be transported in an elevator. As they climb up, he realizes her grip is getting stronger, not weaker. At the first floor, away from what he imagines is the inquisition point of the reception desk, her fingers slide down, extricate his hand from his trouser pocket and interlink with his fingers in a firm grip. As they approach the second floor, she has turned into him, his upper arm now snug in the wedge between her arm and breast. Kedar finds himself racking his brain for any reports of people his family might know currently staying at the hotel. 'Saw your son at Great Eastern, with a white woman entwined around him like a creeper.' Not what he wants to hear from his mother. Thankfully, they pass no one. By the time they arrive at the third floor, Eva's head is nuzzled up against his shoulder and they are walking, climbing, as a slightly clumsy but very happy single unit.

Nearly at the landing of the third floor, Kedar hears someone clipping up the stairs a few steps behind them. His first instinct is to turn around and look, but being with Eva is already having its effect – he is learning quickly – and he fights off the urge. Let whoever it is present himself as a challenge and only then will we deal with it. His mind pauses on the 'we' as he turns to go up the next flight of stairs, actually starting to lead now, but Eva pulls him in another direction, along the corridor. 'We are here, not more up,' she mumbles into his jacket and navigates them past a row of closed, numbered doors. The footsteps following them also turn, but across the landing and away, down the corridor leading in the opposite direction. Kedar sneaks a glance over his shoulder.

The white man, military, also turns to look back at the same time and, for an uncomfortable moment, their eyes meet. By the time Eva undoes her face from Kedar's shoulder and turns, the khaki uniform is walking away, eyes focused dead ahead.

'Air Force but not in Indian Air Force dress, RAF,' says Kedar softly, his uniform spotting having improved much in the last two years.

'Who cares?' Eva is back snuggling into his arm, turning him right along a new corridor. 'Everywhere they are same, men in funny clothes who like to be danger. All over my life, every country, this men with shine buttons and shine guns.'

'Shiny,' corrects Kedar.

'Shiny buttons, sometimes not so shine-y guns.'

They follow the short passage and turn left into yet another corridor. Eva uncouples herself briskly. 'Wait here,' she instructs, and walks down a few doors to one that is open with light coming out of the gap. She knocks and peeps in. Kedar hears a quick scuffle of feet, an obsequious 'Yes, madam!', and a chink of small metal. Eva is walking back now, a key ring dangling from a finger. She turns him around and leads him back to the short passage connecting the two long corridors. There, she stops at a door.

'So, shiny buttons and guns in which countries?' Kedar has been meaning to ask the question earlier but now he pulls it out just to keep things casual, to distract her from the thumping of his loud heart.

Eva opens the door, pushes it wide, bows and gestures like a courtier. 'Please, sir. My little castle.'

Kedar goes into the room. Eva follows him in and shuts the door.

'So, which countries?' Kedar feels like he's trying to turn the wrong key in a lock. 'How many countries?'

Eva comes and stands under his chin. She addresses the dip below his Adam's apple.

'Today we meet is only second time, yes? And at once, already, like a police you want to know all mine secrets?'

Kedar feels her hands bring his head down. Between their bodies, where there was just now none, suddenly there is a small magical space, and then her breath and mouth on his, bridging that space. He feels her fingers tighten slightly on his hair, forcing his mouth open, and her un-English tongue snaking on to his.

As the drizzle scrawls across the night, the last embers are doused on the poet's funeral pyre near the riverbank. Around the pyre, the great man's younger acolytes stand guard through the night, protecting the ashes and bone shards from souvenir seekers. As the rain patters its night-long lullaby on the tin window awnings around Shyambajar, Nirupama sleeps a deep sleep with her arm around her mother. In her father's bungalow in Alipore, Imogen sleeps too, but her sleep is laced with disturbing dreams that taste of alcohol-bile; in the morning, she will remember the soft drumming of water on the trees outside as being twinned with searchlights and air-raid sirens on a rainless night from the other place, far away. In a different part of the city, Andrew sleeps well, his body suffused with a happy hunger.

What happens with Gopal and the gun is going to have to wait.

I know it's dicey, loading yet another crate of new characters on to the story just as the first lot begin to get somewhere, but a hotel's a hotel, and half the fun is peering through doors left ajar and trying to decipher what's going on inside. I remind myself this is one of the best hotels in the world, and these are proper doors, thick teak, with heavy brass handles, doors in command of a proper language of partition – their main role is to stay closed, so, when I get the chance to follow someone into a room, I don't want to miss it.

The man in the RAF uniform, for instance, walks away from Eva and Kedar and heads into the opposite wing of the building. Thinking about him, I have to sift through all the different characters I've retained from books and comics about air warfare in the Second World War and get past their residue. This man has little to do with the ageless English air hero Bigglesworth of the Biggles books, nor does he resemble any of the taciturn, narrow-eyed fighter pilots from Fleetway Library and Commando comics, he doesn't have the eyepatch of the grounded wing commander who, against orders, tigers off in his Hurricane in a suicidal solo attack on a Luftwaffe armada. Despite his sweaty uniform, Squadron Leader Lambert looks most like a misplaced London bank clerk, his middle already thickening from many months of mostly flying a desk, his round face readying a neutral expression to be deployed at other people.

Making his way down this cat's cradle of corridors, Lambert is always reminded of the first time he reported here for work. There was a moment then when he had felt the kind of panic that must have gripped people in dungeon passageways – what if I get lost and no one ever finds me? Now, in this strange oven of a tropical city, he has discovered new fears. It's not the maze that scares him – after eight months, he knows his way by heart – it's what's waiting for him when he gets to the end that makes him slow his stride.

Coming through the daily drill of left turns, right turns and short flights of steps up and down, Lambert reaches an unmarked door in an obscure section of the third floor. He knocks and is let in.

THE OCHTERLONY SUITE

On some nights, the howling comes through more sharply than on others. On these nights, Jeremy Lambert can feel the hotel start to surround him: the whole of the big old cake of a building lowering down on him in the dead of the night. Every room, every suffocating, labyrinthine corridor, every corkscrew of a stairway, all nudging each other as they gather together and try to bury him. When this happens, he has to get up from his desk and walk over to where the others are working, to their rooms, their desks, or their territories marked only by a carpet or a filing cabinet. These aimless, memo-less tours of the suite are painful and difficult, for Lambert is aware that most of the others don't like him very much.

For reasons that aren't entirely clear to him, most of the people in the Section, ranging from Jimmy the gofer to Mr Currie the boss, give him a wide berth except on work matters. The ones with whom he works most closely avoid him most assiduously of all, but about this Lambert isn't too unhappy – he can't imagine what he could possibly have to say to someone like the sergeant outside of work, even though on a couple of operational flights they've worked well together, and he himself can't stand Todd-Cartwright and his toff superciliousness. On these bad nights, the howling playing buggery with his work, Lambert wanders from desk to desk before the thin politeness and shoddily camouflaged unwelcome force him back to pretended labour and deep unease.

There are other nights, though, the ones when he actually manages to tunnel deep into his little patch. On these nights – early mornings, to be precise – he can delude himself into thinking that the group is a sort of family, that he is an important and respected member of the team; that the European parts of the city, the hotel, the suite, the Section, his room at the RAF quarters at Alipore Aerodrome, his desks and his lamps, and, finally, he himself, are all part of a smoothly turning engine; that the warped hatch of the dumb waiter is but a slightly loose small component. And not, in the end, dangerous.

Tonight is the third kind of night, when the two become mixed up, the work and the noise, in an even fight. Tonight, around ten o'clock, he walks in through the discreet side-entrance past the horse-carriages, a surprisingly nice dinner at the mess – fish soup, lamb chops, mash and peas, custard – sorting itself out quietly in a stomach that hasn't bothered him for a while. Climbing briskly up the stairs, he almost bumps into a drunken couple, joined at more than the hip, so to speak, and almost mutters an apology before guessing they are Anglo-Indians, probably from some out of town band with dates in one of the hotel restaurants. Looking again, he realizes that the man is actually, definitely, Indian, and the woman white for sure. This gives him a slight twinge – he hasn't had much to do with girls for a while now – actually, double twinge – white girl with rich local shorty – but he overcomes it quickly. Reaching the suite, he gets stuck right into work the way he'd got stuck into his dinner, and with even more satisfaction. It takes him three hours to go through the material sent from London and other centres; another ninety minutes from the fifteen-minute break at 0100 to read the regional ciphers and intercepts marked for his attention; from about 0245, he has been concentrating on the day's Calcutta cull and become completely engrossed in it.

The prints are sharp and well presented. Despite an excess of lip, Sergeant Deyton is good at his job, clean, methodical, even intelligent, in the way he anticipates what Lambert needs. Today, for example, the labels are stuck on the top right corner of each print – as they should be for all material from within India – and the grammar-school hand is neat, if a bit irritating. The labelling starts with the date: '7 August 1941', then the place: 'Calcutta – Proper', and then the subject: '*Procession/Funeral/R. Tagore, Poet*', after which comes the detail of each photo, including the approximate time the aircraft has made its pass:

> Jorasanko, North Calcutta, home of deceased, 1230hrs.
> Crowdings of tiny dots packing Chitpur Road and spilling into the lanes off the main road.
>
> Jorasanko, home of deceased, 1300hrs.
> Impossible to imagine, but the mass increases near the gates of the mansion.
> Inside the walls, though, the driveway and gardens are startlingly clean of people, a few cars, what looks like a horse carriage, the lorry waiting to take the body.
>
> Ditto, ditto, ditto, 1500hrs.
> Ah, the first melee, photograph taken as the lorry starts to move, the sea of dots blurring where the crowd surges towards the truck.

At 1630hrs.

One last pass over the house: all empty, one of the gates ripped flat, displaying its wrought-iron pattern for the aerial camera, the people all gone, except there seems to be some kind of strange random pattern on the print, specifically contained to the road and the side streets.

What on earth? Sergeant?

Deyton comes without any actual delay, but the impression he gives is that of a man in a pub sauntering over to have a chat. Sir? Not insolent enough for Lambert to get any purchase of rank, but just a whisker outside the off stump of respectful, as Currie might put it. Oh, these, sir? I believe that's the footwear left behind by the crowd. I was talking to a chap I know over at the Home Guards, shifted there for the time being, sir, and he heard it on the police wireless. Thousands of these slipper things, not sure what the locals call 'em, sir.

What they wear on their feet, you mean?

Yes, sir. This slipper-type footwear they have.

Right, thank you, sergeant, you can carry on.

Deyton goes off. On his pad, Lambert scribbles – '*Signs of footwear (abandoned).*' Then he begins to work with his geometrical instruments, calculating the strength of the crowd at various points of the march. March? No, one couldn't quite call this one a 'march', or even a 'procession', more a glacier made up of humans scraping through the valleys of city streets. Something oddly calm about the whole thing despite the odd disturbance here and there, something you could even see from the aeroplane. Something about the way the mass made space for itself, almost eerie when compared to, say, that Maulana fellow's meeting in Lucknow last April.

Now that had been quite something. Far fewer people than this, only about ten thousand or so, but, again, you could actually see the tension from eight hundred feet above, see the way a section of crowd tightened near a police post, see fingers of it spreading in different directions, actually perceive what a nightmare it would be to any civil admin–type hoping to control the situation. Nothing had happened, no riots, no violence – the Maulana and all the rest of the Congress bunch always stressed this, claimed it as an ongoing triumph – but it had been plain to see what a powder keg the whole thing was. One wrong move from someone, a native policeman, a bystander, some religious type in front of his temple, and the whole thing could have – the sound seems to open the gap in the dumb waiter slightly wider.

Ooooooo – oooooooooooooooooooooo – ooooo.

You could synchronize an op with it, Lambert thinks.

Every morning, around 0440 hours, it begins. Fear and irritation shoulder each other as he glances at his watch: the noise had no business in a place such as this, all the pride and pomp beginning to peel away in one corner, his corner, with just enough space between the warp of the metal and the wall to let through the sound.

The machine starts softly at first, but then it settles down into an irregular wail, changing pitch like a siren, almost making words, or, like a large cat on heat, coming and going but never quite going away, and for the next two hours or so it drives him mad. Relief comes only around 0700 when other sounds – traffic, kitchen, waiters shouting in their floor pantries – intervene, come down the chute and drown out the infernal hum.

It's not rational for him to let this one particular noise put him off his work, given the far more prominent sounds being produced in the suite around him: the occasional strafing of typewriters in the billiard room, for instance, or the gravelly chuntering of the shortwave and the staccato of the Morse which comes from the radio room next door; but there's something about it, its timbre, its bass but insistent needling, that cuts through the aspic of logic in which he and the others are suspended; perhaps it has to do with the fact that he shares all the other stuff – the outside noises, the inside noises, the invisible carpet of secrets and unspoken things – with everybody else, but this sound is *his* sound, his alone to bear.

It sends Lambert into the most intense fury that, most of the time, he is the only one who can hear it. The sergeant, Deyton, sitting no more than ten feet away, is deaf to it. Todd-Cartwright is completely bloody oblivious at a fifteen-foot distance, though the filing cabinet which stands between them might have something to do with that. As for the rest, no point even thinking about them, for they are all in other rooms.

Lambert has tried to move, of course, but to no avail. For one, the large light table that stands next to his desk would cause great inconvenience if placed elsewhere. Secondly, the wiring for the telephones had been put in place well before the Section moved in. And you can't suspend work while some worker ant from Signals comes around to change things around, can you?

And. We'd have to cover up all our maps and charts, wouldn't we? No question of letting them actually *see* what it is we do here, is there, squadron leader?

No, sir.

To coin a phrase, squadron leader, there *is* a war on.

Yes, sir, I understand.

I do hope so. Good night.

With which crisp shutting, his current lord and master, the rankless Mr Currie, disappears back into his little office; the 'C&D room' as Todd-Cartwright calls it, though Lambert can't really see it, even via the sneer, unless you counted the daily waterfall of obfuscation as a Cloak, and the ceaseless bureaucratic sawmill as a sort of Dagger. Not that it's any of his business, mind you. He's been seconded from the RAF to do a job for king and sundries, and it's not his to question *why*. His is, however, clearly and emphatically, to question *what*. Therefore, yet again pushing aside the *why* as he pushes aside the gnawing in his ears, Lambert goes back to yesterday's pictures.

Lambert has stopped believing in ghosts long ago and, so far, all of Deyton's attempts to push him in that direction have failed. But on nights such as these, when the machine breaks out of its normal pattern, Lambert has to make an effort to swat the thought away. He stares down at the photographs, mentally trying to stuff a rag into Deyton's mouth, but the man's voice keeps fishing in his ear, an accomplice to the hum coming out of the hole in the wall.

Mmmmmmm, mmmmmmmmmmmm, mmmmmmmmm

I don't know, sir, but my Nan always swore she could hear them better than see them. But at her age it wasn't too surprising, sir, her not being able to see much by then, my Nan, if you see what I mean.

And: Not surprising it's the dumb waiter, is it, sir? Connected to the kitchens, isn't it? Well, it's said they do like to hang about near the food. Apparently, it's the one thing they really miss after, you know... But all old wives' tales, sir, I'm sure.

Lambert wishes Deyton hadn't mentioned food. He doesn't know about the dumb waiter, but there is certainly a ghost in his stomach, the ghost of his long-digested dinner, and he finds himself fantasizing about making a quick trip down to the hotel kitchens, just to see what they might be up to down there.

ROOM 386

There are days when he knows he is master of the world. And there are days when he feels like a second-grade sow eating her own shit. This night is not a night when he is in control, though he also knows it's unfair to whip himself. He knows that a painter cannot paint without paints, a violinist cannot play without a bow. This particular kind of heat would cause his most dangerous competitors, wherever they are scattered across the world, to collapse far quicker, wilt before they got close to producing anything worth the name.

None of this helps. Bonnemaison sits there, watching the fan spinning like a white insect inside the copper belly of a saucepan hanging from her hook. If he allows himself to look to the right, he can see the same insect crawling around his other pans, until his eyes come to rest on the clock, four o'clock she says, and the insect-fan flickers on the clock glass as well, less defined, but there, pushing the clock hands faster than they would like to go, bringing him closer to nemesis.

He turns away from the clock, but the fan traps him again. The bastard completely smudged now but still unmistakable as it multiplies to molest the skins of the aubergines laid out on the chopping table.

Perhaps to put the vegetables back in the cold room? Yes, but the cold room being what it is, they get too cold and then too hard to bring back to room temperature in time. He needs them to be calm, especially the aubergines, and then to work for him slowly across the coming day.

He takes another sip from the small glass. Careful now, you don't want to burn your mouth into ash. He hears a shuffle and turns around to find Salim Ali right there, standing too close to him as usual.

'Mussyu Chef, you go sleep,' the old oilcan murmurs, with the infuriatingly familiar air of a co-conspirator. 'Dorm, dorm. I call you when they come.'

Something in Bonnemaison wants to spit at the man full in his face, except it would be a waste of good, rare, Calvados. And besides, he needs this half-bit slug to work for him all day, he needs him too, to stay at room temperature, even though it drives him mad to still have to say 'Rose-Marie' to the cretin who refuses, even after more than a year, to understand a simple word like 'romarin'.

'It's all right, enh?' Bonnemaison says, as calmly as he can. 'You reste. And you don't call me. I will tell you when the time.'

Salim Ali simpers but stays there, as unmoving as a pockmarked elbow of Normandy rock under a storm wave. It doesn't matter what he is told to do – it makes no difference – at sixty, Salim Ali is the rising star khansama at the hotel, and he knows it. He knows he will be the one to take over this special kitchen once the war is over and the Frenchman leaves. Just as Salim Ali knows this, so Bonnemaison knows that this slippery cockroach is impossible to squash. If he, Bonnemaison, throws him out, he will only destroy the one thin bridge that connects his genius to the babble of sub-cooks under him. Nothing, on the other hand, will happen to Salim Ali, who will go back to the hotel's main kitchen and continue manufacturing the abominable 'Continental' menu that the Piglish bifteks and the native minor rich so love. Salim Ali the khansama, the con-sama, the cuntsama, the—

'Saheb, Mussyu Chef, the meat. We take down now?'

And here, with the deceptive speed of a syphilitic old cobra, the canny bastard has him. Bonnemaison looks at the clock again and it shows a quarter to five. The meat.

Back in Lyon, Bonnemaison would hang his beautiful, local beef for twenty-two days, just as his maître had taught him, but here, in this tropical cesspit, he has worked out after much experiment that the correct time is fourteen days and maybe three to four hours. Don't ask why, less blood perhaps, but it's just the way the local cows behave after they are slaughtered. It is now coming up to that time for the special carcasses they have hung for the dinner tonight and Salim Ali knows it, knows also that the Mussyu cannot take down the meat and start preparing it all by himself.

Bonnemaison curses inside himself, realizing that there is now no way the old cockroach can be kept away when the delivery comes, *if* the delivery comes. He moves away to his office, where he pretends to look at some papers, lighting a cigarette and pouring himself some more Calvados. Salim Ali stands close as ever, and Bonnemaison takes a deep, dramatic puff and then coughs, making a patently fake attempt at keeping his exhalations away from the shit-eater. Once the old man reels back a couple of steps, Bonnemaison commands him: 'Yes, Ali, you can take the meat down now. I will check it in twenty minutes.'

By five-thirty, with the first faint light of the dawn discolouring the clean throw of the heavy lamps over the worktables, the nemesis clock and his own maverick sweat begin to trap the Frenchman in a pincer. That these people can have their poet, he says why not? They have their own garlic, they do semi-acceptable things with their garlic, so why not, he supposes, a kind of thin, squeezed, twisted kind of poetry? Just like their garlic and their vegetables? But, merciful father in his heaven, he just hopes that this epidemic of grief, as if a demigod or a popular president had just died, doesn't interfere with the dinner.

Because you never knew with these people, they were superb at coming up with the most fantastic of excuses, much better than even the Spanish or the Algerians. Like the one boy he had trained with such patience to become his pastry chef: 'Mussyu, my little girl drank milk from a cow which was bitten by a sick monkey. We had to catch the monkey and kill him before the child could become well again, and this took a week, and as her father, I was the one who had to kill—' As he checks the meat, Bonnemaison still remembers with satisfaction the pin-drop silence created by the whipcrack of his slap.

On top of due salary, he had had to pay the boy something from his own pocket before the hotel threw him out, but the frequency of absences had decreased after that and, when they did come, the quality of excuses was much improved. A pity about the boy though, Ram Narain, with his soft skin and large eyes, but after something like that, there could be no... he hears the sound he has been waiting for – the thud of a heavy motorcycle engine slowing to a stop in the lane downstairs – and it's all he can do not to rush to the window and look down. He carries on working, trying to concentrate, but his ears are now tuned to the door of the galley and to the flight of steps that leads up to it from the delivery entrance.

He hears the big man's voice asking for him on the stairs and hears a waiter reply. Bonnemaison tries, occasionally, to navigate through the maze of native languages that surrounds him, but time and his patience are both too short. Today, for example, there is no possibility of his grasping the quick exchange that takes place, but he recognizes the voice and he moves quickly to receive his visitor.

When the big man comes around the door, Bonnemaison is surprised to see him alone and carrying the goods himself. The old chief thief with whom he has made the deal specifically promised him that there would be someone else along with the big man but, at this moment, Bonnemaison cannot find it in himself to be too concerned about that. His focus is completely on the dripping box the man holds in his arms.

'Yes, yes, come, come,' he says and leads the man into his little office. Once inside, Bonnemaison gestures for the crate to be put down, not on the floor as the man is about to do, but on a table where a special space has been created. The big man starts to jimmy open the wood, but Bonnemaison stops him with a gesture. He approaches the crate and bends over it. Once close, he takes a deep sniff, and then another. There is no smell, not the faintest trace of one, which is good. He signals for the crate to be opened.

When the man hands him a tin, the Frenchman takes it in both hands, as if the cold cylinder contains something fragile, like a Fabergé egg. He turns away from the man, trying to hide his excitement, and from a drawer in his desk he takes out a new tin opener he has cleaned and put aside especially for this moment. He starts to work on the tin but stops, thinking the better of it. Then he turns back and reaches confidently inside the crate, picking out three more tins, making sure they are from different parts of the box.

'You wait here,' he says to this large man with whom he has never felt easy, adding, 'Sit. In this chair. I come in five minute.'

Moving out of his office, Bonnemaison walks quickly to the worktable and the six cooking rings that form his own station. He puts the tins down, giving their external labelling and condition only a cursory look; as small beads of condensation begin to appear down the sides, he quickly and efficiently cuts open the lid from one of them. What he sees pleases him, but he remains cautious until he has all four tins open and their contents upended carefully in a pristine roasting tray.

From another drawer he pulls out a clean fork and, with the care of a surgeon, one by one, he cuts into each of the four yellow-white cylinders that sit glistening on the tray, shaving a tiny sliver from each and putting each one carefully into his mouth. He gives a long moment's pause between each sample, allowing each one to move in his mouth, for his saliva to coat, for his teeth to chew, for his trained throat to swallow. Since no one is close enough to see them, the tears that suddenly condense around his eyes remain unremarked. By the time he has stowed away his treasure and started walking back to his office, he is Mussyu Chef again, dabbing the sweat from his eyes on a mid-monsoon day that already promises to be exceptionally sultry.

Back in the office, Bonnemaison has to make an effort not to smile triumphantly at the ugly bear sitting there with his arms folded. Instead, the Frenchman unlocks a drawer in his desk and takes out an envelope packed with rupee notes. 'Tell your Ustaade M'sieu Bonnemaison sahib says it is good.' He hands over the money. The big man spirits away the packet in the folds of the strange winter garment he is wearing, nods and gets up to leave. Bonnemaison suddenly remembers the boy that was to be supplied with this delivery and clears his throat. The big man looks at him, his face expressionless. 'He is small accident, the boy. Next time he will come.'

As the man leaves, Bonnemaison feels a weight lift off of him, as if a malevolent magnet had moved away from the iron filings of his soul, and he almost resists the temptation to go and look out from his office window.

Peering down into the street, he is careful not to let himself be too obvious. The big man climbs on to the back of the motorcycle as the fellow with the nose like an elephant trunk kicks the machine alive. Next to them, in the sidecar, there is a small shivering thing, head huddled in a shawl, and Bonnemaison can't see his face. Ah. The small accident. Which is obviously no accident, but obviously the victim of some illness, some horrible infection. Damaged goods, and therefore not delivered, which was just as well. Anyway, Bonnemaison had to admit he was getting tired of the class of flesh this city had so far offered him, poor boys all of them, with no English, leave aside French. There was nothing to do with them except the act itself, which, after a while, could become tiresome.

Almost as if his mind has confected an alternative, Bonnemaison's eyes leave the departing motorcycle to look at the car that's pulled out from the carriage rank and come head-to-head with his smugglers. Look at *that* now! Young, beautiful, rich, in his little green coupé, swimming in some private pool of happiness, turning his smile at Elephant Nose, raising his arm in a signal before turning his head and reversing to make way. What beautiful eyes, what a beautiful arm that comes out of a rolled-up shirtsleeve, his dinner jacket slung over the passenger seat... Shit! he must have spent the night at the hotel. With his mistress, perhaps.

Bonnemaison turns away from the window, trying to take his frustration off the heat. Therefore, he doesn't see the shawl dropping from the boy in the sidecar, misses the flaring of his eyes as his head hooks around to stare at the driver of the MG, doesn't see the desire stretching taut from the sidecar boy as the motorcycle turns on to the main road and speeds away, misses the rich young man, oblivious of both motorcycle and boy, putting a lighter to a cigarette and then taking it out of his mouth to move the tip across his lips – as if he doesn't quite believe they are still there – before gunning his engine unnecessarily and jerking out into the gathering traffic of life.

Back inside, in what he sometimes thinks of as his studio, the Frenchman hurries back to his gas rings and looks at the clock again. She is benign now, showing eight o'clock in the morning. Thirteen hours in hand. He is a king again.

Bonnemaison reaches up to the row of hanging vessels and brings down a small frying pan. Before he pulls out the tray he has put away so carefully, he picks up one of the empty tins and examines it carefully. The maker's name is one he knows well, a good, reliable farm from near Perigord, but what holds his attention is the strange black typeface that slashes across the bottom of the familiar French label. His German is almost non-existent, but he can make out the words 'OKW', 'Wehrmacht', and 'Berlin', and the small swastikas that bracket the print are all too painfully familiar. Suddenly, he feels his stomach convulse. A small reverse of apple brandy sears the edges of his tongue just before the laughter bursts through.

Salim Ali, standing only a few feet away, is startled by the violence. Why is the sisterfucker Three-Eighty-Six screaming loud enough to break every window in the hotel? It takes a couple of minutes before Ali can summon the courage to go closer, to see if this thing can yield some unimagined advantage.

'Mussyu? Sava, chef?' he waits for Three-Eighty-Six to gasp for breath before slipping in the question.

Bonnemaison looks up at Ali, his eyes streaming, his yellowed teeth flashing. He slams the empty tin hard on his worktable, once, twice, thrice, as if bringing it down on someone's head. He shouts something in French and repeats it, again and again, and then he does something he has never done before and will never do again: he puts his arms around Salim Ali and hugs him and kisses him hard, once on each grizzled cheek. Then he pulls away and shouts the thing again, before gathering up all the empty tins and striding back to his office.

Just as Bonnemaison will never realize that the staff derisively refer to him by his room number, so Ali will never know what the

Frenchman has just shouted: '*We start with this and we take back all of France, you pigs!*' And neither will Ali know what the sealed envelope contains which, twenty minutes later, Bonnemaison hands over to a peon he has had summoned from the hotel manager's office.

By the time His Highness, the Maharaja of Navgadh sits up in his bed and cuts open the envelope from Bonnemaison, the chef is already busy at his station. By the time the maharaja reads the two-line note informing him of the first course of the gala dinner tonight, Bonnemaison is already experimenting with a small sample from his tins and the pungent smell of foie gras being lightly fried is already on its way up to the roof via the exhaust vent above the legendary Paul Bonnemaison's kitchen station.

There is almost no tangible trace of the wonders produced by Paul Bonnemaison in what he would later call his period of great exile. After the war, when asked about his Calcutta years, all Chef Bonnemaison would say was that it was a time of crippling scarcity, and he had to learn to do what he could with very, very little.

I've tried to get hold of the Bonnemaison dinner menus from that time. These menus were legendary, and not just within the confines of the Great Eastern; their fame spread far and wide among the so-called upper echelons through word of mouth, each triumph emulsifying into myth as the war scarcities increased. The problem is, these menus were outside the hotel's normal fare, each one only typed up on the day of the private dinner, naturally without mention of any prices. Some menus would have been thrown away for sure, others might have been squirreled away by worshipful guests, and there was some indication that the management was not eager to broadcast the sheer debauchery at a time when the rest of the population was going through a period of great want.

What I do have is bits of tangential and circumstantial evidence. For instance, there is the story Old Elko tells of tasting foie gras for the first time, which was apparently not in France but in Calcutta. The recording on the tape is clear but the story is fuzzy, blurred by the booze and the intervening years. He may not have made the small oil painting at the time, but it was clearly inspired by that first liverish epiphany.

The picture is part of a bunch of sketches and small studies that had been saved from destruction. Mostly painted between the mid-50s and early 60s, these were little oils on primed wood, the images slapped on to any surface that would bear the primer and paint, sides of wooden crates, scarred chopping boards and sandwich boards, tin traffic signs found abandoned in a junkyard, on the backs of the wooden presentation boxes you got at Christmas. The painting I'm talking about was quite exquisite – the first one I fell in love with – not big, about 6' x 8', done on the flat, reverse side of one of those etched souvenirs from Kashmir, some inlay of a shikara on a lake or something. The background was a roiling mess of burnt umber, blacks and greys, with some mistake streaks of dark maroon showing through, the plate itself was a barely defined disk of a dirty blue-and-white pattern, in the middle of which sat a glowing cream-and-gold slab of what could only be fried foie gras, the edges of brown rendered beautifully, the hard black shadow of the thing bringing it out in almost Rembrandt-like chiaroscuro, as if it was not food but the shuddering, glistening slice of someone's brain you were looking at.

Towards the end, Missus got into the habit of pulling this one out and jabbing her finger at the fat-slicked slab on the plate – 'This is *your* liver, Lord Goose-a-had, your *cooked* liver as it looks right now!' Invariably Old Elko would lurch out of his chair to make a grab for it, bull lunging at red rag, and invariably she'd be ready, whether tipsy or fully two sheets to the wind, always faster and nimbler than him, disappearing the little rectangle before he could get hold of it.

There were other equally lovely ones, so beautiful it almost hurts to look at them. Against no particularly discernible background, flowers, always only one particular flower in a painting – rose, orchid, a bunch of lavender, marigold – and little still lifes of vegetables, sometimes with surrounding context, sometimes without – potatoes, artichokes, then begoon – aubergine varieties typical to Bengal, shining like swords that had swollen up purple – and then karelas, kumdo, kanch-kola, then a superb one of an elongated green gourd, a lau or lauki – what was alternately referred to by both Elko and Missus as 'love-key' or 'low-key'. Sitting there, oblivious to the cornucopia of local vegetables in the food paradise surrounding him, he painted every vegetable he had been missing in recent years. And then there were the little portraits of objects: a woman's powder case, lipstick, a brassiere hanging against a wall as if suspended there by magic, an overstuffed wallet next to an empty coffee cup with dregs, the criss-crossed handle of something that looked very much like the grip of what Americans like to call a 'handgun', as if other firearms are fired by feet or elbows.

Where's the automatic pistol from then?

From the old imagination, dear boy, or, rather, from a story I was once told.

DHAKURIA

First, with great gentleness and reverence, he removes the picture of Ma Kali from his shelf of deities. Then he moves all the smaller pictures and statuettes. Then he removes the red cloth that's nailed to the wall behind the gods and goddesses, revealing a wall of small, old bricks. Carefully, he pries open the bricks to reach the hole, his little safe, and takes out the wooden box with the small, brass lock.

A few minutes later, he's out in the hot sun, a thin film of sweat forming around his entire head. As Gopal crosses Southern Avenue and makes his way to towards Dhakuria Lake, he knows what anyone looking at him will see: a short young man, peon type, in shirt-pant, nondescript chappals on his feet, nondescript cloth side bag hanging from shoulder, the stalks of green lau poking out of the top; a young man just above the poorest class delivering a couple of gourds to someone, perhaps his mother, perhaps some other relative, and hoping to be fed some of the vegetable as lunch, along with rice and fish and a crisp sprinkle of potato bhaja.

He waits at the crossing of Lansdowne Road and Southern Avenue as two cars pass, followed by the racket of a pony pulling an old jhurrie-gaadi, followed by three men on bicycles, masonry tools tied to their carriers. Gopal has thought of taking his own cycle but decided against it; the weight distribution of the cloth jhola on his shoulder would have been awkward and he couldn't risk tying it to the carrier – going over a bump, the contents spilling from the bag, was not a chance he could take.

As he walks past the gora shahebs' rowing clubs into the greenery surrounding the lake, Gopal can feel the round lau bump into the side of his leg. Without turning too obviously, he checks what's behind him and sees nothing; anyone following would have had to make themselves obvious, as there is only this one narrow road leading away from the Avenue and to the concrete bridge that now sits across the chicken's neck of water that connects the eastern part of the lake to the western bit. Gopal strolls across the bridge, forcing himself to walk slowly, almost as if the point of the journey is the walk itself and not any important destination. No one is following him, the traffic cop manning the crossing at the Avenue hasn't looked at him twice; Ustad is away for business in Patna after having expressly told Gopal to take a few days off until the sudden heat from Lalbazar Police Headquarters subsides into some cooler weather.

This is the first time Gopal has got the chance to do the thing he has been wanting to do since early August. Despite the risks, he's not going to stop himself today. Everything is in place, the different factors ranged as generously as life will ever allow them to be, and he is not going to stop himself. Everything is in place, except one thing. What had been in the crate that made it worth killing three men? Three men who were themselves ready to kill?

On the bridge, Gopal suddenly stops and looks east. The eight o'clock sun lays a sheen on the water of Dhakuria Lake that it only gets in this brief period between the end of the post-monsoon heat and the start of winter, but what catches Gopal's eye is a thick branch of a tree at the edge of the lake cantilevering several feet over the water. He has walked past this tree many times, but today, something in the way it catches the light, something in the way the elbow of wood makes a perfect seat, takes him back to Khulna and to a thick trunk that curved over the Kakai River next to his village.

Suddenly, his grandfather's voice calling out across the water, 'Urey porarmukhor betaa! Tor mukhey zaatar baari maari!' Shrill, nasal, from nowhere else but Khulna, 'You burnt-face brat! I'll slap your face with this broom!'

Four naked boys perched on the branch, watching the river flow under them. One of them would start the game, organize his feet and shift into a squat, stick his backside out as far as he could without overbalancing, and slowly squeeze out a shit. They would all watch the first turd drop into the water – plop! – and then the answering plops of catfish as the eely things came shooting to the surface, eager mouths open. Soon, all four would be dropping turds into the water, moving up and down the bouncing branch, trying to score a direct hit on one of the bobbing mouths, watching as their produce was gobbled up by the congregation of maagur. Living creatures will eat anything.

Gopal walks on. Ice, why so much ice for the crate? To stop something from rotting until it got safely to what he now knows is called a rephriz-rator or a colstoraze. So, either medicine or food. Must have been some kind of food, must have come being kept cold at the bottom a ship, must have needed the ice to protect it from the huge change in temperature – 'It will rot by the time you get it to Bombay!' Aurangzeb-bhai had said contemptuously, and then the delivery at the hotel. Yes, food. Living creatures will eat other living creatures, alive or dead or frozen.

Gopal makes his way off the bridge and slips down a path into the forest that marks the southern border of Calcutta. Actually, two arms of the city have grown southwards, one on the west spreading along the river towards Canning and the delta, the other on the east, going a bit further down from Gol Park, but between the two stretches of settlement is this swamp and forest, uninhabitable, owned once by some nawab called Anwar Shah, and now by some Marwari called

Bangur, and it's perfect for what Gopal needs: it's not far from where he lives and it's completely free of people.

Ten minutes' walking brings Gopal to a small clearing he has discovered earlier. Here, he stops and lifts the heavy jhola off his shoulder. He is not sure what he will do on his way back because, if things go according to plan, there will no round lau left to cover the gun. Nature wastes nothing, but he's about to waste three very good, fresh gourds. Sitting cross-legged on the grass, Gopal takes out the contents of the bag and lays them out in a row: three round lau, not the long ones which look nothing like a man's head, a pair of kitchen tongs, the cloth parcel with the gun, and a new notebook and pencil. Today he's going to be a very thorough and attentive self-taught student.

Before he unwraps the cloth, Gopal goes through the few things he knows about guns. He knows which side the bullet comes out of; he knows where the bullets are stored, at least in the Browning revolvar Gaurango has shown him; he knows the lever, triggar, that you have to pull to shoot; he knows the haimmar, the curved thing that looks like a very bent thumb that sticks out from the back of the round bit; the bit that cocks back and smacks into the chamber, slamming the bullet out into the barrel and beyond, 'straight into the sisterfucker's' heart!' Gaurango said, grinning, as he demonstrated with the emptied revolvar. Gopal also knows this precious possession of his looks nothing like the 'chamber' that Gaurango refused to let him handle, except to briefly let him feel its weight. Having taken his own gun out a couple of times, having run his hands over it, he knows it's a far heavier, smoother thing, as if from a completely different world; once explained, Gaurango's revolver is easy to understand – it shows all its attributes as if naked, like a large black metal scorpion. His own weapon is like a man draped in a large blanket, you can't see anything of the body but all the small bumps coming out of the main shape mean something: you know where the head is, where the arms and legs are, and you can sense a mysterious power.

Gopal pulls in a breath and lifts up the cloth parcel. Quickly, trying not to put too much ceremony into it, he removes the cloth and lets it fall, wrapping his hand around the strange, straight handle. He's not a fool, and as he examines the weapon, he instinctively keeps the hole pointed away from himself. In the confines of the little room where he lives, he has been scared to do too much with the gun, afraid it will go off and announce its presence to the people living around him; now he is suddenly free, and he examines it much more confidently.

Holding it in two hands, he first feels the weight and balance; the thing is heavy, almost as heavy as one of the lau, but the way the metal is distributed, he can sense there is something right about the way it weighs. In the darkness of his room the gun has looked black, but now, in sunlight, the metal keeps shifting colour from black to a curious deep blue and back. Keeping the gun flat in one hand, he runs his fingers over the criss-crossed wood of the slightly battered grip, feels the little screws that hold things in place, moves his fingertips over the Ingreji letters etched on to the side, as if someone had a typewriter that could bite into metal. His Ingreji reading has improved over the last year or so, but he can't quite decipher the words and numbers. M1911A1. Pa... tent. '11, '15, '26, then 'S-p-r-i-n-g-f-i-e-l-d, full stop MA full stop, and on the other side, two words he knows, 'Army' and 'Property' preceded by another, 'us', but in capitals with a full stop between the two: U.S Army Property. He deduces that this gun belonged, as guns often do, to some army.

Gopal identifies the trigger as a distant relative of the hook of metal Gourango had yanked with his forefinger, here it is almost like a tiny wall with a curve cut out. Keeping his finger far away from the curve, he carries on his inspection. There's the hammer, at the back as it should be, but a small one compared to the Browning's; maybe the bullets are tiny despite the heft of the thing. On the left side, just behind the trigger area, he sees two different buttons. One button slides back and forth and is quite hard to move; he pushes it forward and then carefully pushes it back. The second button is more like a lever, and Gopal turns the gun the right way up as he gently pushes down on the switch. He feels something hard smack into his right knee and tumble into his lap. The gun suddenly feels a lot lighter. Gopal overcomes the small shock, telling himself no pistol can shoot from two sides, and looks down. The object sitting in the fold of his leg reminds him of the cigarette cases he has lifted, but it's not shiny at all, it's a matte black and the shape is longer. What does have a slight sheen is the brass nose of the bullet poking out of one end.

Gopal puts the gun down on the cloth and lifts up this new object. Using the kitchen tongs, he works with the bullet, trying to prise it out. Metal slides off rounded metal, finding no purchase. After a couple of minutes, Gopal reverts to his trusted fingers, hoping his hand won't get blown off. As he fiddles with it, the bullet develops a life of its own. It pops out and flies away. Another one replaces it, as if by magic. No, not magic... a strong spring somewhere at the bottom. Ah. So this is how the bullets are stored, unlike in the round cylinder of a revolvar. For some reason, Gopal has imagined a small, round cylinder with some very tiny bullets hidden somewhere above the trigger. Seeing the size of the bullet fills him with an odd relief. One by one, he takes out the bullets, the first couple jumping out, but the others coming away in his hand as he gets the measure of the mechanism.

Gopal wipes the sweat from his forehead and carefully retrieves the escaped cartridges, adding them to the small pile at his feet. One, two... eight in all. With the sun rising higher into the morning, he slowly tries to work out how to put the bullets back into their container. After ten minutes, he manages the first one: the trick is to slide it in from the back of the opening while pushing down on it. Now, how to put in the next one? Surely it might explode if he rubs it against the one already lodged inside? There is nothing for it but to try – he's not going to take the chinking mess of a dismantled gun back to his room. Clearing his eyes, Gopal aligns the second bullet behind the first one and pushes down and forward. The second bullet almost flies off but, just before it does, the mouth of the container grips it and it clicks into place, sitting there half out of the box as if it's always been there. Still not quite believing it, Gopal pushes in a third cartridge, and a fourth, until all eight are loaded. As the eighth bullet goes into place, he has an odd feeling that the thing is pulling in two opposite directions, the bullets straining to be let out and yet firmly, solidly, patiently waiting in place for the command of metal that will release them. He shakes the container to see if the cartridges fall out, but no, the yantra is well designed and the bullets stay in place. Now to get it back into the gun.

Keeping the top bullet pointing the way it would need to go – up and through the hole in front, Gopal gingerly slides the container up the hollow handle from where it has dropped. After a few attempts, he slides it in really firmly and it fits perfectly; the releasing lever goes up and the gun is a single unit again, the brain of the man who's made the instrument locking perfectly with Gopal's own intelligence.

Still keeping the hole pointing away from himself, Gopal now shakes the gun to see if the bullet box will fall out. The gun makes small noises, loose bits of metal knocking against each other, but no part of it feels like it will detach itself. It's far trickier to put the bullets into the angled container than into the cylinder of a revolver, and Gopal wonders how someone would reload this quickly during a gunfight.

Still cross-legged, the veins on his legs trilling with the inactivity, Gopal puts the gun down on the cloth and composes himself. Around him, the small jungle buzzes with silence. Birds, the rustle of leaves and the traffic of squirrel-creatures, the odd unauthored noise from afar signalling the absence of other human beings in the vicinity, all this washes over Gopal as he gathers the courage to finally use his precious talisman. He wishes he had put water into an empty alcohol bottle and brought it along, and he wishes he had some food, a banana or some muri. So much has this little construction of blue metal drained him, he realizes he is exhausted before he has even fired a shot.

After a while, Gopal gets to his feet and stamps against the grass to bring back his blood. Moving quickly, he picks up a lau and walks over to a tetul tree about fifteen feet away. There is a fork in the trunk, just about the height where a man's neck would be – an Indian man, not one of those overgrown goras who were sometimes as tall as six feet – where Gopal carefully balances the gourd. The light is odd, coming down from all directions through the leaves, but the pale green of the gourd is clear enough against all the other colours of the foliage. Making sure the lau is firmly wedged, Gopal walks back to the pistol and picks it up. His heart is pounding so hard that, for a moment, he thinks the gun has become heavier. He takes a deep breath and lifts the pistol, not aware that he is using both hands.

Gopal's left hand clutches the bottom of the automatic, taking most of the weight, while his right hand gingerly curls around the handle, afraid to touch it properly. There is a funny loose bit at the back of the handle that can be pressed down, and Gopal avoids doing this, not sure of what will happen if he does. Aligning the pointy bit on top of the gun to the gourd, Gopal squeezes the trigger, not conscious that he has shut his eyes at the moment of squeezing. Nothing happens. The curve of the trigger gives a bit and stops, implacable. Gopal opens his eyes and looks at the gun again: ah, fool, the other thing, the little lever, that must be the safety catch that Gourango said some modern pistols have, 'to stop them from going off into your cock!' Gopal slides the lever down and repeats the whole procedure, lift gun, aim, close eyes, squeeze.

Nothing. The pistol is unyielding.

Gopal tries again, managing to keep his eyes open this time, but again, nothing, the gun is like a foreigner who will not speak in your language. Gopal wonders if the three months of storing has damaged the thing, but he can't see how: everything he knows about mechanical things, and he realizes he now knows quite a lot, tells him that the parts seem to be in good working order, smooth, unrusted. He takes the gun completely in his right hand and holds the grip firmly. With his left hand, he fiddles with the slightly loose bit on top that feels as if it could slide; he notices the little dip where the metal is cut open to reveal the round tube beneath, a dip about the size of a bullet, wonder why that's

The animal gives off the smallest of growls before it breaks into an attacking run across the clearing. Gopal's head snaps up to see a large dog hurtling straight at him and his heart stops. His right hand goes up without any connection to the rest of him and it squeezes the trigger and the whole of the grip as hard as it can. His hand shatters and his arm convulses out of his shoulder as if a giant has wrenched it off. The sound, like a small, flat thunderclap is gone, already weaving its way into the forest, scattering birds out of trees, sending small creatures scurrying.

The pain is excruciating, totally overwhelming, galloping from the right of his skull down his neck, into his shoulder and then traversing all the way down to his right hip bone. As he reaches across with his left hand to hold his right arm, he realizes the gun is still stuck to his hand, which is still attached to his arm, which is still linked to his shoulder. As the first wave of throbbing pain passes, Gopal notices there is silence from the dog.

Trying to overcome the next wave, Gopal looks around, waiting for the dog to get over its fright and return, but there seems to be no sign of it behind the trees circling the clearing. As Gopal massages his arm, he realizes he is avoiding looking down at a particular spot about ten feet away where the grass is changing colour from its bright winter green.

The dog looks like someone has driven an invisible spear through it, as if its body is a pump for spurting blood. Gopal knows this gun can't fire from more than one side, but now he realizes it can make a body shoot blood from two ends. The animal's mouth is open, spewing blood, and there is a gash in the stomach, just before the hind legs, from where another pulsing delivers regular clots of scarlet innards to the ground. It's a big male mongrel, and the bullet has clearly entered the mouth and gone straight through the length of the body, leaving a big hole going out.

As he watches the dog die, Gopal keeps reconnecting the subsiding body on the ground to the thing in his hand. One by one, he goes through all the other possibilities that would have rendered a running animal to this state, a thick thorn branch the dog hasn't seen, someone else with a rifle or a revolver, a tribal with the invisible spear, a bomb inside the dog that has detonated. In the end, there is no getting away from it – the pistol has fired, using his hand as support, and the bullet has hit the dog, stopping it in mid-run and killing it.

By now, Gopal has witnessed a few men dying. It bothers the outside of him less and less, but the animal seeping into the earth wrenches something inside him, a twist of pain that complements the sharp ache he can feel from the recoil of the .45.

He recovers his breath as he waits to make sure that the dog is completely dead. Once everything subsides, he grabs the creature by its hind legs and flings it into the undergrowth, making sure not to step in the little swamp of blood, making sure to avoid bloodstains. Next, he finds a banana tree and tears off a couple of large leaves, using these to pick up as much of the entrail mess as he can. Finally, the only trace left is a very visible smear of blood on the grass, which could be from anything: a fight between two rabid foxes, some strange ritual sacrifice, a dog catching a very large squirrel.

The lau is still in the tree, sitting there patiently, watching the proceedings. Gopal wipes his sweating palms on his trousers and picks up the gun again, but one-handed. This time, he stands side-on to the target as Gourangzeb has shown him and aligns everything, eyes, head, neck, throbbing shoulder, arm, gun wrist, sight. He closes his hand around the grip and trigger and the gun jumps again, sending new pain shooting into the areas already aching. The lau looks back at him, impassive, untouched. The bullet is swallowed by the thick jungle, it sends back no message of impact. As Gopal lowers his pulsing arm, he realizes two things. One, that the slightly loose bit at the back of the handle is there for a reason, as a second safety mechanism; if a person isn't holding the gun deliberately and tightly, the thing won't shoot. Two, that his arm hurts less after the second shot.

As he massages his arm, Gopal debates whether he can afford to use up another bullet. The gun has come with eight cartridges, and now he only has six; should he ever need to use the gun seriously, it's likely he will need all the remaining bullets, especially since he has no ability to handle this bondook properly, since he will clearly need many more than eight bullets to learn how to shoot accurately. Gopal feels the ache subside in his arm and suddenly he wants it back; he wants to see the dog explode, he wants to see the lau pierced and dripping green-white pulp, he longs to feel that great power coming out of his hand, and if this snapping pain in his muscles is the price for it, he is willing to pay it.

With the greatest reluctance, Gopal pushes back the safety catch, wraps the automatic in its cloth and puts it away. Then he goes to the tree, retrieves the lau and adds the three gourds back into the jhola along with the unused pencil and notebook. By time he reaches the bridge over Dhakuria Lake, he's remembering how his mother used to make shukto in Khulna, very different from here in the west of Bengal where they use sweet potatoes with all the other vegetables but, strangely, no lau.

He sees the tree curving over the water, he sees the boys again, still naked, still teasing the fish with their turds, he hears his grandfather's voice again 'Urey gukhekor betaa! Tor mukhey zaata ghoshi di!' Shrill, nasal, now running after him and the other boys, balancing on the hard mud ridge of aal running between two square lakes of paddy. 'You son of a shit-eater! Let me rub this broom in your face!' He remembers the taste of his mother's shukto as she mashed it into the rice and fed him, him still crying from the beating dadu had just given him. Eggplant, karela and lau, all covered with a delicious white paste of mustard seeds, all mixing into the pillow of hot rice, the rice releasing the taste of the vegetables, the vegetables unleashing the taste of the rice.

As the dirt road hardens into asphalt under his chappals, Gopal returns to the city and his normal concerns. By the time he reaches Southern Avenue, he is back to the question of the box that needed so much ice to protect it. What was in that box that men had to be killed for it? Was it more precious than the hair from the dead poet's beard?

SNAPPAGE

> 1435 hrs.
> Second melee, on Harrison Road this time, around the truck with body.
> That was apparently when yet another person tried to snatch some hair from the body.
> After that the frames calm, nothing, just thousands and thousands of people filling the streets quietly, all the way to the cremation area on the bank of the river.

At some point, the body is transferred from the truck on to the shoulders of pall-bearers, and they carry it the rest of the way to the cremation ground.

1745 hrs.
A final shot, not very good because of the fading light, but with the tiny white flares of a few pyres burning beside the water. Little scratches in the dusk, then a gap, a mass of grey people surrounding the poet's pyre, which seemed to be a far bigger glow than the rest of the pyres.

All that, all those people just for this, Lambert thinks. This is their Westminster Abbey, no interment, no pomp of coffin, service or church, no marker of a gravestone, let alone a tomb. Just a body under a great, big, bloody bonfire, with about a hundred thousand in attendance. Wonder what it was exactly that the man wrote, what it was that—

Hello there, Jerry! Working hard this fine morning?

As is his habit, Goodsugar has sneaked up. Lambert looks at him and nods, trying to keep it short. If there's a ghost around, it's this man, he thinks to himself, very aware of the American standing just outside the pool of light falling on his desk. All of them, all the rest of them except Currie, agree that the fellow seems to be very chummy with shadows. As the toff Todd-Cartwright said once – If it wasn't for Monsignor Goodsugar, we'd have a lot more light in here. The lamps are for us, the dark bits are for him.'

The man leans forward to look at Lambert's pictures, almost delicate in his manner, but no less present for all that. They've all more or less decided Goodsugar is genuinely American, for these days, with London picking up all sorts of odd bods of unknown manufacture, one can never be sure. Not done to ask, of course, partly because that's the code and partly, as Deyton has once pointed out to Todd-C within Lambert's hearing – No earthly reason for anyone to tell the truth, is there, sir?

So, here is Irwin 'Bob' Goodsugar, perhaps-probably a Yank, but a Yank licensed by Mr Currie to wander around and poke his cheery nose into everyone's work. Why is he here? There is no clear answer, but his chief expertise seems to lie in the area of wireless communications and codes, seeing the amount of time he spends in the small cabin connected to the radio room. Anyway, not Lambert's to ask why, but he really wishes there was some way he could stop the man from calling him 'Jerry'.

Good snappage today, Jerry?

Lambert hates Goodsugar's off-key coinages as much as he detests the nicknames, but he has decided a couple of months ago that the best policy is to keep all contact as brief as possible. There is, therefore, no civilized way to steer the man away from the grating language and tone. Snappage, indeed. He tries to put on his busiest manner as he replies – Reasonable pictures, Bob, very reasonable.

Goodsugar picks up one of the photographs and turns it over, as if expecting to find something equally interesting on the back.

Quite a shindig down there today, huh?

Quite a few people, yes.

Any rough stuff down there at all, Jerry? Anything your little eye in the air can see, that we might have missed on the ground?

Nothing to write home about. A scramble here and there, which is to be expected, I suppose.

Before he goes, Goodsugar puts down the photo carefully, but on completely the wrong place, on Lambert's desk. In the early days, this used to drive Lambert up a wall. Lambert is a man who worships at the altar of systematic order, and it has taken him a good four months to inch himself back from barely contained murderousness to some equilibrium. Tonight, for some reason, the desire to kill the Yank is back with a vengeance.

A few days later, the murdering of Goodsugar still on his mind, Lambert passes Farquhar's desk on his way to the toilet. Todd-Cartwright and Farquhar are playing finger polo with a slim dossier, poking it here and there, turning the pages back and forth.

They couldn't be ghosts. Not ghosts, then, are we agreed?

No, clearly flesh-and-blood characters. Wot done this.

Flesh and blood is very apt, Alan, very apt.

No, what I meant was...

Well, right, you've got a jetty. Remote. And a decommissioned silt barge for cover from the other jetties, as it also says here. So, secluded jetty with bloodstains, with marks of struggle or, rather, as the report puts it, sudden, brief, extreme violence.

Yes.

And then these bodies float up in the water nearby.

They don't bother weighing them down.

Not New York, so, no.

So... they're only concerned with getting rid of them temporarily, until they can exit.

Exactly.

So they're not particularly bothered about... connections... being traced back to...

To themselves, no.

But not premeditated.

Not premeditated, no, but however many of them there were, they were ready and willing to...

Act.

Act. And not that many of them, from the traces on the jetty, though it was raining by then.

How many?

About double the number of the three dead men, at most maybe six or seven, maybe eight. A couple each to hold down the sailors and one or two to do the coshing and the knifing. Maybe even fewer, maybe no more than five. This place has some pretty hefty nasties, the coppers tell me.

And the dead sods?

Two very large men, one less so. Two white, one less so. A Swede, by the name of Sorensen, a Flemish gorilla, Loop, pronounced 'lope', it says here, and a native called Cutty Sark.

Cutty Sark? No!

Well, spelt k-u-t-t-y... No, hang on, not Sark, s-*H*-a-r-k, so perhaps a 'cutting shark'?

Hang on, I've read somewhere that 'kutty' means 'small' on the Malabar coast. Pronounced 'kootty'.

Kuttee? Kutta? A dog?

No, kootti, small, a smaller version of something. Small shark, then.

Well, a coot, nevertheless. Short, dark, bloated body. Head smashed in, probably with a rod.

And the others?

Post-mortem deems knifed. Sorensen stabbed clean through the heart and the other, this Loop, hit with something and then knifed, gut and then throat.

Many wounds?

Worryingly, no. Pretty precise. Not a crime of rage. Nothing superfluous, no dark frenzy, pretty much the minimum required.

So, natives? Indians? Other sailors, of other nationalities?

The message was from their Swedish ship, ex-Malacca. These three were always trouble and the captain assumed they'd jumped ship and he sailed off, probably feeling relieved, the poor devil. No other vessels concurrently in port with any crew that would fit the bill. Inescapable conclusion, they fell afoul of nasty natives, i.e., some natives nastier than themselves.

Untidy.

Untidy would be one way of putting it, Alan, yes. Not to have any clue is hardly reassuring. But for CID to send this on to us betrays... I'd say... no little anxiety.

A bit worrying that Lalbazar actually parts with information on this.

Not just parts, flags it bloody up! When was the last time they photostatted a whole file to us? Question for us obviously, is this an aberration or...

The beginning of some pattern.

Some spate, some trend.

Through those months, another trend, a far more public one, vies for the Ochterlony Section's attention – a passing phenomenon everyone refers to as 'Paxton'. The utterly ridiculous decoy pawn, the obviously sacrificial little goat of a proposal that M.A. Jinnah has pushed forward for no plausible reason, but one that's suddenly causing all sorts of problems in the sluggish three-way chess game between the government, the Congress and the Muslim League. That this 'Paxton' will be devoured in due time by the big pieces, masticated by the tigers of reality into digestible bone-mulch, there's no doubt. But for the moment, idiotic natives all over the country are babbling madly about an independent Mahommedan state 'after the British leave'.

Deyton puts a question to Todd-Cartwright: Paxton. What does it mean, sir?

It's actually Pack-is-stern, sergeant.

Which pack would that be, sir? The one that is stern?

Well, they're all quite stern, sergeant, all the blighters, all quite stern. None of them have any bloody sense of humour at all, except for the Naked Gnome, but if you pay attention, you can sort of tell from their bloody caps.

Sir.

Yes. So the Congress have these white sailor caps, these floppy, faggoty ones. Then the Mahommedans, this Jinner's so-called 'Muslim' League, many of them wear these Yid skull caps, and a lot of green, and all sorts of sickle moon and star symbols. They're obviously the ones who want this Land of the Pure and Holy, this Packistern. Then the Hindoo hounds have these orange faux turbans, as if they're all bloody maharajas, and red and orange muck on their foreheads. As for the bleeding communists, you will see a predominance of red on their clothing, even though they deign to wear no tribal head decoration or smears.

As the monsoon recedes, Lambert's mind has no place for colour. It's all black and white and lots of greys, different shades of missing grey that have started sending him cogent meanings that are almost as private as love messages, signals as intense as the ones coming from the ghost in the dumb waiter.

By early September, the file on the 8th August dock murders has been sent back to Lalbazar police headquarters, stamped 'NOI' in green – Not of Interest – but, as usual, without the name of the Ochterlony Section, since it doesn't officially exist. The consensus is that the triple murder at Kidderpore is a straightforward crime and unrelated to any nationalist terrorism or any espionage activity.

On the 19th of September one of Jinnah's local associates, H.S. Suhrawardy gives a speech at Mohammad Ali Park in which he lays out his reasons why a separate Muslim nation is both necessary and inevitable.

This time, it's Currie himself who has a question for Todd-Cartwright, and he asks it right in front of Lambert's desk, as if the squadron leader isn't there, or as if he doesn't speak the language.

This Surravardy fellow, this mayor chap.

Yes, sir.

Didn't we have a note on a file saying...

Yes, sir, we did have a note.

Saying he was chatting to Bose's brother, Sarat Bose...

About a united Bengal, post... Yes, sir, exactly.

Post us buggering off, major, you're allowed to say it.

Yes, sir, we did have such a note.

So, we are clear this chap's backing two horses. In public, he's rabbiting on about this Muslim state, while negotiating quietly for a united, independent bloody Bengal which, presumably, would comprise both Muslims and Hindoos.

It would seem so, sir.

Goes to show, doesn't it, major? All these buggers are two-faced, if not three- or four-faced!

A bit like double agents, sir, yes, never know which side they're playing for.

Par for the course for these Indian politicians, major, par for the course!

Sergeant Deyton hears Currie's parting shots as he comes in with some files.

Sir?

Sergeant?

Couldn't help hearing that, sir.

Yes, well, the old man was a bit on the pulpit today.

Sir?

Yes?

Is one to understand... speaking about politicians, is it only these Indian geezers who are two-faced?

Now, now, sergeant. There is war on, you do remember?

Yes, sir.

Todd-Cartwright and Deyton exchange a smile. Neither acknowledges Lambert who pretends to be busy with his work.

It takes Lambert exactly two months from the early morning of the 8th of August 1941 to get his own back on Goodsugar. Recounting the story on tape, he says he will remember the date all his life. He will also remember that it is on this day that he found unexpected allies among his English colleagues, all united in their distaste for the bloody Yank.

On the 8th of October, the occasion is the weekly general briefing and the entire Section is gathered around the billiard table in the drawing room for what Toff-Cartwright calls 'The Monday Morning Chukka', except today is a Wednesday.

At 0930, their weekly quota of two nights' sleep spent, everybody finds their place along the green baize. The rains have gone but the humidity is yet to loosen its grip on the city, and Currie calls the meeting to order while wiping the sweat off his neck with a handkerchief.

An overview of the situation in India and Bengal passes by without causing any undue excitement, everyone in turn putting in their two bits when required. Then, as has happened every week since mid-May, the Section's Great Operation comes up for discussion. The torpor lifts off the group as Currie turns to the gofer from the navy.

Would you be so kind, commander, and organize some tea for us?

Calling the petty officer 'commander' is another one of Todd-Cartwright's inspirations, and it comes from the fact that young Jimmy's main job is to provide an unending supply of tea and sandwiches to the crew without letting any waiters into the main suite.

The Frogs call it commande, as in a restaurant you commande a coq au vin. Jimmy, good chap, commandes tea, so a tea commander, verily a Commander of Tea.

Jimmy the Commander is the only member of the Section not cleared for classified stuff, and Currie's polite system is to send him off whenever the topic is about to become unsuitable for the lad's ears.

As Jimmy leaves, Currie turns a page and asks the usual question.

Now then, major, where exactly are we with Ostrich?

Todd-Cartwright takes his time before answering. Best to be extra careful with Rice visiting, best to be precise in his imprecision.

He's still camped in Berlin, sir. Not been far since he visited Rome in May.

Any closer to meeting...?

No, sir. He keeps trying, but the closest he's got is Ribbentrop. What we hear is that Ostrich went into shock in June, when the Germans opened the Russian front. He was rather hoping both countries would join to back his campaign for Indian independence. Now he's trying to pull the fat out of the fire, asking his hosts for help while insisting the Indian POWs they've turned cannot be used against the Soviets. Not a good position in which to be, you'd agree. There has been some talk of a meeting at Berchtesgaden, but Herr Corporal's been busy and Ostrich is clearly not a priority.

No trace of drama in Toff-C's voice, Lambert thinks admiringly, it's as if he's reading from the food supply report.

Your sources are sure, are they?

Yes, sir, quite sure.

So... the operation is at a stalemate at the moment? Can we say that?

Well, no, not quite. When Ostrich passed through Kabul, we cracked the Italian mission there. In his wake, so to speak, and that's come to fruition. They've given us some very nice stuff, I'm happy to say.

Actually, the triumph is there, Lambert corrects himself. He notes that Toff-C has missed out the 'sir' while addressing Rice, and his voice has shifted ever so slightly into a superior tone. He also notices that neither Toff-C nor Currie make any mention of their man who has been attached to Ostrich since the beginning.

Rice's reply is sharp – Why haven't I received regular reports about this?

Toff-C reminds Rice of the special rules that are in place for Ostrich, rules put in place by London and further underlined by Currie, and by Rice himself: no mention of Ostrich was to travel by radio or telegraph and the paperwork was to be kept strict as well. Unless there was some major breakthrough, the protocol was to pretend the operation didn't exist, even within the services.

If you remember, sir, SOE even had teams waiting in Damascus and Istanbul to intercept Ostrich and we weren't allowed to call them off. We're lucky he took the Soviet route and got through alive.

In fact, whenever Lambert remembers the part he himself played at the beginning of the operation, the strongest memory is of the way the hush-hush was stepped up.

It was early in Lambert's posting to Calcutta. That time Deyton and himself had taken one of the small Tiger Moths, Deyton spotting, Lambert flying, and practised the route for a week before the actual moment. On the day, they'd taken off in the dark from the aerodrome at Barrackpore, with no film in the cameras because the intention was not the capture of traces but to make sure there were none. Using the few dim lights on Lower Circular Road, they had managed to reach their first observation point before first light broke. Once there, Lambert flew in lazy circles, keeping the junction of Lansdowne Road and Elgin Road as his centre. He flew as high as possible while making sure that, between himself and the sergeant, at least one of them could see down the straight lines of both Elgin Road and Allenby Road at all times.

They knew which house to watch, and that the car would probably emerge from the back gates on Allenby Road, but it was still quite tricky waiting for the vehicle to appear and then finding a way to follow it without giving the game away. Once the two-tone Wanderer saloon was on the road, their job was straightforward: to tail the vehicle and watch that it did not let out any passengers. If the car did stop and let someone out, Lambert was to radio the units waiting below and the one closest would go into action. As it happened, the motorcar reached its destination in Bihar without mishap. There were no undue stops, no passenger disgorged. Two aeroplanes, Lambert's Tiger Moth and a Hurricane from 32 Squadron flying much higher, overlapped the car all the way to the railway station of a town called Gomoh. Codename Ostrich was safely delivered to his escort, who was codenamed Sabre, and all Lambert had to do was to turn around and fly back. All in all, it was a relatively simple beginning to an extremely complicated operation.

I think we did well, Lambert had said to Deyton. Was a bit of a help, us knowing where he was starting and where he was going, Deyton had replied, parsimonious as ever with the praise as he looked at the newspaper headlines that unknowingly heralded the first major success of Currie and his team at the Ochterlony Suite.

Goodsugar thumps the edge of the table to make an interruption.

Gentlemen, I know all roads lead to Rome, or in this case Berlin and Rome, but perhaps it would be good to get back to matters outstanding further east? As in, around these parts? Lambert feels the whiff of the American tobacco almost before the voice brings him back from his reverie.

Something in the tone, something in the way Goodsugar injects a plume of smoke into the circle before following it by leaning his bulky body forward, sends off a series of signals to Lambert. Not only is Goodsugar privy, not only does he have carte blanche to go looking over people's shoulders, he is now declaring that he is in a position to steer the meeting away from whatever Currie and Rice might want to dwell upon. This has not happened before, and Lambert's are not the only pair of eyes now trained on Mr Currie.

Certainly, Bob, certainly. Currie brisk and cheerful, as if indulging a favourite nephew, no trace of offence and none of any obsequiousness, but none of the dismissive tone, either, that the man so loved as a weapon. He turns to Lambert.

Squadron leader? What have you got for us this week?

Toff-C slides in before Lambert can reply. I was wondering about those Russian coverts you were looking at from the sludge, actually. I imagine there should be something there, wouldn't you?

The Russian pictures are just a kernel of an idea and Lambert hadn't been meaning to bring up them up in full company just yet. But even as irritation sears through him, he sees the beauty of the pass Toff-C has just slipped his way. Seated immediately to his right, Deyton too seems to straighten up a fraction in anticipation.

Lambert's exposition is precise and systematic. Taking a leaf from Toff-C, he keeps his voice as clean of drama as he can.

For the benefit of Rice, he explains 'sludge', the term normally denoting some kind of waste material produced by a factory, in this particular context meaning the intelligence material deemed extraneous and un-useful by its initial recipients, in this particular case some photographs covertly shot by a Soviet-controlled spy which have made their way to London and then been sent back out to Lambert in Calcutta as they have to other reconnaissance experts in other intelligence cells.

Shot just over a month ago, the photographs are taken with a miniature camera and are of fairly low-grade quality in terms of sharpness and shake. What is interesting is that the spy seems to have got himself on a service aircraft plying regularly between small ports in northern Japan and the shots are taken from a fairly low altitude. On the surface, there isn't much to get excited about in a few blurry ships and port buildings with no obvious naval or military presence. But here, two seemingly unconnected jigsaw pieces have clicked into place in Lambert's mind. Lambert doesn't mention it, but everyone in the Section save Goodsugar is aware that his is an extraordinary memory, and he has remembered some photographs of the same ports taken in 1938 by an English operative pretending to be an anthropologist interested in the fishing communities of Japan's northern island. What is curious in the Soviet spy's pictures is not what's there, but what is missing – in none of the ports are there any medium or large ships.

There are lots of small fishing boats, sir, but none of the ocean-going vessels that filled these ports in '38.

So? So they've gone whaling or whatever. Pressed into the war effort for when they enter the conflict. What's the big deal? Goodsugar suddenly finds himself in a bad temper.

Well, exactly, old chap, pressed into the war effort, but where? We've only been looking into it for a week or so but... Toff-C's drawl pours water on electricity.

We? Goodsugar's cigarette seems ready to explode. We? How many of you? I thought it was only our spy eye in the sky here.

Deyton clears his throat and weighs in.

If I may, sir. Sir, I've checked the shipping reports and all the other stuff it is possible to check, and those ships are up to something funny. They are not where they should be.

I thought your job here was to develop pictures.

Currie turns on Goodsugar. You know we like to keep things flexible, Mr Goodsugar. These men have been chosen for their ability to think beyond their individual disciplines.

Thinking? Well, if you call this thinking, I'd like to know what the thinking is.

The thinking, Lambert suddenly has a voice in his throat, is that these missing ships are on some sort of supply rota in the North Pacific. By which I mean they are carrying supplies to larger ships at sea, naval ships that don't want to be seen coming into port, that don't want to be seen going out in any sort of grouping. The thinking is that the Japs are preparing for something they want to keep very quiet.

I'll tell you what the Japs are preparing! Goodsugar's voice takes on a jeering tone. They are preparing to land those forty thousand men they've got sitting in Indo-China, and they are preparing to land them on your two little outposts, Hong Kong and Singapore!

Yes, but they are also up to something in the North Pacific. Lambert is shocked at how clipped and firm he suddenly sounds.

Meaning, old boy, that they may be planning to land something on you as well. Toff-C's voice is full of sympathy.

Land where from the North Pacific? Goodsugar is now laughing out loud. Land where? Alaska? Let 'em come, they'll freeze their eyeballs off! And then we'll take care of 'em. We'll take care of our neck of the woods, sport, don't you waste your time worrying about us. And if you're going to play solitaire with little pictures, I suggest you find some from a little closer to home!

No offence, but I'm pretty sure of my snappage.

Goodsugar feels a sharp sting on the inside of his index and middle fingers and looks down to see that his cigarette has burnt all the way down. As he lights the next one, his smile rakes the room, starting from Todd-Cartwright, warmly cutting Lambert and Deyton into half, before stopping on Currie the Ferret.

No offence, no offence taken at all, gentlemen. And I do take the... photographs, and, uh, the squadron leader's analysis very seriously indeed. It's just that it's good to play devil's advocate sometimes, you do understand? I find it helps squeeze up the clarifications a little bit better.

Yes, of course, of course. Rice moving his hands nervously through his peppery hair. We must be clear about the clarifications, you're quite right.

Yes, well, do look at the photographs again, won't you, Lambert, and write a memo with a final precis of your thoughts.

Yes, I would be grateful for that, Jerry. And I'll wire my people immediately. These Nips are like rattlesnakes, got to keep an eye on 'em, wherever and everywhere.

Of course, Lambert writes no memo and Goodsugar wires nobody. Over the next few weeks, the memory of the three Limeys cornering him recedes to a small shelf deep in the back of Goodsugar's mental workshop.

He's reminded of the whole thing again just once, in mid-November, when he walks in on Lambert arguing with Currie on the need to push Singapore to blackout. From what Goodsugar can gather, Lambert has just seen a dusk-time picture accidentally taken by a reconnaissance plane about to land at Sing and this has made him anxious.

Lit up like Piccadilly at Christmas, sir, the place is just asking for it. Can we not recomm—

Afraid not, Mr Lambert. This Section is charged with a few very specific tasks, and our brief does not extend to advising on the defence of Singapore.

Yes, sir, but they don't seem to realize they are almost within range of carrier-borne—

I know, squadron leader, believe me, I know. But very sticky about their parish, the brass in Singapore, so put it out of your mind.

Parish. Sticky. Inside himself, Goodsugar shakes his head. One by one, the thought bubbles plume out of it as he walks away. Typical, these people. Won't deal with the danger staring them in the face, and insist on telling us Yanks where we're going wrong, all this trying to pull us off the chairs and on to the dance floor... Take Lambert, with that fairy tale about the missing boats... and then this princeling-type Washington is currently starry-eyed about, whatshisname, Poundbatter, Mountpatter, Battenhatch? This incompetent idiot first cousin of the king... this Admiral Royal Disaster, who's apparently gone and sunk more of his own destroyers than the enemy's in the Mediterranean, now lording it around naval bases stateside, some embarrassing craziness Goodsugar has picked up on the scuttlebutt: apparently Lord Nelson Mountbatten – *that* was his name, Mountbatten! – had toured Hawaii and found Pearl 'ill-prepared for an air attack'.

'Attack from *where,* my Lord Lughead?' Some ornery vice admiral should have asked him, but of course no one did, too polite to just say, 'Listen, Your Lordship, you can try and stampede us into joining your war but it ain't going to work, you hear?'

I look around the apartment, and realize yet again how I've turned the whole place into a replica of the Ochterlony Section. Well, maybe not a replica – since I have no actual pictures of the Section – but a kind of homage to the place, I imagine, an archaeological workshop where one pieces together shards of the past, or one of those police rooms in films where they have photos and maps stuck across the walls as they try and track some heinous crime, track some serial killer, except here we already know who done it – the perpetrator is time with all its relentless trickery and ruthlessness – and we know that time doesn't just kill people, it kills memory as well. In fact, time kills everybody just once, but memory is a victim that is constantly being killed. Perhaps it's foolish, attempting to revive the memory-corpses while knowing fully well they will die again at some point, irrevocably and forever. Perhaps it makes no difference, giving some memories the extension of a second life.

Nevertheless, I have stuff up all over the walls and even across some of the windows, and the dining table and another large desk have been turned into worktables, complete with hanging lamps glaring down upon the material. The stuff is vaguely organized and distributed according to whom it belongs to: the work desk is covered with stuff relevant to Nirupama; the dining table is mostly devoted to Elko, who takes up more space than he really should, and to notes about jazz in the '40s; the sofa is for the goras I know, Imogen and Lambert; the walls and windows have different timelines stuck across them, and so on.

Normally, I don't put on music when I'm working on the project, maybe some jazz from the '30s and '40s when I'm looking at certain areas, but mostly not, because the sound interferes with trying to put myself into that period.

This evening, I'm yet to start work, so the radio's on and Jim Morrison is growling his vacuousness into the apartment. '*I'm a spy... in the House of Love...*' I've never been a great fan of The Doors, or even old Anaïs Nin whom he's quoting, and I can't control what they play on the radio. I turn it off and put my needle back on the correct, undulating track.

There are, of course, no records or photographs of any kind pertaining to the military intelligence cell that occupied the Ochterlony Suite at the Great Eastern Hotel from mid-1940 until about a year after the end of the war in August 1945. At the time, the cell was apparently referred to by different names within the rarefied and highly limited military, intelligence and police circles that knew of it – Ochterlony Group or O.G., G.E. Group, G.E. Section or just Section. In the hotel records, the large Ochterlony Suite on the third floor was shut for renovations at some point in 1939 and never reopened to guests. The personal dossiers of the members of the Section apparently have oblique references to their war service in Calcutta but, again, no details of this time. Though most of his menus are untraceable, there is far more evidence of Chef Paul Bonnemaison's stint at the hotel, signed requisition lists, two employment contracts covering 1938 to 1945, photographs of him at banquets and large parties and so on.

After I finished making an initial inventory of Elko's work, whatever I could find of it, I did look to see if there were any sketches that could match the characters of the Section described to me, but I could find nothing very much. There is one half-done pencil sketch of a bulky, Caucasian man in a jacket and trilby hat at the side of which Elko has scrawled the words 'Ugly American', but I found that folded into the pages of a Graham Greene novel from the late 1950s, *Our Man in Havana*, so I don't think that can be connected to Goodsugar, and I don't think that Elko actually ever met the man.

I do know for sure Missus met him, and how that eventually led to many things, including my being involved with this project. I know Goodsugar was one of the few official Americans in India at the time, even though he was initially pretending to be a civilian, part of the advance party before the whole lot of them arrived a bit later. We know the Yanks were over there in India, about 1,20,000 of them at peak strength, and a whole lot of them in Calcutta. I'm here because they were there. Partly.

I look around me and remind myself that the paintings are the main thing, the reason why I've lowered myself into this tunnel, but then there are the other things, the stories attached to the pictures, stories that led to them being made and stories that came from them being made. Then there are the notes, the tapes and interviews, nominally about the work and about Elko, but actually going far beyond and around; if the paintings and drawings are an old, dilapidated Calcutta mansion, the rest of it is like the trees and plants twirling out of the brick and masonry.

Looking around at the mass of orderly chaos, I feel a spasm of rage at those two. It's those two who are to blame, Old Elko and his Cirrhosis Missus, who was not his wife, nothing like his Missus, more a liver partner than a spouse – 'The only better half I have, old chap, is the half of the glass that's still got something in it!' Those two are the ones who've left me with these foundlings, these unwanted, miscegenated infants of tales, this long, badly itemized, unpaid hotel bill of stories. I realize, yet again, how much I've let those two take over my life or, rather, let the Calcutta of that time, through those two, take me hostage.

Thankfully, there's not too much dust in this part of the world, nothing like in Calcutta, but the stuff that surrounds me does need regular dusting and wiping, and my will to do housekeeping gets stretched to breaking point. And from time to time, I find I also need to tidy up the mess of stories, even if it's just for myself.

For instance, today, in 1977, it's easy to forget that there are many crimes from thirty–forty years ago for which you *can't* blame the Americans. Looking back, there's a tendency now to segue from the Nazis and the Tojo-Japs straight into the parallel, interlocking hells created by the United States and the Soviets, with Stalin providing a kind of bridge of evil between the 1930s and the 1950s, and then Mao starting another arc just where Stalin's tapers off. Crawling under this melee of competing villains, the British and the French get to sidle away into the foliage.

Even when I listen back to the Nirupama tapes, so intense is her anger towards the Americans and the Russians, and her bitterness at the Soviets' different betrayals, that I tend to forget that all that came much later to join her hatred of the Ingrej.

'I still remember the moment. It was in late October of '42, after the big cyclone and the Pujas, and Roma and I had come out of Bijoli Cinema, you know the one with the pillars in front with the round lights on top? That one, yes. We had gone for a morning show, but the lights would have been off anyway, even at night, because of the blackout. I can't remember which film, some Bangla film, obviously, and we were walking down the avenue to the Hazra crossing to catch a tram. It was October, so not yet cold, but even so I wondered why these two women were almost naked. They saw us and started to, I don't know, sort of stumble towards us with a desperation. It's not what beggars did, it's not what beggars do. Normal city beggars, no matter how destitute, would have a sense of where they were, who they were approaching, but not these two women. They were on the road itself, with no awareness of the cars and buses just missing them... Of course, all this I thought about only later, when I thought about it. At the time, I just had the mad idea that these two had dropped from the sky, from some other planet, like one used to read in science fiction stories.

'They were two women and we were two women, but we had nothing in common. We were two Calcutta girls in pretty good health, and these were two... two... I couldn't help checking again and again that they were actually women, two human females.' At this point, Nirupama breaks down into almost sobbing, not something she does very often, and then she controls herself. 'Their eyes were one thing, huge, almost popping out of the head, and the older one already had a distended stomach. At first, I thought she was pregnant, but then I saw her white hair. Their eyes were one thing, but when the younger one opened her mouth, some strange sounds came out which I could not recognize. Rather, I could almost recognize them as Bangla speech but then again, not quite. Roma was also flummoxed.

'What did you say? I asked. The woman repeated something. Then Roma asked. Food? Hungry? Then a shopkeeper's boy passing by started laughing. Arre didi, they are from Comilla, close to where I'm from! They haven't eaten for a week, that's what they are saying. Go down towards Kalighat, there are many more of them, all looking for food! They are everywhere, but I haven't seen anybody else from Comilla.

'Comilla. You know, geographically it's two hundred and fifty miles east from Calcutta, but those two hundred and fifty miles are all river delta, so you have to double that, and then... the two-fifty miles of those days are very different from the two-fifty miles of today, you understand?'

I nodded.

'So... how do these two starving village women from Comilla get to Calcutta in 1942? If you're from Comilla, why not head for Dhaka, a city which is right there? But we never asked them, because it was not possible to ask. You just knew they didn't have too many days left in their bodies. Roma and I pulled out whatever money we had, a rupee and a few annas, keeping back just enough for the tram fare, and gave it to them. We had to make sure the younger one didn't drop the money, Roma made sure she closed the girl's fingers around the coins, and then, and then... I'm ashamed to say, Communist Niru and Congress Socialist Roma, we almost ran to the tram. When we got home, I realized that such had been my panic I had scratched myself badly while reaching into my blouse.

'By the end of 1942, reports from the villages had already started coming in via the Party cadres, but everybody thought this was just – what was the sentence? – "Just another temporary intensification of long ongoing peasant misery." It was when they appeared on the streets, these skeletons whispering in dialects we rarely heard in Calcutta, that the horror became clear. As I said, you could tell they were different from city beggars. They didn't know their way around. You could almost see every big building, every wide avenue sparking a new fear in their eyes. Speaking in tongues we could only vaguely connect to the Bangla we knew. A few days after that encounter near Bijoli, around Shyambajar I again heard very different accents, which I later understood were from Mednipur and Purulia, all the way in the west. It was as if all of Bengal was arriving to collect their dues from Calcutta.

'I took a while to realize this is what the British had done to us, them and the black marketeers, the middlemen who were – and in the Party study groups, we were taught never to forget this – very much Indian. Marwaris, Bhaiyas and Bengalis. Both Hindus and Muslims, and very much Indians.'

That was in 1942, but at the moment I'm looking at the end of November 1941.

Sometimes, the more you tidy the messier it gets.

LANDINGS

For all his bluster, Bob Goodsugar is too intelligent keep underestimating others and smart enough to know when he has reached the limits of his understanding. Over the last few weeks, he has sensed that there is something in the air between Lambert, Deyton and Todd-Cartwright, something in each man's body language, some extra tick in the little hesitations and pauses all Limeys use like pawns in a chess game, something that creates a slight unease in Goodsugar. Something brewing at the back of the suite, but Goodsugar hasn't had the time to try and figure it out.

One morning, early in December, Goodsugar wakes up with a thought sticking in his brain. He can't quite hunt it down, but it's something that's started as a vague dream on the last outskirts of sleep and stayed with him, crystallizing all too slowly across the brushing of his teeth, his showering, and his donning of the slightly thicker suit in deference to the mild winter that is now upon the city. By the time the bearer knocks with his breakfast, he has located Coyote-Skunk Lambert as being at the centre of the dream, but no more than that.

Over his eggs and sausages, he tries to dispel the whole thing, reminding himself that he now always has strange dreams on nights he goes to sleep at a normal time. The previous seven days have been crazily hectic, and last night is the first time in about a fortnight that he has not stayed up until well past dawn. For some reason, something had suddenly relaxed inside him yesterday, as if he had done everything that could possibly be done and the rest was up to god almighty. He felt maybe a bit like a Hollywood mogul who's just finished a picture and is now waiting for the box office to reply. At 5.30 p.m., he had gone to Currie and informed him that he was taking the evening off. After which, he had driven to the Calcutta Swimming Club for a few good, hard lengths, returned, showered and dressed, before going out for dinner and cabaret at the Silver Slipper.

The show at the Slipper had been pretty good: a pair of cockney girls doing a kind of slap-and-tickle routine, with a lone darkie ivory merchant as accompaniment. The guy not bad at all for an Anglo-Indian, and the women even more not bad for a pair of big-titted Limey broads. On the other hand, the full band that took the stage between the acts, also Anglo, hadn't been so great. They clearly needed to be kicked up the butt to deliver more punch. Missing home and craving Basie or Ellington, he had eaten just the right amount but drunk far too much Scotch – almost a full bottle's worth he guessed. Despite the booze, he had made the correct decision in not staying on for the second show. Around midnight, he had tottered into a taxicab for the short ride between Park Street and the Great Eastern, and by half-past twelve he had been asleep.

Now, making a piece of sausage slip around in a turmoil of egg yellow, he almost starts to laugh. Missing medium tonnage from the northern ports. Not mentioned by Lambert after that Monday meeting in October, nor by the other two bastards. Goodsugar had forgotten, remembered faintly, and then forgotten again. Except, he now realizes that he hasn't forgotten at all, just pushed it all to the back of his mind as he's dealt with all the other stuff that Donovan, sitting back in Maryland, has required him to do. Polishing off his eggs and uncovering the plate of pancakes, he is faced with the finished formula of an equation his brain has obviously been working out over the last several weeks.

The first time, smelly Lambert and Deyton and Todd-Cartwright had ever been friendly towards each other was at that meeting, as they constructed the report on the empty Japanese ports. Since then, none of them had brought it up again, despite Currie's instructions to keep the whole Section informed. But the new-found cahootsy stuff had continued, of soft conversations chopped off whenever he chanced upon them in a huddle, of pregnant tones and stifled amusement, all of which has suddenly begun to get under the thick skin of Goodsugar's self-assurance: what if the bastards actually knew something that he ought to know?

Goodsugar walks over to his drinks cabinet and unlocks it. From among the bottles of bourbon and vodka, he pulls out the jar of pure Vermont maple syrup and returns to his pancakes. The last week has been tense for several reasons: the Jap delegation is in DC, negotiating with State, and the rumours are that Roosevelt is trying to secure a peaceful settlement with them so he can free himself up to declare war on Germany. The recent radio traffic from Service headquarters has all been about taking a harder look at the Krauts; after years of rickety neutrality, the Pentagon and his bosses at the Service suddenly want anything and everything on the Germans, not just military stuff, but things like abandoned Reich passports, Americans and other friendly whites who can speak German, anyone who's studied in Germany in the last fifteen years, tourist maps, recipe books, everything.

Ruminatively, Goodsugar cuts a triangular slice from the stack of pancakes. Making sure the syrup has been properly absorbed along with the melted butter, he puts the slice in his mouth and wonders who is trying to break down his door at this early hour.

Which fool of a waiter and where was the fire? Still chewing his pancakes, Goodsugar hauls himself out of the deep armchair and goes to the door. The solid wood is now shaking under the onslaught, and this incenses Goodsugar. He hurls the door open, his choice Indian abuse firing already.

'Kuttey ke bachhey! Kya chahiye?'

The words are well out of his mouth before he realizes that the guy he's just called a son-of-a-dog is not a waiter.

'Sorry, sir, Mr Goodsugar, but it's very urgent! Mr Currie wants you – would like you to come to the Section at once!'

Jimmy the Commander looks like he hasn't slept in months. The rings under his eyes pulsate as he speaks.

'What's up, Jimmy? Who shot who?'

'The Japs, sir. They're going to land.'

'Oh yeah?' Goodsugar wakes up some more. 'Land where, son? Dum Dum Aerodrome?'

'I'm not sure, sir, couldn't tell you exactly, but north of Singapore somewhere. Mr Currie...'

'Okay, you go ahead, go on down and tell him I'll be right there.' Goodsugar shuts the door in the ensign's face and returns to his breakfast.

For the next five minutes, he concentrates on demolishing the pancakes and finishing the coffee remaining in the pot – who knows when he'll get a peaceful meal again. As he wolfs down the food, he calculates many different things in his mind. Squadron Leader Lambert's facial expressions and any knowledge he might be hiding are not among the things he thinks about.

Downstairs, in the billiard room of the Ochterlony Suite, everybody is standing, as if the inevitable arrival of the Japanese invasion, a thousand miles of complicated geography to the south-east of Calcutta, has put an end to sitting forever. Lambert is reading the transcript of the first message over and over again, trying to decipher in the short text of terse sentences what the pilots of the two RAF Hudsons might actually have seen:

0700/SING/HQ SIGNALS - 6/12/41:

MOST URGENT MOST URGENT MOST URGENT STOP ALERT ALL SECTIONS STOP MASSIVE ENEMY FORCE SIGHTED 80 NAUTICAL OFF INDO-CHINA STOP SIGHTING 0535 HOURS STOP STEAMING WEST DIRECTION SIAM STOP ESTIMATED LANDING UNDER 48 HOURS STOP

Lambert checks his watch. 0900 here in Calcutta, so 1000 hours in Singapore and Siam which were an hour ahead. The message has come in just over an hour ago, just when everybody was winding down for the night. The first message has been followed by all sorts of other stuff confirming this was not a false alarm but indeed the real thing. If the estimations were correct, the Japanese would be landing somewhere on the Siam coast in the early hours of the day after tomorrow.

Right, gentlemen, to order please. And I suggest all of you do sit down – this war is going to last for quite a while yet. Currie neat and dapper as usual, his all-in-a-day's-work demeanour completely untouched by the news.

Currie waits for everyone to settle, keeping himself standing while everyone finds their stools and chairs. Goodsugar is the last to join, but today even he finds his place without fuss.

Right. Now, the first thing I want to remind this Section is that this... these landings are hardly unexpected. In fact, this is only one development among the many we have anticipated correctly, so do please let's make an effort, among ourselves and when dealing with people outside this Section, to maintain absolute calm. It is paramount, paramount, not only that there be no snappage of nerve among us, but also that we infect all around us with what I hope is our iron confidence.

May I also remind you that we are not, specifically *not,* a field intelligence unit. It goes without saying that we will have to give primacy to the Singapore theatre, but the cost to our other duties and operations cannot be too great. I am of a mind, however, to stand down some of our internal surveillance within India and deploy whatever that frees up towards our yellow friends and the little bash they're just about to throw. Let's do our best to make their party as short and unpleasant as possible, but let's not be surprised if it continues longer than we hope.

Over the next twenty-four hours, Currie's Ochterlony Section moves smoothly into a higher operational gear. The controlling committee consisting of Currie, Farquhar and Todd-Cartwright quickly puts up a twenty-four-hour duty roster, parcelling out a rota of work, rest and sleep for everyone, with all members being given additional duties to the ones they already have. A part of the master bedroom of the suite, having earlier been emptied of its grand double bed, is now redeployed as a dossing place, with six camp beds being brought in. A wall running along the billiard table is cleared of paintings and a huge composite map of South East Asia – a series of charts that stretches east-west from western India to Indo-China, and north-south from southern China to Ceylon – is fixed to the wall; two Chinese folding screens are arranged in such a manner, in the corridor outside the suite entrance, that no waiter or outsider can catch even an accidental glimpse of what, until then, has been the innocuous looking billiard room. Jimmy the Commander finds himself in charge of two gofers even more junior than himself, two lowly lads grabbed from the kitchen section of the small contingent of Welsh Guards serving in Governor House across the road.

Without revealing too much by way of fact or figure, Currie manages to convey to his immediate subordinates that the Section's resources have had an immediate fillip because they are among the very few who have accurately predicted where the Japanese would attack. This same minority, until now pooh-poohed and ignored, is now apparently in ascendancy: useful while it works, this contrition business. The fine trick is not to the push the gentlemen up there so hard that they return to their normal obstreperousness.

The hours skittle into each other, and by 2030 hours the next day, Lambert is as close to breaking down from exhaustion as he has ever been. Even closer, he reckons, than those hellish weeks in the August and September of last year when he was stationed as a junior cog in the straining gears of the Reconnaissance Section at Biggin Hill. Then, he had felt responsible for each German aircraft that had got through the net, responsible for each ten- or twenty-pounder that had been dropped on southern England. His job had been to fly, to assess the pattern of damage from raids the previous day, and to try and think like a Luftwaffe recce pilot – if you were a Hun scouting about, flight lieutenant, what would look scrumptious, what would look unfinished, what would make you hungry? I don't want you to dawdle over the targets, I want you to fly that Spit jolly bloody fast, as if you were a Jerry pilot about to be bounced any moment, and try and catch whatever you can on your cameras. And then to report back to me as though you were reporting to Hermann Buggering Goering.

For two months, he had flown an average of three sorties a day, going up to four daily in September. He had come back, developed the film, connected the pictorial narrative of bomb craters to what he had been told about possible targets, and then made out his reports. This is different, and much harder. There is no Spitfire to fly jolly bloody fast, for one. There is nothing to fly, in fact, except his overstretched eyes and brain. He starts to say something to Todd-Cartwright but thinks the better of it. Sleep-starved eyes stinging from the cigarette smoke, Lambert puts his scarred voice back into his voice box and carries on punching the keys on the recalcitrant elephant of a typewriter, making sure the carbons are exactly aligned between the paper as he writes out his latest assessments of Japanese air capability in triplicate.

At about 2100 hours, Todd-Cartwright saunters up to him, smelling fresh as roses and murmurs a question: Jeremy, old boy, shall we tell 'em Patani and Singora are good as gone? Or d'you think we should wait until they come to this conclusion themselves and inform them *post facto*, as it were?

It is a strategic question in more than one sense of the word.

The first landings are estimated at around 0600 hours Singapore time tomorrow, a tomorrow that seems as if it's already been here for many hours; in Calcutta, it is now 9 p.m. in the evening, i.e., 10 p.m. in the now dark tropical forests of the isthmus linking Siam and Malaya. Just a bit under twelve hours to go. Troops from Singapore have been rushed north across the border to meet the invasion, RAF planes have made sorties, trenches are being dug furiously in the jungles and the rubber plantations. The battle hasn't yet begun, but between Todd-Cartwright and Lambert there is already a certainty that the two key airstrips will fall in the next few days. Jap planes being able to land from the carriers, being able to refuel and take off from these fields, means that things are shortly going to get very, very hot for the island fortress of Singapore.

The problem facing the two men is that they have, in the past, paid a rather heavy price for being the bearers of bad, albeit accurate, news – contemptuous disbelief, sharp upbraidings, and probably adverse comments on their personal files, though of these they will never be fully sure. Mr Currie, a leader in the classical mould, has taken every credit for their work, when credit has come, and passed on to their heads every bit of brass flak, minor or major. Until a few months ago, the animosity between Lambert and Todd-Cartwright meant neither could do much about this; their new-found camaraderie means that they now have options. Strategic ones.

Well, I've been thinking about just that. I had an idea we could write a short memo saying—

Sergeant Deyton walks up briskly and coughs.

Yes, Len, what is it? The same question comes out of both Lambert and Todd-Cartwright.

Well, something's up. While there is no question of him addressing either officer by first name, Deyton, too, has judiciously begun to dispense with his 'sir's when the three of them are on their own. Something's up for sure, though I can't for the life of me...

Deyton proffers a bottle at them. Just been given this by Mr Currie. Said the three of us deserved it more than anybody else. Also said we would need it. Seemed to be in a bit of a flap, the old man, but not... exactly... unhappy, if you see what I mean. Eyes shining when he hauled me in. Slung this over, said his piece and got rid of me sharpish. 'Dismissed, sergeant!' he said, not something he—

Todd-Cartwright emits a long, low whistle. Lambert turns see the man examining the bottle with great care.

Well, well, well... I'll be damned. I'll... be... bloody... damned.

What is it, Alan? Mind telling us?

What it is, my dear fellow, is extremely good, extremely rare Scotch whisky. In fact, calling this Scotch whisky is like calling a Bugatti a sports car.

Bugatti, sir?

Like calling a Rolls a mere motorcar, he means. Lambert joins the dots for Deyton, who, for once, is at a loss.

This, my hearties, is whisky from a single distillery, unmixed with other, lesser tosh. And if I'm reading this illiterate Scottish scrawl correctly, it says '1921', which means, sergeant, that this liquor has been aging in a barrel for as long as you have.

Born in '16, sir. 18th of February 1916, it says on the paper, which would mean I am—

Don't quibble, my boy! Go and procure three tumblers from the commander, *clean* tumblers, and a jug of cold water. I want a taste of this before Currie comes to his senses and asks for it back!

Lambert asks the obvious question. Alan, what's Currie playing at?

Todd-Cartwright doesn't answer. Instead, he takes off his jacket and puts it carefully around the shoulders of his chair. His eyes stay down, flicking over the carpet as if someone's placed a crossword there. Not quite sure, old boy, not quite sure. He rolls up his sleeves, getting ready for the whisky. The situation hardly warrants a ...even an ordinary bottle of... quite extraordinary of the old man to even... unless, unless...

Both men stand wordlessly, listening to the noises coming out of the radio room where Farquhar is overseeing the installation of a brand-new cipher machine that is to be connected directly to London.

Deyton returns, three glasses stacked in one large hand, a jug of water held in the other. The clink of glass snaps Todd-Cartwright out of his contemplation, and he expertly peels off the wax and pops the stopper from the bottle. Carefully, he pours out three generous drams of drink. He puts back the cork before watering each glass carefully, as if conducting an experiment in advanced chemistry. He then picks up each glass and shakes it in a small circle, mixing the water and the alcohol, before ceremoniously handing one, first to Lambert, then to Deyton, and finally to himself.

Deyton notices that the liquor has gone almost opaque with the addition of water, not something he has seen whisky do before. He makes a mental note to ask the major about this later. He knocks glasses with the officers and takes a sip. A slow, incendiary sensation spreads from the back of his tongue, taking over his throat and gullet. He finds he can actually connect this taste to what he has previously known as whisky, but only if he tries really hard.

To your health, gentlemen! And may this war provide many such moments of triumph for us, no matter how cloudy!

Sir?

The ritual has briefly blanked out the rest of the world, and none of the three has noticed Jimmy the Commander adding a glass-less fourth to their threesome.

Beg pardon, sir? May I ask a question?

Todd-Cartwright fixes Jimmy with a stare that is hardly a 'yes' but short of a 'no'.

Begging your pardon, sir, don't mean to disturb, but can you please tell me where Pearl Harbour is located?

What's that? Lambert's voice is out, much sharper than he intends it to be.

Pearl Harbour, sir. I was wondering if you could tell me...

Why do you ask? It has fallen to Lambert to focus on young Jimmy, which gives the other two a chance to exchange a quick, telling rally of looks. They gauge, a good few moments before Lambert, why Jimmy is carting around the question. Todd-Cartwright answers before Lambert can.

It's a huge American naval base on an island called Hawaii. It's the home port of their Pacific Fleet. Now, lad, has anything happened at this Pearl Harbour?

Is it very far, sir, across the Pacific? Jimmy's second question pops simultaneously.

It is. Very far. On the other side of the Pacific. Todd-Cartwright's reply continues to carry his previous question.

But, but that's imposs—, Lambert almost drops his whisky tumbler, his own detailed calculations over the last three months chopping the remaining syllables off the word.

Well, sir, I had better find Mr Goodsugar. Mr Currie has ordered me to wake him up.

How big? The frog of fire skipping around inside his chest makes it very hard for Deyton to stop himself from grinning.

Sir?

How big was the attack? asks Todd-Cartwright gently.

I'm not sure, sir, but Mr Currie has had to leave for an urgent briefing at Fort William, and he's asked me to wake Mr Goodsugar and inform him that he has just received word that Japanese planes have bombed Pearl Harbour a few hours ago. Said Mr Goodsugar might like to get on the wire to his people.

They can see Jimmy is rehearsing his speech for the Yank, and that he is very scared.

Just received word, did he? Todd-Cartwright picks up the bottle of whisky and smiles down at it. And an urgent briefing, was it, to which he was called away?

Sudden telephone call, must've been, Deyton adds happily.

Well, off you go, then, ensign! Lambert's voice has a tone of crackling command.

And Jimmy? Todd-Cartwright's soft drawl pulls the young sailor back. No need to mention that you've stopped by here on your way, d'you understand?

Yes, sir, no, sir.

All three of them can see through the back of Jimmy the Commander's head, see the look of bafflement increasing on his face as he walks away slowly. Before Lambert or Deyton realize it, their glasses are charged again and the bottle locked away in a drawer in Todd-Cartwright's desk. Without a word being exchanged, the three of them find themselves casually distributed in the vicinity of the door to the master bedroom, well within earshot of everything going on inside.

They are in time to hear Goodsugar's grunt as Jimmy finally wakes him up.

What is it now, goddammit?

Please wake up, sir, the Japanese have attacked, sir!

They were always going to, son. You need to get hold of the duty officer.

Please wake up, sir, the Japanese have *attacked!*

Now you listen to me, you dumb sonofabitch. You will go get a hold of whoever's on that duty roster and you will inform them that the bastards have landed early.

Sir, I've been asked by Mr Currie to tell you that Japanese planes have bombed a place called Hurl Parbour. I believe it's one of yours.

One of mine? Hurl Parlour?

I mean, Pearl Harbour, sir. Pearl Harbour in the Pacific. Other side of the Pacific.

Lambert, Deyton and Todd-Cartwright hear the snap of the light blanket as it's ripped off the bed, and then the thump of two large feet hitting the floor. They can all hear the sound of the big man straightening up, taking up his space in the darkness. Coming now from a height, the voice changes.

Son, if you're trying to tell me something, you better tell it to me.

Sir, yes, sir. Mr Currie.

Currie, yes?

Said.

Yes?

To wake you up and tell you.

Keep going.

Japanese planes. Japanese Air Force planes.

Yes.

Bombed. Bombing raid.

Yes.

About four hours ago.

Yes, where?

Pearl Harbour. In Hawa—

Pearl Harbor, Hawaii, yes. Go on.

Yes, sir. Bombed American naval base... port... home port, fleet...

Son? If this is someone's idea of a Limey joke, I'm going to fry you crisp, you understand?

Yes, sir. Don't think it's a joke, sir. Mr Currie's rushed to Fort William. Ordered me to wake you and tell you.

They hear the thump of a posterior hitting the bunk bed, a scuffle of bedside stuff, a flinty click of a lighter. The voice is now sitting down.

I believe you, son. Thank you. I'm awake now, thank you. Now, do you think you can go get me some coffee?

THREE

Light Dancing

24 DECEMBER 1941

I

LEAVE

Coming out of the night, the smile spreads across his face, out of control, taking him over. Kedar misses her as he wakes up, even as he is aware of waking up, even as he is aware that one day he will not wake up, even as he is aware that he is waking up not just for himself but for others as well. He is aware, as the grin hurts his still sleepy facial muscles, that the smile comes from the same uncanny power, the power that has nothing to do with him, that allowed him to produce that shot he played against Motherwalla, the magical cross-court backhand from an impossible angle that destroyed the Parsi cockatoo's will and won him the match that distant afternoon in August.

'You were a fool, Eva, to leave.' He tries the sentence out aloud and it furs up just behind his throat. He is still half asleep, and his imagination isn't in a high enough gear to manage it convincingly. All the words do is leave him feeling incomplete and wrong, like a quilt that's slipped off in the middle of a deep dream and bunched up out of reach. Beyond the sunlight scraping the mosquito net, beyond the winter-morning smell of the house, beyond the twisting roads that lead from the gate to the port on the river, beyond the river which leaps to the sea which salts into the ocean, is Eva in her ship, together with her going and her moment of departure.

'You wyeare a phool-iva. To liibh.' Rasko places the tea tray on the bedside table.

The ball whistles off from the middle of Kedar's racquet, smacks into the net-cord and bounces back.

'Dada-babu, what is a phooliva?'

Rasko's question is genuine. This is borne out by the fact that he is looking away from Kedar and mouthing the word again, trying to locate it in the shallow drawers of his English.

Kedar's morning sleep escapes, like Eva's skirted buttocks swerving out of the door behind the porter with the luggage, like the water whirlpooling out from the last bath she ran before leaving; the English he had tried to teach her draining away, 'Goodbye, we will see us again sometime, I hope.' The formal wreckage of words underlining the finality of the hotel doors opening and closing, the money he'd lent her spent on the passage to Sydney, the Sikh driver standing next to the taxi, waiting to take her to the docks, the side of her hip sliding into the seat while she held his eyes, the same hips where he had held her, so, too tight he had thought the first time, but no, just as she liked it, escaping, gone like the absurd moment a few days before she left, when he had said 'I am in love' and she had replied 'Yes, but I am afraid I am in leave.' Her laughing, aware that she had made a very bad joke, laughing, hoping to make it easier for him, and, as he hadn't then consciously realized, for herself.

Kedar sits up, pushing back the bedclothes with his legs. He rips out the mosquito net from its tucking under his mattress and swings his legs out, dangling feet fishing for slippers. His torso is still behind the mesh as he snaps at Rasko.

'It's *leave*, you bloody idiot! LEAVE! Libh na, leeeeve!'

Rasko maintains his calm, raises the net from Kedar's face and hands him his tea.

'Liiiibh,' he says, still the scientist, still mulling it over as he begins to roll up the net from around Kedar, flipping the sides over the top where it forms its own hammock over the huge, high bed.

Kedar looks down at his teacup, sees something else even as he feels it, and quickly retrieves the quilt before Rasko's busy hands reach it. Grabbing a part of it, Kedar makes a thick cushion on his lap, hoping Rasko hasn't seen the raging erection rising like a volcano from his pyjamas. Who would have thought the effect of a single banana from Panchpukur would last over four months?

Now safe under his wraps, cup and saucer balanced on top, Kedar begins his assault anew.

'Leave maney jaawa, means to go! Leeeeave! It's a *wa* sound, not a *bha* sound! Leave, cleave, sleeve, all *wa*! When will you understand this?'

'Thiik achhey, thiik achhey, Dada-babu, your brain isn't set yet, have your tea now and we will try later.' Rasko in Bangla can be quite brisk when he wants, especially when he sees a weakness, especially in his younger employers like Kedar and Borun-kaku.

The aroma of the tea opens up Kedar's nose. As he takes a first sip, things start to fall into some kind of place. Rasko's linguistic fumbling actually brings up the unwelcome yet undeniable undertaste of relief at Eva's going. Yes, he was, is, in love, but in no way was he ready to handle the huge rock she would have dropped into the measured pond of his life had she, for instance, said 'Yes, I love you too. Can we be marriage?' The taste of the tea counters the vast and sour tang of what that might have meant, telling his parents, explaining to them, arguing with them, possibly leaving the house and living... where?

Without realizing it, he has moved away from the bed, leaving its trapped night-lanes of heat and dreams for Rasko to release. He finds himself standing next to the French window, looking out at the garden still divesting itself of mist at nine o'clock. The uncomfortable banana between his legs has disappeared, leaving behind a powerful surging of bladder. He greedily gulps down his tea and goes to the bathroom.

When he returns, he finds Rasko refilling his cup, adding milk and sugar exactly as he likes it. As he takes back the cup and saucer, he wonders if the family would have let him have Rasko, whether Rasko would have got along with his new mistress, whether she could have dealt with him properly; Rasko and Eva, two listing boats of 'English' colliding in the midriver of domesticity, in some small flat on Southern Avenue or in Bhowanipur... suddenly Rasko evaporates from the equation, leaving just Eva and himself; the small flat goes too, replaced by the only space they could inhabit, which was her hotel room. Again, the idiot smile comes and stands in the wings, wanting the stage of his face.

The bearer knocking on the door with breakfast, Eva locked on top of him, turning one of her sighs into an impish grin, 'My little prince is hungry you are, yes?', pulling herself off of him quickly and making straight for the door, completely naked, trails of dark brown hair stuck between her shoulder blades by sweat, walking up to the door and looking back at him, hair streaking across her eyes and cheeks – 'How hungry is Prince?' – and turning the key. Him leaping out of bed to scramble into his clothes, her telling the bearer to wait just a minute as the man tries to push open the door, her leaning on the door just enough to hold it, as Kedar tumbles to it barely dressed. The bearer trying to push the trolley in, Kedar saying he will take it from here as she hides behind the open door, shoulders squeezed in, clavicles glistening, knuckles against teeth.

He remembers how naked he felt before that bearer, the knowing look from the man as he released the trolley to Kedar's control, the slight, very slight flick of the eyes over Kedar's shoulder to check the storm-racked bed, the not asking for a signature, and the about-turn down the corridor, obsequiously, dramatically emphatic.

Eva now under him, perverse, head upside down, reaching over to the trolley behind her, trying to feed him bits of buttered toast, wriggling away as he tries to push into her again. Her desire now subservient to her need to tease, to torment, to change the game from straight tennis to some convoluted chess. She rolls him over and gets on top, still playing with him, not letting him in. Without warning, she grabs the tail of the shirt he's still wearing and slowly, deliberately, wipes the head of his wet cock, knowing this will drive him mad. The morning light from the window behind her outlining her waist and the spill of her breasts as she throws back her head and shouts 'I am like Japanese! We have war when I want, and you, Prince English, wait till I want! Till then you eat kipper!'

The windows of this hotel room have framed the monsoon for them in August and well into September, then the sweltering heat and the coming of the first cool mornings in the Bengali month of Kartik that sits across September and October. They are now in mid-Oghrayon which is late October. The monsoons gone from the region, the Japanese attack has been imminent for a few weeks, hanging over people like the first touch of a dangerous fever. As Kedar chews on toast, furious about the shirt and furiously in love, she begins to nip at his sides, moving from one side of his stomach to the other. 'Where?' she breathes between bites, 'where will I come and land?' She reaches up and closes his eyes and he, unwilling to be unwilling, the toast still disintegrating in his mouth, lets her. He feels her take a sharp nibble on his abdomen, 'Singapore?', then she is further down, flicking the tip of her tongue on his kneecap, 'Hong Kong?', then up again, her hair netting her mouth as she sucks the air from his ear, 'Madras?', her voice distant again as he feels her hold him and graze the tip of his penis across her furrow, 'Or, or, will be some parachutes like small suns opening over...' she brings him in halfway and twitches her muscles, 'over...' she goes up and slides down hard, slamming bone against bone, 'Calcutta?'

TERRAIN

'*Prince of Wales*, sunk, *Repulse*, sunk, both gone, yes! Their torpedo bombers had a stroke of luck, yes! But early reverses, part and parcel of history! This has only been going on for? Not even twenty days. My assessment, they will manage to hold the Japanese. In Malaya itself. Japanese are no exponents of blitzkrieg. Then the thick jungle terrain. That should nullify their tanks and aircraft. I think our forces should be able to hold them, at least until the Germans finish the Russia business, which should be by May. Then Hitler's stomach will be temporarily full. Japanese will be facing the monsoon. *That* is when... some peace negotiations can begin. *Perhaps* begin!'

Niru's eyes flare. She stands up from the fire she's trying to light and leans out of the little balcony, trying to see the character who's writing off the Soviet Union with such dispatch. The wall of the neighbouring garden is low enough, but there's a neem tree in the way and, though its branches are almost bare, it manages to make enough of a lattice to obscure the man's face. Through the tree, Niru can see two figures wrapped in woollens. The speaker, speaking entirely in English, is a large, square man wearing a woollen cap with flaps on the ears. He is accompanied by a thinner, smaller companion, head wrapped in a muffler, who is nodding, rapt in attention. The two men are taking a walk around the garden of the big house next door, and she's sure this fat, arrogant fool is none other than the owner of the mansion, Sir Naren Mitter, the famous surgeon and toady of the Ingrej.

We are communists! We will never surrender! she wants to shout across on behalf of all Soviet Russia. But even as her mouth opens, she realizes the absurdity of this. And how unwise it would be to provoke a close friend of her landlord, who, of course, is another be-mansioned and be-knighted Bengali by the name of Sir Braja Bannerjea. She keeps her silence while calculating that these two men, Sir and Sir-vant, will circle back below her balcony in a short while.

The cold is sharp this early in the morning, there is still a lot of moisture in the air, and the clay-and-metal oven-creature is taking its time to light. Niru sits on a low stool and uses a pair of iron tongs to poke the little blaze of paper and twigs through the opening at the bottom. Simultaneously, she blows lightly across the bed of coal sitting on the grate at the top, trying to coax the flames to rise and catch the coal. Small billows of smoke rise through the sharp-edged rocks, swirling off to join the mist hanging over Sir Naren's garden, but the coal remains unrelentingly black.

Niru adds a few more rolls of newspaper to the fire, stoking it as she does, and the coal just begins to ignite as she again hears the two men's voices in the distance. Still sitting, Niru takes a deep breath and starts to sing. The song in her mind is the Bengali version of 'We Shall Overcome', the great hymn of international socialism, but her throat has other ideas.

Tobey poraaaan khuley
tui mukh phutey
tor moner kotha ekla bolo rey!

Then open your soul
and with erupting speech
speak your mind, all on your own!

She finds herself starting in the middle of the song, but she doesn't care, she can repeat the beginning. Like the coal, her voice is taking its time to warm up, but this song, one that she has sung since childhood, is far easier than the foreign march of the communist anthem.

If they don't answer your call,
O unlucky one,
walk alone, walk alone, walk alone, walk alone, my friend!

Niru straightens her back so that she can just see above the balcony parapet. Sir Naren's face is fair, and jowly as a pumpkin. His eyes are small but sharp, and they suddenly acquire a set look, determined to ignore this attacking noise, but the movement of his walking stick now has a martial twitch to it as it smacks down on the grass. Yes, the two men can definitely hear her, and the shorter one can't help looking this way and that trying to locate the person disturbing Sir Naren's morning peace. *Ekla cholo, ekla cholo, ekla cholo, ekla cholo rey!* As the two approach the neem tree, the flames finally coat the charcoal, releasing a thick plume of smoke. A lot of it goes straight into Niru's throat and she begins to cough violently. By the time she recovers, the men are past the tree and walking away. Niru takes another deep breath and continues with all her power.

If they all turn their backs, O hey, O unlucky one,
if they all turn away from the impassable track,

The coughing has made a part of Niru suddenly timid. She stays hidden out of sight as she sings.

Then take the thorns underfoot
and dance over the bloody path, all on your own!

If they don't answer your call,
O unlucky one,
walk alone, walk alone, walk alone, walk alone, my friend!

'Niru! What are you doing, will you tell me? You're scaring the neighbours!' Titir is standing behind her, speaking through a hand clamped on her mouth, her eyes flicking between the crouching Niru and the neighbouring lawn.

'Where are they? Have they gone?' Niru asks in a low voice. Then she resumes singing at her loudest, not bothering about any tunefulness.

If no one heeds your call, if no one comes along,
O unlucky one...

'Achcha, they've gone now, you can stop.'

'Sure they can't hear me any more?'

'Yes, but they went off looking quite alarmed. Were you singing for them? Were they your intended audience? Those two old men?'

'Well...' Niru takes the pot and sets it on the coal, starting to heat up the mixture of milk and water.

'You know,' Titir keeps watching the garden, 'they were staring this way. At first, they must have thought it was me who was singing. Then they looked confused because my mouth was shut, as if I was one of those, how to say in Ingreji? Ventri-loquist! Then I started laughing and they looked very annoyed, especially the big fat man, Sir Whatshisname. I hope they don't complain.'

'I don't care! I could hear him saying the Nazis would finish off the Russians. As if he approved.'

'Oh, so just for that Comrade Nirupama lost her temper? Lost her Party discipline? Ha ha ha ha!'

'I'm not in the Party yet... No, I know it won't be funny if we have to move after just four months, when we've barely settled...'

'Don't worry so much. What can they say? That someone was singing Rabindranath loudly, early in the morning?'

'No, true, but I was really loud.' As the liquid begins to boil, Niru quickly opens a tin, reaches in and drops four fingersnaps of tea into the pot. The milkwater reacts as if stung, rising angrily to the rim, carrying the offending tea with it. Using the tongs, Niru raises the pot away from the coal to make the liquid subside before provoking it again by putting the pot back on the heat. As it starts to boil again, Niru carefully adds two spoons of the yellowish sugar, again incensing the mixture. As she continues this little dance of raising and dropping, the two women's noses fill with the smell of freshly brewed tea. It's as if the winter morning has completed its presence only now, with the addition of this final element to the bouquet of dewy grass, other coal fires nearby, a horse-smell from an occasional early morning jhurrie-gaadi as it passes, and the faint background of combusting petrol from a motorcar engine.

Niru reaches for the tray on which three clean glasses have been kept upside down. The gritty, cold glass surprises her warmed hands, and she almost drops it.

'Achcha, now are you walking alone or are you making tea for everybody?'

'There's enough for three here. As long as you don't mind street tea. And I can make more later.'

'Listen, don't bother about Roma. As usual she has sneaked in to capture the bathroom. She clearly has no need for that first tea. Anyway, she'll wrinkle her nose at your tea, she'll want her shaheb tea.'

'Oho, Titir, if you need to go, just knock and tell her to hurry up, why don't you?' Her grip tightening again around the tong handles, Niru lifts the pot and sieves the steaming tea into the glasses. She covers one glass with a small saucer to keep it warm. 'Tell her the tea's getting cold. That will bring her out, she hates cold tea.'

Titir goes and knocks hard on the bathroom doors. 'Open up! This is a police raid!'

'I'm sorry, sir, but I'm just destroying Congress pamphlets for my friend Nandini Basak, alias Titir. She is the short girl outside making a nuisance of herself. Please! Kindly! Arrest her! She's the one who doesn't support the war!' Roma's voice bounces off the wet surfaces inside.

'Roma, you've been in there for half an hour!'

'Nonsense.' Niru comes in with the tray. 'You've not even been *up* for half an hour.' Niru also knocks on the door, but more gently. 'Your Royal Highness! Please come! Your tea is getting cold!'

There is the clank and slash of metal and water. 'Slave! If you start singing after pouring the tea, it's bound to get cold! I could hear you in here!'

'She was doing it out of loyalty to Soviet Russia. Comrades, we have nothing to lose but our little abode! Now hurry up!'

Through the splashing of water and the swish of sari cloth, a deep voice, much lower than Niru's, bursts into a wetly reverberating melody.

Naai, naai bhoy!
Hobey, hobey joy
Khuley jaabey ei dwaar!

None, there's no fear!
Victory, victory is near!

The locking chain rattles once, and the two narrow wooden doors are flung apart. Roma stands there, resplendently happy, a large smile on her newly washed face, drops of water on her spectacles.

These doors will fall open!

Roma's hair tumbles amok from a loose knot and covers her shoulders.

These doors will fall open!
Your chains will all be broken!

'Oof! Why are you *both* torturing poor Rabindranath this morning? Niru, cover my tea, will you?' Titir brushes past Roma, remarries the doors from the inside, and emphatically slaps on the chain.

Arise from your sleep, the world calls to you!

'Ah, we're having your wonderful street tea. So, what melodrama did I miss? You had a fight with Naren Mitter?'

'No, not all, meaning...'

Roma cradles her tea in both hands as she walks into the little central room they use for everything. Niru follows her.

'Roma, what is *exponents*?'

Roma shifts a pile of books on the little dining table to make place for her glass and pulls out a chair. 'Well, exponent can be someone who explains a theory, but it can also mean—'

'No, not that one, another meaning?' Niru picks up the books and puts them away on a shelf before taking another chair.

'Another meaning would be... someone who does something particular with a lot of skill, mastery.'

'Yes, that's it, that last one. And *terrain* is same as *territory*? No, na?'

'No. Territory is an area. Terrain is the land itself, the actual jomin, the maati, the soil, the local landscape.'

'Achcha, right.'

'What happened?'

'Nothing, nothing. Those two men, Sir Naren and his lackey, were taking a circle of their garden...'

'Hah, yes, I've seen them. Every morning. A small exclamation mark scurrying alongside a large paragraph!'

'Exactly! I think of them as Sir and Sir-vant.'

'So? What happened?'

'Well, they were talking, or rather he was proclaiming, and I just overheard this fine, difficult English.'

'Stop it. Your English is not nearly as bad as you imagine. It's better than your tea, for example.'

'Listen, just because you cook for us more than we cook for you...'

'So, what else didn't you understand?'

'Nullify is... destroy?'

'No. Nullify is to take something out of the calculation, reduce something to zero.'

'He said the jungle terrain would nullify the Japani aircraft.'

'That's funny, because, you've seen, na, that the papers are full of talk about these powerful Japani planes called Zero? So he was saying the jungles would reduce the Japani Zeros to zero!'

'Ah, maybe...'

'He must have meant the jungles would render the Japani war planes ineffective.'

'I think that is what he was saying.' The morning sunlight firms up through the window bars, striping across the table, highlighting a faint layer of dust on the dulled brown polish.

'And so this drove you to singing strident revolutionary songs?'

Niru gets up and finds a dusting cloth. 'Not that. What set me off was when he said the Germans would finish "the Russia business" by May. So I had to say something, na?'

'You did quite right! Let them hear!' Roma grins and takes a gulp of the tea. '*These doors will fall oooopen! These chains will be broken!*'

'Hm. You're in good voice this morning. My tea is that bad, is it?'

'Not as bad as Madam Sarojini's.' Roma gestures quietly to the bathroom doors, from behind which a slightly moist silence continues to emanate. 'In fact, you're improving. Today's tea is quite good. Maybe we should get our Sir-neighbour to insult the Soviets every morning.'

'Thanks. Oi jey, that Sarojini Naidu can make the next round of tea.'

Arise from your sleep, the world calls to you!

As Niru quickly works around the small room, hunting down patches of dust wherever she can find them, Roma hums while flipping through a long notebook, energetically making notes as though she's never been asleep. As she cleans, Niru feels a small surge of elation at this house the three of them have set up. Everything about it seems magically right, everything imparts odd, surprising little pleasures, from the slightly ill-fitting doors at the entrance, the little wooden complaint they make when you open the padlock and push them apart, the narrow corridor that seems to lead straight to the balcony door until you notice the two rooms on either side, the half-light things catch until you open up the balcony, and then the almost-harsh brightness that falls on objects, the few things, bits of furniture they've collected, the whole adventure belonging to the three of them and nobody else.

Niru finds herself dusting and cleaning more than the other two girls, but she doesn't mind. She is still new enough to find everything here exotic, the ageing, dented wood of the doors and windows, the glossy maroon floor that contrasts with the rough white lime-paint on walls, the nicks on the smooth iron bars on the windows, all very different here in south Calcutta, somehow drier, cleaner, more brittle than the constantly worked surfaces of her home in north Calcutta which has its textures lubricated by a different humidity, by long years of daily living amidst a cluster of closely packed buildings.

The first time Roma had brought them here, in early September, neither she nor Titir had known what to expect. Dover Road was right in shaheb-para, a quiet side street off Ballygunge Circular Road. Their location was tucked between two large properties: embedded in a long wall, the gate was a narrow iron grille which looked like it could be the side entrance to a private prison; inside lay a small compound of damp earth carved out of the back garden of one of the big houses. On their way here, they had caught glimpses of the big lawns, gravel driveways and porticos of the huge two-storey houses on Ballygunge Circular Road. Even though it was an adjunct to one such mansion, this place was an island of 1930s simplicity in the surrounding grandeur. There was the parsimony of straight, undecorated lines and a small unpretentious scale that indicated that this cream-coloured two-storey building, while not a servant's quarter exactly, had clearly been built to house some poor relatives or exalted retainers of the big house in front.

Nearly four months later, Niru still remembers the Hansel-and-Gretel thrill of twisting up the wrought-iron fire-escape stairs that lead to the first-floor flat. Opening the doors, Roma had led them into a musty darkness. One by one, she had thrown open the doors and windows, letting the late monsoon light fall on the surprised cobwebs. 'Perfectly good for the likes of us, the floor is quite nice, but please note the absence of marble, of teak or mahogany, or proper wrought-iron work on the window grilles. The smell will go once we've cleaned up and let in some air.' Roma kept speaking but Niru could no longer hear a word she was saying, her eyes were fixed on the shining leaves of a mango tree almost coming in from a window. As she pulled her eyes away, the shock slowly unfolded inside. By stepping through the doorway, she had crossed the threshold into another life.

Moving in, they've made the place liveable, populated it with things, laughter, song and argument, and the spaces in the flat are already linked with different memories. There is the room she shares with Roma, then Titir's small room, the 'mandir' as they call it, the 'temple' filled with pictures of gods and goddesses, a little cell of incense, then this room – which Roma calls the 'drawing room' even though it is no such thing – that serves as the indoor part of the kitchen, dining room and study all together. Two bookshelves, borrowed from an aunt of Roma's, the table and four chairs provided by Roma's Tilu-mashi, Lady Tilottama, the landlord's wife with her memshaheb English – 'You girls will need something upon which you can dine!' The counter, which runs the length of the room from the balcony door, is half taken up by kitchen things and half by more piles of books and papers. The room is illuminated via the balcony and two windows, one facing east, with the mango tree outside, the other facing south with the currently naked branches of a palash twirling in the winter sunlight. Lastly, the best part of the dwelling, the little covered balcony with its neem tree and view of the Mitter garden, where they can cook on the bucket unoon, keeping the smoke and smells out all year save during the monsoons.

This year, the monsoon's stayed longer than usual and brought about many strange things. For instance, none of them remembered to bring a boti, the basic, ground-based cutting implement used in most Bengali kitchens, and Roma had to expand the other girls' knowledge of how to use a kitchen knife. Even after a boti was acquired, the rule they agreed to, at Roma's insistence, was that no food was to be cut on the floor inside the house. In the beginning, Niru found it strange to be standing while chopping vegetables and especially fish, using the knife instead of the boti with its sideways sail of a blade which you hold steady with your foot. For the first few weeks, whenever she was cutting something, Niru's right foot would automatically press down on the floor, the one action married to the other since childhood, impossible to get the correct size of the slice from your fingers without that rhythmic pressure of the toes.

Only slightly less strange was sitting at a table to eat, though she already had experience of this in the college canteen at Scottish Church and the various eateries in College Street. At home, Baba was the only one with a desk, and all her reading and writing was done on the bed, and all the eating on the floor. As Niru's Ma likes to say, 'You can only digest food properly sitting cross-legged on the ground like decent gentlefolk', though, of late, hungry after long days of volunteer work, food has been digesting itself, no matter where Niru's eaten it. Thank god, though, that the Western-style arrangements stopped outside the bathroom. Or, just at the washbasin, which, with its attendant mirror, she had to admit was a useful invention. She certainly couldn't bear using a Western commode all the time, every day of the week.

Almost as if reading her mind, Roma stops humming and looks up from her notebook. The sound of a big splash comes from the bathroom. 'Hear that? That's when she does it!'

'Does what? Roma, she's just upending the bucket over herself to finish her bath. Don't you also do that? I do.'

'You do and I do too! But Titir is the only one who always manages to wet my...'

'Lady Linlithgow! Your *toilet paper!* Told you to keep it high up, on the windowsill!'

'I do! Where do you think I keep it? But I don't know what she does with that bucket, I think she spins it around like a wrestler with an opponent. And she splashes the whole bathroom. I'm sure she drenches everything but herself.'

'How can you be so sure?'

'All right, next time let's insist on watching her. We'll make her keep the door open and inspect her technique!'

Hearing her own words, Roma drops her fountain pen, spraying ink all over the notebook. Niru drops her dusting cloth and collapses on the floor.

'Inspect! Like a committee!' hisses Roma.

'Technique!' Niru gasps back.

The two go into loops of laughter. As one subsides the other starts again, the mirth see-sawing between them.

'Arre! What happened? Why are you two crying?' Neither of them has heard Titir coming out of the bathroom. Both Niru and Roma look up at Titir and go into further convulsions. Niru tries to get up off the floor, but the spasms keep her pinned down. Roma has snatched off her spectacles to wipe her eyes.

'What happened, will you tell me?' Titir's huge eyes are open even wider. 'Why are you crying, Roma?'

Niru hauls herself up only to fall forward on the table as she hears the word 'crying', the laughter turning into staccato coughing. Roma flings out her hands and Niru grabs them. The two girls are both now face down on the table, bodies stretched, hands locked in mutual support as incoherent howls emerge from their hair.

'Oh, you two monsters are *laughing!* You're laughing at *me!*' Titir swings her wet towel over her shoulder as if readying for a physical fight. 'So, what's so hilarious, will you tell me?'

'Nothing, nothing...' Roma and Niru detach themselves and bring their heaving stomachs under control. Roma gets up and hugs her freshly bathed friend. 'Titir... lokkhi shona... why don't you make us some normal tea before I put on the rice? Then I'll go have my bath?'

'No! I'm not a fool, all right? Tell me what you were laughing about!'

Roma cradles Titir's face in her hands. 'Nothing, you know how sometimes someone says something silly and you can't stop laughing?'

Niru quietly moves behind Titir and slips into the bathroom.

'So what was this silly thing? And who said it?' Titir pushes Roma away, refusing to let go of her suspicion.

'I was just telling Niru how she was becoming a Bihari thhela-walla with her street tea.'

'You said she was a Bihari and that set you laughing like two witches on bhang? No, but wait. You laughed some more when I said crying.'

Niru is now standing behind Titir. She takes the end of the roll and stretches her arm in a dancing movement, pulling out the paper as she does. She catches Roma's eye and waves the toilet paper like a battle standard.

'Yes, because...' Roma's face transforms as she looks beyond Titir, '*Niru, stop that*, you'll waste my precious—'

Titir whirls around. Niru sways from side to side, making the stretch of paper billow. Roma goes for Niru, who turns around and stumbles into the bathroom.

'*Give me that!*'

'Listen – stop – it's dry now, but I'll wet it if you—'

RANGOON

Something odd about her, something odd around her, something missing between herself and the rest of the world. She is lying on her left side, left arm packed into her body, but her right arm is on top of the sheet, a long lever bent at the elbow, rising as it goes up the ridge of white cloth. Against the sheet, it looks almost golden brown. Her hand against the man's shoulder, where the sheet stops, looks an even darker brown. Strange, because he spends far more time in the sun. Some skin can take on only so much colour, she thinks, imagining a translucent leather pouch filling with coloured liquid which is also, somehow, sunlight.

The sun is up outside – Imogen can tell by the brightness seeping into the room through the drawn curtains – and it's probably around eight o'clock in the morning. A winter's morning, she thinks and realizes what the oddness is about her. It's a winter morning and she doesn't have on any nightclothes. No clothes at all, which is not something that would happen on the hottest of summer nights, leave aside in England, even in a stifling Paris apartment.

No clothes at all, all body, only sheet. Next to a man who's turned away and sleeping, also no clothes, all gently snoring Andrew-body.

She fights the temptation to lean over his shoulder and look at his face. I know what he looks like when he's asleep, she thinks, I now know that. And I'm going to have to do without seeing him asleep – used to being stern with herself, she manages to cut off the thought.

She suddenly needs to go, and her eyes move from Andrew's shoulder to the bathroom door, which is slightly ajar. Then she turns her head further and looks through the gap in the balcony curtains: a slice of railing, black iron against a slice of smudged white pile in the middle distance. It's as if the mist is powdering Victoria Memorial, making it both whiter and mirage-like; nothing like proper British mist this, nothing like a crisp September morning with soft walls of grey rising from the downs, but a warm imitation created for the visual comfort of the exiled Islanders, for them, and for her, specifically, in her first Calcutta winter. She has always found the Memorial odd, a bad copy of the Taj Mahal, very home, a piece of England that doesn't fit here, with its self-conscious proportions and pompous demeanour, but now she's begun to think of it as reassuring. Try as she might, she cannot imagine a Japanese flag flying from the dome.

She feels a very slight chill as she sits up and scouts around for her clothes. She locates them and maps where they lie: skirt, stockings, petticoat and camiknickers on the carpet, furthest away, right near the bathroom door; blouse and bra on armchair; pullover, first thing he'd pulled off last night, dangling on the wall light where he'd flung it; shoes, whereabouts unknown.

It hadn't been their first time – that had been about a month ago – but the crying had made it seem as though it was. First her, with him inside her, with him trying desperately for levity, and then, after they were both done, him, Andrew, when he'd turned away from her far too suddenly and she had realized. She had reached across and felt his eyes; the smallest, tiniest, most fleeting of triumphs when she found her fingers wet with his tears. She had taken over the clown's job then, made jokes about all the Burmese girls he would soon have, how she didn't see the point of waiting for him while he single-handedly pushed the Nips off the last ledge of the Malay peninsula, all the while replenishing his harem, replacing the Burmese, first with Siamese, then with Malay and Chinese and, finally, with Japanese beauties. He had whirled around just as she was whispering, 'Major Hillcott, I have no time for these crocodile tears, perhaps you should save them for your future victims...' He had pinned her arms down, kneed her legs apart and tried to ram himself inside, but his heart was not in it and neither was his blood. She had felt his body deflate on top of her, with all his weight and all the weight of the call-up. 'That last bit was going too far,' he'd tried feebly. 'You know I'd never touch a Jap woman.' She had slapped him then, but, again, without conviction. They had both tried to laugh, then they had both called in their tears, then they had fallen asleep.

Imogen puts a leg out on the floor. It's a foreign thing this nakedness, not at all the same as when she's on her own, with just her mirror as witness. It's as if everything is watching her: their strewn clothes, the fan on the ceiling, the lamps on the wall, even the Memorial peeping in through the balcony. It's as if she's being examined by everything Andrew and she have ever done together, by every drive they've taken, every dance they've danced, every party they've attended, by every kiss and every embrace, whether stolen in his car or seized luxuriously in this room, by every moment of their lovemaking. When alone, she is without clothes. But now, she is truly and completely naked.

As she walks across the room, she tries to decide which garment to put on first. There is no question of entering the loo with nothing on, yet her clothes now all seem unwelcome, unattractive, uncomfortable. She pauses, caught in a no man's land for a moment, before rejecting them all and going in and pulling the door shut.

The wooden seat is cold on her skin, but the release feels good, the stream quite powerful through muscles that have been unusually exercised, smarting over the soreness she feels down there. Sore but nice, Andrew-aching soreness, which is quite different from the few times in Paris, her first times, with the one she now thinks of as 'the American Boy'. She looks around the large bathroom with its big, frosted window streaming cathedral light and remembers the boy with no sting of feeling. The very first time had been in a tiny, close, windowless, Paris toilet, the culmination of a month of snatched but pleasurable gropings. A party dying outside. Both of them drunk on Dubonnet, both of them clumsy, but the boy, Wade, determined, and Imogen not determined enough. And then there had been a couple of nights in the apartment she'd shared for that summer with two other English girls.

Even before she put an end to it, she had realized the affair with Wade was more about Hemingway and Gertrude Stein than anything else, more about Flaubert, Maupassant and Celine. Though the long preamble had been quite nice, there had been no pleasure in the actual doing of it. All of it had been hurried, all except once – only one moment had stretched and stayed, once when they had kissed for a long time on the steps near Abbesses. Though now, even that had been moved off the small pedestal where she had had it preserved in her mind. Being with Andrew, she feels she has lost her virginity again, or actually, lost it properly for the first time, and it has nothing to do with the physical act.

Standing at the washbasin, Imogen reaches for Andrew's toothbrush without a thought. She has it almost to her mouth when she realizes the intimacy of what she is doing. It's in this, in small things like these, that you actually lose your maidenhood, she thinks, as she spreads the rough tooth powder across her gums.

Brushing her teeth, she counts the times Andrew and she have been together: the first time, at home, one Sunday afternoon when Mummy was away with Daddy in Darjeeling and most of the staff was off; the second time, at the weekend party at that jute mill up the river, where Andrew had pretended to the fat mill-owner host that they were married – damned risky, given this was actually a such a small town, but worth it for the two nights it gained them in the opulent riverside bungalow; the third time had been riskier, in a back room at the Royal Calcutta Golf Club, standing up, a flash of ecstatic lightning leading to no rain, with Andrew bent upon outdoing the fast-fading Wade after she had told him about Paris; then came the gift of this chummery, taken over by the Fort William people for their top junior officers, the understanding quiet but clear that the chaps would be inviting young ladies over from time to time, so, times four, five and last night's six, here, all dependent on the other two fellows being away at their unit camps.

Six times already, in barely over a month. Only six times, but it already feels like a grand lifetime. Six times, each one precious, because now there was no guarantee of a seventh. 'Darling... the old man just told me today: I'm off with the forward mob, Boxing Day. Shouldn't really tell you this, but it's probably Rangoon. Rangoon and then east, I imagine.' She towels her face, wiping away the tears before they can emerge. She brisks and brightens herself and goes out of the door. Right, time to wake Andrew up, wolf down some brekker, and clear off before Gerald and Harry return for their Christmas Eve. Now then, where was that jumper?

She goes to the wall light, walking on the balls of her feet for some reason. She puts one foot on the armchair and levers herself up, reaching for the sweater.

'Very graceful, my love, but I'm afraid you're far too tall to be prima ballerina.'

Andrew is sitting up, his back against the headboard, hands crossed behind his head. This means he can't use them to fend off the little chair pillow as it hurtles towards him. The throw is fast, and he only manages to sway enough so that it hits him on the ear and not full in the face. By the time he reaches the pillow for the return throw, she is on him, pummelling him, pulling his hair, ripping the sheet off him and punching him on his chest and stomach, not hard, but hard enough for him to wince through his laughter.

She straddles him and pulls the sheet back over both of them. Andrew puts his arms around her and digs his nose into the nape of her neck. He takes a deep breath and mumbles into her skin. 'Aaaah, the smell of Snell, the perfume of Snell, the...' She stops him, pulling his head back and putting her mouth on his. Their tongues meet, hers fresh from the tooth powder, his still coated with the whisky from the night before; their bodies relax by mistake, giving up the act for a moment, and their breaths cross and collide. They stay kissing for a moment before Andrew pulls away. He goes back to playing the fool, 'Aaah, the peculiar heady oxygen of Imogen, the atmosphere of planet—'

She puts the little pillow on his face so that he won't see her tears. Not a good idea this early in the morning, on possibly their last day together. She holds the pillow in place with one hand, gently but firmly muffling him, while she grabs a corner of a bedsheet and quickly wipes her eyes. Outside the door, she can hear the bearer setting the table for breakfast, the noise of cutlery being arranged just a tad too loud. The smell of freshly made tea wafts through the door. Not good tea, no longer good tea, only bad tea has the strength to come through doors. Composed now, Imogen flicks away the pillow and cups Andrew's face in her hands. The engagement ring he's given her shines against his cheek. She manages to smile wickedly as she asks the question.

'Now then, major, when were you planning to have that come-around-by-sea party again?'

COLD MEAT

'Iiingleesh, Gogai, Ingleesh ko dharey raakhtey hobey!' Ustad's voice always needles into his ear on the mornings he wakes up in the Frenchman's room. 'Hold on to the English, Gogai! Everything else is fine, but it is the English, the In-gra-ji, that you must finally master!'

But how much English to find in this fetid little fortress of French?

Gopal pushes himself up and quickly gets rid of the covering blankets. Despite the early hour, the room is bright because of the angle of the sun. The windows are shut because of the air conditioning, and they mute the already filtered December light, but at this time of the day the milky sunlight slices into one corner of the room, hitting the wall and the mirror to create a brightness that the boxy space doesn't otherwise have. Gopal looks around for the Frenchman and hears the sound of splashing coming from the bathroom. The big gora's spoor hangs in the air, the smell from his cigarettes dancing a nose-tango with the smell of slightly stale sweat.

Outside room 386, there is the thrum of the hotel waking up, the staff voices shouting confidently now that it's daytime, the clank of the lifts moving up and down, taking the morning service to the guests, the wheeling of trolleys, the sound of the little wheels changing just outside the room, to the left of the door, as they move from the uncarpeted service area on to the thick strip of red that runs through the corridors. Bonnemaison's room is on the border between the guest rooms and the large first-floor staging area where the tea and 'dry' room service such as sandwiches and the like are put together. Though Gopal doesn't know it for sure, he suspects the Frenchman has picked this room because it allows easy access for the boys the gora likes to bring in from time to time. Why otherwise would this man, who could have commanded a space almost as luxurious as the hotel manager's deeper inside the guest area, choose to live at the edge of the floor? As Gopal has now understood, the hotel allows women prostitutes of a certain presentability to pass unremarked, but a pleasure-boy from the streets would cause problems for even the most powerful guest.

'Don't worry about how they look at you, those mother-pimps working there, yes?' Gopal was touched when Ustad had put a sympathetic hand on his shoulder. By now, he had seen the ruthless old tiger send men to possible maiming and death with far less ado. 'Remember, this is as big a job as anything anyone else is doing for your Ustad. It's just that the fruit of this will grow slowly, Gogai, invisibly, and be so big when it falls you cannot even imagine it.' Curious that Ustad, the king of detail, the ultimate master of precise instructions, had given him only general pointers as to what he was to do besides letting the Phorashi fuck him as often as he liked.

Now, after three months, smell and language and the feel of the Phorashi's heavy body all get mixed up in his head, and he has to make an effort to unravel them, to separate, sort and place things neatly next to each other, the way Gourangzeb cleans and sharpens his knives before every job.

First, the man, the big, fat, white Frenchman: Phorashi, which means 'Phench' in Ingreji, which is 'Phransey' in Phorashi. And his things: his language, his food, his cock, his kaaphé, his cigarettes which smell black but a different black from the cigarette the big gora had lit on the docks, the one Aurangzeb and Gourango had dealt with.

His fat wallet that the sisterfucker leaves carelessly on the desk when he goes into the bathroom, a half-open invitation that Gopal is far too clever to take, Ustad's warnings totally unnecessary – 'Gogai, we want the man, not his money! We don't even want the man, we want the world he can bring us, we want *that* gold, do you understand? Don't, not even in your dreams, be tempted to steal small change from this backhole addict!' But Gopal already knows – he's had his man from the beginning. He has seen how Bonnemaison counts every small piece of meat in the hotel kitchen, every cigarette in his tin, every grain of the foul coffee he sifts into his little jug every morning. Gopal knows that every coin and crumpled note stuffed into the half-open wallet has been counted and he knows that Bonnemaison is waiting for the day when one single anna goes missing. But Gopal now also understands that if the Phorashi catches him stealing, he will get rid of him with no small sadness, that the flung wallet is now just a habit – still standard practice on every night they spend together, but no longer the tightly sprung trap it used to be.

In any case, Gopal has become familiar with his own secret wallet now, the one he stole from the pretty boy, and the fat Phorashi's battered money purse, overfull with old bills and scribbled notes, holds no intrinsic fascination. Also, since that day in August when the wallet came into his life, he has gained the important insight that a rich man's wallet is not where his real wealth lies. Gopal has also understood that he is no longer among the very desperately poor who need to attack small personal things such as handbags and wallets, though he does exempt jewellery from this calculation.

Gopal sits there, imagining the rich, pretty boy wearing a thin gold chain around his neck, like Marwari seths do, a thin gold chain and nothing else, his body nothing like a Marwari's, his eyes... '*Allez cocotte!*' the point of Bonnemaison's wet towel flicks the back of his neck bringing Gopal back to reality. He can feel the big man standing over him, drying his crotch, briefly calculating whether he has time for one more bout with him. The bathroom door is open and the steam spills into the room, carrying the smell of lotions and shampoo. Bonnemaison looks at the table clock on the desk and decides against it. He turns away from Gopal, looking for his clothes and using his English: 'Yu go qwikly, eh? 'Ave qvik baath, zen u go! Today I ave a big work!'

'Oui, m'syu,' says Gopal, heading to the bathroom.

'And, écoute!' Gopal stops. He knows by heart what will be said next, and inside himself he repeats it exactly: 'This is not your little shit 'ole in the village, eh? So don't be dirty. And don't put the watter evri-vhere!'

'Oui, m'syu!' Gopal makes sure he smiles respectfully as he says it.

Entering the bathroom, Gopal sees it's in the usual spectacular mess that only Bonnemaison can create. There is water all over the floor, there are flecks of shaving foam on the mirror and the wall, and tooth powder spit marks on the edge of the large washbasin. Gopal knows there will be shaved hair caught in the drain of the basin, as there will be different kinds of hair in the commode bowl and the drain of the bathtub. As he tries to locate a clean towel that has survived the massacre, Gopal once again thinks about human beings.

He has seen the Phorashi at work in his huge kitchen, seen him put together the most delicate constructions, soufflés that would evaporate if you breathed at the wrong time and golden, spiderweb cages of sugar that would crack if you looked too hard. Gopal has seen him move precisely and swiftly, his hands dancing through fires and fine china, aware of everything around him as if he has eyes at the back of his head, anticipating, seeing, smelling and hearing things that nobody else can. He has seen Bonnemaison murderously angry, seen him shockingly gentle and, sometimes, seen him burst into maniacal laughter when a dish or a meal is a triumph of some indecipherable daring.

In bed, the man is usually a slow bullock, his ardour and rigidity directly related to how well or badly things have gone in the kitchen that day. On some nights, Bonnemaison merely does his bodily sums on top of him, all expenditure of muscle and fluid as coldly and offhandedly calculated as Ustad counting the day's take, the big body unconnected to Gopal except for his thick, digging cock and his large, grasping hands; on other nights, the big man reaches clumsily for love, and then, upon not finding it, attacks brutally before subsiding into a strange, hollow tenderness – on these nights, Gopal realizes, the man is happiest when he is done with the churn of lust and disgust, when he is empty and finally just holding him.

Gopal stands on the curve of the bathtub, letting the water smash into him for as long as he dares. He takes the misshapen ball of the lavender soap and cleanses himself of the Frenchman, of his musky, closed room, of his sweaty, closed bed, of his caged growl of a closed language. The magic of this shower will last him more than a week. It will make up for the quick scrubbings he snatches under the tap in the back courtyard behind his little room and energize him in ways that he hasn't fully understood. Squatting under the tap, he will manoeuvre the gamchha tied around his waist, trying not to offend the modesty of the families living around as he soaps and washes himself; here, for five minutes every ten days or so, he can luxuriate in his own nakedness and breathe in the smell of the soap as its foam swirls around him, snaking in and out of his corners, opening him up for the world he is about to face outside.

As he comes out of the womb of the bathroom, a different set of smells goes to war with the aura of lavender essence he has just acquired. After three months, the stink of the coffee in the morning is still the worst thing about this whole business. He now understands that this is not the locally available Polson's 'coffee powder' that most of the ignorant Ingrej drink, but proper Phorashi – Phench – coffee that the Frenchman hides as if hoarding precious gems. To Gopal, it still smells like the strongest of animal farts – the particular pungency you get when you're trying to save a sick baby goat. One day, when the fat man was feeling very warm towards Gopal, he offered him his bowl. The liquid swirled like a small lake-pukur, fetid and brown after the monsoons, and the goat smell bubbled up from just under the surface. '*Tiens!*' said the Phorashi as Gopal tried to hide the retch rising inside him. '*Tiens! Ça c'est la France, tu comprends, mon petit?*'

Gopal comprends a bit now, grasps a few strands of the strange language, understands that Phransey is the bigger and far more noble cousin of Ingleesh or 'Ongley', and that the two will always wage an essentially unequal battle with each other. Being with the gora in this big hotel, Gopal had hoped to learn Ingleesh; what he has picked up instead is the khichuri of English, French and Hindustani that the chef speaks. One of the few English sentences Gopal understands immediately is the Phorashi's favourite expression: 'Thees Eenglish, she is ghiully sheet, eh!'

The Ongley 'sheet' and the 'bon' and 'fomidaabla' of Phransey stand in direct opposition. Once, when Gopal produced a dented but still intact tin of coffee with a certain yellow label from his delivery bag, Bonnemaison almost cried in gratitude, alternately muttering the two words, '*C'est bon! T'es formidable!*', repeating them again and again. That same precious kaaphé had led the Frenchman to make his boy a special impromptu meal from leftover chicken and cheese, something called a graataa that Gopal still remembers on nights he finds himself slightly hungry. That was nice, and he loves the sweet cakes and pastries the cook confects; he has quickly learnt the advantages of putting up with the old man in bed, but this black, liquid morning torture is still hard to bear.

When Gopal is out of this room 386, he always pairs and counters the two foul smells with the two smells he has grown to love, the lavender soap and the smell of the air conditioner after it's been switched off – which the gora usually makes him do at about 4 a.m. in the morning, when the room turns too cold. Of late, the air conditioner gets switched off by 2 a.m. given the cool weather outside, and even though he's thankful for not freezing, Gopal misses that humming smell in the morning.

Today, Bonnemaison has woken early, cheerful, ready to continue the making of the big khaana for tonight's party. The night before, he tried to explain to Gopal the brilliant meal he had planned and already put into operation. Gopal has understood that the meal will be amazing not least because Bonnemaison has managed to source things that others can only dream about, because he has planned with sheer genius within what is available in this wartime colonial wasteland where all the usual imports from Europe have long disappeared. Gopal hasn't tried to understand the 'menoo' in too much detail but, looking slightly baffled as usual, he has quietly gleaned what he needs to know. Last night, he has pocketed the facts he needs, just as he has done over the last several weeks: foreign butter tastes different, has less salt, and is more valuable; 'phrawmazh' is also called 'cheejh' and Phorashi cheejh is extremely valuable; wine is difficult to get, but there are stores of it all over India, in various rajas' and nawabs' palaces and rich men's homes from where it can be bought at a high price or stolen; other hotels also have chefs, not in the same league as Bonnemaison, but who may pay more for some things; on the other hand, what is good here in Bengal, in this hell's backhole of a place, are the vegetables, the chicken and the fish – as good here as anywhere in the world outside La-Bel-Phraans if you know how to pick them; good food doesn't have to be good in quantity, it is the quality that fetches the price at the table.

The only moment when Gopal's ears have perked up about tonight's menu is when Bonnemaison has said, 'And for dessert we will have two… One, a gateaux of chocolate, pineapple and cream, and second, a crème brulee l'impératrice Joséphine.' Because by now Gopal knows his bileti mishti, his sweet dishes, by heart.

In terms of learning to name what he craves, Bonnemaison from his side has only recently learnt Gopal's name. For the first few times it was just a grunt which attached itself to Gopal's body; then came a mix of an '*allez!*', a '*garçon!*' and, in moments of extreme tenderness, a '*mon petit!*'. Since early November, an occasional 'Gopalle' has been added to these, followed a couple of weeks later by permission for the boy to use the shower and drink cold water from Bonnemaison's private fridge. On the days Bonnemaison is in a foul mood, he doesn't bother with English or any of the admixtures with Hindustani or Bengali, muttering along in French as he does his business with Gopal; on the days which are good, he tries to communicate, imagining for some reason that Gopal will understand English better, and his half-cooked Ingreji comes out, garnished with crudely chopped local argot. Today, as Gopal gets ready to leave, Bonnemaison hands him a little paper bag.

'*Prends ça.* This is foh'yu, *ma cocotte! Allez* jaldi now. I 'ave to work for the big khaana!'

'Messi, m'syu.' Gopal nods his thanks as he takes the bag. The chill of the fridge comes through the paper and Gopal guesses it will be one of the Phorashi's chicken preparations from the day before. Despite everything life has taught him about the value of a hot meal, Gopal has now learnt to value these cold little gifts because they invariably surprise his mouth with some strange new world of taste. Holding his prize, he does a small salaam as he backs out of the room. Thinking about the Frenchman's food as he walks down the corridor, Gopal gets a reverse of something from last night, almost as if his stomach understands and agrees with him. The swirl of taste comes from a soup bowl Bonnemaison had handed him. The bowl had been filled with what looked like muddied hot brown water, the smell and power of it shocking for something so thin. The gora had called it a 'khansama', mispronouncing it as 'khonsomey' in his French accent, and this morning Gopal finds himself suddenly craving more of that pungently rich hot water.

As Gopal's feet leave the carpeted area, his feet suddenly realize they are touching a cold, tiled floor. He turns back quickly and goes back to the door of 386. His shoes are sitting just outside, exactly where he has left them last night, with the white socks neatly tucked in as he has been taught. It has been just over three months since Gopal has started to put anything on his feet, and his toes still conspire to gain back their freedom sometimes.

Properly shod now, Gopal goes back down the passage, enjoying the clip-clop noise of the shoe soles on the tiles. He doesn't really understand the logic of the goras and the rich babus – surely carpets were meant to be enjoyed with bare feet, and, if you did have shoes, then surely the main pleasure of wearing them was the beautiful sound they made on the hard floors and the roads. The taste of the consommé in his mouth and the click of his shoes in his ears, Gopal makes his way to the pair of lifts which he is not allowed to use and to the door next to them which opens on to a stairway that leads directly down to the hotel's side entrance.

Inside the massive Everything that is Calcutta, occupying only a small part of the city universe, is this grand and intricate maze, this other Everything; this thing that now sits in Gopal's mind as a vast, living creature of stairs, corridors, walls, light fixtures, windows and darknesses; a whole intricate hierarchy of biped organisms scuttling through its veins, some in random freedom and others in the strict choreography of service; this snake-and-ladder cage of smells and textures and criss-crossing echoes. These backstairs he always regards as his escape route, even though sometimes he's not desperate to escape, or eager to escape only the Frenchman but not the world he inhabits. The sound of his footsteps changes as Gopal prances down the wooden steps, sliding his fingers lightly over the polished banister, skipping a step or two every now and then to change the rhythm of his foot syncopation. It's his ambition to one day sound exactly like the pujo dhaakis, drumming and spinning in their madness as people take the statues of Durga Ma down to the river. Tak-ta-thatak tak-tak-tak, tak-ta-thatak tak-tak-tak, tak-ta-thatak tak-tak—

'Looks like the cook shaheb pushed firecrackers up your backhole all night long.'

Gopal comes to a sudden stop on the last landing before the ground floor.

'Tell us, is that the rhythm in which he bangs you?' The second one has a softer voice, but her wit is far sharper, 'Can't believe that fat pig Phorashi keeps up that beat.'

Gopal grins at the two of them. 'And you look like your thhokes fell asleep on you without doing anything. You both look a bit flat this morning, like two-day-old rotis. Did they even pay you? Looks like not!'

Radhuni and Sheyali. No matter how many times he meets them, he keeps being surprised at the supernatural powers of whoever it was who named them Sheyali and Radhuni. Sheyali is sharp-nosed, indeed like a fox, slinky and dusky, with eyes that slant at you sideways even when she's looking straight at you. And Radhuni is indeed like the spice, 'Light and innocent before I heat up, dark and tongue-burning when I reach my temperature, best to watch out!' She is small, so small she could be a ten-year-old girl, except that huge jut of breasts never belonged to anyone under a full seventeen, and that crocodile smile could only live on the face of a very old whore, a maagi who was thirty at least. There are only two of them, but Gopal feels as if he's walked into a room full of women.

'Ki rey! Gogai gaandu! Now tell us the truth! Why are *you* so happy this morning?' Radhuni puts her arm around Gopal's waist so that her breasts squeeze into his stomach. She likes it when this doesn't have the usual effect, which, with Gopal, it doesn't.

Sheyali points to the packet in Gopal's hand. 'He's happy because he's cut off that gora's prick and he' s taking it home to eat it for the last time. With some kashundi.'

'This *is* where my gora gets his prick from. Want a taste?' Gopal opens the packet and offers it to the two girls as they make their way down.

Both women peer into the paper thunga with interest. 'Ehh maa, cold meat! What meat is it?' Radhuni stands on tiptoe, sniffing the bag suspiciously.

'Sleeping chicken,' says Sheyali. 'Careful when you heat it up. It will get up and start walking!'

Gopal grins again. 'You don't heat it. You eat it cold. That way, it stays dead.'

'Cold, undercooked meat! That too in winter! You'll fall sick!' Both women chorus this with real alarm, making a passing bearer turn around. He looks them up and down but keeps his mouth shut as he's been told – this is the way out for all sorts of non-guests who spend the night in the hotel, and interaction between the staff and those who service customers' other needs is not encouraged. The two women stare back at the bearer, their eyes and bodies saying, 'You can look at us with as much contempt as you want but you'll never be able to afford us – you're just a beggar in uniform.' Gopal ignores the man completely, as if he's invisible.

He takes one more sniff of the bag before folding close its mouth and turning to the two women with authority. 'You know nothing. This is made with wine-brandy and onions, so it warms you even when it's cold. And anyway, for these goras this is not winter, this is like their spring season.'

At one side, just inside the staff entrance, sit a liveried guard and a woman in a white sari who looks like a nurse. Pilferage has gone up in recent months, forcing the hotel to take extra precautions. The man nods at Gopal, not budging from his stool, but the nurse takes the two girls behind a screen and does a quick check. The checking doesn't bother Gopal because he knows these two are there to stop stolen goods from going out of the hotel, not to keep them from coming in.

Mild sunlight smelling of the Christmas cakes and fresh bread from the bakery washes over them as they come out on to the street. Gopal notices a pallor on the girls' faces that isn't matched by their arms and the midriffs that show under their saris. He realizes why he has compared them to rotis: something about the powder on their cheeks reminds him of discs of chapati dough just dusted with flour.

'Make sure the tailor stitches up your backhole nice and tight for next time!' Radhuni moves away quickly, heading down to the main street. Sheyali smiles at Gopal. 'Poor thing, she can't bear to smell the new bread,' she says. 'Bechara, she's worried she'll spend her night's take before she can get it to the mashi!' – with which, she turns and follows her partner.

The bakery smell reminds of a contrasting one. Ustad handing him a plate of freshly fried filluries on the boat. 'Gogai, dhorjyo rukhtey hobey! You'll have to hold hard to patience, Gogai. We don't just want the bread, we want the butter that goes on top, and the whole meal that goes around the bread, remember!'

Gopal walks the other way, heading towards Governor House. Near the corner, he stops at a paan-walla perched in his wall-kiosk and wordlessly hands the man some money and his empty yellow packet of Charminars. The paan-walla wordlessly hands Gopal a fresh packet of cigarettes and an extra stick for the returned empty. The young man takes the loose cigarette and rolls one end around the tip of his moistened tongue to keep the tobacco in check. He looks around, hoping against hope, but of course there is no green, open-roof sports car pulling out between the horse carriages. There is no car and no pretty boy at the wheel, no polite, rich man's braking to let through Gourango, Aurangzeb and the shivering first-time murderer in the sidecar. No using of the pause to flick open a lighter so that the glow lights the beautiful eyes from below.

Gopal comes back to himself, bends forward, takes the end of the slow-burning jute twine that hangs next to the kiosk and puts it to his cigarette, puffing economically until the fire transfers and the smoke fills his nose and mouth. Looking down, in the instant before he straightens, he notices the shoes on his own feet, and a small, solid happiness nudges away the larger but thinner sadness.

The cassette tapes I've recorded for the project are divided by interviewee, clearly labelled with marker and now colour-coded with fresh labels, a different colour for each person. So, for instance, the Elko tapes are a bright cadmium yellow while the Missus ones are orange and the Nirupama ones are, naturally, a bright communist red. Where I have

Elko and Missus together, I've gone for either the yellow stickers with an orange marker dot on them or, vice-versa, orange sticker with a yellow dot. For Sheyali and Radhuni, I've used the same colour, a bright pink, because I almost always have them speaking together.

There is no colour for Gopal, because, of course, there's no way to have him on tape. There may be no interviews of Gopal, but the others, particularly Comrade Nirupama, do speak of him at different times. For example, that comment of Nirupama's, which still surprises me even when I know the reasons for it, when she says she somehow never felt the same contempt for Gopal as she did for other criminals she came across at that time.

But let me not jump ahead. At this point in time, the meeting of Nirupama and Gopal is a while into the future. In December 1941, Gopal is just getting to know the world of the Great Eastern Hotel.

Speaking of the hotel, whenever I think about those years, what comes up in my mind is M.C. Escher and his etchings. Old Elko wasn't too impressed by the pictures of Escher. 'A mere technical trickster,' he called him. 'You bloody Indians *would* love Escher because, for you, he feeds directly into all this claptrap about rebirth and never-ending cycles, all this business, the snake eating its own tail and so on. Escher and all this Eastern so-called philosophy, all this kaal-chukker stuff, all utter fucking poppycock!'

Maybe so, but the way he, Old Elko, used to describe that time always reminded me of Escher's images. Not just the stairways and corridors at the Great Eastern, which Elko always said were like a deadly maze – 'Chasing the Minotaur of desire in order to find it and kill it,' as he said – but also that whole convoluted time which could only come to me in this strange tessellation of stories.

Take the two old ladies, for example, too easy to refer to them as *les deux putes veielles,* though that's what the Big Man actually called them while giving me their location – 'oi duto buro maagi' – but then he also instructed me to make sure I addressed them respectfully, Radhuni-mashi and Sheyali-mashi, 'and watch they don't reach into your pant pockets, into *any* of your pant openings!'

The Big Man also gave me a telephone number, 28-5850: 'Belongs to a neighbour four houses down, but they'll call them to the phone for sure, those two maagis hold the entire neighbourhood in terror. In fact, I shouldn't tell you this, but it's their phone only. They pay for it, cash, but they want a buffer to protect the business and themselves.'

I went home and called the number, my fingers sticking to the holes in the dial because of the humidity. It took ten minutes before Sheyali-mashi came to the telephone, during which I could hear the phone owners cursing the old bitch. They stopped suddenly. An older woman's suspicious voice asked me who I was. I gave her the relevant names, and she said to come and meet them the next Sunday.

It was a hot day in March, that Sunday, and the roads should have been quite empty, but the elections had been called and every other street corner echoed with competing speeches. As I bumped past in my taxi, it was as if I was being passed on from loudspeaker to loudspeaker, the party flags changing from meeting to meeting, but the same metallic voice escorting me, the hysterical Bangla constantly rising up through increasingly impossible octaves. It all seemed a joke, of course – there was no question of the bloody Emergency lifting any time soon. Like everybody, I too was convinced there was no chance of Mother & Son giving up power, but nevertheless the charade felt strangely reassuring.

The taxi dropped me at the crossing of Dharmatolla and Wellesley Road, at the corner of Wellington Square, and I asked my way to the address. Abruptly, I was out of the near-noon sun and into a narrow lane between two shops, being sucked in through a cool, dark pipe. Then into the back door of the rear extension of one of those old Dharmatolla buildings, the front of which might once have looked out god knows where, probably somewhere on to Wellington Square.

Inside, the entrance passage lined with the closed shutters of various small shops, and then, in the central well of the house, little pockets of dwelling, different groups settled around the base of the grand old wooden stairway that led up towards some smudged skylight. On the first floor, a whole family living on the landing, mattresses, dirty, naked babies, cats, dogs, an unoon with the coal embers still glowing. After all my time abroad, I'd forgotten quite how many poor people could fit into a small space. I didn't like being reminded. On the second floor, shown the way through another set of people's homes, all producing a gauntlet escort of different smells, two rooms here, a corridor, visible through a door, a whole age-destroyed apartment, the iron ceiling beams collapsed, the wall separating the balcony half eaten away, as if by brick-eating rats. Uninhabited, except for two cats prowling their ownership through the debris.

A few feet along, a doorway throwing bright light into the dark corridor. Another world, clean, compact, intact, smelling of incense and flowers, some pungent fish being cooked in the back somewhere, and something else I couldn't place. Sheyali was standing just inside the doorway, pretending she wasn't waiting for me, arranging something on the high prayer shelf next to the radio. As I waited for her to turn around, I noticed the sequence of pictures. Saraswati, big in the centre, a smaller Ramakrishna to her right, small Sai Baba on her left, a Krishna from Orissa to the right of Ramakrishna, a Ganesh picture to the left of old Sai Baba, a little further along beyond the Krishna, belonging to the grouping yet a little apart, a framed black-and-white photo of Indira clipped from a newspaper, probably taken in the early 1960s, still with mostly black hair, smiling beneath her dark glasses, folding her hands as she alighted from an aeroplane. On another wall, Tagore and Subhas Bose, twinned for eternity. All of these lit by the straight glare of the tube light above.

'Nomoshkar.' Her tone and expression were those of a poker player stating a bet.

I nomoshkared my hands in return, my best disarming smile fully affixed. I thanked her for finding the time to meet me. She replied saying it was nothing, that there weren't too many demands on her time now that she was old and infirm. I had to stop myself from laughing because the woman in front of me was no older than sixty and looked in robust health. She asked me if I wanted water and switched off the radio, cutting off some Hindi film song. Freed of the radio, the loudspeaker sound from the big meeting in Wellington Square suddenly swelled into the room.

'We Bengalis! We Bengalis! We Bengalis know how to fight and when to fight! We in Bengal have seen a lot! We have seen the blood of our young men and women on the grass of this very park where you stand! We have seen their blood flow in the streets, on Wellesley Street, on Dharmatolla, on Harrison Road! We have SEEN the greed of the heartless British and the massive famine they wreaked upon our starving peasants! Across thirty years of this so-called Independence, of this FALSE Independence, we have also seen the duplicity of our own, bloodsucking, profiteer-class, the business vultures who, hand in hand with this cynical Congress government, have continued to stab into the wounds of our poor, our working, sweating masses, wounds that have never been allowed to heal since the time of John Company! Eventually, it was us that sent the British home! And now, AND NOW! Now we, the working masses of Bengal – and Bihar – will also send home this oppressive, exploitative Indira Company!'

'Eraa jaai chainchaak na keno, maagi-ta oto shohojey jaabey na!' Whatever these people may scream, the bitch won't disappear that easily! Sheyali had taken a look at me and decided I was all right to talk to. 'O kono Durga noy kintu o'r opore haath achhey nishchoi, maayer haath achhey nishchoi!' She's no Durga, but she definitely has Durga-ma's hand on her head, that's for sure!

A young girl brought in two cups of tea and looked at me directly as she handed me my cup and saucer, her eyes framed big by kajol under tightly tied, shiny jet-black hair. It was good tea, strong, milk, sugar, everything – clearly their clientele didn't consist only of Bengali men. Sheyali continued: These people shout a lot, but they don't actually do anything. Why, she remembered, during the August '42 struggle they were nowhere to be seen, it was all Congress boys and girls, and some Forward Bloc people, none of these communists, and certainly none of those Muslim League or Hindu Mahasabha-RSS types, they were nowhere to be seen. Look, I'm not saying this about your – she stopped short, anxious not to offend me – why don't you sit, food will be ready soon, though we don't eat so early on a Sunday.

The chunky old fan clanked above, a veteran, maybe also from the 1940s, still hanging on, out of place among all the decor of more recent vintage. As I sat down, I could see into another room through a half-drawn curtain, a TV playing on a stool against the wall, the antenna on top of it like a sci-fi crown, the dials still shiny, the lightly pregnant screen striated with some dam being inaugurated. Clearly, no one had taught the ladies how to use the contrast dial, and the flickering of the hard blacks and whites hurt the eyes, even from a distance of fifteen feet. There was a brief constellation of figures against architecture. The shadows in the top light were dark grey and black on a narrow scale, popping against three notes of white glare: dam parapet, curving dam wall and crisp khadi. The whole image reminded me of this emerging West German painter called Richter and his paintings based on wartime Nazi photographs. Old Elko was the one who'd first showed me this guy's work in an art magazine – 'Look! Now here's someone doing something interesting!' – for once, no trace of envy in his voice, no regrets about ideas lost to others via procrastination or self-redaction, just genuine pleasure and admiration.

Sheyali saw me looking at the TV and called into the room. 'He's here, shall I bring him to you?' The reply reedy, tetchy, 'Not today, I'm tired, you talk to him.' Sheyali's eyes snapped shut with the irritation that spouses in old marriages develop for each other, her voice muttering, addressing me and her gods and goddesses rather than the recalcitrant Radhuni, 'It's watching all that TV that's tiring you out! It was good when we had to go to the neighbours to watch, and when they used to broadcast only in the evenings! Now they start showing from the morning until eleven at night! And her son's bought her this new TV so there is no escape! Lying in bed all day! Watching a day-long kirtan of Indira-Sanjay-Indira, and sometimes Indira-Sanjay-Rajesh-Dharmendra-Amitabh-Indira! I can't bear it! And she doesn't even hear what it says, not even the songs, she just likes to keep it on for the pictures. So, anyway, you can meet her another time, I'll see she is not tired then!'

'No, no, not to worry, Mashima, please, it's all right. I was just—'

'Anyway, what can they show on this TV-box that we haven't seen with our own eyes? You wanted to know about that time, no? Oh, that month of Shrabon was one I'll never forget, Shrabon and Bhadra, both the months, what you call Agosht...'

'11 Agosht 1942, you're talking about 11 Agosht 1942.' Radhuni's voice was suddenly clear from inside the other room. 'The day the news came in properly about Gandhi and everybody being arrested by the Ingrej.'

'Not the 11th, it was the 13th of Agosht, you're getting old! The arrests were on the 7th, the news spread on the 11th, you're right about that, but they took two days to organize the protests. End of Shrabon, before Bhadra began, though the fires kept burning through most of Bhadra also. But as that day began, in the early morning itself you could feel that Yamraj – you know the god of death, yes? – you could feel that he was prowling around close by, and that he was very hungry. Our night customers also felt it, all the sons of bitches scarpered early when normally you had to give them tea and ghugni and kick them out. By 10.30 you could feel the heat rising, not from the weather, it wasn't raining that day, but it wasn't particularly hot either. You could just feel the heat of the bodies as they poured into the square from all directions, and you could feel the heat of their anger. It's a different heat from the heat of the sun, it's a heat no TV will ever be able to show you.'

Radhuni – 'There were 25,000 people gathered by eleven o'clock.'

'Oooff, chhado toh! 25,000! There is no space for more than 10,000, even if you include the roads around the square, but I tell you, 11,000 of those 10,000 were there by noon. And that's not counting the police.'

The TV suddenly released a crackle of sound, or so I thought until I realized Radhuni was laughing from her bed – 'Police! Those Anglo-Indian mamas didn't have time to bother us for their weekly money for the next two months! Imagine! How busy they must have been, those fuck-sergeants!'

'Ei! Watch your language! He's a gentleman boy, don't use your lower-class language in front of him!'

'*Gentleman* boy! How old is he? Twelve? Get one of the girls to make him older! There's still time before lunch!'

'Don't listen to her... already on her third gin and Fanta! Ever since we've had a bit of money, this is the problem – drinks like a memshaheb in Governor House!'

Gin. I identified the mysterious smell.

'Oho. I should have asked you, do you want some? Ei, I'm going to give this boy some of your gin! He's come from abroad! All the way from Phrance!'

'No, no, Mashima, I won't have any. The tea was good.'

I hadn't mentioned where I'd come from, so the Big Man must have talked to her. I wondered if he'd mentioned the paintings. Sheyali showed no sign of knowing anything about that.

'The thing was, we later heard there was trouble at Jagubajar in the morning. A large crowd had reached there, and the police charged them and also hit them with tear gas. The crowd here knew nothing about it, but the police must have heard about it. At about one o'clock, they charged with their bamboo batons. We were on the roof terrace, but we couldn't see clearly, we just heard a roar as the crowd reacted. Then we smelt it, the tear gas, even before we saw the smoke.'

'Remember the noise it used to make when they fired the gas? When the tin cans hit the road? It was like a haphazard rain, like hail, as if god was flinging thick coins from the sky! Like castanets! Like a kathak dancer high on bhang!' The out-of-sight Radhuni was suddenly animated, all tiredness gone.

Tear gas. There was a series, brush and Chinese ink on rice paper. I've only ever seen two of them in actuality, the rest were gone by the time I met Elko and Missus, only present in photographs, hanging in the background as they entertained someone for lunch, the beautiful natural light in the house throwing a glow on the work. One of the destroyed ones was actually called *Wellington Square, August 1942*, scrawled in brush at the bottom, a large enough brush that you could read the scrawl in the photograph. That day, he'd not been too near Wellington Square, of course, but later, he had gone back to the newspapers and journals of the time, clearly accessed the Indian ones in some library over there and used the photographs as the basis for this series.

He'd done these in the late '50s, well before Richter et al, and not as deftly or realistically, but you could clearly see the photographic quality, the photographic provenance of the images. *Wellington Square* had washes of deep grey for the grass, with the paper left untouched for the snaking clouds of tear gas coming in from both sides, an oriental landscape gone badly awry, with white and grey bodies lying flat in the foreground, a blur of people somehow both static and rushing in the middle distance, the buildings in the background rendered with a few light grey strokes. The painting I was hoping to find here wasn't from this series but from way before. However, the television set and the two old ladies' storytelling folded me into an origami of time, into, actually yes, the rabbit hole of an Escher engraving, into thinking about all the different Minotaurs of desire that people chase...

2

CROSSING

The car doesn't fit into the composition, so he decides to get rid of it. He waves to the driver and calls out.

'Ramshoron! Move my car!'

'Move it where, Dada-babu?'

'I don't care! Take it somewhere else! Put it in the garage, park it behind the Packard! Put it on your head and dance with it! Move it where?... I don't want to see it near that gate, that's all!'

Ram Saran gets into the MG and gingerly reverses over the gravel towards the garage behind the house. Standing behind Kedar on the veranda, Rasko decides to impart an observation.

'There was a time, when that car first came, when Dada-babu wouldn't even let Ramshoron touch the car. Him, who taught you how to drive! He was so upset. And you always parked it so that you could see it from your window. Now Dada-babu has a new love, peyn-tiing, and you don't want to see your old love in your new love, hain?'

Kedar takes the tea tray from Rasko's hands and puts it down on the little table next to the easel.

'You can go now, Rasko. I'm sure you're needed in the kitchen.'

Rasko gauges Kedar's tone and ignores the instruction to leave.

'Now, every morning, you come here and unveil your picture as you would a new bride, na ki?'

Kedar looks at the cloth that's loosely draped across the canvas and the easel, and immediately sees what Rasko means. But to concede that would be another victory for Rasko who's been at him since he opened his eyes this morning.

'Rasko, if you've got brides on your mind then go ask my mother, as in your Didimoni, for some leave. Go back to the village and bother your wife for a few days until she kicks you out again!'

This is a low, cheap blow, because Rasko's wife is pregnant with their third child and Kedar knows fully well that in Rasko's universe a husband isn't allowed to go near his wife while she's expecting.

'Why is Dada-babu saying that? Why are you being mean? I was just joking about how much you are involved in your peyn-tiing! What's it to me? I'm only a servant here, I'm only here to serve you!'

Kedar waits until Rasko's sulking feet slap away out of earshot. Then he takes the old bedsheet off the canvas, careful not to smudge the wet paint. It's very true, this business about the new bride. Whenever Kedar isn't thinking about Eva, he's thinking about his paintings. It now takes all his self-control to not get up in the middle of meals, in the middle of the night, to not stop in the middle of a game of tennis and return to look at whichever canvas he's painting.

And, since it's Eva who is responsible for this state, he often finds the two getting mixed up, his painting and his lost love, his paints and all the colours Eva has snatched up while going. The only difference is, you usually unveil a bride or a lover at night, whereas this thing you unclothe in the full light of morning; and, unlike a woman, with this painting thing you don't always like what stares back at you once the covering is gone. Pleasant or not, the first look of each morning is always a surprise, sometimes big, often small, as if the image has been working away at itself in your absence.

Today, he knows he has made a mistake as soon as he looks at the canvas. The green of his car had seemed wrong all of last evening: the perfunctory dark green slashes with which he'd rendered the bonnet, the badly painted silver highlights of the grille and headlamps, all of it had kept him dissatisfied overnight; the damned car seemed to be sullying the quite nicely captured gate and bank of dahlias, it seemed to wilfully imbalance the arch of the portico and the soft winter morning light he'd struggled to pin down. Today, the dashed-off shape of the MG pulls the game away from him. The arch of the house entrance is still fine, the lines of the gate are still tolerable though needing work, but, suddenly, it's the over-pretty line of flowers and the too carefully constructed gulmohar trees in the background that have become the problem. The jutting rectangle of the car is actually quite beautiful, and it shows up the rest of the elements for what they are – daubings straining for a cheap realism. It's as if he is a teacher and the problem pupil of the class has executed a perfect exam while the favourite students have all turned out to be failures and cheats.

How to start all over again while preserving the accidental magic of the bloody car? Despite his feudal training, he is now too embarrassed to ask the driver to bring back the MG. He doesn't really need it anyway. The car is done, it's everything around it that needs to come up to the mark – it's the painting that's actually the teacher; it's he who is the doltish pupil, all his smug, correct answers from yesterday now rendered wrong and meaningless. How to find the answers in a subject he clearly hasn't studied?

For all the small currents of despair coursing through him, Kedar doesn't for a moment think of giving up. He takes a deep breath and the garden's winter layers envelope him. He can smell the fresh bed the maali has dug for some new plants, he can smell the coals burning in the open unoon behind the kitchen, with the mid-morning tea boiling for the staff, he can smell petrol as the neighbours' driver races the engine of Barrister Patronobis's Ford, he can smell the pungent waft of linseed oil from the paints as he peels off the butter paper with which he has covered the palette the night before. He can smell Eva's mouth as it searches for his, and he can hear her soft voice as her breath trips into his nose, 'Prince, you will come on now. You will breathe. You will live your life now. You are wanting painting, you will paint now! No tomorrow, no next week, but now, like this kiss.'

Now, like this kiss.

He is a blank canvas upon which she makes her marks, tentative, some wrong, which she tries to erase, some accidentally just right, line and tone growing in confidence, building the picture, stroke by stroke, scratch of knife by scratch of palette knife.

That first night in long ago August, all she had allowed him was her mouth against his. She had danced off all his fumbling attempts to undress her and turned the night into one, long, changing, pulsating channel of a kiss. He had learnt very quickly how much of a novice he really was; he had learnt to breathe, as if for the first time; he had learnt in those few hours how to give meanings to his tongue and his hands, give every little movement sensibilities he hadn't known existed. It was only much later, once he knew her better, that he realized how much pleasure she herself had taken while lifting away the last of his boyhood.

The gulmohars are the easiest to dispose, so he takes the colour mixed for the sky and covers them up; he will now have to wait for the light blue to dry before he attempts the trees again, but that's all right, the well-mannered dahlias are now waiting to be chopped down, the gate needs small attentions, the cracked white of the portico arch could bear some braver brushwork. He reaches towards the tin of brushes upended in turpentine, pulls out a tiny No. 2 and wipes from it the last traces of yesterday's paint. He places it next to the palette, ready to be called up for the grille of the gate. Then he finds a No. 8 flat edge and wipes it clean. It's a beautiful Winsor & Newton, from the first bunch of brushes he'd bought from G.C. Laha on the way home from Eva's hotel on one of the early occasions.

'You may be very bad painter, but you will never find out unless you paint.' It was one of her almost-perfect sentences, but he remembers it as a different kind of sentence, inescapable once pronounced: 'You will never find out unless you paint.' And so, one morning after an Eva night, he'd turned left on to Dharmatolla, bumped across the tramlines criss-crossing the junction with Chowringhee, and parked in front of the biggest art material suppliers in India. He'd heard about the famously rude shop assistants at G.C. Laha but the one who dealt with him was solicitous and helpful, perhaps because of the early hour or possibly because he could see money.

'Brushes, babu? Oil or watercolour?'

'Oil.'

'Yes, babu. In which case you will also need...'

By the time the shop porter finished loading it, the small sports car was overflowing with canvases, boxes of paint tubes, tins of linseed oil and turpentine, some pads for sketching, and the mast of an easel. Once home, Kedar navigated through Borun-kaku's lectures on Titian and Raphael, his mother's horrified stares and his father's snorts of laughter. He opened a cupboard and pulled out the brushes and palettes left by his aunt, his father's sister Lotika who died in 1937. Lotika-pishi, who was always known as Delphine-pishi, with her penchant for things French and her obsession with wanting to be a painter. Not that much painting was possible for a tuberculosis patient, but Kedar remembers Delphine-pishi's stories of her honeymoon in Paris in 1921, and the galleries she visited and the artists she met.

The white portico wall now has bold slaps of tree shadow, something he avoided seeing yesterday. Finishing with the shadow greys, he looks again at the lines of the gate. No, wait, attack the dahlias first, otherwise the gate doesn't come into proper focus. Kedar pulls out another brush, another medium size, and begins to play with it. Even without looking at them, he can feel the difference between one of his new brushes and an older French one belonging to D-pishi. The older ones are a touch stiffer when he starts working with them, but there's something about the slight encrustation of dried paint on the handles, the way only the top half of the hairs respond, that he enjoys. Kedar has now realized that he chooses different brushes for different jobs, some things are always done with the new ones and others always with the D-pishi set. There is no logic to it that he can decipher, but then, as Delphine-pishi used to repeat, it's not always a matter for rationality. 'As he grows, each painter develops his own way of holding his brush. There is a basic way, of course, but as your style develops, so does the way you handle your instruments. In fact, your style ultimately *comes* from the way you handle them!'

He remembers Delphine showing him reproductions of the greats, especially her beloved Impressionists – her brother Bulldog-kaku barking interruptions: 'You mean, the Impostorists! Phorashi charlatans, every man jack of them! None in their number, my dear Delfy, who could hold a charcoal to a master like Titian!' – he remembers her describing them individually: 'Monet, now he is like an elephant bathing in the river of colour, a haathi flinging spumes of paint over himself! Some of it sticks, some of it washes away back into the stream', and 'Van Gogh was like one of those naked sadhu-babas you see on the streets, you know the ones who keep poking needles into their bodies? Every mark is like a wound, and his yellows are the colour of blood as he understood it – the blood of the soul not the veins!' and her favourite Cézanne with whom she also infected her nephew, 'Can you see the chopping in the strokes, Kedar? He sculpts his canvas, it's as if he's chiselling out the form from a blank canvas, drawing out the colour, unearthing the lines, can you see?'

Kedar tries to see. He looks at his poorly painted flowers and suddenly longs for the little picture in his stolen wallet, the one of Cézanne's *Jugs and Peaches*. He remembers Delphine in her last days, watching Kedar trying to capture Cézanne's brushstrokes, Van Gogh's fury, Monet's light. 'Darling, don't try to copy! But don't try not to copy either! Don't try, just paint! If you listen through your looking, the painting will talk to you, itself it will tell you what to do!'

'Tell me what to do. Teach me how to make love.' They are standing on the pavement, with their back to Firpo's restaurant where there are no tables available for lunch. When Kedar says this to Eva, it comes out like conversation, like a comment about the hot September afternoon, but there's no mistaking his desperation. It is the fifth or sixth time they are meeting, and Eva has lifted Kedar's hand to her face and taken a deep breath. 'I like this smell of turpenseed – I mean turpentoil – on your hands. I like on your fingers the smell of paint even after soap.' All Kedar can connect with his hands is the memory of holding her breasts the last time they've met. Of her pushing his head away as he bends down to kiss her nipples, of turning him around, away from her as she does up her bra and buttons up her blouse. 'Not yet. Some waiting is good, specially when lady is not ready.' Today, he can't wait, so he says it.

Eva looks at Kedar thoughtfully and takes his hand in hers. Then she glances left and right down Chowringhee Avenue. Without warning, she tightens her grip and yanks him into the torrent of traffic. Before Kedar can react, she is running across the busiest road in Calcutta, tugging him along, her high heels pelting, her little hat askew, his tie wrapped around his neck, his legs now in a twisting sprint. In the screaming complaint of car horns a bus nearly catches them, a taxi driver curses their mothers as he jams down on his brakes, by some trick of shifting space they miss coming under the hooves of a pony pulling a jhurrie-gaadi. And then the traffic from the other direction engulfs them. They are squeezed together as two cars bracket them in mid-overtake, they almost part when a small delivery van nearly cleaves through them, there's almost a riot as Eva makes them leap through the back of a jhurrie-gaadi parked on the Maidan side of the road. As they run past the square water ponds into the grass of the Maidan, Kedar has to keep telling himself that both of them are alive and intact, he has to fight off the part of him that is dead and running in the afterlife. Once they are far enough away, Eva slows down. Panting, she takes him around a tree, leans her back against it and pulls him to her. As his body slams into hers, she takes a fistful of his hair and looks into his eyes from up close. There are tears in her own eyes, but Kedar can't tell if they are from sorrow or laughter. 'There!' she says, kissing his forehead as the late monsoon shower begins to spit around them. 'There! Now you know how to make love!'

The tiny No. 2 brush is into the flowers now, the gate forgotten, the brush having decided that the tops of the dahlias need a bright, almost-white lemon yellow; no sooner is he done, he exchanges the small brush for a palette knife and kneads together a massing of ochre under the white highlights, he knows what he will do next, flecking the ochre with a dark brown to fool the eye into seeing individual flowers, which will develop small underbellies of black shadow which will melt into the bright green sliver of visible lawn. It's risky. The flower bed is the fulcrum of the whole composition, and it will mean hours of waiting and then tiny, difficult work to retrieve it from a mess, but he has lost all diffidence, all sense of fear; he has the measure of the tightrope under his feet. Eva scratching patterns on his naked back with a butter knife, following the lines with her nails and her tongue, mumbling almost to herself, 'Without egg-break, no omelettes...'

The brown and black done, he straightens up and steps back. He can see the picture has transformed completely. The shadows have formed a new club among themselves, ranging from the greys on the wall to the underbrush of the dahlias to the sharp network defining the car grille and headlights. The gate no longer needs any tampering – it is just right, half-drawn wisps of dark metal sitting in a larger penumbra, offset perfectly by the glare of the gravel. The flowers are now alive, but they've moved away from being dahlias into a general, bright, winter-yellow flowerness; they remind him of some other flowers seen in some completely different scene, but he can't think where.

'Baaah! Very nice! Dada-babu has changed the dahlias into gedaa phul! Very nice!'

Rasko is back with another service of Darjeeling tea, his sulk now buried under what seems like genuine appreciation.

'Ah, chaa! Good! Give!' Kedar produces the noise he uses to thank Rasko.

The two of them contemplate the painting as Kedar sips his tea.

'What did you just say, Rasko? What have these flowers changed to?'

'Gedaa phul, before someone takes them to a temple, except that's not how they grow...'

'Gedaa phul are taken to temple *and* funeral!'

'Yes, Dada-babu, I know, temple, funeral, wedding, bou-bhaat, pujo...'

'Okay, okay! What's for lunch?'

'No, no, it must be difficult, I know.'

'What's difficult?'

'No, to draw different types of flowers, each different from the other, a gedaa from a dahlia from a rose, you know. But it will come. Dada-babu is working so hard, it's bound to come, different flowers, different birds that actually look like they are in real life...' Rasko picks up the tea tray, 'Lunch! Lunch is shukto, muger dal, aloo poshto and topshey fish. It's what you like, Dada-babu.'

'Are you saying I can't draw a gedaa phul to look different from a dahlia?'

'No, no, nothing like that, I was just saying how hard you are working...'

'I'm going to talk to Ma. You definitely need some chhuti.'

'Chhuti equal to Ingreji *leave*, paataa means *leaf*, jibon or bechey thaka means *to live*... Dada-babu, you didn't tell me what a Phooliva is? Is it a kind of flower? Or a woman's name, Phooliva like Phoolmati.'

'What are you babbling about?'

'From this morning, when you were waking up...' Rasko changes his voice and intones, 'You wyeare a PHOOL-Iva... to... leave!'

But Kedar is no longer paying attention. He sits down in his chair and pulls a tea table towards himself. He picks up a pencil and a drawing book from the red veranda floor.

'Is Ma around?' he asks without looking up.

'No, I think she's gone out, Dada-babu.'

Kedar nods and pulls out his packet of cigarettes. Puffing on one, he opens the pad to a blank page and begins to draw.

THE BLACK GIRL'S FEET

Niru comes out of the steam embrace of the bathroom and quickly walks to where she has left her slippers near the dining table. Titir is singing as she cooks, and her voice fills the rooms even though she's outside in the balcony.

Kaalo meyer paayer tolaay, dekhe jaa aalor naachon

Look at the light dancing, under the black girl's feet
Look at the dance of light, under the black girl's feet

Roma notices the trail of wet footprints Niru has left on the dark red floor. 'Look! Comrade Nirupama, what a good communist you are, even the traces of your feet are in red! If light dances under Kali's feet, under your feet dances the colour of revolution!'

Niru wants to reply, but Titir's voice has taken over everything.

Roop dekhe daay buuk petey Shib
Jaar haathey moron-baachon

Seeing her beauty, Shiva lays down his body
In whose hands lies living and dying

It's as if the place has been transported to some other location while Niru was having her bath. As she dries her hair, she realizes that what has changed is the light, and the ruling smell now is of freshly cooked rice and spices frying, interfered somewhat by the plume of Roma's third cigarette. But it's as if the sun has taken the raw materials of dawn and cooked the morning itself into a different dish. Gone is the peace of the moment just after waking up, the reassuring station of the first cup of tea, the quiet of the mind before it fills with the clutter of the things she needs to do today.

In the dark lap of the black girl,
Rock the infant sun, the infant moon

Roma puts down her cigarette and calls out to Titir. 'Ei, that panch-phoron has fried enough in the hot lap of your dekchi! I can smell it from here. Put in the shiim now, before the spices burn.'

'Ji, ji, yes, chief khansama madam! Though how you can smell anything over there, while puffing like a train engine, I do not know!' There is the sizzle of the flat beans going into the oil, almost like a beat, before Titir goes back to her song.

Ektu khaani ruper jholok
Maayer ektu khani ruper jholok
Snigdho biraat neel gogon

A glimpse of her beauty,
Just a flash of the Mother's beauty,
A vast, soft blue sky

'You washed your hair? In what you call this cold weather?' Roma turns to Niru.

'Yes, hadn't washed it for a few days. I'm going to Shyambajar this evening and Ma is bound to notice. *What state you girls live in, in that place of yours, I don't know! Do you even bathe properly?* You know how she is.'

'Yes, yes. My Ma likes to attack my clothes more than my bathing, how badly they are washed, how my sari isn't properly ironed...' Roma gestures towards the balcony, lowering her voice. 'I know it's her turn to cook today, and I know she insists, but maybe we should find some way of preventing her getting near the unoon…'

'Leave it, Roma. It's not your level of ranna, but it's perfectly edible, as I hope is mine!'

'Your cooking is fine. You're getting better even, I can say. But our little songbird always burns the spices slightly. And her rice is always mushy. And as for the sugar…'

Niru changes the subject. 'What are you working on? That requires so much smoking before it's even nine-thirty?'

'Kajol-di has asked me to make a precis for her committee from these party reports on the Dhaka riots, so I was reading them. It makes me angry… We are so bent on killing each other when we should be fighting these Ingrej… People just can't see beyond being Hindu or Muslim, and it suits the goras just fine…'

'Well, this lunatic Pakistan nonsense doesn't help. Struggling people who can barely get enough to eat need to stick together, not chop off each other's heads on the basis of some religious hocus-pocus.' Niru says the last three words in English.

'Religious hocus-pocus! Very good, Niru, your use of English words is getting better! Soon you'll be speaking English as well as any of our imperialist oppressors.'

'As well as you, you mean? Yes, well, that will be the day.'

'No, look, we can call it hocus-pocus all we like, you and your Marx Gurudev can call it opium of the masses, whatever, but people can't see all that. *This* is what people want to hear, and Jinnah is giving it to them.'

'I know…'

Niru looks at her old school friend and realizes yet again that there is now a difference of rank between them. Roma, the one who was always the brightest, physically the tallest, the one who grasped the stinging nettles of English with more courage than the rest of them, not least because of her extended family, but still, the one who shot ahead in her understanding of the world, of politics, and not just because of the English. Roma, who could concentrate more than the rest of them, who could digest information and difficult concepts and generously explain them to anyone who wanted to listen. Roma, who always seemed two steps ahead of others, and certainly ahead of Niru and Titir in so many things. Yet, Roma, who would always be Roma, one of her two closest friends. Niru shakes the water from her ears and tries to concentrate on what Roma is saying.

'I mean, I was just looking at the dates across the last few months. Look! Jinnah declares the aim of Pakistan in March last year and it's clearly a gambit, nothing else. Yet Suhrawardy has that meeting in the Town Hall, September 19th, to shout why Pakistan is needed, no, why it is an inevitability! *Inevitability!* When everyone knows it's just a cynical chess move to counter the Congress, that there is *no* chance, ever, that you can separate Muslims from Hindus and the rest… as if it was like skimming cream from the top of milk! So, Mr Suhrawardy, September 19th, Pakistan zindabad! Less than a month later, October 5th, in the *middle* of Durga Puja, Bengali Hindus develop a blood thirst: *You want Pakistan, do you? I'll show you Pakistan!* So, trouble, killing, riots in Mymensingh and Dinajpur, even here in Budge-Budge. Next day, October 6th, more killing, like in a tennis match – it's *my* service now! – in Dhaka. Middle of October, the Damodar River floods but doesn't matter—'

'Harvest destroyed, so many people lose their homes, yes—'

'Yes! But doesn't matter! Dhaka erupts again, barely a week later! Doesn't matter that the danger is coming towards all of you, Damodar is over there, in the west, the Padma is here and it's not flooding, so we don't care! It's more important to kill our neighbours! They killed their Muslims, we will now kill our Hindus!'

'Eijey! Who's talking about killing Hindus now? Is the young Congress leader blessing us with another lecture?' The sunlight is behind Titir and its glow throws a thin outline around her. Her long black hair is open, framing her face and her eyes. The fair girl who can sing so beautifully about the dark Kali. Both Niru and Roma fall silent, startled yet again by the beauty that has taken over their school friend in the last couple of years. Titir's eyes narrow with suspicion. 'What happened? Why have you two gone quiet yet again?'

'No... we were just admiring the most beautiful girl in all of Bengal.' Niru moves to go hang up her towel.

'No! Stop! You're making fun of me again!'

Roma smiles. 'No, Titir-moni, we were actually talking about the communal situation in Bengal. As you asked, who's talking about killing the Hindus? Well, as you know, it's the Muslims, or some of them, but too many of them. Just as some Hindus, too many of us, are talking about killing Muslims.'

'Oh-ho! No, no, no, how bad is that?' says Titir. 'Muslim peasants in East Bengal can freely talk about killing oppressive Hindu zamindars and both of you, socialist and communist, will actually clap secretly inside yourselves! As if *they* have no landowners, no... phyoodall... nawab-zamindars oppressing poor Hindu farmers in UP and Paanjaab!'

Roma smacks the cap of her pen into the table. 'Titir! The point is to stop all killing and all thought of killing! No one is denying that land reforms are highly overdue! But the Ingrej aren't going to do that. Only we can bring them about, and we can only bring them about once we are free, once we have our own democracy, and once we have put an end to this urge to kill each other.'

Niru feels a huge irritation come over her, towards both her friends. 'Neither of you understand a basic point! Poor Indians killing each other suits not only the Ingrej, it also suits the zamindars and the capitalists. If the Empire was to disappear overnight, if the English went home overnight, do you think the killing and hating will suddenly stop? Do you think Ma Kali will fling down democracy on us with one of her benevolent arms? Do you think that no zamindar here, no factory owner there, will keep the pot boiling? Do you think a single zamindar or kulak farmer will part with an inch of land without a fight? Do you think industrialists will suddenly start paying workers fair wages without some fear of harm? You, Titir, are trapped in your ancient tribal hatred for anyone who is not like you! And as for you, Roma, all that your great Congress Mahatma can come up with is his old platitudes about non-violence.' Niru flicks her towel at an invisible Gandhi. 'No single landowner is going to give up his land without a fight. After we win that fight, we can talk about democracy!'

Roma starts clapping and Titir joins her, and the pact of laughter shifts to them.

'Wah, Comrade Majumdar, wah!' says Roma. 'Good practice for your meeting today, yes? Will they let you speak, do you think? In our Congress meetings, women actually get to speak, you know?'

'Listen, Niru, whatever we do or don't do, *your* people are like stick puppets being manipulated from Moscow!' Titir reaches for a hair clip and puts it above her upper lip, making a Joseph Stalin moustache. 'Ei naacho! Dance! Ebar laphaao! Now jump! Now, SIT down!'

'You know, Niru, she's right. At least Gandhi-ji wants a free, united India. You wait until after the war, when Stalin demands Afghanistan and a bit of Northern Punjab from Churchill, and fatso agrees to hand it over! Your... communist leadership... is like a new bride constantly worrying about what the in-laws in Moscow will think of her every act.'

Niru feels the blood rising to her head, but she knows it would be a deadly mistake to lose her temper. The rule between the three of them is to mercilessly tease whichever one of them gets angry. If she lets fly at these idiots, she will have to hear about it for weeks. She composes herself and forces out a smile. 'Well, I'd rather belong to a party that worries about Moscow than a party that is beholden to landowners and mill owners. And as for belief, I'd rather have faith in a revolution than live in fear of curses from non-existent gods.'

Titir grabs Roma's shoulder, points at Niru, and starts jumping up and down. 'Look! Look! We've got to her! She's trying to control her temper, look!'

Niru adjusts her sari and shawl and starts to put things in her jhola. 'You girls have fun, playing hide-and-seek and fantasizing about fairy stories, all right? I've got to go.'

Roma pushes Titir's hand away from her shoulder. 'Ei! Aren't you going to eat? You're not leaving in a sulk, are you?'

'No, no, no. I told you I have to be at a meeting, remember?'

'That sari looks nice, that pink border suits you.' Titir, too, is conciliatory.

'What they will certainly not say to you at the meeting', Roma stands straight and, waving her cigarette, begins to declaim Tagore:

Hey Nirupama, gaaney jodi laagey biho bolo taan koriyo khoma.

O Nirupama, if my song shifts key upon seeing you, forgive me.

Titir adds the second line:

Jhara jhara dhara aaji uttorol, nodi kuley kuley uthey kollol

Streams of rain, nature agitated, eager, waves break out from the lap of the river

Waving their arms in Tagorean dance, the two finish the stanza in perfect schoolgirl chorus:

Boney boney gaahey mormoro shore nobino paata
Shajala pobono dishey dishey toley badolo gaatha

In the forest at the edge of the water, new leaves murmuring song
In every direction, the rain-loaded wind lifts a ballad of monsoon

'All right, all right!' Niru's doesn't respond to the compliments but her tone has softened. 'Remember, I'm going to the meeting, then college. And tonight Ma's called me home, so I'm staying at Shyambajar. So don't wait for me, just eat.'

It takes Niru about twenty minutes to walk from the flat on Dover Road to the address in Sunny Park. By the time she reaches, she has pushed all thoughts of Roma, Titir and Rabindranath to the back of her mind. She reminds herself that it is a privilege to be invited today. Not everybody volunteering for the Party nor all senior members of the BPSF were necessarily asked to attend these meetings. Last week, Tapati, one of the other volunteer girls at college, had come with a message: 'Make sure you are free between 10 and 12.30 next Wednesday. Yes, the 24th. Renu-di has asked a few of us from the Students' Federation to go to her house for a meeting. A couple of senior comrades will speak. And then, discussion. Come on your own and no telling anybody else, understood? Renu-di was very specific she wanted three of us girls to be there. Ten o'clock, 7/1 Sunny Park, in Ballygunge. It's a lane off the main Ballygunge tram road, you should find it easily.'

Niru checks the house number again, and then the name on the white marble plaque outside, just the surname inlaid in simple black letters, no 'Sir' or 'Dr' or 'Hon', no letters denoting honours from the Empire unlike so many of the neighbouring houses, just, simply: 'Chakravarty'. The guard at the gates seems to know why she is here. He points away from the main portico to the side of the house, where a narrow passage leads to the lawn at the back. 'Please go that way, the door next to the gulmohar tree.'

Niru makes her way, cutting across the gravel drive, a strange, disbelieving excitement growing inside. Until now, she has only heard talk of these meetings in various houses across Calcutta, meetings where the leadership of the Party actually engages with selected younger cadres, 'almost as equals' she has been told. Clearly, something she has done came to the notice of the people higher up, though she can't imagine what. She keeps repeating what she has been saying to herself since last week, 'You will just keep quiet and listen, you will not open your mouth at all. If they speak in English, you will pretend to understand, note it down and ask Tapati later.'

At the gulmohar tree, Niru hesitates, considers turning back and walking away. She can hear voices coming past the open door, somebody laughing quietly, the clink of teacups.

'Nirupama! Eijey, esho, come in, come in!' Renu-di has seen her and now there is no escape. Niru bobs her head in a respectful greeting and goes in through the door.

Despite being on the ground floor, the room is bright. One wall of the room is lined with bookshelves filled with leather-bound legal volumes and other books. There are chairs and armchairs of different heights arranged in a rough circle around a low table and a settee. A few of the chairs are occupied already, and Niru recognizes some of the men, all older than her, and her volunteer group. Beyond the chairs, at the other end of the room, a set of windows looks out on to a resplendent garden filled with flowers in full winter bloom. There is a desk at the window, piled with books and papers.

A man sits in the swivel chair, his jet-black hair and his crisp, white dhoti-kurta rimmed by the sunlight coming in, the smoke from his cigarette forming a fine, silvery yarn as it spins up. Renu-di ushers Niru in and goes back to where she has been sitting with two other women on the settee. There is no space for Niru there and she winds her way to the chair furthest from the centre of the group, right in one corner. As she sits down, someone passes her tea in a proper china cup and saucer, very different from the bhaands normal in the Study Circle meetings around her college.

'Tapati is late!' says Renu-di cheerfully. 'She's bringing two more girls, but Nirupama is here.'

'Perhaps we should start?' One of the men opens a long notebook, revealing a short, neat list in blue ink.

'Yes, yes.' Renu-di looks at the man in the swivel chair. 'Will you start? We are going to be speaking mostly about the local situation in Bengal, Bihar and Orissa today, but perhaps you could tell us a bit about London and what the comrades are thinking there? Just to remind us we are far from alone?'

The man emits a short laugh. 'Renu-di, I have been back for over a year now, and I'm still being asked to speak about London!' Niru thinks the man's thin voice doesn't match the confidence he exudes.

'Yes, but a lot of these youngsters have only heard about the CPGB at a great remove. You are the one who can make the struggle over there vivid for them. I think that might be quite... useful.' Niru notes with a spike of anxiety that Renu-di has spoken the last two sentences in English. She can't remember what 'vivid' means and it throws her into a tiny panic.

'You can keep it quite brief, Jyoti. Just let the younger people here experience the human element of the Ingrej. Here, we always tend to see them simply as both class enemy and unapproachable.'

TWO TEAS

The collection is unexpectedly good, especially for a day when she wasn't planning to take any at all. It must be this funny 'winter' light, she thinks, or perhaps everything is just sharper because of the situation, the streets, the people, her own ability to spot good subjects, hard to say. Leaving Andrew's chummery at Victoria Mansions, she has taken the first tram that's come her way, without worrying about route or destination, and suddenly, as happens sometimes, the pictures have begun to come, one by one, as if they've been waiting just for her and her Brownie.

First, there was the profile of the ricksha-puller through the tram window, wonderful, dark, gnarled tree of a man, resting a moment by the side of the road, pulling on his bidi, which made the smoke curl out from under his turban to catch the mid-morning sunlight. Then there was the family crossing the road just behind the tram; she had to lean out of the small window to get the shot, but she thinks she has them: clearly new from the village, never been to the city before, a look of slight panic about the man leading, the wife abjectly terrified by the bustle, and the wake of small children with tiny sacks on each head, as if they'd just moved, lock, stock and barrel. Somewhere approaching Kidderpore, she had the good sense to get off and catch a tram heading back to the centre; she's no wilting memsahib, not particularly cowardly, especially in broad daylight, but the stories of the seedy dock area with its criminals and prostitutes have made the rounds in her head and she wasn't feeling intrepid enough to risk a brush with that world today. The third photograph she'd snapped on one of the jetties at Hastings, a brahmin type, standing more or less to attention, arms raised and hands folded, praying to the holy river, mucky though it was. She thinks the tones might look quite nice, the brilliant white of the man's dhoti, the embroidered grey of his shawl fluttering in the slight breeze, and black barges and bright launches dotting the water in the background. The fourth picture was one she hasn't actually taken, but wishes she had: a flock of river boats moored by the bank, on the deck of one boat a short local in European garb, his back to her, conversing with two very tall men dressed native. Something about the difference in height, something about the way the three of them were standing, drew her eye; but as she raised the camera, the bearded one of the two tall men just stared at her. She was no mem-coward, no, but this fellow had looked like a brigand from the Khyber, ready to leap over the boats and come straight at her. Something about his demeanour told her he was completely unperturbed by the fact that she was a white woman in a town ruled by white men. She had instantly lowered her camera, steadied her sun hat and walked away, hoping the fellow wasn't following her. A quick look over her shoulder confirmed he was not: she could see the three figures stepping nimbly from boat to boat, heading away from the bank.

Another tram has brought her up the Strand and around Eden Gardens. She has walked past the lieutenant governor's mansion – Governor House as everybody calls it – and down Mayo Road with the open green of the Maidan on either side; she has kept her camera well out of sight while passing the tents being put up to receive troops who would be coming in soon, in droves, apparently, and has only pulled it out once she is on a tram which will take her to Ballygunge, where she's lunching with her mother at a friend's place on Mayfair Road. Checking the clouded little number-window in the clanging and the shaking, she sees she has seven exposures remaining after the three this morning and the two probably quite useless attempts last evening where one of Andrew's bunch had offered to photograph the newly engaged couple. It would be typical of life if she, one day, found herself back in London with photographs of a whole circus of Calcutta characters and not a single image of Andrew.

She's aware, of course, that this solitary morning jaunt has purely been by way of passing some of the hours between saying goodbye to Andrew this morning and the ball this evening, which will be their last time together until—

She sees it and can't quite believe her eyes. A man, a boy, but just a torso of a boy who's nearly a man, bumping along the pavement, no lower body, no legs, as if the earth has half swallowed him. Just under where his legs should start is a square board of some thick wood, with small wheels in each corner. The wretched creature is using his hands, pushing against the ground to propel himself forward. Where the pavement drops into a driveway, the fellow pushes himself up, nudges the board over the edge with the stubs of his legs, and then swings back on it with the practised skill of a trapeze artist. Imogen is already off the tram, running on the grass to steady herself before turning around and running back towards the trolleying boy. She is out of breath when she reaches him. The box camera is swinging from her neck like a pendulum. She catches it in mid-swing and opens the leather case before doubt and a sort of guilt insert themselves between her gasps. The boy stops his board, wondering if he's in trouble of some sort. Then he sees the contraption on the mem's neck, recognizes it, and makes a decision to go around her. Imogen tries to move out of his way but only manages to step into his path. The boy rudders the other way at the same time she steps to her left and she finds she's in his way again.

Suddenly, Imogen is desperate to break out of this self-made trap, she is desperate to turn around and run back to the tram, erasing any memory of this ghastly stupidity. She tries to step back, straight back, and finds a pair of hands gripping her shoulders. Before she can do anything about this, the hands have spun her around with great strength.

'SHAME ON YOU!'

The shout seems to be magnified by the woman's bangles, though there aren't that many on her arms. There is a finger shaking in Imogen's face and that makes the bangles louder.

'YOU! SHAME! You are not a being of HUMAN!'

'Now, now... look here, I'm so terribly...' Imogen loses control of her face and the tears burst out, fighting past the words she's trying to stitch together. Her mouth goes into a spasm, repeating the first syllable of the next word like a needle stuck on a gramophone record. 'So-so-so-sorr-sorr—'

The woman, standing well below Imogen's eye level, lowers her voice slightly and corrects her own English.

'Shameful! Are you not human!'

Imogen begins to shake her head, unable to speak. Suddenly, everything about the noonday thorns into her, everything around her, the high sun, the shadows of leaves, the fading red cloth sash someone has tied around a nearby tree, the broken wires of the cage around a municipal sapling, the shiny new blue-and-white paint on a milk booth, another tram passing by, the smell of hair oil, everything. She stares at the young woman who has shouted at her, and takes in that she has spoken in English, and that she is wearing a simple cream-coloured sari with a broad red border. A small red dot on the forehead beneath the tightly combed and oiled hair. She hears a noise of small metal squeaking and scraping rapidly over something, and sees the boy pumping away with his arms, putting distance between himself and the trouble he thinks he has caused. There are tatters of intention hanging off her – somewhere in her mind she was already reaching into her purse for a handful of coins, but she realizes that even that would have compounded the mistake.

The woman is still standing in front of her, arms crossed, eyes staring in unremitting challenge. The bottom of the cloth bag strapped across her chest is jutting out sideways, so tightly are her arms locked.

'Arre leave her be! You've said enough!'

'Yes, look at the poor mem! Even her tears are like white pearls! Torturing a queen like her for a cripple... now leave her be!'

The chorus comes from two old men squatting by the pillar of a dilapidated gate. Imogen doesn't understand a word of their Bengali, but she can tell they are laughing at her and the other woman, both. She opens her mouth again, words of contrition finally formed and ready, but the woman spins around and walks off. The snap of her chappals marks out her contempt and dismissal.

Imogen looks behind her and sees the trundling boy becoming a low dot in the distance; she looks at the two ancient wrecks, who bow their heads and lift their hands in folded greeting, obsequious and ironic at the same time; she sees the woman walking away and knows she can't let her go, not without some apology, some explanation, '*We are not all like that! I'm not actually like that! You don't understand!*' Imogen has to make her understand, and so she follows her, tripping over the bumps on the pavement in her hurry.

She is much taller than the local woman, but it still takes an effort to catch up.

'Hi, I say! I'm terribly sorry, but may I—'

The woman whips her a look and maintains her pace. If this mem now wants a quarrel, she is going to have to work for it.

In her desperation, Imogen decides to speak in Hindi – I've made a mistake, please forgive me. 'Ji… meri galti ho gayi, mujhe maaffkijye!'

'Hum Hindi nahi boltaa haay!' I don't speak Hindi – but said in perfectly clear Hindi. The woman's anger seems to go up a scale; she quickens her pace. Imogen is now almost jogging, tears and sobs returning, making it difficult to see. Somehow Imogen passes the woman, gets far enough ahead to block her, but there's no stopping the oncoming train, so she starts stumbling backwards and back into English.

'I just wanted to say I *understand!* I realized how awful I – my mistake – just before you—'

'What do you understand?' The woman stops and this fills Imogen with a strange fear: now there is no getting away, no quick apology possible. 'You people are understanding nothing!'

'Oh, but I do! It was wrong! I wasn't thinking! I'm – I'm not in my right mind today.'

The woman makes an effort to organize her sentences before she replies. 'You have not been in right mind for centuries. What is so special today?' Imogen's reply-words all go missing. She purses her lips hard, trying to bring this weeping under control. The woman doesn't lower her stare. 'This is how you are seeing us, isn't it? All of us are like half-animal in this, your zoo, this zoo of your owning, is it not?'

Imogen can feel the sun on her head now. She reaches up to adjust her hat but finds it gone. The woman catches this and looks around quickly. She sees the mem's topi lying a few feet away. A stray dog is nosing it suspiciously. Something makes her walk over and shoo away the mongrel; perhaps she is being too hard on this stupid English girl. Victim of her class. Stupid, but not such an amanush that she didn't realize what she had done.

'Oh, thank you so much!' The hat back on her head, the crying drains away from Imogen, leaving sniffs between words.

'You should have water. Do you have water bottle?'

Imogen shakes her head. No. The woman looks around and spots a tea shop. Maybe she should point it out to the girl. 'Then you should have some tea. It is boiled. It will calm you.'

Since arriving in India, Imogen has never touched any food off the street; it's the one taboo of her mother's she has religiously maintained. And then there's Andrew: 'Suicide, darling, and painfully slow, at that!'

'Boiled... oh, that's an excellent idea! Would you... would you mind terribly having tea with me?'

The woman suddenly feels in no position to refuse; the irrational logic has been set in place the moment she fetched the girl's hat. And anyway, as her cadre leader Soumen-da would point out sarcastically, since 22nd June the British are now allies in the anti-fascist struggle.

'Dada, two teas!'

'Yes, for the memshaheb also? Sure?'

'Yes, she will have. Two teas.'

Imogen sits down on one of the benches, forcing herself not to check if it's dirty. The woman sits on the opposite bench. The stall boy comes with the tea; Imogen notices how close his fingers are to the overflowing brim of the funny little cups. She burns her own fingertips immediately and almost drops the slimy clay thimble. Following the woman, she blows on the surface and gingerly puts the cup down next to her, waiting for it to cool.

'What... do you call these cups?'

'They are called bhaand.'

'Baand.'

'No, bHaand.'

'Bhaand.'

'Very good.'

Imogen lifts the bhaand and makes herself sip from it. Her tongue feels seared. Serves you jolly well right, Imogen Snell, for—

'Oh! How very rude of me, I haven't introduced myself. Imogen Snell!'

The woman shakes her hand softly.

'My name is Nirupama Majumdar.'

'Ni-roo-pomme-a?'

'Ni-roo-poe-maa. And you are Imoe-zen.'

'Imm-uh-junn.'

'Imozunn!'

'Yes! Niroopaw-ma!'

'Yes. But simpler is, you may call me Niru.'

SALT

'Gogai, I know you like to eat, but I hope you're also paying attention. If you don't, all those filluries will come out of your stomach when the police slice it open with a razor blade.' Gopal has just bitten into another large onion fillury, and his mouth is full of the deep-fried batter and its oil and salt. The boat moves under him, not helping him as he nods rapidly, speaking through a full mouth as he tries to swallow the hot thing down.

'No, mUstad, m'I'm mlistening to mevery word!'

Ustad smiles, revealing a new gold tooth, a shiny canine to go with the dulled incisor two teeth away.

'Look at this chutiya!' he says to Aurangzeb and Gourango. 'Eats the best food in the land now, all that Phorashi and shaheb whatnot, but still such a glutton for his filluries! A mullah runs only to his mosque! Mother's milk tastes better than a king's kabab!'

Aurangzeb and Gourango know better than to reply. They all sense that Ustad's mood can switch at any moment, turn and capsize this brilliant winter morning into the darkest of nights. Things have been going badly, and the old man's eyes have taken on the look they've all learnt to fear.

'So, which one of you going to explain this business of cow shit?' The smile widens, giving the gold tooth more light. 'No? Why not? Why do I have to do all you people's work?'

Gopal can tell that he's not the only one who has no idea what Ustad is talking about.

'Gogai, do you know how much a bucket of cow shit is worth?'

Gopal rifles through his mind, trying to find an answer. 'I'm not sure, Ustad. Normally, nothing. People collect it from the roads, or the khatal-wallas collect it—'

'Exactly! Nothing! Or, not very much! If the poorest man is desperate, he can go to the khatal and ask the gowala to give you a stack of dried cowpats for two or three paise, isn't that so?'

'Well, sometimes the gowalas sell the dried cowpats in bulk,' Gourango speaks, almost just to say something. 'Sometimes when there's a wedding in a basti and they need the gobar pats for the fuel, to cook a big meal then...'

'Yes.' Ustad's smile disappears. 'So why is there an order in the city, in all the khatals, both cow and buffalo khatals, that for the next two weeks all fresh cow dung must be turned over to the PWD? And why have they quietly told everyone they will pay, hear this, that they will pay, *four whole annas per kg* for good, fresh, cow and buffalo shit? One whole rupee for four kgs of gobar? Hain? Do you have any idea how many cows there are in this city? How many buffalos? Do you have any idea how much money this will come to?'

Aurangzeb reaches meditatively into his mouth, trying to pull out something.

'What's in your mouth?' Ustad whirls on the big man. 'Trying to find an answer, are you?'

Aurangzeb drops his hand quickly. 'No, Ustad, but maybe they need the fuel to cook for all the extra soldiers coming in...?'

'Just for two weeks? What happens after two weeks? They marry off each and every extra motherfucker soldier who's come in? And then? The order says *the next two weeks* only! The order says *fresh*, meaning wet, they don't want it dried! Why?'

Nobody has an answer.

'What was that song? What was that song that lizard of a Baul was singing two years ago? About diamonds selling at the price of cumin? Gogai?'

Gopal knows the words by heart, but he takes his time remembering them. *I went to far countries, to engage in high commerce... I bought good gold and solid silver, after checking it through and through... Fault of my fate, it turned out to be brass, zinc and glass... Now... now my diamonds sell at the price of cumin. Oh Lord, this you do, this you do to the ones you want to cause sorrow.*

'So. Now we have the opposite situation! Gobar is selling at the price of saffron! And not only do none of you know why, you haven't even heard about this!'

'Ustad...' Gourangzeb shows courage. 'Ustad, we've had other things to deal with.'

The old man snaps a look at Gourangzeb and reaches for a bidi. 'You, I'm not blaming. You can only hear so much in jail, especially when the mamas are teaching you music lessons. It's these other two.'

Ustad turns back to Gopal.

'Now, Gogai, what do you have on that paper? Read it out!'

Gopal looks down at the pad in his hand and he makes sure the fountain pen doesn't shake as he uses it to go down his list. He ignores the rolling of the boat as it kneads down the river. He makes sure his mouth is empty and his tongue clear when he speaks.

'In jail: Roton and his whole toli, all eight of them. So all wagon working at Howrah yard stopped for now, for us, but also for all the others.'

'Yes. Inside, but as far as we know, silent. And it's not as if the other's tolis are breaking into wagons of gold either.' Ustad drops his head back into deep meditation.

'Were in jail. But now out: Gourango-da,' Gopal nods respectfully towards Gourango, 'Aziz Mian, Ashraf, Red Kanhai, Jogeshwar, Kishore and his toli of five, Kana Lalten, Salim the tailor, the two Mishra brothers, Savan Kumar and Bhairav Kum—'

'Those four motherfucking Biharis.'

Gopal stops as Ustad holds up a fillury in both hands as if showing them a rare specimen of insect. 'Those madarchod Bihari sons of whore-cunts.'

Not one of the three men watching dreams of pointing out that Ustad himself is a Bihari. Ustad softly rips apart the fillury, revealing the sliced rings of onion lurking inside the golden batter. Then he puts it in his mouth and pulverizes the whole thing. The old man rarely repeats the same abuse thrice, but he does it now.

'Madarchod Bihari, khaanki ka chhele. They sang a lot of thumris for those cockroaches in Lalbazar.'

No one says a word. Their silence bobs to the chug of the boat engine.

'Who the sister-fuck am I talking about?' The voice barely rises, but the eyes whip across Gopal's face to stop on the other two.

'That Ashraf, that Salim Tailor, that Savan Kumar and Bhairav Kumar,' Gopal keeps his voice even, as if choosing from a list of groceries.

'Mishra? Call themselves big brahmins. Singing whore-songs for cops.'

This is a death sentence being pronounced, and not one of the three looks at Ustad as he speaks.

'So where are they now, those two?'

Gopal answers, 'I met them in a tea stall at Moulali crossing, and I told them like you told me to. That you were getting them a permit to travel on a goods train to Patna, a train no one would be watching, and to meet me at that siding tonight, just before eleven, for the train leaving at eleven thirty-five. Told them I would put them on the train with the valid permits. They were a bit shifty, so I gave them the money and told them like you told me to, but I added... I said we knew they had sung a bit about the other gangs to save themselves but nothing about us, and I thanked them from you. Told them you thought they had been loyal and clever but that the other gangs had wind of them talking to the mamas, especially after all the new arrests. Told them they needed to lay low until the train. Said you were talking about giving them a small bonus to take home.'

'Bonus... nice. That was a nice touch, Gogai.'

Gopal ducks his head in thanks and continues. 'I'm more or less sure they will show up. Savan's wife is pregnant, and I've told them they can't contact any one of us but me because of the mamas and the other tolis, so they are a bit—'

'It's things like this that make me stop Aurangzeb when he asks my permission to kill you...'

'So they are a bit nervous, not quite sure what their singing has done to us. They think the cops are waiting to jump on us last and they want to get out before it happens.'

'... which is something he asks me every second day, but I tell him that it's things like this that make me stuff you with filluries. If he,' Ustad smiles at the big Pathan, 'if *he* had said this to these Mishra whore-boys in the middle of Moulali, they would have run there and then. Run straight to Sealdah Station and caught the train to Dhaka and we would never have seen them again.'

Aurangzeb says nothing. His eyes bore deep into the right knee of his crossed legs. His big hands stay folded in his lap, reaching neither for the small cup of tea nor the pile of filluries on the scrap of newspaper next to him. The cawing of seagulls underlines his silence.

'Eiiijey!' The old man throws his voice out to the deck. 'Are you asleep or what? Take this tea away and bring us new cups, it's gone cold!'

The new tea comes quickly. It's always been ready, the man waiting for Ustad's command.

'And bring Gogai some more filluries! Boy's clearly hungry for home food!'

As a passing gunboat hits them with its wave, Gopal retches inside himself. He now finds the filluries on Ustad's boat far too salty. But these fragile complications of fried flour and onion, entrapped by deep frying into tributaries, veins and little bladders of oily batter, are Ustad's way of showing both affection and ownership. Had Gopal's other master, Bonnemaison, made the mistake of putting one in his mouth, he would have screamed, 'This is sheet! Sheet raped by salt!'

After three months of servicing the Phorashi chef, the over-salting is an assault on Gopal's mouth, the same way his ears can't bear it when someone stops halfway while singing a song he's enjoying and begins on one he doesn't like. The only thing he can do is keep quaffing the filluries and hope that Ustad doesn't notice how much he hates them. The first time Gopal had brought in a good pocket-maar's haul, at thirteen or so, Ustad had rewarded him with filluries. A small mountain of batter-fried onion, and no part of the actual takings, Gopal now realizes; a luxury of salt, which was not something a poor street kid came by easily, but none of the gold and money he had stolen.

By now, Gopal has often seen Ustad devour huge quantities of chaanp, plates piled high with shattered bone and mutton, all of it still trembling with the slow slaughter and the eternal cooking in chillies and spices, seen him consume whole sides of baby goat and large pots of beef keema and haleem. He has seen the man put away chickens without leaving so much as a dot of cartilage on the plate, seen the beard part to magically strip fish off its tree of fine bone. It has taken years for Gopal to realize that the simple onion fillury was the old man's own first stop on the train-line of reward when he was young.

'This is sheet! Sheet raped by salt!' Gopal has seen Bonnemaison in his fury upend a whole pot of fish soup into one of the large sinks of the hotel kitchen, the hot liquid splashing and steaming, the chunks of fish, enough fish to feed half a wedding, bouncing off the porcelain. Later, almost as if reminding himself, Bonnemaison has given Gopal a small lecture, 'Sel, mon p'ti, is like a door... 'ow you say, a gate! This salt, it's a gateway to other tastes, but only when it's parfait, exacte. But if there is too much, the gate is bloque, is blocked, but if there is too little then the door does not open at all!' Gopal has taken this lesson and constructed his own analogy. In his own line of work, it is patience that is like salt: if you are impatient, there is serious danger, but if you fail to act when the time is right, you miss opportunities, and that can again lead to grave peril; if you calibrate your patience correctly, new doors open, as if by magic.

'So, you, Gogai, will meet them tonight at the siding at Howrah?'

Gopal nods.

'You will hand them the permits.'

Gopal nods again.

'You will hand them the permits, make sure they see the papers are real, you will tell them to...'

'To wait for the train to leave the platform and go past the siding. Of course, the train will be blacked out, but they have to jump into the fourth goods bogey, which will have its door open.'

'After which you will go. And so, no train, no open door, and you two will be there to give them their final bonus once Gogai leaves?' Ustad looks at the big men.

'Just Gourango. He wants to do this on his own.' Aurangzeb speaks for his partner.

'Those two are big-built oxen. Gourangzeb, I know you were in charge of them, but right now, I don't want to hear the love story of your betrayed heart. This is not about revenge, this is about setting an example, and I want it done cleanly and quickly.'

'Ustad, I have to look after the truck from Siliguri.' Aurangzeb has Gourango's answer ready for him. 'The driver will only be able to leave the convoy after it comes into main Calcutta. He will reach the Kasba godown at ten and he'll have to leave quickly. I will have less than half an hour to unload.'

Ustad pauses to take a gulp of his tea. He wipes his beard with the end of his lungi. He scratches a small itch by the side of his right eye as he waits for a long river horn to die away.

'Show me the list again,' he says finally.

Aurangzeb reaches into the folds of his gown and pulls out a piece of paper. Ustad adjusts a pair of glasses on his nose and peers at the list for a while.

'Gogai?'

'Yes, Ustad.'

'Can you now read this?' Ustad hands Gopal the little chit. Gopal flicks his eyes down the list of items, scribbled in a tortured English handwriting. He parts his lips and mouths the words he's reading. He doesn't need to, but he does. Hopefully, the seasoning of patience is correct.

'I can read most of it, Ustad, but...' he gets up and goes and crouches near Aurangzeb, showing him the paper, 'I can't understand, this, this, this... and this.'

The Pathan looks at Ustad. His face is deadpan, but the act of looking says everything he needs to say.

'Well, what do you expect?' Ustad snaps. 'The chutiya is still learning! Everybody can't read Ingreji phet-phet-phet like you, so tell him what it says!'

Gourangzeb, who can't read, looks out of the window at the procession of trees and buildings on the riverbank. Aurangzeb scowls at the paper. 'That is... bully beef. Twenty crates of tins. Tins of cow meat, made into keema, army rations, bujhli?'

'Yes.'

'And that is... penicillin ampoules, two crates. It's a kind of new medicine the goras have invented.'

'Magic, it's supposed to be. Cures everything but stupidity,' Ustad adds.

'Ampoule?' asks Gopal.

'It's a tiny bottle. You break the tip and pull the liquid into an injection. They're made of glass, so make sure you don't get excited while checking the stuff and put an ampoule up your backhole.'

'Him checking the stuff?' Aurangzeb asks.

'Yes, him. You go to the station. Gogai can oversee three men unloading a truck. Better than having him near blood. Remember what happened at the port that time?'

No one reminds the old man that since the night Gopal was promoted, he has witnessed in total the killing of five men and helped set up the murders of three others, that Gopal, in fact, is quite at home in the vicinity of blood. Aurangzeb looks down at the list again, conceding the argument. 'And this is a kind of sharaab called sherry. Four crates, also army supply, so look for the BIA seals and make a random check that the bottles are closed properly.'

'And that last one?' Gopal's voice is confused and curious.

'That is...' Aurangzeb's eyes squint for a second. 'A-n-t-i-q-u-e-s... that is probably "an teak". The fool doesn't know how to spell. It will be some furniture made from teak wood, like a table or a bed. The things they send nowadays, expecting us to pay for them!'

The windows of the cabin darken on one side as the launch passes below a big freighter.

'Thiik achhey, that's settled. Now what is next?'

'Salim Tailor, and Ashraf?'

'Where now?'

'Waiting. We've got them in a room at Kasba.'

'Those madarchod, Bihari, cock-loving chhakkas. Tomorrow, get someone who can sew, maybe Salim's assistant, that fellow, Imtiaz.

Give him one pair of those doctor's gloves to put on. Make him sew their dicks together, head-to-head. Those Mussalman dicks they think are so big. Then show them to some of the others before getting rid of them. I don't care which hole you want to stick your dick into, but let everybody understand what happens to people who try to stick their dicks into my ass! Let them see what happens to bhainchod namak-harams like these.'

None of the men points out that this will be neither clean nor quick, though everybody understands the example it will set. Ustad takes his walking stick and thumps the tip thrice on the ceiling of the cabin. It is a signal for the man at the wheel to turn the boat around and take it back to the city and the barge near the jetty.

Namak-haram, salt-disloyal, trust-violator – the one who betrays the salt he has received, the food he has eaten, from his master. As the launch starts to push against the water for its turn, Gopal looks at the river and runs through his betrayals since the day that Rabindranath poet died. It's a brief but potentially lethal list: the pretty boy's wallet, itself enough to get him broken legs and thrown out of the gang; then the tall gora's gun, a sure and dragged-out death if Ustad ever found out about that one; and now, today, this latest one.

'Gogai? What dream are you lost in, my golden one?'

Ustad's voice is almost tender. When Gopal looks back, he sees Aurangzeb and Gourango have gone, obviously on a signal he hasn't seen. Gopal is now alone with Ustad.

'Nothing, Ustad, nothing. Just looking at all these new ships that are coming in. The ones with the cannons.'

'Yes... quite something, aren't they?' Ustad lights a bidi, the first one of the day, delayed until now because his doctor has told him to stop smoking. 'But do you know, Gogai, do you know which are the most frightening of these ships?'

'No, Ustad.' Gopal is back on alert, calves tensing, trying to get rid of the pins and needles from his folded legs.

'Well, you would think it would be the biggest ones, wouldn't you? The ones with guns that can throw a shell over miles, the biggest planes also, the ones which can drop the most bombs, han na ki?'

'I really don't know, Ustad.'

'You know, the Germans had the biggest planes, and the most planes, and last year they tried to bomb the Ingrej into dust. You know what happened? The madarchod Ingrej had a few very small but very fast planes, phaaiturr-plane, and they buzzed around these big German machines and the Ingrej shoved it up the fat Germans' backhole.'

'Yes, Ustad, I read about that somewhere.'

'And on the sea, the opposite happened. The Ingrej thought they had the best warships, biggest navy in the world. They thought they owned the samundar. But! The Germans have a lot of boats called submerin that can go under water – you can't see them – and they fire rockets through the water, called torpido! And in the Atlantic, the mahasaagar, they shoved it up the gaand of the British! Torpido after torpido up the gaand of all these Ingrej commanders…'

'Yes, Ustad, I read about that too, recently.'

'Yes, I'm very proud of how much you can read… But tell me, which do you think is more dangerous, Gogai? A large enemy you can see or a small one you can't?'

Gopal's ears flood with the thump of his heart. A reverse of fillury-acid rises in his throat. He says nothing.

'Who started you reading, beta Gogai? In Bangla, in Hindi, in English, who?'

'You, Ustad.'

'Who slapped your face red and made you learn how to write?'

Gopal swallows his lips.

'So, you think I'm getting so old I can't remember things, beta?'

'No, Ustad.'

'*Peni-ci-llin.* Do you remember picking up a box in the godown and reading the word out loud from a label, that time in October? Remember how proud you were? And now, suddenly, you can't read the same word.'

Gopal drops his head and folds his hands in his lap. Obviously, he has miscalculated his seasoning of patience.

'Next, you little dog, *sherry*.'

Gopal remembers before Ustad speaks and disembowels himself mentally.

'You came back from that Phorashi pig's hotel one day in November with a – kya bolta hai – shopping list, remember, in November?'

Gopal keeps looking down as he calculates the distance to the open window. He calculates the leaping up, the jump through the window and the dive into the water, works it all out vividly in a few seconds before accepting there would be no point – if one of Gourangzeb's knives didn't get him first, Ustad's network would track him down in two days. .

'Sherry. You said the pig wanted something called sherry. When I asked you what it was, you told me it was a strong wine that came from Ispain, whereas this... port comes from Porchu-gaal. You wrote down the name and then some good brands.'

Gopal has tears in his eyes when he looks up. The tears are from fear, but he's hoping it will bring out the tiny residue of pity that even this man has to have lurking somewhere.

'Luckily for you, both times that big bullock Aurangzeb wasn't there. Neither was Gourangzeb, who may not read but who is far from deaf or stupid. Otherwise, it would have been hard for even Ustad to save you today.'

'Yes, Ustad, I—'

'Don't open your mouth until I tell you to open your mouth. The kind of mood I'm in, I might cut your lying tongue out and feed it to the gulls. Do you think I don't know why you did it?'

The old man shakes his head in defeat and pulls out another bidi.

'You over-smart little, cock-sucking little submerin. You think I don't understand how scared all you people are of that big Pathan? You think I haven't thought it through that he may start to worry about how much you can read now? When all these years he's been the only one besides me who's somewhat literate in my whole outfit?'

Gopal finds himself hoping the old witch of a bastard can't sense the blood dropping back into his veins, can't hear his heart slowing down to normal. He tries to keep the tears coming, fighting against the relief that's drying them up. His head still low, he nods in furious apology.

'The next time you start to piss in your pants, you come and talk to your Ustad, do you understand? You do not ever again do something stupid like this which puts Ustad into awkwardness, you understand? Let me hear you say it now.'

'Ustad, please forgive me for—'

The slap hits Gopal square in the jaw, knocking him sideways. The strength of the blow is not surprising, but the speed is completely unexpected.

'What exactly is *antiks*, my little submerin?'

'Antiques, means old things, quite valuable sometimes, like furniture and lamps and things like that. I was going to tell you later!'

'I'm sure you will tell me many things later. Now go and wash your face, we are nearly there.'

Gopal totters to his feet which he can no longer feel, the pins and needles now unbearable. As he hitches up his trousers and reaches the door to the deck, he feels as if he has been born anew. Through the opening, he can smell the sooty winter musk of the river.

'Gogai, do you want to die?' Ustad's voice is soft but very clear, despite the loud drumming of the engine. Gopal forces himself to turn around, still bent to get through the door.

'Ustad?'

'There is one thing you are still lying about.' The veins on the old man's face are popping and his eyes are like huge bulbs. Gopal feels his bladder going, but he keeps his voice level.

'No, Ustad.'

'Gogai, are you sure you don't want some more filluries?'

Before Gopal can respond, a huge swat of laughter reverberates in the cabin. Ustad has his head thrown back, mouth open, belly pumping out guffaws, both gold teeth glinting in the shade on the cabin. He can barely manage the words through his wheezing. 'Too... much... salt for my freshwater submerin, no?'

'Yes, Ustad,' Gopal grins wide, 'much too salty for me. I didn't know how to tell you.'

I don't have Gopal on tape but I do have a list in what is probably his handwriting from a bit later, in 1944. Most of it is what you would expect in a list from that time: rice, salt, masur dal, haldi, jeera, milk powder for children, some medicines, scrawled in pencil on cheap, blue-lined notebook paper. Most of it is in Bangla, with 'milk powder' and 'malaria tablet' in English.

When I asked Niru about the list, she told me she had dictated it during one of the times they had dealt with each other during the famine.

'Was that the first time you met this fellow?'

'First time? No, no, I first met him a couple of years earlier, in August '42. I'd immediately labelled him as some sort of an antisocial, some fringe lumpen, petty criminal type. In fact, I'd first thought he was some sort of assistant pimp, you know, a dalal, which is funny when you look at how he began to help me later, during the famine.'

It took some work to get that story out of her, but what I've pieced together from different taped conversations is this:

'By September '43, the famine is at its peak and the pavements of south Calcutta around the Bengali neighbourhoods are filled with people from the villages. Somehow, they knew where to come. They didn't bother trying to go anywhere near the shaheb-paras like Alipur or Ballygunge, or even the paras where non-Bengalis were concentrated, like Bhowanipur, at least not at first.

'In the Party and the Women's Self-Protection groups, we were doing what we could. One of our duties was to go and organize the roadside langarkhanas meant for women and children. We had to make sure that men didn't barge in. We had to make sure the women stood in orderly queues when the first smell of food was enough to make people riot, even in that state. Then, for the ones with the really advanced malnutrition, we made sure to give them only phyan, very thin rice-water, no matter how much they begged for solid rice. Some langarkhanas even had different thicknesses of phyan for different stages of malnutrition. Every day, the same mantra would turn our tongues into pulp – "No, ma, you can't have rice just yet, your stomach is too weak, it will burst and you will die. Drink a bit of this phyan right now. When you are stronger, we will give you rice and dal. No, ma, not even one handful, believe me your stomach will split open." And even then, some of them would go and manage to get a bit of rice from somewhere and collapse in front of us. Writhing and vomiting till their eyes turned up.

'I had my revolution all nicely mapped out, we all did, all the young comrades. We would educate the workers while other comrades educated the peasants. The crises that would lead to revolution would signal in advance with clear flags, they would be recognizable, identifiable from what had happened in Russia or in Spain, or what was happening in China. We knew there would be differences, but they would be manageable differences. This was not part of what we had imagined. Where had *this* come from? What were we to do with this? We were not ready for this. We had not been taught about this, not been trained for this. Every day, I woke up thinking I was about to give a completely unfair exam, for a syllabus that had been changed at the last minute, no, not even that, for a different course, a different *subject* than the one for which I had studied.

'For instance, the hunger was one thing, but you had to watch out for other things as well. The queues would start forming around three o'clock in the morning and a few of us girls had to be there on, you know, on patrol. The food would only be brought around 5.30 or 6, but the women and babies would be in a line, snaking all the way from Gariahat Crossing to the railway station, and sometimes even to the canal market and beyond. Many of the women were almost skeletons, but there were also many with just enough flesh on their bodies to make them easy prey.'

One such early morning, Niru found herself guarding the queue where it petered out at the rail tracks near Gariahat railway station. As she's said on more than one tape, after a while she found she was distancing herself from the people so that she could do her job. 'Eijey! You there! Go back to your place in the queue! Everyone is hungry, you're not the only one! And you, ma, wait! I can see you have four mouths to feed, but there are many more than four little mouths in front of you, wait your turn!'

'After a while, the line just became a human wall that you had to keep propped up, push the women and kids back in, like you would bricks to stop a wall from crumbling, you couldn't let the wall crumble for that would mean chaos, riot, bloodshed – it's amazing how much energy a human body can have even when it's not much more than bones and skin. It's startling. As if a battery has suddenly been plugged into them, jerking them to life from near-dead, suddenly able to claw and kick in order to get to food.

'It wouldn't last long, of course. Sometimes a push or a firm yank, and the person would just collapse, done with living, unable to get up, unable to even open her mouth for a cup of phyan.'

That morning, Niru walked up and down in the near total darkness of the blackout, scanning her section of the queue. Something was out of place down the line, something was extra, and her experience told her what kind of danger it was. She strode down towards the two figures talking to someone in the line. From their silhouettes, Niru could tell that these were men, and well-fed ones.

'They used to be like hyenas circling. They would walk around the end of the queue, because they knew the organizers were mostly at the other end, near the food being distributed. They would pick on the girls, anyone just past puberty who was not completely gone, and the better-looking ones were naturally their first targets. "Eijey, you're really hungry, aren't you? You'll wait for hours here and for what, a handful of rice and some thin dal? You'll be hungry again in half an hour, won't you? Come with us, we'll feed you. Proper food, fish, meat, sweets. Work properly for us and you'll never go hungry again. Come. Come for half a day and see. It's not far, and you can come right back afterwards. We'll give you extra food for your family."'

Niru hurried towards the men, anger mounting, calling out, 'You! What are you doing here! Go!' As she reached them, she raised her arm and pointed away from the queue. 'You two, go away, now! No one needs your badmashi here! Go!' Usually, the men would slink away and wait to come back later. But these two were different. They didn't move. One of them had his hand gripped around the thin arm of a young girl, about fifteen, trying to tug her out of the line. Niru could see the girl was in two minds, frightened, but also wanting to try her luck with the offer. Niru reached the girl and grabbed the man's hand, trying to loosen his grip.

'Let her go, you monster! She's not coming with you!' The man slammed his free hand into Niru's chest, sending her reeling. The other man came and stood right in front of her. 'She said she wants to come with us. Are you envious? Do you want to come as well?'

From the corner of her eye, Niru saw a small blue van stopping sharply a few feet away, a red cross painted on a white circle on the doors at the back. 'So that's how they're transporting them now,' she thought. The man further from her turned to look at the source of the sound and stiffened. He moved his hand off the young woman and grunted to his companion, 'Ei, let's go, leave it, let's go.' The second man didn't turn around. 'Leave it? Why? Take the girl. This bitch won't do anything.'

'Trouble. It's that mother___ Pocket, Shabuddin's guy. Let's go.' The second man whirled around, started, and quickly began to move away as well. A little man had stepped out of the van and the two pimps seemed anxious to avoid him. They tried to walk away, but the man quickly intercepted them. He put his hand on the first man's shoulder and said something softly. They were a few yards away and Niru could only hear the word, 'elaka', area, and then two filthy abuses that she won't repeat to me. The two procurers folded their hands and tried to make themselves smaller. Niru could see them shaking their heads in apology, their folded hands going up and down. The little fellow moved away and came towards Niru as the two men scurried off.

'Nomoshkar, didi.'

'Nomoshkar.'

'Those men were creating trouble here, isn't it?'

'Yes. They're trying to turn all these girls into prostitutes. We won't let that happen. Their situation is bad enough as it is.'

'Yes, I know. Didi, they won't trouble you any more. If anybody else like them comes, you telephone me from somewhere. I will give you my number. If I'm not there, someone else will come and help you.

The man took out a children's exercise book, wrote down a name and number, tore out the page and gave it to Niru.

'All right, I'll keep this. I hope you will help. My name is Nirupama.'

'Ah, achcha, I didn't know your name, didi. You don't recognize me, but we've met before!' The man smiled.

'Have we?' Niru tried to remember. 'Where? When?'

'About two years ago? Wellington Square? Dharmatolla? Tear gas? You were injured in the head and those two girls took you into their house?'

Sometimes it's a wrench when I move from listening to one set of tapes to another, as if I'm changing planets, but then again, sometimes the different worlds make strange gravitational links. Today, I'm transcribing the Sheyali–Radhuni tapes, and this diversion into the Niru tapes has been part indulgence, part diligence, just to remind me where the jigsaw pieces fit a bit later down the line.

The pink label says: *Sheyali-Radhuni – 2 nd meeting – 1 st recording – 27 March 1977.*

At the second meeting, it was a different girl who served us. This one kept her eyes to herself. Maybe it was to do with her character or, more likely, the mashis had come to the conclusion that I was a different kind of trick, that my areas of potential profit lay somewhere above my belt. Maybe it was because I'd gone in the evening that time and the other girl had finished her shift – or perhaps gone off to actually do it. This girl was a bit more rounded than the one from two Sundays ago, but more classically beautiful, a dark Bengali beauty with a touch of Assam, of Burma and parts further east.

As she put down the plates in front of me, it occurred to me that both the girls were what you would call 'shyamla' – dusky – and I wondered whether that was connected to my own complexion or just a coincidence, contradicting my earlier thought about my below-belt profitability.

'We got you these to start with, because you'd said the other day—'

'Ah, Mashima! They look so dangerous! You shouldn't have—'

'They are for us also. You provide the excuse. Otherwise, with this Radhuni's sugar, the doctor would fry *us* in hot oil!'

'Mmeaanh! I'm the *only* one who has sugar, I see!'

'You can't compare my sugar with yours, mine is nothing!'

'Mmeaanh! Nothing! 185 is nothing, is it!?!'

'You just keep quiet! Want me to tell Doctor Babu how much gin and Fanta you've been quaffing? I'll telephone him *right* now!'

It was the first time I was actually getting a look at Radhuni-mashi, who'd remained the acid voice from the TV-bedroom all through our previous meeting. She was like a Luigi Botero portrait but painted by a Kalighat pat painter. The armchair which she occupied seemed in constant danger of collapsing. Her flesh, as it cascaded down, overflowing across the arms of the chair, seemed as though it would make insurrections, break loose from under her sari and a float away in separatist blobs of fat, but it didn't. All of it, all of her, stayed there across the evening, sliding this way and that, but managing to hang on to whatever deeply buried skeleton she must, by physiological rationality, have possessed.

Both of them had put on nice saris, as if it was a special occasion, or maybe it was just that they liked to dress up on Sunday nights, to rev the old engines, as it were. Radhuni's sari was a yellow with a spiky black and indigo border of the kind the Kalighat patuas loved to paint. Her face was caked with make-up, which buried her eyes further and made them seem smaller despite the generous bordering of kajol. There was a glinting orange glass of gin and Fanta attached to the big planet, a haphazardly orbiting moon, circling slowly but regularly from the tea table in front of her, making its way around her belly and chest to find shaky docking with her mouth before orbiting back. I didn't at all intend to think meanly of her. It's just that I wondered how he would have painted her today, or even sketched her, and when I tried to imagine this, my mind began to wander.

Sheyali picked up a curl of onion fillury and bit into it, not bothering to dip it into the little bowl of kashundi next to it.

'You know, people your age have no idea what it was to live through that time you were asking about. You're lucky you've never had to stop and worry about what you might or might not get to eat next week. It's not that we starved, *we* didn't ever starve, not even close to it, we gave the men what they needed, and we had customers who were far from poor, so we didn't starve. But to see so much starvation around you, how to say it, made your hunger do strange things. Sometimes you couldn't eat. Other times you couldn't stop eating. And you always worried that it would come and get you, like an infectious typhoid or a cholera, or like a demon, you know, catch you and pull you down into those poor unfortunates in the street. In our position, we never felt far from them, those who were dying on the roadsides.'

In contrast to Radhuni, Sheyali was sharp, slanted eyes, sharp nose, a fox like her name, though not foxy in the way Hendrix might have described a woman. While Radhuni exuded cheerful good humour, Sheyali in her red sari looked ready to discuss business, even as she went through the hostess protocols. The only genuine warmth she had shown was when I pulled out the two bottles from my satchel; the gin was local, Blue Riband, the best I could find, but the whisky was from the duty-free at Heathrow. Sheyali had smiled when I said 'Scotch'. Then she saw the brand and her face fell.

'What is this one? I have not seen this – Fiddich before... is it a bit, you know, lower than Chivas?'

'It's supposed to better than Chivas and all the rest of them, Mashima.'

'Hm. I can't imagine anything is better than Chivas Regal. Is it less costly, this one?'

'Why! Your brain is melting!' Radhuni interrupted, high-pitched already. 'You always said that Dimple whisky is even better than Chivas, now you are saying—'

'Well, Mashima, it was a bit cheaper, not much, but the man at the London Airport shop told me it was only temporary, because it's a new thing. In a few months, it will be much more expensive than all the normal brands, he said.'

'Hm. Shopkeepers lie, it's in their blood, whether they are in London or Laldanga. But let's see.'

Glasses had come, Fanta for the gin, soda for the whisky, and a beautiful ice-bucket of slightly battered copper, clearly of late '40s or '50s vintage, with an embossed crest of some sort, that I wished I could steal. There was even a pewter peg measure from which Sheyali had poured a parsimonious single gin for Radhuni and stiff double shots of whisky for herself and me. She had then buried the alcohol under copious amounts of ice before topping up the glass with soda.

'Hm. Can't really taste much, except it tastes like shaheb whisky alright.'

'Cheers! Agey cheers bolbi toh!' Radhuni was sharp in her reprimand. 'What do you foreigners say, what is that, chin-chin? Cheers and chin-chin!'

'Chin-chin, Mashima, Mashima, cheers, but I'm not a foreigner, you know.'

Sheyali added more soda to her glass. 'You don't want any soda at all?'

'No, just ice is fine.'

'No water? I can get some water, our water is safe, we boil it twice. It's the same water we use for the ice.'

'No, no, in Paris, I—'

'Yes?'

'Usually drink it just with ice.'

'I thought in Paris they drank only Phorashi wine. And that brandy, what's it called?'

'Cognac. No, in Paris they drink everything.'

'Paris. Ooh, I so wanted to go to Paris one day...' Radhuni finished her drink and plonked the glass down for Sheyali to replenish. 'Maybe in my next life I'll be born in Paris. You know, golden hair, blue-green eyes, a slim body like a curving vine, speaking Phorashi phat-phat-phat!' Radhuni moved within her body and suddenly I could see the curves of a much younger woman. Her eyes filmed over. Her mouth opened and she called out, sharply, 'Eii, Konika! Konika! Are you listening?'

The girl appeared. 'Hyan, ma?'

'Where are the ashtrays? Who will bring them, your father?' The girl started to move, but Radhuni was not done. 'Did I say you could go?'

'No, ma.'

'My cigarettes. Get them from the bedroom. The nice cigarettes, in that gold-and-white packet, those ones. And the holder.'

'Yes, ma.'

'And the matchbox!'

I wanted Sheyali to be fully relaxed before I asked about the paintings, so I made an obvious detour. I pointed to the photo of Indira Gandhi on the wall.

'So! Did you both vote? What do you think of this result?'

In the two weeks since I'd last been to this house, both national and state elections have taken place and India has turned upside down. Mother and Son have lost the elections. They've been routed, in fact, and a new national government has taken over in New Delhi, even as the communists' Left Front has taken charge in the state of West Bengal.

'What can one say if goats bring in an early Eid?' Sheyali's face darkened and she almost spat out the words.

'We are a nation of idiots,' said Radhuni. 'And the worst is this state of West Bengal, we are the stupidest in a very stupid country. This Janata government in Delhi is still tolerable, I'm not such a worshipper of Indira, not like Sheyali, but putting the crown on the communists' head over here? Who gives the treasury keys to the robbers?'

Sheyali let out a laugh. 'Dekhte thhako. Maagi ta oto shohojey jaabey na!' The bitch won't go away so easily, you just watch. 'She will sterilize the whole lot of this Morarji and Jagjivan, this Vajpayee–Advani, Fernandes. With Jyotibabu toh she will do more than just sterilize, she will cut off his...'

'You talk nonsense sometimes – they are all already sterilized, these old men!'

'I mean power-wise, politically she will emasculate them, just give her some time! Getting Delhi back may be tough, but in Bengal toh, these red dogs will not last even three years.'

'But, Mashima, they are talking about arresting Indira,' I said.

'Ar-REST! Mmeaanh! Not so cheap! Not so easy! She's a tigress. She'll get them even while sitting inside the jail. She'll make them eat their own tails.'

'Make them drink their own piss, you want to say, except they are *already* doing that, or at least the old vulture in the Congress topi is!' Radhuni started to laugh at her own joke. The effect was of a planet starting to spin faster and faster, the flesh of her jowls and around her elbows blurring, the eyes even sharper, but now wet with tears.

'Mashima – Mashima, would you both mind if I asked you a few questions and recorded our talking?'

'Hanh? What questions?'

'Yes, what questions? And recorded means?'

Old Elko's reaction had been almost identical when I'd asked if I could record conversations with him and Missus, ask them a few questions. This was in 1970, I think the fourth time I went to see them. He'd replied in that drawl of his, a single eyebrow going up, perhaps on his third pre-lunch drink which made him ever so slightly sharp.

'*Questions*, old boy? What sort of questions, exactly? And what exactly d'you mean by *record*?'

'I took the liberty of bringing along a tape recorder, in the hope that both of you would agree. I just wanted to get down a few things about your life in those days, about Calcutta, and about your work...'

'Well! Well, well, well! The Queen Empress you'd better ask yourself – I wouldn't dare speak on her behalf. And as for yours truly, and my "work" as you so kindly call it... I should tell you I'm not too fond of these modern Gestapo techniques...' He turned suddenly and called out through the window to where Missus was pottering about outside. 'Your Highness! Rani Sahiba! Watch out! It seems we have a spy in our midst! The bugger's a buggist!'

He was grinning as he turned back to me, so I felt relief. 'The bugger of it is... I can't even ask you what I get in return, you little whippersnapper, seeing as you always come so loaded with gifts every time you visit.'

'Oh no, but please! Don't feel obliged to... those are just, you know, it's perfectly normal when you're going somewhere as a guest... We should only do this if you're absolutely...'

'Yes, boys, what is it?' She came in with twigs and grasses magneted to her cardigan, a small rose in her bun, her precious gardening clippers which she'd got from England held like a small weapon, clearly happy after having massacred various growing things in the garden.

'This bloody impostor! Claiming to be a guest! Gestapo! Wants to give us the CIA treatment!'

'You wish to torture His Zemindearship? Go right ahead! With my blessings!' She went into a clownish German accent, 'You vill need some instruments, ja? I vill give you!'

'Not just me. You as well, madame.'

'Look, he's going on about gifts, as if the few things I bring along are some big deal...'

'Well, you *are* a very generous young man, it has to be said. Very well brought up and all that. But why on earth would you want to interview us?'

The first time, a year earlier, I'd come almost straight from New York, just changing planes at London. Landed, plonked down my big luggage where I was staying, tried to telephone in advance and then given up, pushed aside my jet lag, jumped straight on a train out of the city and arrived unannounced. Except, of course, I'd written earlier and had been invited by return air mail letter, so they knew I'd be coming at some point in these few days.

In terms of gifts, my instructions had been very specific: no food, obviously no point carrying coals to Newcastle, and no alcohol – don't encourage them to drink more; duty free perfume for her, specifically L'Interdit by Givenchy and not Chanel No. 5 (so *common* my darling!); for him, jazz records which I was to select according to my taste ('something modern, new stuff'), so four albums, my favourite current Miles, *In a Silent Way*, a Mingus, I forget which one, for safety's sake a mid-period Coltrane, one of the early '60s Village Vanguard ones, from just before he started to really freak out, and then, since I'm not *that* well brought up, something I was sure they would hate but which I couldn't live without, Ornette Coleman's Stockholm concerts, both volumes 1 and 2, just to introduce myself, so to speak, so five records actually. And then there was the somewhat strange direct request in the letter – I was sure there were no children – for a particular brand of felt-tip pens. When I went to Canal Street to get them, I realized these were anything but kids' playthings, these Eberhard Faber permanent markers. I had to carry five black ones and another fifteen in an assortment of listed colours – repeated assurances in the letter that they would reimburse me for these, which of course I was never about to accept.

His eyes lit up when he saw the markers. 'Dear boy! Dear boy! Thank you *so* much! Can't find decent markers anywhere! People say get them from England, but the English don't know how to make marker pens! And as for *this* godforsaken place…'

I had no idea why this genial old coot was so excited by these harsh graphic designers' colours, but then I had no idea about anything very much about them at that point. For instance, I had no clue as to what either of them actually did, except lead this supposedly idyllic life surrounded by beautiful countryside. About how they supported themselves, I'd received contradictory shards of half-information: they both had family money, but actually there wasn't so much, and Missus also had some sort of job that involved travelling; they had a perfect life, but actually it was a perpetual struggle; they had indicated I could stay as long as I wanted, but I was to ignore their politeness – I shouldn't impose beyond three or four days for it would stretch their limited resources; of course, I shouldn't do any silly Americanish thing and offer to contribute, but to make sure with the gifts I erred on the side of the generous, since they didn't have that much.

I arrived in the late afternoon, and the first evening was spent drinking and exchanging basic stories about our respective lives. I can't remember what we ate except that the woman who came to work had cooked something local and delicious, a welcome change from the student's make-do fare I was used to. It was dark by the time I went to bed, and I didn't even bother putting on the light in the room, just took off my outer clothes and slipped myself into bed.

When I woke up the next morning, I realized I was billeted in a small room containing a big library, the bed an island on a small lake of floor surrounded by steep cliffs of bookshelves. The lower books were a strange assortment, lots and lots of paperback novels, Penguins, Fabers, but also thrillers and murder mysteries in English and French, everything from Agatha Christie and Georges Simenon to Nick Carter, James Hadley Chase and Modesty Blaise. A whole orange-and-white row of P.G Wodehouse titles, and then an entire shelf devoted to air-warfare in the Second World War, from those small Observer books of war aircraft of different countries to serious biographies of pilots and air-force generals. A little higher up, a whole series of Graphis Annuals on one shelf, and then a number of big art books of various vintage, Occidental, Oriental and Indian, I noted, my profession kicking in. Another two shelves about the Holocaust, again ranging from the popular works of Leon Uris to several books by Elie Wiesel, two copies of his great novel *Night* in English, and one in French. I stopped peering at the books from nose-distance and found my spectacles.

I was up with the early sun, but the rest of the house felt as if it was in deep sleep. I needed to find the toilet. During the evening, I had used the john attached to the main living room, but before I turned in, she had pointed in the direction of the one assigned to me exclusively. Sort of shown it to me – 'It's through this room, my dear, right next to yours, through there and at the end, the door on the left... you'll find it won't you... I won't step in there in my state, that room's full of stuff and I don't trust myself... but with your young eyes, you'll find it, won't you?' 'Of course I will. Please, not to worry. I'll be fine.'

I put on my pants, opened the door of my room, and stepped into the hallway, feeling the slightly dusty floor. The whole house smelled of cigarettes and alcohol, with only an afterthought whiff of food. The door to the adjoining room was ajar as she had left it the night before, and I went in, my feet already careful. I guess I was expecting the normal clutter of a bohemian house – I'd seen a few of those in America by then – stuff left unattended, just dumped in the extra room, piled up things that had then grown further stalactites of dusty boxes and objects. This room wasn't like that.

An uncluttered window halfway down the room let in a bright July morning's sunlight despite the thin curtains drawn across. The light bounced off the ceiling, showing a more or less clear path to the bathroom door through the neatly stacked piles. As I entered, my eyes focussed through my spectacles and I realized some of the piles were vertically stacked, cloth-draped rectangular frames of all sizes, while other concentrations consisted of paper stacked on tables, of what looked like drawing books and ring binders with brand names of manufacturers of watercolour paper, all piled on top of one another. Between some of the neat stacks were messes of torn-up paper, broken board and shredded canvas, all eviscerated, the guts of material curving on to one another, sometimes revealing colour, sometimes monochromatic marks. I couldn't help lifting the cloth off a couple of the stacks. I opened two or three of the pads on the tables, as carefully as a spy. It took me a while, for my eyes and hurting head to swim through to reach clarity.

'You want to record about what? The paintings?' Sheyali was all businesslike now, even as she poured herself a third shot. I watched as she avoided the soda this time and added two careful cubes of ice before taking a sip. As the whisky attacked her mouth, she quickly put down the glass, pushing it away on the table.

'Maybe a little water, Mashima, maybe add just a little bit.'

She nodded, forehead creased, her mouth clamped with her sari pallu. I'm not sure whether the nod meant yes or no. Radhuni yelled to the girl to bring a bottle of cold water from the fridge.

'So, record why? For whom? HMV will not buy our voices talking!' Radhuni grinned through the cigarette holder clamped in her teeth.

'No, no, it's for myself, so that I can play it back later and make notes. You see, I'm doing some research about the Calcutta of that time, from the years just before the famine up to—'

'So, not about the paintings, just about that time?' Sheyali came back into the conversation.

'No, also about the paintings, of course. I'm looking at different painters of that time, so the paintings are important, and then the time in which they were painted.'

'Oh, we never asked you! What work do you do exactly, over there, abroad?'

'I am... with a college... what you would call a junior lecturer here, so I'm supposed to teach but also to do research and write papers about it. Maybe even a book, occasionally.'

'A book like a golpo?' A novel?

'No, no, a scholarly book... maybe about some buildings.'

'You teach what?'

'I teach about architecture, about the history of buildings, about how they were made, why they were made, how they were used. Also, a course on the history of art, Art History.'

'And they pay you to do this?'

'Yes, Mashima, not too much, but I get by.'

'That's why not yet married, yes?'

'I'm in no hurry. Work is more important at this point.'

'Work! In our time, in a village, you'd have been a father of three or four kids by now!'

'Well, I'm glad that's not the case! I'm not sure I ever want to be a father.' I finished my drink and reached for the bottle.

'All right, you can record, but mainly because Radhuni here wants you to record her singing.'

'What? I never said anything about singing!'

'But I know you. Do I not know you? I know you.'

'I know you too! And you don't know as much as you think! You don't know everything!'

'Really? Really? What don't I know?'

'I never said to this boy I wanted to sing. You didn't hear me say that, so what are you saying—'

I felt panic. I decided to jump in.

'Mashima, Mashima, please don't fight both of you, please, now, just because I said... It's my fault, please let's just leave it.'

'No, no, nothing to do with you! This Sheyali, she drinks and then imagines things. Sing! I never said that!'

'Okay, okay, well, *I* would love to hear you sing, if you wanted to—'

'Eijey, who's inside?' Sheyali called towards the curtained doorway. 'Are you girls asleep? Where is the fish fry for dada?'

'Just bringing it, ma!' the girl called back. Suddenly peace was restored. It was as if neither woman had raised her voice.

'So, where is your machine?' Sheyali also lit a cigarette.

I brought it out of the satchel, my boxy Philips, and made a place for it on the small table. I took out the small microphone from its leather pouch and plugged it into the jack. Then I set up the mic on its little stand, vaguely pointing at Radhuni. The fan was on, which would screw up the sound a bit, but there was nothing to be done about that – I wasn't about to discomfit these two or let anything get in the way of getting them talking. There was already a new, blank C-90 cassette in the machine, and I hoped I'd be able to make out what they said when I transcribed it later, which was all I needed.

'How does this work, exactly?' Radhuni made a gesture of leaning forward. I lifted up the tape recorder and showed her.

'This is the microphone, same as you have in the big recorders. This is the tape. It goes for forty-five minutes, after which I'll flip it around and we have another forty-five minutes.'

'This runs on batteries?' Sheyali asked.

'Batteries or electricity, either.'

'Hitachi,' said Radhuni, peering at the cassette. 'I know somebody who has a Hitachi television their nephew brought from Singapore.'

'Same company,' I said. 'Japanese. Very good.'

'They have Shony also, don't they?' Radhuni looked up at the two girls who'd come in bearing plates. 'Find somewhere to put those.'

'Yes, Sony is also very good. They also make cassettes, but right now I'm using Hitachi.'

'They make everything, the Japanese, don't they?' Sheyali shook her head in wonder. 'Imagine, who would have thought, after the way the Markin destroyed them with that bomb...' She gestured to the girl to bring another small table for the plates of fish fry. I used the distraction to press down the record button and simultaneously push forward the main lever, starting the recording. Best to keep everybody as unselfconscious as possible.

'Mmeaanh! They're not like us!' Radhuni blew a plume of smoke. 'During that time, kids used to chant *Sa re ga ma pa dha ni, bomb phelechhe Japani!*' Do re mi fa so la ti, dropped the bombs have the Japanese! 'But actually we Bengalis still haven't recovered from the bomb of the famine the British dropped on us.'

The white needle moved in the curved little sound level window to show the machine was recording. I left it there and leaned back.

'Well, I'll tell you one thing,' Sheyali smiled into her glass. 'Those slant eyes can make what machines they want, but they will never be able to make whisky the way the Ingrej make it!'

'You're liking this now, Sheyali-mashi?'

'Yes, it took some time, but now I really like it! I think only ice and a little water is the correct thing for this, your shopkeeper was right! But now it's going to my head!'

Radhuni let out a peal of laughter. 'Look at her now! Now she's drunk! And calls me a lush!'

I had to cut them off at the gulch, I couldn't afford another fight, so I just came out with it.

'So, I believe he made a painting of the two of you?'

Sheyali had opened her mouth to return Radhuni's serve, but she changed what she was about to say.

'Yes, he painted us in the hotel, well, not exactly in the hotel – us as we were then, fully showing us as we were then.'

'*Don't* say fully as we were! This boy will think he made one of those paintings with us wearing no clothes...!'

'No, no, no, Mashima, I wasn't thinking anything...'

'Why not?'

'Eijey! You! You don't think we had anything beautiful to show?'

Suddenly, the two of them had me in a pincer, all squabbling forgotten, working together like a pair of hunting animals.

'Yes! You think we looked like *this* in those days?'

'We could have matched any of those women you saw in those foreign paintings, you know, those naked... just that we weren't so shameless!'

Radhuni smacked her glass down, nearly hitting the mic. 'Speak for yourself! To tell the honest truth, I would have happily had a painting of me, full... you know... that I could have looked at today to remember, or shown these know-nothing girls who work here, these stupid little whores who think they are so beautiful they are superior to Dimple or Zeenat!'

Sheyali ignored Radhuni. 'Well, actually, there was more than one painting he made of us. There was one with us sitting on a sofa in one of the suites. Then another one, I remember, of us standing up on a balcony.'

'Not balcony, the terrace on top of the hotel! With Sheyali holding a tennis ball, like a glowing white egg... Do you know that Great Eastern had a tennis court on the rooftop?'

'No, I didn't, no.' Like some detective in a book, I tried to keep all excitement out of my voice. 'Would you still have either of these paintings? I believe he left at least one over here...'

They exchanged a look, not even trying to hide it from me. Then Sheyali answered, 'Oh, people left paintings with us, among other things, because they knew they could trust us... Then they would come and take them away. Do you remember the one Gogai left here for a couple of years, the small one, all wrapped up? Came back and took it away as if it was gold...'

Another rally of looks, now that they had me thinking about tennis. Radhuni concentrated on inserting a new cigarette into her holder. 'I don't know where to look for it... We haven't seen it for quite a few years now, isn't it?' Sheyali nodded. 'May have been eaten away by insects or something...'

Sheyali picked up the tune. 'Dekhthe hobey... we'll have to look... How long are you here this time?'

3

BACKHAND

The way to do it would not be to paint fast, but to paint cleverly to indicate action. And the background in all its stillness would matter as much as the depicted movement, like the racecourse against which Gauguin's horses thunder at you. Here, it would be the orderly row of nets and court lines against the rich green of the grass, the occasional vertical of umpires' chairs rolled to the side, the duller army green of the high cloth which makes a corridor of the courts, and then the trees and the jumble of bungalows beyond the club wall. On this stage would come the blur of tennis whites and white balls; several balls, in varying degrees of suspension; mostly pinkish-white skin in action, leavened with the occasional darker brown arm or leg or head. Again, another thing to counterbalance the smudge of movement could be the statue-stillness of a man about to serve.

The racquet scythes towards the plummeting ball. The marker doesn't quite middle the serve, putting a bit of frame into it, slowing down the ball and sending it over the net with a slight loop. It's an easy enough return for Cardhu Motherwalla, except that he is exhausted and eager to finish the game. He overhits the shot, but the marker miscalculates as well. Volleys weakly when the ball is heading well out of court. Motherwalla doesn't spurn the second offering, puts it away in the bank, deep cross-court, far out of his opponent's reach.

'Bad luck, my boy, bad luck!' he calls, as he prances back to the baseline, the winner having given him some energy.

Then there could just be a portrait of a man about to receive service: Motherwalla, hair parted almost in the centre, sweat staining the lenses of his expensive tortoiseshell spectacles, a wedge of a nose cantilevered over a little black caterpillar glistening above a Pekinese mouth, lower teeth clamping on upper lip, weak chin falling into soft open-collared sports shirt, a typical mixture of quivering nervousness and arrogance. Tall-ish fellow with a complexion of weak Darjeeling tea, right shoelace coming open, perhaps about to trip and do himself some damage. 'Luvv-thurrty, saheb!' The marker shows no emotion as he towels the sweat from his eyes and makes ready to serve again. His stance is perfect, his thin black calves come out of spotless white tennis shoes and socks and disappear into spotless, crisply ironed shorts which look a size too big for his narrow waist. Tucked equally neatly into the shorts is a gleaming white shirt that is buttoned all the way to the throat. His arms and face are dark, but his cap of neatly cut silver hair provides a perfect, balancing contrast to finish the picture. He looks up to see if Motherwalla is ready, bounces the ball precisely twice and then languidly flings it up, as if he has all day to watch it come down. As the ball drops, the knees accordion his black-and-white form into the most feared service in all of Eastern India.

'Just dekhte thaako – fault korbey.' Just watch, he's going to serve a fault. Borun-kaku makes sure he's looking away from the receiving Motherwalla as he mutters under his breath.

'Bad luck, my boy! Just out!' Sure enough, the ball misses the centre line.

'Sorry, saheb!'

'Come on, come on, concentrate now!' Motherwalla commands, 'I want a decent game here!' All his twenty-three years alert inside him, the young man bends forward again and hungrily twirls his racquet.

'Luvv-thurrty, second serve, saheb!' calls out the marker, before taking up his stance. Kedar notices a slight shift in the man's demeanour. The Parsi fool has gone too far with his hectoring.

The ball singes the grass and smacks into the green cloth at the end of the court. Motherwalla suddenly resembles a befuddled waiter bending forward to serve someone a tennis racquet. He shakes his head.

'Didn't quite see that.' Motherwalla turns towards Kedar and Borun-kaku standing at the net and calls out, 'I say, could you chaps see if that was in?'

'In, in!' says Kedar, who hasn't seen anything more than a momentary white blur disturbing the green air.

'Ace!' barks out Borun, underlining the obvious before turning to the marker's side. 'Bahut achha, Mohanlal! Well served!'

'Piptin-thurtty, saheb.' The marker remains unmoved.

The next serve is a rank lollipop, and Motherwalla takes brutal revenge. His return ricochets off a cane chair with enough power to disrupt two other games in progress in the adjacent courts. Fifteen-forty. Game, set and match point. Motherwalla hobbles to his chair to pick up a towel. Mohanlal, the most senior and skilful marker of the club, waits patiently, like a man resigned to the noose around his neck.

'How much do you think he's paid him?' Kedar also keeps his head turned away from Motherwalla.

'Who knows? Five whole rupees?' Borun-kaku enjoys the look of horror on Kedar's face. 'Perhaps even ten?'

'Now, now, gentlemen! Let's try and not be unkind to a fellow member!'

Standing behind them, Andrew Hillcott has spoken very softly.

'Oh, hullo Hillcott! Have you just come?' Kedar turns around in welcome.

'Yes, just. Listen, Lahiri, you can't fully blame the chap, can you? Not if you look at what's sitting over there.'

Andrew has made no gesture to specify his 'there', and none of the three men looks in the direction to which he refers. All three know what they will see if they look through the lob and slice of balls, if they lift their gaze past the white-and-green criss-cross of the tennis club to the terrace of the cream-coloured house just beyond the club wall. Old Mrs Motherwalla has never had a problem with being spotted on the terrace she has commandeered in a friend's house. There has never been any trace of coyness as she sits, servant in attendance, under a large beach umbrella, sipping her pink gins, lighting the cigarettes sticking out of her ebony holder, one fag after another, across morning or afternoon, whenever she's come across the country from Bombay to inspect her son's game. Neither has there ever been any surreptitiousness about the heavy binoculars she briskly brings up to her goggles from time to time.

'Point taken... What did you call her the other day, Hillcott? Mater... what?'

'Mater-gator. My little Americanism. As opposed to allig – I say, don't you *dare* bandy that about!'

'Not to worry, I certainly won't say I'm quoting you.'

'You're a swine, Lahiri. I do hope you know that.'

'Yes, Kedar, you *are* a young swine!' agrees Borun. 'Now that Hillcott's given you license, you'll purloin his brilliant coinage and claim it as your own!'

'Least I can do for a young friend,' says Andrew placatingly. 'Can I buy you two gentlemen a round of beer?' Andrew bows towards the garden bar next to the club house.

'Only one gentleman among the two of us,' corrects Borun. 'But yes, thank you. My appetite for tennis has suddenly... vanished.'

As the two older men turn away from the court, Kedar follows them. 'Now just a minute!' he says, trying to nose between the two taller figures as soon as they are out of earshot of the players. 'Just a minute! Speaking of gentlemen, now *who* was it that regaled us with the scene of Motherwalla being picked up from the club by his... mater-gator? Who was it that kept us in absolute stitches for weeks, mimicking a poor old lady? Was it I, Kedar Lahiri? Do remind me, *gentlemen!*'

Andrew and Borun need no further invitation. With a precautionary glance towards the courts, the two men transform. Borun adjusts his own dark glasses, pushing them slightly down his nose. He pulls out a cigarette and screws it into an imaginary holder eight inches from his mouth. Andrew drops his shoulders, miming the holding of several framed racquets under his arm while he nervously wipes his brow, a handkerchief doubling for a tennis towel.

'*Aaaniiii! Cardhu!*' Borun's voice is low but a shriek.

'Yes, hellyoe mummy, do let's get in the car.'

'*Aaaniiiiii! Cardhu, you idiot!*'

'Mummy... please... car? Let's talk on the way hyome...' The racquets now shift from armpit to armpit.

'Ghelchodya! Bloody fool!'

'Mummy, I tried my absolute best—'

'*Nincompoop, gadheda, ghelchodya!* What tried your best? What tried absolute? The *amount* of money I've wasted and this, aa taaru best chhe ki!' A cigarette is ejected and another inserted.

'The umpire was blind, mummy!'

'*What blind!* What blind, even I could see from *that far* with these Zeiss!' Mrs Motherwalla nearly brains her son with her binocular case. 'All the line calls were ekdum barrabar! Spot on! Tu! *You* were the only blind fellow on that court!'

'All right, mummy, can we discuss this at—' Andrew acknowledges the waiting bearer in his normal voice 'Teen beer lao. Ekdum cold. Becks ka bottle baaki hai ki khuttam ho gayaa?' The bearer confirms the club bar still has a stock of pre-war German beer. Borun resumes hostilities with renewed vigour.

'Don't you dare call me mummy! Next time, I'm *not* taking you to Wimbledon! I'm going on my own! What *Tilden*! What *Perry*! Today you couldn't even have taken a ruddy game of that, that Helen *girl*, that Wills Moody! Even she would have thrashed you six-nil, six-nil, six-nil!'

'I dyoyn't quite think syo, mummy, but please get in—'

Borun pauses to lift his beer. 'Cheers, cheers, mud in your eye!' They toast, producing the soft and satisfying sound of filled pewter mugs colliding gently. All three take a pull, Kedar having to quell his heaving throat before he can let the cold liquid down.

'*Ghelchodya*! *Donkey*! Where did you leave your *backhand*? *In which bloody girl's boudoir, aiii*? Get in the car!'

'And then the chauffeur drives away your "poor old lady" and fils in their Bentley,' Andrew finishes, looking seriously and pityingly at Kedar who is now doubled up and trying not to drool beer.

'Hillcott, I notice you're not in playing kit. Just popped by?' Kedar decides to change the subject.

'Yes, well, thought I'd come in and clear my dues.'

'Dues? Your monthly bill?' Borun looks through the glass bottom of his beer tankard as he asks the question.

'Yes.'

'Isn't it a bit early? Surely not due until the seventh of next month?'

'Yes, well, I might not be around next month.'

'What do you mean?' Borun is now the Admiral of Enquiry, treating the pewter tankard like a telescope, one eye screwed shut, peering through it as he asks the question. 'Where on earth would you be but Calcutta?'

Kedar has spent a lot more time with Andrew, and he immediately understands what this means. Even though they've known each other for only a few months, Kedar has become quite fond of this Englishman. He will miss him once he's gone, though there's no question of his actually saying so to Andrew. He decides to cut short Borun-kaku's obtuseness: 'Another round, gentlemen? Allow me to—'

'No, no, won't hear of it, this afternoon's entirely on me!' Andrew catches the bearer's eye.

'*Aiiin ghelchodya!*' Borun is stuck with the old lady.

'What does that mean, exactly? I always meant to ask. Is it... Hindi? It's not, is it?'

'Well, you know, it's Parsi, which is actually a variation of Gujratty,' Borun climbs on to his didact horse. 'Parsis would say they are speaking Gujratty, but the Gujratties wouldn't necessarily agree... and ghelchodya means...' Borun looks around conspiratorially, 'Kono ladies nei toh, Kedar?'

'No,' Kedar confirms there are no women flouting the 'Gentlemen Only' sign at the entrance of the bar.

'Ghelchodya means a stupid... er...'

Andrew gets to the point quickly. 'Something to do with *fuck* is it? Like the Hindi bahaanchod?'

'Uh... exactly, exactly, stupid... er... fucker, you could say.'

'Not to worry, BL, I hear a lot of that with my men. Question is, how did the old lady become an old sailor?'

'Not sure, not sure at all, but her swearing is apparently famous in the Bombay Gymkhana. Anyone less wealthy and less influential would have had the boot a long time ago, but not a Motherwalla.'

'Oh, and that too. I know you did this explain this *walla* business once,' Andrew turns to Kedar.

'Let me explain.' Borun doesn't let Kedar open his mouth. 'Well, many of these Parsis lot take on a surname to do with their profession, so you have Engineer, Doctor and Vakil, meaning lawyer, and suchlike. Others include their businesses in their name like Ginwala, which is the cotton spindle and not the drink. The Motherwallas were originally called Attawallas because they produced flour, as in atta, the first packed flour in India, first one with a brand, as I understand it.'

'Right...'

'And, when our hero's grandfather split with the main family, he came out with his own brand – Mother's Atta, meaning Mother's Flour, you see – which was highly successful... So, to differentiate himself in the market, he changed his name to Motherwalla.'

'How apt.' Andrew takes the beer bottles off the bearer's tray and fills all the tankards himself. Not something Kedar has ever seen him do before. 'And that leaves the first name. Cardhu?'

'Yes, well, Kaku doesn't know this story, but I do.' Kedar relishes his uncle's silence, but not for long.

'Kedu, you can just call me Borun when in company. No need for Kaku-shaku.'

'And you can just call me Kedar, no need for nicknames.'

'Do continue. Cheers.' Andrew raises his tankard.

'Cheers. Well, when he was small, something like three, apparently this Mother-fellow toddled up to his father's glass of Scotch and downed the whole thing.'

'Good lord.'

'Yes, and since the whisky was Cardhu, that's what he's been called ever since.'

'I see... Does he have a proper first name?'

'Yes!' Kedar takes a deep breath. 'It's... his full name is Ardeshir Jamshetjee Navrozjee Motherwalla.'

'Actually, Lahiri, my dear fellow, it's Ardeshir *Navrozjee* Jamshetjee *Cawasjee* Motherwalla.' The man looks denuded of something until Kedar notices he's in the process of wiping his spectacles with a silk handkerchief.

'Oh, hullo! Game over?'

'Hello... my friend... Cardhu!' Borun washes the name with the beer in his mouth.

'Hullo, Motherwalla! Good game, as we all saw!' Andrew pulls out the fourth cane chair without missing a beat.

'May I?' Cardhu sits down and crosses his legs before addressing the pair of Lahiris.

'Byearaah!' Borun calls out, taking command of the welcome. 'Ektho beer lao saheb ke liye! India Pale Ale, ekdum cold!'

'I say,' Motherwalla rushes the net against Borun, 'were you pretending to smoke that thing out of a holder? From a distance it looked as though you were...'

'Well spotted, my keen-eyed friend! Indeed I was!' Borun is quick on the return volley. 'I was giving these gentlemen an impression of my sister-in-law, mother to young Ked... *ar* here! Thing is, she caught us in an inebriated state the other day...' Borun slips into a fair mimicry of Kedar's mother berating them, the cigarette holder now held in her manner as opposed to Mrs Motherwalla's, the English now flavoured with an upper-class Bengali accent. 'I do nawhtwhant to see my house tarned intu a Rake's Progress! Bujhechho tomra?'

Motherwalla loses interest and turns to Andrew, lifting his beer in a salute. 'Great show, major! You're holding 'em in Siam, it seems! Cold British steel, I'm sure!'

Andrew looks away. Kedar feels obliged to provide the contradiction. 'Not that simple, Cardhu. Hong Kong's gone, and Penang. They are bombing Rangoon. People are already leaving the city in large numbers.'

'Tchaah! Lahiri! Typical defeatist Bengali talk, if you don't mind my saying so! The only people abandoning Rangoon are you people... and the Marwaris, of course. Our small factory there's running like a Mer— like a Rolls Royce.'

No one replies. Mistaking this as a victory, Motherwalla refuels his views with a big pull of beer and continues. 'Hong Kong and Penang! That was just a bad first set, wouldn't you say, Major Hillcott?'

'Let's hope so, my dear chap, let's hope so.' Andrew concentrates on lighting a cigarette.

Motherwalla senses something is not quite right. He looks at his watch and it seems to tell him something. 'Right! Well, thank you very much for the beer! Must be off, cheerio!' With a slight tweak of his spectacles, he is up and gone, trotting away between the flowerpots lining the path to the club gate.

'Bad first set...' Borun makes no effort to keep out the derision.

'Two sets to love and three games down, more like...' mutters Andrew, his face clouding, even as he smiles. 'And the blighters have serve.'

'Hillcott, what will happen should Rangoon...' Kedar leaves the question hanging.

'Fraid it's not a matter of *should*, Lahiri. *By the time* Rangoon falls, let's hope and pray we are playing cricket and not tennis, that we can hold out for a draw, if you get my gist.'

'Is that where you're off to, then?' Kedar is immediately contrite, 'Oh, so sorry, I know one isn't supposed to ask – I shouldn't have.'

'Never mind, don't blame you for being curious, quite natural.'

'Ghelchodya!' Borun growls at Kedar.

'I say, BL, how many dialects *do* you speak?' Andrew is bright again.

'Not dialects, dear chap, they are distinct languages. Well, Bengali, Hindi, or what people call Hindustani, and I suppose this pidgin sort of Parsi. And English, after a fashion.'

'And where did you pick up this... Parsi from?'

'Oh, friends, a few very good Parsi friends with free and flowery tongues. In fact, one of them is in uniform, actually a good friend of my second brother, the one who's been captured in Egypt? Fellow called Sam, slightly junior to Bulldog, Sam who's in the...' Borun turns to Kedar.

'12th Frontier Force or something, I think.'

'Small, tiny chap, but my god, when he laughs it's as if a bomb has gone off in the room.'

'Twelve Frontier? Hmm. I'll keep a lookout. Suspect we'll need a few laughs before this thing is over.' Andrew finishes his beer. 'Any further word from your brother?'

'No, just that one letter through the Red Cross.'

'My mother insists the paper is Italian,' adds Kedar.

Andrew shakes his head. 'Probably standard German paper for all POW letters, if I know them.'

'Well, we shall miss you, old chap.' Borun's voice drops an octave as he raises his tankard. 'No laughter until you return, no Cardhu and Mrs Motherwalla, no—'

'I say, Lahiri, where were *you* that day when we witnessed that mother and son encounter?' Andrew chops into the sentimentality before Borun can fully get going.

'I... er... can't remember now.'

'Probably practising his backhand at the Great Eastern!' Borun switches from maudlin to nasty in a trice.

'No, not really! I hardly play there.' Kedar finds himself colouring. 'Those courts they have on the roof terrace aren't exactly the—'

'Fellow-me-lad!' Borun now booms out in Major Bulldog's artillery voice, 'No one here is suggesting you were playing on the dashed *roof* of the hotel!'

STALINGRAD

Her mother has let her in, given her tea, and gone off to teach her evening class.

'Ma, what should I put on for dinner?'

'Don't worry, ma. Baba got some fish this morning, some nice koi, and I've half fried it. I'll bring back some cauliflower and aubergine, so we'll have dal, cauliflower shobji, fried aubergine and the koi.'

'Have you kept rice from the morning, or should I put some on?'

'No, I didn't make any this morning. Baba had to leave early, some sets being delivered, and I was going to eat at the school anyway. I'll do it all when I come back. You rest.'

'Rest? Why? Every time I come here you treat me like I've been ill.'

'No, it's just that you've had a long day.'

'I'm fine... You kept the fish in the cage?'

'Where else? Do I have a refrigerator like your Lady Whatshername in her big house?'

'Lady Tilottama.'

'What?'

'Lady Tilu, we call her among ourselves, the lady of the big house.'

'Anyway, your Baba said he would be back by six-thirty. I'll be back by eight. And remember to tell Baba to pick up that bill from the ground floor people as soon as he comes.'

'I won't forget, Ma. Go and come back quickly.'

As soon as her mother leaves, Niru wraps herself in a shawl, skips quickly to the top of the stairs and goes out on to the terrace. She's been hoping to catch the sunset, but she's too late. There is still a bright stain on the western horizon, but the city is rapidly sinking into its smoky winter gloom. Downstairs, talking to her mother, she has heard the evening azan start from the big mosque on Chitpur Road, with the other mosques following. The overlapping calls are just fading as she reaches the terrace. After a few moments of silence, almost as if on cue, the first conch shell blows from a nearby house, another shaankh picking up the long honk and then another and another, until she feels she's in an invisible forest, surrounded by trees of rising sound. It's something she always waits for when she's on the terrace at this moment of dusk – her body remembers it since childhood.

As the darkness thickens, Niru can smell the incense from nearby houses. A few minutes later, this is followed by the smell of coals catching as the unoons are lit around the neighbourhood for the evening's cooking. Everything is very familiar and comforting but something is missing, and it takes her a minute or two to realize what it is. Normally, the azan and shaankh blowing would be accompanied by lights coming on in all the houses and the streets below. The blackout imposed ten days ago means the layers of buildings all blend into a dark mass. The yellow glow of the lamp posts is gone – it's as if someone has stolen the lanes below. There are still little rebellions of illumination leaking from a window here, a balcony there, but overall it feels as though someone has taken a massive brush and painted the city black.

Looking around, Niru realizes she hasn't been up here since she moved out to Dover Road in September. Even though she's been missing her parents, she has been glad to see her mother go, giving her this little stretch of time for herself. This terrace has always been her private place, where she could bring up the day's happinesses and sadnesses, the day's questions, and mull them over, sifting through them for the treasure of answers, or for reassurance or solace. She loves the little dwelling the three of them have put together so quickly, but Dover Road doesn't have anything to replace this little empire of solitude, this space which is both enclosed and yet open to the whole wide world, this squarish stage bound by its parapet, where she can hide in plain sight, where she could be dancing or singing inside herself and all that the neighbours would see is the Majumdar girl standing there, looking at the view. Standing there today with a chipped toenail and her feet hurting from too much walking.

Facing west, Niru can see a muted glow from around Dalhousie Square, where the weight of all the lights is still pushing against the blackout. Beyond the diffused brick-and-dome tangle of central Calcutta, she can just about make out two pairs of huge needles poking into the darkening sky. Startled, she realizes that the new Howrah Bridge has actually made a lot of progress since she was last on the terrace. She has heard people say that those needles are the supports from which the huge bridge will actually hang, but it's not something she can vividly imagine.

Vividly. Imagine. She realizes her mind has produced the last two words in Ingreji.

'Excuse me, Imo-gen, but can you tell me what is meaning of this word... vivid?'

She cringes once again as she remembers asking the question. What was the need to ask that mem-girl when she had the walking Oxford Dictionary of Roma? Was it a perverse way of showing off? Of indicating that she was striving to learn English? Was it a roundabout way to try and set up some sort of friendship? How much more cloyingly obsequious could she have been? 'Oh, please, High Princess of Gora People, please teach me your great language!'

The other girl's response had immediately relieved Niru's self-inflicted sting. 'Oh! Vivid. When something is... very alive in your mind, when you can imagine, or remember, something as very real, when you can *vividly imagine* something. But one also uses the word to describe bright colours – the flowers in the painting had vivid colours. Do you see? Right, now your turn! Teach me a Bengali word!'

'Chomotkar.'

'Tchaw-motorcar?'

'Chomotkar. Means something magical, something amaze to you.'

'Something amazing. Chaw-maw- tkar!'

Sitting at the tea stall, they had talked for over half an hour. Niru's eyes widen with a thought: the confrontation that first brought them together was completely forgotten by the time they parted. Neither of them so much as mentioned it while saying goodbye.

'I say, Niru, do you think it might be an idea... Do you think you might want to meet again?'

'Meet? Us... again? That we should meet again?'

'Yes, I'd very much like that, if you would.'

'Yes, I would also like... It would be nice... very much, I mean very nice.'

Niru had pulled out a notebook from her jhola, jotted down her Dover Road address, careful to write in her best English hand, torn out the page and handed it over. In turn, the mem-girl had put down her own address – 5 New Road, Calcutta 27, and a telephone number as well – *Alipore 3535*.

'I am not having a telephone. So I shall send you a letter only.'

'That's fine. I put it down just in case. I'll write too, but for next time should we just make an appointment now?'

'Yes... I can show you, I can show you...' Niru remembers swallowing all the places where she might meet fellow students or other people she knew. For some reason, she didn't want to tell the world about her new friendship, not just yet.

Imogen had noticed Niru's consternation. 'Oh, why don't we just meet here, at this tea shop? Say next Friday... the 2nd?'

'2nd of January? We will be in 1942!'

'Exactly! The new year! When would suit?'

'Suit?'

'What time would be convenient for you?'

'Oh, I think, ten o'clock?'

'Lovely, ten o'clock it is!'

It's a good thing Roma, Titir and she have made the pact about the postboxes, Niru thinks. It was done childishly, they'd decided it as a joke, almost, to have three separate mailboxes hung on the wall downstairs, just where the stairs ended. Three different colours, Roma's was green, Titir's was white and Niru's was red.

'Yes, we don't want to be tempted into reading each other's mail,' Roma had said mock seriously. 'And who knows what secret instructions any of us may receive from our respective parties? We wouldn't want the others to know, would we?'

'Or love letters,' Niru had said. 'Those should be private as well!'

'Who's going to get love letters now?' Titir had raised her eyebrows.

'Most likely *you*!' Roma and Niru had said together.

It was on old joke between them that Titir would be the only one to get married and become a mother, while Roma and Niru would spend their lives as spinsters looking after Titir's many children. Today, however, Niru feels no great warmth towards her housemates. Their comments this morning about the Party have really rankled, stayed thorned inside her, even though the girls often find themselves in a three-cornered joust about each other's political beliefs. Maybe it's just the way someone says something sometimes. The joke about Indian communists and Russia was an old one, but what Niru can't forget is Roma's nasty barb about the leadership being like a new bride constantly worried about the in-laws in Moscow. Now, having moved away from the actual exchange, different things prickle from what got her angry in the morning. The bride comment had provoked Niru right then, but that mean girl Roma had also slipped in something else earlier, something that Niru can't quite remember right now, that really began to bother her during the meeting in Sunny Park.

There is a loud cry from the building just across the street. Niru leans over the parapet to see who it is. The glass panes of a balcony door on the third floor are exposed. The sudden light throws the curlicued wrought iron of the railing into a network of sharp blacks. Beyond the door, Niru can see the two little Sen boys doing a tug of war with a black cloth. There is another shout, and then their mother's hand smacks one of the boys on the back of the head. Sen-babu himself comes into the picture, takes the cloth, and covers the door again. Now Niru can hear both kids howling, the sound carrying more weight in the dark, as if some great calamity has befallen the family. She moves away from the parapet and begins to pace up and down the terrace.

What was it... ah yes! Good practice! When Roma had said, 'Good practice for your meeting today, but will they actually let you say anything? In the Congress, women actually get to speak...' It had taken a couple of hours for that taunt-seed to grow into a plant of proper resentment.

Niru realizes that part of her anger comes from the fact that Roma and Titir were not completely wrong. In the meeting, Niru found herself counting the number of times the Comintern and Moscow were referred to; she counted twenty-four instances in one hour before she stopped. Had someone been eavesdropping, they would have concluded that no thought or action was possible for Indian communists without it having some precedent in Russia, or without some sort of green signal from the Soviet committees. It was also more or less true that it was the men who spoke and discussed things among each other while the women listened. Renu-di had asked a few questions, but none of the other women opened their mouths. Of the four younger girls there, clearly she wasn't the only one who'd taken the vow of silence. No, not true, one girl did speak up, asked a question, but she was cut short by a man's interruption, and her question then forgotten.

But still, all this was irrelevant after a point. Theirs was the only movement talking about the real condition of the vast majority of Indians. Gandhi, Nehru and that bunch could talk broadly about poor farmers, but the CPI was the only group which could scientifically point out, like the second speaker had done today, that 'it can be said without exaggeration that the majority of our peasant brothers and sisters have been in a continuous quasi-famine situation that has got worse since the shortages of 1932, meaning Greater Bengal has been in this state of scarcity for about nine years now'. The man had then gone on to specify, 'Over the last decade, in the years there has been a reasonable monsoon and harvest, the Bengali peasant has managed to eat. In the other years, he has barely managed to eke out an existence.' Bakul-babu, her professor at Scottish Church had also been saying similar things, but it was quite different to hear this backed up by detailed figures and statistics, the whole thing delivered in an unemotional, dispassionate tone. Everybody nodding, some people taking notes, the numbers cascading over her head, as decipherable as a bucket of cold water, but the message very clear: except for a few pockets, all of Bengal, both East and West, has been in a state of food siege for most of the 1930s and the war is not going to make things any better.

Standing in the dark, Niru tries to remember things that were said at the meeting. Just as the man called Jyoti started to speak about the CP in Britain, an older man had interrupted him. 'Excuse me, one minute. Listen, this is for the younger comrades attending for the first time – you may make notes about the issues we discuss here, but make sure you write down *no names* of any of the speakers.' The man's voice was quiet, but his tone was heavy with a certain authoritative weight. 'Also. You must be careful not to make notes about any *strategic* discussions we may have today, about how the Party may want to move forward in this set of circumstances. Notes only about issues and facts, understood?' As the meeting ended two hours later, again a sense of secrecy was conveyed. 'Spread the information around the issues that you've got from here, but remember, don't say where you got it from.'

A big part of the reason, of course, was the fact that the Communist Party of India was still officially illegal and underground. As one of the speakers laid out, their new alliance meant that workers' unions would have to suspend strikes and agitations in the context of the anti-fascist war, that negotiations were on meanwhile between the Soviets and the Western Allies to lift the ban on the CPI, but that these would take time. It was an open secret that the group Niru belonged to, the Bengal Provincial Students Federation, was a front for the Party. The question was how deep the BPSF's links were with the higher echelons of the

CPI. At the end of the meeting, Niru understood that one or more of the several layers between the ordinary student 'foot soldier' and the Party leadership had been removed for her today. As Tapati asked her when saying goodbye after the meeting, 'How does it feel to be promoted, comrade?'

'Promoted? I'm sorry, I didn't understand.'

'Why do you think Renu-di asked me to get you and the other three girls? Where were the others today, you know, all those loud-mouthed boys who know everything, why were they not here?'

'Why?'

'Because they clearly think we are ready to take on more responsibility! I think you'll find your days of merely being a stenographer for the federation are going to end soon.'

Before Niru could think of anything to say, Tapati had jumped on to the tram heading south. As the tram jerked forward, Tapati leaned out of a window, smiled, raised her right hand to her cheek and made a discreet fist. Niru, too, changed her wave into a briefly clenched fist, wishing she didn't have her clutched handkerchief participating in the international gesture of left solidarity.

So, what should she tell her parents? There was no need to tell them anything about the meeting and, no, certainly nothing about that strange, tall mem. Neither Ma-Baba nor the girls.

Imogen. What a strange name. And what a strange thing, the way the meeting happened. Anyway, it was unlikely the mem-girl would want to meet a third time. What did they have to talk about, after all? It was just politeness on Niru's part, and some mutual curiosity that was still not sated after thirty minutes of awkward conversation. What did these people actually think? What did someone like Imogen actually feel about things? From her side, Niru just wanted to get some idea, that's all... So no need to tell everyone about one or two encounters, tell them and risk being made fun of, or her parents worrying that she was getting entangled with strange foreigners.

Niru finds herself looking at the night sky as if for the first time, as if someone has just spilled all these new stars over the amalgamated clump of dead architecture. It's as if the city has come and gone and she is looking at the ruins of an extinct civilization in starlight, the constellations seemingly freshly manufactured in some factory, just produced, and yet, as she knows, actually much older than any human settlement. There is a sudden memory of a trip to Santiniketan with her parents, around the same time a few years ago, for the Poush Mela. Outside the campus, on the banks of the Kopai, the smell of village Bengal in midwinter, the different songs, loud and faint, wound their way through scattered, mist-smudged clumps of date palms. Ma's sudden intake of breath as she looked up and noticed the universe. How she grabbed Niru's hand like someone drowning in a sea.

'Niru, are you up here?'

Her father calling as he comes up the stairs. Something in his voice – does she imagine it? – almost asking for permission to disturb her.

'Hyan, Baba, here!'

She sees his shawl and dhoti-kurta better than she can see his face, and something about the movement of the clothes makes her uneasy. She's seeing him after nearly a month; he was away the last couple of times she was here, busy with a rehearsal. Now, suddenly, she can sense oldness in the way he moves, something amiss with his knees, in the slightly unsure, unseeing way he steps over the little raised band of masonry put around the terrace door to keep out rainwater. He's only fifty-eight, she tells herself, nothing to do with the knees, it's just the eyes that the theatre has aged, everything else is still fine.

'Where are you, ma? Oh, over there! I tell you, this blackout will make owls out of all of us. If the Japanese capture Calcutta and still keep the blackout, we'll run circles around them because we'll have had solid training by then!'

'Baba, you have to get the electricity bill from the ground floor.'

'I've got it, I've got it. Have you heard of any landlord who's shy about collecting his bills? Just as I came in through the downstairs door, "Majumdar-babu, your bill..."'

'Was it him or her?'

'Her, her! Sarkar-babu doesn't do menial work like chasing after tenants! I could hear him doing his evening prayer-paath inside, mauling the defenceless Sanskrit language, while the Mrs stopped her cooking to fetch the bill... Anyway, how have you been? I haven't seen you for a month!'

'Well, I'm not the one who's overworking, doing two or three plays! No, I've been fine, busy with the MA classes and the volunteer work.'

'Ah, right.' Baba pats Niru's shoulder and puts his elbows on the parapet. He leans forward to examine the darkness.

'And you, Baba? Ma said you went off early to fix some sets?'

'It's another adaptation of Chekov's *Cherry Orchard*, much better than the one we did in 1937, and Nitin Babu's direction, so we have had to create a whole grove of mango trees in the background, and a zamindari baari in front. It's looking quite good. I'll tell you once the performance is settled, you girls can come see it.'

'Bakul-babu says Chekhov is essentially a bourgeois writer, but I've learnt to ignore some of his more silly statements about Robi Thakur and other writers. I love Chekhov.'

'That's wise...' Baba smiles. 'So, how are the other members of the triumvirate? You are all managing all right, are you?'

'Well, we haven't killed each other yet, unlike what you predicted.'

'I never said you would kill each other, I only said you might want to.'

'That yes, that happens sometimes. Not kill, obviously, but we do have quarrels.'

'That's normal. As long as they don't fester.'

'Mostly they don't, no. But today...'

'Oho, what happened today?' He turns to her, trying to read her face properly.

'Na, nothing, actually. It's just that... you know how something happens, or someone says something, and it becomes a theme for the day? Same thing coming at you from different people, same thing coming up in different unconnected places?'

'Yes, I know what you mean. So?'

'So, early this morning, I was making tea in the balcony, I told you we have our unoon in the balcony, and I hear this man, the owner of the neighbouring mansion—'

'What's his name, that surgeon, he's on the governor general's council, isn't he? Sir Nalin whatsit?'

'Sir Naren Mitter, yes, him, exactly, and he was talking to his yes-man while taking his morning walk. And I could hear him saying, *pronouncing*, that Russia was done for! That the Germans will have defeated the Red Army by May!'

'Like a doctor's prognosis, was it? Is he now a famous doctor of the war disease?'

'Exactly! So I got angry and started to sing loudly, *Ekla cholo*. There is a tree, and they couldn't see me... I think they got quite scared!'

Her father laughs and slaps her on her back. 'Titir's singing, I can imagine, would entrance someone. Romola or you singing, and singing angrily at that, could be quite scary, yes!'

'It's not good to laugh at your own daughter, you know!' Niru finds herself grinning from ear to ear.

'Right... so then?'

'So then, a bit later, Roma, Titir and I were having an argument, more like a discussion, you could say – actually, it began with me and Roma making fun of Titir's, you know, her tendency to see everything as if we Hindus are always martyrs—'

'No, but the two of you are very mean to that Titir sometimes, even with jokes, even with friends, you have to be a bit mindful that you don't hurt.'

'Yes, yes, but what about them also being mindful of my feelings?'

'What did they say?'

'Oh, Titir started doing a little Stalin-naatok, you know, pretending to have a moustache and saying, *Stand up! Sit down! Now dance!* As if it was Stalin ordering the CPI.'

'I see. Then?'

'No, that was okay, but Roma, your favourite Roma, then said something very nasty – that the CPI was like a new bride constantly worried about what the in-laws in Moscow would say... Oh! *You* also find that funny, do you? What's the point of me talking to you?'

Baba controls himself. 'Look, I know it's not nice, what she said, but there is an element of truth to it, which is why it hurts, right? And it's not as though you yourself mince words about her Congress leaders, is it?'

'No, true, but then, this afternoon at college, one of those stupid, know-it-all boys, one boy in MA second year called Satyen, started lecturing us about military strategy. You know *The Statesman* has this map they update every day, about the battles between the Nazi army and Red Army? So he was using one of those to demonstrate how the Soviets cannot last beyond their midsummer, so July!'

'Ah, another military expert.'

'Yes, so you know, once in the morning, then the joke, then this... it somehow got too much for me!'

There's a sound of a short sharp whistle from somewhere in the streets below, followed by some commotion and someone banging on a door. The door is opened and they can now hear the voices clearly – the Air Raid people asking someone to cover a window properly because a light is showing. After two minutes, the silence returns as suddenly as the sound had come.

Baba shakes his head. 'You know, if you think about it, all of this can drive you mad. Here we are, our town blacked out by one side because the other side may send planes to drop bombs on us at night. We have no enmity with the Japanese, but neither are they our friends. They probably will not come as liberators but as replacement rulers. We don't even know if they will attack us, but it seems logical, inevitable. When? We can't say! In the meantime, people here are contributing to funds to buy individual fighter planes for the Air Force. You were talking about *The Statesman*. Have you seen the advertisements in there? Each and every one of the raja-maharajas is putting out half-page ads saluting the British Empire and offering their soldiers for the war effort. Jaipur, Bhopal, Hyderabad, Rampur, Patiala, Aligaputtu, all of them! Do these soldiers have any say? Of course not, they are mere pawns, doubly enslaved, first under their king and then under the king's king, the so-called emperor. And you, ma, with all your socialism and yearning for equality and revolution, now find yourself on the same side as these rajas and nawabs! It is absurd.'

'Baba. Why are you lecturing me on what we all already know?'

'No, not a lecture! I'm laying it out because I just want you to step back and take a look at the absurdity of the situation—'

'Baba! The situation is that they have already reached Stalingrad—'

'No, Niru, just think about it! For one minute! Let's suppose, and it's not impossible, you know, so let's put emotion aside and suppose that all of Russia *is* conquered by Hitler. What will happen then? How exactly does it affect you? Yes, they have reached Stalingrad. Tomorrow, they will also reach Cairo. The day after, these Japanese may reach the outskirts of Singapore or almost up to Rangoon. So, then what? Do you think we will stop fighting for independence if the Japanese suddenly become our rulers? Are you afraid that if the Soviet Union disappears, the socialist struggle in India will also die?'

Niru finds herself biting her lip, tears welling up in her eyes. Instead of a place where she finds answers, suddenly this dark terrace has become a place of difficult questions. She opens her mouth to answer, but no sensible words find their way. Baba puts his arm around her shoulders.

'Ma... we have our own Indian soul, which you may not believe in, but we do. Whatever happens, our different struggles will continue, and not necessarily in a shape that European logic can recognize. You keep faith in Marx and Lenin, I keep shraddha in Rabindranath, in Saraswati...'

Niru wipes her face with her sari pallu and smiles. 'Tchaah!' she says, pretending derision, but she grips the hand on her shoulder to counter her tone. 'There you go again with all your mysticism! Demi-god and goddess! Rabindranath! Saraswati! And then you'll say Kalidas and Valmiki! And then, can Lalon Fakir be far off?'

Both of them start laughing softly. Baba taps her on the forehead as if she's ten years old again. 'What's wrong with any of them? Especially Saraswati? Surely a good communist should worship the goddess of knowledge, study, sadhana and rigour?'

Ya kundendu tushar haar dhavala... ya shubra vastra avruta,
ya veena varadandita kara, ya shweta padmasana...
Ya bhrahmachyutshankara pramrutibhi
devai sadaa vandita...
Sa ma pa tu Saraswati bhagavati
ni-shesha jaddya apaha...

Radhuni actually sings beautifully. This particular recording is from the third time I met them, not the second time, that night when they got drunk and squabbled, but from the time after that. That was in April, in the afternoon, with kaal boishakhi clouds suddenly capturing the sky and cooling everything, so I could even ask them to switch off the fan. You can hear the thunder in the background, and the occasional crack of lightning. Except for that, the recording is remarkably clean. Also, that was a Tuesday afternoon and not the usual Sunday rendezvous, and Radhuni apparently didn't drink on Tuesdays, so the voice is sober and quite strong.

'Do you know what that was?'

'Something to do with Ma Saraswati...' I knew exactly what she was singing, but I pretended to guess so that I could get her explanation on tape.

'Exactly! Very good! The Saraswati strotra, which I hope you know is a series of verses in praise of Goddess Saraswati.'

'Yes, yes, that's what I thought...'

'She who is pure white like jasmine, with the coolness of the moon, the brightness of snow... who shines like a garland of pearls... in whose hands is the veena... O Goddess Saraswati, please protect me and remove my ignorance!'

'It's beautiful. And you sing it beautifully.'

Sheyali stifled a snort, but her tone wasn't malicious at all. 'Now don't praise her too much! Otherwise we'll have to hear a recording of your praises for the next two weeks!'

Radhuni was in such a good mood that she completely ignored the provocation. 'So, why Saraswati? Saraswati because we,' she circled her hand to include Sheyali and the girls beyond the curtained door, 'not many people know, but all of us, us prostitutes, we worship her... For many of us, Saraswati is our main devi.'

'Oh, really? I see, I didn't know that.'

'Yes, now see the fun. Saraswati is supposed to be one of the most celibate of all the goddesses. And, in a way, we whores too are celibate! We mostly cannot take pleasure in the act of sexual congress, we cannot afford to let our bodies and minds get involved in the rasa of it, you see? For us, it is work, a sadhana, actually a disciplined study, if you like, and even while servicing a client, inside us we keep a distance from the usual results of the act, pleasure, release, attachment, love, desire, all those emotions we keep at bay, we *have* to keep at bay, you understand?'

'Though, of course, you can never let a customer know that,' Sheyali added, 'otherwise you would starve. So we are also, if you like, the greatest actresses. We play a vesh, a role, or slightly different roles, with different customers.'

'And then, the celibate Saraswati is also, of course, the great seeker of knowledge. She is both the one who facilitates learning, vidya, but who also constantly seeks it. And in our sadhana, in our practice, which involves not just the bed things but also singing and dancing, we too try and perfect our art.'

'So, just as all performers and musicians, all scholars and all artists pray to Saraswati, we too keep her as our main deity.'

The clouds rattled and cracked overhead as if the goddess was listening. I remember the hot, blank, sweat-ridden afternoon outside distilling itself into this god-light piercing through black clouds, the dust swirling in the blast of sudden cool wind and also, somehow, in the middle of the city, from somewhere the sharp smell of freshly drenched earth. It had gone very dark, so Sheyali called to one of the girls to come in and switch on the tube light – I made a gesture to say it's all right, that the light was lovely as it was – Sheyali cancelled her instructions – 'Never mind, leave it! Make some more tea!'

There was now a film of dust on the outside of my teacup and on my saucer, as if all of Bengal had decided to come in and join us.

Radhuni didn't seem to be missing the gin at all, she was now intoxicated by some new melody. 'You know, I've heard Bauls sing this song… I don't know it fully, but in this one they say a woman – *meye* becomes *maya* – is Saraswati, the river of secret knowledge, the secret river that links up with all the ones we know on the surface… maya, Ganga, Jamuna, Saraswati… maya, Ganga, Jamuna, Saraswati…

Playing it back, I wish Old Elko could have heard it, how much the old guy would have appreciated this. At first, I can just hear him snap, 'Bloody hell! More of your religious claptrap!', but I know he had a real affinity for north Indian classical, and Radhuni clearly has a voice well-trained in khayal and no doubt all the lighter forms, thumri, tappa, ghazal, something in itself not so surprising in a 'working lady' of her generation. Besides, what am I saying? As they told me themselves, he loved to hear Radhuni sing.

But also, Elko always had this bee in his bonnet about most artists basically being prostitutes. As I got to know him and Missus better, I could go into bits of the house that were out of bounds for the casual visitor and even for most friends. There was a small room, attached to the 'studio' – though we were never allowed to call it that – so an annexe to the room where he did most of his work, which I later started calling his 'puja room'. In its previous avatar, this must have been some kind of a pantry, just off the studio, which itself might have been a secondary dining space or a breakfast room or something. This small pantry is where he stored his paints and fresh paper and canvases, and I only got to see it by accident when he asked me to get something for him, nearly two years after I first met them.

There was only a small window and a small light bulb in the room, and at first, I thought the bits of paper stuck on the walls were lists of things to be bought, a checklist for regular items that needed to be stocked constantly, such as you have in American workshops and garages, and in some restaurant kitchens in both America and Europe. Wouldn't have thought he'd be so very methodical is what went through my mind, until my eye snagged on the list titles and names. On a notepaper ruled with blue squares a scrawl in a thick black felt pen: '*Remember! Essentially prostitutes who produced great art!*' and below this, individual scraps of paper stuck into the wall, sometimes with drawing pins, sometimes held by tape, each scrap with a name: *Leonardo*, *Michelangelo*, *Caravaggio*, one that said: '*Even Rembrandt, yes, even Rembrandt*!' and then another one: 'A working artist, a successful artist, is often a *putain*', underneath another note of more recent vintage, 'So are talentless, unsuccessful ones.'

I brought him the stuff from the room, pretending I hadn't noticed anything in the gloom. But a couple of days later, I raised it with him after lunch, the whole business of artists being prostitutes.

'So, do you believe that an artist can ever be pure?' I tried to put a joke in my voice but didn't quite pull it off. 'Meaning that, ideally, he should not ever worry about the market?'

Missus burst out laughing when I said this. Elko was having his post lunch coffee and he almost spilled it because Missus slapped him hard on his shoulder. 'Puuuure!' she drew out the word like a wail as she doubled and straightened with such violence that I thought she would fall on to the floor.

'Worry about the market! There's no one who worries more about the market than his nibs here, but from the other side of the fence! You should see him, you should be around when he goes into a sulk, *right* under a black cloud, whenever he accidentally earns a bob or two – a rupee and some annas – from his pictures! Do you have *any* idea, mon Colonel Zemindear, how many of us it takes? And the effort involved?' Then turning to me, 'To keep his esteemed exaltedness here coddled in his purity?'

Initially, it was always a touchy subject between us, me and them, Baron de Elko's painting. There were times I felt both of them would have much rather I didn't harp on about 'the bloody hobby' as both referred to it, but always on different occasions, never both at the same time. Then there were other days, moments, when I sensed a strong gratitude from Missus that I was calling the old fool's bluff, when I trampled over his pretence that it was just a hobby, a tic, really, in a life that he'd rather spend reading, listening to music and drinking.

Actually, this began from the second morning itself, on my first visit there. Over breakfast that day, with both of them looking as if they'd dragged themselves out of bed just for me, there were the usual pleasantries.

'Did you sleep well, dear?'

'Oh, very well, thank you!'

'You must have been exhausted, with the long flight and then the train journey.'

'I was a bit, but the air here is marvellous, like a tonic, and I slept really well, thank you.'

'Yes, we are blessed with this air, it's true.'

All this was entirely between Missus and myself, Elko in communion with his coffee, cigarettes and two-day-old newspaper, untruculent but silent, it being too early for him to speak, though I hadn't quite figured that out yet.

After a while, I brought it up. 'I couldn't help noticing that one of you, or is it both of you... you know, the paintings and the drawing books, I mean the watercolour books... I mean the pads... as I went to use the...'

'Oh, not me! That's all him. Don't mind that, just walk through it, won't you? I made sure there was a path through the jungle!'

'Oh, no, that's no problem at all. I was just wondering...'

Elko's silence changed character but stayed unbroken. Missus just gave a small laugh. 'Yes, well, everyone has their dark corners, don't they? You've only just met us and already you want to know all our secrets!'

'I'm so sorry! I didn't mean to pry!'

'No, my dear, it's quite all right. Really.' Missus nodded towards Elko behind his newspaper mask. 'I'm only teasing, and him more than you, actually.' She jumped up to head for the kitchen. 'More coffee for everyone? Yes, clearly required!'

And so, it began to come out. In bits and pieces, dribs and drabs. Occasional light passing over dark corners, sometimes staying, sometimes moving on, like a searchlight in one of those war movies or spy thrillers. As I spent time with them, repeated my visits, some things became clearer, yet others got smudged, erased before my eyes. There was this quite mad and magical old house, with gardens in the front and back, including a kitchen garden. There was the countryside almost outside the gate, just a short walk or a drive away, so brutal in the hot summer, so lovely in other seasons. There was the never-mentioned sense of exile, the lost time and the lost city, that were, to coin a phrase, so far yet so near.

We went for walks. They drove me to small local places for superb meals, and showed me the sights, mostly landscape, very few ruins and such. We talked about what I was doing, my plans for further study, the possibility of doing my doctorate in Paris, about art and history and politics, and, of course, we talked about Calcutta.

I realize now that, on my first visit, he was having one of his periods where he was off painting. Much later, Missus told me that he'd stopped touching his brushes for over two weeks, that just a couple of days before I'd first arrived, she'd had to stop him when she realized he was hauling away a whole carload of canvases and drawings, intending to take them into some field and destroy them. 'Imagine the smoke from that rubbish poisoning this air. You know, they've begun to speak about *environmental pollution*, have you heard of it over in the States? This idea that we are vitiating the atmosphere of the whole planet! Imagine Sir Zemindear's burning detritus contributing to this, all because he can't control his sulking ego!'

Waking up on the fourth day, I found that someone had left a pot of fresh coffee on the table, along with the bread, jam and fruits for breakfast. As I took my cup and went into the front garden, I suddenly smelled a vaguely familiar chemical waft, slight in itself but strong enough to cut into the aroma of my coffee and all the garden smells. Turning a corner, I saw him sitting there on a chair, working on a large piece of white art board with the new markers. I recognized the smell from when I'd uncapped one or two of the markers before packing them. Maybe I'm imagining the smell travelling so far, but I don't think so – I learnt later that those EF markers were famous among graphic designers in New York for their stink, especially when they were new. I avoided going too close, I didn't want him thinking I was poking my nose into his business. He noticed me and waved. 'You found the coffee? Just help yourself to the bread and things. If you want eggs and sausages or something, you'll have to wait for Her Ladyship. I don't have any truck with the cooking, you see. But she should be up soon, I hope.'

That evening was the first time I saw him properly drunk. He'd spent the morning with us, we had our usual pre-lunch drinks and ate together, and then he'd mumbled something about needing to tinker and had gone off, clutching his coffee. I didn't see him until the evening, but when he appeared he was in a ragged shirt and an old pair of trousers, both stained with paint. When he handed me my drink, his fingers smelled of turpentine. 'Right. So, which of these would you recommend I listen to first?' He pointed to the stack of records I'd brought, all still untouched.

'Well, I think the Miles Davis is a classic, so you might want to start with that.'

He picked up the album, slit the cellophane with his fingernail and peeled it off. Switching on the amp, he lifted the lid on the turntable and carefully placed the record on the platter. As the evening progressed, this became my job – 'Would you mind terribly, dear boy? Let's hear the next one, whichever one you choose!'

That evening, he drank much faster than on the previous nights. While I was told to drink whatever I wanted from the bar, I'd noticed each of them had their separate bottles of wine. Seeing him put it away at speed, Missus tried at first to slow him down without actually saying anything. But then, I also saw her give up the battle and up the attack on her own bottle. As they got into their cups, I have a memory of suddenly feeling excluded, as if I was an interloper in a private club of two, and then, yet again, flipping the record around, there was also this feeling that I only put my finger on later – that was the first night where I became just another friend, almost another family member for these two, neither of whom had much in the way of families.

'So... with all this art history you're mucking about with, do you have any ambition yourself, to paint, to be some sort of artist?' They'd both really liked the Coltrane album and we were now listening to it for the second time. I had to wait for a pause in the music to answer.

'Me? Oh no, no! I have no talent and... no craving to draw or paint myself. I love looking at the things, you know, painting, sculpture, architecture, but no desire to... though I did flirt with the sitar at one point...'

'That's natural, I suppose.' Missus nodded at her glass as if she had a full and complete understanding of my life.

'Natural, my foot!' The nasty snap in his voice was unexpected, without warning, at least to me. 'There's no need, absolutely no need to visit the...'

'No, I just meant—' Missus wasn't looking for a fight that evening and she let him cut her off.

'Sorry, you were saying?'

'Well, I do like history, the paintings and the stories behind the paintings, just as with buildings, how they came about, how they came to be made, you know? All the rest, all this new theory and all that is fine, but that's what excites...'

'Oh! *We* have some stories about how—'

'No, we *don't,* my dear!' His voice was gentler now, the waspishness gone. 'No boring old stories, or this chap will jump on his bike and vamoose!'

I hastened to keep the door ajar. 'No, no, no, I'd *love* to hear the stories... and, whenever you felt like it, to see some of your—'

'Oh, bugger all that! You were explaining about this bastard, Kissinger.'

I liked the way Sheyali-mashi pronounced 'Kissinger'.

'Why do I worship this Indira? I'll tell you! Because she took away these sons of pigs', these raja-maharajas' privy purses and because, when Bangladesh came about, she stood up to those Pakistanis, and to those whoresons Nik-shawn and that Kishinjhaar!'

But the Indira-Nixon-Kissinger discussion was from yet another time. In that afternoon recording from April 1977, you can hear the kaal boishakhi rain start to smash down, with Radhuni now singing raag Megh Malhar.

Sheyali then shouting to the girls – 'Have you all died suddenly? Where are you idiots? Shut the windows before we get swept away!'

To the percussion of creaking wood and window bolts being slammed, Radhuni singing *Garaje ghata, ga-ra-jey gha-taa...*

'He used to love hearing Radhuni sing. He didn't want anything else, you know, anything like *that* from us, ever. He'd pay of course, later, discreetly leave some money, but what he wanted was for us to sing. Mostly Radhuni, but he would be polite and ask both of us.'

Radhuni paused in her raag. 'Now, there's no need to be so modest! You know she sings the most beautiful bhatiali and kirton? Far better than me.'

Sheyali puffed on her bidi. Her eyes went away somewhere and came back with a grin. 'Ei, tor money achhey...' Hey, do you remember...

'Ki?' Radhuni raised an eyebrow.

Sheyali turned to me. 'You know, the back stairs at the hotel, at the Great Eastern, they had a great sound. Meaning, if you sang there, your voice reverberated as if in a theatre. I don't know what it was, maybe all that wood...'

'Yes, yes, yes!' Radhuni laughed, nodding hard. 'It was our one bit of mischief after work! Sometimes, as went down those stairs, we would sing loudly! These were only the back stairs, for waiters, guests' servants and various staff people to use, but they were almost as wide as this whole room, and how our voices would bounce!'

'And! Remember that time we got caught by that Manager Shaheb?'

'That Barbora Shaheb! Chief manager! Oh my god! Luckily, he also really liked our singing. Now, see, he liked Sheyali's voice better than mine. Reminded him of his Assam.'

'Hm. He liked my voice better, but he liked better everything else of yours! I remember, I had to sing just on the other side of the door while...'

There is a small scuffle at this point, leavened with giggles, as Radhuni grabs the microphone and then the recording ends.

BALL

Only three whisky sours down, but she's high enough to imagine it's cats fighting. Two cats clawing screams out of each other, she thinks, as if hearing this music for the first time, except there's no denying the sheer joy of their playing.

The MC has announced the tune as something called 'King Porter Stomp', and it has pulled several couples to the dance floor. As Imogen loosens from Andrew and cleaves back to him, she can feel other pairs around them more than see them, feel them opening up like some early industrial contraption, feel them folding back together with the chorus-scrape of shoes, imagine each unit churning out yarn or paper in clackety, nineteenth-century unison.

She can't ignore the pleasure the intertwining clarinets train down her spine. Like two sirens going, announcing competing air raids, she thinks, with the thump of the drums and massed brass thrumming overhead, except they're raining down delight, exultation, freedom of touch, the license to hold her man in public, hold him one last time. Not true, the 'one last time', she thinks, not quite true, not yet. There's still midnight mass at St Paul's and the night afterwards, probably in the car, unless she can sneak him into the house. Then tomorrow. Christmas lunch. After which her stocking will finally empty, leaving her with nothing but a seared tongue.

It's as though the entire ceiling is mined with mistletoe, as if they are navigating narrow channels in order to avoid doing what they most want, except it now hurts when Andrew kisses her, at the tip of her tongue because of that scalding tea with the Bengali girl. Except it's nothing another cold whisky sour won't see to, nothing another kiss from Andrew won't help cure, nothing that will last beyond the last smash of drums tonight.

As Andrew spins Imogen back to himself, the saxophones cut into the clarinets, the piano goes off on a lunatically high jiggle, and she has to stop herself from completely letting go.

Won't do to have the senior officers' wives strafing her with their disapproval, can't be denting Andrew's prospects for a few moments of wanton movement.

There's something else tugging her back, and she realizes it only faintly, like a soft, quick, background tapping on the rim of a drum. The floor tilting like the ballroom of a liner in a mid-Atlantic storm, the little man dancing next to them, twirling around an Indian girl. Being quite sedate by his standards.

Can't do, won't do, to be going wild while right next to them is Larry Lahiri being suave, as much sweat as a seal sunning on an iceberg, playing Latin gigolo to a satin-skinned beauty.

She wishes she had on dark glasses to fight off the glare. The light on the bloody epaulettes, the banks of medals flashing on people who've hardly begun to fight, the outrageous white teeth the Lahiri chap keeps flashing at his partner as he sends her into yet another spin. Not fair the local women should be allowed almost naked waists and her mem-self not. Not that the other girl, that Eva woman, ever had such problems dancing with Little Larry Lahiri at earlier parties. Fully covered in her dated Slavic fashions, but might as well have not been wearing a stitch, the dear, departed, long-embarked Eva. And, despite all his recent, badly underplayed dramatics at his European princess's hasty exit, the little lover-boy is doing *quite* well now, thank you very much.

She can feel Larry Lahiri enjoying himself. She sees his fingers brush lightly over the Indian girl's elbow as he stops her turning, guiding her, ever so oily yet ever so correct. She can see that his touch is much subtler than Andrew's, and how much lighter he is on his feet, she can see that the intense look in his eyes is genuine, almost, and that his body is springy with barely contained excitement – poor, lucky, dusky, musky sari-wrapped dame, however will she fend him off tonight? *Not* our bizny, is it, miss, as her WAAF driver used to say during the last days of that September, there has to be some advantage to this bloody war, doesn't there, miss?

Imogen feels Andrew's hand almost at the bottom of her spine, pulsing through her evening dress, and forgives the world everything except.

The war. Suddenly it wells up inside Imogen. In mid-step, out of rhythm with it all, she finds herself firing off a short burst of laughter – it's out before she can put it back in its pen and Andrew, blessedly good

Andrew, quick of reaction as always, is already waltzing her away from the centre of the dance floor.

'Darling?'

'I'm sorry, so sorry, darling! I just remembered the name you gave your little friend there and I couldn't help myself!' As Andrew rudders them to the bar, Imogen buries her face in her handkerchief as if suffering from a bad toothache.

'Little friend – oh, you mean Lahiri?'

Imogen nods into her handkerchief before starting into another spasm.

'Ah yes, Air Marshal—'

'Andrew. Don't. I shall burst.'

'—Cheddar. Air Marshal Cheddar.'

It had been the little dwarf's own fault, no one else he could've blamed, really. One evening at the tennis club, he'd made the mistake of bragging to them about his uncle, some BIA gunner-type in Egypt, who'd apparently received a special recommendation from the RAF for rescuing two downed pilots from the very jaws of the Hun.

'From Tedder himself, would you believe?' Lahiri had said.

'I say, that's jolly, bloody unusual.' Andrew had raised his glass affably. 'The old vulture's not known to dispense praise easily, especially to those of us who have to crawl around on the ground!'

'Who, darling?' Imogen was bored of war talk and irritated at Lahiri for trying to insert himself into the war effort via some relative.

'Air Marshal Tedder himself!' Lahiri had repeated. 'C-in-C, RAF Middle East.'

Imogen was on her fourth double Scotch and she wasn't having it. She didn't like the boasting and she couldn't stand the way the man kept pronouncing 'east' as 'ist'.

'Cheddar? Cheddar? Impossible, Mr Lahiri. You can't possibly have a General named after a cheese! Whatever next? Admiral Blue Stilton? You must have the name wrong. Or the recommendation, perhaps. RAF love to pull army's leg, don't they, darling?' Imogen had turned to Andrew.

'I'm absolutely certain,' said Lahiri frostily. 'Desert Command sent us the actual letter along with his effects.'

'Good lord, man, I'm *so*—'

'Field Marshal Double Gloucester.' Imogen swallowed the whisky. 'Marechal Camembert.'

Andrew had gripped Imogen's arm so hard she thought he was going to break it.

'No, no, no, no,' it was the Indian's turn to switch on the contrition, 'not *effects*, I shouldn't have said effects, what I meant was, they only sent us the few things they do when someone's taken prisoner. My uncle was captured at Halfaya Pass, you see, a couple of weeks after he received the letter from Tedder. Prisoner of war, now, somewhere in Libya or Italy, probably. We can't tell from his letters.'

Imogen had sneered, but only when she and Andrew were on their way home. 'Saved the flyboys, perhaps, but clearly couldn't do the same for himself.'

'Understandable, don't you think, if you're dragging around a whopping big Bofors gun and trying to fight off a horde of Panzers.' Andrew's voice was on the edge.

'Yes, darling, quite. Anyway, I do think cheese is so appropriate for *all* our brass, don't you?' Imogen had nearly retched at the thought of cheese. 'Or perhaps, butter, given the way Our Enemy's sliced through them all.'

Andrew Hillcott had slammed his hand down on the steering wheel of his car and skewed it dangerously to a stop at the side of the blacked-out road.

Tonight, as Andrew hands her another drink, Imogen remembers the ensuing quarrel and it brings back no taste of satisfaction. The thought of never seeing Andrew ever again mixes with the horror of that memory and the three days they had not spoken to each other. What an utterly stupid, stupid waste of time.

'Dare we venture out again, m'lady, or should we take a pew?' Andrew allows the crowd around the bar to push him into Imogen.

A criminal waste of time, those three days, except, except the making up had been well worth it. Tears, the crossfire of apologies and kisses, all natural stepping stones to final barriers breaking down, leading to bed for the first time. The next morning, as a peace offering, Andrew on how Kedar Lahiri ponged after a hard game of tennis: 'If you promise not to make fun of some poor devil who was actually fighting for us, we can call his nephew Air Marshal Cheddar.'

'Not to his face, I take it?' Imogen had locked herself around Andrew. 'Strictly *entre nous*, I take it?'

'Yes, strictly.' As Imogen smothered him, she could hear Andrew mumble, 'Cheddar smell, definitely. *Old* cheddar...'

The band brings the tune to a crashing end and immediately swings into the next tune with no interjection from the MC.

Savvoy, the home of sweet romance! Saavvvoy, it wins you at a glance!

Gerald from Andrew's chummery leans into them and shouts, 'These fellows aren't too bad, are they? But apparently this Cheddarford chap and his band at the Winter Garden are *quite* something!'

Saaavvvoy, gives happy feet a chance... to dance!

Imogen tries not to bite into the rim of her glass.

Your old form, just like a clinging vine,

youuur lips, so warm and sweet as wine...

'You didn't say Cheddarford did you?' She is shaking.

'No, no, WEATHERfurd! Weather as in current climate!'

Your cheek, so soft and close to mine – deee-viiine!

They are joined by another chummer. Lit up like a Verey light.

'Current primate, did you say?'

'Very much so. Except he's as white as you and me, my boy!'

'Yank?'

How my heart is singing...

'Yank! Yes!'

While the band is swinging...

'Well, they can't afford to monkey around any longer, can they?'

I'm never tired of romping,

and stomping with...

'They're Yanks, old boy. They'll monkey around through this war!'

... you at the Savoy!

'And win it for us, do you think?' Andrew is smiling, but he's waiting to leap upon the reply.

Whaat joy – a perfect holiday,

Saaavvvoy, where we can glide and sway...

'Might do, they might just do, there's no denying it!'

Andrew opens his mouth—

Savvvvoy, let me stomp away – with yooouuu...

—but the man saves himself in the nick of time.

'More accurately, Andy old boy, it would suit us to let them think they've got the starring role. What they'd actually be doing, of course, is helping *us* win it, but we've got to be large-hearted about this, I suspect, and let them imagine *they've* got the best lines!'

'And you see the Russians as...? The chorus line?' Imogen's words shear into a softer part of the tune, just before a trombone solo soars up.

'Oh, no, no! They're *jolly* useful, the Reds! Catching it now, for sure, but once Hitler takes Moscow and Siberia, he'll have to invest a lot of troops keeping them quiet. It's quite a large shire, their little union of Soviets. Which will suit us to a T.'

Imogen can't help it, the words come out of her mouth, a trumpet maliciously interrupting a saxophone.

'Just as the Japs will need a lot of men to keep India quiet, one would imagine?'

The men turn to look at her, each trying to control his expression in a different way.

'I imagine that would suit us to a T as well, don't you?'

The drummer dives into a solo, setting up a wash of high-tinged syncopation, undercut by deep, regular knocks of his big drum, the other instruments flying high escort. Suddenly, along with the drums, Imogen can hear every clink of glass, every chink of a cufflink or dancing necklace. It seems to Imogen as if the men around her can hear it too, the crackling of the Empire breaking up slowly, like an ignited dirigible, crumbling burning debris and ash down upon their lives.

'Miss Snell? Could I have the next dance?'

Out of the glare and clash of glasses, shining brass instruments, spectacles, medals, Imogen sees Cheddar Lahiri standing, it seems, a couple of inches below her chin.

Outlaw Snell surrounded by the sheriff's posse. Indian offering her honourable escape. She turns and smiles lopsidedly at Andrew and the others. Then she turns to Lahiri and smiles at him as well, in the spirit of Christmas giving. 'It would be a pleasure.' She looks again at the Englishmen. 'Excuse me, gentlemen, but this lady must needs dance.'

She leans towards Lahiri's arm but aims too high and almost falls. The little man doesn't miss a step, steadying her, arranging it for her to find a firm link around his forearm, moving her away from the bar and into the swirling couples. Without any effort on her part, she is suddenly in rhythm, finding it easier to move to the music than to stand still. The difference of height has suddenly disappeared, Lahiri is actually not that short, about an inch and a half shorter than her, if that, and he's quite adept, standing just a little further back from her than he was with his local beauty, not trying anything fancy, doing just enough to keep them in the game. After a while, she bends to his ear and says, 'Kedder. You must call me Imogen. All of Andrew's friends call me Imogen and so must you.'

'With pleasure.'

'It's Kedder, isn't it? Am I saying it right?'

'Well, actually, it's Kay-daar. Like radar, but with a k.'

The song has changed, and Imogen recognizes it.

'Caravan,' she says and realizes Lahiri has said it at the same time.

'I love this melody,' she says.

'Good, that means you have an ear for our Eastern music. Or, at least, for Middle Eastern music.' He's pronounced 'east' perfectly this time and Imogen smiles at the left-handed compliment.

After a while, Imogen realizes she's moving the way she's wanted to all evening. The only brass she now cares about is the mass of golden instruments on the stage. She remembers all too clearly that it's always easier to dance with someone you don't care about, someone with whom you aren't involved and aren't likely to be. She notices that Larry 'Cheddar' Lahiri, too, is far more relaxed, with none of the desperation to impress that she had witnessed with his previous partner. For the first time this evening, the dancing becomes purely about the music.

'One more? Or shall we rejoin...' Lahiri relaxes the dancing grip on her hand.

'Oh no, please, I wouldn't stop now for the world.' She looks over at Andrew, still in the thicket of full-dress khaki near the bar, deep in animated conversation. 'I'm so enjoying this band, aren't you?'

'Oh yes, they're very good.'

Imogen adjusts her left hand on Lahiri's dinner jacket. 'And if you're sure you don't mind dancing with a woman with two left feet?'

'Well, that's not in evidence tonight, Miss Snell.'

Imogen is startled. It's not often that men come back with such a quick repartee. 'Imogen, please.'

'Imogen. I beg your pardon.'

The dance is a slow one, and she briefly wishes she was with Andrew. Then she lets it recede into the web of sound, all of it – Andrew, tomorrow, Burma, the bloody Japs, the unexploded eight-pounder that had stalked her since the day she was born, that found her on that last day of September, that had missed 99 per cent of her as the doctors had said, the one that had taken 99 per cent instead of her driver, Aircraftwoman Mildred Glover.

'Mistletoe... cheshta kore jaao, kintu tomar off-stump'er besh bairey, my boy.'

Imogen only hears the words in English and none of the exchange in what she has now come to differentiate as Bengali. She hears the words only because she feels Larry Lahiri's right hand stiffen on her waist and the fingers of his left starting to disengage with hers in mid-dance.

She looks down at the little man's face and she suddenly feels a burn of unease. Lahiri's beauty has disappeared, replaced by the mask of a ferret about to fight for its life. The hands leave her, not a word of apology, almost as if she's not there. Only then does she see the Indian officer dancing with the girl Lahiri was partnering earlier. The girl, clearly panicked, says something quickly in a high voice, including something that sounds like 'da-da' and the word 'scene'. Ending with a clear 'naa' which Imogen guesses is the Bengali word for 'no'.

Without quite understanding how she's got there, Imogen finds herself looking at the buffet table. The parade of food sits pristine, the candlelight sliding off the pewter domes being removed from the dishes.

'What was that man saying?'

'Nothing. There's nothing worse than an Indian in his cups...'

'Oh, come on, Kedar. I'm not as thick as I look.'

'... I should probably say nothing worse than a Bengali. Some Indians can actually hold their drink, you know.'

'What did he *say*?'

'Nothing. Would you care to eat? Shall I fetch you a plate?'

'You can fetch me exactly what that man said. It was something to do with the two of us, wasn't it? It wasn't to do with the... that girl you were dancing with?'

'She's his sister. She's actually all right. She's not to be blamed.'

'Quite. And?'

'Well, the... gentleman... is drunk and he made some unfortunate comments.'

'Such as? Something about us standing under the mistletoe, wasn't it?'

'Well, look, Mi – Imogen, shall we just forget the whole thing?'

'You looked as if you were going to punch him.' Imogen grinned.

'I was just a bit irritated, I do apologize.'

'No, don't see why you should, really. You behaved impeccably under the—'

'The fact is, the chap feels their family, I mean the girl's family, and mine should have clear discussions before any further contact...'

'Ah.'

'In which she and I may not exactly be allowed to be party. About a possible, a possible, er...'

'Betrothal? Engagement? Marriage?'

'Yes, you see, we belong to a particular group – by which I mean a sort of a... a church called Brahm—'

'Well, Kedar, you *were* party to dancing quite vigorously with the young lady. Would that be seen as a bit naughty, especially if your intentions weren't—'

The band sends a crescendo reverberating across the ballroom, almost making the chandeliers shake. Larry Lahiri uses the interruption to his advantage.

'All very cheerful tonight, isn't it?'

'Yes... you know, good old British spirit. But I was asking...'

'We shall all miss Hillcott. But not as badly as you will, of course.'

Imogen is startled at this forwardness. But she's damned if she's going to back down.

'Yes... we all miss people when they leave, don't we? Have you told your potential fiancée about your friend, Miss... what *was* her name?'

'Eva Attali. No, I haven't mentioned her, but it seems quite a few people know we were... er... quite fond of each other.'

'I'm not surprised. You were hardly the most discreet pair one's seen. I remember spotting you at lunch at Firpo's once. You might as well have been—'

'This business of marriage might be a requirement only for our families. The young lady and I may have different ideas.'

'I see, so you feel able to take—'

'I'm sorry, I interrupted you. Ev—Miss Attali and I might as well have been... what?' Lahiri looks up at Imogen. His face breaks open into an unabashed anticipatory smile, half embarrassed, half proud.

'*Your cheek, so soft and close to mine...*' Imogen sways a bit and goes into herself, humming the earlier tune against the grain of what the band is now playing. She is damned if she's going to give this little cockerel the satisfaction of finishing a sentence from which he will only cull admiration. '*... your lips, so warm and sweet as hmmm.*'

Larry Lahiri surveys the scene, seemingly not at all put out by Imogen's dissimulation. 'You've spent some time in Paris, haven't you? Have you ever seen Manet's painting of the barmaid at the Folies Bergère?'

'*... while the band is swinging!* The foelis-burgers? Oh, yes! I have, actually! It's quite stupendous.' Imogen suddenly feels as if she's a drink short. This is not a question she has been expecting.

'How I envy you.' Lahiri keeps looking at the spread of the dancing and the throng at the bar.

'This does remind one of that picture, doesn't it? You're quite right!'

'No, you know, you see,' Lahiri turns to look at Imogen, 'you see, I'm fascinated by how those people, how those Impressionist chaps, managed to paint. Every brushstroke sort of contradicts the other and they all, all the strokes, fight among themselves, sizes, the colours, the directions of the brush. But the moment you stand back, you get a pulsation of the whole person.'

'That's very true.' Imogen looks at the man with new interest. Perhaps the cockerel has something to him after all.

'I've only seen reproductions, mind you. And read descriptions. So it's very much a second-hand—'

'No, but you're absolutely right! That's exactly how those paintings *do* play their magic!'

'I sometimes think it's the same with life.' Kedar looks away and runs a hand through his Brylcreemed hair, disturbing the carefully combed parting. 'When somebody's standing before you, you can only see all their contradictory strokes. It's only once the person's gone, or once you're away from her, that you can form the whole picture.'

'Or him.'

'Beg your pardon?'

'Only once you are away from her... or him... that you can...'

'Yes, quite, exactly.'

'Unless, of course, a person's a Cubist painting. In which case...'

'You can't ever make sense of utter nonsense!' Kedar laughs.

'Would you say Picasso is utter nonsense? Really?'

'Well, not his earlier work, of course. No.'

'But, what about Cubism?' Imogen finds it hard to keep standing once she lets Picasso's paintings come into her mind. She desperately throws herself a lifeline. 'What about the Surrealists?'

'It becomes too easy, doesn't it? If you can just paint what you want, if you can paint an object without adhering to... any of its actual properties, where is the challenge?'

'But I can adhere to actual properties with a click of my Brownie, you know.'

'Yes, I suppose you can, but there you wouldn't have the emotion one gets from the... it *is* a very fine line, you see. If you take Cézanne's last paintings, or Monet's—'

'So, would you say your Eva was a Cubist painting, or have you made sense of her yet?' Imogen uses the shifting plates of her brain to slide in the question.

'Well... I'm still...' Kedar is momentarily flummoxed.

'Do you have a photograph her, by the way?'

'Yes, a small one. Taken a few years ago, in Riga, where she comes from. None from the time here.'

'I happen to have one of the two of you. You didn't notice, but I took it at that picnic in Budge-Budge, at the river house. Sitting on the grass, near the boats. I rather think it... adheres to all the actual properties. Remind me to give it to you.'

Kedar's eyes widen. He avoids looking at Imogen. 'Thank you, yes, I will.'

'Though once Andrew's away, I don't know quite when I shall next see you. I don't see myself spending too much time at the South Club, somehow.'

'Well, if you don't mind, I could send across my driver? To collect it?'

'No, of course I don't mind, Kedar! I imagine you'll be quite occupied yourself, won't you, with the young lady who is, or perhaps isn't, your intended...'

'You call her a young lady as if you were her mother's age! I wouldn't presume to guess your age, but I'd say she's only a couple of years younger.'

Imogen gets a sharp whiff of the cologne Kedar is wearing, and she notes that it doesn't smell anything like cheddar cheese. Obviously, Larry Lahiri perspires less when playing certain kinds of games.

'I'll be twenty-six next January, since you ask Mr Lahiri, and I wouldn't let a man dance with me in that fashion unless I thought him serious. When I was twenty-two, I might have.' Imogen smiles wide to defang the formal address, but she can see the shot has hit home. Kedar finds an ashtray to stub out his cigarette.

'Twenty-six? I see.' He continues to search for an answer.

'God willing. Unless the Japs get here first and bomb us all to smithereens.'

'I don't think they'll be able to capture aerodromes from which they can reach Calcutta. Not by January.' Kedar's eyes widen as he realizes the import of what he has said. He goes into a desperate rescue effort. 'Anyway, actually, I think Andrew's bunch will have pushed them into the sea by then.'

'I do hope so, Kedar. In which case, I'm sure we'll meet again and I'll enjoy watching you dance with your usual wanton abandon'

Kedar looks around and finds the stack of waiting plates. This gives him time to muster a response.

'Look, Imogen, I could dance with her quite freely... precisely because...'

'You feel nothing for her?' Imogen takes the plate that Kedar offers her.

'Well, I wouldn't say—'

'You wouldn't say, but perhaps I can.' Imogen moves ahead of Kedar in the queue that's now forming for the food. 'You don't want to marry her, but you wouldn't mind having a small... *histoire avec elle*, as the French might say.'

'I'm afraid my French is non-existent.'

'A small story with her.' Imogen bypasses the winter soups, French onion and mulligatawny, holding her plate the best she can. She can see Kedar is wondering what he can help her with. He clearly decides it's too complicated, best to leave it to the white jackets standing across the buffet table.

'Ah, yes. Sometimes a smollstori can be quite nice, hein?' Imogen follows the source of the murmur and sees a large, plump man in chef's regalia smiling at them from under a splendid moustache. '*Peut-etre la mademoiselle desirez une petite histoire avec ces scôtellettes d'Agneau?*' The man leans forward towards Imogen, expertly balancing on a serving spoon two beautiful-looking baby lamb chops glistening with sauce and flecks of rosemary.

'Oh, those look lovely, thank – *merci monsieur...?*'

'*Bonnemaison, chef de l'hotel, a votre service!*' The chops slide on to Imogen's plate as if on their own, followed with minimum fuss by a small cake of potatoes au gratin and an exquisite dollop of green mush.

'Ah, so you're Chef Bonnemaison! M'sieur, I've heard so much about you!'

Even as Imogen savours the food with her eyes, she feels the chef's gaze shift to Kedar and stay there as if it will never ever move again.

'And for Le Prince?'

Kedar throws a glance over his shoulder to see who the chef is addressing. He sees no one close enough.

'Muuh'sieur!' The chef draws Kedar's attention back to himself. 'What would amuse your palate tonight? The lamb? Some of this nice fish?'

'Do you have roast beef?'

The chef looks pained. 'Ah, my dear young excellence, the place is full of rosbif, but alas *not* made by Bonnemaison!' The chef gestures with subtle distaste towards the other buffet table which has a parade of all the usual Christmas Eve fare, roast beef, apple sauce, shepherd's pie, mashed potatoes. 'I would be disappointed, destroyed, in fact, if the prince does not try something from my very own hand!'

'Mr Lahiri?' Imogen has to speak before the laughter breaks out of her. 'You do know that Monsieur Bonnemaison is a world-famous chef? I wouldn't pass up an opportunity to sample his cooking! You'll always be surrounded by us rosbifs, but to taste something genuinely French might... transport you.'

Imogen is now looking at the chef, merriment transferring from her to him like crates from freighter to dock. The chef bows with a slight smile, acknowledging he's been simultaneously caught out on two counts: the Englishwoman has obviously spent enough time in France to know that the French nickname for the British is 'rosbif', and she has clearly spent enough time in the beau monde to not shy away from seeing it when a man is attracted to another man. Imogen can see that Bonnemaison's mental abacus has also smacked on to the fact that the young mademoiselle is clearly not romantically attached to the young monsieur.

Kedar is aware he's missing something, but he thinks it's to do with the food.

'Sir, I will eat whatever you want to serve me,' he says gallantly, proffering his empty plate. When Imogen spins around, almost doubling up, Kedar is caught between giving her the help she clearly needs and controlling his plate as it fills up with magically glistening stuff.

'Not to worry about the gai mademoiselle, my prince! She will be fine! Just try, please, first the lambe, then the pommes gratinee, and finally, to clean your tongue and to start again, the puree d'epinards. Since you are clearly from a kingdom somewhere in the Bengale, I don't try with you my fish à la meunière which is a seafish!'

Imogen has turned back to look at Kedar. Suddenly, she remembers that August evening at the club and the small dagger of glass balancing on a gently waving leaf.

Kedar smiles his thanks at the chef and makes to move away, but the Frenchman has just seen someone. 'Just one moment, Prince! I beg a small bit from you, a small bit of time, just ten secondes!' Waving his hand at shoulder height, he hauls the man over on an invisible rope.

Imogen sees something hurrying over. The man is in an evening suit made in 1922 and hanging from his neck is a big, square crate of a camera with an even larger silver bowl on top. 'Yes, chef! I am here!' With speed belying his bulk, Bonnemaison has come around from behind the buffet table and is standing very close to Kedar. 'Quickly, one with the prince and myself!' The man bows and quickly readies his apparatus. A large arm goes around Pretty Larry's shoulders. As the flash blinds him, Imogen can almost feel Kedar being pulled into the acrid aroma of French cigarettes and the smell of some quite expensive cologne. 'One more, with a smile, please!' Bonnemaison's voice marinades Kedar's ear and the second flash punches away the blurred red sight that's fighting to come back to his eyes.

The photographer picks up the spent flashbulbs from the floor and then bows low. 'Your Highness? Highness of…? Forgive me, Highness, but may I beg your card? To which room shall I send the prints? They will be ready by noon tomorrow…'

'You send them to *me!* I will make sure Le Prince sees them!' Bonnemaison dismisses the photographer, inserting himself between the man and Kedar, his face not three inches from the young man's, his cheeks shining with a light film that seems to Imogen to be made of clear egg white and excitement.

As Imogen moves past the fish à la meunière, she can hear a nasal voice which establishes itself over the music.

'Beggars belief, I agree, but he said it was true.'

'No.'

'Tim, I'm telling you.'

'No.'

'He said – he wrote—'

'Not possible, old chap. Laws of matter simply won't allow it.'

'Apparently they do!'

'No.'

'I'm telling you, man! Matilda, gunner obviously punching in the shells, therefore the barrel's red-hot! And therefore, it's soft enough, would you believe?'

'With a bally Nip sabre? No.'

'Yes. Those swords are apparently jolly bloody sharp. Some arcane process they put them through, the blades, since the thirteenth buggering century, apparently.'

'Look, Cyril, as a scientific, rational sort of chap, I am not prepared to accept that a thirteenth-century *sword* can actually *chop* through the barrel of our most modern—'

'Can I point out that the Matilda is not one of our most modern?'

'For god's sake man! That tank barrel is of British manufacture of the twentieth bloody century! You. Are. Now. Not going to tell me.'

'I'm afraid, Tim, I am, yes, I am.'

'That. A. Japanese. Bally, samyou-whatsit, bally sword! A bally blade, after all. Can. Slice. Through. A tank barrel?'

'Several witnesses, apparently. Christians, all. White, our lads, all. Cross'd themselves and ran, he said. Disaster.'

'Because one of their Nip officers managed to – say it again when you're sober, I challenge you, Cyril!'

'I *am* sober, old boy, barely touched a drink since I heard this! We'll need all our wits about us, I fancy.'

Imogen feels a familiar hand on her elbow. Andrew cuts in on the queue.

'And pigs will fly, will they?'

'Hillcott, I can show you the letter! If you read—'

'No need, my dear chap, I've already read and heard a lot of fantastical rubbish. Rommel has an invisible magic carpet, the Japs – hadn't yet heard this particular fairy tale – but apparently the Japs can take the bicycles they've commandeered from the plantations and turn them into amphibious assault craft, ford rivers by pedalling really, really, jolly bloody hard! It's a load of codswallop! These bloody rumours sometimes do us more damage than the enemy himself.'

Imogen finds it difficult to balance the plate as she moves away from the buffet. A bit of the sauce has slipped around the napkin and got between her fingers and the china. The cutlery seems to have developed a life of its own, drumming and clattering on the plate as she tries to grip it. Andrew sees her gone and looks around to locate her. His hand steadies her elbow in the nick of time.

'Darling? Perhaps enough drink for the evening?'

'Just practising, darling. It's what old maidens do while waiting for—'

'Do stop. You've been talking rot all evening. I'll make you pay for it when I'm—'

'Back? Of course you will, darling, of course you will!'

She's now looking out of a slight opening in the blackout curtains on one of the tall windows that line the banquet area. The window is right on the south-western corner of the first-floor ballroom, and it gives on to the junction between Waterloo Street and Cornwallis Street, the main road that goes past Governor House. There is a dark mess of cars and buses on the street below, their headlights dimmed under heavy black eyelids of paint, making little knots of light and creating strange glints off the chrome bumpers and window rims. All the vehicles seem to have their horns blaring, the people inside sticking their heads out and blowing hard on their paper bugles. The cacophony of celebration is so loud, she thinks the Japs must be able to hear it all the way in Malaya.

Trapped between three automobiles trying to go in four directions, a horse-carriage chappie is struggling with his restive pony. One of the cars is a large sports convertible, overflowing with a mix of officers, planters and women. One of the planters stands up in the car, leans over and places his large hat on the pony's head. This adds to the animal's discomfort, and it shakes its head from side to side, trying to get rid of the hat. The carriage driver reaches forward, trying to get the hat off, but every time he gets close, the pony starts and weaves, slamming the man back into his seat. The crowd in the open car seems to find this hilarious, and one of them pops open a bottle of champagne, the foam ghostly white in the semi-darkness. The report of the cork is the final straw. The pony throws off the hat and tries to climb over a car. Imogen's teeth hit bone and she realizes she has finished both the lamb chops without tasting them.

She looks around and understands she's standing with Andrew and another officer in one corner of the dining area. Larry Lahiri is nowhere to be seen. She remembers being introduced to the man Andrew's speaking to, but she can't recall his name, something odd, oh yes, Odd-Cartwright, clearly some dreg from Oxbridge, funny brush of a moustache, quite expensive watch, buttonholed Andrew just a moment ago, or has it been hours? Odd-Cartwright now leaning close to Andrew and dropping his voice.

'By the way, I couldn't help overhearing you there at the buffet table, major.'

'No, well, terribly sorry, but I just can't stand—'

'Quite. I'm not sure where this yarn about the samurai sword began either, though it *is* making the rounds. But you know... you're with the general's group flying out early day after, aren't you?'

'Er...' Andrew hesitates.

'It's alright, major. I'm the one who vetted the list for our backroom people.'

'Oh, sorry to be so slow, you're the *Major* Todd-Cartwright, you're the—'

'Yes, Todd-Cartwright, exactly, seconded to...'

'Oh, right, right, understood.'

'You'll have it in the briefing files during the flight, major, so I don't mind telling you now. Thing is, I'm afraid you weren't far off target about the damned bikes.'

'How d'you mean, exactly?'

'Meaning, what we *can* confirm is that the bicycles have caught us with our pants down and far too often. They've made bloody effective use of them, the Japs. They're not amphibious, no, but they're obviously easy enough to haul across streams and rivers. Gives 'em sharp mobility through the jungle paths, you understand. And that's become rather a large thorn.'

'I've read a report about their use of local boats.'

'Both. The boats and the bloody bikes.'

'While we're ducks sitting on the main roads in our red-hot, soft armour. Not something easy to explain to...'

'Exactly. You've got it cut out for you, I'm afraid.'

Imogen lurches forward, bumping Andrew sideways.

'You know... major... I'm afraid as well! Major... major... what do your briefing papers say about the dangerously pretty Burmese girls... Do you think they may pose a problem to the *mobility* of our manly officers? And...' Imogen takes on the challenge of locating both her feet and getting them to steady in some coordination with each other while finishing her sentence, '... and... what about the local *boys*? *They're* quite fetching too, aren't...'

As Imogen crumples, she senses that Odd-Cartwheel has somehow captured her plate and Andrew has taken hold of her weight before the carpet can have it.

UNKNOWN FRUIT

'So, this Gogai chutiya, he can actually read Ingreji now? What next? Goats laying eggs?'

Kana Lalten's one good eye stares at Gopal, glinting in the flare of the lantern he is holding up. There are three others who've also been assigned lanterns, and the yellow light forms a cage of shadows on the walls of the covered parking area around the truck and the storage room. There are two men on the lorry passing down the crates, and four on the ground working in a relay line. Their labour allows no break in their rhythm when Kana Lalten sneers out his comment, but the eyes of the men holding lanterns train on Aurangzeb's replacement. Lalten hasn't addressed Gopal directly, but there is no question about the challenge contained in the insult. Gopal takes a puff of his cigarette and carries on as if he hasn't heard a word. 'Next. Twenty crates of tea. Bring them down!'

The lorry driver, a big Sardar, stands next to Gopal with a small torch focused on his own copy of the list, ticking off items as they are unloaded. He too ignores the banter, but Gopal can feel the man is tense, and not only because he has to return quickly to his resting convoy of trucks.

'One!' calls the boy on the truck who's known only as Roton's brother. The crate bobs its way from hand to shoulder to hand, out of the truck and into the storage room.

'Two!' As the crate passes Gopal, a whiff of sharp, fresh tea leaves cuts into the general odour of sweat and hanging petrol.

'Three!' The Sardar is tense, Gopal guesses, because he is used to dealing with Aurangzeb and doesn't like this little man who has taken over one of the most crucial jobs in the operation. Other gang members questioning him isn't helping matters.

'Four!' Another crate moves past. The Sardar turns to Gopal. 'You want to check?'

'Not yet,' Gopal replies, still concentrating on the list. He can feel Kana Lalten's eye still fixed upon him from the other side of the line.

'Five!' As the crate passes, Gopal makes up his mind. It takes two more crates before he gets the timing right.

'Eight.' Gopal moves with the speed of a smoke-dancer at Durga Puja. As the crate is slung between him and Kana Lalten, Gopal pushes it hard at the exact moment of its loosest contact between two pairs of hands. The momentum of the box makes it light as it flies through the air. A corner of it slams into Lalten's chest, just below the dip of his throat, just near the heart, sending him down.

Gopal is on the man before the lantern has bounced a second time. His right hand presses down on Kana's throat and the nib of his fountain pen is millimetres from the man's one surviving eye, his left hand ready for the stab into the cornea. Gopal is slightly out of breath, but other than that, his voice is quiet and even.

'I can read very well, Kana... for instance... when Ustad got hold of a copy... of your confession to the mamas in Lalbazar... I read it with him. Do you want me to repeat what you said about the boys in your toli?'

'I said... I said... I said nothing...' Lalten's voice comes out in spasms as he fights the pain in his chest.

'No? That's not what your file in Lalbazar says.'

'Gogai-da, I beg you, leave him.' One of the other men crouches next to Gopal, hands folded in supplication. Kana blinks rapidly, trying to will the nib away from his eye. 'Stupid fucker was just joking, Gogai-da, please leave him.' After a long moment, Gopal pushes his knees up from the shattered glass and steps away from Kana Lalten. He notes with satisfaction that the other man has addressed him as 'da' – 'older brother' – even though Gopal is several years younger. It's the first time this has happened, and Gopal knows that for everyone below a certain rank in the gang, he will from now on always be 'Gogai-da'.

'Go and wash your face, Kana.' Gopal's voice is just short of solicitous now. 'And then get another lantern. Someone give me an aujar.'

As one of the others brushes off the glass shards from Gopal's trousers, he bends down and jimmies open the fallen crate. He pulls out one of the packets and tears off the top. The tea looks as it should, fresh, slightly moist, and with an overpowering fragrance. The crate has stencilled on it the name BENKABARI TEA GARDEN – DARJEELING – FTGFOP.

'All right, get a move on! We haven't got all night.' Gopal goes back and stands next to the Sardar, who now seems much more relaxed despite the delay.

'Two more on the list,' says the Sardar as the last crate of tea is taken away.

'Sherry,' says Gopal.

'Four boxes.'

Just as Gopal has seen various ampoules in Bonnemaison's hotel room, strange stuff that the Frenchman likes to inject into himself, so has he also seen and tasted sherry. Out of all the alcohol with which the Phorashi has plied him, this sticky sweet stuff is Gopal's favourite. As the small crates are taken out, Gopal jimmies open all of them and checks a couple of bottles from each. 'Thiik hai,' he pronounces, and gestures for the crates to be taken away.

'And now there's an almirah. I don't know why they sent it.' The Sardar's voice edges close to an apology.

Two men lift the thing out. Gopal sees it's a half cupboard of the kind in which the shahebs like to keep their clothes – a 'dressar'. Even though the shine is mostly gone, the lanterns make gleaming yellow lines on the edges of the dark wood. The drawers are sealed with some kind of paste to hold them in place, and the corners are padded with jute sacks held in place by thin ropes that criss-cross the wood to hook around the brass handles.

The men look at the thing with questioning eyes, but Gopal quashes their curiosity. 'The shahebs pay stupid money for old furniture,' he remarks, almost to himself but not quite. It provides the explanation the crew needs and all interest seeps out as the dresser is carried into the storeroom.

Gopal puts a coded signature on his list and the Sardar does the same with his own. They exchange the lists, and the big driver gets into the Bedford without further ado. At Gopal's signal, most of the lanterns are put out and the two men open the huge shutters of the loading area and then the gates of the compound. The truck emits a grumble and rolls out into the darkness. Pulling out of the gate, the driver carefully turns into the narrow lane and shifts gear. The headlights come on, their top halves painted black, the bottom throwing a dim light before the tyres. The vehicle disappears, leaving a pocket of smoke hanging in the cold winter air.

'Okay, all of you go now, except for Roton'er bhai, Biswas, Potli and Anath. You four make sure you sweep up and there's no glass on the floor. Then make sure all the lanterns are properly out. I have to check the saman again.'

Gopal goes into the storage room and shuts the wooden doors behind him. He shoots the bolt softly, not wanting the men to think he's scared, and then he switches on the bulb. For a few minutes, he just squats on the floor, getting his breath back and putting his brain in order. Beyond the door, he can hear the chink of glass shards being swept up, but no talk. Good. As he has learnt, there are times when it's good to rob people of talk.

Carefully, Gopal opens a crate of sherry and pulls out two bottles from the crate he is supposed to deliver to Bonnemaison. He peels the off the seal from one and gently pulls out the cork. The smell is as dangerous and inviting as a long story. From a shelf, Gopal pulls down a glass he knows is kept there and, again avoiding noise, pours himself a hefty shot of the dark liquid. The labels on these bottles are slightly different from the ones he has seen previously, and there is a word, prominently printed in dark red, the meaning of which he will have to find out: A-M-O-N-T-I-L-L-A-D-O.

Gopal takes his time, smoking his cigarettes and sipping from the glass. Every now and then, he drags a crate for a small distance and jimmies it open, all with enough sound to convince anyone listening that he is doing what he has been told to do. It is only after a good hour or so, after he's sure the ones who are supposed to be sleeping are asleep and the ones guarding for the night far enough away at the compound walls, that Gopal approaches the dresser. Taking a small blade out of his pocket, Gopal gets rid of the jute and the ropes. Then he works away the dried paste holding the drawers to their slots. Making sure not to scratch the wood, he loosens the top two half drawers and slides them out.

The varnish inside is a different, lighter colour than the dark polish outside. The wood is smooth after years of use and there is a pleasure in the way the small drawers release themselves into his hands, both completely empty.

The first of the big drawers proves more difficult, but Gopal manages to get it out and lay it on the floor. It's large enough to make a bed for a small child, Gopal thinks, spacious enough to have contained someone his size not too many years ago. The paste holding the second drawer takes longer, and Gopal begins to think it's made from some different gummy material. After some time, he feels the edges come free and he gently pulls at the large, open box. The drawer slides halfway and gets stuck; Gopal can feel something is stopping it from coming out fully. As he fiddles with it, he understands what it is: something is stuck below the bottom of the drawer, blocking it from opening fully.

Gopal resists the temptation to pour himself another drink, but he pauses to light a cigarette. He waits, his ears listening for any telltale presence or absence of sound that breaks the pattern of the godown compound on a winter night. Silence, nothing, it's now late even for the mongrels that prowl the lanes. Slowly, carefully, but suddenly sure of himself, Gopal whittles away the paste from the bottom drawer. Once it feels loose, he opens it a fraction, just enough to get his slim hands and wrists inside, and feels the bottom of the drawer above. Understanding dawns along with disappointment. Somebody has nailed a small square of wood to keep the two bottom drawers from sliding open, several nails hammered into small Ls around the wood to hold it up, an extra precaution to back up the paste – incredible how much these fucking goras cared about their furniture. Tired now, Gopal leans back against the wall and looks at his bedroll. Before his other tasks, he has time tomorrow morning to get a carpenter to loosen the last drawer. The winter chill now climbing over his excitement, blankets and sleep suddenly seem to be the most rewarding course.

As he unrolls his bedding and switches off the light, Gopal plans for the visit he will make tomorrow to see the Frenchman. He goes through what he has to take and what the Phorashi is supposed to pay him for the different supplies. The crate of sherry, ten packets of the Benkabari, 'only for ze special guests' as he has been told, and...

How did someone manage to nail such a big piece of wood to the bottom of the drawer through such a small gap? Why so many nails where only four or six could have held the piece, and why not drive the nails through the wood?

His body now protesting, demanding the better sense of deep oblivion, Gopal gets up and switches on the light again. Working carefully, but now with a certain impatience, Gopal gets his arms all the way to the back of the drawer, to the furthest edge of the strange piece of wood. Using a stiff edge of metal that he carries to open locked doors, Gopal peels off the bent nails, one by one until the piece of wood comes loose in his hands. As he does this, he realizes two things: the wooden bit only makes a frame, and the whole thing is actually wrapped in a thick cloth.

As the blocking object drops into his hands, Gopal finds he can open the drawer completely. There is nothing in the drawer save what Gopal is holding, but, for some reason, his disappointment has now gone.

The thing in his hand feels a lot lighter than a slab of wood, and Gopal sees it's not exactly a square but a small rectangle, with a length of about eighteen inches and a breadth of about fourteen. The cloth is dusty but smooth to the touch, almost oily, and it is wrapped around the frame with small strips of gummed paper that Gopal knows is called 'tep'. His heart racing without logical reason, Gopal begins to peel off the strips of tape. After a while, the oil cloth relinquishes some of its rectangular shape and comes off. Gopal finds himself looking at a greyish-brown drumskin of cloth that is stretched under and across the wooden frame, held taut by tiny nails which attach the edges of the cloth to the wood at regular intervals. There are two chips of wood stuck into slots in each of the four corner joins, and a small cluster of words towards one corner, scrawled in what looks like pencil: *Toile – PC – '80* – and a word he can't make out in some language that's not English.

As Gopal examines the thing, he notices the edges of the thick, stiff cloth are almost white. He feels an unevenly bumpy texture under his fingers on the other side of the cloth, and he turns the square drum frame over.

The colour hits him as nothing has done ever before.

It's as if the light of the bulb has just gone brighter, but only on the picture in his hands. It's as if he can pick up one of the pieces of strange red-yellow fruit and put it in his mouth, feel it splitting around his teeth, as if he can pick up the white jug and bring the spout to his mouth and there will be milk in it. And yet, clearly this English chutiya didn't know how to paint too well: only two of the red-brown fruits look real, the others are half-painted, shoddy, little square blocks of colour flung here and there on the curves; and the yellow big limes are painted as if the man is practising how to draw them, as if he has never seen one before; Gopal can see all the marks the fellow has made, each slash of paint clearly visible as if the novice was too inept or too lazy to hide his tracks like a proper artist. And yet, if he yanks the thick tablecloth that snakes between the fruit and the limes, the things will fly off the table like balls and thud on the floor – he can hear the noise they will make. He can feel his fingers curl around the edge of the wooden table, and he can feel the scrape of the grey wall behind the table under his hands.

With a panic he has never known, not realizing that his anxiety is actually a new kind of thrill, Gopal leans the painting against a crate and steps back. From a distance, the spooky thing changes yet again, becomes completely real, like a scene first caught from the corner of the eye that keeps reeling you in. A tall white jug, a jumble of red unknown fruit and big limes on a crumpled tablecloth on a dining table; reflected afternoon light coming from somewhere and playing different games with each object.

Similar to the tiny picture in the pretty boy's wallet except in colour, same kind of black lines dancing... but a real painting. The same kind of painting. The kind of painting someone would carry a small photo of in his wallet, like a picture of a loved one. The kind of painting someone would go to great lengths to hide.

FOUR

Shifting Islands

25 DECEMBER 1941 – 8 AUGUST 1942

AT 9.30 A.M. ON CHRISTMAS Day, 1941 – or Boro Din, Big Day, as it's called here in Bengal – there are huge piles of garbage outside both the side entrance to the Great Eastern Hotel on Waterloo Street and its rear exit on Dacres Lane. Since this is the detritus from a top-class hotel, it is highly organized rubbish. The food waste from the different Christmas Eve parties, both public and private, has been stuffed into about twenty bins of corrugated tin, with only the occasional stalk of a lily or some scrap of greasy paper napkin sticking out from under the lids. This being a cool enough winter morning, you have to be very close to the bins to catch the smell of the rot beginning to form inside.

The food waste is largely outside the rear entrance, and two hotel darwaans watch over it, alert for rats and ready to shoo away any stray dogs. The rest of the garbage is stacked outside the side entrance on Waterloo Street that leads to the kitchens and back offices. Here, the bins exude no smell at all, most of what they contain being burst crackers and paper hats and such, but as the sun ripens in the sky above, there is a heady smell growing from the crates and boxes of empty bottles piled there. People walking past this outdoor laboratory can inhale the cocktail whiff of stale beer, dregs of turning wine and the final fumes from recently emptied whisky, gin and martini bottles as they all heat up together.

While the guards at the rear entrance are waiting to oversee the convoy of handcarts from the Calcutta Corporation, on Waterloo Street an assistant manager and two cleaners wait for the Armenian to arrive in his lorry. As his boys clear the empty bottles, the Armenian and the manager will both keep a tally. Once everything is loaded, the Armenian will sign a receipt leading to an invoice that will lead to a cheque. Every empty bottle of beer will fetch the hotel one anna, sixteen bottles making one rupee, while the rest will be sold at about thirty bottles a rupee. The beer bottles will be reused and, later during the war, people will find themselves pouring lager brewed in northern Punjab from bottles made in Germany, the glass puckering to form the name 'Becks' in Teutonic script. The assistant manager has already counted the empty bottles collected over the previous week leading up to last night's big ball given by the Fort William brass to see off their troops. The total, from all varieties of alcohol, bottles small and large, comes to around 2,000 rupees. Last year, the same manager had done a similar count over the same period and the total had been 435 rupees. The man has heard that there were more Indians invited last night than ever before, but he doesn't for a moment put down the increase of consumption to this factor.

The jamadars of the Calcutta Corporation, who take away the food waste, are a bit late today and the hotel darwaans are getting slightly worried. Rumours are rife that the lower-caste employees of the Calcutta Municipal Corporation, the ones who deal with the city's waste and sanitation, are getting restive. The jute-mill workers' strikes across the last two years and the tram drivers' and conductors' agitations in the last few months have clearly trickled down to these dirty maithors, and it's only a matter of time before the day comes when the city's daily mess piles up, uncleared, inundating the streets under a huge stink.

With six or seven political parties criss-crossing the city conducting their rallies and meetings, all of them promising all sorts of people every kind of ganja and opium under the sun, from voting rights, to removal of caste, to whole independent countries made up of only Hindus or only Muslims, countries from which the goras will magically disappear, what can you expect? It's not a surprise that these maithor bastards think they can take all day to clear bins that were empty on this day last year by 7 a.m. Of course, there are a lot more gora soldier-types in town, so there were probably many more parties on the night before Boro Din, but still, this is disciplined Calcutta and not some provincial backwater like Delhi, Patna or Lucknow where local anarchy finds gaps. Here, ten minutes late is ten minutes late, and two and a half hours late is an outrage.

If you were to stage this as a contemporary play in Calcutta today, you could do a lot with this moment of waiting. For instance, the hotel could be built up of several spare platforms at different heights, with back-projected film or slides to help you change the 'rooms'. You could have a whole soundtrack matched to the changing lights and the exit and entry of characters. You could even perform the play on a field, under huge tents, moving the audience from scene to scene, with actors-cum-ushers sheepdogging people from dramatic moment to dramatic environment; you could even bring in live stray dogs and actual garbage with actual stench to create verisimilitude, but then, to do all that, you'd need to be some avant-garde West German director with an obscene budget from some arts institution in Munich or Cologne. For now, though, we are in the Calcutta of the early forties, where all the two dozen Germans left behind in September 1939 by their escaping merchant ships are either in prison or in hiding.

It's not that Calcutta doesn't have any theatre at this point in history. On the contrary, Bengali theatre at this moment has the most vibrant dramatic groups in India, both professional and amateur. The theatres of north Calcutta in 1941 also have some of the best scenery-makers anywhere, definitely much better than the ones who produce that unrealistic nineteenth-century rubbish for the theatre and film sets in Bombay and Poona. As Nirupama points out in her interviews, people like her father, Niranjan Majumdar, and other set and light designers were doing work that was groundbreaking in terms of Indian theatre. They couldn't match Broadway and Hollywood for the big, shiny numbers, of course, but these designers at the Star Theatre or Srirangan Theatre would have made a pretty good job of creating the area around the staff entrance. They would have made a very realistic, towering white hotel facade disappear into the fly gallery; they would have exactly reproduced the neat lettering above the hotel bakery; they would have brought in a couple of saplings to represent the trees with the wire cages around their trunks, and they would have made a fine replica of the 'footpath' or pavement. All of it would have been very believable for the day, but the designers would probably have left out all of the rubbish piled up on the kerb – this may be the moment when radical modern theatre begins in Bengal, but there are still some things that are considered too obscene to be brought on stage, such as sex and garbage.

Those theatres at that time were striving for realism. But there's nothing stopping us from going briefly into a much older Bengali theatre form, the nakedly melodramatic jatra acting, to contrast with the semi-realistic stage decor. In a jatra, the young smuggler Gopal, alias Pocket Gogai, would have sidled in from stage left and crossed the bakery doorway, whistling casually, carrying a heavy sack from which would come the sound of glass gently clinking against glass. Actually, the orchestra in the pit would have created that sound and then paused exactly as Gopal adjusted the sack to stop the bottles from banging. Another section of the orchestra might have continued to make background effects of whinnying horses and jhurrie-gaadis, the hand-pulled rickshas and thhelas. This being well before tape-recorded sound was used in theatres, there would have been no way to give extra aural depth by adding the faint clamour and horns of the traffic on the main road, just thirty yards further away.

The cruel Phorashi khansama, Bonnemaison, would stand on the steps of the entrance, slapping and kicking a cowering assistant cook as Smuggler Gopal approaches. As they come face to face, their eyes meet with a clash of cymbals. A look of terror crosses Bonnemaison's florid visage, a look that can be seen even in the furthest corners of the audience, and he suddenly ceases his oppressions. Gopal is tall and well built, towering over the fat foreigner with the quivering, pointy moustaches.

One of the four heavy microphones suspended over the floodlights at head height catches the dialogue.

'You rakkhosh! You monstrous, perverted French devil! I have heard about you and your cruel ways! Now, today, you meet your long overdue comeuppance!'

The French devil would recoil in fear and horror as the young hero advanced.

The driver of the small delivery van parks and pulls the handbrake. 'Do you want me to wait, Gogai-da?'

'No, it'll take time here. You go on to Russell Street, you know the Turf Club? Aurangzeb-bhai will meet you there.'

'And after that?'

'Then you go to 300. Aurangzeb-bhai knows.'

'I was asking because of the petrol...'

'There are two jerrycun in the back. Both full. One should be enough. Don't let the mamas see you filling up though, be discreet and do it on a side street.'

Gopal gets out, throws his cigarette at a gutter grille, goes to the rear of the blue van. An official-looking red cross is painted on a white circle across the two doors at the back and there is a padlock holding them shut. Gopal takes out a key, opens the doors and reaches inside to carefully pull down two crates of different sizes, both covered with jute sacking. He locks the door, hands the key back to the driver and carries the crates towards the hotel, careful not to slip on the wet mess around the empty bottles. The van putters away past the row of waiting horse carriages. As he passes, Gopal notices the Christmas smell from the bakery, different from the smell of normal shaheb bread, a sweet and pungent cake smell, coming from those stick-things Bonnemaison calls 'kaanel', and from burnt raisins. As he reaches the doorway, the cloud of stale alcohol from the stacks of empty bottles fights with the aroma of the bread.

The hotel guard and Gopal exchange nods as he walks past, while the 'nurse' ignores him. There is a small area of chessboard marble at the foot of the back staircase, and on it, since last week, stands a small Christmas tree, festooned with shiny, brightly coloured balls and stars. Gopal hasn't seen the big tree near the reception desk but he has heard it described by one of the doormen – 'huge thing, almost as tall as an elephant, hundreds of balls and stars, and tied up with little electric bulbs, blinking like a demon with several night-eyes. Enough wads of cottonwool to fill a hospital, all scattered below to look like snow. Every December, the goras do this. Every year, this monster arrives, orphaned from Darjeeling and sent down from the high mountains.'

Looking at the doorway light reflecting off the red, yellow, blue and silver balls on the spiky little tree, Gopal thinks how they could be rendered by someone making a certain kind of painting. Then he notices the few bits of cottonwool scattered around the bottom of the thin trunk, the stuff already brown-grey from the kitchen smoke, the mess sucking up all definition.

Bonnemaison is sitting in his little office making a list, and he shows neither pleasure nor annoyance at Gopal's arrival, which is unusual. After a while, he gets up from his desk and quickly inspects the tea, smelling it and checking the packets for damp.

'*Ça marche*,' he says and then turns to the smaller crate and points a question.

'Sherry,' says Gopal.

'Ah, yes. If not, our English friends will die even before the Japanese reach here.'

'When the Japanese will come?'

'Who knows! Maybe before the rains, or surely after. It depend 'ow many of them can be killed by malaria before, or 'ow many of the English and Indian *they* can kill before.' Bonnemaison's breaks into a grin. 'Until then, we can dance and hope, hein, my little monkey? Bring this, *allez!*'

As the Phorashi leads the way, Gopal sees there is a real spring in his step. It's as if the man has grown larger overnight, not fatter but more muscular and energetic. The tension from last morning is gone, the nasty spray of jokes dissipated, the serrated temper put away, replaced by a calmer, lower, more confident energy that Gopal has not seen earlier. Since there is no reference to it, since there are no terrified or miserable faces in the kitchen, clearly last night's dinner for the big ball has been a success.

They walk into a service lift and, to Gopal's surprise, Bonnemaison moves the crank to the up arrow instead of down towards the cellar. As the cage goes up, marking each floor with a loud clank, Bonnemaison notes the boy's expression and reaches across and pinches his cheek, but without smiling. 'You think you know everything, hein, my little smuggler boy? You think so, *n'est ce pas?*'

'No, m'syu, but I thinking alcohol is always going down-i-stairs...'

'Not always, my little spy, not always.' As the lift reaches the top floor, Bonnemaison's large hand expertly moves the lever to the stop position, clanking the two sets of grilles into alignment. He walks out, leaving the gates open, disabling the cage. As Gopal follows, he notes this particular corridor isn't in as good repair as the rest of the floors. The paint on the walls is flaking in places. Many of the doors have lost their polish, leaving matte wood with ghosts of room numbers where the metal numerals have fallen off. The brass has dulled on most of the door handles, though not all. As they approach the end of the corridor, the light brightens, sunlight coming in from a set of large windows and an open door that leads on to the terrace.

'You know, they have some very nice rooms on this floor, very... *discret*, but they are on the other side, and on the south side is the tennis court but you can only reach from the *ascenseur* in the other wing. This is... just for a few people in the hotel, these rooms.'

'For to istay?'

'Not for to stay, non. Usually for other... projects...' Bonnemaison winks as he stops at the last but two doors on the left and takes out a set of keys. Standing behind him, holding the crate, his arms hurting a bit now, Gopal is again aware of the Phorashi's bulk. Suddenly, Gopal finds himself wishing he had brought along the gun.

The set has changed and there is a dramatic spotlight on the demon chef as he holds down a puny Gopal, strangling him. As the heroic but powerless Gopal struggles to fend off death, the rakkhosh Frenchman releases an echoing laugh, 'Hah-hah-hah! You puny little smuggler boy, you thought you could fight the great Bonnemaison? Hah-hah-hah! Now you meet your sad end! No one will find you in this great maze! The rats will strip all the meat from your body! Then the ants will carry away all your bones!'

As Bonnemaison fiddles with his keys, Gopal imagines the man talking to Aurangzeb or even Ustad, 'The boy? That Gogai? He left many hours ago! I paid him for the goods, yes, as agreed, and then he left! I wonder where he could have gone with all that monnaie!' No, the Frenchman couldn't imagine he would get away with that. Five months ago, when he was nothing but a small-time pickpocket, yes, maybe, but not now.

Gopal forces himself to concentrate. One lock, then a second, and then a third one that turns three times. Unlike other room doors, this one opens outwards, and Bonnemaison steps back as he pulls it open, revealing another door just behind the first one. The second door looks like it's covered in some sort of grey wool. The chef uses another key and then pushes this grey door inwards. The blast of cool air makes Gopal let off an involuntary shiver. Bonnemaison switches on a big bulb and shuts both doors behind them. There is a small window on the back wall, with thick opaque glass. In the mix of the light from the window and the small bulb, Gopal can now see they are surrounded by a small library of bottles, shelves of them, most of them stacked horizontally, their necks poking out of a square beehive of wood, many of them covered with dust, here and there, some bottles connected with fine bridges of cobweb.

Bonnemaison indicates to Gopal that he should put the crate down. He shows no sign of wanting to commit murder. There is a small, proud smile under the waxed moustache as he turns to regard his treasure.

'I begin this in *vingt-neuf*, in 1929, when I first come here with my maitre. *Normalment*, wine is to keep below the ground, in the cellar. After, even when I was back in Lyon, regularly I send them good bottles and tell them to not touch but keep, *tu comprends*? They would write to me, only the manager and the maitre'd, and sometimes even send a telegramme asking about which bottles to open for some special guest. This, *ma cocotte*, is the real treasure of the Great Eastern Hotel. Not even many of the big, big maharaja-nawab have this collection of wine!'

Gopal takes it all in, the smell of the dust heavy despite the ice-cool air, the small paper labels that hang, tied from the necks of some bottles, many with just the year scrawled on them, a few with some code, in a handwriting that reminds him of the signature on the back of the canvas from last night.

Suddenly, Gopal thinks of a club sandwich that Bonnemaison once gave him to eat. 'Each layer is different! Can you taste? This is the only interesting thing the Americains have given to food! It's not formidable, but it's interesting, the melange of base ingredients!' Gopal then didn't know the word 'ingredients' but he found out the meaning: different kinds of aanaaj and maangsho and diim, each different thing was an 'ingredient'.

Today, in his mind, he tries to balance the clubsanwhich through which he has passed. He has left the godown in Kasba, the first ingridyaant; second, the city streets; third, outside the hotel with its aura of authority and spilled waste; fourth, the chef's domain, the kitchen factory; and then, right on top, just under the toasted bread, where the surprising fried egg provided a completely different taste and texture, this strange treasure house opening off from a dusty, almost abandoned corridor. Gopal tries to bite into the whole sandwich and fails, just as he had with the actual thing. 'Take smoll-bite, it is the only way,' Bonnemaison had advised him. Here, in this cold hospital ward of precious bottles, Gopal now reminds himself of that advice.

Bonnemaison has lit a cigarette and is surveying his gold. He turns to Gopal and narrows his eyes.

'Now, what I tell you, you listen carefully, yes?'

Gopal nods.

'I want you to talk to your Ustaade, yes?'

Gopal reaches into his pocket for a cigarette, pulls it out and bobs his head, asking for permission to smoke. Bonnemaison ignores the gesture and Gopal takes the plunge – he pulls out matches and, for the first time, lights up his own cigarette in the Phorashi's presence.

'Listen carefully, yes? I don't know when the Japanese get here. I don't know if they don't get here, *jamais*, never, but they bomb the city like they bomb Nanking, yes? If they bomb, this room is not good for bombing, it's a disaster. But! If they get here, I don't want those yellow *cochons* to drink a single drop of this wine. Also, if they have Calcutta then you can be sure the Boches will also come here. For them, I would personally poison the best bottles here!'

The big man indicates Gopal should give him a bottle from the crate of sherry. He takes it and wrinkles his nose as he opens it, before reaching to open a case with glass doors and pulling out two glasses. He pours two large slugs, clinks the glasses himself before handing one to Gopal.

'It would be a waste, a big waste, of ten year, twelve year of work! So, you talk to your Ustaade. I have some... possibility of customers... for some bottles, but not here, in other part of India, quite far away. Other bottles I can give you a list and price. So, for my own customer, you arrange delivery of the bottles in special cases. For the other bottles, you find customers, yes? *Tu saisis?* Understa—'

'Yes, understand, m'syu. You want to move all this bottles?'

'Not all! There are nearly eight hundred bottles! So, all bottles, no! Just some special ones! Some we keep for the Americain generals, hein?' He taps his head, indicating that intelligence needs to be deployed.

'Markin? Coming here?'

'Yes. So they say to me.'

Gopal wonders what it would take to come here with Aurangzeb and Gourangzeb one night, hold a knife to the fat prick's throat and take the whole lot. Bonnemaison takes a swig of the sherry and grins.

'Now, listen carefully, yes? In case you think you can come here and take them all in a little truck, yes, in *case* you think like this?'

'*Mais non, m'syu!*' The sliver of French escapes Gopal before he can stop it.

'This wine is worth monnaie because it is very good, no, great, wine! *Du vin!* So why I have this special room? And why not in cellar downstairs? Because this shit city and this shit country is the *enemy* of wine. We don't make for this kind of heat, our wine. I find the cellars too humide, too much wet. A little bit is good, *l'humidite*, but here it is too much! Same with the cold. *Alors*. It is a folie, but I get them, the hotel, to make this room and I make it cool with air condition I can control, and I test after a month, after two month, after six, to see what it does to the wine. Only after, I bring more bottles, the really good ones, understand? Ten days, maybe even five days for some, in bad storing and it is finish, the wine!' Bonnemaison smashes one palm against another, 'It become *vinaigre*, yes?'

Gopal reaches for the bottle of sherry, trying to keep his hand steady. Bonnemaison's large hand comes down on top of his.

'Wait, you little *salope*. Listen!' He removes his hand, letting Gopal pour a second drink. 'So, you sell the bottles, but you don't know how much is the value of each bottle. You get some... little... monnaie, some anna, some paisa, yes? With me, you sell slowly, a few bottle at a time, the rest are here, in the best storing. When you move bottles to, maybe, Bombay, Karachi, Rajasthan, Lahore, Hyderabad or Mysore, I give you special cases so they are okay for three-four-five days on the train. My customers pay me in gold or dollars, and I pay you the share in the same! If... when... the Japonais take Calcutta, this rupee will be just toilet paper!'

Gopal takes a small bite of this information and makes sure to chew thoroughly. There would have to be a lot of trust involved. On both sides. He was now clearly the designated go-between and not Aurangzeb, who would need to be handled carefully, no matter what came of this deal. The Frenchman seems to think they have a network of reliable couriers who can travel the length of the country. They would have to find customers for some of the bottles, but at prices fixed by the Frenchman. Payment arrangements would have to be worked out. Yes, there would have to be a lot of trust.

The Japanese were coming. Money could soon be worth nothing – Gopal has a vision of the little paper thhongas for holding dry dal and spices being made from the big hundred-rupee notes instead of old newspapers. The Japanese were coming, perhaps. But first, the Americans were definitely coming. The Bonnemaison talking to him today is very different from the man who has absently pushed his half-hard cock into Gopal's mouth the night before last. Or maybe it is Gopal himself who has changed overnight into someone else.

'You listen carefully, yes? Becoz I trust you, you understand? You talk about this only to your... Ustaade, yes? No one else, yes?' Bonnemaison puts the stopper back into the open bottle.

'Yes, m'syu, only to Ustad.'

'*Allez, mon chou!*' Bonnemaison shoves the bottle back into the crate, takes the cigarette out of Gopal's hand and dips it out into the dregs of one of the wine glasses. 'Take this downstair again!'

Gopal lifts the crate and follows Bonnemaison out of the wine room.

'And one more thing.' As the chef locks the doors his tone shifts to a growl. 'With wine, you have to listen to what I say. Las'time I ask specifically for fino sherry! Fino! Not this heavy amontillado you have got!'

The Big Man has arranged permission for me to visit the hotel and explore even the collapsed areas. Visiting the place now, I love the vast, flat roof and its high-noon melancholy. I'm entranced by the ghost of the half-collapsed corridor, doors and walls on either side escorting the devastation which is open to the sky, I love the way the light complains over the rotted wood of the doors and the cracked floor, the dust-furred tripe of thick electric wires that hang down from the grimy ceiling and, yes, the ever-present cobwebs. But there is no way you could store decent wine on the top floor of a Calcutta building, no matter how efficient the air conditioning. The heat is most intense here and so is the fluctuating humidity, far more so than in the cellars where a bit of damp can actually help keep very old corks from going brittle. No, the wine won't tolerate it, and neither will the story.

Bonnemaison will take Gopal to show him his precious stash of wine and have almost exactly this conversation, but not yet, not until much later. And the stash will be stored in just such a strong room but deep in the cellars and nowhere near the roof. Today, in his office, the Frenchman finishes checking the crate of Darjeeling from the Benkabari Tea Estate and turns to the crate of sherry. He does snarl at Gopal about it being the wrong kind of sherry before opening a bottle and sniffing it. He makes a face. '*Pas terrible*,' he says, as there is a knock on the door. Bonnemaison pulls the jute covering over the crates.

'Kaun 'ai? Come in!'

'Barbora, chef! Bonjour!' The manager of the hotel comes in and shakes the Frenchman's hand. 'Happy Christmas, maestro! A great triumph, last night, a great triumph!'

'Appy Christmas to you also. *Joyeux Noel*, thank you! Always 'appy to be appreciated!' Bonnemaison turns to Gopal and snaps his fingers, 'You! Boy! Wait outside!'

Gopal ducks his head in a salaam and slips out of the chef's office. After a few minutes, Barbora Saheb pokes his head out of the door and summons an old room-waiter who has been waiting a few feet away.

'Shyam Lal!'

Barbora hands the waiter a bottle wrapped in shiny silver paper with a red-and-green pattern. The waiter seems to know what he has to do with the gift, and he takes himself off. After a few minutes, Barbora emerges himself, clutching a brown paper bag from which poke out the tops of what Gopal recognizes as two bottles of his sherry. As the kitchen staff all stop work and come to attention, the manager strides away, eyes ostentatiously raking the kitchen for signs of dirt and misdemeanour.

HOWRAH

Shyam Lal has been working at the hotel for twenty-five years now, from the year following the one when electricity came to the establishment, and he likes to boast that he can tell the exact time by his feet. This morning, Shyam Lal's aching legs and feet tell him it's well past ten in the morning, well past the end of his twelve-hour night shift which normally finishes at 9 a.m. But today, the 8th of January in the white people's calendar, his feet are also feeling all the hours they have worked since Christmas Eve, a good fortnight ago.

These last few days, from Christmas Eve and the Bada Din through New Year's Eve and 1st January have not been normal. Through the pockets of his black uniform trousers has crackled the largest amount of paper money he has made in twenty years of working as a room waiter. Christmas and New Year's always does bring out the generosity of the guests, even the most tight-fisted ones – who are usually the richest – but the last two weeks have been exceptional. Where people would give him four annas they have given eight, where they would give eight annas they have given whole rupees, the ones who would give the huge five-rupee tips to show off to their friends, those princes and zamindars have flung ten-rupee notes at him. It's almost as if the paper rupaiya is in its last days, about to be replaced by some other medium of exchange. Shyam Lal doesn't mind. He knows he must have collected more than four months' worth of salary and tip earnings in this one lunatic period. Possibly nearly a hundred and fifty rupees, if one was to count all the coins and paper together.

Today, Shyam Lal deposits his last breakfast trolley on the first-floor service area and heads straight for the lower staff changing room. He changes into his pant-shirt and chappals, deftly transferring the final stash of paper cash from a hiding place behind a defunct switch panel into a discreet pocket on his waistband. The coins tied up in a large handkerchief are a problem, there are so many of them, but Shyam Lal isn't one of the hotel's top veteran waiters for nothing. He takes the bundle and puts it on his head, and fixes his uniform turban on top of it. With him, he carries a cloth bag with a clean waiter's uniform inside. As he heads to the door, the coins feel nicely cool on his bald head. He can hear them chinking softly, and he begins to sing to cover the noise – what was that one saheb singing? It's not as though he's doing something illegal, taking home his own tips, it's just that the gateman and 'nurse' at the back entrance have taken to putting pressure on waiters to part with a tithe as they leave, and Shyam Lal isn't in the mood to argue or even wear the envy of those guard dogs, to have them tell everyone else how much Old Baldy has recently earned.

The gateman does a perfunctory check of Shyam Lal's body and the cloth bag. 'Oh, maharaja! Why are you wearing your waiter's pagdi today?'

'Photograph,' says Shyam Lal disdainfully, showing him the uniform in his cloth bag. 'My sister's son is getting married, and they want to see the uncle in his finery.'

'Photograph!' says the guard, eyes opening in wonder. 'Dowry is big, then?'

'Yes, the girl's father is an engine driver. He drives the engine for the Toofan Mail, you know the one that goes all the way to Kalka above Delhi? That one. So what they'll give is very good... so you also have to spend a bit, you see?'

Shyam Lal swings jauntily out into the pavement and walks past the hotel bakery, ignoring the smell of uncleared garbage hanging in the air. He has a good voice, and he allows it some freedom as he moves away from the hotel, keeping beat with the coins rhythmically massaging his scalp.

Just past the bakery, he passes the young Bengali saheb he has seen before. In that third-floor mem's room, but not since the mem left in a hurry two-three months ago. Now putting something in his roofless car. For some reason, now staring at Shyam Lal.

'You! Just a minute!'

Shyam Lal keeps walking, singing as if he hasn't heard, the coins keeping the beat.

'O bhai! You there in the pagdi! Can I ask you something?'

A babu in a dhoti-shirt and shawl comes up to Shyam Lal and tugs at his arm.

'Arre bhai, that gentleman is calling you!'

The babu with his thick black spectacles is on his left, while the young man in the jacket is now accosting him from the right. It's broad daylight, but Shyam Lal is suddenly uneasy.

'Yes, saheb? What is it?'

'This thing you're singing. What raag is it?' The young man is smiling at him.

'I don't know about raags, saheb, I was just singing a tune.'

The babu is now also involved. 'Yes!' He waves an approving finger at the young man. 'Good thing you asked him! I was also curious!'

'It's a raag, isn't it? Are you sure you don't know what raag it is, bhai? I just want to know, it's so beautiful.'

'Sir...' Shyam Lal immediately shrinks into his waiter's persona, 'sir, please forgive me. I just work at the hotel and maybe I heard it when some guest was singing...'

The babu is twisting on the balls of his feet, his black shoes scraping, looking intensely at the ground and snapping the fingers of his left hand, calling his brain to heel. 'Guest, guest, guest... oitaa impossible!'

'Perhaps it was playing on a gramophone, saheb.

'*Impossible!*' The babu almost shouts the English word, his head moving from side to side as if an invisible giant has him on puppet strings.

As the other two watch, the man stops, takes off his spectacles, closes his eyes and begins to hum blindly, more or less replicating Shyam Lal's tune. Then he stops. He opens his eyes and grins triumphantly at the young man. 'Shree. But this is Raag Shree!'

The young man reaches out and grabs the babu's elbows in congratulation. 'Yes, of course! Shree! You are right, moshai! Shree!' Shyam Lal makes to move away, but the babu is now on him.

'You didn't hear this on the gramophone!'

'Babu, I...'

'Are you from Darbhanga?' The excitement seems to be rising even higher in the babu.

'No, babu, I'm from near Banaras.'

'Because... because...' The babu turns to his fellow aficionado, 'This is pure Dhrupad, what he was singing. A dhamar in Shree, and somehow exactly singing in the style of the Darbhanga gharana. Very typical, almost for sure a cheez from the great Pandit Meghnath Sharma! How strange to find a gem in the, in the... in such ordinary soil!'

'I know the name but never actually heard him.' Kedar wrinkles his eyebrows. 'But why do you say gramophone impossible?'

'Because... the Panditji loathed the recording business. He was famous for hating it. Never allowed his voice to be captured!'

Shyam Lal sees the two men engrossed and takes himself off, not worrying about the coins chinking into his scalp.

'Ah. I see.'

'Ah.'

'Wonder where that fellow got it from?' They both look around, searching for the turbaned singer, but the man has been swallowed by the crowded lane.

'Yes... you had to have heard Meghnath Sharma in person.' The babu polishes his spectacles on the corner of his long dhoti-shirt. 'Magical. *Directly* from above. Straight from *god*. I heard him many times, which is why you are lucky I could identify it for you.'

'Yes, I see, moshai. Thank you.'

'My pleasure,' says the babu in English. 'You are most welcome.' He turns on his heel, adjusts his glasses and strides away.

Kedar lowers himself into the MG and pulls the list out of his jacket pocket.

20 chicken patties
20 meat patties (mutton, not beef)
30 cheese puffs

2 kg cheese straws (tightly packed – to be kept)
4 kg sweet biscuits (no shortbread, no coconut)
One dozen chocolate pastries (boats)
One dozen lemon tarts
4 big loaves of bread (sliced)

He sees each item is ticked and is pleased with himself. How a family of six, including perhaps two children, will consume most of this food in a train journey that doesn't even stretch overnight, he doesn't quite know. But his is not to question why, his is but to purchase and deliver. His mind is now infected by the waiter's song. '*Fa-na-ka-ta, faa-naa-kaa-taa, fanakata laa-hey Shiva!*' He guns the engine before putting the car into gear.

Making his way out of Waterloo Street, Kedar takes a quick right and then a left along the tall railings of Governor House. Despite the chaos of the last few days, the big soldiers with the MP armbands are keeping the traffic flowing freely on the streets around the mansion from where the Viceroys used to rule India. As he drives by at 20 mph, Kedar can fool himself into imagining it's the 9th of January 1938, the year he first got his car. The gardeners working on the governor's winter lawns seem not to have moved for three years, except for the sandbags piled high at various points in the garden. It's only when he winds his way around a corner of Dalhousie Square and heads towards the river on Old Court House Street that the real city engulfs him again. As he approaches the warehouses lining Strand Road, soldiers lumber about, stacking sandbags for anti-aircraft emplacements on the roofs of the red-brick buildings. Kedar can almost imagine dirty white barrage balloons rising from ropes, as in London, hanging in the winter sky like misshapen roshogollas. Even before he reaches the corner, Kedar can hear the cacophony. Even before his eyes drop back to the road, he can feel the solid, unmoving mesh of vehicles and bodies clogging Strand Road. Though the exodus has begun just before the New Year, it seems as if the whole city has just had the same idea at the same time this morning: let's get to Howrah Station.

Kedar glances at his watch – a quarter past eleven, the Patna train leaves at half-past twelve. Normal driving from here to Howrah would take ten to fifteen minutes, but today it could take even two hours. There's nothing for it but to try. As he tries to wheedle his way into the turgid flow of cars and buses, a policeman comes up to the MG and raps the front right tyre lightly with his stick.

'Wait for my signal, saheb! I will tell you when to go!'

The touch of the bamboo cane on the tyre feels as if the man has rapped a nerve on Kedar's own knee. He thinks of Borun-kaku, who would have promptly got out of the car and remonstrated with the insolent mama before taking down the number on his shoulder. He briefly considers doing this himself but lets it go – he is not Borun, and he has other fish to fry. As he watches the constable move around the snarl, he remembers the waiter and his beautiful tune. Kedar doesn't have much of a voice but he's not afraid of singing, especially when on his own. As he watches the mama balancing traffic, moving through the maze of vehicles, Kedar tries to match each phrase of the melody to the man's movement. *Aaaa-aa-aa-aaaaa-aaaaa* – the man dances past a grumbling lorry and stops a delivery van just behind; *hmm-hmmm-hmm* – the sun catches the turban as the mama smacks his cane into a ricksha-walla's calf, making the puller first stumble forwards in pain, then backwards in fear; *hmm-hmm-aaaa* – the mama blows his whistle, putting his arm up, palm to the sky, not unlike a classical singer protesting his innocence as some divine melody takes over him; *fanakata laa-hey Shiva!* – the man has an exchange with a Sardar taxi driver, the Sikh leans out angrily and slams his hand against the door of his taxi, the tower of luggage tied to the roof of the taxi shakes and teeters and Kedar wonders if it will fall on the policeman's head. No. The man carries on, sloughing off the abuse spewing from the taxi driver as if a soiled sheet off his back.

All around him, the winter morning is streaked with panic, but Kedar feels strangely distant from it, as if he is the only one who knows the sky isn't about to fall on his head. The singing makes him light-headed and observant. He notes that the mama, too, has a confidence that comes when you're surrounded by people in a state of anxiety that you don't share. After a while, he adds to his analysis the fact that the lowly constable has a superior watching him, an Anglo inspector no less. Standing in the shade of a portico on the right, sola topi pushed slightly back. A clipboard in the crook of his arm, a cigarette in a holder smouldering in front of a thin moustache that cuts across an impassive coffee-brown face. A man clearly thinking about his forehand lob. Kedar calls out to him.

'I say, Errol! Over here!'

The inspector's head snaps around, searching for the voice calling him by his first name. His neck moves like a bird sensing danger, his eyes jagging here and there before he spots Kedar. His shoulders drop in slight relief, and he adjusts his sola topi before sauntering out of the shade to the green convertible.

'You little bugger. What are you doing here? You planning to jump ship too?'

'No, Errol, I'm delivering much-needed rations to a departing family.'

The inspector looks at the tiny rear seat of the car and sees the two large brown paper bags from the bakery of the Great Eastern Hotel.

'Aha. A departing family with extremely expensive taste, I see. Where are they going?'

'Mungher. On the Patna train.'

'Mungher? Oh, I see, *that* family!'

'Yes. Their country estate. Shouldn't be a priority for the Japanese Air Force, or so they hope.'

'Hm. Patna departs when?'

'Half-past twelve.'

'Well, you won't get there, man. Might as well hand over the goodies to hard-working public servants.'

'Such as yourself?' Kedar slips into the voice of a cricket commentator on the radio. 'Inspector E.J.K. Ghose of the Calcutta Police. Whose chief duty seems to be to sit pretty in the shade. Smoking away, while all chaos breaks loose around him.'

'Precisely! I'll... show you my duty, you bugger!' The inspector looks around and shouts out to his constable. 'Havaldar! Idhar aao!'

The policeman freezes in mid-semaphore, turns and jogs over to his superior.

'Take this man's license and make him pull the car over to the side where he can't block traffic!' The havaldar stiffens, salutes, turns to Kedar and then subsides. People about to have their driver's license confiscated do not usually wear such wide grins.

'I'll wire Keya and inform her that you delayed me.' Kedar taps a fresh cigarette on the back of his hand. 'That should make your next tête-à-tête with your sister Deirdre quite interesting.'

Errol Ghose grins back. 'I can also send a telegram to our dear Miss Dutta with some information that would make things quite, shall we say, *quite* hot for *you*, you little peacock!' He whirls on his subordinate and snarls mildly. 'Arre, idiot, dekhta kya hai? Saheb ka gaadi pass karo, jaldi!' What are you looking at, you idiot? Make a way for the saheb's car!

The constable sprints into the melee, waving his stick and blowing his whistle, waving at Kedar to follow.

Kedar nods to Ghose as he lets out the clutch. 'Drink? Club? Friday?'

'Many drinks, Larry-boy! Entirely on you!'

'Tally-ho! Pip pip!'

'Tally-ho!'

As Kedar inches forward, he sees the way blocked by a long Studebaker and two identical Dodge 8s, each flying the flag of a princely state on the nose. All three automobiles are crowned by stacks of expensive luggage tied to their roof racks. Standing on the running boards of the Studebaker and the first Dodge, holding on to the roof racks with one hand, are eight large, uniformed guards in bright yellow turbans, scabbards in their sashes, shielding their masters from the gaze of the hoi polloi. The constable is dwarfed by the giant guards, squeezed by their comically staring eyes, and his inspector's orders have to wait as he lets through the small convoy. Then, struck by a brainwave, the man quickly gestures at Kedar to join in the wake of the mini cavalcade. Needing no second invitation, Kedar guns the MG forward and slides in behind the last Dodge as the constable intercepts the traffic, both arms held high. 'Left Hand Drive', Kedar notices the half-moon of the white plate with black letters sticking out of the rear bumper.

Turning on to Strand Road, Kedar can feel his tyres stutter. It's a sensation he would know blindfolded – when you drive on to one of the few roads in the city that are still cobblestoned, several years after the withdrawal of horse-drawn trams. On a normal trip to Howrah, the cobblestones would soon give way to a very different kind of bumping underneath. But today, Kedar has to wait, the smell of the warm meat patties needling his nose as he manoeuvres to stay in the wake of the princely convoy.

From further up the road comes the noise of glass smashing: a small open lorry with a load of metal poles poking up has gone too close to the cage of a lamp post. Almost in reaction to the breaking glass, a bit to the right, above the roofs of the cars and trucks, Kedar can see the simmering of sparks where the connector of a stationary tram begins an argument with its overhead wires. As he double de-clutches to move the car forward by a foot, Kedar can feel the sun rising towards noon, the shadows pulling in their young. On what is notionally the 'right' side of the packed street, four thhela-wallas struggle toward Kedar, bare-bodied, dhotis hiked tight around their loins, muscles pulsating on and off like electric signs as they strain to pull their handcart over a deep rut in the cobblestones. Behind them, at right angles to the traffic, is a black Renault trying to poke its long nose into the flow towards the station. A little girl wearing heavy gold jewellery leans out of the back window, vomiting, trying to make sure the spew misses her necklaces and silk jaamaa. Kedar glances at his watch – a quarter to twelve already, trapped, no way forward and no way back.

He can't smell the vomit and, from where he is, he can't see any jhurrie carriages. But suddenly, the smell of horse manure and uncleared garbage attaches itself to the vomiting girl, and Kedar finds himself heaving mildly. As he fumbles in his pocket for his cigarette tin, he wonders why the business of love is always connected to nausea.

'Saheb, it is opening up now.' Errol Ghose's constable finds Kedar again. 'If you'll just stay behind the nawab's cars, you should be there in less than half an hour.'

The smell of trapped sweat swarms off the havaldar as he leans in to shout at Kedar. Despite January, there are round, grey shields of perspiration under both arms of the man's white uniform tunic. Kedar jerks back, nodding in as commanding a manner as he can muster before lighting his cigarette and dealing with his pedals. As the traffic begins to turn towards the river, the smell of the huge flower market replaces the sweat and imagined vomit. Habit makes Kedar stick out his arm and spin his wrist to indicate the left turn even though there is no other choice for the cars in his lane. The smell of flowers is soon accompanied by the stench of the water and then a return of straining, stationary truck engines, the petrol stink oddly effective in cutting the nausea. Without seeming to really move, the tide of the traffic washes the MG on to the bridge, and Kedar now feels the familiar bouncing of the pontoons under his tyres.

Through the mess of trucks, pushcarts and horse carriages, Kedar can see the red-brick facade of Howrah Station rising across the wide river and a little to the right. Forty minutes to departure, which should be all right, though Kedar has a twelve-year-old's memory of entangled traffic on this very bridge, sitting next to his uncle on the large, sweaty front seat of the family Packard during one monsoon downpour, where the station stayed at the same tantalizing distance for over an hour while their train to Kalka ruthlessly departed.

Today, up the river to his right, rudely jutting nearly a hundred metres into the sky, are two pairs of steel pillars, a pair on each bank of the river, each with a crane perched on top. For most of last year, these have resembled a pair of gigantic rugby goalposts, the green-brown stretch of the Hooghly swirling between them, the ancient flow majestically unbothered by whatever foolish humans are trying to tinker up on its flanks. The whole city has understood that these structures will eventually hold up the new bridge, but only the few who are intimate with the science of cantilevers can actually imagine a span. Over the last few months, the scaffolding has begun to inch out over the water from both sides, but people are still shaking their heads, waiting for the whole steel madness to collapse.

From the middle of the pontoon bridge, which is much lower, Kedar thinks the two ends look like a huge Durga Puja pandal being constructed from big and small grey bamboos. Barrage balloons hovering above the steel would add to the air of festivity, he thinks. He has heard that heartbroken lovers are already committing suicide off the huge girders poking out over the water. Logically, this seems unlikely, given that the bridgework is surrounded by a heavy military guard on both banks, but then, these are times when rationality goes into headlong retreat. The other rumour making the rounds in club circles is that, even as they build it, the engineers are planting explosive charges in the frame. Should the war ever make it necessary, the mechanism for its destruction will be complete along with the bridge. A taxi coming the other way sends him back to early October, Eva's hand smoothing her skirt to her hip as she slid into the cab. She'd told him her father had been in the construction business in Latvia, with a lot of dealings with Germany. 'So they have a strange word, as only Germans can. My father taught me. *Sollbruchstelle*.' 'Sold-book-what?' '*Soll-bruch-stelle*. It means a planned point, so even when some constructions is collapsing, it will break only where is planned from before. A... planned breaking point.'

Watching the welding sparks make small fireworks off the steel structure, Kedar realizes that perhaps – no, for sure – Eva had planned their breaking point well before she left. A *sollbruchstelle* for the affair, though he doesn't like calling it an affair, even now, when it's clear this is the most accurate label for what they had. Suddenly, he wants to turn the car around, fling the bloody pastries and patties into the water, and drive home. Let Keya and her overpopulated family starve, or eat 'native' food from the stations, fall sick and die, each and every one of the bloody Duttas, especially 'Dada' Dutta, who can die in Quetta where he's been shunted off for training by the army. He wants what he wants from Keya, but more than that he really wants never to hear another idiot female cooing about how their names match so well, 'Keya and Kedar, ki shundor!' Perhaps this should be the unplanned breaking point, well before the K&K construction rises too high off the ground. Maybe—

Someone is banging on the boot of his MG. A long gap has opened up before him, the vehicle in front having sped forward. He turns to see a short, tight, brown bundle of energy glowering at him. Behind the Gurkha soldier, a white officer leans out from the driver's cabin of an army truck, shouting down, flecks of spit flying out his mouth. '*Move* along, y'blllloody fool! Naik! Woh nahi jaata hai to gaadi ko paani mey phenk doe!' If he doesn't move forward, throw the car into the river. The Gurkha stares at Kedar for a beat, as if assessing his weight, before ducking out of sight, obviously crouching down to get a grip on the rear bumper. No rationality at all. Kedar whips around and stamps on the accelerator. Not the Gurkha's to question why, his but to lift and throw. Within seconds, he's nosing into the rear of the Nawab's convoy again, with the army truck growling down his back.

'You're in love, but I'm in leave, my prince.' Eva had only said that after he'd paid for her passage to Sydney, not before. He hadn't thought twice about lending her the money. It was only later, when Borun-kaku pointed out that, even with wartime prices, the sum was enough to deposit one far beyond Australia, that he began to think that she may well have taken advantage of him. The sum he had spent – one thousand rupees – enlarged itself to its full size in his mind. From late October to mid-December, the money rose and fell inside Kedar like a storm-wracked freighter: he was the fool and she was a consummate confidence trickster, an expensive courtesan who'd left after charging her exorbitant fee, her Baltic favours a sight more expensive than the Balkan aunties prowling around Free School Street, but in the same profession; no, it was, it had to be, the beginning of a running account that would continue until death finally did them apart, a minor bit of give and take in the vast project of their love; no, she was a whore, plain and simple, who'd tricked him through meticulous planning, from the first touch, the first invitation up to her room, the first kiss, all cold-blooded, immaculate.

The envelope had arrived in the post three days ago, with a typewritten letter. The paper was embossed at the top with the letterhead of a small American commercial bank, with a sole Indian branch near Dalhousie Square. It requested Mr Kedar Lahiri Esq., to kindly present himself at his best convenience during working hours to collect a sum sent by a Miss E. Attali of Oakland, California.

The office on the fourth floor faced other similar mercantile buildings, though from one angle you could see the afternoon sun falling on a sliver of the park and water tank in the centre of Dalhousie Square. The banker's name was displayed on the brass plate on the desk – 'Raymond J. Hollister' – and the tilt of the reading glasses on his nose formed a disconcerting opaque band right under the man's eyes. 'I have here an example of your signature as sent to me by the remitting party, sir.' The nasal voice seemed to come out not from the mouth but from somewhere behind the man's head. 'I now have to ask you to count the sum remitted and sign this receipt.'

The man handed Kedar a thickly loaded manila envelope with his name typed on it. Kedar tore open the flap and began counting King George's face on the broad, hundred-rupee notes. After he passed ten, he stopped, confused. Hollister raised an eyebrow. 'Anything wrong, sir?' Kedar shook his head and began counting all over again, finishing when he reached twenty.

'But this is *two* thousand rupees,' he said. In Kedar's mind, the money ship lifted off the waves and capsized.

'That would be correct, sir.'

'No, I think the lady has made a mistake.'

'Mistake, how exactly, sir? Were you expecting a larger sum?' Hollister squared his shoulders as if preparing for combat and his 'r's took on a sharper edge.

'No, no, on the contrary, I think she has sent too much.'

Hollister sank back into his droop. 'I'm sure the amount is as per instructions, sir, but let me just verify it here.' He took the envelope back from Kedar's unprotesting hands and put it close within reach. Then he reached into a desk drawer and pulled out three similar envelopes and a thin sheet of paper. Reaching across to a stand on his left, he chose a pipe. Using the mouthpiece as a pointer, he began going down the list typed on the onionskin. The light that fell on the paper from the window behind Hollister was bright enough to show up a list of four names. Kedar could see his name reversed, second on the list. Next to it was a figure: Rs 2,000. Third on the list was the Great Eastern Hotel with a much larger sum. Hollister folded away the list before Kedar could decipher any other names, but the figure next to his own name was clearly the second highest after the hotel bill. Putting away the list and the other envelopes, Hollister smiled. 'All correct, Mr Lairy, all just fine and dandy.' He smiled as he pushed the open envelope back across the desk. 'Guess it's always nice to get a Christmas surprise from the fairy godmother, hunh?' Hollister indicated the printed receipt that Kedar hadn't read and handed him an unsheathed fountain pen. 'Now, sir, if you'll just...'

Kedar signed, trying to make sure his hand didn't shake. Hollister compared the two signatures, nodded, and put the receipt away in a separate drawer. Kedar slid the envelope into the inside pocket of his jacket, and it felt heavy sitting over his pounding heart. He pushed back his chair to stand up, but Hollister gestured with his pipe as he peered once again into the drawer with the envelopes. This time, the banker came up with a sheaf of thinner white envelopes, four of them, all of them addressed in a running hand. He shuffled through them and snapped out one at Kedar. 'I was almost forgetting, Mr Lairy! The old lady has sent you a personal letter as well.'

As the cars push up the slope from the pontoon bridge, Kedar can see the throngs of people around the two station porticos on either side of the main entrance. Some trouble has broken out near the north portico, and policemen are blowing their whistles and charging into the crowd, their long bamboo rods rising and falling as though they are trying to churn up whey from this eddying mass. Things are calmer around the near portico, but only just so, possibly because there are two army lorries quickly disgorging khaki uniforms right in front of it. It's not clear whether the troops are here to control the crowds or embark on trains, Kedar guesses the former until he sees a sergeant start to throw duffel bags and other equipment from the cave of one truck. A queue of jhurrie-gaadis maintains a semblance of normalcy, the horse carriages forming an orderly carousel, dropping off passengers on one side of an oblong island before coming around to the other side, where there seem to be an equal number of people trying to escape from Howrah Station as enter it. Policemen stand along a narrow route they are keeping clear for motorized traffic, arms linked, holding back packed bodies.

As he drives deeper into the convolution, Kedar sees three armoured cars, their turrets with the heavy machine guns poking out, stationed at more or less equal distance in the mass of people. Distributed around the entire concourse in front of the old Victorian building are small clusters of troops – Gurkhas – probably from the same regiment as the lorry that's still trying to clamber over his posterior. Conclusion: some troops are trying to get on trains, while others are here to facilitate their departure. Even as the white-shirted police dance into the crowd, the khaki men remain unmoving and watchful, their foreheads damp under the Gurkha hats with the brims buttoned up on one side.

A group of porters notices the nawab's convoy. Some of them try to negotiate with policemen, while others run forward through the police cordon to try and capture the custom. Two of the porters reach the second car, one of them tries to put a hand on the door pillar to indicate 'This is mine!' One of the royal guards backhands the man with his free hand and the coolie goes flying back into a group of policemen, his red tunic disappearing in a whirl of turbans and white shirts as the mamas smack their lathis into him. The chief of the guards turns and slowly waves his arm to his subordinate, telling him to keep calm. Then he imperiously gestures to the coolies and police, pointing to the arched gateway at the centre of the station facade: the convoy will park inside the station, in the central driveway that divides the platforms. As they approach the entrance, a gora officer comes forward. He throws up his palm to stop the convoy.

'You *can't* drive *into* the *station* today! *Reserved* for the *military*!' The man enunciates each word as if speaking to a child or a dotard. A suited arm comes out of the front right-hand window of the Studebaker. The officer looks at the paper he's been given and steps back. With great reluctance, he waves on the nawab's cars. Kedar curses under his breath. He has no magic permit, and it's now twenty past noon – only ten minutes to go.

'Saheb, saheb! Idhar!' An urgent voice in his ear. Kedar turns. 'A.A.E.I, saheb! Mai gaadi lagaa dunga, saheb!' I will park the car. With a shock of relief, Kedar remembers the Automobile Association decal prominent on his windshield. The association man salutes and proffers a wooden token. Kedar looks over his shoulder for the army lorry following, but it's gone. Three years ago, having to let some attendant drive his precious machine would have been a calamity. Today, he pulls up the handbrake and jumps out of the car. 'Park carefully!' He snatches the token, grabs the paper bags in the back seat and rushes headlong into the great hall that lies behind the south portico.

It's as if he has sprinted into a sea.

Just beyond the Gothic arches, not ten yards into the station, the open floor disappears, covered by a high tide of humanity. The entire hall on both sides of the central driveway wells with people, sitting, sleeping, waiting. Others, whose trains are about to leave, move at snail speed, balancing their luggage and inventing pathways through the unmoving mass. Calcutta is lost already. Everyone who can, rich, poor and in-between, is abandoning the city.

On one side of the hall, there is a roped-off space near the first-class waiting room, and a path marked out by policemen through which the shahebs and Indian worthies can reach the area. Next to the driveway, ropes tied to empty petrol drums cordon off a large square reserved for travelling soldiers. In the driveway itself, there is an open lorry loaded with flowers and people holding dhoop bowls from which smoke rises. Someone's body is clearly coming in from one of the neighbouring mofussil towns, somebody who can afford a cremation on the banks of the holy Hooghly–Ganga in the middle of this chaos. He can see the nawab's Studebaker stuck, crawling behind the lorry, the driver unable to use the horn out of respect, the big guards unable to slap the pomp of death out of the way.

Kedar takes all this in as he tries to find a route to the platforms. As he moves forward, he finds himself stepping on corners of straw mats that families have spread to mark out their temporary dwellings, each group with its entire universe clutched close. Pushing through, he trips over cloth sacks, bedrolls, trunks and bamboo tarazoo cages holding squawking poultry, people carrying their entire kitchens with them, several sacks with protruding iron, the khumtas women use to stir food in pots, and some even holding on to their bucket ovens turbaned with dried clay. His feet sliding on stray bits of guava and banana and god knows what human fluids, the floor shifting under his shoes as if some devil is offering an easy welcome into a one-way underworld. In the centre of this vast mess, he notices his fingers are close to piercing the paper bags he's clutching. He thinks of the day Tagore died, the fortress of banana fronds on the lorry, the dhoop and the chanting, the paste of flowers underfoot. That was the death of only one man, albeit a great man. Today, it feels as though it's the funeral of the whole city. On that August day that now seems many years ago, the mass was united. This now is a mass trying to scatter, tearing off bits of itself, fighting against itself, eating out its own heart and liver.

His panic mounting, the smell of engine smoke in his nose, Kedar works his way towards the platforms, sometimes having to go at right angles to the direction he needs, and once or twice even backwards before another narrow pathway reveals itself. All around him, the cavernous space echoes with sounds, trains releasing steam and warning whistles, the garble of constant announcements on the loudspeakers, car horns rejoining now, the shrill whistles of traffic policemen, voices shouting in panic or fury, all enmeshed in the constant hubbub of thousands of people, all of it bouncing off the high roofs and the skylights from which the midday sunlight falls straight down into this noisy cathedral of soot.

His legs shaking with the extended effort of stepping carefully while trying to move fast, he finally reaches the platforms. An announcement peels itself away from the unclear repetitions in three languages.

'*Delayed departure. 16 Down, Patna Express, will now leave platform eleven at 1 p.m. Delayed departure. The Patna Express will now depart at 1 p.m.*' Still holding the brown paper bags in a tight embrace, Kedar locates the large clock suspended from the roof of platform seven: forty minutes past noon. He would have been ten minutes too late.

On the platforms, a bit of space opens up, space people use as they pelt past him, running for their trains, their faces screwed up with fear, as if the Japanese are already at Jessore. His pace now even, Kedar moves swiftly to the mouth of platform eleven. The engine holding down the Patna Express hisses self-importantly, releasing malicious wisps of steam, but Kedar knows from avid childhood study that this is not one of the gargantuan round-nosed monsters that pull the great cross-country trains but merely a medium engine used to pull trains into the platform. When the train actually leaves, this little fellow will be left behind like a severed thumb in a magician's amputation trick. Only when the track is cleared will it chug backwards and out into the sidings, looking for another set of cleaned bogeys to tug into the terminus platforms. Moving past the heat of the engine, Kedar begins searching for the three first-class carriages. He has not gone very far when a sharp exclamation catches him.

'Look! Look at how little that boy is taking with him! His entire life in two big thhongas!'

A babu stands staring at Kedar through thick spectacles. His wife follows her husband's pointed gaze, her jaws balefully masticating paan, her eyes unhappy and unconvinced. Behind them, towers of luggage teeter on the heads of three porters.

'Look at that, now! Leaving his entire world behind, but so bravely! Disciplined! No slavery to maya whatsoever!' The man continues, completely sanguine that Kedar knows no Bengali. 'A change or two of clothes. Maybe a book or two. Perhaps a notebook and a pen. Bas, that's all! Not even a small attaché! Koto free!' Flinging out the last word in English, he turns to his wife and adjusts his glasses. 'I could have been like that, were it not for you.'

Kedar makes quick sketch-notes in his head, rectangles of suitcases on the porters' turbans, their red tunics twisted, two of them holding the rolls of holdalls from the shoulder, a bistra as they call it, the third man somehow balancing the cases with one hand while carrying a large brass water jug in the other. The woman clutching what looks like a small temple in her hands, with a statue of Ma Kali inside. The man himself quite unencumbered except for the large brown Gladstone bag strapped across his shawl, one of those absurd, new 'monkey caps' clutched in his hand, the ones that cover the whole face leaving openings for eyes, nose and mouth, the thing ready to be pulled on at a moment's notice. As he hurries alongside the train, Kedar decides that when he makes the drawing, he will have the fool with his monkey cap already on.

The fever envelops him as he weaves his way through the crowd. A cluster of people around a TT, nearly suffocating the man as they implore him for last-minute berths. A woman screaming, 'Aami maa ke chhede jaabo naa! I won't leave mother behind! Why do we have to go? They are only attacking Singapore!' and the man – her husband? her brother? – snapping back, 'Singapore-ta irrelevant! You don't know anything! They are also attacking Rangoon, which is closer than Lucknow! Do you know how many thousand people Japani planes have killed in Rangoon? And! Do you know? No! You don't know what is an aircraft carrier!'

On the platform, along the jam-packed third-class carriages, complete chaos: people lifting babies in through open windows; shady-looking men moving along the windows, surreptitiously plucking wads of money from outstretched hands as they pass, clearly touts collecting final payments for having secured seats; people clutching each other as if the planet itself was about to cleave apart, sundering them for eternity. Through all this move the police, distaste writ large across their faces, choosing quite carefully what to see and what to ignore.

A large arm sticks out in Kedar's way, and he tries to move it aside. The arm stiffens into a rod and is joined by another man's arm, the hands locking. Kedar happens to be looking down at the time, watching his steps on the messy platform. Meeting this barrier, he looks up to see who's blocking him. There is a ring of large men in grey-and-gold livery, creating a circle of space near the door of a carriage. A shield of a royal house hangs from a hook next to the carriage door, a different prince from the one whose convoy he's just followed. As he looks along the carriage, he sees the crest repeated, painted over the middle window, indicating that the carriage belongs to the state of Aligaputtu, which he knows to be sandwiched between the borders of Hyderabad and the Central Provinces. Through grey coats and plumed red turbans,

Kedar sees the nawab himself, a short, dark man fitted with a hooked nose belonging to someone three times his size. The nawab is wearing a blazer of the Royal Calcutta Polo Club. The man he's speaking to is dressed in a dapper cream suit with a double-breasted jacket. The two of them stand as if they are on a green at a golf course, each with one hand in his trouser pocket, both fencing the air with their cigarettes, the cream suit sporting an ebony cigarette holder, the nawab one of his own gold-and-grey cigarettes.

For an instant, Kedar feels the jolt of recognition. He has seen the nawab many times, at the racecourse, at polo, at cricket matches; Zulfikar Sarfraz Ali Khan, known to the Calcutta sporting world variously as 'Kulfi' and 'Alligator'; but the man he's speaking to is well known all over India from press photographs and newsreels – surely this is none other than Mohammad Ali Jinnah? Kedar looks again and sees his mistake: this man is short whereas Jinnah is famously tall, and his nose is straight, whereas Jinnah's hooked protuberance, which would more than match the nawab's, is by now an emblem.

As Kedar makes his way around the ring of guards, he can hear the conversation.

'Well, old chap, there it is,' says Kulfi.

'Yes, Your Highness, but no question of Rangoon, er, of these people conceding Rangoon. No question at all, let me assure you!'

'And Singapore? You would say that about Singapore as well?'

'Highness... a temporary setba—No, I couldn't very well say that about Singapore, but...'

'Well, old chap, there it is. You see.'

'Yes, of course, we'll have to see who we...'

'Who exactly is bowling to us in the last innings. Exactly! And whether it is indeed the last innings!'

'*Indeed*, Your Highness, very true, who we find ourselves negotiating with finally! You're quite right, and we must make sure these Congress-wallas don't run us out and hog all the batting, but you *will* give this some thought?' Cream Suit's voice is deep, but his Oxbridge drawl still manages to be softly obsequious.

'Certainly, certainly, *all* of us have to think about this, old chap! All the princely houses who are willing. No choice but! Issmey toh koi nawabiyat nahi chalegi!'

Kedar doesn't understand the last sentence, which is in Urdu, but it triggers both men into a burst of companionable laughter.

'Then, if I may take your leave, Highness?' Cream Suit bows and extends his hand in goodbye.

'By all means, old boy! And, you know, perhaps,' the Kulfi Alligator gives off a small chortle, 'perhaps, we should get used to *you* chaps being the Highnesses, being our openers in the new...'

'Not at all, Nawab Saheb, not at all! We are all *quite* aware of how much we will owe all of you, all our... shining jewels, when the mulq becomes a reality. We'll have to hold our own against these... and all of *you* will be our—'

'Inshallah, old boy, inshallah.' Kulfi steps back towards his carriage as a loud whistle wails down from the big engine at the outer end of the platform.

'Safe and smooth journey, Your Highness!' Cream Suit raises his hand in a semi-salute.

'And to you, dear fellow! Safe and smooth! Safe and smooth! And our salaams to the Barrister Saha—to our leader!'

'Eijey! Where have you been?' Kedar is still watching Nawab Kulfi spring up into his royal carriage when Keya's voice finds his ear. He snaps around, searching for her face framed by one of the windows. 'Kedar Lahiri. Eikhaaney! Here!' He spots her on the other side of the platform, standing with Swati, her older sister. Actually, Keya is crouching slightly and next to her stand three taller boys, cousins, forming a wall that shields the girls from the carriage windows and the oldies inside. One of the boys holds his hand near his waist. Three lit cigarettes poke out from between the curved fingers, making the hand look like an incense-stick holder. He hands one to Swati who has a puff and passes it back. He takes it and carefully hands another one to Keya, who takes a long, greedy drag, her eyes fixed on Kedar.

'Oh, our *hero*! You managed to bring the tuck! Ma was just saying how useless you were.'

'I'll just go and give it to her then, shall I? And mention that I saw you out here, smoking?'

'*Ma* doesn't object! She appreciates cosmopolitanism! It's Baba and Dragon-pishi!'

'All right, in that case I know who to inform.'

Keya pokes the outermost member of the wall. 'Biggles, lokhhi shona? Please take this from our hero and deliver it na, babu?'

'Train is departing any minute,' says Biggles, leaning forward and snatching a quick puff from the third cigarette.

Kedar gingerly transfers the paper bags to the boy. 'Careful, almost tearing. Hold them from below!' Biggles balances the bags, pretending to reel under the weight. 'And let Mashima know who brought them, thiik achhey?'

'Can't open my mouth inside, Kedar-da. They'll smell my breath.'

'Right. Then you can't eat any of this either.'

Biggles grins. 'Oh, in a few minutes it'll be fine. Keya-di, don't forget the paan.'

Keya smiles, flips aside her shawl and holds up a thhonga full of glistening green paan. 'I'll only give you one if you tell Ma later that Kedar came empty-handed. Tell her another friend brought the stuff. Tell her Anshu-da came and dropped it off, had to leave because he was in a hurry.'

Kedar feels a flash of irritation rising. 'Hang it, I'll go in and give it to her myself! Biggles, give that back here!'

Keya puts a hand on Kedar's arm. 'Actually, not a good idea. Obviously we'll tell Ma you brought the food as per the list. But best you stay out here with us.'

'Keno? Ki hoyechhey?'

'Nothing...' Keya starts walking away from the group, beckoning him to follow. A few yards further away from her carriage, she turns around suddenly and he almost bumps into her. He can smell her perfume, and then the Cavendish tobacco as she opens her mouth. 'Dada felt obliged to tell them that we spent a lot of time alone in that room. Belvedere Court party.'

'Bloody swine.'

'No, don't call him that. He thinks he's protecting his baby sister. He just didn't like you dancing with that King Kong woman on Christmas Eve.'

'Bloody swine. I told you. She's Hillcott's fiancée.'

'Kayu, I've put that painting on the upper berth, so be careful if you climb up.' Keya's sister is now hovering near them.

'Which painting?' Kedar asks, immediately wishing he hadn't.

'The one you gave her,' Swati says. 'The one of the palm trees from the balcony. Just refused to leave it behind. In case the Japani come and loot it.'

Kedar finds himself smiling. Swati turns to go. 'Ei, train's about to move, kintu. Bye-bye, Mr Dandy, bhaalo thheko.' Stay well.

'Mr Dandy?' Kedar raises his eyebrow at Keya.

'That's what Ma calls you. Now what we all call you.'

'I see. How nice.' He makes sure they're not watched and lightly presses the round red tiip on her forehead with his index finger.

'What I don't say out loud is that you're *my* Mr Dandy.'

From the corner of his eye, Kedar can see the blue and silver of the train beginning to slide forward. Keya sees it too.

'Safe and smooth journey.' Accidentally pocketed, Cream Suit's words slip out.

Keya grins and quickly puts a paan into her mouth. Then she changes her mind, pulls it out, bites it in half and puts one half in Kedar's mouth, which happens to be open. She pulls up her sari and crosses the platform, running to greet the open door of the carriage as it comes up to her. Kedar can see Keya's father coming to the doorway as she climbs in. He helps her up and she goes in past him. He comes to the door, covering her from sight. A tall man, the Honourable Justice Shekhar Kumar Dutta of the Calcutta High Court, now holding the door handrails and glowering at Kedar, muffler around his throat like chainmail, a pipe clenched in mouth. Kedar bobs his head in respectful greeting but the Judge-shaheb doesn't respond. As the train passes, Keya appears at a window further down the carriage, inscribing the air, furiously making writing gestures. As she smiles, he can see her mouth is now red from the betelnut.

He remembers the half paan still trapped in his mouth, and he waits until the carriage is well out of sight. He finds a wastebin next to a pillar and spits the whole foul thing out, leaf, shards of betelnut, chalk-lime paste, sweet chutney, cardamom, everything, leaning well forward, making sure not to spray any on his shirt front. He straightens up and looks around for a tea stall. Must get rid of this taste. He sees a chaa-walla sitting in a slant of sunlight.

'Chaa dao, bhai! Taara-taari!' Give me some tea, quickly.

'Chaa aar nei, babu, shob shesh!' No tea left, babu, all gone. The man huddles deeper into his thin shawl.

'How can you run out of tea?'

'No one was expecting so many people, babu. Last six days it's been like this. Other thing is, now every son-of-a-pig, dui-poishar chaa-walla in Kolkata has made his way to Howrah. So, in the shops they've raised the price of tea leaf. Every fool is paying their robbery prices, but the tea is still in short supply. I'll only get more around four o' clock, when the big evening trains start leaving.'

Kedar snorts in disgust as he lights a cigarette. The chaa-walla looks at him in sympathy. 'The big stall on platform seven will probably have some, if you want to go there. Not as good as mine, of course.' Kedar doesn't feel like moving. On this platform emptied of trains, he suddenly feels free. Keya, the bakery goods and his painting are safely away. His MG is hopefully intact in the parking area. Eva is snug in San Francisco. The mild sun on this winter afternoon is warming. There is nowhere he needs to rush off to.

He has forgotten to bring the little sketchbook he carries with him, but artists can also make mental notes, he tells himself. He marks the radhachura tree he can just about see beyond a far platform, its bare winter branches looking as if they are coming out from a carriage roof, as if the train will cart it away any moment. He marks the two stalks of clay cups curving out of the chaa-walla's square oil tin, the rims sharp in the light, shadows scooping into stacks of burnt sienna that will now stay dry and intact until evening. From before this, a list from the river: the vomiting girl in her finery, the smudge of imaginary barrage balloons in the sky, the highlights on the absurd masts of the invisible bridge, the sweat on the thhela-wallas' bodies, the mad look on the Gurkha's face just before he ducked down. And, how to render, through all this, the city draining out of the station? *As you can see, everything is not as it looks.* Eva's strange European hand sprawling across the onionskin letter paper. *From the beginning, my words were not very well working, and now I find difficult – difficultY – in using them to explain what I cannot explain. How to explain to you that I may never see my family again, them who I always never wanted to see again, and also my behated country which I now miss so much? About reaching here to my remaining people and knowing, realizing, that I am not alone in this but in thousands? How to explain how I miss you, and only in what things I am able to miss you?* Two small pages later, just above her signature, the last sentence, *Paint, my prince, paint! Do it without fear! You will only discover if you have the painting gift (or not) by doing, but at least you have the gift of being able to want it.* The last phrase, in suddenly perfectly correct English, perfectly accurate, shoots through him every time he rereads it in his mind.

He wonders what would happen if Japanese bombers appeared now, catapulted from some stealthy aircraft carrier lurking off the river mouth at Ganga Sagar. From the tea-bhaands, his gaze moves up to the clear blue he can see through the straight lines of the corrugated platform roofs. He can't imagine bombers screaming down from this, his own sky. The bombers in the newsreels he has seen over the last seven or eight years have almost always been black darts arrowing down against a grainy white European expanse. Almost always German bombers, and then, soon after the summer of '40, the flood of movies showing the RAF fighting back: small, busy pinpricks making larger enemy shapes explode. He tries to imagine the noise the Jap planes might make, red circles on their flanks, like huge, oversized forehead dots. He imagines sticks of bombs hanging over Dalhousie and Strand Road, like rope ladders with the sides cut off. He tries to conjure up the scream of the bombs that he has read so much about, the thump of the explosions people have memorized from the talkies, colonnade pillars smashing, horses rearing up, the ceiling of Eva's room in Great Eastern slicing open as they hold each other in bed, dust pouring out of some broken, cosmic hourglass. The whole hotel collapsing on them, burying them, erasing them forever.

Bhasma bhushan anga lahe Shiva, gangaa shikhar birup Shiva
Kar damaru baajata funakata fanesh bhaari

He finds himself humming the Shree as he watches the train pull out across the tracks, from platform thirteen, rust-red carriages with the yellow stripe across the windows, the letters BNR painted on each carriage – Bengal Nagpur Railway.

'Oita kon train?' He asks the chaa-walla.

'Oita, babu, Madras Mail. Puro chaar din laagbey, pouchhote.' That's the Madras Mail. It will take four whole days to reach.

As the third-class carriages pass, he can see that they are jam-packed with people, some windows bulging with packed jute sacking. Like a chain of metal sausages filled to bursting, he thinks. Four days in that fetid, foul metal prison, people sitting on top of each other, unable to move, Madrasis, Hyderabadis, Mysoreans, Malayalis, and anyone else who thinks they can find shelter in the southern cities. Eating their little flying saucers of steamed rice, but with nowhere to evacuate them because, after the first few hours, the bathrooms would be ankle-deep with faeces and urine. It's not that he has ever experienced this himself, but Borun-kaku's description of his train journeys of pilgrimage to the south have been vivid. 'Kedu Babu, the thing you have to remember is that, despite all this, they are *cleaner* than us, also cleaner *by far* than any Bhaiya or Paanjaabi! You can almost say as clean as... the Japanese!'

As the tail of the Madras Mail clanks past, Kedar notes a solitary carriage just before the brake van, its windows shuttered, bracketed by two flatcars. Each flat with a tarpaulin covering a frog shape – some sort of anti-aircraft guns, Kedar guesses – which he hasn't seen on any of the other trains so far. 'The gift of flight is still not fully old before we make instruments to smash ourselves out of the sky,' he has heard in the commentary of some documentary on air warfare. Wouldn't it be the best joke if the super-clean Japanese were to bypass Calcutta completely and land around the Hyderabad coast? '*You don't know what is an aircraft carrier!'* What if this train were the first one to catch it from a squadron of carrier-borne Zeros as it went chugging around the Bay of Bengal? Kedar imagines being caught inside the rat-trap coffin of those carriages and shudders with small guilt. It's clear to him that nowhere else in the world but India could trains possibly take on this heavy human significance, carry this freight of potential horror.

He had brought Eva to Howrah Station in late September to see the trains. She had been gay on the bridge, bouncing up and down in her seat, adding to the bumping of the pontoon but, as soon as they approached the station, she had frozen. More precisely, she had transformed the moment they heard a long train whistle. 'Please turn car, I don't want to see trains. Please turn, I want to go back now. Please.' When he asked why, she wouldn't reply except with the set mouth and the small shake of the head he had learnt not to challenge. Later, discussing the best option for the journey to Sydney, the man at Thomas Cook had suggested embarking in Bombay from where the ships took a safer, far more southernly route, curving around Ceylon.

'This means one train to Bombay, yes?' she had asked with great, precise anxiety.

'Yes, madam, under three days' train journey to Bombay, quite comfortable if you are in first class, followed by two nights at the Taj Mahal Hotel, the best hotel in India, and then you board the ship.'

'No question of this. No train.' Her eyes staring at a spot on the wall, far away.

Here in Oakland, everything is so big I feel even smaller than normal. They have even a big train carrying cargo crates that goes slowly on a middle of a boulevard all the way to the big cranes for the ocean ships. Some days I am wishing the ship would bring you to me. My small heart next to my small prince in the middle of all this big world. After this clear insincerity, there are a couple of lines she has scratched over, at the very bottom of the page. Try as he might, holding up the paper to different kinds of light, Kedar cannot make out what it says under the redactions. Perhaps they were for someone else – in one of the other letters – and she had realized just in time? Or perhaps there was no will to start the page again? The slanted hand resumes on the next sheet. *I remember the top button open of your shirt, and that silk scarf you so liked to wearing. So tyaansh yes but so lovely, I miss!*

He'd once explained the word 'tyaansh' to her. 'It means for a Bengali to be too much like the British, or like you whites. In manner, in dress, in the way of speaking, too much like a European, like a fake European. Like a brown shaheb.'

He observes himself on the platform. 'Koto free!'

The babu chattering away as if he, Kedar, were a creature from some other planet. How could the cretin not see him as a Bengali? Did he really look so completely tyaansh? Suddenly, Kedar draws himself, a jigsaw puzzle, a self-portrait as the world is being torn up around him: a short, dapper shaheb-ized clown, absurd, in wide, sharply creased cream trousers, ironed shirt of thick white linen, top button open even in winter, brown jacket with leather patches on the elbows, shining brogues – careful, be parsimonious with the white highlights – sunglasses pushing back his hair in the fashion of Hollywood stars. This is how he looks to others. A 'free' man. 'My dandy.' A bloody non-Bengali dandy at that, a bloody fop, a toffee-nosed toff, a Hurree Jamsett Ram Singh, just like the Musholman popinjay in the cream suit. 'Safe and smooth journey' indeed!

It's now obvious to him that Cream Suit was wholly copying M.A. Jinnah's dress, attitude and demeanour, as if he had swallowed the cadaverous Bombay barrister entirely and reproduced him from within. Stomach dropping, horror rising, Kedar cannot slip out of the realization that he himself is also got up in almost exactly the same costume.

In his painting, the two figures stand mimicking each other's posture, each with a hand in trouser pocket, Cream Suit and Nawab Kulfi Alligator spotlighted by beams of sunlight that cut through train smoke. In the foreground is a shadowy, muddily painted mass of squatting poorer people. The envious fool of a Koto-Free babu and his wife are also in the light, at one side. Behind them, porters with their suitcases, like Rajputana village belles holding stacked water pots, but not beautiful – haggard and desperate.

'Thiik holo na, Dada-babu!' Rasko over his shoulder. 'Not quite right! And why are *you* so tall and why talking to that big-nosed raja-shaheb? It's not clear what you are saying to him!' Himself exploding, 'You now want me to make balloons for the words, like in the Superman comics, Rasko?' But he knows exactly what the blighter means. The brush sliding the wrong way, finding errant grooves in the drying paint, refusing to obey him, the canvas too big, his talent too small. 'Dada-babu... maybe your land-escapes are better,' Rasko pronouncing as he takes away the full ashtray. 'Maybe make more of those!' Perhaps the man is right, perhaps this level of work is totally beyond him at present. Walk before you can run. Float before you try swimming. Paint, my prince, paint. You will only discover if.

At least, he has the gift of being able to want it.

He imagines Howrah in the early winter morning, empty platform, tracks heading into the mist, the chaa-walla's tin box with its clay cups unattended, a floating newspaper with big headlines marking another military fiasco in these weeks of ceaseless disaster. Then, Victoria Memorial in a cage of bamboo, the top half brown, the bottom half still white. Then another view of his garden, again a winter dawn, but from the first floor of the house, a dance drama of bare-branched trees beyond the muted flower beds, and at the gate below, huddled in his shawl, the guard with his stick.

He now wishes he hadn't given that painting of the palm grove to Keya. His mother has thrown a fit – given it away to *that girl* – Ma loves that canvas. He has tried to reproduce it but, again, his skill isn't up to the task. He just can't retrieve the particular flukes that went into making that picture. Each succeeding attempt is met with Ma's sniffs of dismissal, Rasko standing next to her and agreeing. 'Thiik holo na! Not as nice as *that* one!' But it's not just Ma Lahiri. Kedar now realizes he needs to keep looking at that painting because, in making it, he had stumbled upon a tiny route into something else, a tenuous bridge out of a trap, a land-escape, a certain confidence with the brushwork, a peculiar balance of colour and form that was somehow very Indian, very Bengal, very much of this land, something momentarily shifting away from a tyaansh mimicry of the great Europeans.

A trace of paan returns around the back of his tongue, bringing with it the mixture of desire and repulsion. Not repulsion, exactly, but a lust that doesn't carry the full taste of desire, a repetition almost emptied of meaning, like making yet another nicely rendered view of his house or garden, whereas what he really wants to paint now is a bigger painting of those chappals he had sketched around Christmas, or to render properly the station and the drama of exodus. Watching Keya leave, he felt a small pang of sadness, but one quickly washed under a wave of elation – he was free to work, to wander the city, with no more duty teas and duty parties with Keya and her friends and cousins, no more choreographed courtship pretending to be true, adventurous, risky, thorny love.

He imagines Keya as she steps down from the train at Mungher. He knows it's a small, proper town in Bihar and not a village station in Bengal, but he imagines her alighting on one of those romantic, desolate platforms from one of Rabindranath's stories, or Bibhutibhushan's or Banaphul's, or perhaps that one by Saradindu. In his mind, he removes the family, the nasty owl of a father, the saw-voiced mother, the malice-breathing Dragon-pishi, the pesky cousins quaffing down patties, the sister who's actually a good sort. Keya gets down alone from the first-class carriage, with just enough time for the station's only porter to drag out her luggage before the train moves off again. The station master is in attendance, of course, and the man does a nomoshkar before quickly taking the wrapped painting from Keya's hand.

In Kedar's imagination, it is evening, the winter sun just starting to set, and Keya's lovely face is lit up by the koney dyekha aalo, the bride-light, the best light in which to show a girl's face to a prospective groom. The shawl has fallen from one shoulder, and her neck glows in the orange rays. Above her, a squadron of warplanes drones away, curving like dots of bridal make-up on the forehead of the darkening sky, their black forms brought out by a necklace of white highlights.

'Fortresses fall, prisoners bow asking for mercy, smoke rises to the sky, victorious armies rejoice, but nothing, no defeat and no triumph can touch the ramparts of her ethereal beauty...'

A portrait of her in exchange for the palm-grove picture. He knows Keya is vain enough to accept this, if only he can manage a proper likeness and do justice to her undeniably exquisite countenance.

Thinking about exactly how open he wants her mouth to be, he looks down and notices a fleck of paint on the right knee of his trousers, the ultramarine blue showing up loud against the faded, light yellow ochre of the cloth. He notes that his older pair of tennis shoes are scuffed and dirty as they move across the station floor, and that it is already too warm to be wearing socks and shoes. Looking up, he spots the radhachura tree, left behind by all the trains. Across the empty platforms, he can now see it's actually on the other side of the station wall. Yellow buds are breaking out on the branches, and a couple of parrots hover around, nibbling at the tips.

'Chaa, chaa garam!' A chaa-walla calls out, looking at him hopefully, but Kedar is not interested in tea, having just had a late breakfast with a nice cup of Polson's coffee. As he walks down platform eleven, he waves off the flies with a folded copy of today's *Statesman*. The bit facing upwards only says 'ISH DEC' and below it 'AVE RAN' both in large black print, but the headline is spread wide inside him, as it is with every newspaper reader in Calcutta this morning. It may not be the shock of the news – which is hardly unexpected – but driving here, it's as if the entire city has eloped overnight. Traffic is sparse on the roads, as if the Sunday has continued from day before yesterday, the boats on the river seem to have hidden themselves, and the covered up machinery suggests the engineers and welders seem to have long ago given up the new bridge as a bad idea.

Keya's lips, slightly parted, as they are when she's considering allowing him to kiss her. Before dawn, it's still quite chilly on the platform at Mungher Junction and she wraps her shawl tighter around her cardigan as she waits for the train to Howrah. The porter squats a little distance away, puffing on a bidi. Pishtoto cousin Biggles, good fellow, has come to see her off, and he looks around the platform, making sure there's no one they know before handing a Cavendish to

Keya and striking a match. As the sky lightens, the plumes of tobacco smoke from the cigarette and the coolie's bidi take on a symmetry. In fact, in the charcoal sketch, there is a third figure – the only other passenger waiting, an official shaheb of some sort, sola topi already on – who holds a pipe in his hand, barely discernible, but in Kedar's artistic decision, yet to be lit, implying a third plume that will join the cigarette and the bidi and, presently, the steam from the engine as it pulls in. Of everything he's attempted in the last two months, Kedar loves this recent small charcoal the most. But it's not a painting he dare make, even in today's world. It will stay hidden away in his sketchbook. A Bengali woman of aristocratic class smoking openly at a railway platform is not something the eyes of society will tolerate – he might as well paint her without any clothes... In fact, yes, a nude study would be far more acceptable.

That image of Keya courses through him, and he has to stand still for a moment. It has been a long time since he has seen a woman fully naked, a long time since he's been lucky enough to make love properly, five months now since Eva left, and a long enough time since he's felt any touch of a lover.

When the Patna Express steams in, he's waiting where the first-class carriages usually stop, cigarette in mouth, one hand casually in trouser pocket. As he watches the blue-and-silver carriages roll past, he remembers a sliding curtain in a village puppet show he had seen as a child.

The last inland letter from Mungher sits in his jacket pocket, smelling of gum from the flap and of flowers. The mixture of English and Bangla scripts elegant, as is to be expected from a student of Loreto House, the best girls' school in Calcutta, but the content of the writing is so wanting in modesty it would draw the strongest disapproval from Sister Siobhan, the principal. Even Keya's professors at Bethune College, used to skimming over the more bawdy bits of Shakespeare and Donne, might blush. A line towards the end broadly lays out the plan, 'I can't bear it here, I have to find a way to come back. My Dida is being helpful, in that she has not been well and is asking for yours truly, her favourite granddaughter. Will wire DG.' The telegram has indeed been sent to Miss Deirdre Ghose c/o Sub-Inspector Errol Ghose: GRANDMOTHER ILL STOP RETURNING ALONE 9 MARCH PATNA EXPRESS ARRIVING NOON STOP CAN YOU RECEIVE ME HOWRAH STOP KEYA. To which the coded reply has been prompt: BROTHER AND SELF WILL MEET YOU AT HOWRAH STOP DEIRDRE – the word 'brother' being the sign that it would be Mr Dandy alone who would be waiting at this platform.

It's quite hot already, winter in full retreat, and Kedar so wishes he could open a second button on his shirt. Coolies barge past him as the train jerks to a stop, and he finds himself standing on his toes, his eyes flicking from window to window, trying to sift through the flurry of red tunics. He passes over the face of a beautiful woman twice before he realizes that this is Keya and that her broad smile is aimed at himself. It takes him a moment to find his own smile – she looks nothing like the painting he has almost completed. By the time he waves, it's at an empty window.

A coolie pokes his arm, 'Do you need a porter, babu?' Kedar doesn't bother to reply as he moves into the small crowd of people coming out of the carriage. The coolie sticks to him and follows his gaze. Without any instruction, the man climbs into the door and takes the two small suitcases from Keya. As she turns around to climb down the metal steps, Kedar is almost overcome by the need to hold her from behind, where her sari parts to reveal the blouse narrowing at the waist. Luckily, before he can move, he is pushed aside by a panicky passenger who has left her purse inside. Trying to get back in, the woman almost wrenches Keya from the steps.

'Aarrey, ki oshobhho!' How rude. Keya's eyes flash at the woman even as she checks whether her own purse is secure. Kedar's arms spread protectively around Keya, but his body is about two feet away from hers. She turns around and looks at him, her face almost neutral, almost completely hiding her smile. After a few seconds, she moves her eyes away and looks over his shoulder at the coolie who is standing patiently, suitcases balanced on his head.

'Make sure the fellow doesn't run away with my cases,' she says in English.

'How far will he run with that load?' Kedar takes the cigarette out of his mouth and casually taps off the long extension of ash.

'They're not that heavy. And don't smoke until we get to the car. I can't bear it.'

'What do you mean?' Kedar gestures for the coolie to follow them and starts walking.

'I'm desperate for a ciggie, so don't smoke until you can give me one.'

'Puro, complete addict, ekta.'

'Addict yourself! Standing there, bidi hanging from mouth like some chhotolok Hollywood gangster. Hmnh!'

Kedar grins and throws away the cigarette. 'Did you have a good journey?'

The MG is parked in the central driveway, and within a few minutes they are going down the slope to the pontoon bridge. Kedar takes advantage of a pause in traffic to light Keya's cigarette.

'What would you like to do? When do you have to be at your Dida's?'

Keya blows a celebratory plume skywards. 'Food! Food! I want some decent food! There is nothing you can call food in that Bihari hole. If I ever see rice, dal and fried fish again, I shall kill myself. And alu poshto, too. You can treat me to lunch at Firpo's.'

Kedar nods. 'Milady's wish is my command.'

'Is that today's *Statesman*?' Keya reaches for the folded newspaper in Kedar's jacket pocket. Her bangle catches on some loose stitching as she pulls it out, and Kedar helps to free her wrist with his left hand. It's their first touch in weeks and it silences them for a moment. Then, Keya gives a small jerk of her head and busies herself with opening the paper but without looking down at it. 'You know, Baba's getting so terribly irritated, sitting in Mungher. He took leave and came with us, supposed to be for his health, but his ulcer's become worse! The old wireless is refusing to work, no one else has a radio it seems, and the papers come three, sometimes even four days late. And those Ingrej district officials are not very forthcoming with the news they receive, not even to a sitting judge of the Calcutta High Court! It took Baba five whole days before he learnt about the Japanese taking Singapo...' Keya's voice trails off as the print traps her eyes.

'BRITISH DECISION TO LEAVE RANGOON – Essential Demolitions Carried Out'

To his left, looking north between the pillars of the invisible new bridge, Kedar can see two large barges with pyramids of camouflage netting rising atop them. On his right, where the water shines in the midday sun, there are two more, one just off the Strand Road embankment and one further down, on the Howrah side of the river. Anti-aircraft guns, their barrels poking up, almost inviting the war to descend upon the city. The sky is now clear and he can see the taller cranes poking up from the Kidderpore docks that are invisible beyond the curve of the river after Hastings. The guns and baffle walls have now got the people of the city into the habit of checking the sky for enemy airplanes, even the ones like Kedar who know things like the range of all the enemy's bombers. There has been no sign of Japanese planes yet, but everyone knows after the quick toppling of Singapore and Rangoon that Calcutta is next on the list and it's now just a matter of time.

'When did this happen?' Keya asks, even though the paper is full of nothing but the details of the loss of the Burmese capital.

'Well, as it says, late at night, the day before yesterday, but who actually knows? News from there also takes a few days to reach here. Must have been some time around two-three days ago.'

Keya switches to Bangla.

'What are your people saying? Will they leave Kolkata?'

'Baba says the further we go from Rajshahi, the further we move from hoping to retain the land. Ma says she chooses to die in Ballygunge. Borun-kaku is talking of digging a trench in the garden, an air-raid shelter he says, but Baba and I are convinced he wants to fight the Battle of the Somme again – but against the Japanese.'

'Aar tumi?' And you?

'I'm... I've been, no, I missed you, definitely, of course, but otherwise I've been quite happy. Been working.'

'Working?' Keya slips back into English. 'Don't tell me a Lahiri has lowered himself to employment? You said nothing in your letters!'

'Let me be inphorming yourself, maidiyaar djyong ledi. That allovaar thees shitty thyere aar menii employed Lahiris.' Kedar stops mimicking a clerk's accent and goes back to his normal English. 'I was referring to my painting.'

'Oh, thaat...! Na, shono, your family needs to think things through. Baba was already saying, already just after Singapore, that we need to think of moving to Delhi, or even Shimla, where Shankha-pisho has that cottage. Baba says he'll have to stay behind, duty as a judge of the high court and all that, but the rest of us, especially Ma, Pishi, Swati and myself, we should go. He's predicting the Japanese will be here by November or December, but life would be hell from long before then. In his calculations, he said they would take Rangoon by April.'

'April? Taaholey toh they are nearly a month in advance of your old man's calculations! So we can expect them here by... August? September? Uncle Tojo will celebrate the pujos in Calcutta!'

'Everything is not a joke, Kedar Lahiri. There is such a thing as the monsoon. They will not advance from Burma until after the rains, but then it will be very quick. These Ingrej are finished. Baba's been dealing with them at the club in Mungher, and he says their panic is so tangible you can cut it with a knife.' Feeling the sun, Keya puts her sari pallu over her head. 'And don't call him an old man! My Baba is one of the most brilliant men in this city. In India!'

'Yes... well, perhaps they should have handed the army over to him. He would have had the Japanese here by May.'

'You've never really felt real love for me, have you?'

Keya is staring at him from the centre of the blue halo of her sari. Kedar notes the grey-white slashes where the sunlight is trapped in the weave of the crisply ironed cotton. He suddenly sees that Keya's face has grown much older, in just two months. He realizes that it can now be a mask for something sharper, harder, something that's perhaps always been inside her, something that he has not yet seen.

He turns off Strand Road, leaving behind the cobblestones, and drives towards Dalhousie Square.

'*Didn't you hear what I just said? What I just asked?*' The girl's voice is now shrill, exactly like her mother's when the lady gets angry, like the occasion when Kedar and Keya were found walking in the Duttas' garden at well past eight in the evening. 'I mean, you can't stand my brother, you show utter disrespect to my father, you have contempt for my mother, you can't bear my pishi—'

'Your didi is all right, Swati is a good egg.' Kedar turns left past the Chamber of Commerce, heading towards Brabourne Road to avoid the checkposts around the Central Post Office. 'I don't mind Biggles either. He's a good young chap.' Keeping himself perversely calm, Kedar delivers the deadliest blow. 'But I really can't stand Bismarck and Clemenceau.' A small lorry full of bricks is backing across the road into the compound of MacLeish & Ferguson, and Kedar is forced to stop. 'Why anyone should keep a rakhhosher moto, perishing huge St Bernard in Calcutta defeats me. It's actually animal torture, not that I care too much about dogs, as you know.'

Kedar glances left to see the effect of his words. The bottom half of her face covered, Keya is now chewing on the end of her sari, trying to control some extreme emotion. Kedar continues with his assault. 'And that mangy little Clemu, that joke of an ancient Pomeranian, you need to send him up to keep his namesake company. That's it! Take Bismarck to Shimla and never bring him back, and put Clemensooo out of his misery!'

Keya is now heaving, making the little MG rock, and a low gurgle emerges out of the sari stuffed in her mouth. Kedar wonders if he has gone too far. The sound is like Krakatoa erupting. The driver stops reversing the lorry, thinking he has hit someone. The labourers standing around the vehicle turn to look at the rich girl in the open car screaming with laughter.

'Not that you care too much about... as we know... oh, oh, oh, poor Mr Dandy... poor, poor, bechara Mr Dandy! Bismy *did* take a patch out of your new trousers, didn't he? Everybody still remembers that at home!'

Keya's hand stays moored on Kedar's thigh as she shakes with the memory.

'No, he did *not*! That bloody canine hippopotamus actually bit my *car*! He took a patch off my mudguard!' Kedar starts laughing himself, as he remembers the hurried end of his first visit to the Dutta house on Short Street.

'I really thought you'd never come back.' Keya's hand softens but does not move from Kedar's leg. The way clear, Kedar lets out the clutch, feeling Keya's hand on his shifting muscles. He takes them on to Brabourne Road, where two more lorries are involved in similar manoeuvres. He stops again and puts the car into neutral. Then he remembers fuel is now rationed and he turns off the ignition, from which place it's a natural transition for his hand to drop and rest on Keya's. His crotch is now bothering him, and he changes the subject.

'Do you know why these lorries are here?'

'No...' The fight has gone out of Keya and her voice is suddenly languorous.

'Borun-kaku's friend Joyesh works at Mac & Fergu back there. They've been practicing air-raid drills every other day. He told us some shaheb realized the cellars don't have enough space for all the staff. So, naturally, the management will have priority. But now, all these firms have to build temporary shelters for the babus and peons, et cetera.'

'Ei shono?' Keya straightens and smooths down her hair. 'Who's at home today?'

'Ballygunge? Everybody. It's like a Sunday. Why?' Kedar starts the car, curves around St Andrew's Church and on to Dalhousie Square.

'Na... I was just thinking... after lunch... but same problem at Short Street. All the staff, your favourite dogs, Dragon-pishi's friend Mrs Talukdar waiting for her husband to reach here from Rangoon. House full, even without us.'

'Well, has this Mrs Talukdar checked at Sealdah Station? You do know they're keeping Howrah clear, but there are many people at Sealdah who don't know where they are. All come in from Burma, shell-shocked. Many in rags, so you can't tell whether they're plantation labour or bhadralok.'

'Now don't be overdramatic! She has word that he managed to board a ship.'

'I thought ships were reserved for women and children.'

'And VIPs. He's the manager of some teak karobaar.'

'Anyway, your servants would—'

'No. Chandrakant's silence, once bought, is pakka.'

'Rasko's, too, and I don't even have to buy it, but... let me think.'

Kedar guns the car on to an empty stretch and brings them next to the long portico of the Great Eastern. As they drive past, his eye is caught by a pattern in the windows of the hotel. He looks again and notes that each glass pane now has a diagonal cross of tape. Keya notices him look up.

'Don't even think of it, Kedar Lahiri! I'm not that kind of... All I wanted was a little time alone, without causing an all-India scandal, so don't get carried away, thiik achhey? Keep that for trysts with your King Kong mem, should you become so fortunate!'

'For when you're in Shimla with Count von Bismarck,' Kedar grins. 'Except, I don't prey on women who are betrothed to my friends.'

'Hm. Have you been meeting her, then?' Keya is smiling, but her mask is back in place.

'Only seen her a couple of times since that Christmas Eve. Once she was having tea at South Club, with Wardle, this friend of Hillcott's, same regiment, who's been assigned to Staff College in Quetta.'

'He'll be studying with Dada, then.'

'Yes, the two of them and three hundred others, yes,' Kedar says. Then adds, but only in his mind, 'All studiedly avoiding the Defeat Bash.'

'Well, the army does select only the bravest and most intelligent officers for Staff College, ones who've proved themselves, so actually, no more than two hundred from all of India and North Africa.' Keya reaches for another cigarette. 'And the second time? When was the second time you saw Miss King Kong?'

'I was driving somewhere, and I saw her with some local girl, walking on the Maidan. No one we'd know. Some girl in a simple shawl. Maybe she's learning Bangla or something.'

'Simple shawl! Just look at *you*, wearing a shirt with frayed collars!' Relief and nicotine make Keya fully waspish again. 'Fat chance they'd allow you into Great Eastern looking like this. If you cared a jot, you would have dressed properly to meet me! I don't think they'll let us into Firpo's.'

'Well, if they don't, we'll go to Peiping and have chimney soup.' Kedar nips away the cigarette from Keya's fingers.

'I really wanted that chicken pie they serve at Firpo's, no spice, no jhaal, just plain old, good old, properly cooked chicken in a nice crust... my god, what on earth is that?'

They've slowed down near Metro Cinema and stopped at the crossing near Whiteway & Laidlaw's, and Keya is pointing to the new structures obscuring the department store's massive show windows.

'They are called blast walls,' Kedar explains. 'The theory is that people can take shelter behind them during a bombing raid. Though I have a feeling these are to protect the damned windows.'

Kedar waits for the traffic policeman to lower his arm. The banging at the back of the car startles him, and he whirls around, fully expecting to see an irate Gurkha. The beggar woman is so frail he can't at first connect the powerful thumping to her skeletal limbs. But the woman does it again, almost not looking at him, not aware where she's hitting the bodywork with her free arm. It takes him a moment to notice the little rat of a baby she has pasted to her breast under her torn sari. The woman looks at him and then finds Keya's eyes. The bone of her arm goes up to her mouth in a slow eating gesture.

'Ei! Jaao!' Run along! Kedar's standard response comes out, but he can hear the chink of small change as Keya reaches into her purse.

'Eita oke diye dao.' Give these to her. Keya hands him two four-anna coins.

Kedar has to turn around in his seat and lean out – the woman's eyes are rolling, and she makes no move to come closer. As the traffic around him starts to move, a couple of cars sound their horns in irritation. Finally, Kedar finds the beggar's hand and he forces himself to touch it, which is the only way he can convey the coins into the dry palm.

He wipes his hand on his knee before gripping the steering wheel. 'Rarely seen one of them so desperate,' he says.

Keya has taken the cigarette back from Kedar as he has leaned out of the car. She pulls on it. 'Baba says the poor will really suffer when the Japanese come. The Japs will hardly think it's their responsibility to feed India's paupers.'

'I hope they do let us in,' says Kedar, prising the cigarette back. 'I'm suddenly hungry now.'

Keya spills a small, mischievous giggle. 'Talking about pies, do you know what I heard? You remember that man, Krishen Wahi? You know, the one who owns those clothing stores near New Market?'

'Him? Oh yes. Punjabi business chap. Keeps trying to oil his way into the club, but people have shown some sense so far. Blocked his bid twice.'

'Well, someone who didn't... ki bolbo... block his bid, was that other mem you were trying to flirt with, ki naam? Eve something, na? Jewish something? Anyway, Wahi apparently told Dada's friend Anshu-da that he had *fully enjoyed partaking of that hot little pie*. Unlike you, darling, it seems he managed to get what he wanted. Even lent her money to pay off her hotel bill and take the ship to New Zealand.'

Kedar remembers the waiter singing outside Great Eastern. When he had scurried away, it had sounded as if he was wearing anklet-bells. He remembers forming the sentence – 'Poor man, robbed of his song by bookish highwaymen!' As they approach Firpo's, Kedar forces himself to retrieve a couple of phrases from that Raag Shree.

LUNCH AT FIRPO'S

The white gloved hand places the leather folder on the table.

'Saheb.' The waiter salutes and steps away.

'Sure about the dessert wine, Jeremy? Last chance.' Todd-Cartwright reaches for the folder.

'Quite sure. Are you sure about the...' Lambert wills his hand to move towards his wallet. A sharp fold in the white tablecloth grazes across his knuckles, burning slightly.

'Not to fret, old boy. The old man was quite clear. This is coming out of the Section's little war chest.' Todd-Cartwright flicks his eyes over the bill, slaps two broad ten-rupee notes into the folder and waves it in the air without turning around. Lambert has calculated the amount while ordering, and it comes to a hefty sixteen rupees and eight annas. Cream of asparagus for him and spinach soup for T-C, one each of the excellent local beckty dressed up as 'Dover sole', a concoction called 'Chicken Rasputin' for T-C, breast wrapped with bits of bacon and a touch of red chilli, quite adventurous, and straightforward pork chops with mint sauce for himself, astonishingly satisfying. Two small pots of crème brûlée accompanied by the best coffee in the city. A six-rupee bottle of very reasonable claret adding a final kick to the tally. Plus, the order of one of their famous chicken pies for Deyton, the sergeant. Rangoon fallen two days ago, all of bloody Burma soon lost, probably. This lunch being Currie's reward for their hard, relentless work through the three hellish months that have followed the Jap landings in early December.

'I say, squadron leader, I've asked Todd-Cartwright to drive around and take a good look at the preparations. You can do city proper later, of course, but for now a close recce, really, around the perimeter, you know, Budge-Budge, Barrackpore, Canning, Howrah, just to see how it looks to the native *public*, to the suburban chappie on the omnibus, so to speak. Must shore up their spirits, you see. And I also thought it might be a good idea for you to go along, in case anything strikes your airman's eye.' Currie had looked down at the maps of the Greater Calcutta area that Lambert and Deyton had marked up for him since early December. 'They've been jolly useful, these night flights of yours. I've even had a thank you from Fort William. If one reads between the lines, heats the invisible ink, they are truly grateful we've taken on the task of pinpointing the chinks in the blackout. Now what we require is a jolly good dekko during daylight. The major concentrating on how the defences might better boost public confidence, and you looking out for whatever pops up as a potential problem if, *if* the Japs do come calling.'

Todd-C and Lambert had left just before dawn and driven around the edges of Calcutta, paying special attention to the southern periphery over which the raids would probably come. Though he had now flown over them at night, almost once a week since December, these were far-flung parts of Greater Calcutta that Lambert had never been to before. It felt strange to see the places redacted by the blackout in harsh sunlight. Small factories sticking out of paddy fields, now enclosed by walls of sandbags; an abandoned old jute plant on the river, with a brand new observation tower hiding behind a crumbling chimney stack, the wood of the cross-struts and ladder splinter-fresh; two fake anti-aircraft emplacements at the edge of an embankment, barrels made from wood poking out of camouflage netting, that almost seemed to escort a listing old ferry as it smoked its way south into the delta waters; another tower sticking straight out of a cluster of mud huts on the swampland to the east.

Lambert looked out for things that would stand out, too white or bright, too contrasting, too tall, not properly camouflaged. The new baffle walls sprouted in all sorts of strange places, some yet to be plastered and painted, the fresh earth-red of the bare brick startling against the moss-covered walls of a godown or the venerable sprawl of a manager's bungalow. Some of the new brick already slapped over with the big polka dots of cowpats, for the existence of which Lambert was now deeply grateful. At one point, the crew gone god knows where, naked urchins playing on an actual anti-aircraft gun, using the camouflage netting as a swing, hanging off the barrel and jumping on the wheels, driving Todd-C to expletives and furious note-taking. Two months ago, Lambert reckoned, the man would have laughed. Lambert remembered the flurry of quips from Todd-C when Deyton and he had raised the business of the Memorial four days after the Malaya landings. But that was before Todd-C's old unit was taken prisoner outside Singapore.

Sweat beginning to trickle behind their ears, they finished their inspection of the city near Dum-Dum aerodrome. Heading back to town, the major pulled over next to a canal and snatched open his map.

'Not much stopping them from simply giving these a wide berth, is there? From sweeping around and coming in from the north?'

'Yes, Alan, except any Jap raider would be at the very edge of his range by the time he got here. They probably won't be able to monkey around too much. At most, a very brief in and out, no more than five minutes over main target, which would be the port. Port being on the southern side, I can't imagine they'd risk a sweep north.' Lambert has patiently repeated the assessment he has worked out over the last month, taking the sortie base not from Rangoon but from a point much closer to the Assam border and from another realistic point in the Bay of Bengal, assuming a carrier force. It's a calculation the local RAF command and others have matched in their own reports.

'All that might well change in a couple of weeks, mightn't it?'

'Yes, well, if the Japanese have an extra carrier or two we don't know about, that they slip past us in the bay. They won't manage to lay strips in the jungle quite yet.'

'Well, yes... but bloody huge bay... and not much navy left.'

It had been fascinating for Lambert to see Todd-C's humour spring little leaks and then capsize completely as things went from bad to worse. In the same period, Sergeant Deyton's sails seemed to have picked up some mysterious wind. The man's grin had widened and his wit had grown more teeth. Last evening, Todd-C had told him of their planned expedition. 'The chief has given us a *budget* for the picnic, so would you, young Leonard, like us to bring you back some tuck from Firpo's?'

'Firpo's, sir?' Deyton's face betrayed no desire or envy.

'Yes, that's where I've booked a lunch for the squadron leader and myself. Loathe to leave you out, but...'

'Thank you, sir, but isn't it officers only, that place? Anyway, I'm getting used to the food Jimmy's been bringing us. It's quite similar to the rations in the enemy's POW camps, I'm told, which should have me in quite good training.' It was a risky joke, given that Todd-C's comrades were now actually in those POW camps, but Deyton got away with it because morally he had the upper hand: it was his way of pointing out that the officers receive better food from the hotel kitchens than the non-commissioned staff in Ochterlony, and that one special meal from Firpo's wouldn't necessarily offset that.

'Yeh tumhare liye hai.' This is for you. Todd-C suddenly notices the waiter and points to the two whole rupees he's leaving as a tip. He even smiles at the man. The difference two months can make, Lambert thinks. Last November, Todd, aka Toff-C, would have left no more than a rupee, if that, and not acknowledged the waiter at all. That slightly ingratiating smile is new, freshly imported from the burning pyres of Singapore and Rangoon.

Toff-C hands Lambert the brown paper bag with Deyton's pie and pushes back his chair. As they leave, Lambert steals one last glance at the battlefield of glass, china and silver scattered across the table, pewter coffee pot still standing, condensation still melting on the empty glasses of iced water. Who knows when they'll be able to make the ten-minute journey again from the Great Eastern to Firpo's, who knows whether this place will be shattered by bombs like the grand restaurants of Singapore, or boarded up completely while awaiting the arrival of new customers with completely different tastes? Lambert is pretty sure of the calculations he has made, but deep inside him is a small file marked 'Unexpected Enemy Advance', a file he has had to reach for quite a few times since the 7th of December.

'Excuse me! *So* sorry!' The woman's voice is high and gay.

'Oh, I *do* beg your pardon!' Todd-Cartwright steps back to let an Indian couple precede them down the stairway. The woman is clearly somewhat tiddly, also carrying a brown paper bag with the Firpo's legend, no doubt also containing a chicken pie. The man Lambert has seen before, though he can't quite place him. Toff-C waits at the top of the stairs, letting the couple reach the ground floor, chattering happily about the lunch they've just finished. Once they are out of earshot, he gives himself the freedom.

'That little bugger there, with his tennis shoes. Quite the Playboy of the Eastern World. Pretty sure he was well in with that Polish minx, d'you remember her at all? Staying at the hotel, pretending to be an heiress of some sort? And now he's clearly chained to this new little lovely... Also *quite* friendly with that Hillcott fellow, that bright staffer from Hutton's bunch.'

Suddenly Lambert remembers following a couple, up a flight of stairs instead of down, back at the hotel last... August, possibly... smell of rain outside. Yes, this same man, with another woman wrapped around him. White girl. Minx.

'Lucky blighter. Is it legal?'

'What? Sleeping with women? Slipping some girl a length? I should hope so!'

'No, I meant, you know, natives and Europeans... er... mingling, I meant.'

Todd-C stifles a guffaw. 'Good *point*, Jeremy! Shouldn't be, at least not with wartime shortages! You'd imagine there would be rations reserved just for us! In any case, I wouldn't imagine there are too many of these pairings, Indian fellows with European women. And as to marriage, I'm not sure you can stop anybody marrying, and I'm afraid all the rest of it is probably just within the boundaries of the law.' Todd-C's spirits have clearly been bolstered by the meal. Lambert joins in the low mirth, but somewhere there is the rub of longing and Todd-C senses it.

'Old chap, not my place, really, but could I...'

They are out on the pavement under one of the porticos lining Chowringhee and the early March heat embraces them. Lambert looks enquiringly at Todd-Cartwright.

'Jeremy. You do know they've got arrangements?'

'Arrangements?'

'Yes. You remember we were discussing it at the last chukker? About the places they've assigned for enlisted men. You remember Currie mentioning specific houses on Ripon Street and off the Central Avenue, close to Chinatown?'

'Oh, *yes*, good god, yes, *oh*, you mean...'

'Well, no, they're for lower ranks and one can't be seen near those, obviously. But there are provisions, quite fulsome and discreet provisions, should one... should an officer also find himself unable to, um, fully concentrate on the war effort, shall we say?'

Lambert is at a loss to reply, and he is thankful that they've come up behind the couple again. There is a small pile of garbage on the street at the end of the portico, smashed green coconut shells, half-masticated straw and horse dung, sodden bits of paper bags made from old newspapers. Clearly the detritus from the most recent garbage men's strike. The dapper boy is helping the young mademoiselle navigate over this mess, gallantly holding her hand.

On the other side of the side street, two men sitting in a strange vehicle observe this manoeuvre with naked concentration. The vehicle is an open motorcar. It seems to have been constructed by a Meccano enthusiast in squares and rectangles of metal, every strut and bolt showing. The body is painted a matte, dark green and there are small numbers stencilled in white along one side of the square tabletop of a bonnet, giving away that this is military transport. As Lambert gets closer, he can see that there is a large, five-pointed white star painted on the green of the bonnet and an accompanying one on the side. Despite a powdering of dust and some flecks of mud, one can see that the brutish, large tyres are still hot from the factory mould, their treads still sharp.

So taken is Lambert with this vehicle that he fails to notice the exchange between the two men and the Indian couple. Todd-Cartwright interrupts his thoughts.

'Astounding. No shame at all.'

'What d'you mean?'

'You mean you didn't see that blonde fellow slowly raise his little cap and smile at our Indian princess? Lecherous isn't the word for it. He put aside the book he was reading, some sort of guidebook to India, chucked his fag, and actually climbed out of the thing and bowed low, as though the little playboy was invisible. The Negro at the wheel merely adjusted his helmet, grinned and chewed his gum. But he was gaping as well, also clearly delighted at the chance to run his monkey eyes over a local beauty.'

'Good lord. Where was I?' The drooping flag on the nose of the bonnet flutters open in Lambert's mind, some sort of eagle unwrinkling from the folds.

'Indeed, Jeremy, what *were* you looking at? And then, the best thing, our playboy was least pleased to see his property being fondled by foreign eyes, so he took a firm grip of the young lady's upper arm and literally *dragged* her away!'

'She went uncomplainingly, I take it?'

'Well, a peal of laughter, and a small return bow to the gallant Yank before turning her attention back to the beau.'

By the time they see the couple again, they are walking away quickly to the row of cars parked in front of the twin cinemas next to New Market.

'What a beauty.' Lambert can't help himself.

'Yes, far more of an exotic beauty than the Polish firecracker, I have to say,' Todd-C murmurs. 'Though, that one was quite fetching as well.'

'Come again, Alan? Didn't know the Polish army had comparable transport.'

Todd-Cartwright turns to look at Lambert with slight alarm on his face.

'Beg *your* pardon, old chap, but what on earth are *you* talking about?'

'The… jeep. I believe that was a jeep, made by the Willys company. Willys Jeep, quite revolutionary, it's supposed to be, *a turret-less tank on four wheels* as one magazine described it. Goes over or through anything. We're supposed to be getting some as well. In fact, the LRDG already have a few, and apparently they're the very devil in the desert…'

Todd-C gulps as if he's trying to swallow several flies. Lambert notices this and lets go of whatever he is saying about the Long Range Desert Group's use of the jeep in North Africa.

Their Austin staff car is parked two away from the playboy's vehicle. As they reach it, they can see the little man sitting at the wheel, shaking his head as if to clear it. The girl slips into the passenger's seat. Lambert's eyes follow her fingers as she flicks them across her full little mouth and then across her temple, pushing back an errant strand of coal-black hair. He catches another glimpse of her equally black eyes just before she affixes a pair of dark glasses to her face. The playboy pulls out, gunning his engine while loudly troubling some local song. Todd-C waits for them to go before opening his door. 'Well, the bugger certainly hasn't made his conquests through melody.'

'No, you're quite right, she *is* lovely, that girl. Quite fair too, for a native.'

'Old chap, we must see to you.' Todd-C pushes back the peak of his cap and lets out the clutch.

Over the next two weeks, as the Japanese continue their advance from Rangoon, Lambert keeps thinking about the Indian girl. One day, soon after the Firpo's lunch, Todd-Cartwright slips Lambert a card. The muddy letterpress says 'Madame Toussaint, Palmistry and Tarot', and underneath that 'Strictly by Appointment', followed by a number of a house on Russell Street and a phone number that's been scratched over. On the back, someone has scrawled 'Opp. Royal Turf Club, only after 9 p.m., no telephone'.

Lambert keeps the card in his wallet, and his fingers reach for it from time to time. It's the 9 p.m. business that makes it impossible, he tells himself. That's just when his work starts. How is he to take off precisely at the time of the day the material starts to come in? Clearly impossible. In some ways, it's easier to imagine what things might be like with that Indian girl. Some odd afternoon in this clammy March, where she and himself find themselves stranded in, say, a hotel room. Perhaps with Japanese bombers roaring low overhead, the city a smoking shambles, the girl's poise gone, her native hoity-toity reserve gone, the dot on her forehead slightly smudged by sweat, her cotton drape coming unravelled, her eyes widening with rising fear. Both in his dreams and daydreams, all of Calcutta coming unravelled, the whole city he has been trying to stuff under the blanket of darkness since early December mercilessly stripped naked, all his work in vain.

It was the peak of summer the day he died, 28 July 1974.

A couple of days earlier, he'd watched me load Missus's suitcase into the old taxi.

'Well, keep out of mischief, you two!' she said, waving goodbye through the window.

'Why, dear comrade?' he cackled, in high good spirits. 'Now why should we keep out of mischief? Cat's away! Mice will play!'

'Why indeed!' she replied, also cheerful, or trying to be. 'You've outlived old Picpisso by an age, so now *why* should you care?'

There was no question of them touching, or any hug or goodbye kiss. In the five years I'd known them, I'd hardly seen them make any physical contact while sober, and the contact while drunk was almost that of two male college chums. If they'd ever had a relationship that involved physical contact, it was long buried in the pit of time, leaving behind no visible traces. Arriving or leaving, I would be sure to get a warm embrace from both of them, but with each other, they were different. Later, I tried to imagine that her eyes were wet. But that wasn't the case at all, or, let's say, if her eyes were wet it was because she'd herself been drinking since just after breakfast, and the gin often made her eyes water. If she'd had any premonition that this was the final adieu, she certainly didn't show it. It wouldn't have taken anything as weighty as premonition, of course, because he was now sliding down quite quickly, and she'd told me that each of the last few times she'd gone off on a trip, she'd been prepared not to find him alive when she returned. Since April, I'd been spending as much time down here as my university work would allow – so that she could go about her political work without having to hang around, waiting for him to die.

'Remember, won't you? The benighted Medicine's visit is fixed for day after tomorrow, for three o'clock.' This was to me. A wave to him, a dab of the handkerchief to her eyes and forehead to wipe the sweat, a light slap on the driver's seat and the taxi pulled away over the bumpy track that led to the road to town.

'She's *bloody* right! I've outlived old Picpisso by a distance! That's right!' He was still cackling, drunk already, barely able to stand. I didn't bother pointing out that old Picpisso, aka the hated Picasso, had died at the ripe old age of ninety-one, whereas it didn't look as though he, El Elko, was even going to make it to his fifty-fifth, which was on October 13th. I didn't point out that outliving someone by a year and perhaps a few months didn't quite qualify as 'by a distance', not quite. I'm not sure, but I suspect it was a joke between the two of them, something they'd built up since the first bout of cirrhosis in '68, something like 'I'm damned if I'll die before that wormy old bull!', and now here they were, using it for gallows humour.

In the previous few months, I could only record him every now and then, depending on his mood. My tape recorder was usually banished from his presence: 'You failed gold digger, you've mined whatever you need from me! Now no more of that infernal tape machine! Just make fucking notes if you absolutely fucking must!'

The fucking notes. And the fucking must.

Over the last few days he'd begun to quote from Tagore, 'Shawmukhe shanti parabar, bhashao torini hey kornodhar', sometimes the English translation elocuted in his Rasko accent, 'Thi oshaan oph peace laays in phront!' Slaaide in the boat, O hyelmsman...' Sometimes Hurree Jamset Ram Singh's pidgin rising out of the crypt of Billy Bunter books, 'There is the dashed sad sorrowfullness, there's is the utter unavoidability of deathness, the separatious fire is burning...' On the day, I'd made lunch, salad for myself and soup for him, which was about the only thing he could keep down, and I was trying to limit his pre-lunch hara-kiris, as he now called his drinks.

'Eat something?'

He'd grinned. 'You eat, my boy. Eat for me as well. May you eat for a long time!'

'You don't want to eat?'

He suddenly straightened up in his chair and pointed to someone behind me. 'Oi dyakho, oi chheley-ta ke!' Look there, look at that boy! 'No slavery to maya whatsoever! Koto free!'

He looked back at me, raised his glass of pastis and knocked it back. His body pressed the eject button, he heaved once, twice and the spew caught me as I was moving towards him. He sank back and went quiet. I tried to pull him forward but I was shaking a rag doll, there was nobody home.

The Medicine, which is how they referred to the local doctor, arrived on the day with perfect timing, not twenty minutes after Elko collapsed. I'd rung his chambers where they told me he'd already left to come see us, and sure enough, I soon heard his little car struggling up the track. He did the necessary examination and confirmed demise. We lifted Elko off the armchair, from where I'd dared not move him, and took him to his bedroom. I pushed aside the bedpan with my foot and we laid him on the bed. A small-built man in the first place, the booze had hollowed him out and lifting him felt no more difficult than carrying a stack of his watercolour pads. I was prepared to be embarrassed on his behalf at the smell, but today, somehow, he didn't smell too bad and neither did the bedroom. The doctor assured me there was nothing I could have done. He reminded me gently that he'd been saying to us, Missus and me, that it was only a matter of time before parts of the maestro's body would cease to function. He was already in the early stages of jaundice from irrecoverable cirrhosis but this seemed to have been a massive heart attack. In a way it was good he had gone quickly, rather than after a long, liver-failing coma.

The doctor scrawled a statement across his headed prescription sheet and signed it. He handed it to me and told me I should show it to the police when they came – if he could please use the telephone, he would call them right away. The police visiting was entirely routine after any death, and here they would obviously need to do the paperwork connected with the death of a foreign national, but there should be no problem. He also made another call. Shortly, the hearse would come to take Elko to the local morgue, where his body could be kept until Missus came back and we decided what to do. Best not to keep him here too long in this heat. Obviously, the hearse couldn't come up the track, but not to worry, the driver and his assistant would take him down to the road by stretcher.

I reached for my wallet to pay him for the visit, as always, but he waved it away. Thank you, but no question of money today. He would be visiting the madam, of course, to condole with her and for any explanations she might want, and I too should not hesitate to call him in case of any issues, but there shouldn't be any. He was obliged to take my leave now, many other sick people in the area, and even other people with the same illness, the maestro was hardly the only one in this region who let the alcohol ride him instead of the other way around.

I went outside just as the cicadas were raising their massed machine-voice in mourning.

This twisting rose from my stomach – I'd let him slip away from under my nose, that I'd failed as a guard and let the thief of death enter the house, that I'd been lax and somehow failed to lock a crucial door or window.

His favourite spiky trees circled me in a chorus of the 'bloody crickets' as he called them. The conjunction of light was among the ones he loved best, the sun just beginning to slant, every element of the hills, rocks, trees and fields just slipping into chiaroscuro, the smell from the brush overpowering, going beyond fragrance into a sharp reminder, as he used to put it, that 'the universe doesn't perfume itself for us, just as it doesn't adorn itself with colour for us – the universe isn't trying to seduce us, the universe doesn't give a fuck about us'. After a while, the feeling was outside me. I'd manage to eject it, as if it was some alien, semi-solid thing the uncaring universe had produced. It was now this live, breathing thing in my hand, some small sea creature scooped up by mistake, or a snail or a crab. For a while, I watched this thing pulsating across my palm, before flicking my wrist and sending it into the rocks. He'd never been under my nose or under my guarding, and the doors and windows had been smashed open well before I first met the two of them.

Sitting among his big-band albums, and the Western and Indian classical records, there was the Hemanta Mukherjee LP of Rabindra Sangeet, published by HMV sometime in the mid-60s. It wasn't a record he listened to that often, but he'd put it on every now and then, just so we could have a laugh. His general opinion of Tagore songs and their rendering was pithy. 'It's an ocean of the worst, sentimental caterwauling, except this Hemanta has a voice that saves it, him and that mad Hemanga, that George Biswas fellow, they're the only two who can make some of the old man's *compositions* bearable.' Actually, there was only one track that we would play again and again, and it would start him laughing almost uncontrollably. Putting it on, Elko would straighten up and grasp a pose, one hand cupping his ear, the other arm rigidly stretched out in song.

'Jei raatey mor duaar guli bhaanglo jhorey...' Then he'd pause and change languages. 'You know, Rasko used to sing this and then translate into English... *Thaa naaight... thaa shthorm... brokoppen mai doors...*' He would laugh through the whole length of the tune, even as he sang it word for word, first in Bangla, then in crude English. He would laugh,

but I could tell every time he played it, he was also close to tears and ashamed to let it show.

After a while, I went back into the house. There were things to be done, such as sending Missus a telegram, and tracking down the old gourmand wherever he was gorging himself this summer and summon him, as instructed by Elko. Thirdly, there was the business of letting his family know, but that wasn't, strictly speaking, in my parish. It was something I could perhaps leave to the Missus Rani Saheba herself, once she returned. I wondered how the family would receive the news in Calcutta, how big the notices would be in *The Statesman* and the two big Bengali newspapers, whether the family would spend any money at all, drawing attention and further embarrassment to themselves, or whether they'd just do the minimum and bury it in the personal columns. I would have to make the one call to Calcutta anyway, and there was also the matter of locating old Rasko and telling him as well, if he was still alive somewhere in Midnapur, as Elko had thought he was. That then left America, which I supposed was my job and not something I should ask Missus to do while she was dealing with her grief.

The house was much cooler than the roasting countryside outside, but yet again I found myself wishing the place had some proper fans instead of the tabletop toys both of them insisted were fine for this part of the world. I walked around where we'd been sitting near the music system, as if that space was separately alive, still populated by Elko and his energy. I looked at the bottle of ayurvedic liver pills, Liv 52, that someone had sent him all the way from Calcutta – 'Well, they've worked! I've lived fifty-four!' I considered picking up the bottles and the glasses, but I finally settled on the bowl of soup that I'd brought out for him. As I took it back into the kitchen, I found myself scooping spoonfuls into my mouth. He might be dead, but I was still, unquestionably, alive. And I was angrily hungry, having got tired of waiting for him to eat before feeding myself, just like Ma used to do when I was a kid.

The passageway from the living room to the kitchen had a small table against the wall bracketed by a couple of broken chairs on which they liked to dump things. The light blue KLM airline bag was still there on the chair nearer to the kitchen, just as it had been for the last year, the

M covered over with a rough square of marker slashes in a darker blue, so that the first two white letters became his initials, which she'd flipped around into LK as in 'LK-holic', and then to 'Elko' or – when feeling generous – to 'El Elko, the third brother of El Greco and El Gecko.'

He'd pointed to the bag only recently, repeating himself, as he was wont to do by the end, 'Last will and testicles, old boy, such as it is, all in there. It's only a small mess, but do help her take care of it, won't you?' Yes, of course. As if I had a choice. Any fucking choice. There was no question of touching the damn thing until she came back, who knew what might crawl out, but also, if there was one thing I'd been taught when young, it was never to reach for what might not belong to you. In any case, it didn't really matter what the bag contained, or what the will might say. Here I was now, facing what I had to do, what I had no desire at all to do right now, what I knew I could not escape from trying to do. I supposed, now that his life was over, I could really look at it as a finished work, in Kahn's terms as a properly ruined – and therefore completed – building. I supposed I could, if I fucking must.

I went into his studio and looked again at the last thing he'd been working on, a dark oil, roughly three feet by two feet, swirling with night mist, with a whitish glow on the left of centre that anyone from Calcutta would recognize, even from the unusual angle. Like many of his other paintings, it was not a sight he'd actually seen himself, it was a rendering of a story he had been told. He hadn't really touched the canvas for days, not very much, just staring at it and talking to it in a low voice, and the paint was already quite dry except in one or two spots where he'd recently added some reflections to the water. To me it looked finished enough, and I was glad for that. I made sure the draping cloth wasn't touching the surface and went back to the kitchen. I was still really hungry.

I'd just finished eating, directly from the pot, when I heard someone calling from the gate.

The two men, with the stretcher vertical between them, were friendly, grave, sympathetic, professional. This is what they did for a living, maybe three or four times a day, on a bad day perhaps eight or nine times. One of the men had a form on a clipboard, his reading glasses were not new and slightly dusty.

'Name of the deceased person, please?'

'I'd better spell it for you.' He handed me the ballpoint and clipboard, and I wrote it down in block letters, surname: L-a-h-i-r-i, and then name: K-e-d-a-r, leaving out the 'Nath' in the middle that he so hated, that was nevertheless on his passport, hoping they wouldn't notice.

'Here you are.'

'Thank you. Profession?'

'Artist. Painter.'

'Ah, like Picasso?'

'Exactly.'

BEACONS

Nearly four months ago now, but that moonless night has accompanied Lambert across the weeks.

When he signs the log before taking off from Alipore Aerodrome, it's 0200 hours on the 12th of December 1941, four days after Pearl Harbor and three after the Kota Bharu landings. The date stays with him, like the frayed, right-hand flying glove that he's worn on every flight since he was commissioned.

Deyton is in the seat next to him, and he waits until the plane is truly airborne, settled and biting into the winter air well above the ground mist before asking. Lambert gives him the permission to smoke. 'Yes, but I'll need it off in a few minutes. We do need to make this as realistic as possible, sergeant. Don't imagine the Nips will be coming in with fags in their mouths, somehow.' As Deyton lights up, Lambert takes the plump Hudson into a climb away from the airfield, crossing the river almost immediately and heading, initially, in the direction of Midnapore and Orissa Province beyond. The Hudson's cockpit 'skylights', the triangular windows fixed above the pilots' seats, seem to push darkness down upon them rather than provide the extra vision for which they're designed. As he climbs, Lambert can feel the air progressively cool through the side slat Deyton's kept open. Gradually, the ground smells recede, replaced by the clean whipping of cold December air mingling with the engine fumes.

After fifteen minutes, Deyton stubs out his second cigarette in a tin he's carrying specially for the purpose. 'I'd say the bus turns left here, sir.' The timing is exactly correct, but Lambert does not acknowledge it. He banks the Hudson and takes it out south over the sea. After another twenty minutes, Lambert flicks a glance at Deyton, who's now looking down at a map with a small torch.

'Yes?'

'Yes, turn now, sir.'

'You can do without the formalities on these jaunts, sergeant.'

'My name's Len, as you know.'

'Turning now, Len, thank you.' Lambert coaxes the stub-nosed plane into a wide 180-degree change of direction. 'Height?'

'Correct, as per our calculations, yes si—yes, by now they would be here, at about 8,000, and coming down.'

Lambert tries to imagine he's flying a Japanese bomber. He puts the aircraft into a shallow descent, his eyes flicking between his altimeter and the spread of dark uneasiness below them which is the Bay of Bengal.

'They might try something different, of course.' Deyton plays with a fresh cigarette in his hand.

'Of course, Len,' Lambert snaps, but as if at a friend, 'but our orders are to get the first suspects out of the way. A Tojo Carrier force gets through RN patrols, such as we can now muster, and sends a terror raid at the sleeping city of Calcutta. Straight up from the bay. Straight in and out.'

'Right.' Deyton doesn't remind Lambert that he was present when Lambert proposed this scenario at the billiard table two days ago.

Below the reconnaissance aircraft, the dim, starlit earth has shifted. It's as if they are now suspended over a mass of sleeping serpents, gargantuan criss-crossed creatures, barely discernible in the gloom, their scales uneven, and should one of them awake suddenly, long enough to rear up and smack them out of the sky. Lambert shakes his head to loosen the accumulation of sleepless nights. The scales running up the snakes' bodies are actually hundreds of small silt islets, and the snakes themselves are the waterways formed by larger, more permanent islands, the whole making up the great estuary where the Ganges disinvests itself into the Bay of Bengal.

'Couldn't see anything marking the entrance to main river,' Deyton notes.

'Might be under the mist. More likely, they've switched off the beacons for some reason. We should check.'

'This point is called Gang-a Sag-ar here.'

'You haven't done your homework, Len. *Gungaa* is what they call the Ganges, *Sagar* is what they call the sea, so where the Gungaa meets the sea. And, to confuse you further, this last bit of the river here is called the Hooghly. Don't ask me why.'

As they fly up the lace of rivulets, thick and narrow, flickering winter clouds escort the plane. Closer to the ground, runnels of winter mist lay their own unmappable tracery over the delta, the lighter grey sometimes mimicking the water channels, sometimes not. Having already done this in daylight, Lambert knows that flying northward, the mince of earth begins to coalesce, the land mass forming almost despite itself, increasing in size and eventually isolating the main channel of the river at the apex of the immense triangle of unstable water and mud. Tonight, looking right, he's hard put to locate the town of Canning, slightly south-east of Calcutta, which is the last large settlement on the Hooghly–Ganges before the maze of jungles and mangroves.

'Can't really see Canning,' voices Deyton, who's also leaning over, trying to see through Lambert's windows. 'D'you think they've put a blackout in place even before Calcutta?'

'Winter. Ferries shut down well before dusk. They're all asleep early, probably. Not too many lights, so the town probably has a natural b.o. anyway.'

Deyton nods and looks at the altimeter. '5,000 now,' he mutters and makes another note. After a little while, he speaks again, apropos of nothing. 'I keep trying to imagine there's people sleeping down there, even though you can't see 'em.'

'Not that many, Len, not south of Canning, though they're trying to get farmers to move there. Apparently, those little silt islands are made up of the most fertile soil on earth.'

'Yes, all the good muck the river's scraped up on its way here.' Deyton's a city man and it shows.

'But they shift, you know, those islands.' Lambert increases the angle of descent a touch. 'Imagine. There you are, old farmer MacDonald, *know this farm like the back of me hand, I do,* and you look over one morning and your whole bloody field's gone off somewhere.'

'Surely they don't go that quickly, do they?'

'No, but you have to keep a beady eye, I'm told. Apparently, you have to keep shifting your cultivation. And then there's the small matter of the tigers. Lots of tigers down there, white and black, not yellow, White Bengals, prowling in the growth. And cobras. And crocodiles and sharks in the water.'

'No wonder it's overpopulated.'

As they move away from the faintly reflecting waters, the darkness shuts around them. Lambert follows the invisible river on the map, bringing them closer to Calcutta. Both men automatically cease to chatter. After a while, Lambert puts the lugubrious Hudson into a circle, once to the left and then, after about five minutes of straight flying, once again to the right. 'Anything?' he asks.

'Nothing I can see.' Deyton is peering at the ground, searching for chinks of light from what should now be the far outskirts of the city, landmarks, anything that would help a night bomber find its way. 'No... nothing so far. No small fires, nothing. Looks pretty good to me. Your side?'

'Not a dot. We should come out earlier next time.' Lambert descends to 2,000 feet.

And then it's there, like a magician's trick.

It's as if they've lifted a covering and slipped under: suddenly the city is spread out ahead of them. A little to their left, the line of mist and river separates the darker, smaller Howrah part on the west from the much brighter sprawl on the east, where the criss-cross of faint, yellow dotted lines mark out the larger roads and avenues. From this height, and at this time of night, it doesn't look like much at all, this 'second city of the Empire'. There are none of the distinctive curves of the waterfronts of Bombay, Singapore or Shanghai, nothing of Hong Kong's steep hills in the flat expanse of the skewed diamond of settlement. Even in the better-lit main city, Lambert can see the light concentrated further to the north, around Central Avenue and north Calcutta, the pinpoints of street lamps gradually thinning out as they come closer to the south, into a darkening maze that Lambert knows is made up half of buildings and half of trees and ponds.

The squadron leader straightens in his seat and pushes back his flying helmet. 'Right. Let's have the shopping list then.'

Deyton turns his torch to the pad. 'Kidderpore Docks, first up, obviously.'

'Yes.'

Heading west again, the Hudson flies over the airfield from which they've taken off and finds the river again. Lambert spends a good while circling over the docks, taking the Hudson down to 1,000 feet and climbing up again to 5,000 while he and Deyton note the features visible from different altitudes. There is a cluster of shipping plainly on display, clearly on offer to any bomber that manages to reach this point, the vessels' night lights demarcating them even through the pockets of mist. At lower height, they can see the snouts of the cranes and the smaller launches and other craft that make up the floating connective tissue of any port. The warehouses are also delineated in the port's night lights, but the small train lines used within the dockyards are unclear.

'Sitting ducks?' Deyton ventures.

'With this illumination, certainly sitting ducks.'

'Noted.'

'Right, I'm going to keep her well under 2,000 from now on.'

'Right you are, skipper.'

Lambert glances over to check Deyton's dimly lit face for sarcasm. He decides he can't see any.

'Next?'

'Across the river, Howrah, factories, railway station.' Deyton looks at the curving band of thick, low mist that has formed over the centre of the Hooghly.

'Bearing north by northwest...' says Lambert unnecessarily. About a minute after he finishes saying it, they are above the massive industrial kidney of the city.

'Imagine this looks a bit like bloody Sheffield,' says Deyton.

'Tropical Sheffield,' says Lambert. 'They make everything down there. I just overheard Currie yesterday, giving security clearance for a whopping big order of flying helmets for the Russian Air Force, double-thick jobs lined with wool, to be made by a factory in Howrah, round-the-clock production.'

'Could they have made the best saddles during the Crimean War? I read somewhere that—'

'No, Len, that would be—'

'Ten o'clock, skipper!' Deyton's voice is mildly excited.

Lambert drops his left wing to look. After a moment, he also sees the small square of light cutting up through the murk. He takes them down for a closer look.

'Temple, some sort of temple is it?' As they circle over the illumination, they can now make out two minarets. 'No, mosque. Mohameddan mosque,' Deyton corrects himself, adding, 'mosques usually being Mohameddan.'

'D'you have it on the map now?'

'Yes, I think so.' Deyton makes a mark on his map. 'My god, that party's going on right next to – we should be able to use that mosque to find—'

'Railway station. Got it. Two o'clock.'

As Lambert tilts the plane to the right, Deyton again leans over to peer through the pilot's window. Sure enough, now that he knows what he's looking at, the faint parallel lines become legible through the mist – the platforms and sidings of Howrah Station. As Lambert circles, Deyton reconfirms the location of the mosque in relation to the railway complex. 'Might as well put beacons on top of the station clock tower, eh? We should strafe that mosque, don't you think, skip?'

'No, that would be wasting precious ammo,' Lambert mutters. 'I'd much prefer stringing them up the next morning as the Japs apparently do.'

'Well, can't rightly do that just yet, can we? Not having declared a blackout yet?'

'That was a joke, Len.' Lambert grins, something no one in the Section has ever seen before. 'A private joke just between us, mind you.'

Deyton avoids an answer. 'Next to railway station, the new bridge construction.'

'Hm. Better go up a bit, don't want to rearrange those precious cranes of theirs,' says Lambert, referring to the two engineers' gargoyles perched right on top of the bridge towers.

Lambert takes them over the brightly lit mosque, climbs a bit, and flies a line that takes the plane over the river again. Try as they do, they can't find the towers of the new bridge in the mist. After a while, Deyton speaks up again.

'Next, further north up the river, railway bridge at Bally, the...' Lambert joins in and they say it together in Todd-Cartwright's plummy accent, *'the bally railway bridge at Bally!'*

Twenty minutes later, eyes now tired from raking the undifferentiated darkness below, unable to conjure up the crucial railway bridge, the two men consider the next item on the list.

'Well, no question we need to bring in barrage balloons right away, day time cover around the port, around all the bridges and both the stations. But that's not our headache. You can light up again, Len, but don't you dare let slip you were smoking over target.'

'Thanks.' Deyton half opens his window, sparks his stick, and releases a huge plume of smoke towards the opening. The smoke gusts right back into the cockpit, making Lambert cough. 'Oh, sorry, skip.' Deyton holds his torch and cigarette in the same hand and cups it just over the map and his pad. 'It says here we're to make a sweep over north Calcutta, looking out for the temples and the big mosque, the Nak-hoda mosque, then down Central Avenue, swing west to Dalhousie Square and then head south along the river.'

'The heights, please, of the tall structures in the area.'

Deyton reads out the heights. Watching his altimeter, Lambert takes the Hudson for a leisurely low circuit over the densest part of the city, very little of it visible tonight, before making his way back towards the pinpoint of light from the mosque near the station, which is now at one o'clock.

Deyton reads off from the list. 'We're now looking to fly over Dalhousie, the dome of the General Post Office, other buildings. The Strand Road directly below us. Then the Fort area dead ahead.'

'Well, I can't see very much, not through this carpet.'

'Full moon would be different.'

'Indeed. But should I tell you what I think we'll see in the coming months, once this mist clears?'

'What do you reckon?'

'The military and white areas will maintain strict b.o. but the native areas will lapse and will have to be policed. People go to bed early in this – what they call their winter – and they stay asleep. Once the nights warm up, it'll be different. The ARW will have their work cut out.'

'You could be right.' Deyton surveys the spread of suspended, opaque moisture from his side of the aircraft.

'Right, are we almost done? I think so, don't you?' Lambert straightens from his window and examines his instrument panel.

'Fort William, Racecourse, the Memorial, the curve of Lower Circular Road, quite long, distinctive, might stand out, Park Circus, tram junctions there and at Sha—at Sham Bazar. Finally, heading east-north-east, the factories on the road to Dum-Dum.'

'You do remember it's called the Jessore Road. You do remember we briefly thought Ostrich might take that route? Rendezvous with a Jap sub off East Bengal coast somewhere?'

'Of course, sir, yes, the Jessore Road, yes, and finally Dum-Dum itself.'

'We're to knock politely.'

'Landing flares, red first, then blue, yes, and hopefully they won't shoot at us as we come in.'

'Not that this crate looks anything like a Mitsubishi, but who knows about their recognition.'

'State of mind, more likely. They could just hear our engines, couldn't they, and open up?'

'Enough of your cheery optimism. You can put a tick on Fort William, brass seem to be behaving themselves tonight.'

'Probably knocked out by their heart-attack pills. After looking at the maps of theatre, after... er... perusing the situa—'

'Oh, my *god...*'

'Fort William – done.'

'*Deyton, what the hell is that?*'

'What, skip?' Deyton feels the aircraft suddenly lift under him, Lambert pulling back the stick and putting the Hudson into as sharp a turn as it will take. As the plane comes around, Deyton flicks his eyes across the darkness below.

'Can you see it?'

As the pitch of the engines slows, Deyton sees it.

'*Fuck me with a feath*—beg pardon, si—'

'That's quite all right.' Lambert has his head almost out of his window. 'Let's confirm it's not something else.'

There's no question of it being anything else.

It's as if someone has dropped a huge, sculpted, glowing iceberg into the murk below. The dome at the centre of Victoria Memorial radiates like a membrane lit from within. They can make out the four corner towers as well as the wide stairs and the platform that goes around the structure. On their second circle, their eyes begin to place the large decorative water pools in front of the building. Even the gravel drive that leads to the gate seems to have dragged some light on to itself.

'You wouldn't need a moon.' Deyton lights another cigarette without asking. 'On a clear night, you wouldn't need a beacon or any bloody lit-up mosque.'

'This would be enough,' Lambert agrees. 'If you got your bearing correct from just off the coast, you could fly blind until you got here, or just in the vicinity, drop to say 2,500, and there it would be. Bob's your uncle.'

'Victoria's your aunt, you mean.' Deyton can't help it. 'Your shining guidepost of white marble saying welcome to Cal-bloody-cutter.'

GLEN PEARL

It takes until mid-January to remove Victoria Memorial from immediate memory, helped by the fact that the Public Works and Air Raid Protection people finally manage to wipe it out visually from the air – at least after dark.

'An inelegant solution, to say the least, squadron leader, but effective. Well done, staying on them about it.' Currie's words of praise at the Monday morning chukker are brief, but Lambert doesn't mind. That morning, there are far greater worries crowding around the green baize of the billiard table.

If the sheer nerve of the Japanese in simultaneously launching two major fronts had been startling in early December, by that point in January – three days after Shojiro's 15th Army has struck northwards from Malaya – the full import is clear. On that one December day, the Imperial Army of Japan had actually set in motion not two but three campaigns: the war against the Americans in the Pacific, the juggernaut rolling towards Singapore and now – even before they had properly sighted the island fortress – the invasion of Burma.

By mid-February, things are black.

'You clown Limeys. You goddam English, Monday-morning chukker-fuckers. *We'll* survive this, but what will happen to the sad-sack lot of *you*? You'll be, you'll be, you *will* be like... dried up rinds of lime in the evaporated gin and tonic of your Empire, won't you?' Todd-Cartwright, just returned from a tour of Burma and Assam, mimics Goodsugar whom he had bumped into in Shillong. In Todd-C's rendering, Goodsugar stresses the word 'empire', pronouncing it em-*Pyre*!

'In good spirits then, Mr Goodsugar? Happy we're deep in it, is he?' Deyton's voice is dry but smiling.

Like a good martini, thinks Todd-C, stirred but not in the least bit shaken. 'Oh, very. In fact, the bloody fellow held up his gin and tonic as he said it.' Todd-Cartwright distributes the last of what they've begun to call 'McCurrie's Glen Pearl' among three glasses.

'I see.' Lambert is less inclined to be generous about the Yank bastard. 'What possessed you, Alan, inviting him to your officers' bar, or shouldn't one ask?'

'Now, now, Jeremy.' Todd-C pauses to pay last respects to his drink. 'Firstly, it's not as though I was inviting him to my regimental bar. Secondly, like it or not, these chaps, Goodsugar *not* excluded, are our allies – probably only chance of saving our bacon, let's be honest – and thirdly, chap might have offered me some nuggets and so it's my job as an intell... d'you see?'

Lambert sees and doesn't. 'So, he just drank you out of hearth and home while insulting us left, right and centre in the middle of a British officers' bar?'

'No, no, *no*, Jeremy! Do stop taking it so personally! This was Assam! The *bar* was just a temporary counter set up in a veranda, you know, bungalow of a plantation, and we went for a stroll around the garden, the two of us. And, I never said our Yank was stupid. If you can imagine it, the bugger actually *murmured* the... insults, as you call them. I like to think of it as banter. Quite softly delivered, mind you. Producing low chortles all the while. Almost made it sound as though he was, you know, being sympathetic, you know, grieving at our funeral. Bloody hard to be offended, to *display* displeasure, if you see what I mean. And you could tell he was worried about the supply lines to the Chinks.'

Deyton knocks back his tiny dram, and it immediately suffuses him with pleasure and courage. 'I don't imagine he did he say anything, sir? About what he was doing with Stillwell?'

'Oh no, no, I never said our Yank was stupid. I was just flighting 'em up to see if he'd bite. He just went on with anecdotes about *Vinegar Joe,* as they call this General Stillborn. Vinegar Joe this, Vinegar Joe that, and made it grandly obvious, as the man's wont to do, how central he, Goodsugar, was to the plot. Let me know that he'd been present at a couple of Stillwell's meetings with Chiang. The mind shudders, you know, vinegar mingling with soy sauce! Hardly news for us that they meet regularly, but *no* details. But, but sometimes, a change of tone is all you need, really, to fit in a piece of the jig—' The sound of things smashing startles them, but they realize it's just an exhausted Jimmy the Commander clearing away another stack of dirty plates from the overworked desks in the Section.

Lambert knows whatever jigsaw puzzles the English and Americans are fiddling with, the Japanese have advanced their Monopoly game with what Todd-C would call 'brio', taking Singapore through a mixture of gross British botch-ups and Nipponese bluff. From December until now, the dice has dropped eerily, perfectly, for General Tomoyuki Yamashita.

Lambert watches Todd-C contemplating the empty bottle of whisky. It has lasted from 7th December to 18th February – just over ten weeks. Initially, the unspoken understanding was that the Glen Pearl would be deployed only when there was something to celebrate for their three-member gang. But from December 7th have unfolded possibly the most dreadful seventy-odd days in the annals of British military history, and the bottle has mostly stayed hidden in T-C's drawer. The few times it has been brought out is when the three of them have got something right, usually against the current of brass-brained thinking. Unfortunately, this means the Glen Pearl has helped 'celebrate' some of the worst disasters of the last three months. This evening, too, the celebration is more in the nature of a wake: Lambert, Todd-Cartwright and Deyton have correctly predicted the loss of Singapore – almost to the day – and it was on the 15th of February, three days earlier, that the clueless General Percival had surrendered. Even more to the point, something is now becoming clear from reports trickling in – the assessments by the three of them are proving far more accurate than even they themselves have imagined.

Over the last few weeks, Currie's face has become even more of a gaunt caricature. The plastering of maps and papers on the noticeboard behind his desk has now reached manic levels of craziness.

'Exact figures impossible, of course, but we can agree, can we, squadron leader, that the troop ratio was likely to have been *less than half?*' Currie has called Lambert to his office to regurgitate analysis Lambert has given him, as if Currie himself has come up with it.

Lambert understands this is a way of conveying to him that he and Deyton have been right all along. He knows that Toff-C's best efforts to convince Currie, Rice and others to pass this along to General Wavell's people have met with limited success. By now he knows that the safest response is to agree with the chief, but he can't help himself.

'Well, sir, *half* is a funny word to be using here. We still say the enemy had available no more than 30,000 men against the known figure of our troops, which is about 85,000 men. So, well less than half, we would hold.'

'Hold, Lambert? *Hold?*' Currie whips away his face and stares out of his window as if he's just spotted a Japanese paratrooper dropping past. Then he turns back to Lambert with a very different expression. 'My boy, do listen.' The lines around the old man's faded brown eyes are almost laced with kindness. 'We have failed to *hold* the thing we desperately needed to hold, i.e., Singapore. You clever chaps spotted the ball early, perhaps, I won't deny that... but... do remember, I did warn the Section at the very start it was going to be a long war. Now, I see no advantage in driving home the exactness of your calculations to our masters. I see no point in reminding them the Japs bluffed that bloody foo—the good General Percival. That, if they'd listened to us, they would never have surrendered 85,000 men to a force of 30,000 who were, as Todd-Cartwright pointed out, also by then probably out of ammo for their heavy artillery. To be absolutely clear, dear boy, there is no point in us *rubbing it in*. Brass *know*, they've got the *point*, they're wiping off this bloody large *egg*, they won't make the same mistake in Burma. One rather hopes! And we've got to stay in their good books so that we can help them avoid these debacles in future. Long war, now, very long war. D'you see what I'm driving at?'

Lambert forces himself to nod. 'Yes, sir, I think I understand.'

'Good, wi... squadron leader, good. Carry on... by the way, did the major offer you any of that whisky I gave him before Christmas? Beginning of December?'

'Yes, sir, he certainly did.'

'Well, I'm sure that's long gone. Another one on the way, once I organize my supply lines, so hold hard! Keep your eye on the snappage! That will be all!'

'Thank you, sir.'

JARL-MOODY

There is no rare whisky forthcoming from Currie in the next few weeks, but none of the three hold it against the old grouch as catastrophe piles upon debacle. Rangoon falls a mere three weeks after Singapore, three weeks in which no one in the Section gets any sleep.

One hot four o'clock on a Sunday in late March, two weeks after Rangoon, Lambert finds himself walking down Russell Street looking for the address on the card. It's not as if he's really going to visit Madame Toussaint's, but he's curious to see the building in daylight.

He stops at the gates of the Turf Club and pretends to be interested in the ornate iron work of the big gates and the almost carnal entwining of the wrought iron in the centre that forms the letters CTC. Just inside the tall railings with locked narrow gates are the booking windows where the punters can place their bets. The races have been shut down after the war began, the huge racecourse, a mile away on the other side of the Maidan, taken over by camping troops, but Lambert knows the august members of the Turf Club still enjoy one of the oldest and most plushly furnished club bungalows in the world, complete with its legendary, huge billiard table. As Lambert looks at the betting boards with their small metal slots to accommodate the odds, he suddenly remembers the twanging voice on the telephone last week.

Todd-Cartwright had called him into the radio room and handed him the receiver of the green telephone. 'A friend wants to have a word.' T-C's face was studiedly blank, and he gave no answer to Lambert's whispered 'Who?'

'Hello? Wing Commander Lambert speaking.'

'You son of a bitch! You made wing commander!'

'Yes, hello Bob, how are you?'

'Don't you frost me with your *how are yous*, you little bastard, not if you want those four Harvards I'm trying to kidnap for you!'

'Oh, thank you, that's terribly good of you, Good—Bob.'

And so it goes, first the business stuff covered quite efficiently, and then the question:

'So, Jerry, buddy, you getting some nooky down there in that overcrowded oven?' Goodsugar doesn't wait for the answer Lambert would never give. 'Listen, let me tell who's getting more pussy than Casanova. In fact, he's getting all the dames on your behalf, on behalf of *all* his men, which includes *you*, buddy!'

'Who? Listen, old chap, should you be—'

'This is now a US army line all the way from here into your fucking hotel, so it's totally secure. No one can tap into this... like you Limeys jacking off listening in on old man Gandhi talking to his Working Committee. So I can say exactly what I like, you hear?'

'Yes, clearly, but—'

'Now, this guy Wavell, we call him Horny Archie around here, and he beggars belief, I tell you! You know, I was just telling Alan, one story making the rounds is that Horny Archie flew into Rangoon just before you guys dropped the ball there, two days before the Japs got there, and what's he doing, your commander-in-chief? They find him in the billiard room, sliding his little cue into some local princess! Tall fella, so he's got her perched on the edge of the table, you understand—'

'Goo—Bob! That's complete rot! That's a cock and bull—'

'Cock and bull is right, Jerry, cock and bull both apply here! This Horny Archie of yours is so hot to trot, so tacked to tango when he wakes up each morning, he can't decide whether to ball somebody's wife or screw one of his own generals!'

Lambert realizes there are two men looking at him, both natives. One is the liveried guard of the CTC, standing just behind the gate, and the other is a man wearing a shirt and hiked up loincloth. This second fellow has a circular basket-tray slung from his neck and balanced at his stomach. Flies buzz over this straw protuberance, nestling in which is an array of rusty, battered tins, some open and some with their lids shut. It's an array Lambert recognizes. The man nods down to the tray and looks at Lambert hopefully.

Lambert starts to shake his head but then glances around quickly, checking the road. There are no Europeans to be seen, no military police, no civilians, no one in uniform. He gestures to the man, pointing to a green, wooden pillbox that stands against a wall, a bit further down the street. The man follows Lambert, looking confused. Lambert inserts himself in the gap between the pillbox and a large tree next to it. He is now hidden from view on his side of the road, and hopefully no one will spot him from the other side. What he's about to do is dangerous and totally against the strict guidelines for all troops, but the saliva now overpowers his mouth. He fumbles as he takes out from his wallet the smallest coin he can find, a four-anna piece, and waves it at the man.

'Hurry up, now! Jaldi!'

The man looks as if he's stumbled upon treasure. He breaks into joyful action. There is a stool made from reeds that's hanging down his back. With a deft movement he brings it over his head and sets the basket contraption on it. As Lambert watches, the man's hands become a brown-tinged blur. He opens a square tin and scoops out a generous amount of puffed rice with his hand. Ignoring the dogfight of flies above his tray, he puts the rice into a large, dented metal mug and proceeds to add things from the ancillary tinnery. Lambert can identify cubes of boiled potatoes, chopped onions, various powders. As the man flicks in the additions, he also vigorously stirs the mixture with a metal implement, producing a dry swirling sound. After a few seconds, he unscrews the caps of different ancient and evil-looking bottles and begins to add liquids. The sound acquires a thick, succulent wetness. Lambert runs the back of his hand across his mouth. After about a minute's frenetic movement, the man stops and looks up, suddenly worried. He waves away the flies and reaches into one of the paper containers the locals use to bring out a shining green chilli.

'Eita kaancha lonka. Cholbe, shaheb?' He waves the chilli at Lambert as a question.

'Yes, yes! Teak hai!'

The man then reaches into a tin and brings out another chilli, a dried, wrinkled red one that looks like the dropping from a large snail. Lambert nods again. Looking relieved, the man puts away both the chillies. Lambert starts to object, until he realizes the chillies are a fait accompli, already in the mixture.

The man adds a final dash of what looks like engine oil that's been reused too many times, gives the mixture a last seeing to, and reaches for the sheaf of flattened paper stuck into the side of the basket. Carefully, he selects the biggest paper he can find, makes a cone from it and slides in the mixture, filling it to the brim and then adding the rest to make a dome on top. Clusters of shiny, wet, puffed rice topple over the edge as he hands the thing to Lambert. Then the man reaches for another sheaf of slightly stiffer paper, bends a square into a tiny, rudimentary spoon and proffers it.

Lambert nods in acknowledgement and hands over the coin held in his free hand, receiving the 'spoon' in return. The man grins as he brings the coin up to his forehead in a salaam. As he makes ready to leave, Lambert stops him with a gesture. The man waits, confused, worried again.

'Teak hai! Wait!' Where he is standing, the man covers Lambert from passers-by across the street. Lambert closes his eyes briefly, preparing for the onslaught, and scoops a bit of the puffed rice into his mouth. Pleasure and pain explode in tandem, the chillies like a fist smashing up from inside his skull, the sharp and the sour bringing tears to his eyes. For the next five minutes, Lambert greedily eats. All the while trying to avoid locking eyes with the man who is staring at him.

This is the second time Lambert has dared to do this. The previous occasion was in winter. This is the first time he has eaten this stuff in the hot season – a completely lunatic, suicidal act. He wonders what he'll tell the doctor at the military hospital in Fort William as he lies dying. Admitting to having eaten this native slush was almost worse, no, it *was* worse in some circles, than confessing to actual buggery. The previous time, Lambert had bought the puffed rice from a stationary vendor, finished and walked away, resisting the urge to ask the name of the stuff, just in case it increased the chances of him trying it again. Today, he justifies it to himself: it might help the medicos to identify the illness should something strike. He engages again with the waiting chappie.

'What's this called? Naam? Kya?' His mouth is full as he speaks, but the man seems to understand.

'Eita ke boley jhaalmuri, shaheb. Jhaal-muri.'

'Jarl-moody?'

'Hyan, shaheb.' The man opens his box and takes out a handful of the puffed rice. 'Muri.' Then he shows Lambert the green chilli. 'Jhaal.' Then he circles the chilli over all the other tins. 'Jhaalmuri.'

Lambert tilts the cone to his mouth, making sure every last bead of rice and muck lands on his tongue.

Lambert's mouth, his taste buds, his upper throat are singing. He throws away the cone and reaches for his wallet again. He finds an eight-anna coin this time and gives it to the startled man. 'Ve-ry-good. You make excellent... jaarlmoody!' This time, the man grabs the coin, flips the stool on to his back, essays a quick salute and begins to move away, clearly unwilling to believe his luck. Then he stops, struck by a thought. He gestures to Lambert to wait and walks as fast as his contraption will allow to the gates of the Turf Club. There, he engages the guard in a quick conversation and returns to Lambert, repeatedly mouthing a word so that it doesn't slip away.

'Shaheb! Shaheb!... Tu-modo?'

'What?'

The man flips his hands over each other, points to the sun, and says again. 'Tumoddow?'

'To*morrow*!' Lambert finds himself laughing out loud even though it hurts when he opens his mouth too wide. 'No, you greedy scoundrel, not tomorrow! Never again! Anyway, *tomorrow* I shall probably be dead!'

As he did the last time, Lambert checks his health and bodily functions very carefully over the next few days. Except for an undeniable sensation of burning during the next morning's bombing run in the toilet, there seem to be no untoward repercussions. It's only a few days later he realizes that he completely forgot his reconnaissance mission and didn't once look over the road towards Mme Toussaint's residence.

By early April, the air in this godforsaken city is well-nigh unbearable. Just when you think it can't possibly get any warmer, the sun turns it up yet another notch. In the mornings, the heat starts to creep in through the shuttered windows earlier and earlier; in the evenings, it hangs around completely unaffected by sunset. The fan in Lambert's bedroom spins uselessly, its motor making a regular, sharp click, like a repeated taunt, challenging anybody underneath to sleep. After a fortnight of this, relief comes suddenly one afternoon. Dark clouds scud in like raiders, curtaining the light, turning most of the sky almost pitch black. A cool wind starts to ruffle the leaves on the trees, and a few minutes later the rain lashes down, the spears of water a completely different substance from the humidity that has chained the body all day long. These nor'wester storms don't last long, about an hour at most, but they cool the atmosphere well into the night, making it tolerable to be outside. By the early hours of the morning, the humidity returns and the whole cycle begins again with dawn.

The hand grenade of taste that's exploded in his mouth transfers to desirous memory, and the unchanged stomach functions give Lambert courage. Every few days, he now finds himself sneaking away to try the different local foods available on the roadsides, drawn to the dangerous smells and colours like a moth to flame. Sometimes, he turns south from the hotel and then east, and finds himself well beyond the Esplanade crossing, down Dharmatolla Street, in the lanes near Chandni Market where Europeans are generally thin on the ground. On other days, he makes his way northward, past Dalhousie Square and into the Burra Bazar, area where the natives conduct their business from small alcoves and perches in narrow lanes carpeted with wet garbage. Here too, you hardly see a white man, which suits Lambert's purposes just perfectly fine.

This festering weather and the sudden change in temperature is notorious for causing all sorts of sickness, making no discrimination between prince and pauper, the illnesses creeping freely between protected European and exposed native. Being fundamentally a careful and methodical man, Lambert brings a system to his outings, fully aware that this April and the coming May are among the most dangerous months in which to flirt with native food. When making a sortie, Lambert usually contrives to go out around a quarter past four in the afternoon, by which time he's had a chance to examine the prints from the previous day's late recce runs over the Burma front and before the second batch comes in from the morning's early aerial sweeps – and which also happens to be the best time for catching a cooling nor'wester storm from the shelter of an eatery.

Whenever he sees something interesting, he first walks slowly past the stall or little hole in the wall. His reconnaissance captures the method employed in the eating and, if there are several stalls selling the same thing, then where the most customers are gathered, how much they pay and, importantly, whether there is a source of water nearby for the washing of hands. Lambert has heard somewhere that the more people eating at an 'establishment', the higher the volume of freshly made stuff, therefore the higher the chance of it being safe. Or safe-ish. After scouting and picking a target, a vendor or a food shop, Lambert attacks, usually side-slipping into the cluster of customers. He has developed a technique of studied casualness, and his gluttony has expanded his staccato vocabulary enormously; he can now differentiate between Bengali and Hindustani, and between those two chief local lingos and all the other messy Indian tongues. Crucially, he can now far better understand the different varieties of pidgin when someone attempts to speak to him in what they consider English.

'Saheb! Aur kachori chalega? Yu aar vawnt mawr?' The man stands over Lambert, his massive naked belly a planet of shining sweat. He smiles seductively as he proffers more of the fresh, hot, puffed things on a dirty tin plate. As the late afternoon shower hammers down outside, the flies make a competing weave of noise around Lambert's head. Some of them dart to the kachoris and are repelled by the extreme heat. Lambert looks down at his plate and sees there is still some of the potato mush remaining. No point in wasting it, in for a penny in for a—'Haan, tchaleggaa!' He nods vigorously. 'Doh or day-doe!' Give me two more. The fat man wipes the sweat from his face with a filthy cloth that's attached to his shoulder and grins, repeating Lambert's command. 'Doh aur dey doe! Saheb, doh ki tiin aur dey dey?' Give you two, or should I give you three? Lambert stays firm. He shakes his head and holds up two fingers in a sort of V-sign. The man deftly flicks two of the kachoris on to Lambert's plate. 'Saheb! Hot!' Lambert knows they are hot, having singed his fingertips many times when poking into the crisp domes. Before he can say no, the little boy helping the fat man has shovelled some more of the potato mush, also steaming hot, on to his leaf plate. Damn the fellow. Lambert has twigged on to the trick from his second visit here: the fat stall owner and the little blighter always keep the ratio of potatoes and kachoris in some imbalance, so that at any given moment you either need more potato mush to finish the kachoris or vice versa. Lambert always has to decide which one of the two he will waste and today, as he cracks open the skin of a kachori, he decides on sacrificing some of the potato mush.

No matter how great the urgency, no matter how powerful the need to assuage his wounded tongue with further lacerations of spice, Lambert now knows he has to hold himself in check after cracking open the kachoris, to wait for a bit for the heat to escape before he eats. Deep inside, he thinks of it as poking out the eyes of a dragon and waiting for him to subside.

Outside the narrow tunnel of the shop, there is utter mayhem on Harrison Road. Under the curtaining rain, two gangs of thhela-wallas, the coolies who pull the bamboo handcarts, are about to slaughter each other. The handles of their respective thhelas have somehow become tangled in the heavy downpour, right across the middle of the road, and together they are holding up two clanging trams, several motorcars pumping their horns and a lorry that's revving threateningly. Pedestrians are shouting imprecations and advice. Two policemen arrive on the scene, stumbling and sliding on the muddy mess underfoot. Without ado, one of the coppers lights into one gang of thhela-wallas with his thick bamboo cane. The other fellow pokes the leader of the other team with his cane really hard in the stomach, making the man double over in pain. Lambert briefly wonders whether he should do something, before deciding his kachori is now cool enough to eat. Anticipatory sweat cutting grooves around his eyes, he folds a bit of the kachori around some of the potatoes shining in their dark brown sauce and begins to bring up the bite to his trembling mouth.

'Fucking bastards.' At first, it's a just a strange noise that doesn't fit into the shouting and brawling, just another hiss among the hissing of stoves, water kettles and rain. It takes a moment before the unmistakable Manchester accent corkscrews into Lambert's ear, straightening his back. 'FUCKing bastards, they're the same everywhere!'

'Leave it, Jack, lad, not ours to jump into.'

'Can't just sit 'ere and let 'em—'

'Yeh, we can and we will, lad. Get involved and we'll have to explain what we was doin' here, in this part of town. Y'know? How you goin' to do that, now?'

The exchange comes from the other side of the thin wooden partition on which Lambert has been leaning. He realizes the Tommies are in the next hole in the wall, in the tea shop he's been planning to visit before heading home.

A third voice joins in. 'Lance corp is right, Jack. No sense in us tryin' to be heroes. I don't want more to-do with the buggerin' MPs, yeh?'

'What's the fuckin' point, then, us doin' all this talking about solidarity with workers all over—'

'Remember what the – the man said today, at the meetin'? Did any of it trickle in, or did his posh talking nobble ya completely?'

'I didn't catch the Indian words, but I got the rest of it, sure, yeh I did. It was English, wasn't it? He spoke like a proper toff, barrister or summat, I wouldn't be surprised.'

'So, when he said a commu... that all of us must fight intelligently, what d'you reckon he fuckin' meant, mate?'

Under relentless assault, the thhela-wallas disentangle their carts and jerk away. The police constables take themselves off. The rain shifts a scale and slows down, still continuing to add to the slimy layer of filth on the asphalt while the traffic struggles along. Without realizing it, Lambert has finished his kachoris and potatoes. Though he doesn't like the tea in this shop, he gestures towards the stack of clay cups that teeter next to the round tub of boiling oil in which the kachoris are produced. The fat man nods and stokes the coals in what Lambert now knows is called a chulha, the hard-baked clay fires all natives seem to use. Like him, the soldiers next door are waiting for the downpour to ease further. One of them seems to be better educated than the other two, more articulate, with more words at his command. Through the cacophony outside, the susurration of the tea starting to boil, the clang of metal on metal as yet another batch of kachoris is birthed in the roiling sea of black oil, the rough, familiar English keeps coming through.

'No Nips chopped off your tank barrels, no, that's bollocks, that is, that story. No, it's your feet rotting in the fucking mud, the leeches in the mud, and the flying shards of bamboo, apparently their little mortars turn it into shrapnel, like a rain of bloody daggers. Forget the fairy stories mate, it's the shock of a bunch of yellow Beelzebub bastards cycling into your rest bivouac from nowhere, screaming *Banzai!*, buggering up your bully beef and baked beans.'

'Beelzebub, lance corp?'

'Name for the Devil, never mind.'

'But it makes complete sense, what the... man said, what he said about it being two imperialist powers clashing and that... it bein' a question of whose fat cats rake it all in, in the end...'

'And, lads, I shouldn't have said *yellow bastards* when I did just now, those poor Jap bastards are victims of the profiteering warlords just like we are.'

'Fuck all that. I'm going to kill them first and feel sorry in solidarity after.'

A part of Lambert wants to get a look at these young Reds in His Majesty's army, but the self-protective forager gets the better of that impulse and he waits in the kachori shop until well after the Tommies have gone. Outside, the onset of dusk and the blackout have made the slippery pavements even more dangerous. As he carefully works his way through the press of people, Lambert puts into practice an elaborate procedure to disguise his spice-tainted breath. Stopping at a bar off Mangoe Lane, he orders half a pint of lager and downs it, even though the watery brew robs him of the lingering taste of the kachoris. Then, he stops at a roadside cigarette-and-betelnut shop and buys a couple of lozenges. He pops these in his mouth and makes sure to suck on them all the way back to hotel, getting rid of them only as he approaches the entrance on Waterloo Street. By the time he's back at his desk, he is sure his breath smells faintly of beer that has been masked by mint.

By mid-April, with the enemy moving forward without pause, Currie has worked further magic with the higher-ups. 'The Yanks are taking over most of this hotel, damn them, but I've snaffled some more space for the Section.' Whether through cajolement or soft threats, unctuous lies or breathily whispered truths, Currie has managed to commandeer the eight rooms immediately adjacent to the suite, in effect capturing a large cul-de-sac on this third floor. As a result, the Ochterlony team's sleeping arrangements have acquired some sense of civility. Farquhar, Todd-Cartwright and Lambert now each have a room, while Deyton shares his with another sergeant. The steep improvement in the standards of comfort is clearly a reward for the critical contribution the Section is making, but it comes at a price. The unspoken command stays very much in place: none of them is to stray far from their desks, none of them is to have very much to do with the Yanks. Despite this, even Deyton's caustic patter is now leavened with praise – he can't stop talking about the shiny brass taps in his bathroom. For Lambert, the large single bed is a huge blessing after the tube and wire pallet in his staff quarters, especially now that his working hours are being sliced up in new ways by the inconsiderate Nipponese. After some effort, Lambert is now getting reaccustomed to sleeping at night, sometimes, and working by day.

'My god, Jeremy, wake up! I think I've got it!' Todd-C looms over him early one morning, slapping his shoulder. Lambert snaps awake, very alert, feeling both resentful and relieved that the Toff has solved the impossible problem they have been wrestling with – retrieving urgent reconnaissance film from the forward air bases as Slim's retreating army crawls back towards Imphal and India.

'All right, all right! So where *do* we find the Harvards then?'

'Bugger the bloody aircraft! Come back to your desk and *listen!*'

Lambert stumbles behind Toff-C in his dressing gown. As he approaches his desk, he can hear it again, the larder ghost. He looks at his wrist and it's 0630 hours. The noise seems to be coming in alternating long and short bursts.

'Can you hear it?'

'Yes.'

'No, no, damn it, man, can't you *hear?* Wait for it... wait... there! He said it again!'

'Said what? He?' The idea that this sound might be emanating from a 'he' porcupines the hair on Lambert's arms and neck.

'There! Shiva! He definitely said *Shiva*, that's one their gods isn't it? Shiva!'

'No, it's not. I mean, yes, it *is* one of their... but this sounds more like *she-boat*, as if it's saying she-boat-she-boat-she-boat... It's not human, Alan, that's some bloody machinery changing pitch! Perhaps one of their laundry machines. You've *got* to get more kip, man!'

Todd-Cartwright is using his finger as a metronome and moving his lips, trying to trap the word he has identified, but the ghost chooses not to offer further help today; the sound turns into a deep plumbing gurgle for about thirty seconds, then into a low fluttering, perhaps a loose metal element hitting against some slowing gear. And then it dies out, leaving things inconclusive.

I have a recording, the cassette is marked '9 Sept. 1972', where Elko's talking and Missus puts on a record in the background. It's an LP of some raag by some minor singer, and as the voice comes on, he snaps out at her: 'For god's sake! I can't stand that caterwauling!' This had already happened a couple of times, and I'd begun to think he hated Indian classical music. But then, one day soon afterwards, I took him some coffee in his studio and he didn't notice me coming in. He was standing before a canvas, swaying and humming, the voice breaking into actual song sometimes. It took me a while to realize he was singing a raag, I couldn't tell which one, but quite well for an untrained voice. He would hum or sing a phrase, pause, go forward and add to the painting, and then step back. Then the humming would start again, moving to singing, all of it winding up the brushstrokes inside him, until he brought them to the point of release.

I put down the cup as quietly as I could. He turned, looked at me and then went back to the painting as if he hadn't seen me.

That evening, I asked him, 'I was under the impression you didn't really like Hindustani, or at least not the vocal...'

'What gave you that idea?' he mock-growled. He pulled out a spool tape from the shelf. 'It depends on who's doing the singing, you see. I just can't stand a lot of what passes for vocal classical nowadays, that's all.' He threaded in the tape. 'Listen to this first. Dagar brothers, so singing Dhrupad, obviously. Raag Shree, recorded in Brussels, 1969. Let's hear just the alap, quite long, but just listen.'

The twin voices spun their web around us for about forty minutes, leaving me quite wide-eyed and addicted. At the end of the alap, Elko stopped the tape abruptly and I flinched. He smiled. 'Good, wasn't it? Not to worry, you can hear the whole thing later, but first...' He threaded in another spool. 'Also Dhrupad, same raag again, Shree, but mark how different it is.'

An older recording, with just a tad more hiss, but very clean nevertheless. A lone voice, a similarly startling range, but with a very different timbre. I could recognize the same note progression, but the phrasing was broken up completely differently, as if in a parallel reality to the Dagar rendition, as if it was the same vase of flowers, or the same tree, painted from a completely different angle in radically contradictory light. If the Dagar brothers gave me deep solace, this recording somehow created the deepest of unease before freeing me from it. When it ended, I asked Elko who the singer was.

'This was Dhrupad from the Darbhanga gharana. This is a man who learnt directly from the great Meghnath Sharma, in fact, he's the only surviving exponent of Pandit Meghnath's style, but see!' He showed me the name written on the tape box and I let out a disbelieving laugh. 'No!'

'Yes! Yes, my boy, yes! That is indeed his name, can you believe it? Astonishing, isn't it? Can you imagine that somebody not Indian could sing like this? Some non-deshi actually singing this with such authority?'

'How...'

'How, indeed! It's a long story, and I'll tell you by and by. But first, one has to ask not how, but why not? I mean look at the bloody Beatles and that Harrison fellow trying to learn sitar from Ravi Shankar! Not a patch on this man and how he's imbibed – no, I'd say ingested – not just the technical tradition but the *feeling* that's central to this, to his, school of Dhrupad.' The old man lit one of his foul filterless cigarettes. 'But, again, you have to ask why not? I mean look at us Indians! From early in this century, so many of us trying to be Monet or Manet, so many Runus trying to be Renoirs, and now not to mention—'

'Oh no! Oh no, no, no! We are not opening that little chest of darkness!' Missus was in the next room, sitting at the dining table, typing one of her political letters, but she'd clearly had one ear trained on us. Now she got up and rushed in, snatching up the cigarette packet from the table. 'Look what you've done.' She blew complaining smoke in my direction. 'You've started him off now and we'll have to suffer his—'

'Madam, I'd thank you to—'

'No, I'd thank *you* to just get on with your work without wasting bile on others.'

'Bile? Bile? I wouldn't waste a single drop of my—'

'Yes, Zemindear, we know!'

I already had an idea of what they were talking about. I'd been into his puja room – his paint pantry – a few times now, and you can call it prying but I'd looked more carefully at all the notes he had up in there. Besides the list of artist prostitutes, there were other bits of paper taped to the wall. One ladder of slips had clearly been put together over some time, one could tell from the different yellowing of the bits of paper, backs of envelopes and bills, index cards and even cigarette packets torn open and spread out.

Souza is a peon of Picasso!
Husain is a hustler!
The Bombay ~~Progessives~~ Submissives! Slaves!

A note in Bangla, which took me a moment longer to read – 'Palao, Paritosh, palao, eder theke duur, eder ghaarey jeyo na!' Run, Paritosh run, get far away from these people, don't go near them!

'Bendre is a baandor!' This one mixed English and Bangla: Bendre is a monkey.

I could see that a lot of these were coming to him in alliteration, probably in the middle of painting, or maybe when he was sitting there getting drunk, and he had to put them down on paper before they escaped his mind. Clearly, he had to hide these away, perhaps from Missus, maybe from visitors, and yet these nuggets of resentment were precious to him. Perhaps they helped fuel his work.

That evening, I'd also had a few drinks, so I was brave. I'd also quietly switched on my recorder, and this part of the recording is labelled '9 Sept. 1972 (II)'.

'But aren't you also influenced by other painters? Don't you also take from Matisse, say, or the Kangra painters, or Kalighat—'

'*Me?* I am nothing! I may *take*, as you put it, but I hope I don't imitate! I try not to copy, that's all! Sometimes you can't help but reproduce a colour combination, or a shape, or a kind of brushstroke, but I try not to slavishly, mindlessly reproduce what has already been done before. It's not easy, and I produce mostly shit, but—'

'But at least it's original shit! We know!' By now, Missus had poured herself a shot of gin and knocked it back.

'Why do you think I get rid of so much of it?' He whirls on her. 'And you? Since it *is* shit, why do you always try and stop me when I'm getting rid of my rubbish? Why do *you* need to hoard this garbage, to squirrel it away like some dalal hoarding rice? Do you think the price will go up one day? Is that it?'

I tried to intervene. 'No one is saying your work is shit. It's not shit. And I don't think it's about the price it may fetch in the future. Surely that's not the only thing art is about?'

'What do you know, bloody whippersnapper, what art is about? What *the fuck* do you know about it? You've read a few books and now you know it all, do you? *Do* you?'

'No, I—'

'*You* think that bloody carpetbagger wrapping monuments in tarpaulin is art! Whatshisname, that Christmas fellow! You weren't around in... you weren't around then, when we saw *exactly* what a monument could be wrapped in, when—'

'Well, it's the context, really. All art is art within a context!'

'Context! Context! You actually think that Korean chap with his stacks of television sets is art! What's *that* charlatan's bloody context, pray tell?'

By then, I knew a little bit about the context of all this.

It was on that visit in October 1970 when I'd first started to record conversations with both of them. Elko had gone off for a couple of days to see someone, a 'friend' in a nearby town, and I had Missus to myself, for which I was grateful, because I needed to ask her a few things.

Piecing it together from that first batch of Missus tapes, I'd got this much: Kedar Lahiri travelled abroad as soon as he could after the war. He was twenty-six when he took a ship to London in May 1946 with a view to joining the Royal College of Art. Kedar found post-War London to be a miserable city, and his time there was not happy – enrolling in the RCA was more difficult than he'd imagined. He enrolled in one of the smaller, lesser-known art schools, but he found the atmosphere stifling and uninspiring. Later, he told Missus he'd signed up primarily to obtain rationing coupons.

Missus shook her head in pity. 'I only managed to reach London in late October, by which time the poor devil was ready to leave. The food was not only rationed but awful. The colour bar and way the English looked at someone of his complexion was angry-making. He had warm clothes all right, but he was shivering from homesickness. Also, he kept saying there was nothing to paint in London, at least not for him. I told him he was acting like a spoilt princeling, but I do think he meant it, nothing in London carried any meaning for him, not for his painting. He kept saying it's like being in a vast, cold, Dalhousie Square, but without the soul.'

Kedar missed the great killing and rioting in Calcutta which was in August 1946. By the time he returned to Calcutta in early December, the city had almost recovered from that, inasmuch as was possible, but the place had changed forever. Actually, as many have pointed out, the city changed with the famine, when the people came in from the villages in '43, and the Hindu–Muslim bloodbath of '46 was perhaps one end to that famine story, not that that story ever ended.

'Though other houses nearby had been attacked, the Lahiri house in Palm Avenue was intact. But Zemindear's parents were another matter. His father was ill, on his way out, and I think his mother was already going a bit loopy. Runs in her family, he says, so no one was surprised. It was terrible for him. Though, in all the mass of misery, the hunger and disease, the refugees starting to come in from the east, he didn't have the awareness to recognize that. He couldn't be away from Calcutta, and yet he couldn't stay there. He couldn't bring himself to paint what was going on or what he'd seen during the famine, and yet he couldn't *not* paint the horror that was all around. I still have his letters from that time somewhere and, even in all the laughter in the writing, he's absolutely distraught. But then, as he kept saying, what was *his* misery compared to what was going on around him?'

The famine and the '46 riots were only part of the story, and for some reason I felt I needed the whole of it, so I kept nudging her down the years.

'You said he went to Bombay... would that be around 1950 or so?'

'Oh lord, yes, Bombay! That was a misadventure if there ever was one! Or the beginning of one, I should say.'

At some point in 1949, a year and a half after Independence, still reeling from grief, Kedar Lahiri took a train to Bombay. The Fort area reminded him of both London and Calcutta, the curving seafront of an imagined Nice – totally off the mark, Rio de Janeiro might have provided a better comparison – and there he contacted a few painters, more or less the same age as him, who had formed a group.

'I'm not quite sure how he met them. I think he knew Paritosh, his Paritosh-da, who knew them, and he introduced them. I think he first met Syed Raza and Ara in a coffee shop around Churchgate, and only later all the rest of them, Husain, that Souza, Gade and all of them.'

The painters called themselves the Progressive Artists' Group and Kedar Lahiri's first meeting was amicable enough. They invited the Bengali to meet the others, and he went to a dinner somewhere in Colaba, which passed off all right as well. Lahiri was polite, quietly inquisitive, he saw some of the work, nodded in admiration, came away with invitations to the painters' studios, of which he soon availed. He kept his opinions about Picasso and some of the Bombay painters' work to himself. The work he liked, he praised with enthusiasm, pretending to be confused or in awe of the stuff he found uninteresting. In a letter he wrote at the time, he says, 'It's all very well to think of oneself as *progressive*, and I can see that the rejection of the Western academy and the Bengal school is unavoidable, but what's the point if you reject Abanindranath and Nandalal but slavishly copy the Picasso of the 1930s and the Fauves' work from 1920s? Is that progress? Or is that perhaps like jumping out of the frying pan into the fire?'

The other important fact to note here is that F.N. Souza was away, perhaps in Goa or perhaps already in London, so he is one member of the Progressives Lahiri didn't meet at this point, though as one of the others told him mischievously, 'It will be interesting for you when you meet Newton. He might take you to task, you know, in a way the rest of us might not.'

On the tape, about four drinks down, Missus starts to chuckle to herself. 'Well, they certainly were a match made in heaven, your Uncle Elko and Mr Newton Francis Souza. Talk about two magnets repulsing each other... I only saw them together once, in Paris, and... actually repulsion doesn't describe it quite, more like an alchemical reaction between two, between two enemy elements, like an explosion, if you see what I mean...'

I didn't see, not then, but later I got the picture, pieced it together, so to speak. It took me a year after talking to Missus to raise the subject with Elko, and that too after both of us were well in our cups one night.

'*What do I bloody care if Ara was washing cars before he became a painter?*' The microphone can't take the assault and the sound seems to tear on the tape. '*Or whether Maqbool Husain was a sign painter?* That's not my, not my fault, not my look out! Not every painter needs to be from some, from some poor, from some... *Amrita Sher-Gil was hardly a pauper girl!*'

'Some people would say it helps the artist depict how the other half—'

'Oh, you're going to take *that* line are you? Like that arsehole Souza? Whatever I can... *depict*... has nothing to do with whether I grew up with a full stomach or hungry on the street! If I can't paint for toffee, it's not because I grew up in a mansion, it's because I haven't opened my eyes! It's because I haven't worked enough at my craft! It's because I don't use my brain! It's because my tiny little mind seizes up when faced with a Picpisso or a, or a, or a...'

Lahiri and Newton Souza had finally met in London, on Lahiri's second trip to Britain, sometime around 1952. Lahiri came with introductions from Raza and Bakre but Souza was, as predicted, not impressed. Lahiri had bought the impecunious Souza lunch and taken him to the bedsit he was renting near Victoria to show him some of his paintings. Souza had said nothing, save that they should repair to a nearby pub. The pub opened at 4.30 p.m., and the two of them had drunk copiously, Lahiri paying. Something had then transpired. By 9.30 p.m., Souza was screaming at Lahiri, first inside, then outside the establishment. The altercation involved the throwing of a pint glass – by Souza at Lahiri, whether full or empty is not known. The encounter ended only when the barman threatened to call the police, with the two men walking off in opposite directions.

'I don't know if Souza actually said this, but what Zemindear claimed was that he called him a *buggering bloody Bungalee*. Before that, he apparently said something to the effect of: *You rich boy! You're talentless! Your job is to buy our paintings and get your rich friends to buy our paintings! If you have so much money to buy paints here in London, buy them for us! Don't waste paint and canvas!*'

'And our hero took this lying down? I don't believe it!'

'No... Elko apparently retaliated with *Goan... ga...* what's that word, ga-something... ah, yes, *Goan gander!* And, and this he's never admitted to me, but what I was told was that Souza stomped off stage left, alone, while our baron exited stage right, in the company of a young lady both men had just met at the pub. The rub wasn't just our Bungalee's supposed lack of talent. Souza is famously, notoriously, what the Americans call *randy*, and he didn't like being rejected for what he saw as this rich idiot. So, not so much about the merits of anyone's art, more about two lustful young drunks squabbling over a girl in a drink hole.'

It's around this time that Kedar Lahiri moved to Paris. There, living in a small studio near Pigalle, his money running out, he produced the small canvas titled *A Rich Man's Son Paints a Car*, a clearly self-referential, cubistic Picasso–Souza spoof. I know the painting still survives in a private collection in America. I haven't seen the actual picture, but there's a small photograph of it, framed and hanging in the grand house where it lives. The photo is pinned to the wall in the paint pantry, among the abuse lists and other notes. There are only a few other photos of his paintings that Elko put up, all of them in that small little back room. Not far from *Rich Man's Son* is another picture, one from his aerial series, the engine billowing smoke, the train crossing a river bridge in the geometry of fields seen from above. Small figures spill out of the train and hurtle down into the water, while the end of the train looks as if it's being split open by something.

Next to this one is a pair of notes.

One is a quote from Beckett's *Waiting for Godot*: 'Was I sleeping, while the others suffered?'

Below it, an answering scrawl, clearly put up quite a while later: 'Yes, you're still asleep and you will never wake up.'

PRECAUTIONS

Lambert returns to his bed, determined to win back some lost sleep. As the side of his face settles into the pillow, the interrupted dream recaptures him. Not the damp pillow but the clammy phone receiver against his ear, the words forming but not getting out, his voice lost before it's quite out of his throat, '... *repeat, it's not an invasion, repeat, no attack, cancel the operation, over...'* At the other end, the agitated officer commanding the special force slamming down the crackling field telephone and pushing himself through the ticket turnstile, looking down at the itemized list of primary targets in his hand, calling out to the men waiting in the caged darkness. 'Move forward! Aagey badho!'

The slaughter begins again, pointless, point-blank, the barrels of the .303s heating up in the tropical night as the rounds pump out, unrhythmic, random because of the hesitations. Despite the muttered prayers for forgiveness that precede the bolts being cocked, relentless. The rifle reports coming through on the phone that's dead. The phone sitting on the dresser in the hallway in Dorset. His mum, also in her dressing gown, holding out a cup of tea. 'Jeremy, darling, it's no point fretting. Every living creature has a given time. Their time's up, darling, and there's. Nothing. You. Can. Do.'

Striped lightning. A large White Bengal charges out of a dark, man-made cave, its head a hot breath swerving around the bayonet, teeth closing around the rifle while the soldier's still thinking, nearly yanking his hands in through the bars. Two other men pull their triggers, rack their bolts in sweat-slipping terror, rounds glance off the iron bars and a bullet ricochets to wing a third man who's standing far back. The animal finally subsides ten feet inside the cage, the broken Lee–Enfield clamped in its mouth, well out of reach. In another enclosure, two cheetahs, mother and cub, trying to leap into the shelter of a tree. A ragged volley of shots. The mother drops like a stone, thuds to the ground, while the wounded cub is caught by the tree, its weight making the branches undulate. Hard mangoes falling from the tree, hitting the ground and bouncing like dud green grenades. In the same cage, or perhaps another, a befuddled rhinoceros bull standing in place, shifting its weight from leg to leg, prancing heavily and slowly as the bullets smack into its hide. The white officer screaming as if it's he himself who's being shot, 'Uska aankh mey maaro, uska aankh mey maaro!' Aim for its eyes! 'Jaldi khatam karo!' Finish it off quickly!

Just outside the zoo walls, a blacked-out seafront with a wrought-iron bench on a thin strip of pavement, like a cliff path in Dorset, but he knows it to be the Marina in Madras. A Catalina seaplane from

Coastal Defence circles high above. A line of threatening ship-dots on the horizon, just where the faint moonlight separates the dark of the sky from the sly, shifting grey of sea, a mosquito buzzing death in his ear, attracted there by the sweat, his voice finally coming out: '*For god's sake, man, don't shoot them! For god's sake, don't shoot! There is no bloody invasion!*' The scalding cup of tea flying from Mother's hand and hitting the hallway floor without a sound. The glass of water from his bedside table rolling on the thick hotel carpet, patch of spilled water spreading. His hand wet, but miraculously not burnt.

One 5.30 a.m. in full-oven May, a couple of days after the fall of Mandalay and Monywa, Sergeant Deyton is standing next to the boarded up dumb waiter, his eyes closed, his head cocked, the sharp greyhound nose almost twitching out of his round face. 'One of their, er, *classical* singers, could it be, sir? Might it be someone playing a gramophone record?'

'Can't be.' Todd-C sipping his tea. 'Would have to be too many different ones, very long ones, and we'd hear them changing over. This goes on continuously. For bloody hours. And it's different every day, slightly different.'

'I've half a mind to ask the hotel people,' Lambert finds himself saying. 'Or, rather, get Currie to buttonhole that Barbarossa fellow, whatshisname, the manager, and ask him to get to the bottom of this!'

But the old man has other, more important things to discuss at the chukker. His white hands almost translucent against the green baize, Currie holds up the report from two days ago, of the zoo slaughter in Madras on 14 April by the paramilitary Malabar Special Police. 'Well, gentlemen, it's clear now that the governor, what's his name, Sir Arthur Hope – Hope, hah! – and the ARP chaps reacted rather too quickly. What a pity our fanged fellows had to catch it in the zoo there. It seems there were some fine animals. Totally unnecessary, obviously. But more importantly, most damagingly, the very point I was making two weeks ago, the public will now see it as a sign of our panic. The tigers and leopards can be replaced, the odd rhino or two brought down from Assam, but people's faith in the administration is another matter.'

'Well, sir, one has to say it *was* panic, plain and simple funk.' Todd-Cartwright snorts into his papers.

'Quite, colonel. Well, clearly the chaps in Madras had heard about what happened in Rangoon, that zookeeper releasing dangerous animals by mistake after the bombing, and the tiger that escaped in Batavia during the Jap air raid. The thing is, again, mind you, not our territory at all, not at all, but one must chip in wherever... the thing is, we simply cannot afford to have similar things happen here in Bengal. So this Section must anticipate, must help nip in the bud, anything that shakes, that shakes...' Currie lets the sentence dangle, unable to pronounce the horror. 'I mean, looking at the wider scenario, we've got that blighter Rash Behari Basu broadcasting from Tokyo, asking everyone to take an oath to make India "independent". Then we've got Bose – beg pardon, Ostrich – who's supposed to have died in an air crash, except it's now clear he *hasn't* bloody died! Then, from our phone taps we know that Gandhi is continuously up to no good with his Nehru–Patel gang, so this kind of thing feeds, *fuels* the—'

Farquhar, who's been an actuary in his life before the war, is eager not to let the most pressing issues slip away. He picks up another folder.

'Sir, we should perhaps also look at how this business of the evacuation routes is...'

Currie's head snaps around. 'Yes, major. White Road and Black Road, is it, that you're wanting to examine?'

'Exactly, sir. The rumours are dama—'

'We don't need to call them rumours, old boy, not between us.' Currie's eyes regain life. 'Fact. Spade a spade. D'you see?'

'Yes, sir...'

'Fact, those separate roads are a fact, as we know. Unavoidable fact, that we need to give priority to our troops and our people. It's not ideal that we have to... oblige... locals... natives... the non-Europeans, if you will, to follow a different route, one that doesn't obstruct our retreat from a vastly superior enemy.'

'Sir, but the locals don't see it in a military light. They're seeing white civilians carrying their entire households, portmanteaus and such on a road that's supposed to be reserved for the army.'

Currie nods wearily. 'Yes, yes, while they themselves are forced to stumble through on a far more... insalubrious... mud track with just the clothes on their backs. I know. White Road and Black Road, we know. The point is, it's unavoidable. There is, and always will be, a different priority given to our own people, whether civilian or military. Firstly. Secondly, we have to enjoin all our various branches, bring home, if you will, that these labels can be very damaging in terms of morale. So, no matter what the reality, let's *please* make absolutely sure there's no further mention, publicly, of the phrases *White Road* and *Black Road*. We should send out a strong memo to this effect. And if this reappears in the press, we should be prepared to swat it down with vigour as dangerous misinformation. Otherwise, the administration could lead itself into real trouble.'

'Well, sir, then there is the question of the routes of the troop trains, once they are back in India.' Farquhar picks up another file. 'Reports of situations approaching riot, from Ara and Patna, after trains passed through carrying injured.'

'Well, not much we can do about that, I'm afraid. The troop trains need the broad gauge and those tracks pass where they do.'

'Yes of course, sir, but are they thinking about *when* the trains pass through sensitive stations? Would it be possible to suggest...'

'Middle of the night, yes of course, and I'm told they're on to it already. It seems the problem is whichever stations the trains pass through in daytime are the ones that proceed to become sensitive. They are trying to better distribute the wounded so that only very few trains are exclusively, er... chock a block... but the number of casualties is so high, as we know, and with the men requiring quick treatment...'

In this heavy monsoon, Lambert's dreams shift like islands of silt.

When Yamashita's army breaks out across central Assam, with the secondary, unstoppable thrust coming from the Arakan peninsula, the game looks well and truly up. The huge map from the billiard room balances oddly across Lambert's gunsights, the two ends sticking out of the narrow Spitfire cockpit, the backing board whipping in the airstream, making the flying difficult. They could have given him a smaller map, a cloth one perhaps, but Currie has been insistent. 'Do keep this one with you, squadron leader, just so's you know where your off stump is, there's a good chap!' His off stump, as Currie calls it, is the pulsating line of the Jap army river-hopping across East Bengal towards Calcutta. As people in the Ochterlony Section and other government departments put their evacuation plans into action, moving files and equipment to Ranchi, Patna and Bhubaneswar, Lambert and his Spitfire have been sent in the other direction on an escort mission.

As he follows the train coming back west from Assam, Lambert realizes that he's privileged to be flying on one of the most beautiful routes in the world. On his right, to the north, the high Himalayan peaks display their unmoving triangular standards of snow, the jagged rock slicing up through the cloud to sail in the sunlight. Below him, the black steam engine chugs ahead, pulling the troop train across sheets of grey glass set in greenish-brown frames. Every now and then, Lambert catches the reflection of a muddy sun in the flooded fields, the disk playing hopscotch over the raised boundaries. Occasionally, he can see the shadow of his own aircraft, with the strange fins in the front where the ends of the map stick out. When he goes lower, the light changes, darkens into a mid-monsoon gloom. When he climbs, he's back in the scudding sun and shadow of low cloud. He would like to stay at this height, within sight of the lovely mountains, but he feels obliged to drop down every fifteen minutes or so to check that his wards are alright.

His r/t is hissing like bacon burning in a pan. He can barely make out the voices coming in, but he's sure he has heard that General Stillwell's been captured and killed. Apparently, the Japs are being particularly hard on the Americans. Apparently, Goodsugar was with the general and his last message was clear: there was no coming out of this alive. Apparently, the Japs are killing all officers above the rank of lieutenant, keeping the junior ones alive only in order to control the captured troops.

The r/t crackles in his ears again, and he feels a pulse of dread. The damn thing has brought nothing but ill tidings. Todd-C's voice is calm. 'Jeremy old boy, more bad news, Jeremy old boy, hold on to your hat, over.'

Lambert quickly tears off a bit of the kachori puff, scoops it into the mug of potato mush he has wedged between his left knee and the side of the cockpit, and stuffs it into his mouth. The kachori has gone cold, but the potatoes are still, miraculously, piping hot, and he burns his tongue.

'Jeremy? This is Alan, over.'

Lambert chews furiously, trying to taste the stuff before it goes down his gullet. He replies, hoping Todd-C won't hear the food in his mouth.

'Receiving you, over.'

'Dacca's gone, repeat, Dacca has just fallen, over.'

'Roger-roger, Dacca lost, over.' Lambert quickly confirms on his map that he and his train are well past the longitude of East Bengal's chief city.

'No difference to you, though. Old man says you're to refuel at Bagdogra and stay with the train until Raipur and Charra Station, over.'

'Charra Airfield and not all the way to Madras, confirm please, over.'

'Confirm, Charra and not all the way to Madras. They shouldn't need escort beyond Raipur. Peel off at Raipur, land at Charra and await orders, over.'

Below him, the ground has changed character, become more hilly. By his reckoning, the train is now traversing Cooch Behar. No matter what fate has befallen Dacca, the line of the Japanese advance is now well behind him. His off stump is marginally safer. He struggles with the map, trying to avoid the tiny nails that poke out of the frayed board, and finally manages to push it out of the cockpit. The board flaps away, the map jinking and plummeting to join the territory it describes. His hands now have room to move, and his sight through the gun markings is now clear. That's far more like it.

Below him, the train engine seems to have picked up speed on the drier tracks. Time to take another dekko. As he drops, the engine smoke spirals up towards him. Freed of the encumbering map, he banks and makes a low sweep around the train.

When he gets low enough, he can see the bandaged arms and legs again, almost spilling out of the windows, and rows and rows of small bamboos sticking out, rods of stretchers that haven't quite fit into the carriages. As he throttles back to let the train slide ahead, he sees the bogey at the back. At the very end of the train is a goods carriage without a roof, bracketed by two light anti-aircraft guns on platforms. Following the carriage, he's careful not to raise the pitch of the Spit's engine, not wanting to terrify the poor creatures more than they already are. The straw piled on the floor of the open carriage, he can see, is becoming more and more trampled with each passing mile, the ropes tethering the animals snapping taut on one side and drooping on the other as the train takes a bend, the two rhinos themselves swaying, sometimes only one standing, sometimes both, never both sitting at the same time. 'They'll be tranquilized, of course, but lightly,' Currie has told him. 'Can't knock them out completely, you see, have to feed them a few times until they reach Madras. Calcutta would have been a different matter, they can stay without food for three or four days, apparently.' The train goes into a tunnel and Lambert has to yank back the stick, narrowly avoiding the little range with its cascade of palm trees. Currie patting Lambert's back for a final time. 'You must see these animals home, Mr Lambert! People in Madras must see and note the quick replacement! Face is all, in this situation. On the home front, face is half the battle!'

Lambert waits for the train to emerge from the tunnel and come back under his Spit. As the last carriage passes by, he sees that something is very wrong. The anti-aircraft gun between the rhino pen and the rest of the train has disappeared, leaving behind only the bare slab of the carriage bed. The carriage next up from the pen has a large hole in place of the end door. In the pen itself, only one rhino – its companion missing. As Lambert tries to dive, something holds him back, as if the plane has developed an obstreperous sail, he looks at his rear mirrors and sees a bit of the map-board stuck to his tail, flapping open violently, stopping him from going lower. The train seems to be like a quick python, its camouflaged rectangles rattling and yawing, a bulge moving up towards the engine, as if the snake has swallowed something too large. The first body is ejected from a window on the left, along with its stretcher. As the train passes over a river, two men jump in quick succession from a door on the right, both missing limbs. They topple into the water and flounder. They disappear and rise again, their bandaged corpses now still. He jinks the plane, trying to shake off the map-board, and he goes into a stall. The speed of the descent shakes off the board and he feels sheer, sheer joy as the aircraft responds, smacks hard into his buttocks and comes back under his control.

He reaches over for the glass of water that he has now placed on a chair next to his bed, just out of reach, so as not to spill it again, and then he tries to dive again, but it's no good. The rain is slamming against the room window and he knows he has to wake up.

Looking at my notes, I try and build a chronology.

As far as I can tell, what he called his 'Air Reconnaissance' paintings – what Missus and I call the 'Aerials' – were made between 1958 and 1962. By the late '50s, Elko has already produced what some critic-biographer could call his first two 'periods' of work – the Slipper Period, and the Howrah–Calcutta Tableaux which one could also call the Hotel Period – though, in reality, the different kinds of pictures are all mixed up and overlapping, many of them being painted simultaneously, until a series or style peters out and new ones take centre stage.

From January 1942 onwards, the first serious paintings start to escape from the early landscapes, portraits, still lifes and such. Thankfully, he's not even aware that that's what these are, these oddities. There is almost no self-consciousness at all, and he's painting some of these 'with the left hand' almost, 'like a runner walking through part of a marathon course, with no belief that I would, one day, be able to run the whole twenty-six miles' as he once told me.

'I was letting out my irritation. Whenever I met an obstacle on some *serious* painting, I would draw something quite different, to free my hand, or so I thought, except what was actually being released, I suppose – perhaps – were my brain and my eye. Such as they were.'

So, the 'Slippers/Chappal' series begins here, drawings at first, then oil pastels and gouache on small paper, before he actually makes an oil of the image, the first one about 36' x 24'. These chappal painting are a precursor, a work you do accidentally that's 'ahead' of your other work, that sticks out like a sore thumb, a sore thumb that grows a hand only later, when you make the works that accompany that first breakthrough and demonstrate what it presaged.

Following the slipper paintings comes *Howrah Station – Exodus*, then the portrait of Keya Dutta, *Koney Dekhar Alo* or *Woman in Bride Light*, then *Vishwakarma*, a large oil of a man bowing before an array of knives at the idol's feet, with small factory machinery looming in the shadows. Then there are the unfinished *Christmas Eve Ball* and *Tennis Club*, both of which are in that madman Massimo Ioppi's collection.

Not all of these are successful paintings, mind you. As with a loose plug, the electricity comes and goes, sometimes the drawing is off, or the compositions are quite derivative and banal. Often, as he put it himself, he's 'fighting off the illustrator standing behind my shoulder', and not alwast successfully. But occasionally, Elko stumbles on to something truly sublime; there are bits of execution that are powerful, startling in an otherwise failed picture, like an embryo being formed in an amniotic mess. While I have no patience with the self-flagellation of his destroying so much of his stuff, I can also see why he sometimes gets so angry with himself, where the intention just cannot find a route to the hand and the canvas.

From the 'Air Reconnaissance' series, this changes. He gets better, more assured, even though his dissatisfaction stays constant. He is also, by this point, leaving behind the Calcutta from which he has exiled himself. Not leaving it behind in the paintings, or in the subject matter – that he never really manages to do, or never wants to – but by now, with the approach of the 1960s, he's reconciled to never living there again.

Though he doesn't quite realize that he will never actually set foot again in the city that so rules him.

There are traps in connecting artists' lives too closely to the work, but it's not a coincidence that this is the time, mid-1958, when Missus finally starts to spend more time in the house, and when he gets to know Commander Gourmander through her.

It's difficult to pinpoint the first of the aerial series. Try as I did, he couldn't ever admit to remembering the sequence in which they came, but I suspect they start right after he makes *Brown Memorial*, which is among the last of the 'straight perspective' war views of Calcutta, and the handful of landscapes of the Bengal countryside to do with the famine and the war. Something in Kedar Lahiri needs to go up in the air, to look down, as if to reflect his constant ache that he was never in the thick of things, that he didn't ever really understand the reality on the ground, never experienced it properly.

In terms of historical chronology, though, you'd have to place the 'Funeral Procession' paintings first. A map of north Calcutta, around Jorasanko, then the Brahmo Temple, then Grey Street, College Street, Hare Street, Harrison Road, the procession is in all these places at once, like a Mughal miniature painting of, say, Akbar leaving for the hunt, chasing the quarry, and then with the kill. Near Jorasanko is a mosaic of tiny dots, slippers, with an Englishwoman in a hat standing in their midst, two beggar children playing; on Harrison Road is a swirl of figures around the truck carrying the body, a man being dragged off, clutching a clump of hair, and not far from him, another man, a rakshas, or rakkhosh in Bangla, who looks like something out of Bosch, a dark figure about to leap, tiger on deer – young Elko himself, being pickpocketed, in precise miniature detail in the diffusely dotted mass. But this is an aside, a detour from the main story, which is Tagore's body being borne to his cremation. The truck disappears as the procession approaches Nimtolla burning ghat, people carry the poet's bier on their shoulders, now you can see the body, now you can't, as it's obscured by mourners leaning out of the balconies and terraces. All the while, at the top left of the canvas, the funeral pyre is blazing away, melding into a lurid sunset on the darkening river.

This simultaneous action recurs in a lot of the aerial paintings. In *Rhino Train*, in the bottom left corner, you have a train, far below, quite tiny, poking into the green patchwork of fields, the track ahead obscured by clouds; at the centre right of the canvas, the track is closer, the train is crossing a river bridge, figures are jumping out of the train into the water, some of them have clearly fallen out, tied to stretchers, the carriages splitting down the middle, as if something is slicing them open. At the top of the canvas, more clouds, the train far below again, stationary, derailed, a rhino running into the flooded paddy fields; above all this, down the sides and upside down at the bottom, almost like the border of a miniature, the high Himalayas rise from a gown of clouds in straight perspective.

It's a beautiful painting, but once I'd seen it, it made me suspicious of all sorts of beautiful paintings. Never again could I trust a lot of layered and sectored colour-field canvases – they always seemed to be waiting to be filled in, missing some story, some visual booby trap. On the other hand, nor could a lot of modern Indian miniature-influenced 'narrative' paintings find purchase with me – with the exception of Gulam Mohammed Sheikh in Baroda – when I saw them much later. I found them far too timid and over-respectful of the older traditions.

At the time, I didn't know what had prompted *Rhino Train,* but I could not get away from the fine veins of violence that streaked through the rich colours. At one level, the painting is about nothing but the landscape, to use Calcutta art critics' favourite phrase, 'a beautiful tapestry', but something is badly awry with the lush green fields and the rivers, the train and track lacerate the landscape, while the train itself is also being skewered and split lengthways. The clouds and peaks bear dispassionate witness. The reason behind the sequence of events remains unclear, and because of this, the painting is disturbing. As an illustration of a story, it fails utterly, and yet it's as specific as a painting needs to be and it hooks you. Or, at least, it hooked me. And Missus.

'I do love that one with the rhinos, train and mountains. That's one of the pictures I'd like to hang on to, actually. You can do what you like with it once I've followed His Lordship. You know, museum, or sell it or keep it, whatever.'

She had come back quickly – turned right around and flown back when she got the news. Getting the message to her on the phone was difficult because she was off on some protest march, but I had her friend's address, given to me for exactly this situation, and even the 'code' we'd agreed for the telegram – *Elko now with Paul and Pablo. Stop.* To which I'd added: *Had final drink just before lunch. Stop. Much love RS*

She came back two days after he died, the taxi bumping up the track. As she entered the house, she paused for a moment and rubbed herself all over her arms and shoulders. Then she stroked down her cheeks and lit a cigarette.

'Anything left to drink, or did he finish it all?'

I pulled out a bottle from her hidden stash and made her a gin with her precious imported tonic.

She was not prone to showing emotion, or at least none of the sad ones, and over the next few days, she proceeded to pack up a lot of her things. I hadn't realized, but she had kept a stack of folded cardboard boxes in the attic, ready for this moment. We expanded them, secured the bottoms with tape, and then she filled them, one by one, with the things she wanted to take with her. We only began to discuss what to do with his pictures on the second evening after her return. Without either of us saying anything, we avoided the den where the three of us would normally sit, leaving the bottles and papers untouched, as if he might come back any moment from a walk and throw a fit that his stuff had been moved. The garden table was right in the path of the warm, slow-setting July sun, and it seemed a good place to sit, where we could avoid being overheard by him, though neither of us was given to any straightforward belief in the afterlife.

'I have one regret, probably quite stupid, but I can't get rid of it. I feel I never managed to convey to him that I took him seriously as a painter.'

'Of course you did! Why else would you keep saving his damned work from the bonfire?'

'Well, he might have seen that as me humouring him, you know, you keep retrieving toys that a sulky child throws into the pond, that sort of thing.'

'Nonsense.'

'No, at first, of course I didn't. None of us took him seriously. Here the whole world was falling apart, and our Zemindear was obsessed about rendering Cézanne-like views of his garden! Van Gogh portraits of his darwaan! I mean, I ask you! Artist? Hah! You had to laugh at him. Twenty-bloody-two. *So* caught up with himself, and his good looks, his clothes and his car. What had he *experienced* that he could use to make art? Indeed, what had any of us experienced? But he had his ideas of art, and we, we had our ideas of politics and of changing the world. All equally laughable, I suppose. But we girls took ourselves oh-so seriously, and this pleasant fop we disregarded completely! Laughed at him! He was *fun*, with a capital, nightclub-neon F!'

She looks down at her hands, confused for a moment whether to smoke first or take a sip of her drink.

'There was that day, August '42, soon after the Quit India declaration, tear gas flying about, police opening fire... *Nothing* happened to him that day, yet something changed. The Kedar Lahiri of that day was quite different from who he became later. Later, I sometimes caught myself thinking that was his last day as Kedar, the spoilt Zemindear-aspiring artist.'

It clearly took Elko some time to distil things from that day. He paints several pictures, in normal perspective on rice paper with the photograph mimicry, some signed in front, some only at the back, with the title *Wellington Square, August 1942*, and these come only in the late 1950s. Then he goes back to more aerial work, for instance *Air Attack on Rail Saboteurs, 1942*, with RAF Gloucester biplanes, like in air comics, strafing dhoti-clad villagers. Then back to straight perspective, brush-and-ink sketches in stark black and white: burning post office, burning wine store, burning tram, burning bus, burning milk booth, no people, pieces of the city segmented into still life, but with flames.

The flames remind me. 'So, the cremation... we are sure about it, are we?'

'Yes, yes, that's what he wanted. *Hold up this body of mine, make it a lamp in your godly home / May the light's flame burn night and day in song*. You know that one, don't you? Not that he believed in... but he did like that one.'

'Yes, I know. Well, I've located this crematorium place that will do it, electric, of course, about eighty kilometres away. We'll have to make an appointment, is that all right?'

'Yes, of course... perhaps just you and me... and I suppose WG, if he can be here at the time. And then, I think, invite the friends for a wake and a meal, and we can all spill our drinks on the urn. D & D should be back from Japan soon.'

'We can ask WG when he gets here. I sent him a telegramme care of his magazine and they got a message to him in Greece. He called, not surprised, obviously, but really upset. Should be here in the next two days. I also informed the family in Calcutta, and got Ma to put an obituary notice put in *The Statesman*, just one from us. The family can do another one if they want, and one for the Bengali papers, though I doubt they'll bother... Have I already told you all this?'

'Yes, dear, you have. It's all right, it'll take some getting used to, him not being there. It's all right.'

'Yes... ah, yes! What I haven't told you: I also got Ma to send word to old Rasko in Midnapur.'

'Oh, right. That poor man, he'll be shattered.'

'Yes, I wouldn't want to be there when he gets the postcard.'

'Speaking of Calcutta, what about...'

'Him, yes. No telephone, obviously, or rather, too many telephone numbers, so another telegram to the one address I was told to use. No reply yet. I've also asked Ma to contact him.'

'Right. And darling? What about... did you...?'

'... California? Yes, I telegrammed. They called, some man, some secretary at first, asking who was speaking at this end, and then she came on.'

'How did she sound?'

I didn't quite know what to say to Missus. I hadn't expected Eva's voice to be so strong, with very clear enunciation, as if she didn't quite trust the international phone line. I could tell she was trying to be calm, sending her tone into a false brightness, with misplaced laughs, and then I realized she was trying not to cry, but doing it in American which was causing her strain. In the last few sentences, her accent slipped and that seemed to ease her a bit.

'Oh, I think she was upset, obviously, but controlled it quite well. Apologized about the time difference between California and here. Still has an accent. It sort of peeped out from under the American one. I wasn't expecting that, not after so many years. *I have great regards for Lahiri, Mr Lahiri... He was very helpful to me, of course, when I was passing through Calcutta during the war, of course, for which I am grateful, still this day. I was also lucky to see him on his start to becoming a great painter... Please, to all of you, my deepest condolence.*'

'Helpful is a good word for it, I suppose! I bet she remains grateful, the hussy!' Missus lets out a snort and a few flecks of gin catch my hand. 'Oh dear, I'm awful, aren't I? I've no right to be catty, not at this time!' She moves a hand across her nose and eyes to censor any unseemly dampness.

'I told her we might be thinking of an exhibition at some point. She said she would be happy to loan us some of the work, despite the agreement. She's sure he won't mind, wherever he is.'

'Wherever he is... yes... and we are here, left holding all his unwanted babies...' She throws her cigarette into the grass, trying to work up some anger to counter the grief. 'Look, Saki, I'll visit, of course. And send money to look after it. But as we discussed, it's all yours for now, darling. I think I'm done with this... neck of the woods, as Yanks would say... done with it for a while. I've *got* to get on, can't waste whatever time I've left!'

'Mashi, do stop talking nonsense! You're only, what...' I've been brought up never to allude to the age of a lady and I bite my tongue.

'Well, yes, not quite sixty yet, I know, but the oral fixation does exact its price, as we see.'

Oral fixation was his word for their joint alcoholism. As I poured myself another drink, I wondered if I'd been infected as well. I turned to her, not able to control the snap in my tone. 'Well then, stop drinking so much, will you?'

But she wasn't listening to me any more. She took a gulp of her gin and began laughing to herself, speaking to someone else. 'But, but, old boy, there were *two* rhinos in the pen... One has broken out... What happens to the other one...?'

DENIAL

'Well, old chap, Gauhati, Shillong, Imphal, Dacca, all still under His Majesty's flag, thank heavens, but a great pity about Stillwell. I'm sure Slim and Wavell, perhaps the Chinks as well, would have wanted your dream to come true. But this morning's ticker proudly informs us that General Vinegar Joe has now arrived safely, and with no little pomp, in Delhi. As if that was some sort of sodding triumph. And we know from Mr Currie that our co-principal, the good Major General Rice, has already met His Sourness.'

Todd-Cartwright looks around to make sure they are alone before settling himself on the edge of his desk. 'But fascinating, old boy, the rest of it, absolutely fascinating.' He picks up a glass paperweight to make his point. 'You see, now Sigmund Freud would say the train is your... er... male wherewithal, and it develops problems, or rather, you *fear* it will develop problems if it enters... enters again, I take it, the tunnel, the... any receptacle of your desires, let's say.' Todd-C turns the paperweight in his hand so that it catches different light. 'Whereas Carl Jung might argue it is, in fact, the rhino that is your joystick. And that it wants to run rampant, no matter what the damage.'

'But there were two rhinos in the pen.' Lambert regrets the literal reply as soon as it comes out.

'Indeed, indeed there were...' Todd-C's sympathetic look makes Lambert feel as if he is cursed with two penises. 'Anyway, no such luck as us packing off to Ranchi or Lucknow just yet. Looks like the rhinos of Nippon have decided to take a pew, haven't they?'

'The snappage does indicate the monsoon's stopped them good and proper. But they're tricky bastards.'

'Actually, I do quite like rhinos. These bastards are more like hyenas. Yes, more hyenas than rhinos, actually. But, regardless, since one's done one's sums, wouldn't you agree our friend Yamashitter's having his logistical leash yanked by his masters? I don't think we're dreaming this, would you agree?'

'I would, yes. They can't have imagined they'd knife through so quickly. My pictures show small columns parked in all sorts of odd places, single vehicles too, as if they've run out of fuel, or, my guess is, the limited supply's been prioritized for the front. I reckon they've actually been caught as off-guard by our collapse as we have. I'd imagine they were planning for a longer scrap. They may have calculated Singapore correctly towards the end, just about, but not Burma.'

'They couldn't have anticipated the walkover in Burma,' Todd-Cartwright agrees, leg-spinning the paperweight almost out of his hand before trapping it again. 'Nor did they, I'm sure, expect such a strong return of serve from the Yanks. But one can never say for sure, can one?'

At the chukker meetings, now held every three days, no one seems to want to acknowledge this sliver of luck poking them in the face. Outside the tall windows of the suite, the strong, continuous patter of rain provides a comforting sound. More reassuring than a wing of friendly bombers, Lambert thinks, as he listens absently to the old man explaining something to Major General Rice, who is down from Delhi for the week.

The early arrival of a heavy monsoon, coupled with the overstretching of his supply lines, has forced Yamashita to pause – it seems for the first time since he landed at Kota Bharu seven months ago. Not only have the Japanese halted in the thick, hilly jungles on the border between Burma and India, they are doing something no one has yet seen them do. As he turns to Lambert, Rice's eyes are both disbelieving and greedy, the unlikely winner of a jackpot. 'So, wing commander, could you repeat...?'

'Yes, sir. Sorties have been difficult in this weather, but the material we've gathered in the last two weeks, roughly from June 20th, indicates two things. The enemy now clearly has a problem with his fuel supply, logistical problem indicated by vehicles—'

'Yes, yes, I've got that, go on, the second thing?'

'They seem to be digging in, sir. Trenches, gun emplacements, fencing around permanent buildings that would suggest they are planning to stay there for a bit. Rain shelters, probably for tanks and armoured cars...'

'So no signs of any planned advance, then?'

'No, sir. All signs are to the contrary. It does look as though they want to see out the rains first.'

'Could it be a pretence? For the benefit of your undeniably excellent recce pilots?'

'Wouldn't have thought so, sir. As I've elaborated in my report—'

'Right, no, I take your point, I take your point. Keep up the good work!' Having gained what he needed from Lambert, Rice loses further interest. Currie and he go back to another ongoing discussion.

'Have you looked at that recommendation from front intelligence units? Delhi staff are quite eager to put it into motion.'

'Yes, well...' Currie pauses to light his pipe. 'We've been speaking about it for some time now, and I don't know if it's feasible. There *are* rather a lot of them, you know, especially the boats.'

'But this monsoon delay would give us the time, wouldn't it? This month, July, and August if not September, two months at the very least? If we could get most of them, say all the bloody bicycles and eighty per cent of the boats, that itself would be hugely helpful.'

'The bicycles wouldn't be as effective here, not as they were in Malaya and Burma, but the thing with the boats is that people depend on them for their daily needs.'

'Hang all that, John. There is a war on.'

'Quite. But the boats are critical in the monsoon. If we could number them, you know, do a sort of census, and start culling them in the third week of August, say?'

'Would have to be earlier in the Assam area, can't mess about with that, but yes, we could cut it finer in East Bengal, I suppose. Staff won't like it, but I could convey your point about the potentially volatile repercussions of confiscation in the current political situation.'

Currie leaps forward in his chair. 'Old chap. Quite crucial the word *confiscation* doesn't enter play!'

'Well, that's what it is, isn't it?'

'No... no... we are not confiscating the bicycles and the boats, we're taking them away, we're... um... *borrowing* them in order to... *deny* them to the enemy.'

'Your point being?' Rice looks impatient now.

Currie taps his pipe on the edge of the billiard table, each tap accompanying a word. 'We could call it... boat... *denial*.'

'Right, the... Programme... of... Boat... Denial.'

'No, no, programme implies planning. We don't want to underline our planning.'

'Policy, then.'

'Policy. Includes the bicycles, of course, but no need to mention that.'

'Policy. Policy of Boat Denial. POBD. Good, I like that. Staff should approve.'

'Shorter. Boat Denial Policy. BDP.'

'BDP.'

'BDP.'

GOLF GREEN

Lambert strikes a match and drops it on the piled negatives, but the damned thing fizzles out yet again. Underfoot, the manicured grass is drowned in monsoon water, and it squelches under his shoes, even as the negatives glisten, intact. The highly inflammable emulsion refuses to catch fire. The labels in Deyton's neat hand stay infuriatingly untouched.

Lambert is standing on a green at the Royal Calcutta Golf Club, four days after the surprise landings in Orissa Province. Against all calculations, Yamashita's army has pulled off a rapid, monsoon-time, river-hopping campaign across the geographical snakes and ladders that is the vast delta of East Bengal. While everyone's been busy staring east, the shock landings on the coast to the south-west mean the enemy is tightening its grip around Calcutta, neither rhino nor hyena but an inexorable silver python, its shining skin dotted with the red sun and striped with the spreading rays. There is now no time to move papers to the various designated temporary headquarters in Bihar and the United Provinces. As he heads for Dum-Dum and the last flight of evacuation transports, Currie's final orders are clear: 'Make sure you destroy everything, squadron leader, every *jolly, bloody thing*. They must have *nothing* that helps them govern these bloody people!' Today, there being a miraculous let up in the rain, Lambert is standing on the golf course trying to burn all his precious negatives. There's been a to-do with the two Yanks, Lambert's been no match for the sergeant and his large Negro, and they've taken away the jerrycan of petrol he was planning to use. As he tries to light a match, his left wrist is still numb where the black gorilla gripped it, a wonder it isn't broken, a wonder he managed to save the girl because they were trying to take her as well.

As he fumbles with another match, he suddenly hears the sound of different engines in the distance, ones with a higher whine than the British and American ones he's used to, not unlike ones attached to a child's Meccano set. But he knows these are not children who are approaching, though many of them will be no taller than thirteen-year-old English boys. Even as he's trying to gauge how far away they are, there's a massed squelching close behind him. His stomach convulses even as his bones lock. He looks over to the girl who's sitting under the awning of the club veranda. She's laughing, her sari dropping wantonly. He follows her look, her pointing finger, he turns around and sees that he's about to be surrounded. By hundreds of them. The horns undulating towards him, black crests on dirty white waves. A moving wall of cows slowly wiping out the wide corridor of grass. The herd comes right up to him, the hooves jack-booting quite delicately. The cattle part around the rise of the green and its attendant bunker and sidle past, gently patrolled by the pair of rhinos.

As the animals pass with their spattered bodies, they leave behind a churned up morass of mud and cow dung on the fairway. It starts to rain again. He can hear the drops hitting the piled-up negatives. As the first herd disappears, he can see another wave approaching in the distance, coming out of the curtains of water. In between, an overgrown mongrel pads around in the mud with a flag in its mouth.

Lambert's feeling of helplessness is replaced by something lighter; he feels freed of responsibility, he has tried to do as ordered, but what can one do about the bloody rain, eh? Maybe he can use something to weigh down the negatives and drop them into one of the ponds. Or, no. Maybe it's time to go. Where's that Indian beauty? There! Sipping a cup of steaming tea in the covered veranda, waiting patiently for him to give up. The sound of the engines has gone, which worries him. After a while, he realizes it's been replaced by a low hum, very close, like the rhythmic thump of a Spandau machine-gun: *Shibu-Shibu-Shibu, Shibu-Shibu-Shibu, Shiiibu-Shibu-Shibuuu.*

'Probably someone *praying,* wing commander! Perhaps some of the hotel's Mohammedan staff, a bunch of them perhaps, doing their morning, you know, whatever they call it!' Currie's pipe vibrates in his mouth like a tiny No. 6 golf iron as he chews out the words. 'I would say leave it jolly well alone. Can't mess about with these people's religious stuff at this juncture. You have several things to be getting on with, don't you?'

Fun-a-cut-a, Fun-a-cut-a, Fun-a-cut-a-laa-hey-she-was!

I threaded in the tape of the Darbhanga Raag Shree on the Marantz, and it helped me go about what I needed to do. As I moved in and out of his studio and the den, I could almost hear Old Elko singing along, as if he was still in the house, drunk, his voice fraying as it reached for altitude but still not completely out of tune. Fucker.

I continued making my basic list of Elko's paintings and drawings, trying to finish it before Missus left. She and I had agreed to break it down into five parts: first, the work that was in this house or nearby, including paintings she had hidden with various neighbours; second, paintings and drawings that had gone into collections, mainly two collections, one in Milan and one in Oakland/Berkeley, plus work sold or gifted to others; third, paintings that had survived or may have survived in Calcutta; fourth, paintings that were destroyed but were documented in photographs, either direct documentation or captured in the background, either by Missus herself or by others who had come visiting. A fifth category covered the paintings that were to be found only in written descriptions in various people's letters and diaries, including Elko's own writing.

'It's not as though we are trying to establish him as some sort of undiscovered genius, is it?' she'd asked one evening, veering close to some tears but not quite reaching there. 'It's not like we're going to go knocking on the doors of the Met or the Louvre, it's simply the mark of a life, the evidence of a life and effort that should not be allowed to disappear without...'

'Yes, exactly. Let's just say we are doing this for ourselves and for the two or three other friends who care. And leave aside the artistic value, people can argue over that, but for me the work tells important stories about that time, about what you people experienced and how he – and all of you – remember it.'

'You little bastard. I daresay you *will* get something out of this in terms of your work! Elko was right, this is why you've been recording us over these years, waiting to make your fortune after we pop it!' Before I could get alarmed, I noticed she was laughing. And wiping her eyes at the same time.

'Well, it *is* my work and I never made any secret of it, did I? And when I started, did I think he was going to... no, I didn't.'

'No, no, that's true.'

'And as for making a fortune...'

She leaned across and gripped my hand tightly. 'No, darling, I was just joking! You've been an absolute rock, and you know how much he...'

Yes, I knew. Knew how much he cared, how much he'd 'taken' to me, how I was like a – 'No, I'm *not* going to fall into that trap of Bangali sentimentality, old boy, all that *you're like a son to me* rubbish! You're *not* like a son, and you're *damn* lucky you don't have me... no, *I'm* lucky actually, that nobody has me for a bloody father!' No, I was like 'a younger friend' whom he'd 'become close to despite the gap in our age'. And yet, now, going through the jungle of his stuff, I felt a searing irritation that I suspect was very offspring-like.

Like prehistoric cave dwellers we were both avoiding touching or moving anything in the den area, as if his spirit was still hovering around, except that I was entering the zone every now and then to change the music. And we were also leaving the studio more or less alone. But it was open season on the rest of the house. Especially their bedrooms, and the kitchen which Missus was attacking and cleaning up with controlled fury.

I was in the studio now, picking up odd bits and pieces, and wiping down the nooks and crannies for dust and cobwebs. Just after I finished, I spotted a black-and-white photograph, 10' x 12', lying half bent where it had fallen behind a worktable, probably a few years ago. I knelt down and pulled it out, cursing because my hands, which I'd just washed, were covered with dust and muck again. Straightening the photograph and wiping it clean, my cursing changed scale, now aimed directly at the old bugger, dead or not. The print was lovely, heavy photo paper, the image sharp, with a full grey tonal range. Two pictures hanging side by side on a wall, lit by indirect daylight, a plush art deco sofa under them, half cut off, just the backrest in frame with its padded upholstery in a classic '30s pattern. To the right of the sofa, a French window, also cut in half but vertically, the out of focus palm trees indicating that it was brightly sunny outside.

I could hear her in the kitchen, her radio on softly, tuned to the BBC, *Desert Island Discs*. I wanted to ask her about this photo but not right now, I'd ask her later. Just then, I wanted to think things through.

I'd first come to know about the American factor when I'd made a visit in the autumn of 1970. On an impulse, I'd just taken the train and come down unannounced. The city was enervating at the time, not least because of a recent break-up I'd gone through, and drowning my weekend with the master Drownists, Elko and Missus, seemed like a good idea. If it wasn't convenient – which was unlikely, had never happened – I could always go back to the town nearby, skulk in a hotel and catch a return train the next day.

Going up the road to the house, I could already hear raised voices, Elko and Missus engaged in total war, scorched earth, carpet bombing, thousands of dead civilians, blood everywhere. Outside, there was another car parked next to their old station wagon. Going in through the half-open door, I confirmed the two of them weren't alone. The audience of one was sitting at the dining table, trapped in a parenthesis formed by Elko and Missus standing on either side of him, both about to trip into grievous assault. Her holding a half-empty bottle of gin as if she was about to smash it and use it as a dagger, him feinting with a palette knife, swiping it in the air, roughly at her eye level.

The man in the suit jumped up when he saw me. With great speed, he moved out from behind the table and came up to me, holding out his hand.

'Hi, there! Amos Rosenzweig!'

'Hi, how do you do, I'm—'

'Oh! Now the bloody Gestapo is here!' Elko flung his knife down. 'How did you manage to get him here so quickly! *How?*'

'Oh, hello darling, what a nice surprise! Good timing! We did need someone to oversee our last rites!' Missus put the bottle down on the table as if she had just been about to place it.

My arrival had clearly sucked the oxygen out of the fight. Both of them managed to look simultaneously disappointed and relieved. Elko excused himself and scurried off to the toilet, while Missus sat me down and explained.

Amos here was on one of his six-monthly visits from San Francisco. He represented several collectors on the West Coast, among them one particular collector who regularly bought Elko's work. Amos came over twice a year to help select works for the collection. Usually, Amos would come and go through whatever Elko had done recently, photograph a few works, and go off to visit other artists. In the meantime, he would post the photos back to the US and await a response. A couple of weeks later, he would call or post back small prints of the works he wanted to buy, in effect reserving them. A few days later, he would return to pick up the paintings and drawings. This time, Elko had managed to destroy two of the five pictures the collector had approved for purchase – painted one of them over with slashes of black paint, and burnt a really nice large charcoal drawing along with a bunch of other paper works.

'Oh no. Which ones?' I felt my own anger welling up, but I was careful not to let it show, this bonfire did not need more fuel.

'By the way, Amos, I'm *so* sorry about the Gestapo comment! It's just a silly nickname we have for this young man here! Simply because he does watch over us!'

'That's no problem at all, I understand.' Amos turned to me. 'You're obviously familiar with the maestro's work?'

'*I hate that fucking label, "maestro"!*' Elko was now skulking in the studio, obviously listening to every word.

'Yes, yes, and I know what he's produced recently. I was here a month ago, so at least until that point.'

Amos was a tall, thin man, balding, and he had to push up his glasses before he fanned out five photographs on the table. The full-size colour prints, clearly copied from slides, had that dirty, counterfeit feel about them, but the images still came through strongly.

Three of the photos were of small still lifes: one of a half-eaten toast on a plate where you could see the granules of sugar embedded in the butter, that typical chini-toast you got only in Calcutta; the second was a turgid green banana against a dark background, again from memory, again from Calcutta; and the third was a beautifully rendered peach that I'd seen him make when I was last here.

'These are intact,' said Amos, who had begun to sound to me more and more like an unctuous accountant. 'And these are the ones that are...'

There was a charcoal drawing, two lovers entwined, again a variation of something he made from time to time, just to free his hand, especially when he hadn't painted for a bit. The last one was something else, an image he'd begun to explore over the last few months, this time an oil on canvas, about three feet by two feet. At the bottom of the picture, there was a carpet of bones and food mess, the bones a mix of human and animal, and above it a gang of soldiers, men of unclear race in unspecified uniform, though most likely American, circling around two women in saris. The men were leering, the women clutching each other but defiant, all their faces slightly smudged but somehow conveying clear emotion. The bones and mess formed a platform for the image, but then, growing smaller, continued as a border around the rest of the painting. In the thing you could see trace elements of Kalighat pat, echoes of Francis Bacon in the way the figures were painted, with the bones and spilt food moving from realistic to a filigreed border pattern reminiscent of Indian miniatures.

'Why don't you take him for a walk?' I looked at Missus and nodded in the direction of the studio. 'Just twenty minutes. Try not to kill each other.'

She looked at me doubtfully but got up nevertheless and went to the studio. I could hear some low conversation, and then the two of them went into the garden through the studio door. A few moments later, I could see them from the window, walking away from the house and up the hill.

'The ones that are gone are gone, Amos. There's obviously no replacing them, but let me see what I can do.'

I went into the storage area behind the kitchen, a room that Elko never entered. I moved some crates and jars and pulled away the cloth from a canvas I had hidden there. I'd put it there over a month earlier, and I hoped that the paint had fully dried by now – it had. I brought it out and showed it to Amos.

'Oh wow! Oh my god! Where in hell did you get that from?'

'He finished the one you liked and then immediately started on this second version. He finished this, looked at it for three days, and then threw it into the garden one night. I found it and, er, gave it a safe home. I actually think this one is better than the one he painted over.'

'I agree, I agree... and I'm sure my, my principals will also agree, but is it okay to just—'

'Yes, absolutely. It's signed at the back. Just wrap it with the others and put it in your car. They—'

'They need the money, I know. I'll just pay her the full amount agreed and hope you can send me a similar charcoal drawing later?'

'Yes, of course. And if you could please arrange for decent photographs of all these for their records? And all the earlier works your collector has acquired? Do send two copies of each photograph, and I'll make out the provenance certificates for each one and send them back to you. I'm trying to help them stay organized, if you see what I mean?'

'Yes, of course! Sure thing! Though we've not talked about the certificates until now because of the agreement.'

'The agreement?' I couldn't control my expression.

'Oh, so you don't know. Well, I'm sure they won't mind my telling you. Mr Lahiri only agreed to sell his work to my client if she – if they – agreed not to sell any of the paintings on, or even show them publicly anywhere while he is alive.'

SITTANG DUCKS

'*Sittang* duck! Poor bugger Smyth was... a Sittang duck. Can I... utter... that, Jeremy? May I say that, without anybody...?'

'Yes, Alan, you may. There's no one here to eavesdrop. The Yanks have left. The place is empty.'

'You do mean the *joint*, don't you, old chap? The g-g-g-god-goddamn joint is clear!' Todd-Cartwright toys with the last shreds of crispy Peking duck, pushing the meat away with the fork in his left hand, pulling it back towards him with the pair of chopsticks clutched in his right. Suddenly, he notices Lambert again. '*How*, how can you be so sure, Jer-Jeremy? How can you be *certain* the joint is clear?'

On his way to the toilet, Lambert has casually checked the adjoining booths and they are untenanted. In the open part of the restaurant, on one long table, there lies a massacre of dirty plates and empty beer bottles. A narrow carpet of bones shines on the floor behind the chairs. Sitting in their booth, Todd-C and he have had to put up with the Yanks shouting across lunch. Lambert has heard one of them declaring loudly he'd read somewhere that the Chinese consider it an insult if guests don't throw the bones over their shoulders. 'Whatddya mean with puttin' the fuckin' bones on the side-uv-yrr plate? Y'tryin' to say I don't got no srrvants to clean up!? *Fuck* you, geddouta my house – geddouta my *palace*!' Eight men laughing loudly, glass smashing, a harried matron flipping aside their booth curtain to look in, eyes narrow slants, checking to see if these two goras, at least, were behaving themselves.

'Yu wan something?'

'Some more rice, please, garçon, and two more beers.' Todd-Cartwright flicks his wrist ever so gently, as if he's letting flight a cricket ball.

'And...' Lambert hesitates.

'Go ahead, Jeremy! Heart's content, I said!'

'One more Peking duck?'

'Duck now finish. Calcutta chillie chicken?'

'Why not? My friend likes to eat! A plate of Calcutta chillie chicken!'

'Two beer, chillie chicken, same rice?'

'Same rice.'

The woman is cautious about the rice, and understandably so. At the outset, she had offered them a choice, 'No normal rice now, rice price high up. You want old type rice, cost more. New rice, not so good, from Madras, cost less, but not so good. Depend how much you want eat.'

They have wanted to eat – or at least he has, while Todd-C attacks the beer – and now Lambert is monitoring the behaviour of his stomach. Except for his bladder pushing, all the troops seem to be asleep. At the back of the restaurant, the floor outside the door marked 'WC' is slippery with muck patterned with filthy GI boot prints. Lambert opens the door and finds himself facing a narrow backyard inundated in the unceasing downpour. The ground is covered by two inches of flowing rainwater, and across the shallow flood, he can see the men's urinal through the half-open door of a tin shed. Lining the side of the yard are rusting drums overflowing with food rubbish. As he crosses the yard, trying his best to minimize stepping in the water, Lambert sees one of the mounds of garbage move, as if possessed of life. A thin, curving tail shoots out of a pyramid of greyish rice, erect, vertical as a periscope. It vibrates for a second, searching for enemies, and then disappears again. Shaking with horror, Lambert forces himself into the shed and then out again as quickly as possible, watching out for rats all the way back to the booth.

While he's been away, Todd-Cartwright has arranged the bottles and plates in a pattern legible only to himself. He welcomes Lambert back with a noble nod of the head.

'Now then, Jeremy, what do we now know about Smyth's mistake?'

'That it was only one in the middle of many. Middle of the north and south of many.'

'Exactly!' Todd-Cartwright begins to arrange the bones on his plate in another elaborate pattern. 'Precisely! But...' He pulls four empty beer bottles to one side and makes them stand to. He moves the two half-full ones to his left, muttering 'India'. After pausing a bit, he looks up and grins. 'Right! Let's start from the... start, shall we? 8th December, Malaya landings, buffoons, Percival, 'Pop-off' Shenton, Thomas 'Australian ostrich' Bennett.'

'Benighted Aussie austrich,' Lambert agrees.

'So... Singapore gone by 15th February. Probably, *probably*, couldn't have held it, but still, ignominious, eighty-five thousand surrendering to thirty thousand.' Todd-C smacks an empty bottle off the table, but it doesn't break. He peers down at the bottle in wonderment before continuing. 'Then! Next! Burma! Now when did it start, again?'

'January 18th,' provides Lambert.

'Ah, yes. Shojiro's 15th Army. But Horny Archie sets the field completely wrong, doesn't he? Fr'instance, he... Wavell, orders Smyth *forward!* But, as Smyth's foreseen... he has to retreat. Had he ever written about war, a story straight out of P.G. Wodehou—*Night* of 21st February, Smyth's division has to cross over single file on *one* narrow planked bridge over Sittang River.' Todd-C piles up curved pork ribs, attempting to make a bridge, but they fall over. 'Exactly!' says T-C as if he's proven a point. 'Lorry jams on bridge. Holding everything up. Japs attack. Division's number two has to blow up the bridge. They lose half the men. Not Smyth's fault at all. He was a *Sittang* duck, trying to get his division across a bridge narrower than a virgin's—'

'Virgin's...' Lambert agrees, popping another fried prawn into his mouth.

'Out of respect for your feelings, Jeremy, we won't *specify* a virgin's what, what?'

'7th March,' says Lambert, anxious not to interrupt the Japanese advance.

'7th March, indeed! When we had to blow up the Burmah Shell refineries, we knew the game was up!' Todd-Cartwright starts picking up the bones with his makeshift fork-and-chopstick crane and dropping them from a height into a used-up serving dish. The bones bounce into the shallow pool of leftover sauce, and a fleck of liquid catches Lambert on the side of his nose. 'Nothing Alexander could do, nor the CIC. So. Cheerio, Rangoon!' Todd-C gently pokes one of the beer bottles until it topples over. 'By the end of March, Air Force gone, *gone!* The remains of it *back* behind mummy's apron in Assam! To protect her!'

'C'mon, Alan! The boys gave a good account of themselves!' Lambert's voice rises a fraction, but Todd-Cartwright pays no attention. Lambert takes a swig of beer and swallows the insult to his RAF.

'Slim, Burma Corps, on the run. In th'meantime, Vinegar Joe's on the rampage—'

'What was that they said after Singapore?' Lambert slams down the beer mug and opens his throttle. 'Never before have so manyyyy!'

'So manyyyy...' acapellas Todd-C.

'Been fucked about by so fewwww!'

'Fucked abouuuut!'

'And neither the few or the many...'

'The manyyyy!'

They finish together, '... have... *fuck... all... idea...* what to do!'

A photograph of Chiang Kai-shek on a Chinese calendar stares at them from the booth wall. Chiang is in full peacock military regalia, and Lambert thinks the epaulettes seem too big for the shoulders, like the claws of a dragon about to yank him up and devour him. The medals seem like some artillery has pounded into him, drawing out wounds of starred silver. Clearly, the little ferret will outlast everyone else.

At one side of the cubicle, there's a little window on to which the rain lashes. The windowpanes are crossed with tape covered with Chinese letters. Taken from packing boxes and affixed, Lambert knows, with rice paste, because he's read the ARP reports. The cheap glass panes shake under the onslaught, rhythmically, like whores being given a seeing to, Lambert imagines. The rain's hitting so hard, it seems to be attacking the frail Chinese characters, almost bursting through the glass. The smell of dead food, soy, chilli and overcooked chicken is suddenly overpowering. Lambert remembers the rat and almost retches.

'House of cards, we. Us.' Todd-C's head droops over a piece of chilli chicken that he's holding.

'Rice paper. White Road and Black Road indeed.'

'Rice paper. Smoke, mirrors, cheap and thin deceit... No, come on, dammit, some of the chaps acted honourably!'

'I think the rub is in the *some*, Alan.' Lambert strips the meat from another chicken wing.

'The rub... is in... you're absolutely right! That *some of the* gives us away! Tell me something, Jeremy old boy? How is it that you can quaff this chilli stuff when you blanch when I order something slightly spicy at Firpo's or Max's?'

Lambert thinks about this as he chews. Close as he is to Todd-C, he can't let on about his street forays. Todd-C wouldn't be able to help himself. Sooner or later, he would take the mickey out of him with the others. 'You see, I can't bear spices in our own food, when my tongue expects home. When my mouth expects... abroad... I can be more, more...'

'Adventurous! And let the devil take you on the thunderbox!' Todd-C revives and distributes the last two pieces of chicken, one each.

As he swallows the chicken, Lambert finds himself craving one of those local ice creams which are perfect for cutting the taste of spicy food. There's a specific name for them, what are the damned things called? Some sort of 'fee'. Amalfi? No... cool-something... ku—

Todd-C looks at his watch. 'I don't know about you, old chap, but I really should get going.' The drink has left his voice. The curtain parts, as if the restaurant woman's been standing just outside waiting to hear these words. She pointedly puts down a small tray with the bill and waits, arms akimbo. Todd-C lets out a low whistle as he examines the bill. 'Two whole rupees for three servings of old-style rice.'

'Very hard to find. After monsoon, more expensive. Three order rice, maybe two rupees four annas, maybe even three rupees.'

'Three rupees! For three measly plates of rice?' Todd-C can't keep the incredulity out of his voice as he slaps down some notes. The woman goes away to get the change. Todd-C continues to shake his head. 'I say, Jeremy, did I ever tell you about this conversation I overheard between the old man and the general?'

'Depends which one, Alan, not sure.'

'Last week, when Rice was down for the post-monsoon plans. They were discussing the grain supply. Rice – I say, Currie, about the food stocks for front line... Currie – They seem to be holding, normal monsoon wastage, but nothing of concern. But good thing you brought it up again, I wanted to ask about the civilian situation. Rice – Yes? Currie – Well, what are your chaps doing about the ri – about the grains, you know, what d'you reckon we can do about the ri – about the shortfall? Rice – Do you mean the bloody rice, Currie, the shortage of rice? Currie – Er... yes. Well, for god's sake call it rice then, no need to be coy, call a spade a spade and rice, rice!'

'Call a spade a rice!' Lambert shakes his head.

'And a curry a Currie!'

Outside, on Free School Street, Todd-Cartwright starts to look for a horse carriage. 'Are you coming, Jeremy?'

'I thought I'd take a wander around the Memorial and the Maidan. 17 Squadron have just come in with their new Hurricanes. They're parking around the racecourse, I'd better take a look. Thanks so much for lunch.'

Todd-Cartwright ignores the thanks as he hails a carriage. 'You'll always keep walking around the maidens, Jeremy! My regards to the Queen Empress!'

OUTPUT

'Here it is smelling just like a village. Suddenly.'

'It does smell quite strongly of something. Quite unplea—what *is* the smell?'

'You have never been to Bengali village, have you?'

'No. Must say I haven't.'

'Even here in city, many places they are doing it, where they have the khatals, the cow stables, cow... sheds.'

'Cows? This is the smell of cows, is it?'

'Output of cows.'

'Output... you don't mean milk, surely?'

'No, no. After cows are digesting the grass, the output they leave behind on ground.'

'Cow *dung!* Oh!'

'Yes, you see, people are collecting and putting on the walls of their houses. You know, these round-round, they put. Then, when dry, they use for cooking.'

'Are you saying they *eat*—'

'No, no, no! No, no, no! They use for fire, like coals, but this is free. Dry cow... dung is very good for making fire. Some people even mixed with coal dust falling from goods trains. Fire for cooking, for heat in winter, for other things, you see, such as making melted metal objects.'

'My word.'

They look at the dark block in the middle distance. What they can see is a massive cube of mottled brown partially obscured by the heavy, monsoon green of the surrounding trees. Through the trees, they can see that the top of the block is covered with sheets of dirty black tarpaulin fastened with blackened ropes. A tarp-covered dome of mud rises from the centre of the cube, accompanied by four smaller mounds, each with its own shroud of black, one on each corner of the structure. From where they are standing, near the corner of Middleton Street and Chowringhee, it seems as if the pile is an island commanding a sea of olive green and khaki. The regular waves of military tents begin just across the road from them, from just beyond the makeshift fence of dark green corrugated tin, and stretch all the way over the disappeared Maidan, seemingly to lap up against the cluster of the mottled block. They can see only the tops of the tents in the foreground, poking up above the fence, and the small unit marker flags fluttering in the breeze, but they can both sense the rhythm of the orderly, triangular rise and fall of tenting as it disappears out of their vision, the flags becoming smaller and smaller as they recede into the distance.

'Niru, are you saying the... stuff... keeps smelling even after it has dried?'

'Normally, it should not, no. But perhaps the rain and heat has brought out again the – brought out the smell again.'

'Well, the breeze is certainly coming past there... I never realized... Heavens, they must have needed vast amounts to cover the whole building. A lot of... output.'

'Of many cows,' Niru agrees.

'What do you call it? Is there a specific name for it when it's dried?'

'Same name, when fresh or when dried. It is called gobor.'

'Go-bawr?'

'Yes, gobor.'

'Niru, can I ask how are you so certain?'

'Uhh, I am sorry but, please, what is haiyuso?

'Beg your pardon? What's hai... oh! No, sorry, spoke too quickly! How, are, *you*, so, *certain*?'

'Oh! That they are covering whole Victoria Memorial with cow dung?'

'Yes. There was no mention in the newspapers.'

'You see, that is their war silence, of the papers, they are silent on many things, this is nothing. Some of us are working with poor people, so it is common knowledge for us. In end of December last, authorities are beginning to buy gobor from all Calcutta khatals. Large amounts, at very high price. Very strange. Why they are doing this... why *are they* doing this?'

'I see.'

'For three weeks, lorries are coming and taking away all daily production... daily output of all cows' gobor. Also of all buffaloes. First, we are thinking they need for cooking, for so many new soldiers who are coming. But! They are asking – authorities are *demanding* – that gobor is fresh. They will not buy even one-day-old gobor, only still fresh…'

'Still wet, you mean?'

Niru feels a tremor run down the length of the tall woman standing next to her.

'Yes, yes, exactly. And then we heard… we are hearing from workers hired to put it, that they are covering Victoria Memorial with this gobor. Covering very quickly as possible.'

'As quickly as possible.'

'As quickly as, yes.'

The low clouds above them begin to thrum with a strange, hoarse-voiced thunder. After a moment, Niru spots them: one, two, three, no, four fat, loud dots, insects cutting across the sky, louder than any insect has a right to be. The cluster wheels, the dots separate, first becoming birds, then aeroplanes. The first one banks into a sharp turn, and its wings briefly seem to catch fire as they trap evening sunlight that is invisible from the ground. The roar of the engines grows louder as the first plane comes low over the dome of the Memorial, its whirling nose aimed straight at the sea of tents. The thing comes even lower and raises its snout, hanging for a moment before it drops out of sight behind the Maidan trees. One by one, the other three machines follow, twin rods unfolding from their bellies, like puppet dancers opening their arms, the noise of the engines changing and dying soon after they disappear, as if the neem and gulmohar trees had swallowed them whole – glass, metal, canvas, the painted rings on the sides, everything including their angry sound.

Imogen remembers the bamboo scaffolding going up around the Memorial in late December, just after Andrew left. Remembers going past the cage of curved and knuckled cream-yellow lines jesting with the rigid, straight marble of the Edwardian pile. She remembers missing the view she had of the Memorial when waking up in Andrew's chummery, its bright, reassuring glare as it caught the morning sun. She remembers driving past at the time, around the turn of the year, and noting the slow cascade of brown gradually obscuring the building. Remembers thinking, later, that the white being covered over was a portent of the increasing absence of Andrew, the letters becoming rarer in direct proportion to the growing bad news from the Burma front. The last one she'd received was in the middle of May, two and a half months ago. Uncensored, because it was carried by one Andrew's fellow officers, it has a line in it that doesn't leave her alone – *They're all over us, like these bloody malaria mosquitoes, and I'm not sure we've got any cure...* Very unlike Andrew to say that, or to say that to her sitting so far away, knowing that it would increase her anxiety. Perhaps he'd been preparing her.

'Are you thinking of... shall we have some tea, Imogen?' Niru carefully forming the grammar, sensing the mem-girl is temporarily elsewhere.

'What? Oh yes, tea! Of course! Good idea.' Imogen turns to Niru and gives her a wide but empty smile.

As they begin to walk away from the restricted area, Niru points northwards. 'I think we have to walk a bit, there is no chaa shop nearby, but—'

'No, no, allow *me*. Would you mind having English tea? With sandwiches and cake? It's quite nice.'

'No question of allowing!' Niru finds it even more difficult to form the sentences while laughing. 'I would like very much to try! But how much will it cost? I have not much maa—' She sees Imogen is smiling properly now and shaking her head vehemently.

'Allow, Niru, meaning allow *me* to *pay*, to treat you, not allow the ingestion of English tea!'

'Oh, I see! What exactly is ingeshun? Like a medical injection? Or when, like, stomach is upset?'

'No, to eat or drink something. Opposite of output, a sort of antonym.'

'Antony?'

'Intake is better.'

'Output opposite is intake?'

'Exactly. I know quite a nice place for tea, Flurys, do you know it?'

'I have heard of it, of course. It is quite... well-known.' Niru hesitates as she remembers Roma mentioning the prices in that place.

'So!' Imogen claps in her best headmistress manner. 'Two ladies in no hurry, shall intake tea and cake at Flurys!' Then she pauses and shakes her head. 'Actually, no,' she claps her hands again, more softly this time, just for herself. 'Two ladies in no hurry... shall intake, at excellent Flurys, some tea and cake!'

'Excellent!' replies Niru, her repetition stable on the two wheels of Roma and Imogen.

EVENING PATROL

Lambert walks down Park Street, the beer in his head, the chilli chicken still breathing fire inside his mouth. The sense of extreme repletion he feels is mixed with an unease that he can't quite pin down. There's certainly no trace of that immediate rebellion in his innards, none of the tiny, morse code convulsions that signal his intestines are unhappy with what they've been given to process or are about to do something about it. He *has* quaffed too much Chinese grub, but no alarm bells, all hatches happily shut. No, perhaps it's something Toff-C said over lunch, but the beer has made his head slightly fuzzy and he can't put his finger on the thing.

The busy street with all its fancy shops and restaurants is washed in a watery monsoon afternoon light – 'The sun with many petticoats on,' as Toff-C describes it. Two big buildings rise on the south side of the street, a full seven storeys high. Looking at them, you could be forgiven for thinking they've been transplanted from London, from Oxford Street or Southampton Row. The pile called Stephen Court rules the corner of Park Street and Middleton Row, a stack of obviously spacious, round rooms, like a massive hinge, sending the rest of the architecture in two directions, down both streets. On the Park Street side, the facade has thick, decorative pillars in the middle where the cream-coloured paint is soaked through and chipping slightly in places after three months of heavy downpour. The large balconies on either side of the pillars are veiled with thick chiks, the dark green slats slick with unevaporated moisture. The windows are all crossed with paper tape, as if some large child-monkey's been playing noughts and crosses up and down the building but forgetting to use the noughts. Empire Mansions, the next leviathan along the street, has an arcade that covers the pavement. Drooping tarpaulins cover the first-floor terraces above the arcade, the evening cocktails having moved indoors for the duration. Above these, again, the face of the building interrupted by chiks and crossed windows. At the ground level, Park Street has possibly the largest concentration of classy bars and eateries in the Indian Empire, or so Lambert has heard. But war and rain have muted their splendour. The procession of neon is hard to imagine now, with the signs all trussed up under tarp and jute to protect them for the long years they will likely need to be dormant. Lambert's tidying eye notices odd bits of dirt and grime the war has allowed on to what should be spic and span and smart. He imagines these revelry places will stay open to serve the Jap troops, just as the reports say they have in Singapore, but then, here the Nip bastards will also have to keep the bright lights under wraps against RAF raids from the airfields being prepared in Bihar and the eastern United Provinces, a thought he finds vaguely satisfying.

Lambert remembers the neon trapezing along just before Christmas, the pompous buildings forced to join hands across the street by strings of Yuletide lights and lanterns, the reflections slashing the tooting, celebrating cars. With a slight pang, he remembers complaining about the absence of blackout to Mr Currie. Looking back, his panic had seemed premature in November, prescient after the 7th of December, and premature again as the Jap bombers failed to materialize across the first half of the year. As he crosses the road, heading towards Russell Street, he hears the screech of brakes before he sees the large car that's about to run him over. He skips out of the way, his eyes raking those of the driver and the portly passenger on the back seat, both native, both mouths open to send epithets his way, both tongues held as they realize he's a white officer. As the car barrels away, he realizes there was something odd about it. Ah, a pre-war Benz, but the star on the bonnet removed and the star on the grille covered by a too-large number plate.

Lambert realizes he thinks of last year's Calcutta as a completely different city from the one he's traversing now. The city, or even just the bits that he knows, has changed shape in some subtle way; it's not even outwardly things like the taped windows and draped signs, it's the way people now hold themselves, the way they walk, the way chaps now avoid mentioning certain things, specifically the pre-war past or anything happy to do with it, or saying too much about the future and any possible happiness that may be waiting there. It's as if everybody has been distilled into the narrow present, with the darkness pressing close on either side. And it's not just us, Lambert thinks, but the natives as well who possibly feel this, though he can't quite tell with his almost non-existent local lingo.

Coming out of the Empire Mansions arcade, Lambert turns left into Russell Street and realizes what it is that's been bothering him. Earlier this afternoon, Toff-C and he had taken a horse carriage, a jhurrie-gaadi, from the Great Eastern to the Chinese restaurant. At the five-way crossing at Esplanade, they'd become embroiled in a huge scrum of traffic: trams, bicycles, cars, horse carriages, all trapped in a heaving knot, three traffic policemen in the middle of the maelstrom, one with his pugree comically askew, trying to beat everyone and everything into order. A few feet away from them, a wizened little brigand of a jhurrie-gaadi driver, urging his horse forward, face to face with a large Packard. As car and horse inched towards each other, the chauffeur had punched his horn, making the pony whinny and rear backwards. The brigand, giving up, spat at the pony and whipped him to move sideways, shouting something that sent all the locals into much merriment, a phrase in which Lambert thought he heard the name 'Wavell'. As they finally pulled away, Toff-C and Lambert could see everyone was laughing together, the brigand, the driver of the car, two of the policemen, other locals, their own jhurrie-walla. Toff-C, who had some proper Hindustani, tapped their driver on the shoulder. 'Voh aadmi kya bola?' What did that man say? At first, the driver refused to answer, shaking his head and trying to hide his smile, but finally he replied. 'Kuchh nahi, saheb, voh ghoda ko chillaya ki tum Wavell ban gayaa sa-lla!' Todd-C looked away as if he'd been slapped. 'Alan?' 'The bastard told his horse, *You've turned into Wavell!*'

Almost as if on cue, Lambert spots a dark statue of a rearing horse through the heavily taped plate glass of one of the antiques auction houses on Russell Street. A dulled metal horse rampant, surrounded by the bric-a-brac of a fading empire, china services, porcelain cherubs, stained mirrors, towers of stacked teak and mahogany furniture. Looking away, he tells himself that perhaps not everyone is trapped in the present. No doubt, for many of these Indians, the war has conjured up some idea of an imminent independence, of a different, happier future that is coming soon. Fools. The Japs would slaughter thousands of them, and they would die screaming, missing us, missing the bloody Union Jack they hated so much.

Passing the Turf Club, Lambert automatically scouts around for his accomplice in crime, the muri-walla, but today he doesn't see him. Lambert remembers the encounter with the man, roughly three months ago, that set him off on his food adventures. He realizes that his alimentary lust now makes him associate different parts of the city primarily with different kinds of food. Russell Street and the Turf Club, Madame Toussaint still unvisited, will always be the muri-walla and that first burst of chilli; upper Chowringhee – Firpo's and the pork chops better than his mum's; Burra Bazar with a whole host of street goodies, the chaat, the kachori and potato mush, all the different samosas; Chitpur Road and Park Circus – the heavy, oily, Mahomeddan grub, all meat, that beeryani rice redolent with animal juices; Chinatown and the Tung Foo place on Free School Street with the differently spicy Chinese nosh. And then there's all the mind-boggling variety of fish that he keeps hearing about from the lower ranks, for which he's going to have to buck up the courage and venture further afield, to the stalls near the fish markets at Raja Bazar in the north and south to the edge of Ballygunge.

There's a growing sound of air-engines and he glances up at the broken monsoon clouds. No, it's only the Hurris from 17 Squadron returning to Red Road from their evening patrol. He'd know that sound anywhere, except in this thick air he fancies those Merlin engines sound a wee bit different. He suddenly remembers the Wingco in charge of the Hurricane squadrons at his aerodrome in Sussex bristling when his new Spitfire was delivered. 'This is all very well for your fancy footwork, flight lieutenant! But remembaah! Nothing like a Hurricane on your side when you're a few too many wickets down! Nothing like a stout, solid, bloody Hurricane!' It's as if he's thinking back to a different war from another era. Or a parallel war. Just as there are parallel cities here, just as there are parallel foods, there are also, yes, different, parallel wars. He begins to count them: the European war with Germany, the war here against Japan, the war, no other word for it, between Britain and subject India – all of these further knotted by the bloody Russians, and now the bloody Americans, fighting their own wars which are, yet again, different from all the wars he's fighting.

So many cities here, all coexisting, he can't stave off the thought, each fighting a different war. The phrase 'on the same side' not the same for everyone. Goodsugar's drunken voice again, Goodsugar who's imminently about to land back upon them, the nasal sneering twanging the phone line, Yank aircraft growling behind him: You do understand back home they don't give a skinny skunk's spunk about Europe? Jerry? Wing commodore? Buddy? You do understand that? We hate the goddam Krauts, sure, but what America really wants is to bite into these yellow sonsabitches. And you... Limeys... you fucking Mountfattens... will either help us or you will get out of the way of our due, Lord-ordained repast!'

Due repast. Different hungers, different repasts. He remembers his dream about Goodsugar being beheaded by a samurai sword. He wonders how he himself would fare in a Jap POW camp here, and whether there would be a muri-walla available just outside the barbed wire fence. Would the Nips in the towers open fire? With what money would he pay the fellow? Anyway, no muri-walla today and he feels relief, he really doesn't need any more food, what he needs is—

Two shots ring out from somewhere and Lambert ducks. Low calibre shots, but a bullet is a bullet. He crouches behind a postbox, trying to locate where the gunfire is coming from. Two more reports, accompanied by a gay English voice. Not shots, but someone clapping.

A laugh. Lambert straightens up, trying to look as normal as possible, as if he's just picked up a dropped pencil. It doesn't matter, no one's noticed him.

The clapping has come from the couple walking past, just across the road. At first, he sees just their heads, an Englishman walking with an Indian girl. Then the two pass between parked cars, two women, actually, a tall white girl with short mousey blonde hair, a much shorter local girl with a black braid and a folded umbrella, all very jolly, heading towards Park Street, neither of them a patch on that beauty leaving Firpo's all those months ago, just after Rangoon.

A STRANGE SANDWICH

Niru takes another bite of the strange sandwich. It doesn't taste of much, but she's beginning to like the repeated surprise of the crunchy, peppered cucumber hidden in the thin pillows of soft bread-butter. She's used to cucumber in lengthwise sticks, salted, of course, but with a squeeze of lime, raw onion and green chillies. These thin, round slices with just salt and pepper feel odd, as if notes in a tune are missing, but then the whole thing is strange, to be sitting here in this deluxe place with this mem-girl, in her nose the aroma of what she now knows is 'Darjeeling' tea, on the starched white tablecloth before her, white china plates imprinted with the name of the place – Flurys – in blue, and the same calligraphy embossed on the dull silver of the teapot and the little things holding the milk and sugar. Even the cubes of sugar are a novelty, and she has to stop herself watching them melt in her cup, stop herself from thinking what a waste of effort it is to make these beautiful little cubes knowing their fate is to disappear into some hot liquid like ordinary sugar.

'Death is inevitable. Everybody dies. It's the one truth from which there is no escape, true! How do you say it again?'

'Mrityu anibarjyo.' Niru fails to swallow the bite of sandwich before speaking, not sure how to laugh in this place, the mirth trying to come out as the mouthful tries to go in.

'Mreetoo... oh, you *mean* thing, do stop making fun of me!'

'Not of you, not at you, *weeth* you! My English is so bad, how I can make fun at you?'

'All right! Again! Mreetoo... awning-barge-ho?'

'Very good!' Niru decides none of the adjoining tables are paying the slightest attention to them. 'It is mriTYU awnibarJYO.'

'Mreet-you, only bar joe.'

'Yes, better. We will practise and you will be able.'

'Anyway, so sorry, I interrupted you, you were saying...'

Niru takes a sip of the alien tea to soothe her throat. Then she continues the story about her professor Bakul-babu, and how in his lectures he would say only two things are inevitable, 'In Bangla, we have a saying – *mrityu anibarjyo* – death is inevitable, to which I would ask you to add *proletariat biplab anibarjyo,* the only other thing that is inevitable is the proletarian revolution.' When Imogen asks Niru if she agrees with her teacher, Niru plays it safe, replying that the teacher is a great scholar of Marxist philosophy but she's not so sure about revolution being inevitable.

'But you *do* have a revolution of sorts going on, don't you? So what does your professor think of this Mr Gandy, then? What do *you* think of My-*hat*-ma Gandy?'

Niru looks around quickly before answering. 'Of him, I think... *my hat!*' she says, triumphantly repeating the dismissive phrase Imogen has taught her. 'I am meaning, all this so-called non-violence will not bring us freedo—' she cuts herself off, but Imogen immediately pats her on the shoulder.

'Oh, no, look, do speak your mind! I would want independence too, were I Indian.'

'Perhaps you should want it even if you are British.' Niru smiles and her eyes show no remorse this time.

'Quite. I suppose I do see your point, but...'

'No, I am meaning, sorry, I *mean* if you take... take as a given... that independence is the correct goal... then you have to, you know, that some violence will bound to be required.'

'You mean what Gandy and the Congress are proclaiming won't work, this non-violence?'

'Has not yet. And there has always been violence resistance also, throughout, by poor people.'

'Vio*lent* resistance.'

'Violent, pardon me.'

Niru reaches for a scone and puts it gingerly on her plate. 'How to eat this?'

'Oh, you break it open, cut it open with a knife, if you're being proper, then butter it, this butter is rather good, almost pre-war, wonder how these freebooters manage to find it.' Imogen demonstrates with another scone. 'And then clotted cream if you were back home, before the war, but obviously not here, and then heaps of jam.'

'Hips of jam?' Niru tries to imagine how jam could have buttocks.

'Yes, heaps, lots. At least that's how I like my scones.'

'Violent resistance, you know, there can be all kinds of different violent – of violence. You know, there was one story I heard when I was growing up...'

'Yes?' Imogen sees Niru is shaking her head, furious with herself, obviously biting her tongue hard. 'Oh, don't stop! For now, I'm putting friendship before king and country, I promise!'

Now Niru has opened her mouth wide to bite into the scone. At the last moment, she pulls away, putting down the scone. Blushing, she covers her face with her hands and shakes her head, trying to stifle some awkward merriment.

'But do go on, seriously, I won't be offended on behalf of the Empire.'

'No, it's not about Empire so much... it is... improper story, that's why I cannot!'

'Improper? How do you mean?'

Between exploratory bites of the scone, Niru tells the story. In the 1920s, there were peasant protests in Bengal, not so much against the British but against the zamindars, the big landlords who exploited the farmers mercilessly. The British administration naturally backed the rich landowners against the peasantry, and the police began to put down the protests with great violence and widespread arrests. In one area, people realized that a local foreman was informing the police via the zamindar about what the protesters were planning. One night, the informer went to the zamindar's mansion for a sumptuous meal. As the wicked man was returning home, the peasants caught him and tied him to a tree with his back facing out.

'Oh dear, I'm not sure I want to hear the rest.'

'Yes, you are right. I will stop.'

'No, no, no, now I have to know! Please don't stop. You can't.'

'Well, let us say they tortured him badly.'

'Oh, I know *that!* But what exactly did they do to him? Why tie him up, chest against the tree?'

Niru feels a heady rush, as if she is diving off a high cliff into a deep ocean. What on earth is she doing, sitting in the most high-class tea shop in the city, talking such nonsense with an English girl whom she hardly knows? Her mouth full of strange tastes, new combinations fighting each other, her head spinning, oscillating between extreme awkward shyness and great elation, she decides to continue. She has come up against the fullest limits of her English though, and in her mind, she translates and arranges each sentence before speaking it aloud.

'So they, as I warned, improper, so they—'

'Oh, never mind proper or improper!'

'So they took off his dhuti, what men wear below, instead of long pants, around the legs, you know?'

'A doe-ti, yes... *oh* my god...'

'So, in that area of Birbhum, it is famous for this red ants which are biting terribly. And this tree was near some big ant mountains.'

'Anthills. Oh, no... so they... they *didn't...*' Imogen's fingers are rigid, as though she's playing piano on the tablecloth.

'So, yes, so they then put the honey on the man, in all the, you know, in all the areas, all the impro—what you may call the private parts, especially behind.'

'Oh bloody hell.' The curse escapes before Imogen can stop it.

'Yes, very bloody and like hell. Then they just left him and went away.'

'Did he die? He must have, the poor bast—'

'No, he actually survived. Someone heard his screamings and saved him but not before...'

'Not before the ants got to him.'

'Yes, not before the ants reached him and spent some time with him.'

'What were your thoughts about the dirty pictures, darling? Show? Not show? Keep for later?'

'Not show... not sure. If we've agreed to not be limited by *what he would have wanted*, then I would tend to include them. Though perhaps not initially in Calcutta, perhaps just here, as part of the larger...'

'Quite. I do think it would be a great pity to keep them squirrelled away. Some of them are truly lovely.'

The dirty pictures Missus is referring to are drawings that Elko kept making across his life. Very few of them ever made it to becoming actual paintings, and most of those he destroyed. He used to call them his dirty pictures because there were things there that he could not imagine ever showing in polite society, especially back in India. He'd tried to destroy a whole bunch of them before he died but I'd managed to stop him.

One of my favourites of these was one he'd made in black and red ink, a village scene consciously drawn in the style of Nandalal Bose's flowing lines: a corpulent man, wearing nothing but a singlet, has his hands tied around the trunk of a tree; his backside is completely exposed and his face is distorted as he screams with pain; all this is in black lines but the little dashes, unmistakably ants, that crawl up the man's legs and into his anus are drawn in red. Scrawled at the bottom on the right is a title – *The Informer*.

Then there's one of a couple in a hotel bed, making love while a waiter stands patiently next to the bed with a loaded breakfast trolley.

There are several versions of a view from the windows of a first-class train compartment. Two passengers on either side, faces obscured by newspapers, cups of tea steaming on the little window table, one of the hands holding a smoking cigarette along with the edge of the paper;

through the windows, morning light falls on rail tracks and beyond them is an open field in the hinterland of a town, dotted with squatting figures who are clearly defecating.

He could never draw starving bodies, but he tried to draw every other 'obscenity' and grotesquerie he had seen or experienced. Some of these drawings came not from fascination with the horrific but from love and from the awe of love, of it being able to exist in times such as people were living through.

Then there were the drawings, mostly pencil, some conte and charcoal, of a woman in the throes of lovemaking, seen from above by the lover, hair and spectacles askew, very recognizably someone he could not expose to the leering gaze of Calcutta society.

'He should have married that Keya Dutta,' says Missus, sifting through these. 'She had money, she could have supported him, her Zemindear, helped him remain a dandy. Maybe they'd both be alive right now.'

'You had some money. You supported him for all you were worth. But he's still dead. So perhaps... try not to think along those lines too much.'

'Yes, darling, but we were both *unmoored*, don't you see?' She's feeling the need to state the obvious, using her emphases to explain things to the child I still am for her. 'Both unmoored! Him cut off by his family, basically orphaned for his obsessions, and mad me, with all *my* obsessions, also cut off from *my* family, all bridges burnt, or well, most of them anyway! Perhaps he would have thrived in his Zemindear world, being waited on hand and foot by that chap of his, Rasko... that Keya would have had staff, well, before she – but systems, structures, big house like his own. This life here, I completely believed him that this is the life he wanted, but it whittled him down terribly. They didn't design or train him for this, Ma and Pa Lahiri and all the ancillaries, and in the end, there was a steep bill for that.'

'I think he wouldn't have been half the artist he turned out to be. Not in one of those houses, not with those pressures, family, cars, clubs, class, Keya. I believe she was quite a handful...'

'Dear boy. Are you saying *I'm* not a handful?'

'Yes, of course you are, but the two of you're not together, not in that way.'

'Weren't together, darling. Weren't ever. Were never. We mustn't be shy of using the past tense now.'

After the death of someone you love, it's funny how the past tense comes and puts its cloak over you. And not just the past that is now forever affixed to one who's gone, but all the different pasts that could have been theirs. I remember the one meeting I've had with the surviving Lahiris, his uncles Bulldog and Borun, and think – at least here he was whittled down, back there in Calcutta he'd have been chopped off. It makes my blood boil, the way they referred to Missus, neither of the venal bastards able to say her name even though by now they both knew it very well.

I'd gone back to Calcutta in the winter of '74, a few months after Elko had died, for my annual visit home. Against advice, I'd called and made an appointment to go over to Palm Avenue, to the Lahiri house, for tea. I'd been received by the plump and sleek Borun, dyed hair, dyed sideburns bigger than the sharp little Lahiri nose that I recognized, imported checked shirt tucked over the belly into terry-cotton flares which created walking problems he hadn't fully solved. A wealthy man in his early sixties trying to look young and 'with it', all of it absurd to my eyes, with the fake cherry on top being the chipped cut-glass English accent.

'Oh, hello, hello, you're the chap... you're the young chap, aren't you?'

'Hello, nomoshkar, yes, thank you for...'

'Not at all, not at all, anyone who looked after Kedu is most welcome in this house. Come this way. We'll sit in the garden. Chhot-da will join us shortly. I must warn you, though, we are both a bit pressed for time at this moment. Not that we don't have time for a cuppa tea with...'

As we walked through the hallway, he flicked his fingers at a servant, indicating we should be served in the garden at the back. We walked past an open door through which I could see a messy room, a large double bed on which lay a pile of what looked like amplifier wires, with a large Creedence Clearwater Revival poster stuck to a wall. Borun saw me glance into the room and immediately called out to the servant in Bangla.

'Ei, shut that door to Ani's room! If Boro Shaheb sees it, he'll blow a fuse! And open the windows and switch the fan on inside, that smoke smell is awful!' As we walked out to the veranda, I could hear him muttering under his breath, 'God knows what these young people think they are doing. Father's hotel is all very well, but there are limits. They don't understand limits. Boundaries. No responsibility.' For a few moments, I thought he had forgotten I was there.

We sat down at a glass-topped wrought iron table on the lawn. Borun lit a cigarette and offered me one, which I declined. The servant appeared with a tray from which he unloaded the tea service and a small plate of Flurys biscuits.

'So! What's it like over there? Are you enjoying your life there?'

'It's okay. There are ups and downs, as there are everywhere. But I like my job...'

'Which is teaching at a university! Does it pay well?'

'Well, not as well as some other professions, of course, but yes, I get by.'

'Ah, yes, to be young, unmarried and free in... ah! You're not married, are you?'

'No, no, I—'

'Good! Keep it that way, *keep* it that way! Enjoy life while you can! *Take* the bull of youth by the horns! That's what Hemingway would advise you! Kedu used to love Hemingway when he was young. Kept quoting from...'

'Hemingway? Hemingway!? Borun? Are we outside? Why are we *outside?* We've routed malaria in this garden, have we?' The voice sent shivers up my spine. For a moment, I wondered how Elko had come back and found us here in Calcutta.

'No, Dada, I just thought tea in the garden might be a better...'

'Hello, how d'you do? Lahiri.' Bulldog was about the same height as Elko, with the same voice box and the same glinting eyes, but that was it. As he approached us, the invisible pilot-car of Old Spice preceded him.

Here was a man in his mid-sixties with the battering-ram energy of someone half his age. His handshake was like a punch, the open paw hitting and gripping my hand painfully, the pumping action almost yanking my six feet two inches down to his five feet six. Here he was. Force of nature. Lahiri. As though no Lahiri had existed before him, and none would after. No extra sprinkling of anything in the introduction, no first name, obviously, and no mention of his rank at retirement, which I knew to be a disappointing lieutenant general, one of the two contenders, along with Harbaksh Singh, shunted sideways to make way for Manekshaw to take over as C-in-C in 1969.

'Borun, what are we drinking?'

'Tea, Dada.'

'I know, *tea!* Which tea?'

'I asked for the Benkabari first flush...'

'Fine!' Bulldog turned to snap his fingers at the servant to pour the tea. Then he pulled out his cigarette holder and inserted a 555 into it as if inserting a bullet into a pistol. With the first puff, his eyes were trained back on me.

'So, can you confirm again that my nephew died of, what would you call it, of an alcohol-related condition?'

'Yes. The last thing was a sudden heart attack, as in my letter to you, but the doctor was clear that everything was affected by the cirrhosis.'

'Hm. Quick was it, at the end?'

'At the end, yes it was, quite quick. He collapsed in my—'

'Right. Understood.' Further details were clearly unwelcome.

'And you, er, cremated him and all that, as you wrote?' Borun seemed to be ticking off some list in his mind.

'Yes, I and—'

Bulldog raised his arms and clapped hard in front of his face, killing both the mosquito and my words. 'You and that – yes, we understand.'

'That woman he was living with!' Borun slurped the words out through the teacup at the edge of his mouth.

'Er, yes, the lady and I—'

'Right.' Bulldog was drumming the cigarette holder against the edge of the glass table. His eyes darted around the tea service and biscuits, searching for enemies. 'Right. We are grateful, of course, that you carried out the last rites of my nephew. Very grateful.'

'Very grateful,' chimed in Borun.

'Now, my dear fellow, what do we owe you?'

'Owe? I don't understand.'

'The cost of the whole business. Funerals over there are not cheap, I know, so how much was it? What does it come to in Indian rupees, do you know?' Clearly, Bulldog thought this was the whole reason for my seeking a meeting.

'Oh! The cost! Oh, no, no, no! That's all done, all taken care of, there's no question of asking you for—'

'Look here, young man. I'm quite busy at the moment. So can we do without the usual bhodro Bengali beating around the bush?'

'Yes, please just say. We are happy to cover it. Cover any reasonable amount.'

I felt like a cup and saucer being firmly pushed off the edge of the table. What I had come for and what these two imagined were in two separate universes.

'I apologize, I should have explained when I telephoned.' I took out my own cigarettes and defensively lit one, trying to slow things down. I took a drag and turned my rising anger inside out like a sock, forcing my voice be as unctuous as possible. 'I came to pay my respects, of course, to both of you gentlemen. As also to the house where Kedar Uncle grew up. But I've also come to make a request.'

I took a breath, flinching for interruptions, but none came. 'As you know, Kedar Uncle was a painter of some note, and I am involved in documenting—'

'Of some note? *Was* he? I haven't ever heard that.' Bulldog's eyes had become smaller in suspicion. This was not previously reconnoitred terrain.

'Well, he did have some mentions in the papers, but that was before he left, or perhaps soon after, but about twenty years ago... We haven't seen anything lately.'

'Yes, well, we are hoping to redress that. You see, there is a fair amount of work he left behind in—'

'Yes, it was always his hobby. He got it from my sister, Delphine. A bloody obsessive hobby! So he continued this… *hobby* while drinking himself to death, did he?'

'Well, he left behind quite a serious body of work, and I'm trying to put together an exhibition of a selection of the paintings and drawings.'

'Good lord! An exhibition where? Surely not over there? And… surely not over *here?*' A look of alarm had replaced the look of suspicion on Bulldog's face. He clearly wanted his dear nephew dead and buried and the file closed. A show in Calcutta would make the questions re-emerge – why did Kedar Lahiri leave his home and the city? Why did he never return? What was his relationship with his family? I decided there was no point fudging the answer, let these two deal with it as they would.

'Well, yes, first over there and then, hopefully, here as well, perhaps at the Academy of Fine Arts or—'

'But, but, he has no *standing!* We have never heard of Kedu as a painter! You mentioned the Academy of Fine Arts, but we know Lady Ranu quite well and she has never mentioned—how can he suddenly be seen as an impor—' Borun was intent upon trying to convince reality to change colours.

Bulldog's back had straightened. He glanced at his watch. 'Well, right-ho, wonders will never cease! Now, what is it you want from us? I should make it clear that this family is not in a position to contribute…'

'No, I just wanted to ask if there are any old paintings of his that are still with you? Any paintings, drawings, you know, drawing books, anything in the house? It would be useful to piece together his childhood and growing up.'

'I don't think so…' Borun started shaking his head vigorously, but stopped abruptly when Bulldog smacked his cup and saucer down on the table.

'No! Nothing of his remains in this house! We had a parting many years ago. As you may know, it was not a pleasant parting, and my nephew took everything that was his to take, everything he wanted to take. The rest we threw away. We *threw* out everything he left behind! It was a fumigation! No space for garbage in this house! None! At the time he said—'

'Never coming back! He said he was done with us! Ashamed of us, his own family!' It was as if Bulldog and Borun were passing the ball of anger between each other, raising the tempo with each pass.

'We transferred his *share*, all that was due to him, and that was bloody well that! Sorry to speak ill of the, of the... but there was no space in this family for a wastrel who wouldn't pull his weight and earn honest money! None!'

Elko's recounting of the whole thing was a bit different, but he actually didn't say much about all this. It was Missus who laid it out in more detail for me, based on what Elko had told her at the time of the rupture.

On that evening at Palm Avenue, I quickly got up to go. But the two fuckers weren't done with their kicking.

'You see, you see... sorry, forgetting your name I'm afraid... but not all of us had the luxury of spending our life cavorting with sundry memsahibs and occasionally, occasionally, dabbing a bit of, you know, a bit of paint on a, you know, canvas!'

'Tchhaah! Oita chhado! The *cavorting* wasn't the problem! In fact, in that regard I was proud of the boy! My brother feels he's been deprived of cavorting in his life! Especially with white women! Ha, ha, ha! No! It was what you did once the damned high jinks were over for the day, or the night, as you will!'

'Yes! You can't spend the day like some drooping pansy, looking at flowers in a garden! Or roses in a vase!'

'Borun, I'd drive carefully here, if I were you! Picasso can hardly be called a pansy, it's not that all painters are—'

'Well! Well! If you can make the kind of money Monsieur Picasso made, then it's a different matter! I agree!'

'Or this bugger Hussain.' Bulldog had squeezed himself into a better mood by defecating on Borun. He snapped his fingers at the servant and gestured pouring from a bottle. 'Oi Beefeater's ta aano! Aar tonic, aar ice bucket! Teen-tey glass!' He turned back to us. 'This bugger Hussain. I was over at Motherwalla's the other night. They've just bought a new Hussain, you won't believe what they paid for it.'

The winter dusk was falling, and Borun's money headlights came on. 'You know about all this art business, do you? Would you say... would you say Kedu's, er, paintings, would fetch a good price? You know, anywhere near, say, this Hussain fellow's...'

I was still standing as the servant appeared with the drinks tray. Bulldog gestured grandly for me to sit down. 'Have a gin and tonic, won't you? You do drink? Let's raise a toast to that young stud, Kedu. Gone too soon!'

'I do drink, but I won't today, thank you. I must take your leave. Thank you for the tea.'

The answer to Borun's question was a 'no', but I left without replying.

'Set a little cat among the pigeons, did you, darling?' Missus had travelled to the house to meet me after I returned from India. The first thing she'd done was pull out three bottles of Gordon's gin and several bottles of tonic from her suitcase to help with the debriefing. 'Set that greedy pair thinking about money, did you? Was that wise? Might they not discover new-found love for nephew Kedu-Zemindear and come chasing after imagined millions?'

'I doubt that they will. Bulldog called me a couple of days after I met them. I'd given Borun the neighbour's number in Jodhpur Park.'

'Oh! And?'

'Oh, he was very apologetic for losing control when I met them. *I suppose we were angry, one is often angry when someone you care about dies and leaves you. I suppose we always imagined there would be a reconciliation at some point, who knew the blighter would just up and die on us. This was always his house, we – I, at least – never wanted him to leave.* So on and so forth...'

'What utter lies. The moment his mother died, those two bastards made it impossible for him to stay on there. She died in '55, old man Lahiri had already gone, I think in '53. Intestate, or at least very messy. Despite being a leading barrister, he'd left it all to Bulldog to sort out fairly. I think they were all grateful Bulldog had returned intact from being a POW and was rising like a rocket in the new Indian Army... And our Zemindear couldn't be bothered to look at all the legal stuff, too busy raging at the art world, at himself, and going back and forth between Europe and Calcutta, so the two darling uncles, the bloody kakus did him out of it, out of his one-third, but huge money at that, and then put conditions for him to live there. They knew he would never agree. Swine.'

'Well, our maestro was foolish too, wasn't he?'

'Indeed, both too naive and too arrogant, if you see what I mean.'

'Yes, that's well put. Well anyway, I made it clear to his lieutenant-generalship that what we were doing was essentially a labour of love. And that vast sums from sales of the paintings were highly unlikely. He seemed to understand. Offered money for any exhibition we wanted to do in Calcutta.'

'How noble of him. Fucking thief.' Her eyes closed involuntarily. 'How fucking noble of them.'

Most of the first bottle of gin was gone, mostly drunk by Missus. We'd eaten well and she was dry-eyed still, but the swearing was a sign the firewater was getting to her. As quietly as I could, I slid away the bottle and went and hid it. Then I began to clear up in the kitchen.

Missus had taken a ferry and then a train to get here. I'd thought she might appreciate some Indian food. I'd made rice, dal and her favourite phulkopi, marrying the cauliflower with the fresh mustard seeds I'd just brought back. The dal too had fresh jeera and haldi from my new supply, and the kitchen was an oasis of home smells in the surrounding expanse of the cold, dry winter you get in these parts. But Missus was nothing if not occasionally contrary.

'Darling! Can we possibly keep all this lovely food for tomorrow? At the moment, I just want a simple sandwich, in fact, not that simple, what I'm craving is a club sandwich! Now, what's the closest you can manage to a proper club sandwich?'

She knew I was resourceful in the kitchen, and as it turned out, I managed quite well. I had good local bread, eggs, ham, though no bacon, some cooked cold chicken, and tomatoes and lettuce from the village supermarket. I also had mayonnaise and sharp local mustard. I made us the best sandwiches I could, knowing it was crucial to get some food into her stomach.

Putting food away in the fridge, I realized I not only had notes on Gopal talking about a club sandwich, but also Niru on tape, speaking about the first time she ate the thing.

ONE FOR THE ROAD

'Smell is different again, here.' Niru looks around with wonder in her eyes, because many more things than the smell are new and not at all like at Flurys. Lots of new smells, but also the naked, sexless plaster babies hanging in the corners between the pillars and the ceiling. Not just tea or coffee, there are people clearly having alcohol at four-thirty in the afternoon, mostly gora men, from what Imogen tells her mostly Markin – all officers – and she can smell the odd fermentation from the foaming mugs they lift to their mouths. In contrast to the oppressive heat outside, it is startlingly cool here, cold even. The old wooden ceiling fans revolve slowly overhead but the pleasant temperature is provided by air conditioning, a strange phenomenon that she will never get used to. The light too is different, the windows overlooking the first-floor terrace over the hotel portico heavily taped and not as tall as the ones in Flurys, the illumination inside much more dependent on the little chandeliers, even though there is still quite strong daylight outside, the twinkling crystals seeming to proclaim that this is a place where everything is available, that the establishment depends only on itself and not even on the sun.

Their table is larger than the one at Flurys, and the tea service is somehow even more lavish. The pewter – not silver as she has learnt – is beautifully polished but without any self-advertising embossment, though the china plates do have a discreet crest of the hotel. The tablecloth is thicker than at Flurys, the cutlery heavier and the food seems unfairly enhanced by all the quiet opulence.

The waiters, too, are different. The manager and maroon-jacketed staff have immediately been deferential when Niru and Imogen have walked in, with not a single sideways glance at her, this clearly not-rich Indian girl walking in with the memsahib. The focus is obviously still on the white girl whose natural habitat this is, but if this is the person with whom the young English lady wishes to take tea, theirs is not to wonder why. They are, as always, at the service of Miss and her guest. This is quite unlike the white-jacketed ferrets at Flurys who looked Niru up and down, who made it clear without a word that they were attending to her under duress, serving her despite the fact that she was lowering the tone of the place. There is no tone as such to this place, it is even more expensive than Flurys – as Imogen has let slip – yet clearly more able to encompass the different sorts of clientele it sees daily. As to the new smells vying for her attention, Niru has identified the sweet stink of the beer from the description Roma had once given her, and as to the acrid smell of the fatter tobacco, different from bidis and normal cigarettes, what a lot of the Markin are smoking, Imogen tells her they are cigars, most probably from Cuba. Unlike at Flurys, where the bakery was the queen of the olfactory realm, the food smells have to fight their way through the thicket of alcohol and tobacco odours that overwhelm the Tea Lounge at the Great Eastern Hotel. European or Indian, there were far many more women in Flurys. Here, there is clearly more of a male presence, Niru notes, or at least eight anna to eight anna, as her father would say, meaning half and half.

The walk with Imogen around the permitted parts of the Maidan and Chowringhee has made her hungry. Niru is curious about the different kinds of food on offer, but she doesn't want to be asking constantly like some village yokel. From what she can tell, there are cold as well as hot items being served. As at Flurys, they are eating cucumber sandwiches and fragrant little savoury puffs, but she can see other tables being served these dark brown patties wedged between roundish buns and accompanied by piles of thick alu bhaja that she knows the Ingrej call 'chips', and also tall, teetering sandwiches that seem to have outgrown their stature, lanced by toothpicks in order to keep them together, as if someone has fed them too much sandwich material and then harpooned them for the customers. And then all sorts of sweet dishes, cakes and pastries. And then there's the large, pink man sitting on the table just behind Imogen, his hat placed between the knife and fork across him like a dining companion, being served a stack of what look like really thick porothas, except she can smell some magically sweet fragrance, probably coming from the brown syrupy sauce which the waiter pours over the stack. Oh, if only she could go to each table and stick her nose into—

She almost smells the music before she hears it. The first sounds are quite soft, a tripping of some piano notes, the playful mischief of some deeper plucking, almost like a rudra veena, and then a woman's voice on a microphone, salted yet honeyed, almost whispering, almost talking rather than singing, some words, unclear to Niru, as the voice possesses the melody and passes it on to the orchestra.

Niru twists around to look. Her back has been towards the small dance floor, and she hasn't noticed the band getting ready. As she turns, three men raise golden instruments to their mouths and blow. There is a drumming man behind everybody, sitting possibly on a stool, and he hits his various drums very softly, a stick in his right hand while his left works with something that looks like a small broom that creates a brushing sound which you have to strain to hear. The woman, white or possibly Anglo-Indian, wearing a long Chinese dress, comes in again, her voice much louder this time, more loaded with the tune.

'Oh! Music! What is she singing?' Niru sees that Imogen is suddenly animated, her torso swaying slightly, a finger tapping her glass in rhythm. There is a shuffle of feet, chairs are pushed back, and three sets of men and women walk on to the dance floor. The men hold the women, one hand on the waist, the women's hands on the men's shoulders, the other hands linked, and they start to move around. Just as she has seen in the Hollywood movies.

'*A man is. A two-face. A worrisome thing...*' Imogen interrupts her humming and turns to Niru. 'She's stating the obvious, really, but in a very nice way, that chaps tend to be cads – that men... will betray their women and leave you sad. I'd forgotten, Saturday is always a sort of *thé dansant* here, a tea with dancing. I do hope you don't mind? It's quite fun!'

'Not at all, I don't mind, I like just looking.'

'Quite. Me too. Though with Andrew, one always danced – dances. We *love* coming here.'

'You were here with him last when?' The question slips away from Niru before she can fully think it through.

'Oh, ages. December, last December.' Imogen looks away and settles her hair.

Niru kicks herself. Sitting here, she's been tossed around by conflicting feelings and now this has added to the eddy. She really enjoys being with this older girl who is so different from anyone she knows. She's hungrier than she likes to admit, eager to know about Imogen's world, her life, to absorb all the experiences and stories that drop into their conversation. And yet she has the common, ingrained suspicion of anything foreign, of anything that is different from what she has grown up with, from all the different learnings she has firmed up until now. It bothers her that she has not been able to tell anyone about her meetings with the mem-girl, as if it was a shameful secret. In her college circles and Party meetings, the British, the Ingrej imperialists, are an enemy second only to the Indian capitalists and their agents, the bourgeois Congress, and that too, for the moment, because the Soviet Union needs the alliance. The only English you are allowed to like are communists like Spratt and Bradley of the Meerut Case, and some English poets from the nineteenth century. Certainly, there is no question of taking tea and sharing snacks with anyone who is even vaguely connected to the Empire's administration, and this girl is clearly deeply embedded in the imperial set-up – her father working for the governor general, her mother distantly related to the family of the infamous Lord Curzon who divided Bengal, her fiancé an officer in the army.

Besides, she, Niru, mustn't get used to this – twice in four days in an unaffordable, luxury tea place full of goras and the local rich. How would she ever be able to return the treats? No one has actually explained it to her, but Niru senses clearly that this is how one could get seduced by the way of life, the very assumptions and ideas one opposes. And yet, with this English girl, things are simple, decisions are easy and natural, there is a powerful force to the cheerfulness they bring out in each other. 'Let's compare, Niru, oh do let's! Flurys and the Tea Lounge! I'd love to know what you make of the Great Eastern. I've heard they're about to hand the whole pile, or most of it, over to the Yanks. So this might be our last chance, perhaps. After this it might be, you know these infernal signs you see everywhere: *US Forces Personnel Only*. Then we'll be stuck with the Grand, which is *much* less nice!'

'... Blu-uu-ues! In the ni-ii-ght!'

The song ends with a crash of drums and brass. The couples part and applaud the band, and the rain, now falling hard on the windows, seems to join them. Niru notices Imogen is spending a long time wiping her nose with a handkerchief, or pretending to, as she surreptitiously also wipes her eyes, clearing them of unwanted moisture.

'Perhaps we should not have come here...'

'No, Niru, no! Improper – incorrect – thinking! You were quite right to be curious! Mrityoo awning-barge-ho, yes, but *all* human progress comes from curiosity! I'm jolly glad we are here, now stop fretting!'

Another smell, one that competes with Niru's Darjeeling tea – Imogen has decided to order what she calls a gee-anti, something alcoholic in a funny, tall, straight glass, with some faint bubbles and a green wedge of lembu, and this is the second one the waiter is unctuously sliding under the tall girl's nose.

'Are you sure you won't try one? I don't want at all to offend your religious...' Imo, with her hand on Niru's arm as she orders the first one. Niru, her hand quickly on Imo's hand to reassure, 'I have no religious. It is just that I have never. And would not like to at this moment.'

'Quite. Well, I'll go ahead then.'

The band begins another song. This one is faster in tempo, and the three couples are joined by two more. The dancing seems slightly different, the feet moving faster, the men and women parting from their formal embrace, just linked by the hand, and then rejoining. Imogen swirls her drink with a thin, pencil-like stick made of glass. Fretting, fret. A new word that Niru has to be careful not to confuse in her mind with phetey jawa, to tear. Imogen, on an earlier day, about Andrew: 'I mustn't fret. I know he'll show up somewhere or the other, I know him. I would know if something terrible had happened to him. Maybe he just hasn't been able to write... especially if he's caught up in that chaos around Mandalay...'

The chaos around Mandalay. March and April. In this early August, all of it seems a long way in the past, though the ceaseless rain seems to have fused the months together. Across her meetings with Imogen, she has discovered that the girl is engaged to this officer Andrew who is in

Burma, and that there has been no communication from him since late April. Between April and the end of July, fairly comprehensive lists of prisoners of war have reached relatives in Calcutta and elsewhere, but there is until now no word about Andrew. Yet, Imogen doesn't have the air of someone in mourning for her lost love. In fact, once or twice she has let drop that there are signs that Andrew is still alive somewhere and not yet captured by the enemy either. Niru hasn't been sure whether this notion is based on some fact or whether it is delusionary, but she has known not to probe further – after all, she is not that close to the foreign girl.

The band moves smoothly from one melody to another, this one even faster, with quite a catchy beat. The floor is now quite filled with dancers. Imogen laughs and grabs Niru's hand. 'Come! I know you won't drink, but shall we dance?'

'Dance? Who?'

'Us! You and I! Come on!'

'Oh, no, no, no! Not – I cannot!' Her heart sinking, Niru notices that some of the dancing 'couples' are actually made up of two women.

'Well, you know, it's quite all right for two girls to dance occasionally, especially now there's a war on and there is this man shortage.'

'I, uh, hyan, yes, I understand, but I cannot! I don't know how...'

'Oh, it's simple, I'll teach you! I'll play the man!'

'No, no, no! I cannot! Please excuse me, but I...'

'All right. Perhaps another day.' Imogen is laughing now, pleased at how flustered Nirupama has become.

'I do not think I can ever! But thank you!' Niru reaches for the teapot.

'It's just that I do love this song... *When the shark bites... with its teeth, dear... scarlet billows start to spread...*'

Niru finds herself tapping her foot under the table. The song is infectious, even though the words, something about knives and sharks, are unclear. She is watching the movements of the singer in the red sheath when the waiter appears again. '*Fancy gloves though, wears Macheath dear... so there's not a trace... hmmm... of red...*' When she looks down, she sees that her tea is gone, replaced by a tall glass filled to the brim with something fizzy, mirroring the fresh drink in front of

Imogen. She opens her mouth to say something but is interrupted by the quarrel of drums and wind instruments that end the song. The bandleader shakes his trumpet, takes the microphone, thanks the audience and says they will be back shortly. As the musicians disperse, the pianist offers the singer a tin. The woman plucks a cigarette and puts it in her mouth. The pianist flicks a lighter under the tip and a slight orange glow lights the woman's face from below. Niru realizes the girl is very beautiful, despite the thick make-up and deep scarlet lipstick, maybe Anglo-Indian but with a trace of Chinese, what the Ingrej call 'Oriental'.

'Well, my dear, look what we've got!' Imogen is smiling at Niru.

'But why did you order one extra drinks…?'

'Oh, *I* didn't order these. We've clearly got an admirer.'

'Admirer?' Niru is thoroughly puzzled.

'Go on, have a taste! If you don't like it, we can always summon more tea.'

'No, no thank you, I have had enough tea…'

'Good. No more tea this afternoon.' Imogen knocks back the remnant of her previous drink and raises the new one. 'A toast! To… red ants!' says Imogen. 'To red ants up the…' She leaves the rest unsaid.

Niru feels a rush of blood climbing to her head, as if she has already imbibed some alcohol. She raises her glass. 'Red ants!'

'To red ants!' says the large man sitting behind Imogen, raising his mug of beer at them.

As Imogen turns to look, the large man reaches across for the hat lying across the table. He sweeps it over his head before lifting it away with some irony. His blue eyes bulge with amusement. 'I hope you ladies don't mind. I saw how much you were enjoying the music, so I took the liberty of ordering you another round.'

'That's *so* kind of you. Thank you very much, but my friend here doesn't drink.' Niru feels the sharp tang of the tonic suffuse her mouth just as Imogen says this. The cough that explodes out of her is part embarrassment, part laughter, part gin.

'Well! It seems she does now!' Imogen and the man say the same words at exactly the same time.

'The pleasure is entirely mine, ladies. If I may... Irwin Robert Goodsugar, consultant attached to the US Army. A pleasure to be at your service. Please call me Bob.'

'Oh, how do you do. Imogen Snell.' The mem-girl reaches out and firmly shakes the Markin's hand.

Niru forces herself to look at the man and raise her hands in a nomoshkar. 'Nirupama Majumdar.' Her name sounds strange to her as it comes out of her mouth, as if it's picked up a slight infection from Imogen's accent.

'Miss...? Snell.' The fat man pointedly looks at Imogen's engagement ring. 'Miss Knee-Pamela. Hello.'

'Ni*ruupawmaa*.' Louder than she wants, but it comes out correctly this time.

'Just call her Niru, it's simpler.'

'I beg your pardon. Miss Nero. My hearing is not what it used to be. Assaulted by too many aircraft engines. Pleasure to make your acquaintance, both you ladies.'

'Well, thank you *so* much for the drinks, Mr Goodsugar.' Imogen turns away from the man and engages Niru. 'What was that you were saying?'

It takes Niru a moment to realize Imogen has chopped off the conversation with the fat man, and a couple of beats more to understand that both the accepting of the drinks and the termination of niceties belong to an accepted code of exchange about which she knows nothing.

'I like that song, but I could not understand it. Something about sharks and teeth and blood...?'

'Pardon me for interrupting again, couldn't help overhearing you, Miss Nero.' The pink man leans towards them again. 'The song is called "Mack the Knife", Louis Armstrong got a big hit out of it a couple of years ago. But originally written by a couple of Krau— German gentlemen... The words in the German original were by this theatre fellow, Bert Brett... who had to leave Nazi Germany in a hurry because Hitler wasn't too fond of him.' Niru can see that a slight frown has occupied Imogen's forehead. Clearly the Markin has broken the behaviour code, but he continues regardless, his enthusiasm obviously quite genuine. 'But forget the words, the tune's the thing, the tune's the thing, and the beat, that's where the gold is in this song, and the music's by Bert's partner Kurt Weill… Kurt Weill and… Brecht! That's right, not Brett, Brecht, Bert Brecht! Both escaped the Nazis, and I believe they are in Los Angeles now, working for the studios.'

'Oh, but I *like* the words!' Imogen's own passion overcomes her annoyance. 'They are jolly important! I've actually seen the play in Paris, in French actually, at a cabaret, and it's terrifying, but also quite funny in a macabre way, quite wonderful!'

'You are knowing the words in French?' Niru takes another sip from her glass, unaware she is doing so.

'Oh! No, no, I didn't mean to show off! I mean, I do speak a bit, but I went and found the English translation in a small bookshop. The play is called *Threepenny Circus* or something… a musical, and this is the opening song.'

'About a very evil man… you're right!' Goodsugar continues nodding as he gulps his beer.

'Ber*tolt*, I think is the full first name.'

'The evil man is called Bertolt?' The only thing Niru can understand now is the nice taste coming from her glass.

'Berr*tolt*! That's right, Miss Snell, you're quite right! *Berrr*ttolt *Brrr*eshht!'

A new song breaks their conversation and Imogen turns back again. The Markin goes back to his beer. Niru notices he is meticulously writing something down in a small notebook as he twirls a dead cigar in his left hand. A man is now singing in place of the girl, and he enunciates his words in such a way that Niru can actually understand them, something about 'she's proud to be walking with him', something about 'he wears a pair of silver wings'. She imagines a man walking on a foreign street, with a big pair of wings coming out of his shoulders. She imagines the woman described by the male singer looking at this man with admiration. It doesn't fit, somehow. Then she looks down and sees that her glass is almost empty, and she is feeling good and light in a way that she has never felt before.

Somehow, all her concerns have become like pet dogs, and she can treat them the way Roma treats the Labradors at her parents' place – they bark and lick, but they know who has the real power. Physically, too, her body has changed, in some way become looser inside her sari, as if there is a thin but unyielding layer, an atmosphere of freedom between herself and her petticoat, between her and her bra and blouse, between her shoulder blades and her pallu. She couldn't do anything as unwise, as stupid, as dance with Imogen, but she could easily, now, find the courage to stand away from the table, to actually stand by the dance floor and openly clap to the beat should Imogen be dancing and should she ask her to do this. Except Imogen isn't doing any such thing. Imogen is saying something to the fat man, and he is offering her a cigarette, in a packet rather than a tin, and Imogen is taking this cigarette and letting the man light it for her. A nod, clearly of 'thank you', a return nod from the man – 'no mention' – except only Indians say that in reply to a 'thank you', and he turns back to his notebook as if he has lost all interest in the two girls.

Niru feels a sharp pang that she takes some time to identify. She realizes what it is. She feels both panic and shame knocking at her door. Together. Both wanting to be let in at the same time. She realizes she actually wants another drink but doesn't know the route to asking for one.

The Anglo-Chinese woman is back at the microphone, reeling out a beautiful rendition of Billie Holiday's 'Travellin' Light'. Niru is now swaying slightly to the rhythm and occasionally tapping her glass with the swizzle stick. Something changes in the sound of the glass meeting the stirrer and she looks down. Imogen feels huge pleasure watching the Indian girl's face as she sees that her empty glass has been replaced by a second gin and tonic. Will she leap? Will she demur? Imogen stops herself from laughing, laughing simply with pleasure, the memory of the first time she got drunk in college adding to her general sense of mischief. Much as she enjoys being in this girl's company, Imogen has strict sectors in her head, two lists titled Can Laugh About (around Niru), Cannot Laugh About (around Niru), and she tries very hard to stick to what these lists ordain though, occasionally, as for instance today, she does slip up.

'We did not do for this one!' says Niru, suddenly meeting her eyes.

'I beg your pardon, my dear?'

'First one was to red ants, this we shall dedicate to what?'

'Oh... *you* say, it's *your* turn to say the toast!'

'Toast... oh, yes, *this* kind of toast! Yes!'

'Yes! Go on, then!'

'To... the... to freedom to dance! With who you want!' Niru raises her glass a few inches from the table. Imogen reaches out and lifts Niru's arm higher.

'To dancing! With whom-*so-ever* you wish to! With whoever you want to dance with! To the freedom!'

Niru gingerly clinks her glass with Imogen's, clearly afraid she'll break it. Imogen smacks her glass against Niru's again, more firmly, just to show her how it's done. The tide of music swirls around them again.

Among the things Imogen has proscribed for herself is showing any amusement at the way Niru always keeps her money inside her sari blouse, reaching, it seems to Imogen, publicly for the most intimate part of herself every time she has to pay for something. Imogen has acted it out before her mirror, fiddling with her brassiere to fish out some shillings, and each time it's sent her into fits of giggling. Then there are the constant collisions between Imogen's English and Niru's fledgling speech, though here there is a little give and take, since Niru also laughs at Imogen's infelicities with Bengali and Hindi. The third thing that needs to be handled with care, not with kid gloves exactly, but with *care*, is the whole business of love and romance and the mention of any physical aspects – she has seen Niru blush and become paralysed merely upon hearing the word 'kiss'. 'In some ways, more puritanical than a Victorian dowager,' Imogen would have told someone, except she finds she doesn't mention Niru at all in her own circles. She would have told Andrew, of course, but Andrew isn't here. Andrew not being here is the reason why porcine, over-friendly Yanks can feel free to send her drinks. Andrew being neither here nor really there is the reason why this particular song, 'Travellin' Light', takes on more than one meaning, Andrew, not here but travelling light, so to speak, hopefully, somewhere.

On the other hand – cheer up, old girl! – one of the best things about which she can laugh with Niru are the pomposities of older people, no matter whether European or Indian, especially men of all sizes and colours, and Imogen knows Niru and she will laugh about this pushy Yank at some point.

A year ago, who would have imagined, her having tea with someone in a sari, an over-particular young thing with stumbling English and constantly busy hands wiping crumbs off the tablecloth almost before they fall? Which one of her school or college chums would have imagined that she, Messy Snelly, would rapidly become fast friends with someone who would make sure to put her teaspoon back on the saucer at exactly the same angle – pointing straight away from her – after stirring her tea? And yet, Imogen senses something quite uncatchable moving around underneath all of Niru's obsessive tidiness. It's the strangest thing, the friendship with this Bengali girl. It's as though she's friends with one edge of a large wood, where she knows some of the trees and small paths, but with most of it stretching mysterious and inaccessible beyond the first, welcoming bit.

Andrew is the only one she can imagine telling all this, except, of course, had he been here, she and Niru may well not have become such friends. With the other English people, her parents, others, she can't escape Andrew and his absent presence. Walking around Calcutta with Niru, Imogen is always aware of other worlds, other sadnesses, other wars and sorrows that dwarf her own potential tragedy. The meetings with Niru keep her from going spare with her Andrew-anxiety, help her get off the dark merry-go-round of worries about who she is and what she's doing here.

She looks down into her glass at the wedge of lime nestling among the disappearing ice cubes, at the bubbles spinning in their random dance between ice and lime and glass as the fizz in the tonic dissipates. The things you can get used to – she remembers hating the taste of the local tonic when she first arrived in India, the war making it impossible for people to obtain proper Indian tonic water from England. Now, she knows the tonic at home won't taste right without Andrew there with her, unless he's there drinking with her, his eyes and his voice bubbling with laughter and love. But she knows she mustn't tempt fate, or trigger its rage in any way. She knows if Andrew were actually lost, the chaps in the regiment would let her know, just as they've let her know that she doesn't need to, doesn't *yet* need to, treat herself as a war widow. A hint, a smile, over a G&T for her, usually a beer for whichever fellow who's invited her for the drink. 'Do hope you're all right, old girl?', and then odd details: they swarmed over us like locusts – but we are working out a pesticide – there might be a few of our chaps, you know, who've deliberately stayed behind enemy lines – diciest job in the war – will let you know as soon I hear something, you must trust me – trust, trust, trust – the t at the end dropping off like a leper's little finger, this bloody war, this bloody love becoming a truss.

The song ends in applause. The band bows, the woman drops into a quaint sort of curtsy. There is a moment where silence blankets the room before the hubbub of talk and cutlery take over again. Niru's eyes are caught by something behind Imogen, and the mem-girl has to wait before she can turn around to look. The contrast in voices is startling, the fat Air Force man's words channelled entirely through his nose, the other man's timbre low and soft, almost a growl coming out of the floor.

'You took your time, Jones. I was wondrin' if you were coming at all.'

'I'm sorry, sir. Took a while to get the sarge to...'

'Saturday afternoon? What did he want? For you to get busy with five-course chow for some general?'

'No, sir. The thing is, the whole unit is under discipline this weekend. The boys got a bit wild last weekend and we're CB till two Sundays from now.'

'Sounds bad, buddy. What did you bucks get up to? Wreck some temple? Lift some local broads? What?'

'Something like that, sir. Not a temple, sir, there was a social evening at one of the clubs. Anglo-Indian dock engineers have a club in Kidderpour and... well... seems things got a bit out of hand. Not me, though, I wasn't even there, which is why the sarge made me an exception today, why I got me a day pass.'

Imogen turns as if searching for a waiter. There is a tall Negro standing at the Bob-fellow's table, uniformed, hair cut very short, boat cap in his pocket, a long left arm curled around a dark leather case probably containing a musical instrument.

The Yank grins through a lit cigar. 'You're a good boy, huh? No hanky-panky for Corporal Jones, huh?'

'Well, sir, I was on dinner detail that night. Not a five-course, but the generals flew in that evening with a Chinese…'

'Ah, yes, gotcha, I remember. Work dinner. Stillwell, Chennault, Chiang's air supplies man and a couple of our Lime—RAF brothers-in-arms.'

'That's right, sir.'

'Air Commodore Gilmour and the other guy, the air commodore for supplies.'

'I guess so, sir, that sounds about right.'

Imogen has turned away, not meaning to eavesdrop, and with the Bob-fellow she doesn't even need to – his voice is like a sharp little drilling machine. What whets her curiosity is that she can barely make out what the black soldier is saying, even though he's clearly speaking in English.

'What'd they eat?'

'Well, we got a local Chinese chef for the Chinese general, as we usually do, and the usual for the General—'

'Vinegar Joe *Meatloaf* Stillwell, we call him. And not for nothing! No women, very little liquor, but the man can eat. Bet poor Chennault ate nothing! Deaf as a block of timber! Bet he heard nothing and ate even less!'

'No sir, General Chennault actually asked to be served the Chinese…'

Goodsugar calls out to someone. 'Hey, Fenton! Over here, buddy!'

The Anglo-Indian band leader hurries over to the American's table.

'Good afternoon, Mr Irwin, sir! How are you, sir? Did you enjoy the music?'

'I did, yes! You boys were in good form over there! And that girl… Clara?'

'Yes, sir, Clarissa Rodriguez.'

'Great pipes on her, really great pipes.'

'She sings quite well, sir, thank you. I've been training her, you see.'

'I'll bet!'

Fenton gives off a high-pitched arpeggio of a laugh. 'No, no, Mr Irwin, nothing like that…'

'No, I just meant clearly great coaching. We should try and get her over stateside after this little shindig is over… see what we can get out of her in a proper studio.'

'That would be wonderful, sir, if you're serious!'

'Well, look, we'll talk about that later. This here is my boy I was tellin' you about. Byron Jones, best damn horn player in the CBI theatre! He's been on the Armed Forces Network a few times, with the unit's band, haven't you? This is Mr Fenton Greaves, king of the Hooghly Highballers, the resident band here.'

'Hello, Mr Jones. We actually fill in when Jojo Suarez Orchestra is on tour. When Jojo's here, we are the second band, of course.'

Nirupama can't take her eyes off the very short dark man shaking hands with the very tall hobshi.

'Hello, Mr Greaves. Please just call me Byron.'

'Just call him Byron!'

'Like the poet, isn't it?'

'That's right, like the poet. Byron here is a poet of the cornet.'

'Major Goodsugar is very kind. I just like to blow a little bit, that's all.'

'And you please call me Fenton, just Fenton, please.'

'Sure. Pleasure.'

'Pleasure, pleasure, Byron, pleasure! Now, you would like to see the main stage at Maxim's? If the place is empty, you don't even need the microphone over there. You can just try it out!' Fenton points to the case in the tall man's hand.

'Sure, that would be swell, if that's okay with you…'

'Yes, yes, yes, of course it's okay! We are honoured, in fact, to have a proper, you know, a real jazz, you know…'

'And also allow me to introduce my new friends here, these two ladies...' Goodsugar turns to include Imogen and Niru as if it's the most natural thing in the world, completely aware of their interest through the feigned looking away. 'Miss Snell and Miss... Nero-paw—'

'Nirupama Majumdar. How do you do.'

'Oh, hello. Imogen Snell. Your band was delightful this afternoon.'

'Thank you very much, ma'am. Fenton Greaves. Honoured, my pleasure.'

The Negro soldier nods respectfully at the two women.

Imogen returns her attention to their table, indicating with her eyes that Niru should do the same.

'You were saying we haven't had a toast with this drink... but dear me, it's nearly gone!'

Niru looks down at her own glass and wonders why the waiter has replaced her almost full drink with the dregs in somebody else's glass.

'Never mind! Down the hatch!' Imogen knocks back her gin and looks around for a waiter. For a moment, Niru is reminded of a stork she has once seen on a trip into the countryside. When the waiter arrives, Niru realizes Imogen is fully intent on ordering yet another drink. Niru also understands that no one has tampered with her glass.

'Imogen! Please! I cannot any more drinks! No!'

'Last one! One for the road!'

'I have to meet my parents. They will smell me.'

'We'll find you something sharp to eat, on the street. That will cover it.'

Before Niru can formulate a response, the waiter is swinging around their table with his shiny silver tray. Despite having seen them being placed, there is some magic about how the two full glasses are there, demanding an audience.

Looking up, Niru notices that Goodsugar and party have disappeared, also as if by some sleight of hand, for she has not seen them go.

'A final toast for the afternoon! To what shall it be?'

'Err...'

'I shan't propose one to king and country, keeping your feelings in mind!'

'No... but, yes! To the great queen under the gobor of the holy Indian cow! And buffalo! Not-holy buffalo!'

Imogen's eyes widen at the cheekiness. The shy Bengali maiden is clearly approaching blotto. Imogen feels the satisfaction of a job well done.

'All right then! To go-baw!'

'To *goborr! Goborr!*'

'Hear, hear! To go-baw—'

Imogen senses something has suddenly changed about the lounge. She looks around quickly. Niru thinks of the stork in the paddy field. Imogen's eyes narrow, then widen and then narrow again. Something is not right around them.

People are leaving. All of them seem to be in a rush to pay their bills and leave all at once, which is strange. No one raises their voice, there is certainly no shouting, in fact, no discernible rise in the level of noise around them, but the quality of the chatter has changed.

Niru, too, senses something is amiss. She wonders if she has crossed some invisible line, some unspoken rule about not drinking so much. She sees several people waving for the waiters, some of them making quite abrupt signing gestures in the air. She notices the waiters and stewards are all moving about with great speed, nodding responses to customers, one or two of them almost jogging to the tables with bills ready on their trays.

Imogen deciphers something strange about the change in atmosphere. The tables with Yanks seem untouched by whatever is going on – the American airmen and officers are continuing to drink and eat, laughing and talking as if they are in some other plane of existence, while the tables with the British uniforms are emptying briskly, the officers whispering to each other, the women looking slightly anxious as they gather their purses. It's as if some secret message has been passed around, communicated only to the English and the hotel staff, leaving the Yanks more or less oblivious.

'Memsahib?' The waiter stands before them, holding his tray, his hand covering what is clearly the bill, ready to offer it or take it away depending on what Imogen says.

'What's happening? Why all the rush?' Imogen asks him, not bothering with any Hindi words.

'Memsahib. I don't know. Something. Some trouble in Bombay. Maybe. I cannot say.'

'*Bom*bay!? But Bombay is on the other blood—on the other side of the country!'

'Yes, I cannot say, memsahib, I don't know, I just heard something.'

Imogen has straightened up now, forehead creased, lips pursed, looking around for someone proper to ask. The waiter excuses himself and goes, summoned to another table.

Imogen is looking in another direction when Niru sees the Anglo-Indian bandleader and the woman singer hurrying to the stage, him saying something to the singer with great animation. As they pass their table, Niru finds her voice, speaking quite loudly.

'Hello, please, excuse me!'

The man stops, almost annoyed at this Bengali girl.

'Yes?'

'Can you please tell us? What is going on?'

Imogen turns back. 'Oh, hello again! Yes, what *is* this commotion all about, would you be able to...'

Greaves' body becomes even shorter, immediately dropping into obsequiousness.

'Yes, well, ma'am. I'm really sorry, but it seems that bloody bugg—beg pardon, that stupid Gandhi fellow has created some trouble in Bombay today.'

'Oh? What sort of trouble?'

'He... beg pardon, ma'am, apologies, don't intend any offence to you, he's supposed to have declared that the British should quit India. Can you believe, he actually said those words, *Quit India!*'

'Oh, I see. Yes, I can quite believe he would have said something like that.'

'Yes, ma'am, quite unbelievable... quite outrageous... The fellow actually said this at a large public meeting... and so they've arrested him, of course, and all the other Congress bugg—all his other leaders, Nehru, Patel, the whole jingbang lot!'

'Oh my god, so that's why...'

'Yes, that's why, everybody is expecting trouble. Maybe even riots.'

'All over India, I imagine.'

'Exactly, ma'am. Last thing we needed, what with the war on and all, last thing!'

Outside the taped windows of the lounge, it's coming down quite hard now, dark, invisible rain, smacking into the glass panes as if some cosmic drummer has gone crazy with his set of drums. It's now quite chilly in the lounge, but Niru notices there is a film of sweat on this Greaves' face. The half-Chinese woman seems untouched though, completely uninterested in any of this. Niru finds herself admiring the way the woman doesn't even look at them, and by the way she takes a drag on her cigarette and blows out the smoke, sending it, it seems, into another universe.

FIVE

The Long Flag

13 AUGUST 1942

I

THIS RIVER LISTENS TO NO ONE

They all stand at the water's edge to see him off as he gets into the boat. The thing on his head nearly topples off but his uncle catches it in the nick of time and gives it to his mother for safekeeping. His father is preoccupied with the route the boatman will take; they have to reach the destination before a certain time, before certain stars in the sky lose their alignment, about this there can be no argument, no negotiation. The boatman is truculent – *I can only say about my boats… I'll get you to the big boat in the time I promised… Can't guarantee what happens after… That river listens to no one.*

As the row of boats moves away down the water lane between the tall grass, Gopal turns and waves to the people who are not coming with them. Ustad and the Phorashi stand next to each other, waving back. Behind Bonnemaison, he can see Aurangzeb, even taller, right at the back of the small group, but the Pathan doesn't wave, he just looks. He can't see Gourango anywhere and this worries him.

There is mist. Even though the season is Sarat, when there should be no mist. The monsoon has gone, taking with it the moisture curtains it hangs on the wider waters, and winter is a month away, which is when the mist should really descend. Now an untimely ball of grey-white winter mist blocks the narrow passage ahead of them and it keeps receding as they get closer, playing a game with the prow of the boat. There is mist but there is none of the accompanying cold. He can feel himself sweating under all the layers of unfamiliar clothes. His mother keeps smacking away his hand every time he tries to loosen the buttons on the shiny panjabi. She keeps readjusting the folds of his too-crisp dhuti, as if keeping a doll in place or protecting the idol of some goddess before a puja begins.

They come to a corner in the passage and the boatman stabs his pole into the grassy bank to turn them right, almost at a right angle. Suddenly, the water under the boat feels freer, more powerful. The channel widens, the grass banks dropping away into the mist. The women on the boat behind them blow conch shells. On the last boat, three other women stand up and do the 'ulu', sending invisible birds flapping away in the grass. As they pause in their sharp, staccato wailing, the other women blow the conches again. The smell of the water has changed, and Gopal knows he will have to leap now or it will be too late and escape will be impossible. But his mother's brother seems to have read his mind – his hand is firmly around Gopal's thin, ten-year-old arm and there is no chance. Maybe when they transfer boats, maybe then.

But as the boat pulls out on to the big river, his mama's grip actually tightens, as if he can see every little thought flitting about in Gopal's head. The mist thins into wisps and then hardens into a curved dark wall. Their boat knocks into this wood, creating a watery reverberation. A bamboo ladder comes down through the mist and settles between the seating slats of their boat, the seeped water at the bottom lapping around the twin poles. The rungs of the ladder lead into the rising wall. Voices shout down from the larger boat – be careful – pay attention to any old people climbing up – the river is rough today.

The river listens to no one. No chance of escaping, none. Above him, his mama climbs, still gripping his arm. Under him, his father pushes up on his buttocks, trying to be careful not to crush the dhuti. And then he is in the dark belly of the massive water monster, his head swimming with the smell of hair oil, camphor, hot mustard oil, acrid bidis, different kinds of sweat. As his eyes adjust, he sees there are already two other boys like him in the boat. They are also dressed in wedding clothes, the topor cones unsteady on their heads, surrounded by their families. Clearly the stars are in alignment for lots of little lambs being led to the slaughter.

On either side of the passengers, rows of men sitting, wearing almost no clothes, bare legs stretched out before them. Thick poles in each man's hand, stretching away out of small square windows. At a shout, the men begin to move in unison, forward and back, forward and all the way back until they are almost lying flat, full fold forward, and back. The huge creature begins to move, almost against its will at first, and then more easily, made obedient by the even bigger water outside.

Directly above Gopal's head, the soft drumbeat of the sails snapping the wind, the squeal of ageing wood as the masts twist in the sudden sunlight. Out of the window nearest to him, Gopal can see the oar rising out of the water, flicking off water, dipping out of sight again, rising again. Beyond the oar, he can see Ustad's launch, Aurangzeb and Kana Lalten standing on the deck as it putters along. Still no Gourango.

Still no her, she who'd promised she would save him.

The launch falls behind, the rowers pulling away. The sweat now makes free with his head, carving around his ears and sliding down his neck. The starch of the panjabi bites into his armpits. The dhuti crawls into his crotch. His mother smacks his hand. The sun goes, but it stays hot.

From the big boat to a smaller boat. From the sea-wide expanse of water to a rivulet. From that boat to a cluster of even smaller noukos that hold only five people each. In the small boats, single file through a water channel to another big river, almost as wide as the one they've just left behind.

The village no larger than a lane in his own village, a cluster of huts pushing loosely against each other on an island in the middle of a vast sea which is actually a river. The island alive, like some very large animal, with boats nibbling at it from all sides.

The mist finds them again. The sweat doesn't leave him.

... Despite losses... Soviet Red Army... holding off a heavy German onslaught... city of Stalingrad over the last five days.

The itching between his shoulder blades is unbearable.

In the Pacific... American First Marine Division... landed at Guadalcanal... Solomon Islands, to the north-west of the Australian...

And, finally, General Bernard Montgomery has taken command of the British Eighth Army in North Africa following the loss in an air crash of General William Gott.

The morning news bulletin in Bangla pulses over the neighbouring houses as well as the cluster of dwellings that people have built inside the ruins of the old mansion. As his eyes open, Gopal both curses and thanks the neighbour babu who likes to listen to loud radio sitting on his balcony. The curses are for breaking the morning peace with all this useless news of battles in distant corners the world, the thanks for helping Gopal to find a simple route out of the nightmare.

Gopal rolls out his sweat-roiled khaat and reaches for his gamchha. He looks at his watch taken off a drunken Markin airman by one of Ustad's pickpockets – 7.15 a.m. The van will be waiting for him in a lane near Gol Park at 9 a.m. Just enough time to bathe and get to the alu-kachori shop for a quick breakfast.

He shakes his head clear under the water from the tube well... carefully puts away the fancy lavender soap he has taken from the Phorashi's precious hoard of pre-war *savons*. In his little kholi he's sweating lightly by the time he's putting on his clothes. First the jangia, with the little pockets he has got sewn near the middle for hiding small things and paper money. Then his banyan, to soak up the sweat. Then the wide, loose, trousers, again with special pockets that he can reach quickly. On top, one of his shirts that look cheaper than they are, at first glance just an ordinary cream-coloured cotton shirt, loose, a bit big for his thin frame, but actually made with good cloth that is airy and absorbent. A pen, again, ordinary, black in colour, but actually a nice old German Pelikan with a solid body and a good, fine nib, not that he uses it to write anything but lists and accounts. A comb through his hair, resisting the temptation to put in a smear of the precious Brylcreem he uses in dry weather. It wouldn't do to look too well-maintained with the people he deals with. On the other hand, his days of looking like a poor street boy are behind him for good and he's happier for it, far happier than he could have imagined before his promotion a year ago. For the day's work, no shoes, just ordinary chappals, but with treads the cobbler has gummed on using thin slices of tyre tread which help keep a grip on the monsoon slime that's all over the roads right now.

In his right pocket, a wallet, a cheap one, never the one he got from the pretty boy. In his left pocket, a small notebook, along with his pen his only weapon for dealing with the different sorts of low-life types he will meet today. The last thing he does before locking and leaving is to touch the picture of the rampant, dancing Ma Kali, at the bottom, where her grounded foot is painted. Touch, prayer, hands passing on his head, blessing himself on her behalf.

As he walks out of the old ruin in which his basti is located, he wonders why his feet feel like they're recovering from a cramp, and then he remembers them curving to grip the slimy rungs of the bamboo ladder going up to the big boat. Shave, bath, clean clothes, but as he walks, he feels as though he's still wearing the dream. It stays on him like an extra skin, his ten-year-old self still on him like an extra film of sweat, that Khulna, those rivers, enveloping him like the humid morning air.

As he goes down the side streets of Hindustan Park, his mind slowly returns to the present. On that day, going to the small island, he had prayed for a reprieve; for months before the day itself, he had prayed to her. Today it occurs to him, yet again, that Ma Kali did help him escape, just not when he wanted and not in the way he wanted. She did help him in her own way, and so here he is.

He hears their voices and his heart sinks. He slows down. The one thing he was afraid of today was coming across them. Avoiding them was not something he could pray for, and now here he is. He looks for a lane leading away from the boundary wall of the big camp, but the detour would be too long. And he's not sure he wants to avoid them anyway, not sure at all, so he keeps walking.

There are four of them, working on an open drain just outside the fence of the big camp. Four of them, an interpreter, and three local maithors. One of the maithors is climbing out of the drain, half covered in grey-black slime, his loincloth so blended with his body by the muck that, for a moment, Gopal thinks he is naked. The other two maithors, dark brown skin interrupted only by dirty white loincloths, help the man out of the hole. The Markin officer takes a torch, a huge torch such as Gopal has never seen, and squats down, just outside the spill of sewage around the manhole. He focuses the light into the depths of the hole, points to something with his cigarette and says something to the other soldiers. Gopal cannot ignore that the Americans are also without any upper clothes, except for the white officer, who's in a tight white ganjee with half sleeves. Gopal's eyes range once again over muscle valleys he has never seen on any Indian man, on the upper arms, around the abdomen, where the absurdly flat white stomachs disappear into the olive-green army trousers. The Markin kaptan comes to some understanding in his head. He flicks his cigarette to one side and stands up. He taps the half-caked maithor on the shoulder and points again inside the manhole. There is no thought in the Markin's touch, none whatsoever, leave aside any restriction or revulsion. If these people have a caste system, it's a very different one from the one Gopal understands.

'Look, buddy, you gotta turn that valve there, turn it to the right, you understand? Two turns to the right! You gotta... that's it, attaboy!'

Gopal can feel the kaptan's large hand on his own bare shoulder, not just a tap but a full grip, and it sends a shiver through him. He suddenly remembers the bodies of the men rowing the big boat in his dream. For a flash, his mind replaces the Khulna boatmen with these Markin who are all over the city, both gora Markin and the big, dark habshi soldiers, black and white sitting alternately, pulling and pushing, their abdomens glistening with sweat. Behind his rational understanding, he had come to believe that the Everything already contained all there was to be desired, but now the city even has these previously unimaginable bodies, and that too on full, shameless display.

The fact that the Americans are completely uncaring about who sees them naked from waist up has caused different kinds of commotion and talk. The women from the proper houses haven't stopped expressing their shock at this brazen behaviour by foreigners who should know better; it was one thing for the city to be filled with the naked torsos of the working men who serviced the better off, whether it was the ricksha-wallas, the thhela-wallas, the men who swept the streets or these maithors who dealt with the gutters, the garbage and the night soil, but you would never see a self-respecting Indian soldier or a British Tommy with his shirt and ganjee off, not in the city; what did these GIs, gora and Negro both, think they were doing? Gopal has even seen mothers cover their daughters' eyes as they've passed these naked Americans. On the other hand, in the working-class women and especially the various whores Gopal knows, the hushed gossip has been about how big the Markin are at the business end of their abdomens, huge, apparently, with the habshis apparently even bigger than the white boys. Gopal has not yet met anybody who has actually done the business with a Markin, white or black, but the vivid descriptions based on immediate hearsay have driven him crazy. As he forces himself to walk on, away from the work gang, his own penis hardens as he thinks of a large Markin pipe emerging out of one of those olive-green military pants.

His dream from the night changes from the nightmare it was to something else. From the mess of city smells, he extricates Khulna, the smells of his childhood nibbling at his mind, of the wet wood of the boats, of camphor being lit, of the sweat flicking off the rowing bodies, brown, white, black, all mixed up in the same rhythm.

In an image of a man walking down a south Calcutta lane, you would not catch any of these thoughts, dreams or smells. The trees on the road leading from the Lakes to Gol Park are heavy with last night's rain and their leaves gleam in the monsoon light. Dwarfed by the competing kinds of green, Gopal is a small slash of cream shirt and dark brown trousers, a wavy mimicry of the two colours marking his reflection in a puddle on the road.

HARA-KIRI

He's tired of the green. It's as if the trees and foliage have been washing themselves in green, like elephants bathing in a river. Cascades of green that defeat his eye with their variety, their trickery aided by the shifty monsoon light moving from muted grey, almost to sharp sunlight and back, changing direction and strength, the clouds constantly shuffling the angles from which the light attacks the garden. There is absolutely nothing here for a Monet or a Cézanne to hold on to, no pause of light to aid any visual verisimilitude, and everything for a Van Gogh to drive himself to lunacy. There is a reason, he thinks, that those master bastards prospered in a temperate climate where the light stays the same for long periods of the day. True even of Gauguin, whose basis was what he carried from home. The tropics could never have *given birth* to Impressionism, because you simply cannot overlay human impressionism on the all-encompassing, overpowering impressionism of the tropics. There is nothing here for a painter because the vegetation and light are already doing it all, and there is no honest channel through which a painter can add to it.

As he paints, the leaves and branches grow irritating alien voices.

'It's political suicide, I tell you! What do the Japanese call it? That ritual of theirs?' He hears Borun-kaku trying to be authoritative.

'You mean hara-kiri?' His father, superior, sceptical, always the tallest tree, always looking down, even in his tone.

Borun slaps his leaves against the monsoon wind: 'Yes, exactly! Political hara-kiri! Or seppuku! Group hara-kiri, group seppuku! That's what this Gandhi gang has just committed, all of them, the old man, Nehru, Patel, Azad, what's that Madrasi, Rajaji, all of them!'

Kedar almost has the hang of that mango branch, it's almost too easy now, except this rainy season light makes it slippery. His father interrupts: 'Oh, I don't know that you can be so sure. They must have known this was the likely outcome. They're not that foolish, they must have a plan. Or at least a calculation, or must have had, I suspect.'

Kedar has a plan, but he's not sure he has the courage.

Borun-kaku has certainty: 'No plan, no plan, this was the – hah! – the *non-violent* version of the charge of the Light Brigade! Into the valley of political obliteration rode the Congress cavalry...'

'Tchyaah! No, no! Not so easy!'

'Yes, yes, yes, Dada! Cretins, complete cretins! But good for Subhas Bose! He must be celebrating wherever he is! The field is now open for him to come back and—'

'Come back how, Borun? How exactly does *that* popinjay Boshu *come back*?'

In a sense, the painting is moving towards completion. The composition works, while managing to avoid the tired foreground–background variations Kedar sees so often in the salons and group exhibitions around the city. The colour scheme is fairly unusual, a limited palette of greens, greys and browns, the hues made heavy by the muted light. In a way, the canvas is not dissimilar to the ones he has painted over last winter and after, but he can see he has grown since then as a painter. The rendering is far more confident, the extraneous nonsense more or less left out, the greed for the pretty and the decorative successfully fought off, each included element standing up for itself.

The expanse of the lawn is framed by one of the arches of the porch, the trees, driveway and gate providing a nicely busy boundary to the large curve of sodden grass at the centre, the puddles of rain mottling the green, deftly believable without being overdone. There is no clean blue in the picture, and almost none of his favourite reds and yellows, as if he's a patient on a diet who's not allowed oil or his favourite chillies. Even the black, which he secretly thinks of as the salt in any painting, is strictly reined in, used just so. As he works towards finishing the canvas, he can already hear the positive words from the small circle of people who are allowed to appraise his work and pronounce upon it. And yet he works sitting under a drizzle of dissatisfaction, as if he's yet again a boringly gifted child, solving an arithmetic puzzle of the kind he has bested many times over.

This morning, all the talk of politics, all the overheated newspaper headlines have added to his sense of irritation. Him, Kedar Lahiri, the only be-stilled sailing ship while all and everything around him is in some turmoil of progression. Him, bhetu Bangali, cowardacious, scaredy-cat Calcuttan fop, rabbit-hearted runt, tap-dancing on the pavement while everyone around him is leaping into the rush of traffic without a care.

'Tchyaah! Come back how, Borun? How exactly does *that* popinjay Boshu *come back*?'

'I'm telling you, Dada, it doesn't take a military genius to know that the Japanese are coming as soon as this rain stops. There is no staving them off. And, once they capture Calcutta, they will fly your Boshu-Bose back from Germany post-haste. They will not even wait until they take Delhi. Imagine the propaganda triumph! Those effete Congress-wallas are in British jail while the unchainable Bengal Tiger strides proudly into Governor House.'

'More like a peacock than a tiger! I saw him take oath as mayor in '28. We all admired him then. Foolishly, I now must admit. The man is a pompous ass. You do know your Boudi's mother's side are distantly related to the Boshus?'

A smudge of brick brown on the garden wall where the plaster has fallen off, a smudge of dirty yellow in the flower bed where the winter flowers have long been dead. Subhas comes back through the trench. He digs through all the way from Berlin and worms up suddenly in the Lahiri garden, in Palm Avenue, in Ballygunge, shining sword in hand, behind him the legions of Indian prisoners of war freed from the camps where the BEF has been interred after the Blitzkrieg. Kedar lets one part of his mind imagine what it will, schoolboy drivel, adventure stories, as his brush finds its way around the canvas which is not dry enough from yesterday.

Since the fall of Rangoon in early March, Borun-kaku has been going on about digging a deep trench in the garden, right through his sister-in-law's lawn and flower beds. It started as a joke: 'Boudi, Dada, this is exactly what the Ingrej will do in all their mansions and bungalows as a defence against the Jap invasion! They don't know how to do anything else! They are still living in Ypres and Somme, you see, and we should consider doing the same! We wouldn't want to stand out, would we? From the air, our garden should mingle with the patterns in the neighbouring gardens!'

'There are no Ingrej around here, Borun! The nearest European house is the Van der Waerds five houses away, and the nearest English are on Mayfair Road!'

'Ah, that is a pittance of a distance for a Japanese reconnaissance plane! Nothing!'

'Well, surely we should show them we are not hostile?'

'You are *not* digging any trench in my garden! I don't even want to hear this as a joke! Do you *understand*?' Kedar's mother is incensed, as if someone was speaking of cutting open her child. Which, of course, leads to the joke acquiring a strange longevity, especially when Boudi is out of earshot. 'Young Kedar! What say you? Is today a good day to start our digging? Your Ma has gone to her mamabari in Girish Park for the day! We may not finish by the time she comes back but it will be, what do you call it, a fait accompli, bujhli?'

Over these last few months, Kedar has made patient little noises to indicate he's indulging his uncle, but with no intention of committing to any joint programme of hara-kiri. Today, however, he feels differently towards his mother. As Bertie Hurree Jamset Ram Singh Wooster might say, the stretchability of his patience vis-à-vis the mater has surpassed the point of breakation, with the attachation of oodles. Or, as Rasko might put it, 'He hajh hyad inaaff.'

The trouble had started two days ago, when his mother brought up The Subject.

'Does a mother have any right at all? To expect that her only child will bring home a decent bride? And by some reasonable age? The talk is that this war will last another six to eight years, and then, of course, one can't get married until the Oxford degree is finished, so that's another three to four years, so will you only get married once I'm gone?'

'Ma, I am not even twenty-three, which means you are forty-eight. By god's grace, you are in excellent health. Now, no one is going to murder you, and no Japani is going to bomb this house. I have only a BA degree from Calcutta University, and no current prospect of employment. And anyway, you are much better off without some pesky daughter-in-law eating your head. In fact, you are not – god did not design you – to be a mother-in-law. You should realize that.'

Mother switched from the mixture of Ingreji and Bangla entirely to English. 'I'm certainly not designed to stand around watching my only son go gallivanting around town – like some Playboy of the Eastern World – with that... with that ghastly Dutta girl.'

Today, more and more Kedar can see the point of a deep, long diagonal trench eviscerating his mother's damn lawn. It would be so perfect, as if the lawn had committed hara-kiri. The idea is impossible to avoid.

'I beg your pardon, Ma?' Kedar had also switched to English. 'What? What did I just hear you say?'

'Well, just because they are also Brahmo, and just because they have money, those cannot be the only criteria, can they? And, anyway, that chit of a loudmouth has announced everywhere she doesn't believe in marriage! So what, I ask, is my son doing with some—'

'Your son is simply trying to lead his life! Without being imprisoned by people like you who are trapped in the swamp of the nineteenth century!' The teacup nearly cracked as Kedar smacked it down. The toast slipped off the plate on to the place mat. The chair, pushed back hard, squealed against the floor. It was a good thing Baba and Borun-kaku had gone off to office. The curtain of the kitchen door devoured Rasko who was standing in front of it with a rack of fresh toast. The maalis stopped chattering in the garden outside. So, it seemed, had the birds.

The cold, half-eaten toast was put back on the plate.

'I can't believe you're creating a scandal out of the two or three times I gave her a lift!'

'No one can create a scandal out of you giving a girl a lift twice! The scandal is created when you risk the mob to deliver chicken patties to her at Howrah! When you give her the one painting of yours that your mother actually likes.'

'I got that painting back for you, didn't I?'

'The scandal is created when the two of you are seen lunching – drunkenly – more than once – at Firpo's. The scandal becomes a fact when that over-proud judge father of hers catches you... catches you both at night... doing I don't want to know what in the dark... in that car of yours outside his gate!'

'We were not doing anything!'

'That's not what Shekhar Dutta told DR at Calcutta Club!'

'What... what did he say to DR-kaku now?'

'I don't want to hear my son being called a scoundrel, a good-for-nothing scoundrel! Scoundrel, your *daughter!*'

'Stop calling her names!'

'Oh? It's all right for Shekhar Dutta to call *you* names! But I can't speak my mind about that awful girl, is it? *Stop-calling-her-names,* indeed!'

'Stop calling her names!'

'So! If you care about her more than your own mother, then can we say—'

'No! You can say nothing! No! We are just...'

'Oh, just friends, is it? A deep friendship, I take it? Like brother and sister, is it?'

Kedar finds his brush clawing two diagonal lines of dirty brown across the wet green of the lawn, right through two of the three beautifully achieved puddles. He reaches for the tube of burnt umber to squeeze out more paint. The tube is completely crumpled and only the last smear of pigment escapes the mouth. Kedar rolls the tube tight, as he has been taught, the thin tin sharp against his fingers, but nothing more comes out. He has now ruined his painting, but he can't avail the solace of completing the scarring. Looking down at his paint tubes, he sees he is also very low on yellow ochre and black, the other two colours he will need to paint the trench.

Damn it. Perhaps he can telephone G.C. Laha and get them to send someone over. Looking at it rationally, the green of the lawn needs to dry a bit more, so this is perhaps a good thing. Perhaps he can work on another part of the picture, perhaps he can move to a sketchbook without letting the canvas gnaw away at him.

He finds himself in the hallway, standing over the telephone table, wiping paint off his hand with a cloth. He lifts the receiver and waits for the operator to answer.

'Number please?'

'Dharmatolla 238, please.'

He can hear the operator talking agitatedly to the woman next to her as she transfers the plugs. Normally, there might be some pleasantries, especially if you've spoken in English, a cheerful 'connecting you now, sir' or some such, but today the operators are clearly busy, and he just hears the ring as the call connects.

'Hallow?'

'Is that G.C. Laha?'

'Yes, G.C. Laha Art Supplies.'

Kedar can tell from the voice and the accent of the Bengali that it isn't one of the owners at the other end.

'Listen, can you quickly send me—'

'No deliveries today, not possible today.'

'Why not?'

'No one else here, there's only two of us and I've been told to shut down the shop.'

'What? Why? It's only a quarter to eleven!'

'There is trouble all over town. There is a big crowd in Jodubajar and the police—'

'Jodubajar! Jodubajar is miles away from you!'

'Arre, babu, you don't know. There are processions all over the city. Jodubajar, then Harrison Road, and a huge rally at Wellington Square, just down the road. Heavy police everywhere. Also military. People are expecting big jhamela. I'm just waiting for someone to bring something, then I'm to shut the shop and go.'

'Wait! How long are you open?'

'I just told you, babu. I'm just waiting for someone who should be coming any minute... All the other shops on Dharmatolla are shutting down now. There is sure to be jhamela all over. We are all probably shut for the next few days, it looks like.'

'Wait! I'm coming! Just keep three tubes each of burnt umber, yellow ochre and ivory black ready in a packet! I'm Lahiri Babu speaking!'

'Oil, toh?'

'Yes, yes, oil!'

'I'll have to see... but, babu, I can't promise I'll be open when you reach.'

'Just wait for me!'

'Please hurry, babu. Saying again, I can't promise.'

Kedar looks down at his clothes. He's still in his night-time kurta pajama but perfectly presentable for Calcutta streets at this time of the year. No, at least change to trousers, and from house slippers to tennis shoes, make sure you have wallet, cigarettes, matchbox, car keys.

People scattered in different parts of the large house, no one else around nearby. Hopefully it'll be the same on the other side. He picks up the receiver again.

'Number please?'

'Minto Park 168 please.'

This Anglo girl seems to have more time. Over the chatter behind, he can hear her humming a tune as she finds the correct slots for her wires.

'Urgent call, kindly hurry.' Kedar can't help himself.

'Whole city's urgent today, sir. I'm trying only.'

'Thank you, sorry.'

'Is it a number on Short Street, sir?'

'Yes, that's correct.'

'Taking some time, sir, there's a fault over there because of the rains.'

Finally, the ring. The phone picked up as if someone has been waiting next to the instrument. Keya's voice in his ear.

'Hello? Roma? Where are you?'

'This is not Roma.'

'Mr Dandy! Why are *you* calling now?'

'Umm... about this evening...'

'Yes, yes, I'll see you at Treasure Island. Six, six-thirty.'

'Yes... was just calling to...'

'Yes, now go. I'm waiting for Roma to call. The whole town is about to explode. Don't go out for a few hours, in fact, until you come to—'

'I'm going to Dharmatolla now. Have to pick up some painting stuff.'

'Dharmatolla? Worst place you could go today. Don't. Paint later. Practise your tennis or something.'

'Don't be silly.'

'All right, suit yourself. I'm going to disconnect now. Roma should be calling about something urgent.'

QUIT AND RID

In the future communist India, who would be the whites, how many whites would there be, who would still be welcome to return? She immediately discounts imaginary Russians, who she realizes she doesn't actually think of as white – though that's completely illogical, she realizes – and brings herself back to the only gora person she knows, who's presently sitting next to her , who still hasn't quite got the hang of how to sip tea from a bhaand without burning her fingers, or spilling it on her dress, even after nearly eight months. But she, Niru, after those same eight months, can now easily think of a phrase like 'hasn't quite got the hang of'. She, Niru, now has the hang of that phrase, so to speak, and other such similar phrases.

In fact, the other day, she surprised Roma when she said in perfectly correct English, 'I find it difficult to grapple with that idea.' The sentence just slipped out in the middle of an argument, quite naturally, albeit in her strong Bengali accent, and her friend gave her a quizzical look, as if to say 'Now, where exactly did you learn that?' For a moment, Niru was tempted to tell her, to confess about the whole quite absurdly secret friendship she had developed with Imogen, but something held her back. Partly, it was just the pleasure of having a mystery weapon up her sleeve, Imogen as a secret genie who provided her with magical linguistic wealth, not to mention a very different view of the world from the ones found among her friends' circle. But perhaps it was also the fear of a traitor being caught out; as if her associating with the English girl was a betrayal of their group and the one common political point on which they all agreed: the need to rid India of these Britishers.

A fly zigzags from Niru's tea bhaand to the golden band on Imogen's finger, pauses there, before rising up to attack the English girl's left nostril. A tram clangs by, its roof rods almost brushing the heavy hanging leaves of the trees under which their tea shop is located. Such are the strangenesses being visited upon Calcutta by the war that the chaa-walla has hardly glanced at Niru and Imogen when they've sat down on his benches next to the tram terminus, on the small circle of trees and park at Esplanade. Imogen has noticed Niru's crisp cotton sari, cream-coloured with a yellow-and-blue border, and commented on it. Niru has returned the compliment on Imo's light summer frock with its paisley pattern. Imo has laughed at the fact that the trams leaving the terminus pass so close to the benches that a passenger could lean out and snatch the tea or samosa from one's hand. It's odd – this is possibly the noisiest point of the entire city and yet, here they are, two girls, one Bangali, one Ingrej, sitting unremarked in this little oasis of shaded calm as the metropolis swirls around them.

'Imogen? What exactly is the difference between *quit* and *reed*? I am somewhat confused.'

'Quit and reed? I don't see the connection. To quit is to leave or give up something, whereas a reed is a plant, those thin things that grow out of water… Oh! Silly me, you mean—'

'I mean r-i-d, rid, get rid of.'

'Yes, yes! Sorry! So, to quit is to leave or move away from, as Mr Gandhi says he wants us to quit India, as in, leave the country, give up this habit of Empire, at least as far as India is concerned. And rid is what you want to be of us: *many Indians want to be rid of the British*. I want to *get rid* of this old pair of shoes. I want to *be rid* of these flies, or Niru wants to be rid of Imogen, as in she wants to divest herself of Imogen's company!'

Niru involuntarily grabs Imogen's arm. 'But I don't want to be rid of you!'

Imogen returns the clutch of Niru's hand with her own on hers. 'Niru-*pawma* doesn't want to be rid of Imogen, who's as thin as a reed!'

'You read me correctly!'

'Very good, *touché*! Oh, Niru, that's actually excellent!'

'Khub bhaalo! Eita ekdom thiik bolechho!'

'Er… exactly! Cube baloo! Aik-dom!'

The chaa-walla who runs the stall watches the two odd girls burst into laughter yet again. God has granted him a good old age and now, in his seventies, he imagines he has seen everything or, in any case, seen a lot, but life still has a way of surprising you. Who could have told him that on a hot morning in the rainy season, a pair of girls on their own, one clearly a local student and the other a thin mem, tall as a taal gachh, would sit down and do adda at his tea shop? For all purposes, like two student boys, except for the absence of smoking and the hands triumphantly dropping to adjust the crotch folds of their dhutis whenever they've made a clever point.

Behind him, he feels the weight of the Maidan now filled with military tents all the way to Victoria Memorial. From there, in the evenings, soldiers come to have tea, again different, lower class, even though white, some not even white but hobshi, speaking in many different languages he used to think, until someone – one of the dhuti-wearing students – told him they were all speaking different kinds of Ingreji only. These soldiers now added to the customers he's always had, the office clerks, the shop boys from around the busy crossing and students, both boys and girls, but mostly boys. And now this odd pair. What next?

Niru realizes there is something strange about the traffic today. She's engrossed in what Imogen is saying and it takes her a while to work it out in the back of her mind – a lot of people seem to be making their way into the mouth of Dharmatolla Street and heading towards Wellington Square at its other end. The buses and trams are also full going that way but, oddly for this time of day, quite empty coming the other way. It's almost as if the Congress-wallas' big meeting is sucking people into some dark hole, ensnaring them with a magnetic pull, never to let them out again. She tells herself she's imagining things, but then she notices something else. What's that armoured car doing, casually parked next to the white mosque, blocking the lane of traffic next to the pavement? Broken down, has it? While one of the crew has his head under the engine hood, the other Tommies stand around the machine, smoking and laughing. They look quite relaxed, as if they are lounging around in their cantonment, but for Niru their presence sends off a little alarm bell.

'Is there something odd about the town today, or am I imagining it?' Imogen, too, has smelled something different in the air.

'It may be the meeting in Wellington Square. They were hoping a lot of people would come and it looks like, yes, there will be maybe a lot of people actually.'

'A meeting to...'

'Protest the arresting...'

'... of Gandhi and the other leaders?'

'Yes. Because of this stupid Quit India that he has declared.'

'I know, I know... But how stupid was it, actually? Quite reasonable from his point of view, many would say, many of you In—'

'Well, this is not the time. At this moment, everybody needs to be united against fascism forces which is greatest danger to mankind...'

'True, but—'

'… and one of their main Congress people, one main leader, Subhas Bose is even now hob… hobnobbing with Hitler and Mussolini! They say he has left the Congress, but how can we say for certain? This is the Congress, they always like to have both cake and eat it also.'

'To hunt with the hounds and run with the hares, yes…'

'Sorry, I didn't…'

'Never mind, another saying with a similar meaning to having one's cake and eating it too.'

'I see.'

'But, Niru, isn't that understandable when you're fighting a huge empire? You're naturally tempted to use everything and every available ally, aren't you? I mean, look at your communists – they seem more loyal to Moscow than to India!'

Niru bristles and feels her face going into a frown. She tries to stop herself, but Imogen catches it.

'I'm sorry, I hope I didn't say anything, you know, anything to offend…'

'No, no, not at all! I mean, it may feel like that from outside, *we* can feel that about Communist Party of India, but perhaps they are not so un-loyal to India…' Niru can tell from Imogen's look that the 'we' she'd inserted has shown up as an impostor.

'Disloyal, not un-loyal. I see, yes,' says Imo, not at all seeing what Niru wants her to see, yet seeing what she wants to hide. 'Are you quite close to some communist people then?'

'Not close, exactly, but I know some people who may be in the Party.'

'And they're now officially allowed to be…'

'Yes, the ban was lifted on July 23rd.' Niru kicks herself for revealing she knows the exact date.

Imo smiles and pats Niru's shoulder. 'Oh, good. We wouldn't want your friends to be underground forever, would we?'

Niru is about to say something about it not really being her concern, but suddenly she notices the small crowd forming, a few feet behind Imogen. A bunch of clerks and shop boys all loudly talking over each other. 'What nonsense! I haven't heard any aeroplanes!' 'I tell you they're saying the fighter plane came down and machine-gunned the crowd!' 'They're saying, they're saying, they're saying! They are clearly on strong opium, whoever they are!' 'Exactly! It's not possible! They wouldn't machine-gun their own police! And the mamas, with many gora officers, are in there among the crowd! I saw them riding past on their horses this morning heading towards Moulali and Wellington.' 'He's right, you're right, there's a been a bad lathicharge. And tear gas.'

Niru's first thought is her Party's secret translation office, which is just across the big crossing. For no reason, she suddenly remembers the man's voice, selling flowers supposedly from Rabindranath's last journey, almost exactly a year ago. Then there is Akash-babu repeating again and again that they mustn't even think about the office or ever go to it during normal working hours, so she tries to put it out of her mind.

'People have heard three-nought-threes. There has been gunfire, that much I can tell you.' 'Several people injured, some dead, that much I can tell you is true.' 'The crowd is trapped in the square, people have nowhere to run, it's like Jallianwala Bagh, and the police are firing tear gas from all sides, even at each other. That's the news that Mantu just brought.' 'Which Mantu? That Shalimar Lunch Home Mantu is a simpleton of a gossip monger!' 'No, no, this is cyclostyle shop Mantu, he's quite reliable.'

Roma and Titir. Roma already there at the square. Titir supposed to come from her parents' house in Shyambajar and meet up with Roma – she sees her watch saying 11.30 a.m. – sometime around now. Niru is now standing up without realizing it, standing next to the chaa-walla and paying him quickly. Imogen also throws her clay cup on to the pile next to the benches and stands up. As she turns away from the tea stall, Niru realizes she has quickly translated for Imogen what the men are shouting, but not the import of it.

'Imogen, I'm sorry, but I must go! I must rush quickly.'

'Where to? Surely you're not going *into* that—'

'Yes, no, I have no choice. My two friends will be there, and they may need my help.'

'Which friends? Pardon me, I don't mean to—'

'No, no, just these two girls I am living with, Roma and Titir. One day we will introduce you.'

'But, darling, how on earth will you find them in the melee? You haven't a hope, with all the stampeding! All you'll do is get yourself into—'

'No, no, I will be careful, I will be very careful.'

'Look, let me come with you. Two are better than one in a situation like this.'

'No, no, no, Imogen. For you it might be dangerous in another way. The people are quite angry with... with...'

'The British, you can say it, I understand.'

'Yes, exactly. They may not see that you are with me, just see you as one mem, you know, one of them who is firing at them, or like a spy or something, you cannot say.'

'But, Niru, I so hate to just let you go off on your own!'

Niru pats Imogen firmly on the arm, starts to move away, and then changes her mind. She reaches for the Ingrej girl and puts her arms around her. The muddle of arms and shoulders is awkward because of the difference in height, but for a brief minute the embrace is perfect, mutual, tight, warm. Niru's nose in caught in Imogen's lavender-smelling frock, before she parts and moves away.

'Promise you'll be careful!'

'Don't worry. Really, please. I will try and telephone you from my neighbour's house this evening, or if that's not possible I will definitely send you postcard by tomorrow.'

NOT NOT OPEN

As she crosses the road, a reverse of the strong milky tea rises in her throat. Away from the shade of the trees, the morning has suddenly turned uncomfortably hot. The band of her wide hat forms a ring of sweat around her hair which feels matted and dirty. On her arms, she can still feel the light abrasion of Niru's crisply starched sari pallu, in her nose the petrol fumes now pushing away the sharp smell of Niru's hair oil, the crush of the city trying to erase the warmth of the too-quiet Indian girl.

She makes her way past Whiteway & Laidlaw and then left, down the big road that runs parallel to Dharmatolla, weaving through a throng of people who all seem to be walking at her in some strange, barely contained panic When she reaches Bourne & Shepherd, she's startled to find that the largest photo store in the city has still not opened, despite the clock pushing towards noon. There are two men standing in front of the sliding grille stretching across the shop windows, and one of them recognizes her from her previous visits.

'Good morning, madam!'

'Good morning. Can I ask why you aren't open yet?'

'Not not open yet, madam, now closed, closed for today.'

'I'm sorry, I don't understand...'

'Opened right time, madam, but now shut. Too much trouble is happening, Jodubajar first, and now Moulali and Wellesley Road. So, very dangerous.'

'Oh! I see.'

The second man chimes in, somewhat cheekily, 'Madam, do you have car?'

'No, I don't, I'm afraid. No car.'

'Then, madam, you please take one taxi and go home fast. Big crowd coming maybe and police tear gas and, and maybe...' The man puts an imaginary rifle to his shoulder and makes shooting sounds.

'Oh! Right! Thank you! Do you know where else I can find some Kodak Plus X?'

'Not today, madam, all store are shut!'

Imogen nods an acknowledgement and begins to stride back to Chowringhee. There are some smaller photographic shops past Metro Cinema which might still be open. Also, that is where she's most likely to find a taxi in this mess. As she heads back to the big avenue, it seems as though the torrent of people is now thrusting her forward. She walks past Whiteway & Laidlaw again, this time noticing that the big department store is also being shut quickly. The same with Metro, the box offices deserted, men pulling together the grilles, imprisoning the tensely embracing Cary Grant and Joan Fontaine on the posters.

Even as she searches for an open shop, she realizes she's doing it to distract herself from worrying about Niru. 'I will be careful...' How the blazes is one to be careful if a bloody great horse is charging down on you? Or if somebody starts shooting at you?

Past Metro, the small photo stores interspersed with the gun and ammunition shops are all shut tight, the layers of the grilles and wooden slats all padlocked. Back at the big Dharmatolla crossing, she sees people are now gathering in small knots. There is a small crowd near the chaa-walla where she and Niru had met. Across the road, at K.C. Das, the big sweet store, a man stands on the steps of the store entrance addressing another group, rhythmically pointing his arm skywards and then straight ahead. North of the crossing, the armoured car near the mosque has been joined by another one, with a third vehicle positioned across the road pointing the other way. There are no soldiers milling about outside, but each car has a man sitting in the turret, unsmiling and watchful.

The sirens cut into the clang of Esplanade crossing from far away. By the time the motorcycles appear from Central Avenue, rumbling into sight past Statesman House, the already thin flow of vehicles has obediently parted and moved to the sides of the road. Two policemen jerk up like modern dancers, gyrating on the little platform in the middle of the crossing, arms raised, trying to halt the civilian traffic from all directions. A convoy of trucks goes past, the big white five-pointed stars on the sides already spattered with mud and monsoon grime. The US military police bikes leading the convoy barrel straight through the crossing without waiting to see if anything is coming from the left or right. As they pass, Imogen can see the Yank soldiers sitting inside the trucks. In each vehicle, two men facing out, looking at nothing, weapons ready, and behind them a glowing network of cigarettes in the tarpaulin-covered gloom. After a while, there is the sound of more heavy engines, but coming down Bentinck Street. Good old British lorries this time, uncovered, probably deliberately. In the

Bedfords, Highlanders standing rigid and facing out, their red berets absurd in the monsoon heat, their rifles very visible, staring at the passers-by as if daring them to meet their eyes.

Just as the traffic weaves itself back together, two more trucks come pelting down Central Avenue, their horns going in a staccato warning. These are obviously older vehicles, commandeered from some local owner, and as the suspensions bump over the tram tracks, Imogen can see the black soldiers packed in the back, hanging on to the frames for the non-existent tarp. Unlike the cocooned GIs or the fierce-looking Scots, this African lot look like they are on their way back from a highly successful picnic. Laughing and slapping each other's backs, a couple of the men doubling up at some joke, completely uncaring, as if they were in some parallel reality. As the trucks clatter past, Imogen is sure she can hear the sound of an African drum, a beat she recognizes from her time in Paris, a liquid, circling repetition that reaches directly from the ears to the feet, but then she is not sure, not sure at all, that she isn't imagining it, or the wall of distant voices that has formed somewhere on her right.

She turns to look. At first, she can't make out anything, finds no source for the shouts or the panicky hubbub on which the louder voices are carried. All she can see is that the long, straight, Dharmatolla Street seems to have almost completely emptied of people. Then, in the middle distance – she smells it before she sees it – is a stationary tram with smoke billowing out of it. When the smoke clears, she can see there is an orange pulse of fire deep inside the first carriage, behind the open balcony with the driver's seat. The gusts of smoke rise again, bigger this time, and the tram and the road are briefly obscured. As the smoke clears, there are suddenly people all around the burning vehicle, mostly men, some women clutching the fronts of their saris to be able to run better, a couple of schoolboys leading the crowd, sprinting in front of everyone in their flapping shorts, satchels held above their heads as if for protection, all heading straight at her.

There is a clattering sound, like very loud castanets, and the road sprouts about a dozen small cans, bouncing off the asphalt, eddies of smoke jetting from them, smacking into the wrought iron pillars of the arcades. Once her eyes have deciphered the projectiles, she can suddenly see more of them curving in the air above the crowd as if chasing it, some of the canisters falling right in the middle of the rush of bodies. Under the pelting feet, the tram tracks are streaked with red, and she can see some people slipping and skidding on the blood.

For some reason, her eyes start to sting, and it takes her a long shutter of a moment to make the connection between the bouncing cans, tear gas and her eyes. Bodies are now jostling into her, not caring how hard they bump past, running in all directions. She realizes where she is standing has now become the worst place possible, a small corner railing at the edge of the pavement hemming her in, stopping her from moving on to the road, leaving her nowhere to go except into the onrushing riot. She desperately wants to move, but her feet are soldered to the ground. She wipes her eyes, desperately trying to see if any of the running women is Niru. She feels someone's hand on her wrist, someone trying to snatch her watch, no the grip is too tight for that, and then she feels another arm around her waist, dragging her away, and a voice in her ear shouting in English, shouting at her to run.

2

LONG FLAG

The sweat cuts into the corners of his head like a very light knife. A mark here, just behind the ears, a pair of stinging rivulets around the eyes, a wire of liquid where his jaw meets the neck, all communicating to different parts of his body as if by some wireless – an outbreak of perspiration around his mouth seems to set off a small bath down his spine, his armpits, glued shut, feel connected to the wet tangle of his hair, the damp spaces between his fingers seem to be talking directly to the ones between his toes. Gopal is used to sweating in the hot weather, but today is different. Today is as if the gods have yanked the oil press an extra half-turn just to see what more they can squeeze out of the living body, and in the middle of this, this fool, his van driver, is chattering away about the wrong thing.

'Gogai-da, what is this we keep hearing about rice? These mad prices aren't going to come down? Someone said they're going to keep rising...'

Rice is the one thing Ustad doesn't want anyone to talk about too much right now, and he has told Gopal and the other toli leaders to kill off any discussion.

'Only a child or an idiot believes everything he hears in the bajar,' Gopal grunts. 'The rice from Burma has stopped so the prices have gone up, that's all. In two months, they will find other sources for rice and the prices will come down.' By now Gopal has practised the lie often, and he hopes he sounds convincing.

The shop to which they are heading is on Keshto Nag Street, near Calcutta Medical College, and the delivery procedure is simple: the little Ford van pulls up to the pharmacy, the driver honks and turns into the little lane at one side of the shop; in the lane, the van turns around and parks behind the pharmacy owner's car, obscured from the main road; the shop boys come out with a couple of jute sacks and quickly put flattened carboard boxes into the van; in exchange, they take full boxes and put them into the sacks; the van drives off. Gopal just has to make sure the right boxes are put into the sacks. The boxes bear the labels of locally made biscuits, but hidden inside them are boxes of much better quality, clearly marked as medical supplies for the US army, boxes that one of Ustad's people at the docks has lightened from the Markin ships' unloading with the help of a well-compensated quartermaster.

The heat and sweat aside, Gopal has been really uneasy across the climb of the morning. The streets feel wrong, people are not where they should be, there is something awry with the sounds, all of it odd in a way that is outside of Gopal's experience. But there's nothing to be done – in a shaky market, with all sorts of wild competition popping up, the supply run has to be constant and reliable, this Ustad has driven home to all of them. 'These Markin are like a lactating sow with no piglets, leaking all sorts of goods everywhere, to anybody and everybody. They don't care who they sell to, and they don't care what happens afterwards. So today there's one fool, tomorrow another joker, all offering all kinds of things – Ummerican things! Now too many of them for us to stamp out, but if the buyer knows he can regularly rely on us for genuine stuff, he will get rid of the riff-raff himself.'

As his eyes flick across Wellesley Street and the side streets they are passing, Gopal keeps a bored, impassive face, making sure he conveys no nervousness to the driver who is already jumpy since they've heard about the Jodubajar trouble at their previous delivery stop. The van goes over a bump and something grazes his knee. Gopal looks down and sees a vibrating metal bit curving out of the side near the door.

'What's this?' he asks the driver.

'Oh, that. That's from when we had that small accident last week. I was doing a round with Aurangzeb-bhai when a Markin military truck bumped into us, side on side. He was a big monster, trying to avoid something on the other side, maybe a ricksha, he swerved into me, probably didn't even notice he'd hit us. I got angry and began to chase after him, but Aurangzeb-bhai told me to leave it. Not much damage, just a little dent outside and this thing poking out inside. I've got to get it fixed. There's just been no time these last few days.'

'Hm, yes. No point getting into a fight with the military. They just give you a chit and send you to their transport department, even if they've actually hit a person, and it takes months to get any compensation.'

'The Markin are the worst, though. They drive like animals. I've heard they've killed lots of people.'

'In their country they have big roads, and they drive on the wrong side of the road, on the right, so that's their excuse.'

Passing the S.N. Bannerjee Road crossing, Gopal notes that the pavements are almost empty, as if something has swept away the humans from the roadside. On a wall on the right there are three identical, freshly printed posters, '*British Quit India!*' they proclaim in sword-curved Bangla script. The plaster is suffused with rain damp, and the posters are already crumpling and sliding downwards. Far to the left, somewhere near Elite Cinema, Gopal can see a couple of military vehicles, a lorry and an armoured car, but no troops visible. On Wellesley Street, where they are driving, the silence is louder than ever, underlined by how big their tiny two-stroke engine sounds.

The driver starts on the rice business again. One can tell he's just trying to make conversation to cover his nervousness, but that doesn't help Gopal's irritation.

'I don't know, Gogai-da, you're saying about alternative supplies, but the news from the villages is not good... It seems in many villages, at least in Faridpur, everyone has sold *all* the rice grain to the agents, even each family's own yearly stock...'

A fly writes a quick, indecipherable scribble across Gopal's vision before settling on his left temple, just on the border of his vision. Swatting it away, he manages to dislodge a small reservoir of sweat straight into his eye.

'The stories coming in are that people are getting worried about finding food—'

'Arre, bokachoda! India is a big place, there's lots more rice in other places! The day you and your children don't have enough to eat, tell me! Until then, concentrate on your work, understood?'

'Forgive me, Gogai-da, forgive me... A mistake... Won't say again...'

'Forgive you *what*? I don't know *what* you idiots listen to, what rumours someone pisses into your ears, what nonsense you swallow as if it's some pandit's jupp-mantra!'

North of the S.N. Bannerjee crossing, the streets are now completely empty, the shops all shuttered, as if for some long season of siege. Gopal notices a signboard in English – *Hotal Pakistan* – which someone has scrawled over with some sticky black substance. Across the road, the board for *Jinnah Biryani House* has escaped with a few faint marks, the correctionists clearly having run out of redacting material. A few shops down, a sign that has been recently torched, but he can just about make out the ghost letters rising out of the charred wood – *Azad Pakistan Tea House.*

'Look at that,' the driver says, shaking his head. 'People are truly going mad these days.'

'Oh, these are those Hindu Rashtra chutiyas, using the trouble of the last few days to create more trouble.' Gopal bends his head to light a cigarette. 'But then these type of katuas are also chutiyas, proclaiming this nonsense Pakistan-shakistan to provoke people...'

'What, Gogai-da?' The driver is nonplussed. 'No, I meant look over there, straight and on the right.'

As the driver slows down, Gopal looks up to see what the man is pointing at. Further up Wellesley Street, someone has hung a huge Congress tricolour from their building. The flag seems to pour out of the top floor balcony of a six-storey house, like a Baul's alkhalla, saris and dhutis and odd bits of cloth stitched together to form the orange, white and green stripes cascading down in a long drape over the balconies below and stopping just between the second and first floors. Two mounted police are trying to pull it down, both standing in their stirrups and grabbing at the cloth that's dancing in the breeze, just out of reach.

Whatever wind is moving the flag, it doesn't reach the van. The stinging in his eyes grows sharper and Gopal reaches for the cloth he keeps behind the seat to wipe his face. As he turns, he sees the driver has already wrapped his head with his own gamchha, leaving a narrow gap through which to see. He sees the man's eyes are streaming with water and realizes what is happening. As he quickly wraps his head, he wonders about the sharp pain and how the tear-gas can be stabbing him in the leg. He hears but doesn't see the horse's front hooves. Then the rear ones are right in front of his face, slamming down on the bonnet of the van, sending the protruding metal piece into his calf again, just as the driver kicks the brake and the windscreen comes and smacks his head.

Eyes spinning, Gopal tries to right himself, but too quickly. The dizziness pushes him back and his nose is filled with a new stink which he knows is not blood. He reaches between his legs, not quite accepting he has pissed in his pants, but everything there is dry. The only wetness is on the outside of his left leg, below his knee, where he has been gashed. He understands he is smelling the driver's urine and not his own, and that seems to be the most important thing. The sound of hooves crowds his ears, he ducks instinctively, but the horses gallop past, this time missing the van.

Two more mounted police join the mama who has nearly trampled them, all three chasing after a bunch of young men who seem to have appeared out of thin air. The group pelt straight towards the two cops who have now jointly pincered an edge of the flag with their bamboo lathis. The chasing police shout out and the two turn to look, dragging the flag with them. The running men scatter as they see the new pair of police horses. Two of them go left under a portico and disappear into a lane. One of them runs straight ahead in pure panic, as if blind. Of the three others, two turn back, hoping perhaps to go wide of the chasing horses. The two mamas with the flag try and come forward, the fabric still caught in their raised lathis. As they charge, a section of it tears and comes down, right on their heads.

Watching the two cops struggling to untangle themselves, Gopal notices the last of the men quickly look around and make a decision – sensing attention is turned away from him, the fellow quickly slips behind a horseless jhurrie-gaadi, on to the pavement and into one of the roadside garbage baskets, drawing the lid over himself. It doesn't help him. The two cops have spotted him through the mess of the flag cloth, and they canter over to the basket. The savagery with which they start bringing down their lathis on the basket tells Gopal how very aware the mamas are of people laughing at them from behind the windows all down the street. As he manages to sit up fully, Gopal sees a third horse-cop join the two, all three of them almost fighting with each other to get at the man in the garbage basket. The horses whinny, the mamas shout, now exultant in their rage, bits of rubbish fly in the air as the man struggles to escape the blows. A bit of a banana leaf catches the muted sunlight as it arcs into the air, yellow-brown rubbish mulch spreads on the slate-grey pavement stones, an empty coconut shell shoots out from below the stationary carriage, rolling to a stop on a tram track. The man's light cream kurta begins to get streaked with red, reminding Gopal of the buffalo sacrifices he's seen.

His head still ringing, Gopal's chief thought is to get out alive, and he grabs the driver's shoulder and shakes it. The driver whimpers, tries to move, and collapses back in the seat, holding his chest where the steering wheel has hit. The sound of more horses turns Gopal into a statue. A gora officer brings his mount to a stop right next to the van. He gives a sharp blow on his whistle. One of the mamas, a light-skinned Anglo, peels away from the garbage bin and trots up, saluting as he does.

'Listen here, Gilbert! Tell your men *not* to get caught up! There are others getting away!' Gopal can make out almost all the words the gora bastard is shouting. '*Leave* your mark on them, but on *as many* of the buggers as you can! I'm going around to Dharmatolla Street now! Carry on! Good chap!'

The Anglo salutes again and wheels his horse around. The gora sets off down the side street on the left, the one from which the horses have come. Neither has paid any attention to the van or the two of them inside.

In a minute or so, the horses have disappeared. A moment later, a door opens. Three men and a woman come out and carry the limp, blood-soaked body of the man into the house. Far down Wellesley Street, Gopal can now see commotion and smoke, but around him the streets are empty again.

I reckon it's one of the worst paintings he ever made. He was clearly drunk or disturbed when he made it, or perhaps both. Everything is wrong about it, the intention, the colours, the rendering. It's clear he doesn't know what he's doing with this thing technically, and it almost feels as if he doesn't care. All there is, on the canvas – it's an oil, three feet by three and a half feet – is the urge to slap down the incident. Some things are successful, no doubt. The flying banana leaf is actually beautiful, almost a still life pasted on to the rest, except it has motion, and likewise, the empty, hairy coconut shell shooting out from under the horse carriage is also acute in its execution – you can feel the velocity, the bumping of the dented half-ball as it rolls across the road towards the tram tracks. One of the mounted cops is also powerfully painted, you can't quite see his face, but you can feel the frenzy in the bend of the raised arm, the pressure of the thighs squeezed against the horse's flanks.

As to the rest, most of it is a mess. The half-visible body of the bleeding man in the garbage basket is as if from a different painting, a fish, streaked with entirely predictable rings of blood, the other two mounted cops are also badly drawn and unfinished, as if Elko couldn't bear to think about them, even after the gap of several years. The buildings at the back are shoddily done, as if made by one of those mediocre watercolourists that are rife in Calcutta, the oil paint thin, stingy in its strokes, the lines lackadaisical in their observation. The flag though, is a thing of utter beauty. A long, exotic flower torn apart, one bit hanging out of the balcony, the other floating down, both sections dancing, the three main colours transparent, a deep green from the darkest Bengal vegetation, a grimy white that is somehow vibrant, and then the saffron orange, as if a lurid monsoon sunset has been sliced into a strip and joined to the other two. Amidst all this, a smudge, a dark blue dash of the charkha in the white, a strange inorganic device, chopped up and trapped in the coil of the strange petals hanging in mid-air. In all of this, you can see the cloth, the saris and the white dhutis that have been stitched together to make the thing.

When Sheyali first showed it to me, I found myself trying very hard not to let her see how much I wanted to just snatch that painting and run, how close I was to offering them every penny I could muster for this messy crash of paint.

'You like it, don't you?' Her voice was suddenly soft. 'It's not what you were looking for, but you like it.' Forty years of dealing with her clients, she was a hawk for spotting different kinds of lust. I couldn't have hidden my desire, not without preparation. A missing beat of breath would have been enough for her, or a widening of the eyes, and she had me nailed.

The recorder was still running at this point, and you can hear my consternation, even in the silences. You can also hear the whirr of the fan but not Radhuni's soft snoring as she sleeps in the next room.

'Mashi, you said you had another one as well...?'

'Yes, Radhuni found it the other day, after you asked. It's quite dirty and has a few holes in it, but I told the girl to clean it.' On the tape, there is no trace of my heart jumping, my clamping down on my words before they come out – I hope she hasn't cleaned it with water?

Sheyali summoned the girl, who went away and returned with the second painting. There was no sign of any water or soap, thank god, though the canvas had blackened and you could see bits of fungus in the dark bits. This second one was from a few years before the flag painting and was by far the more finished piece of work, but within a certain received idiom. I wanted both the pictures, but I was far more interested in the flag one.

I did a switcheroo, as Modesty Blaise and Willie Garvin would call it in the comic strip – I lavished the praise I felt for the flag-mess on the double portrait, while playing down the excitement I felt for what I'd started thinking of as 'The Accident'.

'Ooh, this one is truly beautiful!'

'Can you tell which one of us is which?'

Of course I could, the likeness had followed them through the years of entropy, and it wasn't just the physical likeness. In the painting, I fancied you could see the young buds of the different attitudes these girls would carry forward into life, the personalities they would distil out of their young selves. The picture was half Cézanne, which Elko would have been happy to hear. What would have made him less happy is if you'd pointed out the influences of Picpisso and early Souza, or Fucking Neutered Sauzage as he used to call him.

Light from the left, a corridor stretching behind them, actually more a wooden-windowed bridge, small squares of panes in a green grid, perhaps from the top floor of the Great Eastern, and the two girls clearly standing, even though the frame is cut off just at the midriff. Their faces almost mask-like, but not quite, the eyes alight, their breasts forming a collective, four linked undulations under the thin saris, with the white tennis ball in Sheyali's hand making a fifth round shape. And then the hands. Sheyali's darker hands, her left holding the ball and her right almost taking the cigarette out of the frame, as if trying to hide it, Radhuni's fairer hand having just released her cigarette into the grip of her round, full mouth, the lips pursing around the stick, brazen, smiling through the pucker. Their eyes are alive, but different. Radhuni's are wide, smiling, challenging. Sheyali's eyes are not small, exactly, but starkly interrogative – Who are you? How much are you worth? What will break open your bank? Which one of us will it take to break it open, or what combination of the two of us? If you unfocus your eyes, two figures loaded with light menace, one in a red sari, one in yellow, reducing the corridor behind to a green-and-white halo, an aura of straight lines in a world where nothing is straight.

I paused to put aside the flag and horses as though I was completely done with it and kept turning the double portrait this way and that in the light.

'So… you're right, it's not in very good condition, but perhaps I could get it repaired—'

'Ei, don't you dare discuss anything about that picture of us without me!' Radhuni's voice interrupted her snoring with warning. 'He gave it to me, not you, don't forget!'

'Eeeaaanhh! Gave it to you! He gave it to both of us!'

Actually, Elko didn't give it to either of them. I know because he mentions the double portrait in a letter he writes to his friend Rudro in September 1948: '… I wish I could say I envy you your Tour of the Continent, but I don't. The memory of that bloody bastard of a London cold is enough to make everything in this sorry place seem wonderful –

even the business of having to go to G.C. Laha yet again, needing things they just don't have, simple things like decent primer for canvas, (lots of pre-war canvas stock, but no bloody primer, so useless, water water everywhere...), lots of reds and blues in their oil paint drawers, but for some exclusively god-known reason, no greens, browns, ochre or black in decent brands! *Did the painters eat them up?* I asked and the boy just gave a laugh, verging on insolence. No, I don't miss London a jot, or if I'm truthful, I suppose the only thing I really miss about it is being able to walk into that shop near the British Museum and buy any material whatsoever. Bombs, defeat, German occupation, near civil war, nothing has dented the European production of art materials! But here it's as if the warring countries have infected us with a kind of post-war paint rationing, something they have long left behind, but one that will stay with us, it looks like forever... I know you are not particularly interested, but let me mention that, after returning, I've managed to make three or four decent *toils* that I don't actually hate. One is a portrait of those two girls I told you about, those two *ladies of the night* – though they seem to be equally busy both day and night – (and no, before you even raise your eyebrow, NO! I am NOT one of their clients!). I finished it at their *house* – left it to dry – couldn't possibly move it – and they've hung on to it, even though I can tell neither of them really likes it – I suppose the (supposedly) wealthy babu will have to pay them something to extricate it, which I will do when I have my next saline drip of pittance. You will no doubt argue that giving them money makes me some sort of... a client at a remove.'

Sheyali became businesslike and called out to Radhuni. 'Why don't you wake up and have some tea? Then come and sit here. Later don't say I did this and that without your agreement!'

'I'm getting up, I'm getting up! Ask for some tea.'

Sheyali went calling for the girl. I pulled the camera and exposure meter out of the bag, and placed the double portrait on a chair so that it caught maximum light from the window. I put the meter at different points over the surface to check the exposure, adjusted the camera settings, and crouched down to take a few pictures – a few of the whole painting and then some frames of details, the hands, the tennis ball, the eyes.

'So... how much do you think this is worth then?' Radhuni was standing right behind me, and I nearly dropped the camera.

'Oh, Radhuni-mashi!' I looked up at her and she smiled at me. Behind her, Sheyali came back into the room.

'See, it's like this...' I struggled to my feet and found my cigarettes. 'By itself, it's hard to say how much it's worth exactly. You see, he's not very well known, even in India. What I want to do is collect as many of his paintings as I can, select the best, and have an exhibition, a show, of the work. I would also write something to go along with the show, maybe try and convince someone to do a small book, which is called a catalogue. Then, with this painting and others that are in bad shape, I would get them cleaned up and the holes mended perhaps, or not, and then see. If the exhibition is successful, then this one might fetch some price. Or it might not, it might take some time before the value of his paintings goes up. You don't have to sell it immediately, I could just give it back to you after the exhibition, and you wait and sell it later, that's also possible. But you'll have to keep it carefully, if it deteriorates any further, it will have no value at all.'

'We know a couple of artists...' Sheyali says.

'... And just like him, they're always broke.' Radhuni snorts out a small laugh.

'Well, no, that's not true, he wasn't always...' Sheyali picks up her cup of tea.

'Not always, no, but for a boy from a rich family, he didn't always have, you know, enough money.'

'Anyway, these painters we know, they are always complaining that rich people in Calcutta are highly stingy when it comes to paying for art. So why should they pay for some unknown dead painter?'

I don't want to give them false hopes, but neither do I want the two paintings to disappear back into the recesses of the house. I have to dangle something.

'I was thinking of having one exhibition here, but also one in Paris.'

I can tell by the way both of them look away into different corners of the room that they hadn't thought of this.

Radhuni is the first one to regain her bargaining face. 'So, we would have to trust you... to take this painting to France and bring it back?'

I was about to reply that the Big Man would stand guarantee so they needn't worry, but Sheyali poked Radhuni on the arm. 'No, no, what are you saying? He's a good boy, you should be able to tell by now!' She turned to me. 'But if you sell it for us, how much will you charge?'

'Charge?' For a moment I was lost.

'Dalali – what part of the price will you keep for yourself?' Sheyali's tone was suddenly flat, businesslike. She had dealt with many good boys in her life. 'We should fix something, no? In case we loan you the painting and agree to let you get the best price for it?'

Dalali. The agent's commission, the middleman's profit, and also the pimp's cut.

'If I get a good offer, I would first contact you and ask you if you agree to that price. Then I would deduct from that the cost of repairing it and transporting it.' I hadn't thought about any of this, and I was shocked at the firm and clear story coming out of my mouth. 'From what remains, I would take 15 per cent for myself and the rest I would give to you.'

Sheyali took a drag from her cigarette, slanted her eyes down and nodded with some internal satisfaction – she had made the pimp, or the mark, put his cards on the table.

'What do you think?' She looked at her partner.

'You say?' Radhuni smiles.

Sheyali turns back to me. 'Why don't we just sell you the paintings? Two thousand rupees for both, fifteen for the picture of us and five hundred for that one with the horseback mamas.'

LANDSCAPE

The shop boy is yanking the two sections of the grille together just as Kedar reaches the shop. Kedar's hand starts to go between the sliding sections, but the man doesn't notice. Kedar jerks his hand away at the last moment as metal slams into metal. The man looks at him as if he's a lunatic.

'Ki chaan? Dokan bondho!' What do you want? The shop is shut!

'Bhai, I just telephoned a little while ago, about the tubes, oil paint...'

'No chance today, babu, we are shut!' He slides a big padlock into the grille and turns the key with ferocity.

'Oh yes, yes, it was me that spoke to you!' An older shop assistant at the back of the shop recognizes Kedar. 'What colours were they, again?'

'I just need three tubes each of ivory black, burnt umber and yellow ochre... and also two of sap green, no three!'

'What brand, babu?'

Kedar hesitates, thinking, but the man answers his own question. 'Take them all in Talens! We are on the very last of the good Dutch maal! You won't see more for a while, if ever!'

'Yes, Talens is just fine!'

While the junior shop boy begins to insert the wooden slats that go behind the grille, the older chap quickly yanks open drawers in one of the dark mahogany chests that loom at the sides of the shop. He plucks out the colours, almost without looking. 'Sapgrin three, ochre holud, two... how many black did you say?'

'Three – no give me four!' Kedar feels the crowd rushing past behind him, people banging into him as they pass, and his hand instinctively goes around the wallet in his pocket.

'Ivhoryblak, four... You're Lahiri Babu, aren't you? Saprgrin, three. Oijey, that Palm Avenue house, right? In Ballygunge. I've been to your place many times, to deliver material... Three baant umber, three ochre!' The man slides the tubes into a paper thhonga and the thhonga into a thicker envelope with the G.C. Laha design printed on it. He ties the whole thing with tight winds of a jute string.

'Ei! Give this to babu!' He flicks his wrist and the packet flies towards the man in front.

'Here, babu! Now we must shut the shop!' The junior hands Kedar the packet through the grille.

'How much?' Gripping the packet in left hand, Kedar starts to tug at his wallet with his right.

'Never mind the money today, babu!' The man inside has turned away. He calls out over his shoulder. 'We have no place to put it! I'll remember precisely next time you come. Or when I come with the next delivery.'

The shop boy slams the last slat almost on Kedar's face, leaving him staring at a wooden wall.

Something pointed pokes him hard between the shoulder blades.

Kedar begins to wheel around in fury but finds himself hemmed in by the slow torrent of the crowd. Once he manages to turn, he sees what has assaulted him – two coolies are trying to manoeuvre a sewing machine with its heavy stand above the heads of the crowd. One of the wrought iron legs is what has landed the blow.

As he feels himself being pushed along in the press of people, Kedar suddenly finds himself back in Tagore's funeral procession, his kurta almost being torn from his back, the smell of incense climbing up his nose. He feels the nausea rising from a year ago, but the smell is actually different, of something burning somewhere, and he wonders why he is crying for Rabindranath today when he shed no tears on that day.

A few feet down the pavement, something loosens the crowd and Kedar's feet find the space to run. There's a din – a storm of human voices, but accompanied by some erratic metallic percussion, as if a huge machine has burst open somewhere, spewing ball bearings on to a factory floor.

'Gaaa-aas! Run! They are firing gas!'

Above the melee of heads, he suddenly sees a surreal vision. For a few seconds, it's an oddly decorated pillar sticking out at the corner of the big crossing, silhouetted against the sun glare of Esplanade. Then he realizes it's a woman, a white woman in a hat trying to wipe her eyes with a scarf, the sunglasses perched on the brim of her hat giving her a double pair of eyes. Stupid creature, why doesn't she just put on her—

'Miss Sne—*Imogen!*' He grabs her wrist and she resists violently, but his other hand, still clutching the packet of tubes, hooks around her waist in a rugby tackle.

'Run! We've got to run!'

He drags her away from the corner. She stumbles along for a few steps, just following the good sense of the words, and then she recognizes him. They both yell at the same time.

'Oh, *Larry*, it's *you!*'

'It's *me*, Larry! Don't be scared!'

They're running together now, buffeted this way and that by the crowd. His hand on her elbow, guiding her, moving them off the pavement on to the road, avoiding a tangle of people under the Metro Cinema portico, then back on to the pavement. Eva Attali suddenly smiling in his ear, 'But no one told you to *die* for your art, my prince! And that too with this long English girl!' He nearly slips on the wash from a spilled drum of lime paint while Imogen crosses it in a stride. A woman in a sari with a bright orange border, screaming – *Lokhhon! Lokhhon! Where have you gone? Where is my son? Where is my baby?* – then Eva again: 'You told me, wasn't it, that painting and waiting go together? You should have waited at home! It's too early for the paint of your life to dry so soon!'

Despite the panic surrounding him, today things keep pulling Kedar back into the past. Passing Whiteway & Laidlaw, he has another sharp jab of memory, of the beggar woman banging on his car, the day he picked Keya up at Howrah in March. He wonders whether the wretch is still alive and finds himself looks around for her, which is absurd. The whole width of Chowringhee Road is filled with a confusion of people pelting in all directions, like ants from a broken nest, he thinks, or like a mess of colours running on grey paper, and he wonders how many people's paint will dry today. He catches a strong whiff of petrol even though the motor traffic seems to have completely disappeared. His nose opened by the gasoline, he now smells all sorts of things, sweat, stale food smells, rose and musk attar coming off from some passing woman, the smoke spoor from the matchstick going out in his hand as he somehow manages to light a cigarette. Too late, he remembers his manners.

'So sorry! Would you care for a—'

'Not just now, thank you!' Imogen shakes her head in wonder at the little man jogging next to her, juggling a paper packet, a tin of cigarettes and a matchbox, fag bouncing in his mouth. Kedar catches her looking. He can't help grinning back through the cigarette clamped in his teeth.

They both break into the laughter that comes from relief.

'Larr—Kedder, this is tremendous fun, but can I ask where exactly we are going?'

'Oh! To my car!' He stops himself from coming out with a nasal Humphrey Bogart drawl. 'It's parked just near New Market, in that lane next to Firpo's. Not far!'

'Oh, right. Thank heavens you saw me... Do you think you could give me a lift to a taxicab somewhere?'

'Oh, no, no, I'll just drive you wherever you need to go.'

'No, look here, I couldn't possibly drag you out of your way, not with all this going on.'

'It's no trouble at all, and anyway, I think the taxis have all gone home for the day.'

It's true. There's not a single taxi among the cars coming to a halt next to the Grand Hotel arcade. The massed slap of running feet is cut into by a coda of screeching brakes, the drivers furiously trying to turn around before they become engulfed in the onrushing crowd. In a trice, the avenue becomes a cubism of cars and vans at right angles to each other, horns blaring, drivers shouting, fenders grazing grilles and headlights. In the middle of the arcade, at the entrance of the hotel, there is a pocket of calm, with armed soldiers lined up on the pavement to keep the way clear for military vehicles. Kedar and Imogen move on to the road. As they run past, Kedar can see sandbags piled high in the courtyard beyond the closed gates and more armed soldiers watching from the first-floor terrace.

'*Shoot* some of these blighters! What are you bloody standing there for? Come on!' A large, fat Ingrej, face red, light-coloured shirt and shorts smudged with dark patches of sweat, standing between the two rows of soldiers and exhorting them. '*Shoot-sumvem*, I tell you! That'll teach 'em to riot, the little bastards!' His planter's hat topples off, hit by his own waving arm, and he bends down to pick it up, the curses becoming more obscene. Kedar can swear he can smell gin-breath blasting out of the man's mouth. The soldiers remain unmoving, as if the fellow's not there, but Kedar notices this is a white battalion. Today, clearly no native troops have been deployed to guard the second largest hotel in the city.

'Not a good moment to pop in for a beer, I don't think,' pants Kedar. He pulls Imogen back into the shade of the arcade and then lets go of her elbow, the immediate danger having passed.

'No, no point getting shot for a drink.' Imogen gives the joke a serious colour. 'They're very jumpy in there, I'm sure.'

'Can't blame them, I suppose.'

'No, well...'

Imogen follows Kedar around the corner to the row of parked cars. As they slow to a walking pace, she gestures to his cigarette. 'May I? Would you mind if I...'

'Oh no, of course!' Kedar reaches into his kurta pocket for the tin of Players.

'No, no, I'd just like a puff, actually.'

As Kedar hesitates, Imogen wonders if she's broken some Bengali taboo. But then he quickly hands over his cigarette. As she takes a drag, Kedar finds the keys to his car.

'I'd like to shoot that beast though, that drunken pig.' Imogen says it almost to herself, but Kedar can see that a deep anger has caught up with her.

'Waste of a bullet, I'd say. Chap like him, probably soon drown in his own gin.'

'True, how true. I'm sorry, I was a bit...'

Kedar is seeing her properly for the first time today. Sharp nose. Blue eyes and mouth set seriously now. Unruly blonde-brown hair escaping from below the hat, oddly elongated neck covered with freckles. Somehow, her goggles are still perched on her straw hat. Right behind her face is a huge image of Bette Davis on the hoarding above the entrance to Lighthouse Cinema, which adds to the cascade of eyes, making it six. Bette Davis's round face framing Imogen's long face, her thick lips coming out as extensions of Imogen's hat brim. Two completely different species collaged together, two—

'Kedd—Larry? Are you all right?'

'You can call me Kedar. You're getting the hang of it. Andrew nearly had it pat by the time he left.'

'You were staring, as if you'd seen a ghost...'

'Oh, yes, sorry! The ghost of Bette Davis, right behind you. Made an odd combination. I was thinking how different you look...' Kedar holds open the car door.

'Yes, well, there's a good reason why I never developed ambitions towards Hollywood.'

'No, not at all, I just meant the shape of your face is very different from – it wasn't a comment on—' Kedar busies himself with the ignition.

'Oh, we *know* what shape of face you prefer! Andrew and I were remarking on the fact that—'

'I paint a bit, you see, so I tend to stare, at things, faces, you must forgive me – what do you mean?'

'Well, you know the Eastern European miss in whose company we used to see you, what was her name, Evelyn? And then the girl I first saw you with on Christmas Eve, from around here, isn't she? The one whose family you thought might be manoeuvring you towards betro—I thought I saw the two of you again more recently, somewhere... let me think... Anyway, we were remarking upon the fact that they are both very lovely, but of a certain type of beauty...'

'Oh, I think they are very unalike!' Kedar reverses out of the row of cars and changes the subject. 'What brought you here today?'

'Oh, I was meeting a friend. We were to examine shoes on Bentinck Street, but she had to go off to find someone who might be caught up in the trouble around Wellington. And then, I was hoping to buy some film for my camera, but no luck, shops are all shut.'

'Ha! And I came into this circus to buy paints and only just managed to get them. Chap almost shut the slats on my hand.'

Kedar decides to go past New Market, avoiding Chowringhee. They drive past the twin movie theatres of New Empire and Lighthouse and turn right along the side of the old market. Something moves in the corner of his eye and Kedar looks up. Someone has put little Congress tricolour flags out of each of the high Gothic ventilator slits, and they flutter cheerfully in the slight breeze, their orange, white and green contrasting with the red brick of the building. A small spotter plane circles above, not directly above them but a bit in the direction of Wellington Square where the trouble has sparked. The parking lot in front of New Market is completely deserted, as if a plague has come and swept away all humans, leaving behind a few abandoned vehicles. Kedar feels a stab of worry about Keya, but he knows there's nothing he can do about it right now. He hopes Keya and her idiot friends are away from trouble, girls like that crazy Roma and her two footnotes, that tiny, pretty doll Titir, and that other one, the serious wallflower who never speaks and whose name he can't quite remember. His kurta sticking to the seat, he works through the gears and takes the back lanes towards Park Street.

'So where exactly do you live, Imogen?'

'We are on New Road, just off the Judges' Court Road. Isn't it terribly far, though?'

'I know it. You're hardly taking me to the far end of the world.

Reaching Park Street, he turns towards Chowringhee again, but that crossing is blocked. Beyond the police picket, he can see abandoned buses and trams. Wandering through them is a bent figure which could be the beggar woman, or someone very like her, baby, lost, no one to beg from. In the distance, way across the Maidan camp, a barrage balloon spins in the breeze against the towering monsoon clouds. He makes a U-turn and heads back down Park Street, then right on Camac Street. He straightens his back to get some wind between cloth and skin, grips the wheel more firmly, and steps on the accelerator to take advantage of the entirely empty straight road.

'New Road… Your parents' house, isn't it?'

'I'm afraid it is, yes. I'd ask you in for a drink but…'

'No, no, not at all. I wouldn't want to intrude.'

'It would be no intrusion at all! Least I can do after causing you to go so far out of your way. It's just that Mummy isn't a very friendly bird at the moment. My uncle – her brother – he's commanding a destroyer on the Murmansk convoys… and she hasn't heard from him for some time…'

'Oh, I see. In any case, I'm not dressed to meet…'

'Yes, I'm so sorry, I didn't recognize you at first! I've never seen you in your native—I mean this kind of shirt, what do you call it?'

'It's called a kurta across India, but here we call it a panjabi, as in what Punjabis wear, don't ask me why. Yes, I just ran out to get my paints before Apocalypse… and I must be getting back before I lose the light.'

'The light? Oh, the painting! You're anxious to get back to work! I'm quite impressed you're able to carry on while all this is…'

'Yes, a bit ostrich-like, I admit. My family think me quite mad, but I suppose they're happy I'm not out on the streets trying to single-handedly win freedom for my country.'

'Well, it would hardly be single-handedly, would it?'

'No, I meant with the recklessness of some young Turk who thinks he can do anything and everything.' Kedar suddenly realizes he is actually quite anxious about Keya. No way to get out of dropping this English girl all the way across town, but he wants to get back to Dover Road as soon as he can to wait for his female young Turk. 'You know, it's all very well to stand up for your ideals, but then you have to… you have to address reality as well… no matter how omnipotent you think your youth makes you. If you see what I mean?'

Imogen opens her mouth but swallows her words.

At the junction of Camac Street and Lower Circular Road, there are two policemen waving traffic to go east. A little distance behind them a police van has again blocked the road to Chowringhee. Kedar pulls to a stop in front of them.

'I need to take this memshaheb to her house in Alipur. What roads should I take?'

'Babu, everything around here is blocked. No traffic allowed on Chowringhee now, all the way to Kalighat and Rashbehari.'

'You mean I can't go across from Elgin Road?'

'No, babu, it's all blocked after the mess at Jodubajar this morning and now the big jhamela going on at Wellington Square. What you should do is go all the way down Lansdowne Road and go past the Dhakuria Lakes to Tollygunge. Then, take that road from near Tollygunge Club, the one heading towards the Mint, do you understand?'

'Yes, I think so.'

'From there it should be okay. Shaheb-para toh, so they will have good bandobust there. Lot of army is out as you can see.'

'Yes. All right.' Kedar nods to the havaldar and pulls away.

They drive to the big water tank at Minto Park and turn right on to Lansdowne Road. Here, life seems almost normal, as if they've fallen through a rabbit hole into another city. There's still not much traffic on the road, but everything is as if on a Sunday or a public holiday. As ever, the big mansions are hidden behind their frontage of palms, neem, mango and gulmohar, but some of the front gates are half open, the guards standing around outside, the servants on their afternoon break coming in and out. A small group of people stand clustered around a coconut seller's trolley, haggling around the piles of pointed green spheres. A couple of schoolchildren run down the street, their satchels banging awkwardly against their backs. On the first-floor balcony of one of the bungalows, Kedar notices a white woman in a wide-brimmed hat, daubing away at a canvas on an easel. There is the brief rise of some recognition of a kindred spirit, but it goes away sharply, as if his entire body has rejected it – that's not what he does, she is not doing what he does, he can't quite say why, but what he does, in a similarly appointed house, on a similar easel, is very different.

'I don't know whether I should ask, but...' He hesitates, caught out, the words having escaped without passing the roadblock of thought.

'Andrew? Oh, that's quite all right. I'm not sure where he is exactly, but I do believe he's all right. It's good of you to ask.'

'Oh, right, jolly good to know, thanks. One never knows whether one should...'

'I know, I know, it's quite awkward, but then the whole bloody thing is quite awkward.' The curse escapes despite herself, but it makes them both relax.

At the junction where Elgin Road and Rowland Road meet Lansdowne, there are more policemen than usual. After the crossing, they pass smaller bungalows and buildings standing right on the road. Imogen looks around curiously.

'What is this area called? I don't believe I've ever been around here.'

'This is Bhowanipore. We've now left behind the European area, so it's not surprising you haven't been here.'

'Bhow-vannipore... is largely Bengali, is it?'

'Quite mixed, actually. Mostly Bengalis, but now also a lot of Gujaratis, traders from western India, and quite a few Shordars – I mean Sikhs – who have their car-repair workshops here. This is where I come to get this little beast of mine seen to.'

'I see... So which is your favourite part of the city, can I ask?'

'Well... I like my own neighbourhood, of course, Ballygunge, Palm Avenue, Mayfair, you've been that side I'm sure?'

'Yes, of course.'

'Then, parts of the old town are very picturesque, north Calcutta, Shyambajar, and around the river, but I wouldn't want to live there. Too crowded, too dirty, really.'

'If you weren't living at home, where would you want to live?'

'Well, I like being at our family estate in Rajshahi, but only for a few days at a time. No, I do like living in Calcutta, but I don't know... maybe one day I'd like to spend a while in Provence, the south of France, for a few years. To paint.'

'The south of France?' Imogen can't help a startled laugh. 'Provence?' Kedar makes a note that she pronounces it as Pro-vonce and not as he does, rhyming with 'hence'. 'Why France?'

'Why France? In one word, Cézanne. I would love to try and paint Mount Sainte Vict—'

'Mont Sainte-Victoire? It's lovely there, certainly, but why would you go all the way there to paint when you have all this?' Imogen waves her arm to include the surroundings. 'Look! How lovely all this is!'

Finally confronted by some traffic, the car has stopped at Poddopukur. Kedar tries to see the scene through Imogen's eyes. Ranged around the square tank of water, there are buildings of various vintage, from the early nineteenth century to more recent ones, with art deco pretensions. The paint is yellow and white, with one or two showing up old red brick. There is stucco, some small statuary poking out of the crenellations, balconies jutting out of the facades. On the water tank, there is a new building of the swimming club, its corrugated tin roof slanting in the muted monsoon light. From one side, a swimmers' jetty thrusting into the pond. On the other side, just next to the low iron railing, an audience of variously interested palm trees leaning towards the water. Kedar tries to imagine what Manet might have made of this, how Utrillo might have rendered it, what Cézanne would have done, and he only comes up with impossibilities.

A TASTE OF BLOOD

The pulsating human wall pushes her in the wrong direction. A man's elbow comes right in front of her face, so that she doesn't even see the hard mosquito that stings her on top of her forehead. She goes blind. As she begins to fall, her main concern is that her dead body shouldn't be trampled by the crowd, that her Ma-Baba should have something intact to cremate. The ground doesn't come. There seem to be people under her, between her and the asphalt, and then people on top of her, also toppling, burying her in a grave of sweaty, dirty bodies that she can feel but not see.

The pain comes a couple of beats later, as she struggles to push herself out of the tangle of bodies, looking for space to lie down and die peacefully. It's as if she's a bell and the pain is the clapper, ringing her from both outside and inside, tonking inside her head, just behind her eyes, then travelling up, tapping hard on her skull, and then down her spine in a steady, regular beat. She's crawling on all fours now, scraping along the road, but her legs and knees are braided up in her sari – not responding. She's dragging her body forward by the sheer strength of her arms and hands, and she can feel her palms getting cut into shreds. She blinks and blinks and suddenly there is light, a red film through which she can see that she's almost at the footpath, nearly about to wade into a square of dirty water where the hydrant is dormant.

Hands grasp her tightly under her armpits, hands that seem to know what they are doing, and they pull her up. Her head is spinning wildly, but she notes that she is still breathing. The sari and petticoat have loosened from around her legs, and they are now doing what they are told.

'This girl can walk! Get her away from here, quickly! And you two! Go help that man over there! He's much worse, I think his eye is gone.' The woman's voice is also clear in what it's saying. 'It's okay, ma, it's okay. Just a cut on your forehead. That always bleeds a lot but it's nothing to worry about. You'll soon be all right, don't worry!' Niru smells and hears the paan being spit more than she sees it. The woman's betel-scented breath is very close to her ears. 'Just go with this girl, ma, she'll take you inside. What all you girls from good families are doing in the middle of this, I don't know! Hare Krishno, Hare Krishno!' The paan-breath woman passes her on to another pair of hands. 'Sheyali! Take this one inside, wash her head and face, put some clean cloth on the wound and make her sit down. Give her water, but nothing else for now. Then come back. There are many more here who need help.'

'Hyan, Mashi, doing!'

Niru's feet are unsteady, but she can walk. The older woman has said she can walk, so it must be true. The second woman's hands hold her firmly as they move out of the sun into the shadow of a lane going off the footpath between two shops. Her head is still spinning, and fresh blood is pouring over the bits that have become sticky on her face. The woman holding her takes her to the sitting-ledge outside an old building hidden inside the lane and sits her down. She takes water from a pot and quickly washes Niru's wound, before stemming it with a bit of a torn sari dipped in disinfectant. The sharp sting helps Niru focus. 'Here, press this hard against the cut and hold it there while I wash your face.' Niru feels the rag become wet with blood, but then the bleeding seems to somehow stop. The girl – she's only a little older than Niru – quickly but carefully wipes Niru's face with another cloth, making sure to lift off the blood from the corners of her eyes and around the nose. She smiles as she wipes Niru's mouth. 'It's odd to taste your own blood, isn't it? I too split my head once and I remember the taste of my blood. I didn't like it at all!'

The girl fills a tin glass with water, pushes Niru's head back gently and holds her hand under the chin. She gives Niru small sips, as she would a child. Niru indicates she can drink on her own and the girl hands her the glass. 'Don't drink it all in one go, only a little bit at a time, all right?' The girl pushes Niru back gently. 'Just lean on this pillar and sip the water. I'll go and see what more hell is going on out there. Don't worry, one of us will be back soon. And Mashi's even sent word to a compounder to come with medicines.' The girl helps Niru adjust her sari. Niru notices the girl is dark and quite beautiful. She wonders why the girl has alta and so much make-up on in the afternoon.

As she rides the dizzy spells, Niru feels there's something really important that she has misplaced, something she's forgetting, and she feels her anxiety rising. The girl's make-up reminds her – Roma, lipstick – Roma. Where is Roma?

Slowly, Niru pieces together the last forty minutes in her spinning brain. Imogen – tea at Esplanade. She had left Imogen and walked quickly up Dharmatolla Street. Near Jyoti Cinema – the first block of crowd – people circling slowly into themselves – a pack of panicked goats. She could hear talk of lathicharges – but clearly no bullets fired, no tear gas either – obviously just stupid rumours. As she tried to work her way through, gaps formed in the crowd – like patches of skin that are hairless, she remembers thinking. Nearer the Wellesley Street crossing – more people – focused the other way – towards Wellington Square which was just beyond the crossroads. The signboards on shops – some damaged, bent, one or two burnt, for no obvious reason. Imogen's entreaty – '*Be careful, won't you, dear?*' – then, across the line of heads, on the other side of the crossing, Roma with her friend Keya – a glimpse of Roma's animated face through the blur of bodies, then Keya with her hands around her mouth to amplify her voice – the other women shouting – Roma's arm with the Longines watch, raised, fist moving in cadence to some slogans. Roma's arm – no Titir anywhere – dear Roma not being careful at all. Niru had started to move towards the two girls – shouting to get their attention – but her own voice was inaudible to her, snatched by the roar of the crowd. She could no longer find any trace of Roma, but she saw the mounted police converge around the spot where Roma's group of Congress girls were gathered. The white uniformed arms shot up, holding bamboo rods. They came down hard. *But surely they can't be beating women? But surely they can. They are.* A strange new anger welled up inside. Niru's arms and legs suddenly developed crazy energy. She was now trying to swim through the sea of people. Trying almost to skim their shoulders and the tops of their heads. Whatever it took to get to her friend. Whatever, jaa kichhu, whatever.

Her head was pounding, the blood sloganning in her ears, and she didn't hear the dull cracks of sound, though now, sitting crumpled on the uthon, she remembers them clearly. In the crowd, as she struggled just to stay in the same place, the air was suddenly filled with heavy mosquitoes, hard insects buzzing by – not mosquitoes – tear-gas shells, she now realizes. The police must have fired from very close – clearly one had hit her smack in the forehead – but what has hit Roma? Titir she hasn't seen, but Roma she clearly saw in the melee across the crossing – there is no possibility that the horse cops have missed her – none. Roma hit, but how badly? Her eyes sting with a trickle of new blood – it comes to her that she has dropped the pad of cloth she was holding to her head – she sees both her hands are clenched by her side.

'You little ass-fucked goatfucker! What have you done to yourself? Hyan?' Niru can hear the made-up girl's voice coming down the shady lane well before she sees her. 'Who told you to be out and about on a day like this? Couldn't you have stayed in Gate-Ishtaan today, sucking that Phorashi's—'

The girl cuts her voice as soon as she sees Niru sitting there. Limping next to her is a short, scrawny boy, quite dark-skinned, but not nearly as dark as some of the Markin Negro soldiers. Even as he hobbles forward holding his left knee, the boy has quick eyes. He takes in the whole clearing in front of the building, the uthon, Niru herself, who has quickly put back the cloth to her forehead, and the doorway behind her leading into the old building.

The girl helps the fellow sit down and lean against the pillar on the other side of the steps.

'These were nice trousers but now they're torn.' There is regret in the boy's voice, but no mention of his wound.

'Just feel Ma Kali's mercy on you that the metal didn't cut you somewhere higher! That babu outside has certainly lost his eye!' Niru sees the girl has a big pair of tailor's scissors that she must have snatched up from one of the shops in the lane. Without fuss, she now snips away the bottom two-thirds of the left leg of the trousers, carefully cutting just above the bit where the cloth is pasted on to the skin with blood. 'All right, now straighten your leg as much as you can,' she mutters. 'This will hurt a bit.' The boy grimaces slightly as he obeys her, his foot vibrating with the effort. The girl puts down the scissors and wipes her eyes with the end of her sari. Then she yanks hard at the severed cloth, and it strips away from the skin with a wet, tearing sound. The boy's head snaps up, but his clenched mouth emits nothing more than a small, sharp yelp.

Throwing away the sodden tube of cloth, the girl calls up into the house doorway. 'Eijey! Who's in there? Radhuni? Are you coming with the ointment?' Another female voice answers, and then a short, round, beautiful girl appears, holding a tin medicine box and a roll of gauze.

'Here, take.'

'Can you put some ointment on this girl's head, I'm dealing with Gogai here.'

'You know I can't bear to see blood! I'll hold the box for you!'

'Oh, you stupid bi—listen, I don't need you to hold the box. Just put it down and go to the road and see if that kid has gone to call the compounder. Our hero warrior here is going to need that big tetanus injection, so I hope the man brings it.'

A beautiful, mischievous smile fights through the tension on the plump girl's face. 'Gogai-gandu! How are you doing today? You're used to injections in the wrong places, aren't you? This one will be a bit thinner and sharper, that's all!'

Gandu. Niru has to struggle for a moment to recognize the dirty word. The first girl flares her eyes at the second, nodding in the direction of Niru. The second girl clamps her mouth with her pallu and patters away down the lane.

Niru's head has is spinning a little less now, and she makes an effort to stand up. The girl stares at Niru. 'What are you doing?'

'Listen, I'm all right, I have to go out and find my friend—'

'Go out? You don't know what's going on out there. They were firing in the air, but now they are pointing rifles straight at us. People have even heard armoured cars are coming with machine guns. You can only pray for your friend, that's all you can do right now.' As if to back up the girl's words, there is a crack of rifle fire and Niru finds herself swaying again. The girl pushes her down gently.

'Don't worry. That was in the air again,' the boys says. 'They won't fire into the crowd that easily, they're just trying to frighten everybody.'

'How do *you* know, Gogai?'

'It's the echo, Sheyali-di. It only sounds like that when you shoot into the air. And no screams. If they were firing into the crowd, we would be hearing screams by now.' There is a quiet authority about the boy, and Niru feels like believing him.

The boy turns to the first girl. 'Sheyali-di, does anyone nearby have a telephone? I need to make a phone call.'

'Phone call! Who's waiting for you now, Gogai, with their heart in their mouth? Tell me!'

'No, just to my malik's people. I was in the van, and I've had to push it to a spot in that lane next to Shankar Sweets. Also, the driver is hurt, much worse than me, probably needs to go to hospital. Luckily, I found someone I knew in a workshop down that same gully, and he's stretched out there.'

'Hospital, forget! All the hospitals nearby are going to be full of emergency people right now. How badly is he hurt? Maybe we can get the compounder to go see him.'

'I think his rib is broken, but he's breathing normally so he should live.'

'Right... now telephone... Well, Das-babu's shop down Dharmatolla is the nearest, but you can't go there until things calm down.'

The throbbing in Niru's head has come back, and she pushes the back of her skull against the pillar to try and make it stop. The girl, Sheyali, notices Niru and smacks the boy on his shoulder.

'Gogai, can you walk up the stairs? We need to take this girl upstairs and make her lie down until the compounder comes. He'll also bring your injection. Then we'll see about the telephone.'

Niru starts to protest, but Sheyali has gripped her under one armpit and raised her to her feet. The boy takes her other armpit. Niru knows she should react to a male touching her like this, without any by your leave, but she can't fully work it out. Both people's hands feel firm and necessary, and she allows them to take her into the house.

It's much cooler inside the doorway. There is a dark passage that leads to a meadow of light, a courtyard, at the centre of which is a grand staircase leading up. As they approach the stairs, Niru's head falls back a bit and she finds herself looking up at what must have once been a big skylight covering the square gap in the roof. The glass panes are all still there, some a little dirty, and the floor under her feet feels clean. Going up the steps, she can smell incense that is joined a little further up by the waft of recently cooked food. Fresh rice, some fish and spices fried in good-quality oil, maybe some vegetables in poshto, though she may be imagining this because she hasn't eaten for a while. As they reach the first floor landing, the food smell grows stronger and she feels a wave of nausea fighting off her hunger. She closes her eyes. Without quite wanting to, she leans back, letting her weight slide on to the two people supporting her.

'Yes, the noise of tear gas is quite different from the sound of firing, but you know what? The two are forever linked in my head. Like a marriage, like a husband-wife, one always coming after the other. It was always like that. In fact, it was three things, three kinds of sound. First the charge with lathis, the mamas on foot and on horses, the people shouting as the sticks cracked their bones, then the puja-dhak drumming of the gas cans, *tak-tak-tak, takta-tadak*, and then, everything else failing, the 303s cracking out. Like metal whips, as someone said at the time.'

This is the fifth recording from that summer of 1977. Lunch is over. Sheyali has settled down and lit a bidi. Radhuni is snoring in the next room.

I didn't come here for the story of the riot of 'Agosht 1942', but it has become a theme because of how they first met Niru. And they need to tell me about it.

'We were on the rooftop terrace that day, trying to see what was going on, but when the gas reached us and our eyes began to stream, we came down, came inside. By which time people were already running into the lanes off Dharmatolla Street, some of them injured by the canisters. At the same time, the mamas started firing in the air. Mashi was still around then, god bless her soul, very much around, and she was watching the whole situation from the balcony, sari pressed to her nose. She ordered us girls to go downstairs to help people. I can still remember her going from room to room, banging on the doors. 'Ei, tora kaaj bondho kor! Nichey jetey hobey! Kaaj bondho koro shobai!' Stop working, you girls! We have to go downstairs! Stop your work, everybody!

Sheyali starts to laugh quietly as she remembers this. 'One customer, this one man, was very angry, made the mistake of shouting at Mashi through the door. She just went in and started slapping him until he ran out half clothed! *The country is burning and you can't stop fucking for two minutes!* – sorry, using that word, but that's how she was when riled up – once that man ran out, none of the others complained, many even got dressed and began helping with the wounded. A couple of them had finished and thought they would get a freebie because of all the commotion, but no, country burning or not, Mashi kept strict accounts and collected when they came next, whether it was a week later or a month! She was quite something, that woman!

'So, we began to pull injured people off the road. There was this one man, the can had hit him straight in the eye, I'm sure he lost that eye, and then all the others, some just had their limbs broken in the pile-up of the crowd, can you imagine? Like what happens at Kumbh Mela or Ganga Sagar sometimes – a mountain of people collapses on you and there is no escape!

'It was only later that we heard the sound of the serious firing over all the shouting, *dhai, dhai, dhai!* And then it didn't stop, like they usually did after firing one or two rounds, sometimes firing in the air. This time, it continued, and from the screams we knew they weren't just firing in the air. *Dhai, dhai, dhai! Dhai, dhai, dhai!* When it continued, we knew this trouble wasn't going to pass so quickly. No, we just knew it wasn't.'

Sheyali's eyes escape her for a moment, go wandering elsewhere. Radhuni's snores change pitch on the tape, becoming more laboured, as if she was listening to us in her sleep or seeing the same scene in her dreams.

'You know, I want to say that everything changed after that day, or after the next day when people actually began to die in the police firing – by some miracle, no one actually died that day of the first protest, 13th August, but no, the customers kept coming, and we did everything the same way, bed, khatir, eating drinking, singing, everything.

'It's only later you realize that that day was the beginning of a kalyug. The trouble continued for two months, erupting again and again in different parts of the city, in different regions of Bengal, like a fever travelling over different parts of a body. Just as the trouble subsided, there was the cyclone on the coast, at the time of Pujo, in October, devastating everything. Right after that, the bombs dropped. Must have been a gap of a month at least, the Japanese planes came in December but it feels like it was right after the cyclone, and the cyclone right after the Quit India fighting. The Japanese came, just four–five days, and maybe only three bombs actually hit the city, the rest were on the docks, but everyone who had come back after running away in January 1942 started to leave again.' Sheyali gives off a small laugh. 'You know, we spoke a lot of Hindi in those days, because we had at least as many Marwari and bhaiya clients as Bangalis, you know, also some Punjabis, some Sardars and Sindhis, but after that January, for about a year and a half, we hardly spoke anything but Bangla. Everyone who had somewhere to run away to ran away, you understand?

'The hotel, too, changed, Great Eastern. Suddenly it was taken over by the Markin and entry was restricted. They preferred the Anglo girls and the chinky ones from Nepal and NEFA, those stupid white Markin officers, so no chance for us deshi girls. And, maago, did those girls make money! And chocolate and those, what do you call them, stockings, silk and nylon, and tins of their Markin funny food! People talked to Barbora, the manager, on our behalf but there was nothing he could do. It was, how do you call it, a *monopoly*, for the Anglo and chinky girls. Barbora would send us customers, to come here, but as for going to the hotel, with the air conditioning and those nice bathrooms, forget it!

'It felt as if all of Calcutta was one big whorehouse, you know, with places coming up here and there. Who knew the city had so many whores and so many brothels? They came up suddenly! Ripon Street, official place for the Ingrej "lower ranks", places in Free School Street for the other forces, special houses in Sonagachhi for the Africans, different places for the American Negroes, one fancy house in Russell Street for all the British officers. There was no end, we couldn't tell whether they were here to fight or to... do, you know? And, as if all this was not enough, the soldiers were also jumping on any woman they could find on the streets. Not until 1945 did we go back again to Great Eastern, and then it wasn't the same.

'So, the bombs drop. People leave in hordes. And then, just as we are catching our breath, the real thing starts.'

It's only when she reaches out and strokes my cheek that I realize she's crying. There is a sliver of panic, where I run through a checklist in my mind: I have both the paintings safely with me. I have paid them what they asked. My ticket back to Paris is ready to be picked up at Sita Travels in Camac Street. There is nothing she could possibly want from me now, nothing she could gain from...

'You sweet baby boy, you weren't even born then, how can I even explain to someone like you? You know, we women who are in this... profession... we grow a way of looking at ourselves, at our own bodies. Sometimes we look at our bodies from a distance, as if they are precious instruments, a tool that will feed us and our children, and we tend to our bodies, take care of them the best we can.' The tears are now shaking out of her. 'After that time, after those two-three years of the famine, you know, some of us could not bear to eat too much, we could not bear to look at our too well-fed bodies...'

HOME SAFE

She realizes she is very hungry.

'Darling! I've been frantic—'

The clang of the gates shutting have brought her mother out into the portico.

'It's all right, Mummy! I got a lift home! I'm absolutely fine.' Imogen strides over and gives her mother a peck on the cheek.

'Papa called, he was terribly worried as well. The whole place up in flames and you nowhere to be found! I'd better telephone him. Or you might.' The worry drawer is shut, the annoyance drawer pulled open.

'Would you call him? I'm desperate for a quick shower. This heat—'

'Where *were* you, darling?' Her mother follows her into the hallway.

'Silly me. I chose today of all days to go to Chowringhee.' Imogen goes into the pantry and opens the refrigerator, looking for a bottle of water. 'I wanted to buy film for my camera, but everything, simply everything, was shut. Luckily, a friend saw me just as the trouble was starting. Very kindly drove me home, so no mishaps, Mummy dear. You can tell Papa his daughter's home safe.'

'You didn't get caught up...?' She hands Imogen a glass.

'A bit. Masses of people pelting down Dharmatolla Street and then around that cinema, Metro, but we left before the tear gas—'

'Tear gas! Heavens!'

'I only caught a whiff, Mother.' Imogen gulps down the water and fills the glass again. 'Quite ghastly stuff. But we were away before it—'

'Darling! What on earth is *that*? You aren't bleeding, are you? Is that blood?'

She looks down at her dress where her mother is pointing. There is a shiny line of green just below her waist on the right. At first she's alarmed, wondering where she might have caught the wound and how blood could be turning green, but then she lifts the dress and smells it.

'No... Mummy! No heart attack please – it's just paint! Oil paint!'

'Are you sure?'

'Yes, Mummy, look, blood can't be green, can it? Not even *my* blood! It's the friend who gave me a lift. Luckily spotted me in the middle of the crowds. He was carrying some tubes of oil paint in his hand. One must have split when we were running to his car.'

'He drove you back, this chap? Who's he, again?'

'A friend, Larry Lahiri, friend of Andrew's actually, very nice chap from the Tennis Club.'

'Oh? A local fellow?'

'Quite. Little Bengali chap, but if you closed your eyes, you'd think he was—'

Her mother turns away, the matter closed. 'I'd better go and phone your father.'

'Yes, do stand him down before he sends out the cavalry.'

Her mother stops in her tracks, turns, irritation drawer falling right out of the desk. 'Really, Imogen! It's not a matter for hilarity! Papa's been at Governor House all morning, with Sir Herbert and all the rest of them. He's got quite enough on his plate without having to worry about his—'

'– errant, vagabond daughter.' Imogen liberates a stick from her mother's tin of 555s on the telephone table. 'Yes, I know, I know. Please tell Papa I'm *so* sorry, I had obviously no idea all these processions were going to... Where are the matches, Mummy?'

Her mother hands the matchbox to Imogen before speaking into the phone. 'Governor House, extension 12, please.' After a pause, 'Yes, good afternoon, may I please speak to Mr Jonathan Snell? This is Mrs Snell speaking... yes, Mrs Snell... Oh, hello, Captain, yes, look, I wouldn't want to disturb, so may I leave a message? Yes, thank you, please tell him his daughter is home safe. Precisely, our daughter's back and she's fine, yes, thank you so much.'

In the shower, as the lukewarm water needles over her, Imogen remembers coming home after her attempt to follow Tagore's funeral procession. It's only just over a year ago, but it feels as though five years have passed since then. There was a hatred of Calcutta when she first came, and a boredom with the place that she finds very difficult to imagine now. Even with Andrew gone, the city feels as if it's hers, hers and Andrew's, their place, and this makes it more than bearable. Even in her missing of Andrew she realizes that she has not known him anywhere else, and she can't imagine what it would be like to miss him in any other place. Last August, she hardly knew any Indians. But now, between Niru and this Kedar Lahiri, she almost feels as if she has entered a few local circles. It's as if she's grown a new skin, an armoured one that inures her to people's staring, and she realizes that spending time with Niru has helped a lot in this regard. Without ever making it obvious, Niru protects her, creating a shield with her looks, with the language of her body, and for this Imogen is grateful.

Downstairs, the garden is a disorderly traffic jam of different green growing things. The gin and tonic makes her mouth feel sharp and alert, the glass cold in her hand. It's as if she has jumped through space and landed on another planet, galaxies away from the cauldron of Chowringhee and its pall of fear and tear gas.

She wonders if the plants are exactly the same in Burma, if the tree trunks twist in the same sinuous ways over there, if the air weighs down with the same monsoon heaviness as here. Where has she seen these greens before? Nowhere. She has never seen them other than in Calcutta. The paintings of Gauguin and Le Douanier Rousseau sort of remind her of this garden, or vice versa, but the greens and yellows and the unlikely plants and flowers are not the same, and someone needs to do them justice in paint. Maybe some artists are painting them, grappling with their forms and colours with intensity, but a sweet fop like Kedar Lahiri is unlikely to be one of them, him with his eyes starry about Van Gogh, Monet and Cézanne.

'Darling? Did I mention that I've heard from Uncle Hugh?' Her mother is sitting at a desk just inside the living room that looks out on to the rear veranda.

'No, Mummy, you haven't! Is he all right, then?'

'Yes, all seems fine, I've just had a letter and it's pretty recent. He's back in port, wherever, been there for a few days now, it seems. They did have a U-boat attack on the way back from Russia, but luckily his destroyer wasn't involved.'

'Right. Good-oh! When does he go back, can he say?'

'Not really, but I get the feeling he's home for a while.'

'Oh, that's wonderful, Mummy.'

'Yes, it is, isn't it? These moments of respite we get are so precious.'

Imogen goes back in and pours herself another drink.

'I keep remembering that summer with Uncle Hugh, when was it, '38? We had such fun, didn't we? He kept joking about the war that was coming, do you remember?'

'We did, yes, and the two of you drove the rest of us mad, speaking constantly in your infernal French accents.'

'Speaking of letters, Mummy, has Granny heard from Jean-Christophe recently? You did say some mail was trickling through via Portugal?'

'Not for a few months, no. But in the last letter, Granny did say everything with the cottage seemed fine, as much as it can be under the circumstances.'

'Well, at least the Vichy French are not the Germans.'

'No, and Pétain it seems is—'

The peal of the telephone interrupts from the hallway.

'I'll get it. It must be Papa.'

'No, let me speak to him, darling. I need to discuss some things and he may not have a lot of time.' Her mother is up already, and Imogen turns away to look at the garden again.

Perhaps, after the war, if she and Andrew manage to... No, it's tempting fate even to think of the phrase 'perhaps, after the war'...

there's a lot of war still left, a lot of waiting and hoping still to do, and she had better pace herself.

'Darling?' Her mother is back, worry drawer open again, quizzical drawer half open underneath. 'It's for you. A Lieutenant Colonel Todd… Cartwright asking for you.'

The glass develops a life of its own and slides out of Imogen's hand. She doesn't hear it smash as she moves towards the phone.

3

HEADACHE

By the time Gopal reaches the river, it's quarter past seven in the evening. Gaurango's man drops him off at the river near Metiabruz and asks for further instructions.

'Just take the motorcycle back now. Do you have enough petrol?'

'Yes, Gogai-da, just about enough. The two trips ate up a lot...'

'I know. Just go straight back to the garage.'

Gopal's phone call meant the motorcyclist had come all the way from the dock area to Wellesley Street with a replacement driver. He'd then picked up the injured fellow, taken him to a doctor, and then come back to get Gopal. Driving slowly through the streets in the blackout, the side of his stomach sore from the big injection, each bump sending pain through his bandaged leg, Gopal had the strange feeling that he was no longer in Calcutta but in some other place altogether.

By the evening, people have dispersed from the processions. No curfew has been imposed yet, but the city has taken on the air of a ghost town. Every now and then, Gopal thinks he can smell a whiff of tear gas, some residual stink of cordite, but he knows he's imagining this.

The route they took from the centre to the bend of the river at the city's south-western edge was circuitous, circumventing the vast, fenced-off military area around Fort William, the Maidan, the racecourse and Victoria Memorial, while also avoiding the main roads where they heard police and military checkposts were stopping vehicles for spot checks, looking for political troublemakers carrying arms and explosives. Near Kalighat, he stiffened upon hearing the clip-clop of horses. Looking down a side street, he saw a jhurrie-gaadi rattling away, no driver visible. The hair stood on his hands, but he asked the driver to stop. Looking again, he just made out the bump of a head, clearly a kid, someone's assistant driving the carriage. With the engine off, a pack of dogs came out, barking and howling at them, stopping only when the motorcycle was out of their territory. Crossing a big road west of

Alipur, Gopal saw two armoured cars stationed in the distance and then understood they were guarding the Mint. By the time they reached the river, the rain had sharpened from the drizzle that accompanied them most of the way.

As the motorcycle thuds away, a man with a half-covered torch comes forward from the dark gully leading to the riverbank.

'Gogai-da? This way.' He holds out a closed umbrella which Gopal refuses. The man leads the way down to the bobbing cluster of moored pleasure-boats. As they cross the narrow decks, the wood underfoot is slimy and slippery, swollen from several weeks of heavy rain. From every direction come ambushes from different water smells and, from boat to boat, the aroma of food being cooked, the unoons now kept strictly under the covered portions because of the black-out. Beyond the boats sits the launch, its hull a harder black against the ghost grey shift of the dark river.

When he briefly takes his eyes off his feet, looking up across the wide water Gopal can see the gloom on the other bank punctuated at regular intervals by the dirty white smudges of barrage balloons pulled down for the night. He has heard somewhere that they take them down at night and in the rain because the things are great conductors of lightning. To Gopal, they look like rotting, oversized vegetables lurking in black leafage, painted by someone who's lost all sense of proportion. Flecks of rain sting Gopal's eyes. A boat horn calls out across the water. A launch cuts slowly by, the craft eerie without any lights. There is a small temple on this near bank, and he can hear the evening kirton coming from it. The sound of the prayer and bells from the darkened dome send shivers down his spine.

'Achcha, Gogai-da, I'll go?'

Gopal realizes he's standing on the last boat, right next to Ustad's launch.

'Yes, go.' Gopal raises his good leg and hauls himself up on the launch deck. Two men help him up.

'Aha! So our lame soldier has finally made it back to the camp! Come, come!' Looking at the dark doorway, Gopal can only see the glint of Ustad's teeth.

Down in the cabin, the double curtains drawn behind them, Gopal's eyes adjust to the throw of the three hurricane lamps. Ustad sees Gopal looking around for other people and laughs again.

'It's a busy time, Gogai-babu. You're not the only one who's had a difficult day.'

'No, Ustad, I just wondered where everybody was. I'm sure there's a lot of work.'

'Sit. Tea?'

Gopal shakes his head. 'I've had a lot of tea today, it's all right. I just wanted to tell you—'

'Yes, yes, I want to hear. But maybe you could do with something a bit stronger than tea, no?'

'I don't understand, Ustad.'

The old man reaches behind him and brings forth a bottle and a glass. 'Ei!' he calls up to the deck. 'Get a matka of water down here!'

A man comes down carrying a clay pot and a brass ladle. He places it near Ustad and goes off.

'Rum? You know what rum is, don't you?'

'Yes, Ustad, but I—'

'It's all right, Gogai. No need to be shy in front of your Ustad. You think I don't know you've developed a taste for alcohol? You think I expect you to transport so many different kinds of bottles and not taste anything?' Gopal avoids looking at Ustad, but the old man can see him trying to work out if there are any traps here. 'It's all right. If I'm offering it, you can have a drink in my presence. You can even smoke. You're big now, all grown up, and I need to talk to you.'

'Ustad, I can listen without—'

'I'd prefer you to listen with. I'd like to see if you can concentrate properly on what I'm saying while drinking and smoking like a grown-up man. Which is what I now need you to be. Take that child-Gogai you still hide behind and throw him in the river. His time has passed. He is dead.'

Gopal sees Ustad pour a hefty measure of rum into a large, cheap, ribbed glass and then top it up with water from the pot. The old man pushes the glass towards him and leans back. 'Use the coconut shell over there for your cigarette ashes, don't burn my boat down.'

Ustad spreads a small piece of cloth on the wood and reaches for the box where he keeps his smoking stuff. Gopal has only seen him do this a few times before, and he realizes it has happened either when the old man is very relaxed or has something very important to discuss. Utsad takes out a chillum from the box and places it on the cloth. Then he unwraps the paper around a rock of charas, breaks off a piece and sticks a small skewer into it. With the other hand, the old man flicks open a silver lighter and holds it under the skewered piece. There is a sharp assault of hashish as the sap catches. The nugget is briefly allowed to burn before the old man crumbles it and packs it into his chillum.

'Drink! Don't get ideas about trying my intoxication. It won't suit you.'

'No, Ustad, I was just marvelling at how skilfully you—' The old man stares at Gopal, forcing him to pick up his glass and take a very small sip. The chillum is lit, and pungent smoke creates a halo around the old man's head. Gopal has never seen anyone but Aurangzeb smoke in front of Ustad. He waits for the old man to take another pull before taking out his own cigarettes.

'So! A lot of people out on the streets today. Thousands. The mamas must have been very scared.'

'Yes.'

'And when they get scared, they go crazy. I'm told there were the usual lathicharges and tear gas? But this time there was also shooting? No one seems to have died yet, but that's only a matter of time.'

'No one died? The one man I saw them beating up, I wouldn't have given much for him being alive.'

'No reports yet. Of course they could be hiding it, but tomorrow, once their bullets find a few people, there will be no hiding place for them.'

'Yes, I think people will be out again tomorrow. It felt, I don't know, like just the beginning of something...'

'It is, it is. And not just in Kalkatta. They may not allow the papers to tell us, but I'm sure it's happening all over the country.' Ustad hawks into a brass bowl kept for the purpose. 'So tell me, what happened with the van today?'

Gopal recounts the whole thing, including his short conversation with the driver about rice. When he describes the flag getting entangled with the policemen's heads, Ustad starts laughing.

'Remember what I'm saying, Gogai. That tricolour flag is going to keep coming down on all our heads for a long time to come. Not just on these horse-riding cockroaches, but on all of us, mark my words!'

'Ustad, what about this Pakistan business?'

The old man stops laughing. He looks away and sighs. 'Gogai, how old are you now?'

'Ustad? You know better than I do, but maybe twenty-two?'

Another boat horn calls across the water. Ustad waits for the wake to elbow their launch and die out before continuing. 'All right, let's say you're twenty-two. And you've been with me since you were about nine or ten, yes?'

'Yes.'

'So, you should have learnt a few things about life, hain? Now, have you ever seen two Marwari businessmen bargaining in Barabajar? You have, yes? So what are the basic things about bargaining? The things that any bania child knows by the time he is ten? One, always offer less than you are willing to give, and always ask for more than you are willing to settle for, yes? Next, always let the other person think you have someone with a better offer just around the corner, even if this sauda, this deal, is your last chance to save your children from death, yes?'

'Yes.'

'Then, next, if the whole bargain is getting too focused in a way you don't want, what do you do?' Ustad gestures towards the glass. Gopal obediently takes a sip. 'You create a distraction to break that focus. So, for example, if you are arguing about the price for ten bolts of high-quality silk, you also bring into the discussion twenty bolts of rough-woven cotton, even though you have no interest in buying or selling cotton cloth, and say you will pay – or take – a lumpsum price for the silk and the cotton or whatever. Then, once your opponent has taken the bait, you gently start walking backwards in your bargaining, bringing both of you back to a different place than when you started the distraction. Do you understand?'

'Not completely, Ustad, but I'm trying—'

'Arre, that sisterfucker Jinnah is not a lawyer for nothing, and that too a Gujarati Khoja lawyer! Do you know what they say about the Khoja shopkeepers in Barabajar? That eight Khojas out of ten are honest and an honest Khoja is worth his weight in gold, but a crooked Khoja is more dangerous than the worst Marwari or Sindhi – he will convince you to drink poison as if it was your mother's milk.'

'So, this motherfucking Pakistan is just such a distraction! Like the twenty bolts of cotton! Look, there is no chance that the Ingrej will leave so soon, not unless the Japanese put a bamboo up their backside. Then, if and when they leave, they aren't going to just pack up one day and go away. Any zamindar about to sell his land squeezes his peasants and fields before he sells. Exactly like that, they will twist as much juice out of us as they can, and this will take years. A zamindar squeezing his land needs jotedars, foremen, who also benefit from the process, and the chief jotedar profits the most. Now Jinnah was a third-ranking sub-jotedar trying his luck to be one of the top ones by using this Pakistan gambit. That is what the sisterfucker *was*. Until about one week ago. Now, suddenly, one can't say. Unless the Japanese come in and kill all of these leaders, these chutiya Congress monkeys may have handed Jinnah half the power the Ingrej will distribute in the future. But don't worry, Pakistan is as likely to come about as... me turning vegetarian and putting on a brahmin's thread.'

The talk of becoming vegetarian reminds Ustad and he calls out to the curtains. 'Ei, how long before the food is ready?' 'Soon,' comes the reply and the old man loads another chillum. Gopal uses the pause to take a bigger gulp of his rum, still trying to work out what Ustad wants to talk about. He can really taste the rum now, and feel it too, as the alcohol sears through his stomach, reminding him that he hasn't eaten anything through the day except the two shingaras that Sheyali-di had got for him once the trouble died down. As the air fills with hashish smoke from the chillum, Gopal feels the pain coming back in his leg wound, sharp, but not as unpleasant as it was in the afternoon.

'Aurangzeb has made a new contact in the docks. This is someone who works for the Australian shipping people. You know they have troops here as well, from Australia and Nyujhiland, also some pilots in the Air Force. But not much coming from Australia in this direction. What is interesting is when those ships return from England or South Africa on their way to Australia, then there are electrical supplies, alcohol, other things that we can move. Aurangzeb has a list, in English, you should look at it tomorrow. See what we can dispose locally and what needs to go out to other parts of the country.'

'Yes, Ustad.'

'You know... Gogai, has it ever occurred to you? Those sisterfuckers also have ports, the southern ones in Vizag, Madras and Trivandrum, and also the big ones in Bombay and Karachi, yes?'

'Yes...'

'But how is it that I still supply to Bombay and Lahore from here? To Hyderabad?'

'How, Ustad?' Gopal is suddenly finding it hard to concentrate.

'Because... we are still the most important port in all of Asia! Earlier, there was us and Singapore, but now that Singapore is sitting in the air with a long Japanese bamboo up its backhole, it's only us! We get ships docking that the others don't get! We get all kinds of saman, a variety of goods that the others don't get! Now we even get the ships that would stop in Singapore... Ah! Bring it, bring it, our Gogai is dying of hunger!'

Two men bring in the food and put it between Ustad and Gopal, placing a copper thali in front each of them. One of the men starts to serve, but Ustad waves him away. 'We'll help ourselves, just keep the parathas and kababs coming.'

It's a meal typical of when the old man is happy: two or three kinds of kababs, rotis and parathas, with the main dish being the best mutton biryani Gopal has ever eaten until now, accompanied by raita. Some papad. No fripperies like dal or vegetables. Gopal waits for the boss to load his plate before serving himself, but once he starts eating, he eats almost feverishly. A cool wet breeze winds its way into the cabin from the curtained windows, and for a few minutes, Gopal allows himself to think he's in heaven.

Mid-meal, Ustad takes a bit of rice and meat in his fingers and holds it up towards Gopal.

'Listen, boy.'

Gopal's hand stops on its way to his mouth.

'You know, I've seen various unexpected things turning into gold across my life, cloth, jute, coal, different kinds of industrial metal, iron and steel, and medicine, especially when the last big war was ending and there were all these epidemics here, but I never thought I'd see the day when ordinary rice would become rare.' The old man waves the food in his hand and puts it in his mouth, chewing it slowly before speaking again. 'Gogai, it's about to happen. Two months, four months from now, we are going to have to become like a modi, selling rice to this hungry sisterfucking city.' Ustad takes a small bone out of his mouth and puts it on the pile already on his thali. 'There is going to be, *there already is*, a rice shortage. People are saying it's because the Burma rice has stopped coming, people are saying it's a temporary price hike that can happen in a war, you've heard all this, yes?'

'Yes, I have. Why, just today this fool driver was asking me—'

'Not a fool, Gogai, *not* a fool! There's a reason I've ordered you people to not discuss the rice shortage. But people are not fools, they are beginning to sense something is wrong, they just don't know how bad it's going to be and for how long!' The old man takes a swig of water from a glass. 'I'm telling you, from what I'm hearing, it's going to be very bad and it's not going to become all right too soon.'

'Is that so, Ustad?' Gopal stops himself from reaching for more food. He realizes yet again that he hasn't been called here just to eat and drink.

'Look, Aurangzeb can't see it, and neither can Gaurangzeb. They just don't believe there could be any serious money in dealing in coarse rice, but you have a fresher mind and I need you to understand what's happening. Because we will need to be prepared, be ready, well beforehand. We will need to be sitting *in* the compartment with tickets already bought, not trying to scramble on to the train with everybody else, fighting to get on as the gaadi steams away from the platform!'

Ustad gestures to Gopal, indicating he should continue eating. Gopal takes a few mouthfuls, but his appetite has lost its edge. He lifts his glass to drink but finds the rum is over. The old man asks him to hand over his glass and pours him another large drink. Then he starts to talk about plans, about how to procure rice and where to store it. Hoarding will be widespread, and when the crisis grows, the police will start to make raids.

'This is why we have to get into this business quickly and secure the best storage places, because the whole game is about making sure the rice doesn't rot while we wait for the price to go up. And you know... we will have competition. I've heard even Suhrawardy's men are suddenly talking to people who have decent godowns and warehouses. Imagine! Imagine what kind of profit people are smelling if the sisterfucking deputy chief minister of the Bengal state is looking to become a black marketeer!'

The light from the lanterns licks through Gopal's glass. His stomach feels very full, but his head feels strangely empty.

Ustad says he knows just the people for the job of storing the rice, two different Marwaris, one who has a goods depot north of the city near Rishra, and another who has a riverside godown in Howrah. There would be a different arrangement with each of them. Ustad lays out the details and Gopal tries to understand them, but his mind finds it difficult to grasp what is being said.

For a moment, Gopal feels the launch has left its mooring and started to move down the river, the rain drumming on the roof overhead and, through it, actually drumming on Gopal's head. He almost reaches out a hand to steady himself against the hull but stops just in time – it wouldn't do to let Ustad know that the combination of alcohol and hashish smoke has got to him.

'Gogai? Ei, Gogai? Where have you gone? Are you drunk?'

'No, Ustad! Just a bit tired, that's all.'

'Is your wound hurting?'

'No, Ustad, I was just thinking about rice... When I was a kid, back in the village in Khulna, for weddings we used to have boats filled with rice, whole boats of rice, dal, fish, meat, torkaari, all but the poorest families would manage this, at least for a wedding. And now to think...'

'Achcha? But wouldn't the pots break when the boats moved, wouldn't they knock into each other?'

'No, no, Ustad, no pots! People would clean the boats thoroughly and then pour the rice or dal or fish jhol right into the moored boats! Then they would bring the food to the meal in pots, like that... Wedding food would have that wet wooden boat smell, and the boats would smell of food and spices for days!'

Ustad shakes his head in wonder. 'You motherfucking Bengalis, I tell you, I will never stop being surprised by how many different ways you people fuck food!'

'It tasted nice, Ustad, trust me. It was the best food, fresh, pungent—'

'Dhut-teriki! Have some more rum!'

'No, Ustad, I've eaten, so I'm full. Can't drink after eating.'

'Hm. That is what Americans do, I've heard. They drink only after eating their dinner. While you're like the Ingrej and us desis, who will drink themselves stupid on an empty stomach but never drink after eating!'

'From what I've seen, Ustad, all these goras drink all the time. Day and night, before, during and after meals.'

The old man lights a bidi and listens to the hard knocking of the rain. Gopal tries to keep his eyes open, watching his glass move slightly with the gentle rocking of the boat.

Ustad lets out a long breath. 'You know... this rice is like a headache, it's like breathing giving you a headache. You can't avoid it, there's big money to be made, and you can't just let others make it while you sit with your hands under your arse. But you can't forget you are making this money because people are going to starve and others are going to be very afraid of starving.'

Gopal says nothing. Ustad gets up and slaps him on the shoulder. 'Go and sleep. I've told them to add a mattress in the other cabin. We can talk about this tomorrow.'

As Gopal lays down and pulls a sheet over himself, the wound reminds him it's there, but the pain is not unbearable. Soon, the American officer is taking care of it, taking off all of Gopal's clothes before putting on a new bandage. Then he kisses Gopal for a long time. It seems impossible for the rain to get harder, but it does, just as the Markin gently turns Gopal over. Gopal reaches behind him to find the Markin's big, sweet cock, his hand feels small as his fingers close around it, and he places it where

TOOFAN MAIL

He feels he can slide in, and after a moment's hesitation, he does. Keya's jaw snaps up, and her glasses loosen from her face and fall, first on the bed and then on to the floor. Kedar can make out that they haven't broken.

'Don't worry,' she's still working to control her breath, 'I can get new ones.' Her fingers tighten on his forearms. 'Don't stop.'

Kedar disobeys her, pausing while he's at the deepest point inside her. Freeing his right hand, he strokes away the hair from her face, some strands refusing to move, pasted on to her temples by sweat.

'We aren't the Toofan Mail, are we? This time we can take our time, can't we?'

'Oh, you cocksure bastard, you bloody cocksure bloody dandy – listen, is that *door bolted*—' the last two words turn into a moan as he pulls back and thrusts again, the starch of the crushed, pushed-up petticoat suddenly rough against his wrists, a completely different colour of touch from the extreme heat and the softness that rules the centre of his being.

Kedar is aware of the fan clanking above their heads like a witness, he can see Keya's upturned face in the dim hallway light coming through the half-open door, he can feel the rivulets of sweat running down the valley of his spine, the moisture mingling with his drenched shirt, running free where the cloth has puckered up, and he can now feel Keya entirely, her pleasure, her hesitation, her panic and her eagerness, everything gripping the rigid reduction into which his body is distilled.

He waits for her to push against him and pull away slightly, to start to tease him, and when this doesn't happen, he's confused. He realizes he has one hand near her mouth, waiting for her to bite and suck on his middle finger, and wonders why she hasn't done that yet. Then he remembers this is Keya and not Eva. That Eva is long gone. He moves his hand back to where he can support himself better and goes back to controlling their joint rhythm.

New day, he tells himself, new canvas of love, her skin very different, far smoother than Eva's, new marks, new challenges, she raises her head to kiss him, her tongue far less practised than – new confusions replacing the memory of old ones, his hand tugs at her sari, trying to remove it from her shoulder, Keya pushes herself up, helping him, his hand undoing her blouse hooks, reaching for her brassiere, fumbling as if he's a beginner again. The joy of realizing that, perhaps, he'll always be a beginner, an eternal novice at this.

She half sits up to help him get rid of her blouse and bra, he slides out momentarily, and then pushes back in before putting his mouth around her right nipple.

'Ei, eto jorey na!' Hey, not so hard, she laughs.

'Sorry, madam!' He eases up with his teeth and tongue, this is not, he is not with… Something different about making love in Bangla, or partly in Bangla, something deliciously shameful about it, yet something that fills his heart in a way the struggle with another's language can never do. They move awkwardly, first just him, and then, gradually, the movement twinning as she begins to respond. He lifts his head, and their eyes meet. Keya is smiling, her mouth made helpless by pleasure, her usual mask of hauteur fallen to the floor, somewhere next to her glasses. He thrusts again, also helpless, wanting to wait, to hold back. A rain-laden breeze ruffles through the trees outside, lifting the curtain from the bars on the window. An electric storm spikes through his body, her fingers tight again on his arms, her gasp in his ear as he suddenly pulls out of her, the smell of the talcum powder on her skin, his nostrils against hers, the taste of her mouth very different from when they began.

'Tumi – tui – ki…?'

'Hyan, I'm afraid so. Couldn't...'

'Wait? But I didn't want you to, I'm happy like this.'

'But...'

'But what?' Her voice is tender, slightly muffled by his hair. 'I'm not like all those foreign women, Kedar Lahiri, reaching climax in seconds. We are not on the Toofan Mail, are we? It will happen when it does. In the meantime, I'm happy like this.'

They lie there, him collapsed on top of her, their stomachs breathing against each other in mismatching undulations. He thinks of just disconnected jigsaw pieces: joined together, separated by fleeting doubt, about to be re-connected. His breathing deepened by the exertion, he inhales her, all of her, capricious, cactus-tempered, quick-witted, lavender-powdered, ruled by prejudices, fundamentally generous, in the corners of her warmth the faint lurking of sweat. His eyes are shut and he feels the two bodies almost as if he is a third being formed from the conjunction of limbs and breath. They lie there, a whole different contraption from himself and Eva, a new device not quite correctly assembled yet, but with the full possibility that it will work again and function better.

Outside, the rain begins to come down – an actor entering on cue. Keya starts, pushes him off and sits up, all the languorousness gone.

'The windows!' She leans over to the floor, eyes slightly unfocussed. Kedar finds her spectacles for her. Standing up, they both hesitate: clothes first or the windows? Most of the windows are shut for the blackout, but they've opened a couple to let in some air. Kedar is able to move quicker, and he goes off to the kitchen, buttoning his trousers. Once he secures the windows, Keya switches on the lights. She stands at the dining table, lights a cigarette, and pushes the packet towards him. He wants to put his arms around her again, but he can see she has moved into a different mood.

'Listen, Dandy, what should we do about the sheets?'

'The sheets?'

'Yes, you fool, the sheets on Roma's bed, we can't just leave them there!'

'Oh, damn. The sheets.'

Quickly, they run through the various options. They could soak them, but then why have they put both sheet and bed cover to wash? And at this point on a rainy day? When are the others coming back? Keya is not sure, but she thinks Nirupama was going to her parents' in Shyambajar and Titir was going to meet relatives in Howrah. Roma was supposed to rendezvous briefly with Keya at Wellington Square, but Keya couldn't find her. If at all, Roma would be the only one coming back here tonight. She is party to this dalliance, she just doesn't know the full extent of it – and Keya would like to keep it that way.

'I've got it!' Kedar smiles. 'We'll spill some tea! Rasko says if you spill tea on the bed you have to soak the sheets immediately, otherwise the stains don't go.'

'Not bad, Kedar Lahiri. Clearly this... activity... has got your brain to start working!'

'Yes, like, like you know that crank we put into the engine when the car won't start? Like that!'

'Well, that should be me, then, shouldn't it?'

Laughing, they fall into each other's arms, but after a moment she pushes him away.

'I'd better make the tea.'

'Yes, she might be back any moment.'

'Tell me, I don't suppose you know how to make tea, do you?'

'Of course I know how to make tea! I mean... I know the general principles of tea-making quite thoroughly, but...'

'You know, they guillotined people like you in the French Revolution, and for good reason.' Keya moves to the kitchen counter, searching for the tea things. In a minute, she has the stove on and water on the boil.

'See? I knew that! I know you first have to boil water!'

'And then?' Keya adjusts her glasses like a schoolteacher. 'Tell me. In order for us to stain the sheets properly, what kind of tea do we require?'

'Er... what do you mean?'

'Do we need Ingreji tea, with some faint trace of Darjeeling leaf? Will that do the trick?'

'Umm…'

'Or do we need proper boiled deshi tea, with milk, and possibly sugar, for complete realism? If the latter, then how do you make that?'

Kedar watches as Keya drops a large amount of tea dust into the boiling water, adds milk and sugar, and lets the mixture turn a solid brown, lifting the pan and returning it to the fire as he has seen chaa-wallas do on the street. They pour the tea into two cups, criminals attending to detail, overturn one on the bedcover and sheet before quickly yanking it off the mattress, and then find a bucket for soaking. There is enough tea left over to actually drink, just about a cup each. The rain now smashing down full orchestra, they sit a polite distance across the dining table and sip their chaa. After a while, Kedar reaches into the satchel he has hung on the chair.

'Do you think it's all right to have a drink here? I've brought along some whisky.'

'Titir's not coming back, so it should be fine. She's the only one who wrinkles her nose. But perhaps we should wait until Roma gets back. Let's wait for a bit anyway, it's only seven o'clock.'

Kedar puts the bottle on the table and pulls out his sketchbook and pencil case. He takes out a pencil and starts to absently make marks on a fresh page. Keya goes into her own thoughts while she smokes, and watches the black paper and crossed tape vibrating on the panes as the rain thrashes the windows from outside. As her profile becomes steady, Kedar's lines find firmer purchase and the sound of the lead going across the paper changes, to contrapunt against the beat of the rain.

'Ei, Dandy-lion?'

'Hyan, ki?' He glances up and looks down again.

She keeps looking at the windows, as if speaking to someone else. 'Today was the third time, no?'

He looks up and nods, his eyes in a question.

She continues, 'First time, Short Street, April, where vain but innocent Miss Dutta gives up her honour in exchange for a portrait. Second time at Palm Avenue, was it already a month ago?'

'Yes, a little more than a month. But what are you getting at, exactly?'

'Second time better than the first time, third time better than the second time, it has to be said, so this could become an addiction, couldn't it?'

'Yes, hopefully, so?' Kedar remains unsure of what to say or not say.

'But what does it mean? Does it mean anything? How many more times do you think we'll make love?'

'Er – what—'

'Now, don't say stupid things about forever and eternal love and all that rubbish. It doesn't suit you.'

'What do you mean it doesn't suit me? Do you think I'm incapable of serious—'

'Serious feelings? Perhaps, we don't know, we may find out. For now, I just think you should wear your shallowness with pride.'

'Thanks.' Kedar lights another cigarette while glaring at Keya. 'Thanks, I'll keep that in mind.'

She hasn't meant to hurt him. The impulse was to speak her mind, to ask the questions that have bubbled up. She gets up, looks through the kitchen cupboards and finds two glasses. 'They won't have ice here, we'll have to make do.'

'It's all right, I'm shallow enough to drink whisky without ice.'

'The water should be cold, though.' She pours two drinks and tops them up with water from a sirahi. She hands him his glass and leans on the edge of the table where she's right over him.

'Cheers, Mr Lahiri.'

'Cheers.' He clinks glasses, takes a swig, puts down the glass and goes back to his drawing, all without looking up. The clay of the sirahi has absorbed the monsoon air, and the water is indeed cold. She puts her hand in his hair and tugs gently.

'Look at me.'

He looks up, still baleful.

'Ei, shono, listen, you know I was joking about shallow and all that, yes?'

'Hm.' Her fingers still in his hair, he takes another sip and looks up again. His face lights up with a grin. 'As long as you don't call me shallow in all matters.'

She pushes his head away in mock revulsion. 'You animal. It's still hurting... there... but not in a bad way.'

'It gets better with practice.' He bites his tongue, but five words too late. 'I believe,' he adds lamely. There's a split moment where she almost flings her glass in his face, but she stops herself and whirls away. He starts to get up, expecting to chase her to the main door, but Keya merely goes back to her chair.

'I'm sorry, Keya, I didn't mean to, I shouldn't have said – what I mean is—'

'It's perfectly all right. You did inform me that you have had some... practice... in this previously.' All the softness has gone from her face.

'I just meant...'

'I know. The more often we do it, the better it should get. I understand.'

Kedar is bankrupt of useful words. He finds himself drumming his pencil on the edge of the table. Keya's voice is flat. 'So, I never asked you. How was it, with that Polish mem?'

'Latvian.'

'Oijey same thing, Evelyn the Slav, the one you were, um, sharing with Krishen Wahi and god knows how many others. How was it with her?'

Kedar kicks himself again for telling Keya about Eva. It had slipped out the last time, in Palm Avenue. Lying in his bed, Keya had needled him again about chasing the much sought after 'Bulgarian mem' and he had felt obliged to reveal that he hadn't exactly failed in his chase. The noise of Rasko returning from the bajaar had electrified them out of bed, and he has avoided providing further details since then. Later, he was hit with the realization that Judge Dutta's legendary forensic skills as a barrister had passed down to his daughter. Keya had sensed something more between Kedar and Eva from the outset and, gently, using pride as bait, she had reeled him in like the stupid male fish he was. An attendant realization: new to this or not, Keya was clearly less affected by the so-called 'afterglow' than he was, and had deliberately used the state of bliss to trap him into confessing.

'Well, you know, what can I say?' Kedar tries to go back to his sketching.

'I'm sure you can say a lot.' Keya goes and opens half a window. 'And don't try and hide behind some gentlemanly etiquette. I'm sure you've shared copious details with that ghastly uncle of yours, your beloved Borun-kaku, so why spare me now?'

'Borun-kaku! I'd never tell him anything! He's so... he's so *inept*, he becomes so ridiculous around women that it's embarrassing! If he even *sees* me with some fema—'

'He starts dancing the khemta naach, yes, I noticed the other day at the club.'

'Exactly.'

'But you, Kedar Lahiri, cool cucumber Casanova of Calcutta, are a different kettle of fish entirely, aren't you? So how *was* it with that woman?' Keya seems to be enjoying the cross-examination. She reaches across for his glass and pours another drink for both.

'Well... I can hardly remember, it was just a couple of, you know, once or twice, a couple of occasions.'

'Oh? Is that what you'll say about me? Twice or thrice, so unmemorable you can hardly recall?'

Kedar remembers Keya's been at the protest meeting and hasn't eaten all day. Some food would cushion the whisky.

Keya continues, 'And, if you're to be believed, that you didn't lose your... innocence... on some visit to Sonagachhi, then your dalliance with this hot, east European pie was your first time, am I right?'

'I've never been to Sonagachhi. I don't visit prostitutes. And Latvia is *not* in eastern Europe, it's one of the Baltic—'

'So how could you forget about her so easily?'

Suddenly, Kedar remembers returning home from dropping Imogen, not wanting lunch, and asking Rasko to make him a ham sandwich to bring along. He pulls out the packet and puts it close to Keya.

'Sandwich. Ham sandwich. Khabey?'

'Oh yes! I'm quite hungry!' Keya extracts a thick triangle and bites into it. Her mouth engages with the bread and meat for a bit, but then she continues, 'So? You were saying? About this Latvian lady?'

His mouth full of sandwich, Kedar shakes his head. He wasn't saying anything at all.

'You'd better not have picked up something from her, Kedar. I can't afford to have—'

'Do stop talking nonsense! What do you take me for?'

'I don't know what I'm doing with you, really. You're not much better than these soldiers you know, these GIs and Tommies.'

'What? Are you saying I've molested you?'

'No, I meant besides the molesting and actual rapes, these creatures are also going around in gangs to various, you know, houses of ill repute. Who was it who was saying, was it Baba? No, Roma, in fact, that there is a real concern about venereal dis—'

'Keya! I have not visited any houses of ill repute! And she was *not* a prostitute!'

'Yes, well, that's what you'd like to believe, I suppose.'

'And anyway, she left nine months ago!'

'Leaving our poor Dandy heartbroken, one can see.'

'Well, I admit I was quite upset just after she left. You see, the passion was quite mutual, I'm sure of that, and I thought we were—'

The look in Keya's eyes stops him mid-sentence.

'Kedar Lahiri. Do you think I want to hear about your passion, as you call it? I have *no* wish to know sordid details of your past, thiik achhey?'

Kedar feels as if a far superior player has coaxed him through a rally, all the way to one side of the court, before leaving him looking foolish with a precise shot into the other corner. Suddenly, all the pleasure of the lovemaking has disappeared. He finds himself wishing Roma would return so that they can say their hello-goodbye and leave. He goes back to sketching, but starts a new one of window bars with rain on the dark neem tree outside, trying to catch the argument of highlights from the bulb in the kitchen and some other illumination also breaking the blackout from nearby.

Keya has opened up her diary. Sandwich in one hand, she's making some calculations with a pen. Something in her demeanour makes Kedar flip back the page and go back to his drawing of her. Her mouth is now pursed, and this annoys him slightly; he makes a quick sketch of this new mouth on the left page and goes back to the main drawing.

'Today is 13th August. The Red Army departed yesterday. So... twenty-eight days, give or take one or two...' Keya looks up and smiles. 'We can keep meeting here, but you can next have your way with me only between the 9th and 12th of September. Mone rekho, don't forget to mark your calendar.'

It's as though their exchange has never occurred, the acid from her side completely washed away, gone with the subsided rain. He takes a moment to fully grasp what she is saying, double-checking to make sure he's not stumbling into another faux pas.

He smiles back. 'Red Army. Ah. Do your friends know you refer to your, er, monthlies, as the Red Army? How does Comrade Nirupama feel about that?'

'No, heavens no! Of course Niru doesn't know! But that's what Roma and I both call them. It's just between us. Don't you ever dare...'

'Yes, since I regularly discuss menstruation with your female friends, I must be careful not to let this slip, yes.'

She throws the last crust of the sandwich at him. 'Keep quiet! You know what I mean! Not the others, but you might start joking with Roma some day and—'

'Yes, yes... You haven't noticed, but I'm very careful around Roma, very careful not to go into certain areas, even though we like to joke about many things.'

'I did notice you were quite scared of her, yes. Always on your best behaviour.'

'No. I'm on my best behaviour around Titir and Nirupama, not around Roma.'

'That's true, actually.'

'Tell me, do those two have any sense of humour at all? I've never really seen them, you know, let their hair down, so to speak.'

'You want Titir and Niru to let their hair down for you?' Kedar continues to draw without replying. Keya gets up and starts to walk up and down along the dining table as if trying to work out a mathematical equation. Her tone changes. 'No, well, I do like Niru. I think she can be quite funny, but that's around us girls. Around strangers, I think she's a little shy, no, reserved – reserved is a better word. She takes time to make up her mind, she's… cautious, but once she's decided something I think she's fearless, even more so than Roma. Actually, I don't know if I like Niru, it's more that I admire her. She has a tremendous ability to concentrate, and both Roma and I suspect she's one for the long course, not one to get easily derailed.'

'My god, surely that's a lot to read into someone who hardly speaks?'

'Oh, she speaks, Dandy, she speaks, just not around your type of people. I don't agree with all the communist thinking, but she doesn't often spout Party line. I keep getting the sense she has something the rest of us don't have. That Titir is too impulsive, too beautiful, too aware of how beautiful, and she's not an intellectual at all. Roma is the opposite, too… cerebral. Everything is from here.' Keya taps her head.

'Am I an intellectual? Do I give any indication that I'm capable of thought… or am I just a male Titir?' As Keya bursts out laughing, Kedar wishes he hadn't been drinking so quickly.

The girl's mirth shades from derisive to loving, and she comes around and cradles Kedar's head, pulling it into her chest. 'No, my Dandy Zemindear, reading a few books doesn't get you the license to be called intellectual. But you *are* quite intelligent in your own way, much more so than Titir, and you contribute… other things, shall we say?'

'Such as?' Kedar's voice is muffled, but she can feel him laughing against her breasts. She moves away and finds the cigarette packet.

'Such as, how can I put it?' She takes her time to light the cigarette. 'You… infect me with the possibility of joy. And I don't mean just all this…' She waves her hand over herself and towards Roma's room. 'I mean, when I'm with you, the way you are, the way you take enjoyment in everything, *from* everything, like a zamindar extracting maximum tax from his peasants, I mean *that*.'

Kedar tries to be offended, but he can't help the grin. 'That sounds like communist thinking.'

Keya doesn't respond to the joke. Her cigarette has gone out and she lights it again. Kedar find the glow of the match in her thinking eyes very beautiful.

'So, is your Ma happy she got that painting back? The palm trees?' The cross-examination is back in her voice.

'I'm sure she is. But she won't show it, it's not in her nature.'

'Well, at least I could put that thing on my wall without attracting comment. The portrait...'

'What about it? You can't put it up?'

'No, Kedar, I can't, I couldn't. It says too much. It's as if I'm unclothed in that picture and you're looking at me fully naked. I had to hide it.'

'But... but I worked so hard on painting that sari!'

'It's a little bit of sari and a lot of face. And neck. The sari might as well not be there. It's as though the painter knows what I'm – what I look like without the sari.'

'But... but I didn't! Not fully, not when I painted it!'

Keya starts laughing again. She starts to come to him but stops herself, shaking her head.

'Ohhh, Dandy, Dandy, whatever shall we do with you? *I worked so hard on painting that sari!*' She pulls up a chair next to him and sits down. He reaches for her hands and she pushes him away. 'Listen, shono, listen. It doesn't matter how hard you worked on painting that bit of sari, and the sliver of blouse and the suggestion of shawl, people can also see how lovingly you've painted the face, thiik achhey?'

'Oh. Yes, I see.'

'So. I hid the canvas behind my dressing table, a little to the side, turned to the wall. But two days ago, Ma decided to come in and oversee a thorough cleaning of my room while I was out.'

'Oh.'

'Yes.'

'So?'

'So she found it! Oita ki? What is that? And she could read your... bloody... stupidly cocksure signature also. *K. Lahiri '42*!'

'Oh!'

'Yes.'

Keya gets up and starts pacing up and down again. After a while, she prises open another window. 'I can't bear it in here, it's so stifling.'

'Careful, we don't want a warden coming here.'

'They can't see this house from the road. Too many trees, it's all right.'

'So, your Ma...'

'No, not my Ma, *your* Ma! What has she been saying about me to people?'

'What has she been saying? I don't know, but she told me your Baba said something to DR at Calcutta Club, something about me being a scoundrel. She was furious. She may have... retaliated somewhere. You know Ma.'

'No, I don't know Mrs Sukanya Debi Lahiri and I'm planning to keep it that way. I'm sorry about my Baba, but just as you can't control your mother, I can't control him either.'

'So, when your Ma found the portrait... is it still intact? Did she burn it?'

'No, she took a pair of large tailor's scissors and...'

'What?' Kedar almost doubles over.

'Typical, typical, Dandy. All you're concerned about is your little work of art! Never mind what happens to the poor subject!'

Kedar takes a swig of the whisky. Keya can see new sweat has broken out on his forehead and she takes pity.

'It's fine. The painting is fine. I snatched it back from her and made sure she didn't damage it. After all, I don't know how many painters will paint my portrait. Not many, I suspect.'

'Do stop fishing for compliments. What did she say?'

Keya doesn't answer him. 'Zemindear? If you were completely free and had no constraints of money, what would you like to do in life?'

'Why don't we go back to your question of how many more times we'll make love? That was easier.'

'Kedar, try and be serious for once.'

The rain has stopped, and the air is no longer that cool. He takes his time to answer. 'Well, I've always wanted to go and paint in the south of France. And maybe a bit here, the landscape around the Madras-

Pondicherry coast, I'm not sure why, maybe I just want to see those southern temples. And then perhaps spend some time in Mexico.' He runs out of steam. The future is obscure, but he doesn't see it as a problem or anything to be feared. He shuts the sketchbook and puts it on the table. 'What about you?'

'I'd like to stay here and work.'

'Work, maaney? What do you mean? Why would a girl like you need to work?'

'Work politically, I mean. There is a lot to be done.'

'Well, surely independence will come sooner or later? Say after the war, say they defeat the Japs and Germans, no guarantee, but say they do, and then a few years, so say in ten or twelve years. What then? What would you do afterwards?'

'If it does come, there will be a lot more to be done afterwards. In fact, much more than what we can do now.'

'I see.' He can tell she knows that he doesn't see at all.

He reaches for his sketchbook again, but suddenly Keya is there, leaning down towards him. Her lips prise open his mouth, her tongue learning quicker and quicker. After a while, he tries to pull her down on his lap but she pulls away, holding his head in both hands to keep it steady.

'Listen. You keep dreaming of Paris. I'll stay on this Toofan Mail.'

I get mugged by the cold as I come out of the airport terminal. I've only got on a light jacket that felt sweaty even to hold over my arm as I caught the flight from Dum-Dum. Bombay, where I changed over to the international flight, was the same: hot, cloyingly muggy, the jacket or any warm clothes making no sense whatsoever in the hothouse of the international terminal with its recalcitrant air conditioning. Outside Santa Cruz Airport, someone had blacked out a huge hoarding advertising Indira's twenty-point programme. Each of the twenty points was violently redacted using something very like tar. It was ugly, but no one had replaced the hoarding and it felt deliberate.

The flight was what it was, the stewardesses oscillating between racist and snobbish in a way only the French can manage, their service calibrated first to the colour of your skin and then to the quality of your clothes. The immigration at Roissy, now of course named after that sulky vulture de Gaulle, was the usual hurdle: first the look reserved for the Republique's colonial subjects, then the surprise at the Indian passport and my identity card that verifies me as a junior professor at Nanterre, then a shrug – now I have seen everything, what is the world coming to? – and then the stamp on the page, like a second shrug.

In all this, I've forgotten to put on the sweater I'm carrying, one of Elko's oversized ones that Missus has given me. So, coming out of the terminal, the cold hits hard. Men, women, little dogs, cars, buses, everyone and everything is releasing smoke from their muzzles. The early morning spring chill is redolent with newly combusted gasoline.

I don't usually take taxis, but given that I'm carrying drawings in two heavy suitcases and a thick roll of paintings in my hand, I have no choice. Standing in the taxi queue, I go through the list again, the five oils, rolled up, to be put back on stretchers and repaired: *Woman in Bride Light*, *The Long Flag*, the double portrait of Sheyali and Radhuni, the portrait of Rasko and the Palm Avenue garden view.

The taxi driver and I both chain smoke silently, all the way into the early morning city. The cab drops me in the Marais, at the corner of Rue Rambuteau and Rue de Temple, and I haul my suitcases into the courtyard of the building. The concierge is a nice woman and her 'M'sieu! You are back from India!' is genuinely welcoming. I haul the first bag up the narrow staircase, while she guards the other, and then I come down for the second one, cursing Elko, cursing all the stupid packets of spices I've brought.

The apartment is surprisingly warm despite the fact that the heating's been off since early February, but I suppose that's the advantage of being on the floor below the top one, with large windows which trap sunlight. I line up the two suitcases in the living room and look at them with irritation. I desperately want to crawl under the blankets, but the fridge needs supplies and I know it's better to get the initial shopping out of the way before I collapse into untimely sleep. I'll feel much better if there are coffee and croissants to greet me when I wake up. I turn on the radiators and go down again.

Passing the cafes, I breathe in the acrid tobacco air, balanced by the whiff of fresh coffee and bakery products. I could get what I wanted quite close to home, but I'm married to my little Algerian shop in Les Halles for general food supplies and the adjacent *boulangère* for the bread, and so I cross the big road, Rue Beaubourg, and make my way past the massive construction site that is no longer a construction site. The Inside-Out Monster was opened by Giscard just before I left for Calcutta, and I haven't had the chance to go inside yet.

I'm walking past the massive cobblestoned dip in the ground that leads into the museum when the two girls catch me. End of shift, hopeful for one last trick on a slow night. One fake blonde, one brunette, miniskirts both, both toppling forward on high heels. Both high as kites, god knows on what.

'D'you have a light?'

I give them my lighter without offering to light their cigarettes.

'Busy this morning, *cheri*?' the blonde asks me. She sounds German.

'No, but I need to sleep.'

'Never good to sleep on your own, you know that, don't you?' says the other one.

'I'm looking forward to it.' I take my lighter back and start to walk away.

'*Connard! Petit pédé!* Asshole of the Marais! Shall I fetch you a boy then, maybe?' Still the brunette. The blonde is walking away, scanning the streets. 'Anyway, you probably fuck like a baby rabbit!'

I look back at them and remember the Rupali story, the one that Elko said Radhuni had told him. The laughter comes rushing before I can control it. The two girls turn around and spit out abuse, both in French and English, thinking I'm laughing at them. I'm desperate to tell them it's not that, but there's no way to do this – the situation has its own walls. The brunette takes a step towards me and flings her lit cigarette at me. '*Fuckeeng-neegur!*' It almost misses me, catches the shoulder of my jacket and a spark nearly flicks into my eye, but still I can't stop laughing. I'm back in Paris but my cloak of Calcutta is surprisingly thick.

Elko's voice in my ear again. 'This is a story from the nineteenth century. There was once a babu, let's call him Haren-babu, who had a very settled life. Every morning, Haren-babu would say goodbye to his wife and go to work as a senior clerk in an office in Dalhousie Square. Every evening, he would come back, have his dinner and go to sleep. One day, on the tram to Dalhousie, Haren-babu became overly engrossed in his newspaper and missed his stop. When he realized, he got off at once, intending to take the opposite tram. Life, however, had other plans. Looking around, Haren-babu found he was in a strange neighbourhood. Unlike in other parts of Calcutta, the women here were very present and very forward in the way they looked at you. Haren-babu realized he was in the infamous Sonagachhi para, the city's great red-light area, and he had to get out quickly. He began to walk fast, looking for the tram stop.

'"Ei, babu! Where are you going?"

'Haren-babu looked up towards the voice coming from a balcony above him. He found himself staring at the most beautiful vision, a gorgeous, voluptuous young woman who had a wicked smile on her face.

'"Ei, babu! Won't you come up? My name is Rupali, and my rate is one thrust, one aduli."

'Along with other body parts, Haren-babu's eyes also became enlarged. Accounts clerk that he was, he quickly made a calculation. An aduli was only half a rupee, so how much could a session come to? Not much at all! Life would not give him another opportunity like this.

'"Ek thaap, ek aduli, thiik toh?" One thrust, one aduli, sure, yes?

'"Yes, babu! Come up for the pleasure of your life!"

'Haren-babu went up to Rupali's room. Quickly, they both took off their clothes and the girl lay down, all her young splendour on offer. On a stool next to her bed was a notebook, open on a blank page, and a pencil. As Haren-babu climbed on top of her, the pencil in Rupali's hand hovered over the blank page. Haren-babu started to thrust. The girl started tapping the pencil on the page, rapid as a professional typist, putting dots upon dots, one for each thrust. After a glorious few minutes, Haren-babu's dam burst and he fell to the girl's side, his heart racing, exhausted and exhilarated. Rupali was unmoved, sitting up in bed, carefully counting the dots on the page. When she informed Haren-babu how much he had to pay, all his happiness seeped away.

'He grabbed the notebook from the girl's hand and counted the dots – Rupali's calculations were impeccable. Haren-babu's heart began racing again, but differently. Haren-babu took out all the money he had, but it was not enough. Haren-babu then gave Rupali the watch and chain his wife's family had given him at their wedding, but that wasn't enough either. Finally, despite much pleading, Haren-babu had to part with the precious gold ring given to him by his wife.

'There was no way Haren-babu could attend office after this. With a heavy tread, he made his way back home, preparing to face the destruction of his life at the hands of his wife, his parents and their entire joint family. As he entered his own para, Haren-babu passed the tea shop where the local ruffians liked to gather.

'"Arre, Haren-babu! What has happened? Why are you looking like the sky has fallen on your head?" The man asking the question was named Jhonta, and Haren-babu had never liked him nor the jeering looks the man would give him. However, today was a day for doing things he had never done before, so Haren-babu sat down and let Jhonta buy him a cup of tea. As the tea went down, the sad story came out. At the end of it, Jhonta smiled a wide smile. "So! You need to get your watch back and your ring, am I right?" "Yes, but how?" asked Haren-babu. "Well, leave that to me. Just tell me how much cash money did you give this girl?" "Ten rupees. It was all I had."' "Ten whole rupees!" Jhonta smiled even wider. "Well, now look, if I got back your watch and ring, would you also pay me ten rupees plus the tram fare?" Haren-babu nodded vigorously, disbelievingly. Jhonta stood up. "Her name was Rupali, you said?" he confirmed and went off.

'At Sonagachhi, Jhonta went and found Rupali at the busiest time of her working day, which was late evening.

'"My name is Rupali, and my rate is one thrust, one aduli."

'"Ek thaap, ek aduli, thiik toh?" One thrust, one aduli, sure, yes?

'"Yes, sure!"

'Jhonta went up and took his time taking off both their clothes. Then he adored Rupali's body the way a man should, with expert touches and kisses until she was trembling with desire. When she lay down, pencil hovering, Jhonta caressed her entire body tenderly before entering her with a powerful thrust. Rupali cried out in pleasure. Her pencil tapped once on the page and went up again, waiting. Jhonta did not move. The pencil hovered, waiting. And it waited.

'"Eijeyyyy! Why aren't you thrusting?"

'Jhonta smiled his wickedest smile.

'"Tomar naam Rupali, ek thaap ek aduli, thiik toh?" Your name is Rupali, one thrust one aduli, is that correct?

'"Yes…?"

'"Amaar naam Jhonta, ek thaap ek ghonta." My name is Jhonta, one thrust per one hour.

'By late that night, Haren-babu was back home with his watch and ring. Jhonta slept happily, having collected twenty whole rupees, ten from this side and ten from that, and some free warm and tender time with Sonagachhi's most famous denizen.'

Back in the apartment, I put away the milk in the fridge, leaving the tin of coffee and croissants on the kitchen counter. Ignoring the daylight strengthening outside, I change into my sleeping clothes, climb into bed and pull the blankets over me. As I slide into the no man's land between sleep and wakefulness, between my skin still smelling like Calcutta and my nose breathing in Paris, I start thinking of the three-year-old airport complex at Roissy-Charles de Gaulle as being like Haren-babu, bucking away at your attention like a speeded-up cartoon movie, with the Centre Pompidou perhaps being like Jhonta, everything visible, the pipes and veins inside out, proudly turgid and unmoving in the soft centre of the avaricious city.

Away from the fortress of sleep, architecture doesn't yield so easily to simile – not like landscape – and when I wake up, I can see that CDG = Harenbabu + Centre Pompidou = Jhonta doesn't quite add up, but no matter, it's not as though I'm going to put that in a monograph. It is pleasing, however, to see Elko's little watercolour hanging above my bed, the painting about 4' x 6' dwarfed by the mount and the oversized old gilt frame in which I've put it. A big, black, polished four-poster bed cut off by the edge of the picture, rumpled sheets and a pillow that's been doubled up, just recovering from being tortured. Next to the bed, a small bedstand upon which is an old style khata-notebook, the red of its cloth binding visible under the open pages. Across the pages lies a pencil. A freckling of dark grey graphite dots spread randomly across the two pages, as if someone had started making the dots in a systematic manner and then lost control.

It's past three when I wake up, and the May sun is beginning to push aside the cloud cover over the city. I fill the kettle, put it on the burner and find the can opener for the coffee. The strong aroma released from the tin finally makes me happy to be back here – barring the first few days, the absence of any real coffee is one of the worst things about visiting Calcutta or India. I make a strong pot in the cafetière, pour the coffee in the bowl, add milk, and take it out to the little balcony.

The first time I'd seen this view, I'd shaken my head in wonder. That shake of the head comes back to me every time I come out here, even if it's several times a day. You can marvel at my luck at having landed this place – I certainly do. Rather, I regurgitate my gratitude to the late Kedar Lahiri and to the very-much-around Missus that they introduced me to the mad Dominique and Dominic, wife and husband, older hippies with the 'h' silent in the French way. D&D who were independently and jointly wealthy enough to have this place in the Marais, and who, bless them, preferred to headquarter themselves in Goa for most of the year, and on their farm in the Loire when they returned for three months in the summer.

'They ate Paris,' as Missus would say every now and then.

'They ate Paris with vim and vigour,' Elko would agree.

'You ate Paris,' Missus would say to D&D.

'Yes, we ate it. Not all the time, but most of the time we ate it.'

'But how can you possibly ate Paris?' I'd asked, kicking myself for falling into the h trap.

D&D had explained. Every place has its best period and then it passes. The best of Paris was long over, finished around the mid-60s, well before the upheavals of '68, though it might return a few decades later. Right now, Goa was at its best. Once the world discovered it, it would be time to move on, but right now, being based in Goa and oscillating between

Anjuna, Auroville and Banaras was the best possible life anyone could have. In any case, D&D weren't about to return to Paris in the next few years, and then too, not to the apartment in Rue Rambuteau unless someone found a way to put in a lift up to their fifth-floor flat. If I wanted it, I could have it. No rent, I just had to cover the utility bills.

'*No ascenseur, no me*. I ate those stairs. Especially in winter,' explained Dominic.

'You just ate being old,' corrected Dominique.

'You can't be old at fifty-five!' said Elko, who was then fifty-two, I think.

'Oh yes you can, Zemindear! Look at you!' said Missus.

'Anyway, the best Indian food is to be found in Bengal,' said Elko, finishing another glass of wine.

'Ow would one know? Your this Bengal never has any food!'

There was a deadly silence, but Dominic got away with it because he was a close friend of Elko's.

So, here I am in this apartment with a great view in a city famous for great views. Looking more or less straight south from the balcony and the windows of the living room, I can see the dome of Hotel de Ville, and beyond that the profile of Notre Dame. Looking north from the one window in the bedroom, there is a criss-cross of Paris rooftops with the République just out of sight. Looking south-east from the kitchen windows, again rooftops, but poking out above them, the faintest whisper-brush of the golden figure on top of the Bastille column.

Looking west by north-west has become interesting over the last few years. When I first moved in, the focal point was the cactus needle of the Eiffel Tower, the ultimate exclamation point of the city, the signifier of everything Paris, but the excavation for the museum began just after I moved in. The parking lot was already gone when I came, and they'd also destroyed those old pavilions on one side, but you could still see the Eiffel then. In a few months, this disappeared as the long, flat-topped cage rose from the mud and concrete. I myself quite liked the criss-cross supports, the gerberettes and massive funnels curving up, but thank god Elko never lived to see the thing completed. For all his modernism, Elko was a classicist of a sort, not the type who would appreciate the innards of a building, like its water and electrical pipes, pasted to the outside and painted in bright colours.

It's standing here, looking at the view, or sometimes when I go up to Montmartre and Sacré-Cœur or even to Belleville, that it hits home that Calcutta is a sort of anti-Paris. Or the other way round. Calcutta has no heights from which you can admire a view, no hill from which you can see the elbow bend of the Hooghly, or the domes, such as they are, of Victoria Memorial or the General Post Office. To experience the sprawl of the city, you have to imagine it, or fly above it, which is a totally different thing. As for the ordinary views, those without a height, which even flat, low-built cities should have, Calcutta doesn't do too many of those, not unless you're on a terrace on top of a tall building.

In any case, there are times in this overload of occidental beauty when I miss that view-less city, and I suppose this apartment is a homage to my anti-Paris.

I've kept the other views clear, but on the three connected windows that look towards République, I've stuck a long sheet of clear acetate and laid a timeline on it with heavy blue marker, not just to help me remember – I know these dates by heart – but, call me perverse, also to paste them over the face of this city.

The sheet is longer, but the first line, in blue, begins at 1939, with the first vertical mark coming at 7 August 1941 – *RT Dies* – then comes Dec '41 – *Jap invasion begins* – then the dates for the Japanese victories, 15 Feb '42 – *Singapore* – and 8 March '42 – *Rangoon* – then March '42 – *Cripps meets Gandhi, mission fails* – 8 August '42 – *Quit India* – 13 August '42 – *Wellington Square…*

It's wasn't just Elko who took a shine to the Eberhard Faber markers. Buying them for him, watching him use them, I've developed my own relationship with the damn things. Just before 13 August '42, a new timeline begins, this one in a black line below the blue one above. July–October '42 – *Boats and bikes confiscated, rice procurement reaches peak* – December '42 – *Widespread rice shortage, famine widespread* – and then, across 1943 and 1944, repeated in Bangla script, the Bengali words for famine: *mannantar, aakaal, mannantar, aakaal.*

Officially, the famine was acknowledged only in March 1943, and by

September 1944 it was deemed to be over, but my black line continues into the late 40s. From early 1945 starts another line, this time above the blue timeline, this time in what else but red. This red line accompanies the blue line all the way through the August '46 Calcutta riots, past 15 August 1947 – *Partition/Independence,* where I've added Elko's coinage '*Partipendence*', and then goes past it with the label *Tebhaga–* all the way to 1951. At 1952, all the lines terminate, primarily because that is where the third window has its frame and the acetate sheets don't work so well pasted on walls.

Speaking of views, time and again I find myself falling into this trap of wanting a clear sight line down the years, but real history doesn't provide you with too many open boulevards. Away from the acetate sheets, pinned on a wall I also have these charts – another attempt, from a different angle, to get a handle on how things began. Like some obsessive cop detective, I've tried to map critical days across those two years in the lives of my suspects, and I now find myself adding some new initials and notes to this:

7 August 1941 –
– Gopal 'meets' Kedar (KL tape int, GM conversation/notes)
– Kedar meets Imogen + Andrew; start of Eva time (KL, IVS, tape ints)
– Now clear – first day Lambert sees Kedar + vice versa (KL, WG, tape ints)
– Niru tells home she's moving out (NM conversation/notes)
– Gopal 'promoted' (GM, conversation/notes, WG tape int)

24 December 1941 –
– Niru – first Party meeting (NM conversation/notes)
– Niru + Imogen 1st encounter (NM conversation, IVS tape int)
– Imogen – last day with Andrew (IVS tape int)
– Imogen + Kedar speak at the Ball (IVS, KL, tape ints)

13 August 1942 –
– Hara-kiri Trench in garden painting + GC Laha (KL tape int)
– Gopal van accident (GM conversation/notes)

– Niru + Imogen – Dharamtolla – Bourne & Shepherd (NM conversation/notes, IVS tape int)
– Niru – tear-gas head wound (NM conversation/notes, S&R tape int)
– Imogen hears from Andrew (IVS tape int)
– Kedar + Keya D (KL tape int, NM conversation/notes)

After this, there are a couple more pages, but they are less covered with writing and markings: 24 December 1942, 2 and 3 January 1943.

After 13th August 1942, my 'research' turns into narrative mince and the structure disintegrates in my mind. Things, memories, facts, all start to blur and it's like watching a dealer shuffling a deck of cards faster and faster, or like being on the Toofan Mail, the Storm Express, as it picks up speed through the fields: the landscape in the distance is readable enough, but things closer to the eye whip by before you can fully register them.

NEEM AND MANGO

Not that many fires, but the unnatural gloom magnifies each one. The biggest is towards the south, on her left, but she can't see it because houses nearby obscure the actual blaze; something big, burning fiercely, flinging a pulse of illumination across the tops of buildings over a large radius. Then, a swathe of disturbed darkness. Then, directly between her and the river, four flickering points, probably pyres of trams and buses the fire brigade hasn't yet managed to put out, but the line that's formed reminds her of illustrations she has seen of landing lights for aeroplanes. So much for the blackout, Niru thinks. If the Japanese bombers choose to come tonight, they will find a scattered Diwali welcoming them. Nearer, around Shyambajar, there are smaller glows in the lanes, almost subterranean, where people have clearly decided enough is enough and lit small bonfires in defiance of both Raj and rain. In the half an hour Niru has been on the terrace, she has seen two of the small local fires put out and three new ones flare up on the atlas of darkened north Kolkata.

Her wound gives a sharp stab under the bandage, and she reaches to hold on to the parapet. The grit she would normally feel is now covered by the thin satin of monsoon moss. She waits for the pain to hit a second time, but it doesn't come. The compounder who stitched up the cut at the women's house in Dharmatolla had told her that the wound would take a few days to heal. 'It's the skull, which is full of blood, so it's normal that it bled a lot, but there's no real danger. Don't worry, it only needed four stitches. They will only leave a slight mark on your forehead, your future husband won't even notice!' An oncoming laugh had opened her mouth, but the wound hurt sharply and she'd swallowed her mirth. Now, the cut starts to throb slightly, it seems almost in rhythm to the flickering fires. A part of her is at each fire, helping to ignite it, to keep it burning in the face of the police and the air-raid wardens. Yet another part of her is rushing to put each one out – you can't give the fascist air forces easy targets!

The moment she returned home, her mother tried to tuck her into bed. It took a lot of convincing from Roma and her father to let her come upstairs to her terrace. – Ma, I rested for a full three hours in that house before I came home. – Mashima, she's telling the truth. I bumped into her at the tram stop and I thought she was wearing a handkerchief on her forehead just to keep the sweat from her eyes. She was completely normal. – Listen, let the girls go to the terrace for a bit, Niru will feel better if she gets some fresh air. – Mashima, I'll take her up and then come back to help you with the cooking. – No, no need, don't leave her alone. I don't want her falling down from dizziness. – Ma, I told you, I'm not feeling dizzy. It's just a small wound from a tin can. Can you imagine if I was a soldier at the front, this would be nothing! – Well, you're not a soldier at the front, and this front at home is dangerous enough for me. It's a blessing from Ma Kali none of you girls got shot today. You can go, but only for a few minutes, understood? – Listen, don't get so worked up. I'll just finish this bit of the model and go up, then Roma can come down and help you with the cooking.

Niru remembers how she used to love helping her father make models of his sets when she was younger. Most designers in Bengali theatre would make drawings or watercolour sketches and build the sets based on those, but not her Baba; he would make the drawings, discuss them with the director, and then actually sit and make a small model with cardboard, glue and paint, which father and daughter would carefully transport to the carpenters' workshop in a ricksha. 'You see, it helps everyone when you see the whole thing in three dimensions, when you see it from above,' Baba would say. Today, she looks down on the city and tries to imagine it as a set on a vast stage.

In the foreground is the jumbled spread of low buildings, two, three or four storeys high, the dwellings of the so-called 'middle class'; here and there, looming out of this geometry of terraces and balconies, more strongly flecked by the fires, are the high peaks of the rajbaris, the large zamindar mansions with their Europe-mimicking domes, turrets and plaster curlicues, around which these neighbourhoods have come up; further away, she can barely make out the plateaus of the British buildings around Dalhousie Square, and the more recent blocks of the tall office buildings, two or three of them as high as twelve whole floors; beyond those, far in the distance, at the centre of what would have to be a massive painted backdrop of lowering clouds, are the pillars of the new bridge that will connect almost directly with the Howrah Station; she can't see the pillars in the gloom of the blackout, but she can sense them – over the last two years, she has got used to them rising inexorably above the city skyline.

Somewhere in the intricate maze below, the day has unfurled, a play of highly contrasting acts: the fun, innocent morning of meeting Imogen; being suddenly sucked into the whirlpool of the Congress protest; then being squeezed out on to the shore of the footpath where these strange but kind people received her; and then, and then, that strange house at Dharmatolla.

'Tui thiik achhish?' – Are you all right? – Roma had just gone down a few minutes ago, but now she's back.

'I'm fine. It's hurting a bit, and if I tell myself I'm dizzy then I feel slightly dizzy, otherwise not.'

'I think you were lucky today, we both were.' Roma joins Niru at the parapet.

Niru agrees: 'Yes, lucky, true, though at the time I was seeing Baba-Ma lighting my funeral pyre. Anyway, why are you back? I thought Baba was coming up?'

'He's having an argument with your Ma, so they sent me back up.'

'About what?'

'About you, about us. Living independently was bad enough, they should have stopped us. Now we are taking even more risks every day. Your Baba was pointing out that hundreds of girls were at the meeting today. In any case, you would have gone from here. And still come back with your head split open. But Mashima is not yielding.'

'This argument they have every few weeks. Ma doesn't understand that the time for them stopping us is long past. Maybe not for other parents with girls our age but—'

'But for your parents, yes, and also my parents, all that protecting business is gone.'

'That's true, but you know, when I saw the police lined up today, on their horses, and with all their lathis and rifles, I thought, *No one can protect me from this*, you know? Did you also feel that?'

'Yes, at first. But I think I was standing closer to the police, and after a while, Niru, it was impossible to not see it. They... were... scared. The police on foot, the ones on the horses, the gora officers on the horses and, I daresay, even the horses themselves.' Roma pauses and looks around restlessly. 'You know, seeing their fear gave me courage. They are afraid of me. They are afraid of me when I'm part of this big a mass. Do you see?'

'I can sort of imagine, but I only saw the fear on our side, and the terror of the gas and lathis.'

Roma looks furtively at the door to the terrace. 'Ei, speaking of fear, we'll hear your Baba coming up, won't we?'

'Yes, yes, don't worry. Anyway, he knows. I think they both know.'

'How? *You* told them? You *didn't!*' Roma gently nudges Niru to move a little to the left, where trees hide them from most of the surrounding terraces.

'Roma. You're like a daughter to them, yes? So they notice things as they would with me. And Ma has a good sense of smell, Baba not so good, but Ma's nose is pretty sharp.'

'Oh god... do they think you also...?' Roma looks around once more before extracting a cigarette packet from the folds of her sari and lighting up.

'No. I told you, Ma can smell.' Niru waves away the smoke. 'Uff. As if there isn't enough smoke over the city today.'

'It's the smoke of revolution, comrade!' Roma lifts her head and points upwards with her cigarette.

Niru starts to shake her head but stops herself. 'You know, I feel like I've taken one of those tablets doctors give you. You swallow it and nothing happens. And then the effects start, half an hour or even later.'

'Maaney? You head is hurting? You want to go down?'

'No, no, no. Nothing to do with the wound. As I told you at the bus stop, these women took me into this house. I didn't realize it at the time, but today is the first time I met a... prostitute – prostitutes, actually – and I'm a little shocked at how normal they were, how normal it was to talk to them, just ordinary, decent, women who were going out of their way to help a stranger like me... I'm a little shocked and, I don't know, a little ashamed. I don't know what I was imagining earlier, subconsciously, as though prostitutes would be some kind of she-demons. It totally exposed just how *bourgeois* I really am!'

'It's true, you know. I was also thinking that we've escaped this bubble – parents, home – but we've just put ourselves into another bubble that's only slightly less cut off from the real world.'

'Then, then there was also this man, actually this boy – again, at first nothing, no realization, just a straggly rat of a boy, and these two women also treated him like a kid brother, bullying him and laughing at him, but later something else emerged. In my reeling head. If you looked past the joking, you could see the women had a kind of suppressed respect for him. I don't quite know how to put it, he was clearly carrying some other power, some other knowing, in his body.'

'What do you mean knowing? What kind of knowing, do you think?'

'Well, for someone of his... class... he seemed to know a lot about rifles firing and tear gas. Then, I was resting upstairs, in their... house... but not sleeping. And he was talking to the old lady who was clearly the owner of the place, the one everyone called Mashi. They must have thought I was asleep, they were talking quite close by. And this boy was assuring the mashi that he would get them three mawns of good Gobindobhog rice and ten litres of fresh mustard oil in a few days. Three mawns of Gobindobhog! In these days! So he was clearly connected, no, clearly *immersed*, in the black market, he also had that kind of knowledge, but that is still not what I mean by *knowing*... Maybe he gave off a sense of having experienced things that you or I cannot imagine. Something like that.'

'Hm.'

'I don't know about you, but I think I have the imagination of a child. I always imagined prostitutes to be like, you know, over-made-up apsaras, lots of jewels and a certain look in the eyes, and likewise, black marketeers were these large men with scars and moustaches...'

'Prostitutes, same with me. I suppose we've both looked at the same book covers, Saratchandra books and then the cheaper novelists, but black market and smuggling people I always imagined with their faces covered in shawls, with just a sharp nose coming out, something nineteenth-century like that.'

Saratchandra's novels remind Niru of Titir. Roma and she have always teased Titir that she looks like a Sarat-babu heroine. 'Listen, I hope Palash is all right. She wasn't at Wellington Square, right?' The three of them have decided the give themselves code names from the trees outside the Dover Road house; Niru is Neem, Roma both Aam and its English, Mango, because her brain is half-Ingreji, and Titir is obviously the most outrageously beautiful Palash.

'Your brain's clearly damaged. I've told you twice already. She's gone to Howrah to see her uncle. There was no question of her coming to the meeting. Too crowded, too much hurly-burly, sweat.' Roma looks around the neighbouring terraces to make sure no one's within earshot. 'Ei, Niru, listen, I meant to tell you earlier, and don't tell Palash, but I think Keya may be meeting her beau again. At Dover Road, I mean.'

'Oh!' Niru starts to giggle helplessly. 'That peacock Kedar Lahiri?'

'Yes, yes, the same Mr Dandy. I told her where we've hidden the key, today's hiding place, so she – they – should be there now.'

Niru's hand goes to her mouth, trying to stifle the schoolgirl inside. 'Do you think they'll do something, you know, like *that?*'

'No, no, Keya is not stupid. Maybe a hand here or there, you know how people do, maybe some kissing and what they call *petting* in English. That fellow, he wouldn't have the courage to try anything more, he's such a milksop!'

'Milksop! Milksop?'

'Weak, effete, like a girl! Though, I shouldn't say, I don't know, he *is* a man after all...'

'And Keya? That girl might have ideas of her own, you know!'

'You're right. I hadn't thought about what Keya might do.'

Niru controls her giggling and turns her head back to the fires dotting the darkness.

Roma continues. 'Speaking of being lucky today. I don't mind if I never find *love*, I'm just happy to be alive. Anyway, on the subject of men, and prostitutes—'

'Yes?'

'You know, Aloka-di has made friends with these mems? One of them is the wife of the editor of *The Statesman* and then some Mrs Emily Shawcross who is also quite high up, married to someone in the Bengal administration. So, she was saying, Aloka-di, that they were planning a meeting of like-minded women to do something about these soldiers. Today's business reminded me. She said, *We can't let them treat every woman in the city like a prostitute*, and then she corrected herself – *We shouldn't even let them grab the prostitutes the way they are grabbing girls everywhere!*'

'What would the meeting achieve?'

'Well, there is a plan to bring out a procession, to ask the administration to act and stop the assaults on women, write letters to the lieutenant governor, the viceroy and to the army command... Aloka-di wants people from all the different parties to participate. She asked me to ask you girls and any others you can think of.'

'Only women?

'Only women, yes.'

ONLY WOMEN

Only women, only women
Only women on my mind!

I'm lovelorn and I'm blind
I'm lovelorn and I'm blind
Since my baby left me
I've got, I've got, I've got
Only women on my mind!

Only women, only women
Only women, only wom-en
Only women on my mind!

The two Gandhis are dancing a sort of swing, their silk loincloths held together by clusters of safety pins. The female Gandhi is wearing an additional strip of cloth – ostensibly to cover her bosom – but here the pins have already begun to fail, and Imogen can already see more than she wishes to. The woman also has on a bald toupee, clearly acquired from some theatre suppliers, along with a false moustache that owes more to Douglas Fairbanks than the Mahatma chap, while the male Gandhi is actually bald but with a blond moustache which seems to be all his own. Both of them sport round, toy spectacles that keep sliding down their noses as they gyrate across the floor.

The band is clearly American, made up mostly of Negro servicemen, with one Yank on banjo and another on the piano, both more or less managing to keep up with the black fellows. The flat is anything but small, but everything, the band mostly of blacks, the raucous blues music, the crowd melded together by the pall of smoke, the rise and dip of drunken laughter, reminds her of Paris and the tiny apartments with the all-night parties from what now seems aeons ago.

The dancing area in front of the band is demarcated by the ghost rectangle of a large carpet that's been rolled up to reveal the parquet floor. Dancing alongside the twin Gandhis, there's a Napoleon paired with a Cleopatra, a Turk in a fez entwined by a very parsimoniously attired Snake Goddess who Imogen recognizes as the Dutch local manager of Shell and his wife, and then there are the Nabob of Alligator and his favourite queen, both turned up as harlequins in their red-and-white chequered silk body suits, both so tiny compared to the Dutch couple that, for a moment, Imogen has wondered why children have been let into the party.

On the telephone that afternoon, Todd-Cartwright had given fair warning that the post-dinner party might be 'a bit on the outré side, hope that's all right'. Imogen had released a loud peal of laughter, triggered by sheer relief that there was no bad news about Andrew. 'The wilder the better, Alan, the wilder the better! A girl needs some distraction in these grim times.'

Todd-C and his driver had driven up promptly at the promised half past nine. The car had then joined others in the convoy with the armed escort, and they had made their way under a hard drizzle from Alipore towards Hungerford Street in the Minto Park area. Imogen was dressed comparatively modestly as a flapper, and she was relieved to see that Todd-Cartwright had also chosen a slightly conservative costume with a judge's gown and wig.

A few minutes into the drive, the pleasantries over, Todd-Cartwright reached across and made sure the glass partition between them and the driver was firmly shut. Then he filled his pipe and lit it, before reaching into the top of his gown and pulling out an envelope. Holding it, he looked out of the window, sending pipe smoke against the rain-spattered glass. 'Dear girl, what I'm about to do is highly, highly irregular.' Imogen's eyes widened. Todd-Cartwright's voice sank into a mutter, as if trying to convince himself of something. 'Shouldn't really… but then, everything about bloody Burma is irregular.' He turned to Imogen, waving the envelope. 'You are to… read this carefully, because you'll only have this one opportunity. I'm afraid I've read it as well, had to, just to make sure there wasn't anything, that might, you know... Once you've finished, I'll have to have it back.'

'Oh god, Alan, what is it?'

Todd-C gestured towards the driver. 'We'll discuss it later. As much as we can, which is not a lot, I'm afraid.' He took a folded sheet from the envelope and handed it to her, along with one of those small torches with the half-painted beams that people used in the blackout.

My darling,
I hope this manages to reach you.

Andrew's handwriting.

The note was short, barely covering a single page of the onionskin letter paper she'd bought him before he left. She gobbled up the words under the wavering beam of the torch. Then, fighting the nausea, she read it again. And again.

'Got it I hope, dear girl?' After a few minutes, Todd-Cartwright held out his hand.

'Yes. I don't suppose I could keep...'

'Afraid not, my dear.' She handed the note back and watched as Todd-Cartwright brought a match to it. He waited for the thing to catch properly before putting it into an empty cigarette tin he was using for an ashtray. Together, they observed the paper whiten, then blacken, and then the black flecks crumble to join the ash. When she looked up, they were passing the long curving fence of the racecourse and she remembered driving past here many times with Andrew.

'Ladies and Genn'l'mn! I now present to you Mr Fenton Greaves and his band, Fenton and the Hooghly-Woogies!' As the band changes over, the lights in the drawing room area are doused, leaving only a spotlight focussed on the MC. 'And! I now present to you!' The new drummer peels off a drum roll. 'The one and only! The *supreme* exponent of cabaret in all of Asia! The sinpareil, the sinuous, the sensuous, the *sensational* Miss... Nylon Jenna!'

The MC moves out of the light. Two clicks of the drum rim synchronize perfectly with a long, stockinged leg jackknifing into the circle of light. A drumroll and a woman's derriere, sheathed in what looks like cat skin, undulates through the spot and back into the darkness.

A leg comes back into the circle and begins to vibrate in time with the drums.

> *My love, no language can really cover what I must now convey to you, words such as 'apology' and 'sorry' feel like absurdly inadequate impostors.*
>
> *Darling Immy, from this moment on, you have to start forgetting me, forgetting about me and us and everything we had dreamt of. I don't for a moment imagine it'll be easy, but you need to wipe out all traces of me the best you can and move on.*

Imogen has heard about this dancer, Nylon Jenna. Of mixed parentage, father reportedly Irish-Arab, mother some sort of Bengali, like 'a complex and deliciously effective cocktail' as someone has described her. The stage name is apparently a perversion of some Bengali name meaning 'blue eyes', and indeed the blue peepers are striking, set against the rich black hair and dusky complexion.

As the tune grows, Nylon Jenna begins to slink through the spotlight, different segments of her body playing hide-and-seek with the watching crowd. There is a voice singing, and it takes Imogen a moment to realize it's not the dancer. As the chasing spotlight washes over the musicians, Imogen recognizes the woman from the afternoon at Great Eastern, that singer – what was her name – Clarissa something. Imogen suddenly feels trapped in a game of cat and mouse between dancer, singer and spotlight, an extra player in a three-way game. Something's missing, she needs something, she looks down at the glass in her hand and sees it's empty except for dregs of ice.

Glass full, the gin and tonic spilling over her fingers, she wanders away from the bar, looking into other rooms. Imogen has been in flats such as these before, spacious apartments built in this area for the executives of the big British companies, and she marvels again at the generous divisions of space – the corridors, the dining room which seems to be having a separate party of its own, bedrooms with balconies, the high ceilings and long windows. In a smaller sitting area, four women of varying age, all dressed as flappers like herself – no, even older, like some sort of nineteenth-century European aristocracy perhaps – two of them playing with small furs in this heat, all watching a Chinese man who's showing them some card tricks. They speak to each other in one language and address the man with a strangely accented English. It takes a moment for the penny to drop: these are the White Russians she has heard about, women from the Tsar's extended family who escaped and settled in Shanghai. They've had to up and leave again, managing to get out just before the Japanese captured the city. She looks at their 'costumes' again and realizes they are not in fancy dress at all – they are dressed in their actual finery from the old days; that long coil of braided pearls the oldest woman is wearing is actually genuine, as is the tiara sitting on a younger woman's head. Todd-C has already identified the Chinese man as they've come in: he's a close associate of Tan Kah Kee of the Millionaires' Club, Singapore – another one who's managed to get out just ahead of the Japs, just before the fall of Sing.

It seems the only one who doesn't think he can escape the Japs is Andrew.

> *... you need to wipe out all traces of me the best you can and move on.*
>
> *I can't tell you very much about what we're doing – even this letter is madly risky – but I know that the chances of any of us coming back are well below non-existent.*

'What does he mean by non-existent, Alan? How can he be so sure? Surely—' In the car, the outline of Todd-Cartwright's wig moved as it caught some dim light and she understood that he was shaking his head.

'Listen, old girl, the truth is I don't know. I couldn't tell you even if I did, but I don't. But if Hillcott's saying what he's saying, you have to take him seriously. From everything I do know, I can tell you the situation over there is... dire. If they break through in Assam, with east

Bengal already in a civilian mess… Anyway, look, desperate times call for desperate measures. I can tell you we're throwing simply everything we can at the bastards, and very little seems to be having any effect.' He looks at the rain marbling across his window. 'Once this monsoon goes, we're going to be in the thick of it.'

'Yes, all right, but where exactly is he? I know, I know, you can't tell me! But, since there's this hiatus, why couldn't he take some time off and come tell me face to fa—oh, my god, I've got it! He's not at the front, he's over *there,* behind their lines, isn't he? He's *in the fucking jungle,* isn't he?'

Todd-Cartwright forced a short, loud laugh. 'I really… don't know how you surmise that, Imogen but I wouldn't get carried away with that Beau Brummel stuff. War is far more tedious than you imagine. For instance, all I've done today is pore over registers of confiscated boats, poor bloody villagers' boats, can you imagine!'

'Yes, but Andrew's not in an office looking at registers, is he?'

'True, my dear girl, but try not to feed… what did someone call it? Try not to feed the furnace of anxiety.'

She's now on a large, dark balcony surrounded by even darker trees, with people being careful not to smoke towards the outer side. Her own outer side is having a polite conversation with two Indian men, boxwallahs both, both utterly unimaginatively dressed as princely types, both clearly trawling for women, neither able to decide whether she is worth pursuing, both stretching their bodies and craning their necks as they try and stay at her eye level. Inside her, the long-burning anxiety has been pushed to one side – the sentence forms in her head: 'And she's now flying blind above the pit of abandonment and despair.'

'Miss Snell, do you play bridge, by any chance?' One of the men asks. 'We'd be jolly pleased if you joined us at Calcutta Club, Saturday or Sunday, whichever suits…'

'Capital!' says the other fellow. 'We could ask Daphne to make the pairs…'

Imogen looks around for an escape route and, as if by magic, Todd-C appears at her side.

'Can I get you another? What are you drinking?'

Imogen turns to him with ill-disguised enthusiasm. 'Oh, there you are! Yes, please. Whisky, I think. In fact, I'll come with you!' She nods goodbye to the two turbanned idiots and sways alongside Todd-Cartwright. 'God, Alan, thanks for being the cavalry. I was about to visit harm on unsuspecting natives!'

'I saw. I've met them before. Not bad sorts, just... you know.'

'Yes, exactly.'

'What were – did you catch their names?'

'Oh lord... one was a Sengopper and the other was a Dasgopper, both Bengali, I think.'

'Oh, yes! Ratin Sengopp*ter* and, let me get this right, Babba-tosh Dasgopp*ter*. Dodo and Bunny to their friends. Bright, rising stars in the boxwallah universe. Between them, they'll probably own the place after we leave. Dodo Sengoppter is with the Bird mob and Dasgoofter is, I think, with MacLeish and Ferg—oh, here's Jeremy! Wing Commander Jeremy Lambert, Miss Imogen Snell.'

'Wing Commander! Lambert! Hello!'

'Miss Snell.'

'Imogen, please!'

'And likewise, please, Jeremy.'

Imogen thinks tubby, balding men shouldn't wear kilts, even as fancy dress. She puts on a warm smile. 'Are you with the fighters flying from Red Road?'

'Ha! No! If only he could... Jeremy and I fly desks alongside each other!'

'Yes, watching each other's tails!'

'Speaking of which, our mission tonight, if I might enlist you in this, Imogen, is to find young Jeremy some—'

Lambert has found a gap to the bar. 'What are you drinking, Imogen? They have some exotically flavoured vodkas I can recommend.'

The vodka cocktail is far sharper than Imogen has expected, the liquid darkened with the infused tamarind, but the real shock comes from the green chillis which have left no visual trace. Once she recovers from the first sip, however, Imogen can't help taking one more and then another. 'So, yes... a club within a club, you could say...' She's only half listening to Todd-C explaining something to whatshisnamenow. 'Yes, you saw that chap in the bowler hat? Exactly. Lockhart. He's behind all this... Got ticked off a few years ago when Saturday Club got shirty about some actresses he'd invited... Started the 300 Club... He also included Indians, which was impossible in most of the bloody clubs, but only the right sort obviously...' By the time Imogen finishes her drink, she realizes they are sitting at one end of the long dining table which is a chaotic marching ground for glasses and plates of decimated canapés. Just as she's wondering if she has the legs to reach the bar and get another one of these excellent drinks, Lambert offers to procure another round for everyone. Which is very nice of him. But after this, she must find Andrew and drive home with him. Where the devil has he gone now?

With the second vodka drink, the twin tastes are familiar, like old friends, the sweet element, probably some syrup of lemon and sugar, like a handrail guiding her up the alternating steps of chilli and sour. 'So, yes, Lockhart and Sergei the Russian brigand, they began the 300 and then decided they needed something as a, as a subset, if you will, of more select, you know, crowd, so you have this, the Diaghilev Club, named after the famous ballet fellow, Sergei Diaghilev. Our Sergei was not only his namesake but apparently one of his principal dancers back in the day before the Great War... and they have these irregular dos, with no small help from the Yanks, as is obvious...'

Andrew, she remembers, is gone. Sucked into this new great war. *I hope this manages to reach you.* She turns to Todd-C but finds his chair empty. She sees him speaking to a Yank airman at the other end of the table. She looks over to the other fellow and finds him looking deep into his glass... *Start forgetting me, forgetting about me and us and everything we...* Water, she must have some plain water.

Approaching the bar, she gets caught up in a knot of people dancing in a circle, the harlequin Alligators, the Cleopatra and a Tin Man from the Oz movie. Two of them grab her arms and start whirling her around with them. 'Ooooh!' screams the Queen Alligator. 'I haven't had so much fun since Antibes!' 'When was that, Highness buddy?' asks the Tin Man. 'A full four years ago, old chap,' replies the Nabob Alligator, puffing a bit, 'we're in August, so, in fact, exactly four years ago, but feels like a lifetime!'

A lifetime.

> *It's indescribably selfish of me, perhaps, but I know I won't be able to do my job here unless I know I've been truthful with you and stood you down. God knows this bloody war has made me do some horrendous things but, really, this letter is the most difficult, terrible thing I've ever attempted.*

No, you bastard, you could have attempted to have a life with me. She pulls out of the human whirlpool and gasps for air. Bloody Antibes. A bile of memory comes up – making plans with him to go to the Riviera after the war. Delayed honeymoon. Not far from Granny's place in the south of France. Must show you that coast.

She must have water. There's a throng around the bar. Can't see a way through it. They must have drinking water in the kitchen. She works her way past Todd-C talking to the Yank... no, the Yank's now been replaced by that fellow from the London paper, she forgets his name.

'I know you can't discuss operational stuff, man, nor am I asking! What I'm saying, Alan, is that I'm *hearing*, yes, that there are many districts, especially in the east of the province, where the food's run out. Where the men have all left to look for work. Village upon village where there are only women left behind. Can you tell me—'

'I can't, old boy, I really can't discuss any of it.'

'Only women, children and old people left behind. Is that just a wild rumour?'

'It's not my patch, Hugh, but in *principle* I wouldn't give weight to hearsay, you know? War is a fecund time for rumours, and often things aren't nearly as dramatic as you Fleet Street boys...'

A nice big refrigerator, one of those huge American jobs, with a man crouching in front of its open door. The girl standing next to him with a hand on his shoulder, balancing on one leg as she adjusts a shoe with the other. Barely going past his head, even in those absurdly high heels. The one who'd been singing for the cabaret dancer's act. Clarissa, mixed blood, but primarily Chinese, or somewhere there, Malaya perhaps. Panic rising, Imogen sees something moving under the woman's dress, something moving high up the back of her leg that the girl seems to be unaware of, and she opens her mouth to warn her. The man laughs, 'I bet I can find it, baby! What'll you give me if I find it, huh?' The woman laughs back. An intimate laugh. 'Find it and we see. Maybe I give you what you want. But stop trying to find other things first.' She jerks back, but softly, still laughing, pushing out the man's hand from under her dress.

The man stiffens, looks around at Imogen, and almost falls off his haunches. The woman lets off a louder squeal of laughter. Imogen reels back and holds on to the door jamb.

'Oh, hello, I'm so sorry, I...'

'Oh, hello there. I do believe we've met. Miss...' This is that Negro soldier with the Yank at Great Eastern.

'Imogen Snell. Yes, of course, with Mr Goodshaker, and you are Mr...'

'Jones, Byron Jones, I—'

The difference is startling between the uniform and the evening suit the man is wearing now. She reels again and places him again – the spotlight had caught him playing the trumpet behind the Nylon dancer.

'I was just trying to find some water.' She finds she can't move from the doorway. Her hand seems to be glued to the door jamb.

'Oh, I think I saw a jug.' The man stands up and moves further into the kitchen. The woman takes over, squatting and rummaging through the refrigerator.

'Here you go.' He fills a glass and hands it to Imogen.

She drinks down the whole thing. 'Oh god, thank you so much!' The man fills the glass again. She manages another half before she has to stop.

'Found it!' The Clarissa woman stands up, triumphantly holding a bottle.

'Heh, heh! I knew that thing couldn't hide from you too long!' The man starts looking around for glasses. 'These ain't the right ones, but they'll do!' He looks at Imogen and raises his eyebrows. 'Would you care to join us for some champagne, Miss Snell?'

'Oh, thank you, but I don't know if I should!'

'You should, you should!' says the woman gaily and hands the bottle over to the man. 'You know, he got it from a maharaja. He liked his playing so much he gave him an actual bottle of Taittinger!'

As the liquid fizzes over her tongue, all she can taste is that it's cold.

'Cheers, ladies!'

'Cheers!'

'Cheers, cheers! Thank you! It's been ages since I've had bubbly!'

The music is now loud in her ears, and it's not jazz. Somebody is singing, a man, American, possibly black, no, certainly black, but... She points at the man and then at the woman, trying to make calculations. 'That's not you... singing... obviously, and you're not playing, because that's not you playing, you're here!'

...I've got on my Great Eastern shoes,
I've got the Calcutta Blues!

Now the gal done left me,
The malaria done got me,
My de-li-ri-um's on the loose,
And the heat's like a wet noose,
I've got the Calcutta Blues!

She pushes the lever hard, and the thing flushes satisfactorily, the water gushing down as if directly connected to the rain drumming down above. She finds her feet and looks for the door, but she can't see it. Oh, there it is. She yanks it open and finds herself staring at shelves with neatly folded towels and rolls of toilet paper. Not this one, then. She should have noticed the knobs weren't a door handle. She tries another door-like thing, but it's locked. Panic rising, she looks around, notices her glass balanced on the washbasin and takes a steadying swig from it. The other door reappears on the wall from where it had gone AWOL. She turns the latch, goes through, and pulls the door shut behind her.

She had come into the bathroom from a well-lit corridor, but now she's in a dimly lit bedroom. The visit to the WC has sobered her a touch, so she corrects that with a gulp of the drink. The whisky jolts her despite the amount she has drunk.

It's a large bed, with small reading lamps on either side. A mountain landscape hangs above the bed – even in the low light, the lurid colours of the lower hills stand out, crowned by what could only be the high Himalayas, light pink and orange as they catch the last of dusk or the first light of dawn. To her left is a Chinese screen, behind which something seems to be moving. The door out of the bedroom must be to her right, and she's sure she can find it.

'So, are you the poet Tagorey? Is that who you are?' The woman leaning back against the headboard is dressed in stylish rags, tastefully browned in patches to indicate dirt. Under the smears of street urchin make-up, she's clearly white, probably northern European. Imogen can't place her accent except that she's not a native English speaker. The man lying on the bed, propped up on his elbow, has his back to Imogen and his cassock is hiked up to his knees, revealing his calves and bare feet. 'I could be Tagore,' he says, 'but given that I am Russian, I am more likely to be Tolstoy, no?'

'Are you Tolstoy then?' The ivory cigarette holder catches the light as the woman takes a drag.

'I could also be Roerich, of course.'

'Who?'

The man points to the mountain landscape hanging above the woman's head. 'The man who painted that. Also Russian. He—'

The Chinese screen starts to totter, accompanied by the cries of some strange animal that's obviously in distress. Imogen backs up against the door, alarmed. An animal with twin throats, high pitched cries and low growls, rising in intensity.

Wanting to help the creature but too scared to do so, Imogen starts to move further away. The woman on the bed notices her and points her out to the man. He turns around and smiles, slowly raising a hand in greeting. The two of them start to scream as though they've just discovered laughter, completely oblivious to the trapped animal which—

The screen crashes to the ground. Imogen finds herself staring, unable to shift her eyes. The bald woman is on her back and completely naked, the white silks of her costume having fallen to one side. Her eyes are glazed, and her face is tilted back. Her moustache is awry, and she has obviously hurt herself because she's bleeding a ring of brown hair from under her skull. Her legs are wrapped around the man, who is also completely naked except for the loincloth bunched up around his waist. His torso is pumping slowly like a bellows, and his shiny head is buried between the woman's breasts. Next to them is a small table with a statuette of a Chinese dragon. On its snout, the dragon seems to be wearing two pairs of round spectacles.

She finds nobody serving at the bar. When she leans over to look behind it, she finds that all the alcohol has been removed. Clearly the party is over. Clearly she needs to find Todd-C quickly, before he leaves her behind. She moves from room to room, weaving her way through the much-depleted crowd, a vague disquiet rising.

'Miss Snell! Imogen! Are you all right? We've been looking for you!' It's the RAF chappie. In his kilt.

'Oh, hello, err...'

'Jeremy.'

'Jeremy. Of course. I'm fine, thank you. I suppose I should be going...'

'Yes, I've been trying to round everybody up. Now that I've found you, I've lost Alan! Typical.'

She sees an almost full glass of something sitting on a side table, a cigarette smouldering in an ashtray next to it. She picks up the cigarette and takes a drag. It makes her retch. To counter the retching, she takes a gulp from the glass. Some sort of spiced rum. It punches her in the head, but it stops her from wanting to vomit. She remembers leaning out of Andrew's car and throwing up just outside her gate.

'You know, Jeremy, I'm not sure how to put this but...'

'But?' Todd-C has appeared from somewhere and he's holding her gently by the elbow.

'Oh, Alan! Have I made an absolute fool of myself? I have, haven't I?'

'No, my dear, you've been fine, at least around us. I'm sure you've been absolutely fine.'

'Well, the thing is, I'm bloody... three sheets to the blotto. Can't... can't possibly... home... not in this state...'

Todd-C is speaking to the Negro trumpet player. And it's Jeremy who's now holding her up. The trumpet fellow says something about a suite at the hotel. About Mr Goodsugar being out of town but him having the permission to use the rooms. 'The keys? Oh, I've got the keys, but I don't need 'em tonight!' She notices Clarissa standing a few feet away, waiting.

'Imogen. There's a solution. Jones here, good man, can get you into Goodsugar's suite. No one's going to be there tonight, so it's all yours. I'll arrange for you to be dropped home tomorrow. What do you say?'

SIX

Convex and Concave

14 AUGUST 1942 – 20 DECEMBER 1942

IF YOU HAPPENED TO BE flying in a small aeroplane over Calcutta on the morning of 14 August 1942, the first thing you'd notice would be the plumes of smoke rising from different parts of the city. If you were flying at, say, eight hundred feet, your Tiger Moth would feel the slight buffeting from the wind that had carried away the last of the rain clouds from yesterday, the same wind that was turning the thinning plumes of smoke into wiry grey wisps, bending them at the very top before dispersing them into the atmosphere.

As your aircraft came above the southernmost group of plumes, you could follow them down to the black gashes in the wide avenue from which they were rising. As your eyes adjusted, you would see the burnt shells of trams and buses in a vaguely straight line going past the unmistakable Victorian brickwork of the market in the south of the city known variously as Jaggubajar or Jodubajar. On the other side of the brick frontage, you would see the skewed cross-hatching of corrugated tin roofing that made up the actual, very un-English bajar with pools of water collected on the narrow pathways between the roofs. Unlike on a normal morning, the market and the avenue would be almost devoid of people, the curfew still in place in most parts of the city.

Flying north for a minute or two, you would find yourself over a fortress of mottled mud buttressed by bamboo scaffolding. After a moment, you would recognize the dome and turrets of Victoria Memorial draped in black tarpaulin and cow dung. Perched at different levels on the grids of dirty bamboo, you would see small figures in loincloths. You would be able to make out that, curfew or no curfew, these men were working, scooping fresh brown lumps from buckets and flinging them on to the walls of the building, covering the patches of marble where the rain has washed off the natural camouflage.

Continuing northwards, you would find yourself flying over a sea of brownish-green military tents stretching away in orderly waves, the grass between the rows trampled into black mud. Turning slightly north-east, you would find yourself following the main north-south avenue again. This stretch of it is called Chowringhee and it joins up with Esplanade and Dharmatolla Street. At the big crossing, you would again see plumes of smoke, burnt-out trams, a couple of small trucks and some cars that were unfortunate enough to get caught up in the disturbances of yesterday. Again, you would notice the absence of people, save three army pickets and an armoured car with a manned machine gun visible on top. At this height, and at your speed, it would not be possible to differentiate the bloodstains from the general monsoon scarring of the road surfaces.

At that point what might remain of your flight is a circling sweep west over Governor House, the river and Howrah Station before you begin to descend over the racecourse that is also now crowded with tents and camouflaged war equipment; the aircraft, still turning, pointing north again and lining up with the straight stretch of Red Road on which it will land. Before all that, however, just as you bank left from the smouldering mess of the five-way crossing at Chowringhee and Dharmatolla, you would fly over the sprawl of the Great Eastern Hotel with the warren of cabins and storerooms on its roof terrace.

Alternatively, you could begin with a flight from the north of the city, from where you might see a slightly different picture. If you took a heading of south by south-west from Dum Dum Airfield, you would soon leave behind the hinterland, with its mosaic of factories and water ponds, and be juddering over the five-point crossing at Shyambajar. You would see that the roads around the big traffic circle are deserted. Stretching below you would be the road-net of a city from which people seem to have been erased. From this point over Calcutta, you might not see the smoke rising from Jodubajar, far to the south. From here, it may seem as though fire and rain are both gone, leaving traces that are too fine to draw into the frames of the story.

What you wouldn't be able to discern from that height is the unusual silence that has stretched over one of the noisiest cities in the world and that this very temporary silence is made up not just of collective fear but also of a fully ignited mass rage that will take months and a special set of events to douse.

Continuing down Belgachia Road, you could bank sharply left as you came over Central Avenue. Following that wide stripe of road, you would spot the occasional moving dots on the treeless pavements, one or two people defying the curfew, maybe a pack of dogs running free, loping across the tram tracks in the middle of the boulevard, and then the army pickets increasing in number as you approached the government buildings and commercial buildings around Dalhousie.

You would cross the river, the cockpit windows rattling in the breeze coming over the water, and take the plane in a curve over the almost completed new bridge and Howrah Station. You would then come back over the Hooghly, perhaps flying over Governor House to slow down over the Great Eastern. In this approach, you would spot the dull olive-green vehicles lined up outside the hotel, the roof and bonnet of many of them painted with the white five-pointed star of the US Army.

In either case, whether flying in from the south or the north, looking down you would see a section at the southern end of the hotel's terrace fenced off with high netting to protect a rust-coloured surface painted with a familiar design of neat white lines. With the sun strengthening towards what is sure to be a sweltering noon, on this rectangle of red-brown you would see two figures engaging in short dance movements, yanking their shadows this way and that in the jerky choreography of a game of tennis.

From the smack of the gut strings, the ball climbs and curves over the wire netting. Lambert's eyes follow it as it drops, obeying the parabola initiated by the racquet until it passes the jut of the hotel building. It then develops a will of its own, plummeting straight down towards the lane below. The furry white orb parts company with the stained whitewash of the hotel and becomes a planet against the dark grey of the road. It hits the asphalt and comes back up, the dot enlarging and receding and enlarging again until it bounces quietly towards the hooves of a pony tethered to a jhurrie-gaadi. Before it can go under the horse, there is a blur of rags, a small child running to the ball, trying to grab it. The ball evades the first snatch, but the kid traps it on the second attempt, down on all fours now. The boy moves away from the jhurrie-gaadi, protecting the ball from the disinterested pony. A few feet down the street, he stops, looks around, squats down and brings the thing to his mouth, teeth ready.

Lambert's stomach tightens as the boy bites into the ball. The boy's head jerks back in shock, the dirty white wool unyielding, the hard rubber underneath hurting his teeth. But he doesn't give up, turns the thing and looks for another opening. This time, the kid tries the seam, trying to suck it open, but the ball repels him again. The face turns upwards, and even from this distance Lambert can see the enlarged eyes, wide, staring at the sky, uncomprehending. The kid's stomach heaves, trying to bring out a howl, but he can only manage a scraping of breath, not something Lambert can actually hear, yet he can. After a beat, Lambert realizes it's his own breath that's replicating what is beyond earshot.

A woman, not old, yet ancient in her movement, comes out from behind the row of horse carriages and bends over the howling boy. She takes the ball from his hand, examines it, smells it, and then flings it away towards the runnel of water at the edge of the road. She grabs the boy's arm and drags him back into the shadows.

On the acetate of my window timeline, I've used string to hang tiny photo prints I've made of whatever of Elko's work I've found in their house or retrieved from elsewhere. Each year of the timeline has two or three pictures, most representative pictures of the work he was doing at that time, that's to say as far as I've been able to establish the dates.

On the stretch of the famine years, 1943–44, there are very few pictures by Elko. Before and after these two years, it's all entirely him on the window, but hanging from those two years are examples of work by other artists – small reproductions of the famine drawings of Chittoprasad and Zainul Abedin, interspersed with cut-outs of Sunil Janah's photographs taken in the famine districts, and even a couple of reproductions of Somenath Hore's early drawings. A few images of Elko's work from that time are interspersed with these, but not too many. The collection of famine images makes for a strange contrast: Chittoprasad, Abedin, Janah, Hore, with Lahiri the odd one out, with the weakest work of the lot.

It's in 1942 that Kedar Lahiri first starts to try and sketch the people who are coming in from the countryside and camping on the streets. The first mention I find of this is in October 1942, in a letter he writes to Eva:

From the middle of August, when the police shot down those protestors, the city has been at war with the Empire... for the last two months, there seem to have been more days of full curfew than normal ones... no sooner is one protest quelled (what the officials like to call 'a riot') than somebody puts a bomb in a milk depot, or burns down a wine store... the whole country has been like this but, as usual, Bengal and Calcutta lead when it comes to displaying public rage... I find myself imagining the fire of the larger war ringing us, a circle of untouched ground around Calcutta, and then an intense blaze spreading from the centre of the city, moving outward as though trying to join forces with the surrounding inferno...

... Now, just as the protests seem to be dying down, a new, quieter calamity is making its way into our lives...

... if the city is at all my subject, if one can clumsily call it 'the landscape of the city', then that landscape has now begun to change rapidly, at least in the Bengali neighbourhoods of the town. The other day, I was walking on Hazra Road and I saw that an entire section of the footpath (what your Americans would call the 'sidewalk') had disappeared, swallowed up by a cluster of people who had begun to just live there. The wall of their 'house' was the wall of an empty plot that lined the footpath. The floor was a spread of some rough cloth on the pavement concrete, the roof, such as it was, consisted of some pieces of rusted tin and dried palm fronds supported by bamboo, providing a minimum of covering over the head. This family of fifteen or twenty people were conducting the act of living, of domesticity (living in a house, though I'm sure you know the word by now) right before us, the passers-by, the people looking at them with horror and distaste from their dry and secure houses, the cars driving by. The only things missing from this caricature of a 'home': I couldn't see where they would go to relieve themselves and I couldn't see any food being cooked. As I wandered about, trying not to look as though I was prying, I overheard a local lady trying to speak to them. It was with difficulty one could understand what they were saying; I could see the lady having the same problem; they were speaking Bengali all right, but it was almost unrecognizable as the language I know. However, there was no mistaking the desperation in their

> *speech and in their bodies. They hadn't eaten properly for a long time. After a while, I realized what was really odd – in the middle of the morning most of the children were lying down under the 'roof', unmoving, and next to them lay the older people...*

From the taped interviews with Elko, from his letters to Eva and other sources, I've gathered that the young Kedar Lahiri starts trying to draw these 'street people', keeps 'trying and failing' as he puts it himself. For instance, there is a scrap of a page from a drawing book, slightly worm-eaten. At the top, there's a fountain-pen sketch of a figure lying on a pavement, so heavily redacted with cross-hatching that you can barely make out the figure under the slashes of spitting blue lines. What survives the scratching out is the scrawled date – 'Oct '42'. A little below this mess is a clean pencil drawing of a teacup and half-eaten pastry with the Flurys logo on the plate. Next to it is another vignette – a woman's hand holding a cigarette next to an unfinished mouth – which is most probably a sketch of Keya Dutta.

FLURYS

'You'll be fine, Niru. Just stay and finish your tea.'

'I'm not sure... these waiters, you know.'

'There's nothing they can say, don't worry. The bill's being paid. You're a lady of leisure. You have a right to finish what you've ordered.'

'Yes, but...'

'Come to think of it, with that bandage, you look more like a murderous pirate than a lady. They'll be too scared. Just don't pull out your cutlass, there's a good girl!'

'I will try not to kill them.'

The two of them squeeze hands across the table, helping each other suppress the giggles.

The blackout drapes have come down on the semicircle of tall windows at Flurys, as they do at 5 p.m. every evening. Sitting at one of the window tables, Niru watches Imogen pay the bill, nod at the waiter and snap her purse shut.

'Must rush, my dear! See you soon, I hope!' Imogen picks up her hat and reaches across to squeeze Niru's shoulder, which makes Niru's bandaged forehead hurt slightly. She then strides to the exit, where the doorman opens the inner curtains to let the memsahib into the temporary blackout cubicle. Imogen slides between the curtains and vanishes, as though she's part of a magician's trick. Niru imagines her pausing momentarily in the complete blackness before the second doorman opens the outer curtains, releasing her on to a darkened Park Street.

Niru herself has a few minutes before she makes her way to Chowringhee to meet Titir and catch the tram to Shyambajar to spend the night with her parents. She stays anxious – this is the first time she is in one of these shaheb places without Imogen for protection. In her mind, she checks again that the bill has indeed been paid. She owes nothing to the bad-tempered waiters, nothing to Flurys. She reminds herself that, in fact, it is they who owe her the time she will take to finish her last cup of tea and the remaining bit of chicken patty. She has requested Imogen to ask for their glasses to be filled with water so that she doesn't have to say anything at all to the waiters – she can't bear the thought that they may refuse to give her even water – to even give her water – once the mem has left; although Imo has scoffed at the idea, Niru doesn't have the courage to test things here.

The flashily dressed man sitting two window tables away seems to have no such hesitation. He snaps his fingers at a waiter. 'Eijey, you! Two more chocolate boats, and another pot of coffee.' He checks the time as he turns to the look at the girl sitting across from him, and Niru marks both the expensive watch and the gold cufflinks on the pulled-back sleeve of his shirt. The girl is about Niru's age, twenty-one or twenty-two, and she is wearing a lot of powder on her face. Her tiip a red dot island in the middle of an unnaturally cream-white forehead. Her Dhakai sari is clearly new and not cheap. The man says something to her in a low voice and she smiles and titters, lipstick glistening on her lips. The man says something else, and the girl nervously touches the small pile of college books she has kept like a protective moat, a little to the side of her plate. The man notices the gesture and his hand leaps to trap hers on top of the books. Niru finds herself shuddering slightly with disgust.

She forces herself to look away, but there is no escape. Her gaze catches on a table of four, two Markin officers talking to two Anglo-Indian girls, though talking is perhaps as wrong a word as can be to describe what is taking place. Each Markin sits next to his girl, one's long arm hinged around one girl's neck, the other one's fingers clasped on the second girl's shoulder, pushing up the short dress sleeve and kneading the upper arm, both men's mouths close to the girls' ears, the waiters walking past as if the table is unoccupied.

'We're surrounded by them, their farms are right next to ours, but we manage.' Two older mems sit on Niru's left, speaking softly to one another. The one with the small rug of silver hair pasted to her head repeatedly pokes a breadstick into her swirl of butter without eating it. 'They're quite – how can one put it – *quite* primitive in their ways, but we manage to rub along somehow. We're Scottish, you see, I suppose you could call us Transvaal Scots, though that rings oddly I always find, and those people are who they are. I find everything about them, you know, the way they do things, their language, their customs, all very... crude is perhaps too harsh, but I think we manage quite well in hiding our... distaste, if you like, yes, the slight distaste one always feels for...' The woman brings up the breadstick and bites into it with a sharp snap.

Niru feels her ire rising as she overhears the mem's clipped English, but something gives her pause. Maybe they are not talking about Indians.

'I don't suppose there is any question of er, mingling, er, lines, is there?' This woman is shorter, more round, and her greying hair sits under one of those ridiculous little topis Englishwomen love to sport.

'Of intermarriage? With Boers? Good god, no!' The silver woman's eyes widen as she almost chokes on her breadstick.

Boers, so South Africa. The mem is talking about Dutch settlers in South Africa.

'That, my dear, would be about as likely as one of us marrying a black, or a coo—or an Indian, or one of *them* marrying a kaffir! Though one does hear instances every now and then of one of them, you know, trotting off into the veldt. As my father used to say, "They may be white, my dear, but they are far closer to these savages than to us!" You can't say this too loudly nowadays, of course, but my father actually fought in the Boer War, you know, and he wasn't about to mince words, not in the privacy of his home.'

Niru looks down and sees there is a congress of small insects around her teacup. Her heart jumps with elation. She looks up and sees the same specks flicking around the ceiling lights and finds herself smiling. Shyama poka. How would she explain it in English? The small insects, 'bugs', that appear just before Kali Puja, indicating that all the various hot seasons are finally over, that winter is not far away. One or two of them settle right on the old wound on her forehead, and she flicks them away.

'Bearer!' She calls for the waiter firmly, ignoring the ache as she cuts the Black Forest pastry into half. Certain kinds of arm movement still bring back the pain where the bullet has chewed into one corner of her left elbow, but she has learnt to live with it. The waiter ambles up and she asks for some more water and reminds him that they are still waiting for the hot chocolate. Outside the tall windows, the October light is fading and, despite the air conditioning, the lights inside the tea room keep attracting more and more poka. She places half the pastry on to the child's plate, but smacks his hand lightly when he reaches for it.

'What did I tell you? Is this a chom-chom?'

'No, Ma.'

'Is this a rossogolla?'

'Fork, I have to use fork for cake, not hands.'

'Correct.'

The boy takes the fork and gleefully stabs the cube of pastry, making the icing fly.

'Saki!'

'Mistake.' This, in English.

'What mistake? Are you a five-year-old?'

'Sorry.' He continues to reply in English.

'How old are you?'

He goes back to the safety of his Bangla. 'You know fully well, how old I am.'

'Then eat properly, like an eight-year-old.'

'Yes, Ma.'

She watches him as he scoops up the cake, using the cake fork like a spoon. At certain moments she can unmistakably see the boy's father, but from other angles the man disappears, just as he did that December day in '44, into his own magic black box. The intermingling of lines. She was sitting at this same table all those years ago, in 1942, right after that bloody August–September, when the two mad-looking old mems were talking shamelessly about South Africa. She had only properly decoded what they were saying once she had relayed the conversation to Imogen. Little could those ladies have imagined how many different ways human 'lines' would mingle in the coming years, though now South Africa stood naked before the world, with its apartheid declared so soon after the war, when Hitler's ashes were not yet cold. But then, how different from those old mems was her own mother? How different was Titir?

'You let that Negro rob you of your honour! That hobshi animal raped you and you are actually going to have his baby? Niru, have you no shame!?' Roma's hand flashed before Niru could reply. A clash of bangles and then the report of the slap, Titir's pretty face snapping to one side, almost like a cracked china vase. Niru suddenly between Roma and Titir, trying to keep them apart. Roma-she-said-it-to-me, Roma-she-said-it-to-me, she-said-it-to-me-Roma, she-said-it-to-me-not-you, she said-it-to-me, Roma, now enough, now enough.

Good thing Keya and that Dandy-Lion Lahiri had dragged Roma away then, put her in his ridiculous little car and taken her away. Titir inconsolable in Niru's arms, choking on her own sobs.

The first time the hobshi's hand had brushed hers. Accidentally, in the hotel room, both reaching for the ketchup. No different from any other stranger's hand. 'Excuse me, Miss... I do beg your pardon.'

'It's all right. Please don't mention.' The words had slipped out wrong, the ones she usually deployed to reply to 'thank you', but the big man seemed to understand correctly. This encouraged her to add a sentence: 'It is Miss Niru. My name.'

'Miss Nero.' The man nodded courteously.

'Niru.'

'Miss Neeroo, I beg your pardon.'

Across the next few months he'd get it wrong in several different ways, until he got it right and pronounced it like no one had before, and like no one ever would again, but on the night they were trapped in the Markin officer's rooms, the black man avoided addressing her by name as far as possible.

It took long time before that hand did anything else, before they touched again. She had already seen him play, but after that night, later, she saw him play before an audience for the first time, the fingers on the valve buttons, creating many more notes than seemed possible with just three digits. Then she saw him, and those hands, doing things to the Anglo-Chinese girl that she wished she'd never seen. And then, finally, more than a year after the first accidental touch, her fingers managed to lose themselves in the large knot of his hand. As to the jettisoning of her 'honour', the complete opposite of robbery, that had taken even longer, and it wasn't even in the same universe as the things she was to see later, once the peasant war started.

She reassembles the whole thing in her mind, sort of timing each scoop of memory with the boy forking up his cake. The first time the two of them had seen each other, at the tea-dance in the Great Eastern, which she still connects with the headache she'd had the next day, what she learnt from Imogen to call a 'hangover'. In the next few days, things with the Quit India business had moved so fast, she completely forgot about the mountain of a black man. There was the protest at Wellington Square, the blow from the tear-gas cannister, then trying to locate Titir who had never gone to Howrah, and then the business of getting her out of jail. Then there was the chain of upheavals that followed, the firing and the curfews stretching from August all the way into October, 'August Kranti' they now liked to call it, August Revolution, except even then she and her comrades had understood it was anything but a real revolution.

She and Imogen had met here in Flurys once, just after Durga Puja, with her forehead wound still fresh, and then, for more than a fortnight, they had communicated by postcards, somewhat erratic in a city where people were constantly putting incendiaries into postboxes and setting fire to post offices. Once, she managed to place a phone call to Imogen's house, Alipore 3535 – she still remembers the old number after eleven years because it was so easy – but Imogen was out. A week later, a postcard from Imogen indicating when she would be home. She'd called again, and by then the trouble seemed to be dying out. 'Oh, Niru, do let's meet! I've been missing you so terribly! Let's go and do something fun! I know things must be awful for you in so many ways, what with this terrible cyclone and everything, but do let's get out? Tomorrow, then? Let's break out of our cages, shall we?'

Until the mem-girl said it, she had not thought of herself as being in a cage. Once she'd said it, though, she could not see herself in any other way. The next afternoon, she locked away her Party work in a drawer and took a tram to Dalhousie Square through the cool late-October afternoon. The plan was to meet at the Great Eastern and go to the Tea Room, but with a mutual promise that this time no alcoholic drinks would be consumed. The plan went well until about six o'clock.

This time, Niru noticed, was different from that afternoon in August. The first warning sound was the bell of a fire engine, the slow tolling of the gong completely out of rhythm with the screech of tyres as the driver accelerated, braked and then accelerated again. Soon, the rumble of more vehicles, heavy official ones, not normal traffic, and this was enough to alert everyone at the tables of the Tea Room. The waiters moved in smoothly with the bills for the few non-Americans there. This time, some of the Yanks also got up and went to the windows, peering through the tape to try and see what was going on. This time, Niru knew how to interpret the sounds coming from the street: the single firecrackers were rifles being fired in the air, the irregular bursts of metallic drumming were tear-gas cannisters falling on the asphalt and tram tracks, then there was a dull explosion which was probably the petrol tank of a vehicle exploding. She knew these noises by now, but they sounded very different from inside the hotel walls.

Within minutes, Imogen and Niru were out of the Tea Room, part of a group heading for the main doors. In the lobby, an American Military Police sergeant put his arm out to block their way.

'I'm sorry, ladies and gentlemen. You cannot exit from this exit.'

'Why on earth not? From *which* exit can we exit then?' Niru could sense the annoyance in Imogen's tone.

'I'm sorry, ma'am, we've had to seal off the main entrance. The situation right outside is dangerous.'

'Right. So what should we—'

'Well, ma'am, if y'all just go sit somewhere, that'd be best. We'll let you know soon as it's safe to leave. Might not be for a while though.' The big MP turned away to stop others.

'I think there's a side entrance.' Niru couldn't quite see the man, but by now she could recognize an upper-class English accent with its spice-fry of entitlement and disdain. 'I suspect we can go past the nightclub and burrow out near the bakery. Dashed if I'm going to stay holed up here, with all these bally Yan—' Someone shut the man up before the Markin sergeant could hear. The whole bunch, all six or seven of them, turned towards the corridor leading to the club.

Niru had never been deeper inside the hotel, not beyond the Tea Room. In her memory, the corridor to the side exit stretches much longer than could have been actually possible. A clear memory of feeling that this was some strange smelling, oddly organized foreign country, right here in the middle of her messy city. On the walls, portraits of old English lords and ladies, fox-hunting scenes, Imperial war triumphs, each illuminated by its own small electric lamp, the shades made of curved brass that hid the bulbs and focused yellow light on the dark, shiny canvas surfaces. Every now and then, a brass flowerpot on a white marble plinth, all the pots empty, as if someone had stolen the flowers. Lifting her sari and jogging behind the striding Imogen, Niru felt a flash of panic, as though she was being drawn into one of those dungeons she had read about, the castle all grand and fancy above, hiding a dank, dark, claustrophobic maze of hell underneath.

She forced herself on to other thoughts. What will we have here, when the Ingrej have finally gone? When there is no longer any place for plush hotels for the grotesquely rich? Would the place be burnt to the ground? Or would people find a use for the huge building? Government offices? A college, perhaps? Or a hospital? Yes, a hospital, Niru's vote would be for a hospital, the city desperately needed more hospitals.

Imogen suddenly stopped and Niru bumped into her, almost knocking her over.

'So sorry, Niru! My shoe's come off!' Imogen bent down, trying to adjust a strap. Niru stopped. The other people had gone, disappeared, leaving just the two of them in the corridor. A staccato wail of sound hit the walls and bounced off past them. Niru instinctively covered her ears and ducked. Some new kind of infernal siren, or maybe the screech of some new weapon that the Ingrej had deployed against the crowds. There was a break in the sound and then it started again, softer, longer, the sharper notes less frequent as the lower ones smeared into each other like the soft parts of a malfunctioning machine. Not a siren, almost musical.

Imogen straightened. 'Oh!' A smile broke out on her face.

Not almost musical, actually music. Something singing, something crying violently, teto – bitter – an ugly fight between notes, but also sweet in parts.

'Oh! Oh my god, I do think it's...' Imogen was looking at a huge pair of doors on the left of the corridor, one of them half open, and Niru realized this was where the noise was coming from.

'Imogen, what...' The mem-girl gripped Niru's arm and pulled her towards the big doors. To the right of the doors was a brass plaque, about the size of a tea tray, with a single word engraved in curving script – Maxim's. As Imo dragged her to the open door, Niru could see her own arm and two bangles reflected in the mirror-shiny plaque. Her nose was hit by a mixture of smells – tobacco smoke, the ghost whiff of various meats cooked in onions, butter and other Western whatnot, the spoor of cologne and alcohol and old, dead, air conditioning. At the time Niru received this mixture as an accompaniment to the crazy racket blasting out of the doorway, this was the smell of that sound. It was only much later, once she got to know the place properly, that her mind could carry out a forensic separation of the components.

At that moment, she struggled to free herself from the grip Imogen had on her arm, but this only made the mem-girl tighten her long fingers. 'Shh! Niru, do shut up and listen! It's that man I told you about, that trumpeter!'

The sound stopped abruptly, as if someone inside had heard them. But then there were the thumps, perhaps of a hand hitting something metallic, and the notes began again. It dawned on Niru that this was some sort of musical phrase, quite long and complex, which somebody was practising again and again. By now, Imogen had wrapped herself around the closed door with her head poking inside. Niru tried to stand on tiptoe to see over Imo's shoulder, but the mem was too tall. She then leaned forward past the other girl's waist so that she could also take in whatever was going on.

The place was empty. But all the lights were on, the chandeliers, the wall lights, the low lamps suspended above each table, making the banquettes, chairs and tables look naked. The big hobshi was alone on stage, his back to them, body swaying back and forth, his shoulders hunched, and the sound was emerging from his mass. The man half turned with a change of phrase, and suddenly she could see the shiny tubes entwined in his massive hands with the golden bell flowering out. The sound shifted as he moved from one position to another, louder, softer, changing shape, flooding over everything even without a microphone. Every now and then, the man's left hand brought up what looked like a small lid to cover the mouth of the trumpet. This was the thing muddying the notes, muffling them, taking off their sharp edges. When he took the lid away, sometimes slowly, sometimes abruptly, the sharp sounds seemed all the more clear and harsh, tripping out in cascade after ruthless cascade.

Niru found herself pressed hard into Imo's upper arm, unable to take her eyes off the man. Behind her, the group of Ingrej rushed back from the side entrance, clearly thwarted from leaving, but she was only vaguely aware of them.

After a while, Niru noticed a plume of smoke coming from just out of her sight. She leaned further into the room to see who it was. She recognized the Anglo-Indian bandleader from that first time she'd been in the Tea Room, on what everyone was now calling the 'Quit India' day, 9th August, which suddenly felt like many years ago. The man, she couldn't remember his name, was sitting at a table to the left of the stage, smoking and writing in what looked like a ledger. Every now and then, he would look up when the hobshi coaxed some new outrage from his instrument, but then he would go back to his accounting, showing no other reaction. On his part, the big American showed no sign of wanting any response from the Anglo, playing on as if the other fellow wasn't there.

By this time, Niru was beginning to concede there was a tune in the flurry of notes, some structure, some progression, which the man would suddenly chop off, starting again, some phrases repeated exactly, others twisted differently, as if trying to find something, rummaging through the melody with an intense and relentless dissatisfaction, the trumpet emitting quick phrases, music, but also – she couldn't avoid the thought – farts, burps, screams – then whole rippling ladders of sound, the rungs festooned with colour, snakes and ladders of sound, the shades alternating, altering, mutating, the same phrase again and again, and then progressions, drops leading down different paths, producing impossibility after impossibility.

In one of the pauses, Niru had a flash of comprehension. She had always tolerated her father's devotion to Indian classical music, to 'khayal' as he always called it, but without really understanding it. Now, suddenly, as after a blow to the head, she could see what her father had been listening to across all these years.

'Well, hello, if it isn't a pair of true aficionado ladies.' The cigar-voice was very close behind them. It was Imogen this time who banged into Niru as they both jumped back.

'Oh, hello, Irwin! I'm sorry, we didn't mean to eavesdrop, it's just that we were passing by and—'

'No matter, no matter, come in! Let's go in! I'm sure Jones will appreciate an audience, Fenton doesn't really count.' Goodsugar gently took possession of both the girls' arms and steered them through the door. 'Hi there, boys! Lookee what I found here! A couple of stowaways!'

Fenton pushed back his chair and stood up, trying to find his smile. The hobshi just nodded briefly and looked away, wiping his face with a handkerchief. Niru could sense he wasn't pleased to have his practice interrupted.

'Well, don't mind us! Keep going! All hell breaking loose outside, ain't no reason we can't have some fun here, right?'

'What's happening outside, Mr Goodsugar?' Fenton also pulled out a handkerchief to pat his brow.

'Can't say for sure, all I know is that the Injuns have their warpaint on, in their thousands, and His... Majesty's armed forces have opened fire in more than a few places.'

'Bloody not again! I thought the buggers had finally quietened down! Beg pardon, ladies, beg pardon.'

'Well, sport, we are staying out of it. This here hotel now being under US control makes it neutral territory and we've got the building secured. This is one of the safest places in town because – never forget! – the good ol' US Army always protects its booze, broads and billeting!'

Coming through the big main doors this time, Niru had noticed the Markin soldiers standing guard outside, but she hadn't realized the whole hotel had been taken over by them.

Niru looked around the place, forgetting to hide her curiosity. So, this was one of those infamous 'nightclubs', those dens of Western sin and gora debauchery so hated and derided by the morality monitors of pure Bengali culture. With all the lights on, it looked like a slightly strange restaurant, with most of the seating facing towards the stage, a kind of mix between an expensive eatery and theatre. She noted the thick leather-covered upholstery on the banquettes, the polish of the chairs, the heavy glass ashtrays on each table, and in one corner, a cluster of small, silver-shiny buckets on stands.

Fenton's voice interrupted her wide-eyed survey. 'Actually, we'd better clear this place. They'll need to get it ready for the evening.'

'Are you open this evening?' Imogen tilted her head quizzically. 'I wouldn't have imagined you'd get too many customers with all this going on outside.'

'You never know, Miss, you never know, all across the last two months, since August... people come from all corners of the city. The port people, the army people, no problem, the RAF chaps from Dum Dum and Alipore, also European civilians, they get lifts, from Ballygunge and Alipore, just jump into army vehicles, not to mention all the American pilots back from Assam for their R&R. People get tired of sitting around in a curfew, you know?'

People. Niru thinks about who these people are. She doesn't say anything about the many Indians, also people, who also get tired of sitting around in a curfew. She can see the logic, even as she questions it – we people have created the situation for curfew, so it's our load to bear, the 'Europeans', the Ingrej and the Markin, the goras, these people, are blameless victims. They are people, we are not people, we are less people.

Goodsugar chuckled through his cigarette. 'Anyway, now that this joint is full of our people, that's potentially nearly three hundred captive customers courtesy the US Armed Forces!'

Niru saw that Byron had started to pack his things. That peculiar sound again, when he pointed his trumpet downwards and thumped it to release the spit.

Goodsugar had taken Imogen to one side. Closer by, she could hear Fenton talking to Byron. 'Jones, man, I know you've been trying to convince her but I can tell you, she won't like all this fancy stuff. Can you just stick to regular? This Clarissa of ours, you know, she doesn't like too much attention, you know, to be going away from her. Also, people here, man, they won't understand, they won't *get*, you know, what you're trying to do. What with this war and all, people want what they're familiar with, they want the regular stuff, with maybe a bit of new thing here and there, but not too much. Your new style, maybe just keep for your American radio programmes.'

'You know?' Goodsugar added for Fenton.

Imo turned to the hobshi, 'Mr Jones, can I ask? Which tune were you playing? Was it just the one? I kept thinking I recognized it, but I couldn't quite—'

'It's called "One O'Clock Jump", Miss. It's one of the standards here, for Mr Greaves' band.'

Goodsugar: 'One of Basie's big hits.'

'Yes, of course. It was superb, what you were doing with it.'

'Jones is... superb, you're so right, Miss. But it's not how we play the tune. Technically, you know, we just can't match these American fellows. He treats tunes like Meccano. You make something, you take it apart, and with the same parts, you make something else, you know, completely different.

Goodsugar asked the question that had lit up in Niru's mind. 'Say... what is Meccano?'

'It's an engineering set for children,' supplies Imogen. 'Don't you have them over there? Some sets can be quite advanced... But no, Mr Fenton, not Meccano surely, that takes away the idea of any...'

Byron and Niru simultaneously: 'Feeling?' Their eyes flicking around to meet for a second.

'No, no, no,' says Fenton. 'I have never seen as much feeling as in this bug—in Mr Byron's playing. The fact is, people can't bear too much of this kind of feeling. They need plain comfort. Entertainment. What they are used to. Smooth stories. And, you know, that's what we've got to give them. Night after night. I can't be as free as him.'

The child sucks up the dregs of his chocolate milkshake, his straw making a sound that irritates Niru beyond reason. His lips are nothing like his father's, and the pulling on the straw completely the opposite of blowing on a trumpet, but there's something that reminds Niru of the American. Maybe it's the intense concentration the child brings to the task, maybe it's the furrowed forehead. 'I can't be as free as him,' the man had said about Byron, and that's exactly what she'd always felt about him, she could never be as free as him, with his music, with his women, with his ability (she knew he had orders to go home, she knew he had no orders once he got there) to pack his bags and just go and never come back, to not even write, not once.

'Ma, why does it say "So Long, 1955" here? Why was 1955 so long?' The kid is looking at the cover of an American magazine.

'So long, means goodbye.'

'No, it doesn't, Ma! So long means it's very long, something is very long.'

Roma answers for Niru this time. 'Yes, shona, it does mean that, but in American, when Americans say it, it also means bye-bye. As in, *so long till I see you again.*'

Niru wonders yet again if that man is still alive somewhere. Not that she believes in all this hocus-pocus, but she can't get rid of the feeling that if he'd died she would know somehow. He would have figured out a way to say goodbye.

'Mango-mashi? It's been so long since we have come to Flurys,' offers Saki.

'That is a correct English sentence.' Roma claps so loudly that people at the other tables turn to look at them. 'Well done!'

'And we need to say so long to it soon, so hurry up with that cake. Mango-mashi also has to go.'

Niru finds all this Christmas nonsense beginning to gnaw at her, the decorations strung across Park Street outside, and inside Flurys the big Christmas tree with its multiple paws of cottonwool, its stupid lights blinking at all the customers. Christmas crackers lie destroyed on their table, where the boy has gleefully torn them open. She's glad to see the child polishing off the last of the cake.

'Okay, so long, Mango-mashi.'

'No, come on, what do we say in Bangla?' Roma puts her hand into the boy's hair and lifts his head.

'We say *aashi.*'

'What does that mean?'

'It means I'm coming... just coming back.'

'Yes, it means, kindly allow me to leave so that I can come back quickly.'

'Yes... hyan.'

'And when you say *aashi, Dida* what does your grandmother reply?'

'She says *esho, shona.*'

'Meaning, come back soon my golden one, come back quickly, yes?'

'Yes. Please come back soon. It's very old-fashioned. Why can't we just say bye-bye? Or goodbye?'

Niru opens her mouth to cut short the rally but swallows her words. Roma continues the game as she disposes off the bill and wraps her shawl around herself.

'Because we are like that. We are Bengalis. We don't like the whole thing of leaving, and we like to come back. So we do away completely with the business of going away.'

'To the so long.'

'To the so long, to the bye-bye, but not to the au revoir, or the auf weidersehen or dosvidanya...'

'Mango-mashi, how many languages do you know?'

'Bangla, Ingreji, a bit of French, a very small bit of German, I can pretend to know bits of a few others...

'That's three and a half, or maybe two and then two halves,' Saki counts on his fingers. 'Hindi?'

'Hardly. Only enough to talk to the ricksha-walla.'

'American?'

Roma bursts out laughing. Niru finds her own smile cutting through her mood of annoyance. She slides back her chair and gets up.

'Saki, now tell us what you know!'

'I know capitals of countries and states!'

'What was Calcutta once important for?'

'It was the capital of India!'

'Which India?'

'Come on, Ma! British India.'

'What is the capital now?'

'The capital now is Delhi, actually New Delhi.'

'And Calcutta is the capital of?' Roma jumps in.

'The state of West Bengal.'

'What is Bombay the capital of?'

'The Bombay Presidency!'

'And what is the capital of—'

Saki interrupts, jumping up and down as they reach the door, 'Wait, wait, I know! The capital of Madras Presidency is Madras!'

'—the United States?'

Saki pauses, wrong-footed. 'Umm, we don't need to know that for another two years, Ma. World Geography is in class 8.'

'But still. I was showing you a map the other day, wasn't I?'

'Umm, Washington? New York?... No, no, wait, I know! Tchicago!'

'It's Washington DC. And remember, I told you, it's not *Tchi*-cago but *She*-cago.'

'Chicago.'

The first time she herself pronounced Chicago correctly was in Goodsugar's suite at The Great Eastern.

They had left the nightclub, Maxim's, and gone back to the lobby to see if things had died down. They hadn't, and the MPs were still not letting anybody leave. The trumpeter had made his excuses, nodded to the ladies, and disappeared. 'Gone to pretty up for the evening,' Goodsugar had explained, while offering them a drink at the hotel bar. Niru compared the bar to the other spaces she had experienced in the hotel. If the Tea Room and Maxim's imposed on you a certain kind of bright, spreading space, this bar did the opposite – it was like a long cave with very little light, where people could bring out their hidden things without other people being able to see. Niru remembered both Imogen and the American ordering something called whisky sours. She had refused alcohol and they had asked for her to be given something called a Virgin Mary, which was made from spicy tomato juice.

'Would you ladies like to call home?' Goodsugar had asked, and Imogen had immediately taken up the offer, placing a brief telephone call from the bar.

'We have no telephone at my house, at my parents' house.' Niru had explained.

'I see. What about neighbours? Anybody close by?'

Niru shook her head. There was one connection a few houses down, at the big Sen house, but they didn't like to be disturbed unless it was an extreme emergency. She didn't remember their number, and in any case, she wouldn't have called them to say she was trapped in a fancy hotel with strange men.

'My parents are not expecting me today, it's all right.'

'Swell! You're free to have fun then! Say when you want to put live ammunition in that drink!'

Niru had looked at her nearly full glass and wondered what the man meant. Settling back, Imogen had explained. 'What Mr Goodsugar—'

'Please! Irwin!'

'What Irwin means is that you should tell him if you want them to make you a proper cocktail with alcohol in it.' She turned to the man. 'I'm afraid I'm breaking the pact I made with Niru. We'd agreed there would be no drinking today.'

'Ah! But you hadn't reckoned on the little shindig outside, had you?'

Niru had kept her resolve through the evening. As the mem-girl and the Markin put away a series of drinks, she had hung on to the glass in front of her, refusing even a refill. As the two goras talked, Niru went through the scenario again and again: her parents were not expecting her home that evening; they did not have Lady Tilu's phone number and no way of getting in touch; nor were Roma or Titir likely to worry – Roma was in Santiniketan for a few days with her friend Keya, Titir was visiting her people in Howrah and only coming back tomorrow, so there was no one waiting for her at Dover Road. The only question was if, as looked likely, they were forced to spend the night here, where would they stay? And, wherever they stayed, how would she explain it to Titir tomorrow? Could she make up a plausible story? Another friend's house? Could she tell her not to mention it to her parents? Roma, yes. Titir, no – that girl couldn't keep anything in her stomach.

It was difficult for her to follow everything Imogen and Goodsugar were talking about, but she understood they were mostly discussing jazz, the local radio station the Markin army had set up which seemed to be called Voo-two-zee-you, and the differences between jazz clubs in New York, London and Paris. About how music programmes recorded here were being broadcast in America and England. Something Goodsugar said stays with her down the years: 'You've got to remember a lot of these farm-boys have never heard jazz before they got here. Before deployment, these hayseeds had no idea that any such thing existed, no

Louis Armstrong, no Benny Goodman, no Basie, no Ellington or Ella, nothing! You could say they knew less about jazz than Niru here, you who've had the good fortune to live in a, in a… in a cosmopolitan city!'

Around 7.30 p.m., Goodsugar noticed an MP sergeant standing just outside the bar and went over to him. After a brief conversation, he returned. 'The news is the trouble's still continuing in different parts of town, so they've shut down this whole area around the government buildings, everything from Esplanade to the river, and up north to Brabourne Road and Bad-a-bazaar. There's also a curfew around Howrah Bridge and the station. Curfew lifts at dawn and not before, so looks like there's no way home tonight for both you Cinderellas.' Imogen looked at Niru to see how she was taking this. Goodsugar patted Imogen's hand. 'Now, look, it's okay, you're both welcome to stay with me. I have a suite courtesy Uncle Sugar, so there'll be no need to crowd each other, you can each have your own bed. Jones may need to use the couch after he's finished at Maxim's but you won't mind that? He's a good fella, doesn't snore much, not yet anyway! Only thing is this is on the QT as you English say, Imogen, 'cause the authorities don't like the idea of coloured personnel sharing quarters with… you know…'

'With Europea—with white people?' Niru can't stop herself.

'Er, precisely.'

'So what about me?'

'Women don't count – I beg pardon, Niru, I mean ladies are exempt from the official scheme of things.' Goodsugar smiled at having saved himself. Niru noticed he'd stopped using the 'Miss' before both their names. She hoped this was an indication of friendship and nothing else.

Presently, Goodsugar found out there was a movie showing in the ballroom for all US staff and the three of them made their way to the screening. The movie that comes up in Niru's memory is *Casablanca,* but she knows that can't be right because that was the first film she saw with Byron and that was in New Empire Cinema, sometime in 1944. What she firmly remembers, though, is the screen on a stand on the stage for the band, the small 16mm projector and a man changing the reels on a platform in the middle of the rows of chairs, the crackle of sound from the single loudspeaker next to the screen, and the rays of the projector catching the flat cloud of cigarette smoke as the screening progressed. She's also sure about the short films that preceded the main movie: one showing how the Americans were pushing back the Japanese in the Pacific, with shots of factories producing airplanes and artillery shells; she remembers being awed at how huge the factories were, and even more startled that the shell factory seemed to be populated entirely by cheerful women workers wearing headscarves and men's working clothes, costumes she later learnt were called overalls. The second short film was very short indeed, almost an advertisement, aimed at US servicemen in the 'CBI theater', warning them not to venture into areas that were prohibited to them, not to fraternize with local women, to avoid commenting on local politics or anything they found strange, such as a religious custom, say, in case they hurt local people's feelings.

Niru felt that she had understood an important difference between how the Americans and the British saw the Indians around them. For the Markin, the local population were a bit like animals in a jungle, or an open zoo, mostly friendly creatures, but who might charge or bite if provoked. This was quite different from the deeper entanglement that the British had with Indians, where both the hate and the love were stronger, the mutual understanding deeper.

She remembers only half watching the film while wondering what was going on outside. Amidst the whirr of the projector and the pall of tobacco smoke, she felt a bit trapped. Yet, in a way, she was also relieved that she had no choice in this situation. As white people romanced each other on the screen – had it been Fred Astaire and Rita Hayworth? – as they danced and laughed and exchanged dialogue with their funny nasal speech, the roll call repeated itself in her head: Ma-Baba – home, Roma – Santiniketan, Titir – Howrah. She was sure the Party comrades would be keeping their heads down, their instructions being to keep away from these demonstrations for a false independence, which were, in effect, agitations against the anti-fascist war. So, everyone she cared about should be safe and out of harm's way. She wished she could go somewhere and adjust her sari, but she was nervous about visiting the ladies' toilets, worried about sticking out. Looking around, she couldn't see any other deshi women, or at least no one else in a sari. On the other hand, all eyes were on the screen and no one was looking at her at all; perhaps her discomfort was entirely in her own mind. This was joined by the discomfort of trying to imagine how they would all arrange themselves in Goodsugar's room.

When they finally made their way upstairs to the fourth floor, Niru saw that what the American occupied was actually a series of rooms, like a small flat in the hotel. Niru remembers wondering why he kept calling it 'my sweet' and it was only later that she understood the word as 'suite'.

As the Markin showed them in, her forehead wound started hurting, almost as if her body was allowing the pain to reintroduce itself now that she could perhaps lie down. Niru had never been in a hotel room before, never even imagined one with any vividity, and she was shocked by the scale and the luxury of the suite. Her father had taken her and her mother to see one or two English productions when they had played in Calcutta, and each room of the suite looked like a set from one of those plays, the furniture set on a proscenium. It was as though she was looking on to another world, except she was in it, one of the actors. As used to happen whenever she walked onstage into an installed set of one of her father's plays, she found herself being very careful where she put her feet, alert that she should not touch anything or disturb any of the props.

Navigating around a sofa and chairs, she approached a window and found she could look through a gap in the blackout curtain and the crossed tape on the glass. Outside, instead of a painted backdrop or a cleverly hidden spotlight, she could see the dark streets, and make out the gates of Governor House with the cream-yellow arches topped with lions. Power seemed so absurdly close by, within touching distance, and so normal.

'Welcome to the cabin, folks! Holler if I can get you something. Alcohol, Coca-Cola, lemonade... Anyone hungry?'

'Niru, would you like to use the...' Imogen was suddenly aware of how strange all this must feel to Niru.

'Yes, please, the bath—'

'Of course, there are two, one in the bedroom and – why don't you just use the one here, that door on the left.' Goodsugar pointed with his cigar.

Niru hurried to the toilet, shut the door behind her and looked for the bolt. There wasn't one. The chances of one of the others coming in were non-existent, but something in Niru would not allow her to proceed without locking herself in. A small panic mounting, she searched for a lock until she saw the little knob below the door handle and managed to turn it.

The bathroom was bigger than the room she shared with Roma at Dover Road. There was a light with a flower-shaped shade curving over the sink mirror, and Niru caught a glimpse of herself as she walked past to the commode. After she had finished, she went back to the sink. She took her time washing her hands, running both taps and watching her fingers move around the small rectangular ship of porcelain. The mirror showed her a strange Bengali creature in a foreign space. Her hair was all right, still slicked down, the sari was now properly back in place, but things on her internal shelves had shifted and some were teetering on the edge. The prickle of discomfort ranged across her skin, moving from face to arms, down her stomach and legs and, as she looked in the mirror, she could not meet her own eyes for too long. After a while, she turned off the taps, the white cap on the left one marked with a red H, the one on the right with a blue C, and looked for something on which she could wipe her hands. There were two clean tiny towels hanging from the brass spokes next to the sink and she used one, feeling simultaneously quite daring and quite stupid for feeling that. When she remembers this, her memory is tinged with the fragrance of the creamy soap she used, a smell somewhere between lavender and leather, though she's not sure if the smell is overlaid from a later moment from the same or perhaps another bathroom at the hotel.

She doesn't remember how the time passed immediately after that, just that Goodsugar had ordered, and the waiter came into room with a trolley on which there were three silver-coloured domes. The man took the domes off, revealing three plates, each with a small triangular tower. It took Niru some time to recognize the things as sandwiches, so different were they from what she had eaten via Roma or the delicate cucumber sandwiches introduced to her by Imogen. She struggled with her club sandwich, watching the different ways in which Imogen and Goodsugar negotiated theirs. Finally, hunger overcoming decorum, she took the leap, choosing the American's method and opening her mouth wide to take a bite of the thing. Imogen had dismantled hers with a knife and fork, and this allowed Niru to see a cross section of what she was ingesting herself: toasted bread, fried egg, strips of very salty, crisply fried pig meat – bacon – tomatoes, a slice of grilled chicken, lettuce and some white sauce she later understood was named mayonnaise. Accompanied by tomato ketchup sauce, into which you dipped the whole construction.

She has no memory of how the sleeping arrangements were distributed, just a memory of a memory of later realizing that Goodsugar had employed subtle skin-colour segregation: Imogen to have the second bedroom, herself on the couch-bed in what she now thought of as the drawing room, 'and Jones can have the sofa', the meaning of which took time to trickle into her head – the hobshi trumpet man would be in the same room as her, but about eight feet away, sleeping on the long divan.

By the time there was a knock on the door, Niru was sitting on the couch-bed, half asleep, one of Goodsugar's books in her hands that she was no longer able to keep open. Imogen and the Markin were in the main bedroom, playing records on the gramophone, drinking and laughing, a smell of warming varnish that Niru knew was coming from the record player. Goodsugar came out of the bedroom and opened the door. The big man saw Niru behind Goodsugar, and then Imogen standing in the bedroom door.

'Sorry, Mr Goodsugar, I didn't realize... I can maybe go sleep—'

'No, no, it's okay, Jones, just put your butt down over there, these ladies won't bother you!'

Niru remembers the awkward laughter washing all around her. It's the first time she heard the black man's laugh, low, almost a growl; Goodsugar's chortling coming through his nose, pleased at his own joke even though very aware he had created some unease; Imogen pealing, high and drunk. Niru searched for an answering laugh inside her but couldn't find anything. She remembers thinking that everyone except for her was very drunk and the trumpet man the least drunk of the three.

Goodsugar pointed to a trolley where there was a bottle of whisky, glasses, water, and what Niru later learnt were called ice bucket and soda siphon.

'Help yourself, maestro! No Bourbon, I'm afraid, you'll have to swing with what we got.'

'Scotch is fine, boss. Thank you.' Jones walked over to the trolley and made himself a drink. 'Ladies.' He raised the glass in a small salute towards Niru and Imogen before taking a sip.

Niru remembers noticing the contrast between this Jones's sharply white teeth and his dark brown skin and thinking that his eyes looked quite safe. Not counting her father, until that point Niru had never ever spent the night with a grown man sleeping in the same room. Here was not only man, but also cigarettes and whisky, but the sense of panic she was anticipating never came. Years later, she would have the same feeling of missing panic when she and two other women ambushed a police party near Koyra; once you were in it, once the stock of the rifle was against your shoulder, the metal of the trigger warm against your finger, panic could only wave at you from outside the window, like a person wanting to be let in, but without much hope.

On the stage of Goodsugar's suite, someone had switched off a couple of the lights and the living room was lit only by two table lamps, one next to her and one near Jones's sofa. Imogen had gone to sleep with a cheery 'Goodnight, all!', Goodsugar was in his bedroom, tapping something on what sounded like a small typewriter, and the black man was looking deep into his glass, seemingly lost in his thoughts. It was a good moment for Niru to get under the light blanket and go to sleep, but something in her mind kept getting in the way. She kept feeling she should say something to this man before going to sleep. It would be more natural than hiding behind awkward silence, it would show that she was not scared and that this was normal for her. It would counter all the nasty talk she kept hearing among her circles about these Negroes, it would be in keeping with the inspiring spirit Paul Robeson evoked among the Party—

'Is the light bothering you, Miss Nero? I can turn it off. Just say so.'

'No, no, not bothering at all. Good night.'

'Good night, Miss.'

She found the switch for her own table lamp, pulled the blanket up to her chin and closed her eyes. Goodsugar's typewriter stuttered beyond the half-open door of his bedroom, the same opening allowing the sickly-sweet smell of his cigar to wander out. The air conditioner had a whirr that kept changing every now and then – later, she remembered the grille and the flattened letters forming the name Kelvinator – sudden sleep weighing down her eyelids.

Her dreams broke equally abruptly, her eyes snapping open when she heard the strange animal close by. What was it? Where was she? What was this strange, cool clamminess on her arms and neck? It took her a few moments. Hotel. Sweet. Suite. Markin Goodsugar's rooms. Living room. Air conditioner. The trumpet man, asleep on the couch a few feet away, nostrils flaring as the snores made their way out from some deep subterranean place in that big body. She found herself trying to smell him before she moved, sniffing quietly like a deer in a jungle, as if the man's spoor would reveal the extent of danger she was in. Niru caught herself quickly, remembering her disgust when an aunt of Roma's had said something about these American Negroes smelling different, 'like animals, not like humans, like in the zoo', the disgust transferring to herself as she realized that, in some part of her, she had internalized this racialist nonsense. There was no smell coming from the trumpet man that she could make out. Or wait, yes, the room had a general smell of cigarettes and cigars and whisky, and some concentration of that did seem to be emanating from the sleeping man. Not an animal smell, but a gora smell, a Markin smell, fancy hotel smell.

Someone had drawn open the window curtains, and cloudy daylight changed the room completely. The space now had a context, the sense of buildings outside, crows cawing somewhere, traffic, cars, horse hooves, tram bell, ricksha bell. Her city connected now to this foreign space. She swirled out of the blanket, adjusting her sari, her mind already looking for Imogen. Both bedroom doors were open, there was no one there except for her and the hobshi. She quickly made her way to the bathroom and locked the door. Her face ambushed her from the mirror. She was still recognizably Nirupama Majumdar, her parents' daughter Niru, her friends' friend Niru, tree codename Neem, still a junior comrade of the Party, still everything she had been at this time yesterday, but something had changed. After a moment, she realized it was only the background, what was behind her in the mirror, the shiny brass, the white enamel and polished wood, that was making her feel like a traitor to something, like a spy who had been caught out. She pulled her eyes away from themselves and washed her face, drying it on one of the small towels that seemed to have remained crisp and fresh. All the time she was in the bathroom, she avoided looking again at the mirror. Maybe if she un-saw herself she could later convince herself that none of this madness had happened.

When she came out, she saw the piece of paper that had been folded and placed on the little side table next to her couch, a big N scrawled on the top fold.

> *Niru, darling,*
>
> *There's a 'convoy' leaving for Alipore and I must jump into one of the cars. You have to head the other way but Irwin will arrange that, so not to worry, you'll be just fine! Promise you won't be upset that I've scurried off?*
>
> *See you soon!*
>
> *Imo*

She can still remember the taste of the panic breaking through, the spike of fury at Imogen, a clear taste rising in her mouth, accompanied by the unfamiliar bile from the strange sandwich she'd eaten the night before. What was she to do now? Clearly, the curfew had lifted and things were normal outside, but that outside seemed so far away – how was she to get there? What would people say when she left the room?

How would they look at her? Would someone arrest her for illegally spending the night, or, worse, imagine she was one of those women who—

'Good morning, Miss. Did you sleep all right?'

'Oh! Good morning!' The man was awake, sitting up on the couch, having slept in his shirt and trousers, the shirt still tucked into the waistband, but the sleeves rolled up.

'Yes, my sleeping was all right, just fine.'

'Glad to hear that, Miss. From time to time, I've had people complain about my snoring.'

'I didn't hear at all.' The man was smiling and Niru found herself smiling back.

'Glad to hear that. When folks complain, the only thing I can say is take it up with my granmaw, if you can reach her up in the Lord's heaven.'

'What is granmau, please?'

'Oh, my grandmother, my daddy's mama. She was the big snorer in the family and I guess I got it from her. Can't escape heredity, can you?'

She had only a vague idea what heredity meant but she wasn't going to ask, not twice in two minutes, and have him thinking she was a complete boka idiot.

She has a memory of someone knocking on the door, of a waiter bringing in breakfast, of tasting strange food, eggs like she had never had before, shards of bacon, and her first pancakes with some syrup that she first thought was some strange nolen gur, fresh liquid jaggery, somehow there out of season, despite winter being a few weeks away. In the dainty white porcelain cups, no tea but coffee, black and incredibly bitter, until the man, Jones, suggested she add sugar and milk. She ate, all the while glancing across surreptitiously to see how Jones himself dealt with his food.

For a big man, he ate quite delicately, using only the fork, making neat combinations of the different foods with each forkful: scrambled egg and bacon, bacon and small triangle of pancake, pancake triangle and egg, every now and then sweeping up the sweet liquid or runny egg with the more solid pancake or bacon. He was clearly hungry; at first, she could hear him masticating the food through a mouth that was slightly open. Then he seemed to realize he was in polite company and made sure to shut his mouth after delivering each forkful into it. After a while, she became aware of his hands and fingers and noticed that the palms had serious blisters and there were odd cuts on the fingers. A few moments later, she also became aware of him becoming aware of her staring.

'I beg your pardon... I was just looking at hands, your hands. There are many injuries. Because of trumpet?'

'Hah! No, Miss Nero, because of the skillet! You know, the frying pan? I'm a cook in this army, my real job is cooking, so the stuff gets real hot sometimes, you know? And these cuts are because of knives, from when you have to cut real fast. No matter how good you are, sometimes the knife slips. And pans, sometimes the pan handle is too hot, so...'

'Oh, I see.' Having seen him play, she could not imagine him doing anything else, and certainly not cooking at a fire.

'Yeah, that's right. Sometimes I get surprised myself.' He put his empty plate back on the trolley and searched for his cigarettes. 'You know, you have that festival? For the god of work? Bisho – Bishokorm, something?'

'God of work... oh, Bishwakarma! Yes!'

'Well, this was my first time, and I put both my favourite griddle pan and my horn at his feet. Hope it works. Hope He blesses me so that I can leave the pan and stick to the brass!'

'Mr Jones, I'm... not sure any gods are actually existing... but the only thing deserving to be worship is work, is genuine labour.'

'I know about that! If you come from the South Side of Chicago, you sure know about that!' She remembers his laugh as he replied. It was the first time she heard him laugh like that, soft, unworried, a laugh that wasn't looking over its shoulder. Their eyes had been meeting and moving away, but this laugh pulled her gaze to his and held it. She felt her back straighten, and her hand catching her sari pallu as it started to slide down.

'Please, you call me Byron.'

'Mr Byron?'

'Just Byron is fine, thank you.' She had never paid attention to the Romantics in Eng Lit, and she couldn't connect this Byron to the Lord Byron of the 'She Walks in Beauty' poem.

'Then just Niru. Please.' She felt ridiculously brave saying it, as if setting sail in a boat on an open sea.

'Neroo.'

'Nih-ruu.'

There was another knock on the door. A young white soldier who Byron referred to as 'my friend Jim'. This Jim handed them a note from Goodsugar who was already in his office upstairs. The same transport would take both of them where they needed to go.

Outside, there were people on the streets, and traffic, but very few people and fewer cars. Coming out of the hotel, when she adjusted her earrings, her forearm felt pasted to her upper arm and blouse. Her whole body felt sticky in fact, all the corners of it gummed up, and she recognized it as the effect of having spent a long time in air conditioning. Instinctively, she had hated air conditioning, and now she was angry with herself for having been trapped in it for so long.

The jeep was waiting at the side entrance of the hotel, on Waterloo Street. The driver and his companion were also Negroes and they nodded to Byron in recognition. One of them pulled down the top of a front seat and gestured to the bench seat at the back. Niru pulled up her sari to climb in, followed by Byron. The driver asked where she wanted to be dropped off and she told him. Byron clearly didn't need to say anything. As the jeep made its way on to the main road, she noticed that everything was oddly quiet for 9.30 in the morning. It was as if the streets had been washed by something, some strange energy that didn't allow the usual number of people to stick to the pavements, an energy that had temporarily swept away large patches of normalcy from the centre of the city. Later, she would recognize it, the way people walked carefully, watching out for trouble, the absence of laughter, of calling or shouting, as if everyone was being watchful of their own behaviour, almost of where they set their feet, in order not to set off any chain of events that might be uncontrollable – she would see it again in 1946, with bodies littering the streets, and again after the riots in the 1960s, but today this was simply a continuation of what had started a few weeks ago, after that rally at Wellington Square.

At Esplanade, some of the shop signs had been torn down since she'd last been there. A little way down Chowringhee, there was the burnt shell of a bus, still smelling of torched rubber, metal and wood, and a bit later, just past the Lower Circular Road crossing was the charred skeleton of a tram. Just before they turned left on Elgin Road, she saw a man sweeping tear-gas cannisters from the road. As he pushed them up to the pavement, another man loaded them into a sack, both of them overseen by a police havaldar. Wartime metal shortage. Clearly, the cans would be taken somewhere to be refilled. Byron wasn't sitting too close to her, but as the vehicle turned, his knee tapped against hers and she felt a shock at the solidity of the muscle. When it happened again, the man muttered an apology, and she shook her head in response – it's all right. Otherwise, they exchanged no conversation. The further they went from the hotel, the more her body adjusted to normal temperature, the more she felt as if she was slowly peeling off some unwanted layer from her being, unwanted yet now, somehow, unavoidable, something to which she would have to return.

They drove from Elgin Road into the serpentine lane of Rowland Row and out on to Ballygunge Circular Road and the new fencing for the garrison that had now taken over the Ballygunge maidan.

'Ma'am? You'll tell me where to stop?'

'Yes, just a little bit further please. Just at that bus stop.'

She got off quite far from the house, around the corner, just before the road turned eastward towards Dover Road. Best not be seen getting off from a Markin army car, the neighbours were curious enough as it was, about her and the other girls. The driver's companion offered her his hand, but she didn't take it as she balanced on the metal step. Safe on the ground, she turned to the soldiers.

'Thank you very much,' to the front seat. And then to the back seat, 'Nice to meet you. Goodbye.'

'Nice to meet you, Ni—Miss. You have a good day now.' He extended his hand.

She reached to shake it, and her palm and fingers disappeared in a warm engulfment. The jeep smoked away, heading south, presumably towards Hindustan Park and the big Markin camp near the Lakes. As she walked back home, her hand could still feel the blister bumps on the hobshi's palm. It felt as if the cuts on his fingers had actually cut into her own skin.

She remembers remembering those hands when Kanu's Ma returned after a night at the floating police thana at Koyra, in '49. 'Did they dishonour you?' the women asked. Kanu's Ma just shook her head and held out her trembling hands. 'No, just this.' The superintendent visiting the thana didn't have time for fripperies like rape, he was there to get information and he had worked at that all night. Kanu's Ma's palms were a suppurating mess of burns from where the superintendent had stubbed out his cigarettes, one by one.

From before that, she remembers wrapping another comrade's body in a plain sheet so that the family would not see the constellation of bullet holes across the girl's torso. Her comrade and friend – local nickname, Shada Bagheen, White Tigress, tree nickname Taal, Palm in Ingreji. She was only one of the victims of the punitive raid ordered by the superintendent on Niru's Santhal village.

Superintendent Binayak Dasgupta was the first man that Niru killed in cold blood, so to speak. Actually, he was the only man she ever killed by herself, before helping the others deal with the other three policemen within a few minutes. Officially, the Movement did not condone revenge of any kind, no violence that didn't further the cause, but in this case, the area leaders looked the other way, treating the ambush on the police jeep as a forgivable mistake, or a mistake, in fact, that boosted morale among the district's peasant cadre at a very grim time.

Niru and her comrades had planned to target only the superintendent. They had foolishly assumed that, once Dasgupta was dead, the other cops would turn and run. In the event, they had to deal with the entire party – there was no other way to negotiate with the two Sten guns that started spitting at them once the opening shots had felled the officer. She remembers being quietly surprised at how steady her own hands were when she pulled trigger for the first shot, when she racked the bolt and put another bullet in almost the same spot in the khaki chest.

Watching the boy's hands holding the comic book, she notes how big they've grown. They're sitting at their favourite window table at Flurys, a still cold mid-February furring the morning sunlight outside. Looking at the child, she wishes she had photographs of him sitting on this banquette on the seven or eight occasions across the years they have come to this pastry palace: first, as a baby in her lap, then with his little legs sticking straight out while spilling ice cream, then the legs dangling, cake or pastry marking the mouth, and now, almost too tall for the sofa, his heels drumming on the floor as he reads, only tangentially interested in the food, the steam from the cup of hot chocolate catching the sun as it rises to curve off his angled spectacles.

'Saki, eat that patty before it gets cold.'

'Eating, eating...' The boy turns another page of the little square comic, completely engrossed in the story about British and German fighter planes. There's no deity she believes in, so she prays to the chance dice of the universe, prays every day, that the only shooting and killing her son experiences in his life is in the pages of comics and books or on cinema screens.

She takes a sip of her tea and looks again at her watch. Saki cuts off a bit of chicken patty with a fork, pushes it through the tomato sauce – ketchup as she keeps reminding him to call it – and puts it in his mouth, all without looking away from the page. Chewing, he keeps his mouth closed as she has taught him to do.

The world is a terrible place, full of dangers, no doubt, but looking at this boy, no one would immediately worry about him attracting violence or warfare. In the school satchel hanging from his chair are two more comic books and two proper books, one in Bangla and one in English, all to be carried along like an oxygen supply, in case he finishes one and runs out of reading material. The excessive reading has begun at the age of nine. By ten, the glasses have come, much to Niru's dismay and her Ma-Baba's amusement – after all, if a Bengali boy doesn't read extensively which boy will? But for Niru, the thick glass lenses mean the boy will never be able to safely play cricket or football, bringing along the fear that he will be an unhealthy bookworm all his life, not the Bengali boy *she* wanted to bring up.

'Ma, will you stop looking at me?'

'I wasn't looking at you.'

'No, it's very disturbing.'

'I was just looking at this new type of comic book of yours.'

'Ma. You were looking at me. Do you have nothing else to do? Shall I give you something to read? How long before Mashi comes?'

'She should be here any minute. No reading once she is here, understood? She wants to talk to you as well, not just me.'

'I'll talk to her nicely. I talk to all your friends nicely. Just let me finish this now.'

Just outside the curve of Flurys' bay windows is a small, raised semicircle platform of grass and flowers tended by the cake shop; a strange island of polite greenery in this busy, most completely Westernized street of the city. Just beyond that, the pavement also turns from Park Street into the start of Middleton Row. Niru tries to remember how it was in 1942, when she first came here, and finds her memory struggling to push aside thick black-out curtains. Today, a lot of the English shops are gone, for instance, the milliners on the other side of the mouth of Middleton, and the big furniture store diagonally across Park Street, at the corner of Free School Street, has changed owners: instead of the old, familiar 'George Roberts & Co.' the raised, white wooden letters on the green signboard now say 'Thadani Bros.', while the legend below remains exactly the same 'Exclusive Furnishings and Home Fittings'. The people walking down Park Street are still recognizable – the coat-shirt-pants and kurta-pajamas could be from any big town in India, but the mix of saris of Bengali weave and the men in dhuti-panjabi-shawls could only be found in Calcutta, and this movement of pedestrians pulsating a slow-motion anxiety could only be from her city. By now, she has been to Bombay and Delhi several times and even once to Madras for the CPI, and even after she left the Party, for various labour union conferences, and she reckons the crowd in each city has its own specific 'handwriting'. How much that has to do with the much speedier Bombay buses and trams, or the maddeningly wide roads of desert-like New Delhi, she doesn't know, or whether it is actually the ricksha-pullers in Calcutta that give the game away, but—

'Hello, hello, hello!'

Niru whirls out of her chair and locks her arms around her friend without even looking at her. A pair of arms encircle her equally tightly. As her face is pushed up against the neck, the perfume climbs into her nose.

After a long moment, they part.

'And... who do we have here? Oh my word! Where has my baby Saki gone? Kidnapped! Replaced by this young man! Ki chawmawtkar!'

'Hello, Imo-mashi, how are you?' Saki has put down his comic and come around the table, smiling shyly.

It's only when she sees them hugging that Niru understands how tall the boy has grown in the three years since they last met Imogen. That he's already almost a head taller than herself hits home from a different angle when she sees that he's almost as tall as the Giraffe.

They sit down, Niru now sitting next to Saki, both of them facing Imogen. The Englishwoman raises her finger to pause proceedings and brings up a packet from the large bag she is carrying in place of a purse.

'Saki, these are for you. I do hope you like them.' She hands the boy a gift-wrapped packet. 'And, madame, this is from both of us for you. Just a small gift, so don't make a fuss.' Another, smaller packet is passed across the table.

'Thank you so much, Imo-mashi.' Niru notes with satisfaction that Saki is using his best, proper English, and not the mixed patois of Bangla, Hindi and Ingreji that he and his friends bat around between them.

'Thank you, Imogen. There was no need! And I have no present for you as yet.'

'Gifts often don't have anything to do with need! And you've always given me something before I leave.'

The boy opens his parcel. Pushing aside his empty plate, he lays out the contents on the table.

'What does Carand... Ache... what does it mean? Does this box contain pain of some sort?' The boy grins at his own joke. Imogen lets off a peal of laughter.

'No, darling, no ache or pain, at least not for you, I hope! No, it's Caran d'Ache, French, so the *ch* is actually a *sh*, caran *daash*. It's just a good make of paints and pencils and suchlike. I think they are Swiss and not French. The man in the shop said this was just right for someone your age.'

The boy gingerly cuts open the cellophane and peels it off, savouring the small sound. He takes the crumpled material and smoothens it at one side of the large pencil box, reluctant to let go of any part of the gift. He looks for a while at the picture of the three oversized pencils on the shiny tin lid, the pencils red, blue and yellow against a background of deeper blue, and then he prises open the lid. Both son and mother draw in their breath at the glistening array of twenty-four colour pencils.

'Oh, Imogen, you should not... this is too much for this boy! It's too expensive a gift!'

'Well, it's from both of us, not just me. Saki, your Mama thought this would be a good thing to start with, rather than oil paints or some such. He thought it would keep you more free to explore, and he would know.'

'I really like these. I don't like to paint because it gets very dirty and messy. Pencils are much cleaner.'

'So how is Mama Painter Moshai?' Niru asks the question while looking around for a waiter she can summon.

'Oh, the Zemindear! He's fine, I suppose... fine after a fashion, you know? He misses home terribly, but he'll never admit it. He denies caring a jot for Calcutta but, you know, all his work, all his paintings are still about this place and that time.'

This place and that time. The words sing oddly in Saki's ears. He quietly pulls out a notebook and pencil from his satchel and, keeping them under the edge of the table, he scribbles down the phrase. The women don't notice as he puts back the notebook and returns to turning his new pencils so that the silver lettering on each is facing the right way up. It's only after a while that he notices the paperback that is the second component of the gift. On the cover is an old-fashioned Christian-type painting and on top is the title: *Vasari's Lives of the Painters*. Ma and Mashi are completely caught up in their conversation, so he just opens the book and turns to the title page where there is a beautifully symmetrical scrawl of green ink.

For my dear Robi Nagasaki Jones-Majumdar,
In the hope that you will enjoy reading about the lives of these great Renaissance artists so that you may one day better enjoy their work when you see it.
With best wishes,
Kedar Lahiri (your 'Keda-mama'),
27/1/58, Paris

Saki turns the pages, starts to read bits of the book and is immediately bored. Who wants to know the biographical details of obscure Italian painters and sculptors? There are many other books he so badly wants, and he wishes someone had asked him, but he knows he can't say anything, he knows he has to show pleasure and gratitude. And even the pencils. He loves the way they look in the box, but he has no urge to start using them – maybe he can sell the set to one of the other boys in his class who genuinely like to paint, though Ma probably won't hear of it.

Imogen's tea arrives, and while pouring it, she sees that Saki has opened the book. 'Darling... I don't know why Keda-mama sent you that dull book, I think it may have been a kind of joke, though your Ma says you devour everything you come across in print.'

'He does! It is impossible! He will not do his schoolwork, but the other day he came across some golfing manual from 1932 and he was just going over it for hours! Golfing manual! As if he will any day play this, this...'

'Horrible bourgeois sport?' Imogen finishes for her friend.

'Imo-mashi? Can I ask a question?'

'Yes, darling, of course you can.'

'Why is that you are Mashi, meaning a sister of my mother's, when Keda-mama is Mama, meaning a brother of my mother? It should be Mashi and her husband, so Keda-mesho, no?'

Both women ignite with laughter, and Saki feels his ears burning with unexplained embarrassment. Imogen reaches across and squeezes his shoulder. 'My love. I'm glad to see you're not precocious about everything.'

His mother smiles at him in a way he has rarely seen her do of late. 'So, Saki, you see, a man and a woman can live together without being husband and wife. Abroad, it's allowed everywhere.'

Imogen picks it up from there. 'Equally, just because a man and woman live together doesn't mean they *are* a couple, d'you see? Meaning they may be a couple, as in, in love and like husband and wife but without the marriage, or they could just be friends who live together.'

'Like as if you and Ma were living together? Or like two men living together? So with no love and romance, just friendship?'

Imogen grins. 'Well, yes... though, again, just because it's two men living together or two women living together doesn't always mean—' Niru smacks Imogen lightly on the arm.

'Imogen, let him digest one lesson at a time. Some things can be kept for later.'

'Of course, yes, sorry!'

'What for later, Ma? No, I want to know now! I'm nearly thirteen!'

'Yes, Saki, you are all grown up now. So, did you understand what I was saying? That Keda-mama and I are not married? We are friends who happen to be staying in the same house? And, you know, sometimes we fight like lunatics and other times we sort of get along.'

'But you were saying about—'

'So I was saying, just because two men or two women are living together doesn't mean they don't ever fight. And sometimes the fights are very similar to a husband and wife fighting. Grown-ups are like that.'

'Oh my god! What is this?' Nirupama has torn open the wrapping on her presents. Saki sees that for her there are two books instead of one, and a lovely little orange-coloured box with embossed lettering.

The bottle Niru pulls out from the box is exquisitely made, the gold-coloured liquid and the chiselled glass sparkling in the sunlight. 'Is this perfume? What will I do with this costly perfume?'

'Why, wear it, my dear, wear it occasionally!

'But I have, I have no occasions where I can...' Saki can tell his Ma is caught between smiling and irritation.

'Ma? What are the books? Can I see?'

Niru puts away the perfume and examines the books. 'Oh! How nice! Rosa Luxemburg in a language I can understand! Thank you! And...' She picks up the second book, Saki can see it has a colourful cover, an illustration of different kinds of food on plates. Even the lettering looks like it's made from some kind of edible string – *A Certain Taste in the Sunlight: An Exploration of French and Mediterranean Food,* but the author's name means nothing to Saki.

'And this...? Oh, this is your that friend, he finally wrote it!'

'He finally found a publisher, yes. He finished it a couple of years ago, but initially people weren't convinced it was different enough from the books of Elizabeth David and that lot, but finally someone took it. I brought it because you are interested in different kinds of food and it's also nice travel writing.'

'And now he is famous?'

'No, not quite, but he has regular columns in two London magazines and an American travel digest that comes out of the Midwest, so he can keep doing what he likes best, travelling and eating. Currently, he's down in Portugal.'

Saki quietly goes back to his war comic. The women's voices blur in the background, his immediate attention taken up by the rattle of air cannon and the damns and blasts of pilots' curses in the speech bubbles. At one point, a shrapnel of conversation cuts into his universe, something about Zemindear – which he now understands to be another name for Keda-mama – drinking too much, and Ma tapping Imo-mashi on the arm and speaking in her you-haven't-done-your-homework tone, 'My dear Imogen, you also are drinking too much, you know.' And another shard, some recounting of Keda-mama taking a load of his paintings in a car and burning them all in a field.

'Was that after the *Marg* magazine issue? Or after the exhibition?'

'Oh, the exhibition he laughed off: "Who gives a fig about a show selected by an ignorant Indian second attaché in Brussels? Naturally he would select all his Bombay friends! Though Paritosh also had two canvases exhibited, which was good." But the *Marg* issue hurt because it was about Post-Tagore Bengal. They had the Calcutta Group, you know that Tagore fellow who hates his family, Subho, then Rathin Maitra and your namesake Nirode Mazumdar, then Prodosh whatshisname, others not in the group, but no mention of our maestro, Lahiri.'

'I saw that issue at a friend's house. I noticed Painter Moshai was not mentioned.'

'Yes, they had all sorts in it, didn't they? Theatre people, dancers, artists, even this fellow, this cinema chap...'

'Satyajit Ray.'

'Precisely, him, but he didn't mind any of the others, just the painters and sculptors, and even there he was fine with Paritosh and Shankha being there because their work he quite likes, but as to the rest... he was furious, threw the magazine into the fireplace, though it was only September and we hadn't started the fire yet, and then he didn't speak for days. I tried to make light of it, you know that Groucho Marx joke about not wanting to be a member of any club that would have him? I tried that. It didn't work. And then, early one morning I heard him loading the station wagon. He was trying to be quiet, but he was so blotto, the quieter he tried to be the more noise he made.'

'So, you...?'

'Oh, I went down and took away the car keys. Then he began to open the jerrycan of petrol to pour over the canvasses, *while they were in the car!* So I had to wrest that away as well, and the bloody matches.'

'Oh my god. He could have set himself also on fire.'

'Yes. I didn't care if he immolated himself, like one of those crazy Buddhist monks, but the car and the house I did care about.'

'And the paintings.'

'Well, yes, I suppose.'

'And you do care about him also.'

'Well, on some days I—'

'Imo-mashi? What is blotto?'

The two women start, suddenly remembering the child is present. Niru starts to shush him, but Imo takes the bull by the horns.

'Blotto, my love, is when someone is very, very drunk, when someone's had too much alcohol to drink.'

'Ah, I see.'

Imogen's eyes alight on the comic Saki has put down.

'What's this you're reading? *Gladiator's Glory*? It looks violent.'

'Oh, it's about the Second World War. There is an RAF pilot who flies in these very old planes, Glou-sester Gladiators, you know a bi-plane fighter.'

'Glo*ss*ter, darling, Gloucester Gladiators, yes, I know them.'

'And so he keeps getting shot down by superior Luftwaffe fighters, not once but twice, but he survives.'

'I see. And then?'

'And then, and then the Hurricane fighters come and he is given a new Hurricane to fly. And with this Hurricane, which is as good as the German Me109s, he shoots down a lot of the German planes, proving he's a better pilot than the Germans...'

Imogen is smiling.

'You know, we have a friend, your Ma knows him as well, and he actually used to fly Hurricanes and Spitfires during the war.'

'What? Shotti!? Really!? Even Spitfires?' The boy's eyes widen.

'Yes, indeed. You can meet him when you come visit us.'

The boy's excitement deflates rapidly.

'I don't know if I'll ever go to foreign. Ma has no interest in going outside India.'

'Well, perhaps you can come on your own then.'

'How? Ma just wants me to circle around her, as if I am some Sputnik and she is the earth.'

Niru feels her temper mounting, irrational, hard to control. 'Never! I never want you to be some satellite of mine! All I say is if you don't do your schoolwork properly, then you will never—' She chops off her own sentence.

'Anyway, I would rather be a bomb than a satellite!'

Imogen is patting Niru's shoulder, turning to the boy, smiling at him. 'Saki, perhaps you can be like a spaceship that flies away on journeys and comes back to circle for a bit.'

'Come back to here? Why?'

'Why ever not? It's your city after all.'

'Here nobody shoots anybody! It's boring!'

Nirupama can't help herself. 'How do you know? How do you know no one shoots anybody here? Do you know every corner of Calcutta?'

'Well, do *you* know anyone who's shot someone?'

Niru keeps quiet. Imogen claps a hand over her mouth, but the boy doesn't notice. 'See, Ma, see? You don't! This proves my point!'

Imo starts to laugh uncontrollably behind her hand. Niru's anger evaporates even as she grabs to retain it, and she can't stop herself from joining Imogen. The boy glowers at them, not understanding what joke he has made, that has set them off so, where everybody is now looking at them.

The waiter notices the two women laughing, the mem and the ordinary Bangali-type lady. Then the mem takes out her camera and takes a photo of the mother and son, making them sit closer, the boy protesting. Then the two women argue, each vying to pay the bill. Finally, the mem pays the bill, and they go. Except, just outside the glass doors, the boy asks for the mem's camera, and she gives it to him, explaining how to use it. The boy makes sure to put the camera strap around his neck, so the thing doesn't fall. The two women pose next to each other in front of one of Flurys portico pillars, arms around each other's shoulders. The boy carefully lifts the camera to his eye, makes adjustments, and takes their picture.

TWO PHOTOS

I still remember the smell of the camera's leather casing and the light abrasion the knob left on my thumb when I forwarded the film to take a second shot.

'What camera is this, Imo-mashi?'

'It's a Contax, Saki. German. I was told it was quite good, and I can't complain. Can you manage?'

'It's fine. Do you mind it's made by Germans, your camera?'

'Mind? Oh, oh, ha, ha, ha, no!' Imogen grins and shakes her head. 'My dear, what is one to do when the old enemy makes the best cameras? The Leica is famous and so is the Rollei, both German, and now apparently the Japanese are coming out with really good ones as well!'

'Like their fighter planes!'

The print came back from Imo-mashi much later, once she had gone back and got all her rolls processed.

By now I had different names for my mother. There was a letter from the CPI addressed to her where the name was Com. Niru Majumdar, Com for comrade, so she became Com. Niru. By now I also knew she and her friends had tree codenames, hers being 'Neem' and so another variation was Com. Neem. Then, when I was feeling especially cruel, there was just plain Nirupama, unleashed in the same tone Dida used when she was angry with Ma. The woman I sometimes called 'Com. Niru' looked at the picture after reading the letter. Then she handed it to me as I was cutting out the precious French stamps from the envelope.

'Look, Comrade Mother, what a good photograph! I wonder who took it?' Two ladies standing there against a pillar of the small portico at the Flurys entrance, squinting slightly in the sunlight, the dark-skinned woman in a Bengali cotton sari and shawl, the white woman in a paisley dress and light cardigan, arms around each other's shoulders, smiling happily. I'd managed not to shake the camera, so the picture was actually in quite sharp focus and you could see everything without anything being too bright or too dark. I was quite pleased with my effort. Niru took the picture away without releasing any praise in exchange. Instead, as mothers tend to do, she remembered an old crime she should have forgotten.

'You do realize you shouldn't have gone on that time, about Japanese and German war planes and how "good" they were?'

'Yes, Ma, you already ticked me off then, after Imo-mashi left!'

'It was not a game for Imo-mashi and others who actually lived through the war and attacks from German planes. It was not a... comic book for them, you understand?'

'Yes, Ma. How many times will you tell me?'

I've now got that photograph here, in Paris. Leaning against the wall next to the fireplace there's a piece of wood that looks like it could be a Brancusi sculpture. It's actually the huge wooden airscrew from an early Supermarine seaplane prototype, a precursor to the Spitfire, that someone had given D&D. Maybe I'm slightly perverse, but I've got that print of Niru and Imo tacked on the wall right next to it. On the other side of this beautifully shaped piece of wood, I've got a much smaller photo, probably taken in 1947 or '48. Unlike the Flurys photo, the resolution is fuzzy and there's even a very slight shake from whoever was operating the cheap box camera. Nevertheless, you can really feel the presence of the two smiling women. Niru and Keya, the pallus of their saris stretched tight across their chests in the style adopted by militant cadre in those days, almost like bandoliers to go with the rifles both of them hold at their sides.

The rifles are vertical, the butts clearly resting on the ground out of the frame, no bayonets; at first glance you mistake them for sticks, but then you catch the slight glint coming off the metal parts and you recognize them as Lee–Enfield .303s, with a strap curling around Keya's hand. The small photo has been carried around a lot and it has creases where it has been bent. There are traces of decay at the edges where damp has eaten away at the silver of the print, and bugs have turned the bottom right corner into a filigree of rotted paper.

However, all this abuse had been pressed flat by the book from which it fell out, the pages preserving both image and damage for some more time. On one of my trips home, when I was helping her clean up the Jodhpur Park flat, I opened an old trunk and started taking out the books inside. I was slapping and shaking them to force out the deadly book-eating worms that rule Calcutta, when the picture fell out of a book called *Hunger* by Knut Hamsun.

'I haven't seen this one before, Ma. Is this during Tebhaga? Who's this with you?'

Niru came over and peered over my shoulder. 'That's Keya.' She reached for the photo. 'Give, I'll throw it, it's completely riddled. The poka will get into other things.'

I pulled it away from her. 'No, wait, let me at least *see* it properly!' I examined the print and then turned it over to check for live worms and eggs. There were none.

'So this is Keya-mash—' I stopped myself. Though she saw me as a baby, I myself had never really known Keya enough to think of her as a mashi. On the other hand, I now connected the face to sketches and photos I'd seen at Elko and Imo-mashi's.

'Yes, that's her, or that's her during the Movement. She looked very different before this time, very different here in the city where I first knew her. She didn't know how to shoot, didn't want to learn either, tried once and the recoil hurt her shoulder so she gave up. 'My bare hands are enough!' She used to joke. The rifle was borrowed for the photograph.'

'Can I keep this one, Ma? Since you're going to throw it anyway?'

Niru shrugged. 'Yes, I don't need it. I remember very well what she looked like, what we both looked like then.'

NEW EMPIRE

Lambert first sees her in the flash of the bomb on the Manor. It's as though hers is the only face that's lit up by the explosion, those beautiful eyes widened, that rich black hair made darker by sudden highlights, the mouth slightly open as she reacts to the old pile going up in flames. Everything recedes back into darkness, but he keeps looking at the spot to which his gaze has been pulled. There's a little more light at the end of the movie, when the fighters pass over the hole in the church roof, and he confirms it is indeed her. By the time 'God Save the King' comes on, Lambert has lost all interest in the screen. He only stands up when the others around him do, craning his neck as he tries not to lose sight of her, but she disappears nonetheless. He and Deyton are one row behind, and he can now see that little playboy chap but not her.

As he leans forward, Lambert becomes aware of other people looking in the same direction. The grainy black-and-white Union Jack flutters on the screen as the anthem unfolds scratchily – *him victo-ri-*

ous, happy and glo-ri-ous, long to reign over us – and Lambert realizes that the girl has remained seated. This is causing some reaction among the largely European audience in her vicinity. He can see the playboy fellow glancing down now and again and then looking ahead, pretending nothing unusual is taking place.

As the lights come on, people begin to shuffle out of the rows and start going up the steps towards the exits. Amidst the slow exodus, a knot of people stays unmoving around the Indian couple. Out of the hubbub, Lambert can hear a man's voice clearly addressing the rich boy, 'Listen here. Tell your wife. She has to. Stand. Up. For. The National. Anthem!' A woman's voice comes back sharply, 'And you listen to me. I will *not* stand up! It's not *my* national anthem!' Lambert is startled at the clear diction – he has only heard the girl giggling in a mixture of tongues at Firpo's, in all his fantasies he has not imagined her speaking such cut-glass English.

'How dare you! You unpatriotic, ungrateful, un...' The first man collapses into furious, incoherent burbling. A woman's voice, also clearly English: 'She should be put away for treason! There's a war on!' Lambert feels Deyton tugging at his elbow and realizes he's holding up his row. As he moves away, Lambert can hear the playboy trying to quieten the girl down in their own lingo and the girl break into derisive laughter. Another woman's voice, all broad Mancunian vowels: 'These people just don't understand, do they? We should let the Japs loose on them!' The girl's voice again, louder, still countering the first man. 'Madam, why don't you tell your husband that *you* need to pack your bags and leave! And take your unwelcome anthem with you!'

For a moment, Lambert wonders whether he should intervene. Perhaps the couple are about to be assaulted. 'Leave it, Jeremy, they'll be all right.' Deyton seems to read his mind. 'Lucky it's only toffs and not a bunch of drunken Tommies, eh?'

Sure enough, a few minutes later Lambert spots the pair in the foyer outside. While the playboy is dressed properly, he can see the beauty is in a sari, like many other Indian women now breaking the 'European dress only' code for the Dress Circle. Physically they look none the worse for the wear, but they're clearly arguing. Lambert manoeuvres himself towards the stairs, wanting to be close to the two as they go down to the main doors, but Deyton reads his mind yet again. 'I think our lovebirds are going to the bar. Do you fancy buying me a pint, then?'

The bar at New Empire is one the longest in the city and currently not very crowded, but Lambert and Deyton contrive to find themselves a spot not far from Playboy and Beauty. 'Fifteen minutes to last orders, saheb.'

'A pint of IPA and... what whisky have you got?'

'We have bourbon, sir, Old Dixie, then we have Canadian Club, in Scotch we have Dewars Vat 69 and Johnny Walker.'

'A large Dewars, ice and soda.'

'Thank you very kindly, Jeremy.' Deyton brushes off a fleck of popcorn from his one evening suit and looks around. 'Best place if you don't want your drinking disturbed by food or music, eh?'

'Indeed, it is.' Lambert makes a small gesture to quieten Deyton so that they can eavesdrop properly, but he doesn't need to bother – half a drink seems to have made the young Indian Miss even more voluble. And there's enough English in the conversation for it to be perfectly understandable.

'Let them, then! I don't care! Aami aar paarchhi na!'

'But I *do* care! I don't want to get arrested for, of all things, not standing for their bloody anthem! And become a laughing stock on top of it! Bhagat Singh went to the gallows for throwing a bomb, what did Kedar and Keya get arrested for...? Ridiculous!'

'Yes, of course! Only the topmost kind of revolt for our Zemindear! You know... perhaps you should do something truly heroic! Perhaps you should get shot! Like Matangini Hazra! That would obviously look the best in the obituary notices!'

Tamluk, Matangini Hazra, it's been in the news, and besides, Lambert has read the Intelligence Branch reports. It takes him a moment to connect the name she has pronounced to the one he's been reading on the page. The last name is more or less as he's been saying it, Haz-ra, but the first name seems to be Ma-*ton*-gini and not Ma-tan-gini.

Matangini Hazra. Age at the time of death: between 70 and 75. Cause of death: police firing. Time and Place of death: about six weeks ago, some point at the very end of September, just outside Tamluk Police Station, Midnapore District in the west of Bengal. The official reports say the policemen fired in self-defence at a charging crowd and this Hazra woman regrettably caught a bullet. Competing accounts in the local papers are claiming otherwise: the old woman was apparently marching at the head of six thousand women, aiming to reach the police station and take it over 'without violence' when she was shot thrice, including once in the forehead .

All hell breaks loose after this in Tamluk. The place becomes a no-go area.

Currie – Wing Commander, can we get some aerial recce from Tamluk?

Lambert – I don't have the aircraft, sir.

Currie – You're in charge of air surveillance for a reason! Find the planes!

Lambert – Can't, sir, unless we divert from operations over Assam and Burma...

Currie – They are running an 'independent India' in that bloody district! Do you understand what that means? If this particular suppuration spreads, we might as well pack up and go home!

Lambert has seen some police intelligence reports that directly connect the growing scarcity of food to the increase in violent protests in the Midnapore area and, to a lesser degree, in other districts in Bengal. He has read the various administrators' comments in the margins, the handwritten scrawls nibbling at the broad column of typed sentences. The pages and files have begun to gouge out a new kind of anxiety to add to the network of older ones already in place. He knows he's not the only one who feels this. As Todd-Cartwright has taken to repeating, 'Patriots with something in their stomachs we can handle, but the hungry ones are a nightmare.'

The playboy seems to have convinced the beauty to lower her voice and speak in lingo. The two of them are sitting with their heads almost joined, exchanging strange words in low voices, making each other laugh. Lambert knocks back his whisky.

'Drink up, Len. Time we left.'

ONE-THIRD

'Saki, who was Matangini Hazra? And where was she from?'

The quizzing always comes out of nowhere, without warning, but I am a willing participant until I am about fourteen.

'Matangini Hazra was a freedom fighter. She was also known as Gandhi Buri, Gandhi Old Woman, because she believed in Gandhi's non-violence. She was shot by the police in 1942, while leading a procession at Tamluk, in Mednipur. When the police fired warning shots, Matangini went ahead of the procession, carrying a tricolour and calling to the policemen not to shoot. But still they shot her. She died still chanting *"Vande Mataram"*, the song about Mother India.'

'What happened then?'

'The people were angry and they also became violent.'

'Very good. And what was the Tamluk Jatiyo Sarkar?'

'The Tamluk National Government was formed by the people of Tamluk area in the west of Bengal. They kept the British away and ruled independently for nearly two years, from 1942 to 1944. Eventually the Ingrej defeated them, but this was an inspiration for the Tebhaga Movement two years later.'

'Te-Bhag-a. What does it mean, Saki?'

'It's the name of the movement in which you fought! The farmers' movement! Against the Ingrej and then against our own government! The andolon for food! It's said to have lasted from 1946 to 1947 but it went on even after that.'

'Yes, but what does the word itself mean? Can you tell me?'

She explains it to me more than once as I'm growing up, the explanation increasing in complexity over time.

'So? Te-Bhag-a?'

'Tey-bhag is tiin bhag – three parts – or one part of three parts.'

She points to the large, empty aluminium plate on the dining table in front of me. 'So, say I am the zamindar and this thhala is one of the many pieces of land I own. Imagine that I own about a hundred pieces of land like this, maybe even more, yes? Since I'm a rich zamindar, I don't like to do any physical work. Yet I need someone to grow rice for me on all this land, okay? So, I rent out each piece of land to a family of—?'

'Chaashi!'

'Farmers, exactly. And the family might not be small like ours, which is just you and me, but maybe five, six, or even ten people. So, I say to this family of farmers,' she points at me, '"I allow you to live on this land and grow the rice" – Saki, do you know how hard it is to grow rice?'

'It's very hard. It's hard work. In the sun and rain, you have to work. There are no holidays.'

She puts the scoop into the rice box, four times, and makes a small mountain of dirty white on the thhala, the wave-scrape of dry grains continuing to murmur as they slide against the metal. She spreads out the rice so that it covers the disc completely, leaving only the upturned rim. 'What I, the zamindar, say to you, the chaashi, is this – I'll let you do all the hard work to grow the rice, but in return, since it's *my* land, you have to give me half of whatever you grow every year. Thiik achhey?' She puts the edge of her hand into the rice and pulls from the halfway point of the thhala. Rice piles up on her side of the plate, leaving a half-moon of grains covering my side of the aluminium. 'Remember, this is not the only piece of land I own – I have *hundreds* of such pieces of land – and I get half from each and every piece, understood?'

'Yes.'

The flat was on the first floor of a small building in Jodhpur Park, at the very southern end of the city. There were open plots on both sides of the house, and lots of open fields and ponds around the colony. Sparrows would come in and out of the flat, stopping sometimes to peck at the thhala of rice. I was around nine when we left Dida-Dadu's house in Shyambajar and rented this place – three rooms and a kitchen large enough to accommodate a small dining table. Dida constantly muttered about how Niru had always deliberately chosen to live as far away from them as possible. Ma always replied that it had nothing to do with Dida and Dadu – her work in the new refugee tenements and villages just south of the city made it more sensible to rent something close to those areas. Also, a new English-medium school called South Point had just opened not far from Jodhpur Park, and Ma had used Roma-mashi's connections to find me a place.

Roma-mashi also code-named Mango-mashi. Titir-mashi, who we met less often, also had an old codename, Palash, but I never used that name for her. And there was the other name and tree codename that we didn't mention that often. Some roots of clarity took time to grip in my mind and I had to ask again and again as I grew up.

'So, Ma, if you and Mango-mashi and Titir-mashi were such good friends, why were you not in the same party?'

'Everyone sees the world differently, na, babu? So even with three or four close friends, each might see the same situation slightly differently, isn't it?'

I loved Roma-Mango-mashi or, as I sometimes called her, Romango-mashi. She and Ma would teach me all sorts of nonsense when I was five or six. There was the doggerel from the time when the city was bombed, there was home-made nonsense stuff, there was Tagore:

'Saki! Sa, re, ga, ma, pa, dha, ni!'

Me: '*Sa, re, ga, ma, pa, dha, ni! Bomb pheleychhey Japani!*' Do, re, mi, fa, so, la ti! Dropped the bombs have the Japanese!

Roma: Saki, what does Com. Niru say when she wants to eat fish?

Me: 'Kohima tey koi maachh koi ma?' Where, ma, is the koi fish in Kohima?

Roma again: Saki shona, what poem did Robi Thakur write in honour of your Ma?

Me: He didn't write it for Ma, he wrote it before and Dida-Dadu named Ma after it!'

'Yes, but still, what's the poem?'

'Hey Nirupama,
If today I make mischief by mistake, then forgive!
The black shadow of clouds fall on your two black eyes,
Deep black thick curly hair wears a white garland
The new monsoon places its offering at your feet!'

I was older when Niru explained about the Women's Self-Defence Association.

'Mahila.'

'Mahila.' Women.

'Atma-Raksha.'

'Atma-Raksha.' Self-defence.

'Samiti'

'Samiti.' League

'Together it makes?'

'MARS.'

MARS was formed by women from all sorts of background getting together to protest and organize against the attacks by Allied soldiers on Calcutta's women. From this, the women from the Communist Party got the inspiration to take part in other kinds of resistance in the villages. When the Party decided to agitate for a fair share for share-croppers, their women volunteers were also central to the struggle in...

'Tebhaga.'

Once again Com. Niru points to the rice she has spread to cover the thhala.

'So, half the rice for the people who actually grow it, and half the rice for the owner of the land.' She drags a finger across the middle of the thhala, dividing the grains. 'Now, for centuries, farmers accepted this as fair. They worked the land and grew the rice. If the land flooded and a lot of the crop was destroyed, too bad, the landlord still wanted his half of whatever amount of rice would have grown in a *normal* year, which means a year in which nothing went wrong. If there was no rainfall that year – what is called a drought – and very little rice grew, too bad, the landlord's share was unmoving. Do you understand?'

'Yes, it's unfair to the poor farmers who do all the work.' Living in Calcutta, I hadn't seen a proper farmer in my life, or not since I was too young to remember, when Ma had apparently taken me into the villages a few times before she stopped that work.

'And what are these farmers called, the ones who don't own their land but work on the landowner's fields?'

'Bhaag-chaashi! In English, share-farmers – share... *croppers*!'

I learnt these answers very quickly, but as I grew older, I began tampering with the expected replies.

'Yes, Ma, it was unfair to the sharecroppers, but the zamindars did *own* the land!' This was me at about fifteen, trying to provoke her. What it got me was an introduction to rudimentary Marxist thought and the labour theory of value.

'That's exactly it, babu, that's exactly it!' She would turn around and find an empty tin on one of the kitchen shelves. 'I, zamindar, own this piece of land. What is the *value* of this piece of land? In the capitalist system, if this same area of land was in a city, the zamindar could sell it for a certain amount of money. Or he could build a building on it and rent out flats to make more money. But land in the countryside? It either lies there fallow, being used by birds and animals, or someone has to put in the shrom, the labour to grow something from it.' She would take some of the rice from the thhala and put it into the tin. 'You understand, babu? The value of the land *only comes from the work* someone is putting into it: tilling, planting, keeping away birds and insects, harvesting and threshing to finally to give you your rice!'

Me at eight: 'But, Ma, I'm not asking them to do this, I don't even like rice so much! You know I like ruti and luchi and porotha!'

She bursts out laughing. 'No, *you're* not asking them to do it, the zamindar is! Just as some zamindar in Punjab is asking the farmers there to grow the wheat for your ruti and luchi! And the rice is grown because everybody but you, all the people of Bengal except for Robi Nagasaki Majumdar, need their rice, which is our main food! So, as I've explained, a lot of people died in the Bengal Famine from 1943 to 1944, a lot of farmers and their families starved because the British took away the little rice there was in those years to feed their soldiers on the war front.'

'But then, the zamindars should also have starved!'

'They should have, but they didn't. Neither did the people in the towns and Kolkata who had a little bit more money. You know why? Because, just as rich people have far more money than they need in the banks, the zamindars had huge stores of rice. As for the privileged in the cities, they had enough money to pay the crazy prices on the black market. It's simple, Saki, the less money you had, the less you ate, and that is still true today.'

It took me some years to grasp all this properly, the explanations simple when I was seven or eight, more complicated when I was sixteen.

'What I mean when I say the British took away the rice is this: the administration sent procurers into the villages, middlemen licensed to pay a much higher price than normal for the grain. The villagers' eyes widened. They even sold the grain they stored to make sure they had food all year long. As for those who refused to sell, the procurers and police had orders to take their rice anyway. Many though, were fooled by the money they got. "Oh, we'll just buy more from the next village," they thought. Except the middlemen had taken all the rice from the next village and the one after that and the one after that! Suddenly there was no rice grain to be had in the most fertile rice-growing region in the world, and panic began to spread among the peasants. The little money they had made went into buying back their own rice from the hoarders – at many, many times the price.'

'But couldn't they grow more? If it is such a fertile region?'

'You know it takes time for things to grow, right? It takes months for a crop to grow and ripen into a phawshol, a harvest, right?'

'Right.'

'So, rice grows two or three times a year, depending on where your land is. And if you run out of edible grain at the beginning of that cycle of sowing and reaping, you're out of luck. And then, on top of that, you know what?'

'What?'

'You know that in many parts of Bengal there are more rivers than roads? And what the Ingrej did was to take away everyone's boats and bicycles because they were scared the enemy would come and use them to cross the rivers and move through the fields. The Japani had done this in Malaya, so the British were terrified. They didn't care what happened to the people whose lives depended on those boats. With the boats taken away, many people couldn't reach the fields they'd sown. You know, people died for lack of food while looking at fields full of ripened paddy? There, just out of reach across the water, all the rice you might want, waving golden in the sunlight...

'The poor farmers soon realized that it didn't matter whether it was the zamindars or the British, the wealthy and powerful would rather let poor people die than share even a small portion of their stocks. So, once the famine receded and the world war was over, the sharecroppers started to make a demand. What was it, tell me?'

'They wanted a larger share of the rice they were growing!' I'd reach for the half-mountain of rice on Ma's side of the thhala. She would push my hand away, quite firmly. Then she would spread out the rice, again covering the plate. 'Instead of giving half to the zamindars, the sharecroppers said they would give them only...?'

'One third! 33 per cent of 100! Tebhaga!' By twelve, I could mimic my maths pie charts and make three exactly equal divisions of the rice on the plate.

'And did the zamindars and the government agree to this?'

'No, they brought in their goons and the police. Together, the thugs and the cops began to beat up the farmers.'

KHICHURI

WG picks up a small handkerchief of the ham, holds it up against the light to admire its translucence, and drops it into his mouth. He communes with it for bit. Once his mouth is empty, he speaks.

'*Jambon de Bayonne! Quelle* bloody bliss!'

'You old glutton. Anyone would think that you'd never eaten it before in your life!'

'Well, my dear, it does feel like that! *You* try spending three months in the pigless Maghreb!'

Missus just about avoids snorting into her glass of wine. 'A starvation sojourn, was it? You don't seem to have lost much weight, I must say.'

'Oh, no, no, no!' WG wipes his mouth with his napkin. 'Some of the best nosh I've had in my life, I dare say, but, *helas*, pork was thin on the ground and I do miss my...' he reaches for a disc of the saucisson and peels off the rind.

'What about the rest of it? Surely you'd have got a lot of all this.' I point to the table which is covered with plates of salad, olives, tomatoes, ratatouille, anchovies, cheese, cold cuts of pork, bread and tapenade.

'Oh, yes, Saki, yes! Everything you see here, except for the good cheese, the pork stuff and, of course, nothing like...' WG raises his glass of wine to let the sunlight shine through it. 'I'm glad we got this and not the rosé, local though that might be. Nothing like a crisp, flinty Pinot Gris for a Provençal lunch!'

I clink glasses with WG while Missus reacts in mock alarm and moves away the bottle of red she has ordered for herself.

'Of course,' WG continues, 'it all tastes quite different over there, the olives, the oil, the breads, the...'

'Anyway, you were saying...' I try and nudge the man back to the subject.

'Ah, yes, so, yes, they were, actually, I kid you not, as our Yank friends would say, *actually* called Currie and Rice!' He pauses to glance around from under his panama hat at the Cézanne tourists on the surrounding tables, but no one is paying any attention to us. 'Currie, as I told you, was the man who ran the Section, a civilian but my direct superior, and Rice was at the lower end of the top brass in India, tethered to HQ in New Delhi, first under Auk and then under Wavell. Brigadier Rice. Fat little fellow, not the brightest searchlight in the battery, no, but he held on to the job, which was a kind of liaison between the brass and intelligence groups like ourselves. In fact, Alan – Todd-Cartwright, that is – once told me a story about Currie and Rice discussing the food supply situation during, I think 1942, though I have no idea if it's true. Apparently, at one point Rice snapped at Currie, "Damn it, man, if you mean rice say *rice*, don't beat about the bush!"'

'Good policy, not beating about the bush!' Missus waves her cigarette at WG, dropping some ash into one of the small plates, 'Saki's question, Jeremy, was...'

'Well, you know, Imogen, I can't *answer* that! Truth be told, I can't remember, not after all these years. But! Even if I'd been privy to, privy to, um, how the decisions were made, I'm still not at liberty to *divulge*, d'you see? I've already told the pair of you more than I've told anyone, the two of you and Larry, enough to get me into trouble should...'

'To Zemindear!' Imogen raises her glass to the skies and knocks it back without waiting for us.

'To Larry Lahiri, wherever he may be in the great atelier above!' says WG and raises his glass.

I follow. 'To Keda-mama!'

This is the second time after Elko's passing that we are meeting Jeremy Lambert, otherwise known by Elko's coinage 'Wing Gourmander'. WG, as Imogen calls him, had come to Elko's cremation in Marseilles. I've met WG earlier a few times with Elko and Missus, her enjoying my embarrassment as she introduces us: 'Saki, d'you remember the time you used to devour those war comics? And how excited you became when I promised you I'd introduce you to someone who'd actually flown Spitfires in the war? Well, meet Wing Gourm—*Commander* Lambert, Jeremy to us, and he can tell you how he wants to be addressed, perhaps Uncle Jerry?'

'Just Jeremy, old boy, how do you do?'

'I'm Robi Majumdar, but here I'm called Saki.'

'Hello, Saki. Spitfire man, are you? As long as it's not Hurricanes! We can't have that in an upstanding young chap!' At which both the Englishman and Elko burst into chortles, making me feel twelve years old again.

I struggle again to connect this portly man to a young fellow who could not only fit into a Spitfire cockpit, but actually take the thing into all sorts of dives and loops. Nevertheless, this is what I've put together from Elko and Missus, and from the meetings with WG where I've been present: Jeremy Lambert is an RAF reconnaissance pilot stationed in Calcutta from 1941 to early 1946; he becomes friends with Imogen during this time and he also meets Niru; when he's posted out, Imogen and he lose touch; retiring from the RAF, Lambert finds a job as an airline pilot with BEA plying European routes; at some point, he begins to write small sketches about the meals he eats in Europe; this leads to him giving up the pilot's job and becoming a full-time travel and food writer for various British and American magazines, joining the new trend started off by people such as Elizabeth David; at some point around 1956–57, on one of his jaunts to France, Lambert bumps into Imogen and Elko, the friendship revives, and Lambert becomes a regular visitor to the house in Provence; unsurprisingly, this is the point when Elko begins to make his air-reconnaissance paintings; Jeremy Lambert is now well known, placed somewhere at the lower end of the top brass of British food writers.

As Imogen already sensed during the time in Calcutta, Lambert, Todd-Cartwright, Goodsugar and a few of the others were involved in some sort of backroom hush-hush work; the passing years and copiously emptied bottles of wine lead Lambert to drop his guard and release a few nuggets about what went on in the Ochterlony Suite at the Great Eastern Hotel during the war years, but he still tries to prop up some Hollywood flats of secrecy.

'I really can't confirm where the rice decisions were made, you know, to not release back to the public all the bloody big stockpiles of grain we had sitting and rotting, in the Botanical Gardens for instance, bloody great piles under tarp, in the godowns, god knows where else. Nor do I know who first thought up the business of taking away the bikes and the boats. *We* certainly looked at the detailed reports from the rout in Malaya. Other departments would also have read them, obviously, and it was clear the Japs had simply slaughtered us with their infernal mobility. It didn't need a Napoleon, you know, to think, "Ah, let's make sure the Nips don't do that to us again," d'you see?'

I saw and I didn't. A trio of customers sitting under another umbrella caught my eye, perhaps triggered by the mention of Japs and Nips – a man and a woman, elegantly dressed, with a younger woman, perhaps their daughter. Clearly 'Oriental', most likely Japanese. The man picked up a bottle of wine and made a point about it before filling the women's glasses. The girl ducked forward in a slight bow. All three of them laughed. The wife picked up a brochure about Avignon and began to read aloud in a voice I couldn't hear.

'May I suggest that these decisions were probably, in a sense, made collectively?' WG took an olive pip out of his mouth and placed it precisely in a pile at the side of his plate. 'You know, handwritten notes accumulating on the margins of the typed pages, inconclusive discussions around committee tables, things firmed up based on what was left unsaid... a bit like the flavours coming together in a stew or soup... and a soup it was, I can tell you, all the ingredients hurriedly simmered in a thick stock of panic.'

'What an apt analogy, Jeremy! A stew of pure funk leading to mass starvation! You really must put that down somewhere!' The sneer slides from voice into action as Imogen pours the dregs of a bottle into her glass. Then she lifts up two empty bottles and semaphores them to a waiter.

'*Oui, madame?*' The garçon comes over.

'*Du vin, s'il vous plait. Encore. Les deux, le blanc et le rouge.*' Missus turns back to WG.

'Do you remember old Irv Goodsugar's joke about SEAC, what was it?'

'SEAC?' WG is confused for a moment. 'Well, SEAC stood for South East Asia Command, formed in '43 under Mountbatt—'

'Mount*farting*, as Goodsugar used to call him – oh yes, *got it*!' Missus puts her arm on my shoulder, sticks her face close to mine and goes into a bad American drawl. 'Lissen, Jerry, buddy, you know what we think SEAC actually stands for, dontchya? Save! England's! Asian! Colonies!'

WG is off on an internal journey somewhere, distant food beckoning to him. 'Speaking of soups and stews, what is that wonderful gruel you Bengalis make, what's the name again? Ki – Khi—'

'Khichuri?'

'Khi-*cha*-ri! Yes, of course! Imogen did you know kedgereee comes from khichari?'

'Yes, Jeremy, and mulligatawny comes from that Madras-water thing, I know, you've told us a million times.'

'Wonderful stuff. You just don't expect that complexity of tastes from an unprepossessing circle of mush, do you? But then you put a spoon of it into your mouth... and boom! You know, my boy, I first started with your humble jaarlmoody and then gradually worked my way through all the, all the maddeningly, you know, all the street grub you have! It was only a few weeks before I left that I actually tasted food you Bengalis make at home!'

'Well, you must go back and remedy that.' I hope he won't pick up the insincerity.

'Oh, I don't know, I don't know... I'm not sure I can bring myself to go back... You see, it's not geographical, it's more about going back to visit the person you used to be when you were there, and I'm quite happy not to meet that Jeremy Lambert again.'

I wasn't expecting so much depth from this WG, but Imogen is unmoved by the honesty.

'But you'd developed quite a taste for Bengali beauties, hadn't you? Perhaps you wouldn't mind meeting one or two of those again, *n'est ce pas, mon ami?*'

'Well, just the one, as you know. Not that there was any chance of, you know, that being anything more than an utter fantasy, not with young Mr. Larry's lady love...'

Imogen fills her glass and then empties it. 'Did you and Elko ever speak about it? You did, didn't you, that once when...'

'Oh, yes, he was, how shall I say, very sporting, *sporting*? Is that the right word?'

'Well, I don't know, Jeremy, I wasn't there, remember?'

'Well, yes, I mean, he understood that a beautiful woman such as her would draw the attention of other men, of many other men, he took that as a given, at least seemed to, in retrospect.'

'Quite, yes.'

'But he never did tell me how she, um, how she—'

'Went west? Copped it? Died?'

'Yes. He didn't want to talk about it, he said. What I understood was...'

He hadn't told Lambert, but he had told me.

PETITES MORTS

Some faint noise might have sliced into my dreams, the cut waking me up fully a few minutes later. Provence can get pretty cold in the autumn, and my blankets had pushed themselves below my knees. I got up and headed for the toilet, but I was aware that was not the only reason I'd woken up – something wasn't quite right with the sleep of the house. I walked past the stacked canvases to the loo, checking everything there. I came out and went for a look around the rest of the cottage. By now, I knew my way around in the dark and all seemed normal until I came to Elko's studio. The door to the garden was ajar, which it shouldn't have been. Outside, the old Hillman Estate was missing, but I could still smell heavy petrol fumes from when he'd over-gunned the engine, as he would when he was drunk, which meant he hadn't been gone long. I briefly considered waking Missus, but I knew she'd be pretty gone herself. I went back in, put on my clothes, and pulled the bike out of the shed.

The freezing seat speared into my rear, so I was forced to ride raising myself off of it every few seconds. Even through gloves, my hands were soldered on to the handlebars by the cold. Where had the old bastard gone? As I bumped down the path from the gate, faint predawn began to aid the bike lamp. Both Missus and I had marked that he liked one particular field more than others for his periodic pyre ritual. The ownership of that patch of land wasn't clear, so nobody could really make a fuss about the fire and, as Missus had tartly remarked, the slope made for a nice view of the surrounding countryside. 'Even in this, Zemindear needs to make a dramatic picture. I should just let him burn the bloody things and photograph the fire. Maybe *I* could claim to be the real artist then! Photographer artist! Title of arranged photograph: *Burning Paintings against Provençal Landscape*... or just, *Vanity*.'

I took the trail up the small hill from where one could see a large sweep of the area below. The wind at the top was nasty, but I didn't have to spend long – there he was, heading for his field, the tail lights bumping out a tiny Morse code of red as the Hillman fought its way along the country track.

Luckily, the route to where he was went mostly downhill and I reached him in ten minutes. By then, he'd pulled the stuff out of the car – large sheets of paper and tied-up rolls – and arranged them in a kind of crumpled tepee, ready for the sacrifice. He was on his knees, head and torso inside the back of the station wagon, rummaging around for something. As I got closer, I could hear him cursing in a mix of tongues. The body jerked, and something flew out of the cavity and landed in the grass. A tin they used for storing spare petrol on long trips, cap missing, clearly empty.

'*Merde*, baanchod! *Putain!* Fucking bokachoda *gazoil!*'

I suddenly felt I was in a Jacques Tati movie, except it was sharply chilly and I wasn't laughing. He hadn't heard me approach. I laid down the bike and walked up to him, my anger mounting.

'Looking for something, Chief?'

The thin body went still. Then he slowly extricated himself from the car and stood up. His face was smeared with muck and dirt, and something was stuck in his hair. As he stared at me, he began to shake, his eyes showing wet in the thin morning light.

'How the hell did you get here?' He was trying to swallow the crying.

'What the fuck do you think you're doing?'

He reached into the car again and came out with a rag with which he began to wipe his face. His hand was still unsteady, other bits of him still shaking, but I could see he was sobering up quickly, as he could sometimes. He patted his jacket, looking for cigarettes.

'Got a light?'

'No.'

He went around to the glove compartment and came back with a box of matches. We both lit up.

'I forgot there was no petrol in the can. No tube either, otherwise one could've sucked out enough from the tank.'

'Of course.'

'You'd rather I immolated *myself*, don't you? Both of you would, rather.'

'At this moment, I would certainly help enthusiastically. Fuck you.'

He laughed. 'You've never said that to me before. I'm glad. I've always felt you were too polite, too held back.'

'Aar ki bolbo tomakey? Ei shob bandramir ekhono kono shesh nei!' What else do I say to you? Carrying on with all this monkeying about, even now.

'Shesh hawbey jokhon shesh hawbo, I suppose.' It will end when I end.

I switched back to English. 'You selfish, self-obsessed asshole, you do realize you don't end with your end? You might be out of it, but the rest of us have to sort out the you that's left behind, and you understand that takes time and effort?'

'Precisely, dear boy, precisely! And that's just... what I was trying to do... some clearing up, some housekeeping, burn the rubbish so that you don't need to!'

'Oh, Keda-mama, don't worry about the rubbish, leave that to me. I'll take pleasure in burning whatever needs to be...' My eyes stopped on the pile of drawings. '... Let's see what you were trying to burn this time... dekhi ektu?'

I started towards the tepee and Elko tried to hold me back. 'Oh, no, no, no, *leave* this stuff! You head back. I'll put those back in the car and bring them home, I promise!'

'Promise!' I prised away his fingers from my arm. 'I don't give a damn about your promises.'

He came behind me, still trying to divert my attention. 'Saki, look here, there's such a thing as privacy, surely?'

'No, fuck you. You've drunk away any right to privacy.' I began to sift through the drawings.

I identified them even before I looked at the first one because of the plastic sheet that he had flung a few feet away. I lifted up a few of them and laid them out on the dried grass next to each other, large drawings, many quite graphic, of a man and woman in the act of making love. Then I untied a roll of smaller ones which had the same subject and laid those out too. I examined the display for a few moments before turning to him with feigned surprise.

'Why the coyness? This is 1973, not 1943.'

'Well, dear boy, you never know how others, you know, people who were around in '43 for instance, might see them! So I thought it better to...'

'No one here's going to raise an eyebrow. You mean people back home, in case *they* ever see them?'

I didn't let on to Elko, but I had already seen many of these. He'd been away for a few days once, probably on one his assignations, when I'd gone into his bedroom to look for something. The mattress was askew on the bed and a corner of an opaque plastic sheet poked out from underneath. I almost didn't look under the sheet. For some illogical reason, I assumed it was there to catch possible incontinence, like the rubber sheets in hospitals, and I started to push it back with minimum touch. The sheets of paper under it had other ideas, however, and a wedge of them slid out. I tilted the mattress off the bed and went through the whole lot before putting them back and making the bed.

That morning, as I helped Elko put the drawings back in the Hillman, I could see he was still agitated. I'd stopped him from destroying his work before – with and without Missus – and there would always come a point when he would give up the fight and subside; today was different, he was quiet but still quite agitated about something. I, on the other hand, could feel my unspent sleep clawing at me, and the nastiness slipped out.

'Look, don't worry so much about these ones, they aren't that remarkable. Lots of people around, producing this sort of sophisticated smut. In fact, we can probably sell these as anonymously made erotica and make some small money. Let's make sure to erase any signatures – that way no one will trace them back to you.' He stared at me with helpless hatred as I tied the bike to the roof carrier. 'I don't know why you're getting cross,' I continued. 'France is the only place where these would have any value… okay, let's say western Europe. In any case, don't worry about them ever making their way to Calcutta. Or California.'

The station wagon laboured back up the farm track to the road leading to the house. I could see it was an effort for him to deal with the steering and gears.

'Do you want me to drive?'

'No, thank you! I'm fine. This old wreck has had its day, that's all. You must convince Missus to get a new motor afterwards, you know, once there is no fear of me smashing it up.'

I didn't reply. We both knew he was a far better driver than her, especially if you were to compare their drunk driving.

A copse of cypress trees watched us pass by. He jerked back from the wheel and shook his head. 'They *are* shit, I know. Whenever I made these, I was just trying to bring back something for myself, you know, memories of a certain kind of happiness, I suppose, but not only of bed, but everything that becomes attached to that… exchange. You know they call it *La petit mort*, these French? Orgasm, I mean. And… it does feel like that… as though you've died and gone to heaven… you know what I'm talking about, of course?'

'Yes, I'm twenty-eight. I suspect I may have experienced that once or twice.'

'Joking, dear boy, joking! I know about that Canadian girl, Her Ladyship's told me. And this new Moroccan love interest as well.'

'Yes, but you were saying.'

'Yes, so, Eva was the one who taught me the phrase, and when she left, *petit mort* took on another meaning for me. I was even younger than you are now, much younger, and I found myself thinking that every serious parting, sundering, was a kind of small death.

'Of course it's a banal idea! Bloody cliché! Bangla poetry is full of it as you know, biroho, the parting experienced as a dying, the separation felt as half-life or non-life, and so on. And it's universal. For instance, you have Cole bloody Porter and all that "every time we say goodbye, I die a little"… and when Eva left, I was young and foolish enough to die a *lot*, but, but, to make that mistake twice? That takes special talent!'

He was still drunk, talking almost to himself, but he was slurring less and less. We were nearly at the house now, passing the gate with the small board they'd put up in a nod to this English habit of giving every cottage a name.

'You could argue that it was I who left, but that's taking things very literally, isn't it? By '46, when I first went to London, Keya was gone for all purposes, moved from the Congress to the CPI, her true and final love. We'd meet every few weeks, secretly, but it was all confined to those *trysts*, and the business of doing it. Which, I'll admit, was well worth the effort.' He waved towards the pile of drawings in the back. 'But she'd hardly speak of her political work, and she wasn't very interested in my painting, my hobby, as she called it, joking, but I suspected not entirely in jest. But me, despite myself, I'd fallen in love. Or what I thought was love, which, as we know, is often hard to tell apart from the real thing. At least for some of us. As Eva had put it when I told her I loved her, "But I am in leave!", and Keya too, was by then in leave.'

He parked the station wagon, got out slowly and opened the back, reaching for the drawings. I stopped him. 'Keda-mama, leave those. I'll put them away later.' I had no intention of letting him get his hands on them ever again, but if he understood this, he gave no sign. 'Okay. You can just find a corner in the studio or the back room. Do you want a coffee? I think I might have a cup.'

He carried on with the story as I put on the kettle.

'By the time I came back from London, Keya was spending most of her time in the villages, she and your Ma, both. I think I've mentioned before, I hadn't seen you at this point. But Keya had told me there was a small, live product being looked after by Niru's parents in Shyambajar. And these girls would return to Calcutta, what, once in two-three months perhaps? And never usually at the same time. So in those two-three years, I met Keya perhaps four or five times a year, always fleeting. Sometimes... to me... the lovemaking would feel as though she was stocking up on necessary supplies before returning to her real life in the villages. Sometimes it would be the opposite. Very real and desperate, an affirmation of her real life. Which was with me. Before she went back to the unreality of her revolutionary dream.

'She'd usually send letters with Niru when your Ma came for her visits – it was deemed too risky to put anything in the normal post – and sometimes those letters felt more real than our actual meetings, it was strange. Niru would telephone when she was back, and we'd meet. I wasn't allowed to keep any of the letters. Niru would hand me the letter. I could read it and reread while we were together, and then I'd have to burn it in front of Niru before she left.

'Your Ma loved the grub at Flurys but she didn't really like going there, so I'd bring her a little box or two, savouries, pastries, and for some reason, their ordinary cucumber sandwiches, to which she was particularly partial. We'd meet in Victoria Memorial, or on the Hastings riverside. Sometimes, very rarely, she'd come all the way down south to Dhakuria, to the Lakes.

'It was at the Lakes that she told me about Keya. It was the first time she brought you along. I was waiting in the MG, where the buses terminate at the Gol Park roundabout. Niru got off the bus, but with this bouncing brat in tow. She didn't say a word, neither did I, and we drove to the Lakes. I knew about Keya already. Her sister Swati had called me with the news a couple of weeks earlier. In any case, the news had spread quickly in our circles. The story her father and family put about was the same concoction I'd got from Swati – Keya had been doing social work in 24 Parganas and got caught in a village fire, trying to help some Santhal tribals save their huts. Everybody knew the truth was, at best, only adjacent to the story, but no one dared ask anything publicly. No one in Calcutta society was going to question Shekhar Kumar Dutta, who was by then a Justice of the Supreme Court.

'It's a four-minute drive from Gol Park to the Lakes, you know, but Niru didn't say anything, just sat there holding her sari to her mouth, and it felt like one of the longest drives I've taken. She'd put you in the back and there you were, jumping on the seat, beating the trunk and shouting merrily. I was worried you'd fling yourself out. I kept wondering why she had agreed to mind this three-year-old when she was meeting me. It's only when she did something, something motherly and proprietorial, like wipe your nose with the edge of her sari or something, that I realized that you were *her* kid, that *this* was the child Niru had produced—'

'In sin and scandal. Yes, got it.'

'Your Ma – Niru – did she ever tell you how Keya died?

'No, she hasn't, not really, not clearly,' I replied. 'All she'll say is "we lost her in the struggle", and once or twice she let slip about her being killed, "when the police got Keya" or "when they killed Keya..." I've asked, but she won't go into details. You know how she can be, if she doesn't want to part with some bit of information, she just won't.'

'So, this was when the Party had sent Niru and Keya to work in South 24 Parganas. Not many city cadres were sent to the villages, and city women would have been even fewer, but these two girls were clearly marked out as exceptional... exceptional exactly how, I can't say. I mean *I* found them exceptional, each in her own way, but I doubt the Party and the woman who was in charge, one Comrade Tapati, I think, would have recognized exactly the same qualities, except the fierce intelligence was obvious. And I suppose commitment to the cause would have also mattered.'

Through the lifting fog of sleep and anger, I realized he'd never actually told me any of this clearly. He and Missus had alluded to all this from time to time, but all three of us had always circled around talking about it directly, the two of them not sure how much I knew, and vice versa.

'The Santhals trusted very few of the city cadres, but Keya and Niru were two they did trust. Keya told me they used to call your Ma "Cheel" – kite, like the bird of prey – because she was very quiet but when she moved it was always very decisive. Keya they called "Shaada Baghin", white tigress, because she was so fair. Apparently, they would laugh while calling them these names, but there was some element of truth in it.

'At some point, the police began to make these punitive raids as reprisals for any action the farmers took against the landowners and their thugs. Every time there was a tip-off that a mama-party was about to raid their villages, they'd take some old oil or soot or something and blacken Keya's face and arms so that she wouldn't stand out from the tribal women. Niru was deemed dark enough to pass as a Santhal, but Keya needed the disguise. Then, two cops were killed in their area. Niru told me later that their cell had nothing to do with it. A large part of their work was trying to educate the women in basic hygiene and things, and in politics of course, obviously politics according to Uncle Joe and Aunty Comintern. For this, they would have study groups and put together songs and rudimentary theatre shows for the villagers, things like that. In fact, when their movement turned violent from early 1947, the Santhals tried to avoid taking up arms, except for the traditional bows and arrows that they used for hunting and self-defence, but the Party cadres brought in guns and knives and started to use them.

'So, two policemen are shot when they challenge a cadre group passing through the area. In retaliation, the police burn villages and shoot tribals. Niru is away somewhere else during those two or three days. Keya, who never took up the gun, never learnt to shoot, is in the village. The Santhals are expecting to be beaten up, some of their men arrested, the crops seized from their stores, you know, the usual stuff that's been happening until then. But that night, the police give no warning, they just set the whole bloody village on fire. The tribals run, the waiting cops, the fucking bastards, open fire.

'We were sitting on a bench at the lake, and I was playing with you, balancing you on my knees and making you jump, which was the only way to stop you flinging yourself into the water. Niru, I could now see, was exhausted with everything. She was like a house with its outside walls intact, but through the windows you could see everything collapsing inside, everything collapsing inwards.

'Niru told me she got back to the village the next day. She found Keya among the bodies they'd laid out, identified her, washed off the blackening from her face and arms, informed the network that Comrade Shada Bagheen had "made the ultimate sacrifice" or however the commies liked to put it. Then she sent a message to Keya's sister Swati.

'Sitting in Delhi, when he got the trunk call, apparently all the Judge Shaheb wanted to know was the exact condition of his daughter's body – are there any visible injuries on the face and arms? None? All right, then the mother could attend the cremation. The Adivasis kept her in a cool place until her cousin Biggles came and collected the body from the village. They did a quick cremation at some nearby ghat, Biggles, mother and sister, no one else. They didn't allow Niru to come, but before Biggles took away the body, he requested Niru to make sure the white shroud covered everything except her face and arms, so that the ladies didn't see any of the bullet wounds.

'And that's one of the ways, my friend, by which we finally get disposed off.'

Sunlight had begun to poke in through the windows and now it rimmed the left side of Elko's face. He moved to sip his coffee and caught his own reflection in a framed picture above the dining table. He turned his face to the sun, screwed up his eyes and intoned Rabindranath: 'Raat koto holo? Uttar meley na.' He turned back to me and translated, as though I couldn't be trusted to understand Bangla. 'How deep into night are we? There is no answer... or... maybe, how far gone is the night? No reply comes.'

'Petite bloody mort, indeed.' He shook his head as if to shake off some memory. 'You see, I always saw them as two very different kinds of death, Eva leaving, and Keya... disappearing. For instance, I never cried when Eva left, it would never have occurred to me. But that time at the

Lakes, it just punched me in the stomach. I broke down in sobs. And you know what my abiding memory is from that moment?' Suddenly Elko started laughing silently.

'What?'

'You, baby Saki, sitting in my lap. At first, you were quite rightly alarmed. And then,' Elko leaned forward and started patting my cheek. 'Then you started stroking my face gently, saying, "Kaandtey nei, goe, kaandtey nei."' Don't cry now, dear, don't cry.

IF MY EYES COMMIT CRIMES

The drawings are in pencil or charcoal, soft charcoal in the early days and the more recent ones in hard charcoal or conté. Across the years he's used a variety of materials, and you could almost do a biography of his just based on the different kinds of paper. A lot of the early ones are on the typical paper that you find in the G.C. Laha drawing books of the time, smooth sheets, now yellowing a bit, some of the edges deckled by insects. After the war years, he becomes more confident, for the first time valuing his drawings for themselves, including these 'offstage' ones. He begins to indulge himself with European paper that has started to appear again, and there are forays on larger cartridge sheets, 120 gsm or 200 gsm. In 1946 and again in '51, he comes West and to the attendant belt-tightening. From this period, you find large, dark gestures scratched off on the cheap, light brown newsprint sheets which ateliers in Paris and London used for drawing exercises that were meant to be chucked. Then there are little ones on postcard-sized watercolour paper, mostly in pencil these, a few with a fountain pen, later even a few with ballpoint pen, doodled perhaps to plug distractions between serious work. Finally, there are more recent ones, where he's used good, thick sheets meant for print-making and proper painting, mindfully working the charcoal with the grain of the cold-pressed and rough surfaces; the application of fixative spray indicating perhaps that he hadn't intended these to be cremated in a field, at least not when he'd just finished them.

The faces and bodies are almost never clearly delineated, but if you look properly, you realize it isn't always the same pair of people involved in the act. Often there are repetitions of movement, or the way a pair of arms goes around the other body or the positions of the heads, but as you keep looking, you can start to identify different pairings. The relationship between the bodies also varies in terms of scale: sometimes the man and woman are roughly proportionate to each other, sometimes the man is much larger than she is, sometimes he is almost like a baby monkey, clinging to a much bigger energy. The space around the bodies also changes, different surroundings, different kinds of light, various objects, sometimes quite sharply defined in contrast to the amorphous coupling. The furniture and objects are chiefly placed by way of an internal framing within the image but, if you look carefully, things akin to information start to emerge. In a few of them, I can recognize the trees outside the windows of the Dover Road flat because Niru had described them to me – the sun streaming through the mango tree, the neem being slapped about by rain, the palash rich with flowers.

Some of the drawings have words scrawled on them, odd shards of text, like 'wanna hold your', 'we'll ride them some day', 'tongue taking a trip' and 'if my eyes commit crimes, forgive'. Occasionally there are attributions, like the word 'gyre — W.H.A' or 'we were a strange contraption — Amichai'. Mostly the writing is in English, occasionally Bangla, sometimes you can read the words clearly at others they are barely discernible as words, lost inside the marks.

In some of the drawings I fancy, I can see traces of the rooms in the Dharmatolla kothibari, in some the reference is obvious – almost like a production photograph from a film set, the frame divided roughly in the centre by the width of a wall and closed door, with musicians playing on one side and a couple going full throttle on the other. There are three or four drawings where I'm pretty sure I can identify a young Sheyali in various stages of undress, in one of them a rounded shape in the background which could be Radhuni. At other times, the context becomes more plush; there is the four-poster bed at the house in Palm Avenue almost warping under the onslaught of carnality, sky and sea turned upside down, the rolled-up overhang of the mosquito net like roiling water above the storm below.

And then there are the very different textures of the Great Eastern. The hotel emerges through the details, the bedside lamps, the view outside, of the road full of traffic, service trays with half-finished food and drink, or ashtrays of different vintage, cylindrical old tin ones with the embossed hotel logo, cut glass ones, polished steel ones with the letters G.E.H. engraved in copperplate on the rim between the dips to hold the cigarettes.

Sometimes I think I recognize Eva, sometimes Keya. In one of the smaller drawings, there is a waiter standing at the open door with a breakfast trolley, Eva, definitely Eva, naked, hands covering her laughing mouth, hiding behind the door. There are variations of a couple crossing Chowringhee in front of Grand Hotel, in one, they are fully dressed in early '40s Western clothes and the erotic charge is palpable, in another version, the couple's bodies are a blur, they could be clothed or naked, you can't really tell, while everything around them, the buildings, the cars and buses, the jhurrie-gaadi with the big-eyed horse bearing down, is sharply recognizable as a street scene. The thing I love about this one, the thing that's different about it from most all the others is that here the electricity of desire comes from their clearly rendered faces, a young woman and man looking mischievously at each other, oblivious to the whirl of the world that surrounds them.

The peculiar problem with a lot of the charcoal ones is that they are doubly smudged. There are the wipes and the softening of the shapes that are clearly intentional, and then there are the smears and redactions that have come from the paper sitting under a mattress where Elko has perhaps vigorously participated in the very act that he's drawing. From time to time, I wonder when exactly he found the pockets of time to add these inadvertent smudges. It was obviously never spelt out, but I'd come to understand that the unspoken agreement between Missus and Elko was that neither would burden the other with their amorous liaisons. Since Elko was always in Provence, this meant that Missus presumably took care of her needs when back in England or on her travels, while our maestro either went away to play or had lovers over only when he was alone in the house.

At some point, I start to differentiate Eva and Keya in the drawings by the presence and absence of the sari in the drawing; the sari, either worn by the woman or flung somewhere, draped on a chair or crumpled on the floor. But then, the woman in the Western dress becomes someone else, someone not Eva, perhaps vaguely Oriental, while the male figure also changes shape, becomes bigger, bulkier, yet with a certain grace. And then, as I keep sifting through the drawings, the same male figure, with a sari-woman of whom all you can see clearly is the forehead with a little tiip. The man, a kind of vibrating shadow that can't be Kedar. With a woman who is not Keya.

One of these has lighting flashing in the sky, the spike of white just outside the window carving its light into the entwined couple. Looking at the drawing from an odd angle, I suddenly see the words in Bangla, quite small, almost hidden under the hotel bed:

Heroe aakashey duur koney koney
bijuli chomoki uthey khoney khoney
Adhiro pobono kishero lagiya aashichhey dhey

The penny drops. The long flag of Rabindranath engulfs my head. I know the poem of course, and the full stanza that goes:

If my eyes commit crimes forgive,
Look, constant lighting sparkles in every corner of the sky
Lightning peeps in through the window, what does it see?
Why does the impatient wind come gusting so?

Not there in any of the drawings are the first two words that begin each stanza of the poem — *Hey Nirupama*.

I whirl around towards his studio and snap out the question: 'You old fucker, you were trying hard to distract me that morning, weren't you? After I stopped you from burning these? Some of these are you imagining Niru and Byron, aren't they? That's why you were anxious I didn't look at them too carefully, tai na?'

I've turned to shout at him, but no words come out of me. It's 1976 and he's been dead two years.

BHAAV

I can't ever ask her where they finally – where they made their rendezvous or assignations, or however they thought about their meetings. At core, after everything, I'm a Bengali son and she's a Bengali mother, and we don't, we *can't*, talk about things like that.

It was obviously not in the American barracks at Hindustan Park. In any case, Goodsugar made sure Jones was 'promoted' in his billeting, got him off his cooking duties and got him a room in a 'guest house' rented by the US Army in Kyd Street near New Market, much closer to where he'd be playing most nights: the joints in Park Street and Free School Street, not to mention the Grand and the Great Eastern. But it couldn't have been here either. According to Niru, there were several billets for white GIs around Kyd Street and Sudder Street in the better buildings. There were also a couple of houses reserved for the black soldiers, adjutants and batmen to high-ranking officers who needed to live close to their masters' rooms in the two big hotels. As was standard, the white soldiers had bigger quarters and more amenities, while the houses for the blacks were what Niru described as 'glorified dormitories for privileged Negro soldiers'. I wanted to ask her if she had ever been inside, but it soon became clear she hadn't. Byron had told her the 'rooms' were just compartments separated by wooden partitions, with a strictly enforced 'No Ladies Allowed' sign at the entrance.

The other possibility was the girls' 'commune' at Dover Road. While this might have been perfect for Kedar and Keya, it would have been impossible for a uniformed GI, and a Hobshi-Negro at that, to be wandering around the houses in that area. Also out of the question was the Karnani Mansions building, which was reserved for the Yanks' very top brass in the China-Burma-India theatre. Which, of course, left the Great Eastern or, more specifically, Goodsugar's suite at the hotel.

Cleaning the Jodhpur Park flat, another item appeared, this one from inside a ring file of old bills and documents.

'Ma, what's this?'

An old identification card, with a small passport photo stuck on one side above the typed name: *Miss N. Majumdar, Official Translator*; a circular embossed stamp cutting into a corner of the picture, the letters curving through Niru's forehead, '*U.S. Army, CBI*'; below this, a barely decipherable name scrawled under type saying 'authorized by'.

'Is this Goodsugar's signature? I didn't know you worked as a translator for the Americans?'

'Of course I didn't do any such thing, but it was the only way I could get into the hotel. By the end of '43 they were very jumpy, the Markin, and they tightened the security at the entrances. If I wanted to be there with Imogen, or, or hear him play, then I had to have this card.'

She said it as if it was the most unremarkable thing in the world for a card-carrying communist to also be carrying a card allowing access to one of the US Army's main billetings for their senior officers. She carried on wiping the shelves. Her back was turned to me, but I could see her body had stiffened with some memory.

'Would this give you access to Karnani Mansions as well?' The espionage fan in me couldn't help follow a possible spy angle – my mother the secret agent.

Niru turned and stared at me. 'I have no idea. Why would I need to go to Karnani Mansions? The only local girls who went there were the...'

'I only meant if there was a party there or something. Jeremy told me he attended some wild—'

'I did *not* go to any parties with those people. It was just that I made the mistake of... the foolish...' She didn't complete her sentence. She also didn't raise her voice, but I could feel her anger now, almost in my bones. She'd called it a foolish mistake before, and when I was younger she'd taken great pains to try and rewind that and explain to me that she never thought of *me* as a mistake, just the involvement with the man she almost never referred to as my father.

My mother didn't ever fully believe in romantic love, I don't think. The word she used was not 'love' but the Bangla 'bhaav', as in 'amaader bhaav hoye gelo', which is not 'we fell in love' exactly, though neither does the literal English translation – we developed feelings for each other – quite cover it adequately. So, bhaav: in this context, less than proper love, and yet, definitely more than just warm feelings, in this particular case, well short of any urge towards a full commitment to a marriage or lifelong togetherness, but passionate enough to overcome the huge barriers of both bourgeois Bengali shame and what Elko always called the Indian communists' 'Stalinist-Victorian morality', in this case, recklessly desirous enough to produce a baby, as in crazy enough to produce me.

My Ma. And him. Try as I did, I could never quite connect the two of them visually until Elko's drawings forced me to. There is my mother, Ma, Niru, Nirupama, Com. Neem, Comrade Mother. And there's him, the never-was-there-father, Byron, Byron Jones, BJ, the not-Bijon. She has no photograph of him. I kept asking for a picture of him through my childhood and received different replies as I grew older. When I asked at fifteen why she had no picture of my father, her answer was simple, and finally truthful.

'The only pictures of us together, he had. He borrowed some other soldier's little box camera, and one day we went to the Lakes and took some photos, we even asked some passing babu to take a couple of shots of us. Then, before he could get the film processed, his unit got orders to pack up and move out. He left soon after that and I never saw the photos. He promised he would send.'

'And he didn't leave behind a single photo of himself?'

'Now I regret it, mainly for you. Maybe I wanted him to prove he still – still cared about me once he was back home. So I told him to send one of him in America, once he reached home – him in his Chicago, along with the ones of us together, and he promised. As you know, I never heard from him again.'

There is one photograph Imogen has, of people celebrating something at Maxim's, probably New Year's Eve 1944. The party of American servicemen and their girls are brightly lit, but the flash doesn't quite reach the band playing in the background. The suited men in shadow are dark, but Indian dark, the woman singing is fair, 'Chinese with mixed blood' as people always described Clarissa, and then there is the taller man, slightly bulky, with a horn covering most of his face, who's clearly a different dark than the rest of the band, even in black and white. Or is he? Maybe it's just a trick of the light. The hair is close-cropped, pretty close to an army crew cut, so you can't see whether it's straight or curly, the forehead is high, a proper, broad forehead that I think I've seen somewhere else, and I wonder where until I realize perhaps it was in the mirror. I find my eyes trying to rummage through the photo to try and see his eyes – that thing you do when you move your head in front of a two-dimensional image, trying to look around a corner in the frame – but it's no use, the bell of the trumpet obscures the rest of his face and that's that. 'I'm sure that's him!' insists Missus, as though I'm doubting he ever existed, but that doesn't help. 'Thanks, Imo-mashi, it doesn't matter, not that much.'

The truth is there are days when it doesn't matter at all and others when it does. Once Niru told me about Byron Jones, or 'Jones' as she always calls him, I tried to think of myself as a black American. It didn't work. I was thirteen by then, and because my mother had drilled this into me, I knew who the real 'blacks' were in Bengal and India: the lower castes, the tribals, the farmers, the factory workers, the people who had to beg on the street. So for a while, my mind had an ongoing short-circuit — I was neither black nor not black. Then, around fifteen, like a few other boys around me, I discovered American music, pop first, then blues and then jazz – the music played by the man who was never referred to as my 'father'.

From having straight hair as a child, my hair had suddenly gone curly in my teens but that was not necessarily un-Bengali. From time to time, especially when I was younger, I looked for the 'Negro' in me, distilled into some cool black jazz guy, but I never found him. From time to time I put Paul Robeson's face on my imagined father, and then, for a while it was Miles Davis, Miles who actually looked quite Bengali in his early twenties, and then it settled on a smudged version of Coltrane, mainly because it was his music I loved the most. And, except for my hair, forehead, eyes and height, I can see I've gone on my mother. When I was about seventeen or eighteen, I tried to do some visual sums, mentally subtracting from my features elements that were Nirupama, or Majumdar family, or recognisably Bhattacharjee, as in Dida's family, and seeing what remained. It was no good. The Bangali elements were everywhere and they kept waylaying me from different angles. In college in America, no one ever saw me as black but in Europe, especially France, for some reason things are different.

To schoolmates my name was Robi Majumdar, no Nagasaki, no Jones. And father? Father's dead, died soon after I was born – typhoid, sometimes when I slipped up, malaria, for some reason never cholera. Father's full name? Biplab Kumar Majumdar. Biplab – Revolution. My mother had a brush with the Revolution and I was the result. I had a whole legend about his 'family', Thakurda, Thamma's names, background, no, I never met them, just as I never properly knew my Baba ... Well, what's your Dida-Dadu's family name? Also Majumdar, funny no? Yes, it was useful that both sides were called Majumdar, my Ma didn't have to change her name.

Actually, once I reached teenage and Nirupama told me more, I began to think my mother began to love some music and that's what produced me. She was not normally a man-foolish girl, but this time, for this musician fellow, she briefly became one. After Niru told me about the card, a sentence was added in my mind. My mother briefly checked her emotions into a hotel, and it gave her this baby.

SA RE GA MA PA DHA NI

In Lambert's dreams, sometimes the hotel becomes a ship, an ocean liner that can be sliced into by sharp reefs or holed by torpedoes. Its lights dimmed, this liner sails at an angle, slowly navigating the treacherous, storm-wracked night sea of the city.

By December 1942, Currie's empire has expanded from the Ochterlony Suite to include adjacent rooms of the wing. The central air conditioning that covers only some rooms in the hotel has been extended by a conduit to cool this whole wing. The Americans having taken over most of the rest of the hotel, Currie has had his work cut out to protect the Section and its workings, but there is now access to a dedicated elevator, an old service cage at one end of a small corridor, that goes down to a discreet exit at the back of the building. There are British soldiers manning desks round the clock, one just inside the downstairs door and one at the normal third-floor entrance to the wing. Given that a number of spies have been identified at the Grand Hotel, Japanese pretending to be Chinese, Germans pretending to be other kinds of European and even American, no casual person can now approach the wing, much less walk by the doors of the suite and other rooms.

In Lambert's milder nightmares, the Ochterlony wing is a sealed-off part of the ship's bridge – when the torpedoes hit home below the waterline, the rest of the passengers and crew manage to escape, but no one thinks to tell Currie and his team. On some nights, all of them drown, on others, some of them survive. On yet other nights, the ship disappears, playing no role in the more seriously devastating dreams which have more to do with aircraft.

In one of these dreams, Lambert is in his dress uniform standing at attention on the tarmac at Dum Dum Airport. Chiang Kai Shek takes off in an American Dakota after shaking hands with Jawaharlal Nehru. As the Chinese generalissimo's plane rises from Dum Dum, another flight of aircraft appears on the horizon. These planes start to land, one after the other. The red rising sun circles shine briefly in the noon glare as the Jap bombers turn off the runway one by one and taxi towards the airport buildings. Nehru has disappeared, as have Goodsugar and all the American planes and staff cars.

The lead Japanese aircraft is a Nakajima Ki-34. As the engines are turned off, a Japanese officer opens the door at the rear of the aircraft and the short ladder is pulled up to it. A couple of junior officers come down and snap to attention on either side of the steps, as you do only for top brass.

A general emerges from the aircraft and slowly comes down the steps, past the saluting adjutants. Yamashita stands there, a large man for a Japanese, legs spread wide, shiny Japanese boots on American ground markings, and looks around with the air of a new owner surveying his property. His long samurai sword poking out almost horizontally behind him, he looks like some strange, exotic, avian creature – a fat, round bird with a very thin tail. After a moment, another high-ranking Tojo appears in the dark doorway, two prickles of light just catching his thick round spectacles. The man ducks as he comes out of the door frame, though, given his height, he really doesn't need to. Even from the distance of a hundred feet, Lambert can see there's something odd about this little Jap. His uniform is slightly different, and in the sunlight, you can see he has a much darker complexion than the others, not yellow but brown. Brown to the point of being almost native, in fact.

In fact, completely native.

Subhas Chandra Bose stands on top of the metal steps, crouching and blinking in the sunlight of his homeland, smiling and waving. A crowd of locals engulfs the aircraft. More Japanese soldiers have jogged over from other aircraft. They beat back the mob to clear a path for Bose, who walks through them smiling, waving, folding his hands and giving military salutes. When he reaches the waiting convoy of vehicles, he stops, takes off his spectacles and wipes his eyes with the back of his hands, sweat or tears it is not clear, before ducking into a car.

One evening in an early December nosing into 1943, an amused-looking Todd-Cartwright bounces up to Lambert and Deyton at their desks. 'Well, well, well, chaps, look what I've got for us.' Todd-C holds up an object wrapped in a newspaper that can only be a bottle.

'Have we thrown them out of Assam then, sir?' Deyton looks up from labelling a sheaf of photo prints.

'Not quite, not quite. What young whippersnappers like you don't understand is the principle of carrot and stick!'

'You're right, sir, I'm not sure I understand.'

'You won't, the wing commander might, I'll give you both a clue. When he gave this to me, Mr Currie said it was to celebrate El Alamein and the Ivans imminently about to strangle the Boche at Stalingrad. But, he said, said Mr Currie, that we have a long way to go in our part of the woods, and this is an early Christmas present to encourage all of you to keep up the good work.'

'Meaning it's an advance against expected delivery of goods, Len,' Lambert adds.

'Well, sir, looking at our latest stuff, I rather think it might be more like a last tot for the condemned.'

'Might be, might well be... Anyone seen the commander? We need to find some glasses.'

On the Burma front, the expected post-monsoon Japanese assault hasn't materialized. Instead, the reconnaissance reveals that Yamashita has sat in place, building up his forces. The thinking in the Section is that the ongoing local riots and growing pocket revolts since August are softening up the civil administration in eastern India. If these continue, some of the army might need to be diverted to bring them under control. On top of this, the huge cyclone in late October has been heavy, especially in Midnapur and 24 Parganas districts, leaving the coastal villages smashed and the ground sodden. In case the Japanese were planning to land there, it would make sense for them to wait, both for the unrest to grow and the ground to firm up.

The attack is now expected sometime in January or even early February, and plans are in place to counter it. The operation to confiscate local boats and bicycles across Bengal, having taken from June, is finally complete. When the Japanese do come, Calcutta and its volatile, hostile population are to be rapidly abandoned. Bengal's civil administration is to be distributed between Patna, Ranchi and Cuttack – in the bureaucracy, the native babus have been given orders to collate their most important files and be ready to move with them at a moment's notice. In the meantime, the army's main HQ will transfer all the way to Lucknow. The idea is to force the enemy on to the flat open Bihar plains and destroy him there.

In Lambert's dreams, Calcutta is sort of an open city for a few days before the bulk of the Japanese army arrives to reinforce the forward elements already in place. Todd-C, Deyton and most of the Section have been evacuated. For some reason, Lambert is the one left behind to participate in the formal surrender. He has been informed – in his dream he is not sure by who, Goodsugar perhaps – that he will not be beheaded like the other British officers as long as he maintains decorum and shows due humility. His RAF dress uniform smelling after days of wear, the smell mixing with a trace of cow-dung, he is now standing at attention on the gravel driveway of Victoria Memorial. Netaji Bose and two Japanese generals stand on top of the marble stairs leading to the main entrance of the building. They seem to be waiting for someone. A big Mercedes convertible crunches up the gravel to stop at the bottom of the stairway. A white man in a black military uniform gets out and prances briskly up the steps. In disbelief, Lambert sees the Nazi swastika fluttering on the nose of the Mercedes, the same symbol, black in a white circle against red, on the black-costumed man's armband, the double lightning symbol on the man's collar.

The SS officer gives a double salute, first the Hitler arm jab and then a normal military one. Bose and the Japanese salute back. All the men shake hands. A civilian Japanese official in a suit murmurs something to the generals, and all the luminaries arrange themselves in a line facing the audience of seated civilians and ranks of soldiers. A woman standing just below the stage pushes forward four or five little girls in saris edged with the Indian tricolour. The girls come up shyly and begin to garland the generals. The SS general bends forward to receive the yellow garland. Then he straightens up, snaps out another Hitler salute and folds his hands in a nomoshkar, smiling warmly at the girl as he does. The watching civilians spontaneously burst into applause. The woman in charge of the girls gathers them as they are about to step off. She says something to them. The girls all come back, line up in front of the generals, their backs to the audience. Like a trained dance troupe, they first bend forward and do a nomoshkar, then they straighten and bow again, this time in perfect Japanese style, and finally they straighten up and send their little right arms stiffly into the air, bangles clinking, returning the SS man's salute. There is further applause from the audience, and Bose and the generals also join in. The girls run off, giggling in shy triumph.

A new dream overpowers the previous one and puts Lambert back in his hotel room. The woman's sari has somehow become tangled with the bedsheets, and this is making it difficult for Lambert to take the damn thing off. The more he tries the more complicated it gets and the more she laughs. Finally, desperate, he reaches to unbutton her exposed blouse, but she pushes away his hand. 'No, no, no, Jeremy, you have to do this correctly! Sari first, then everything else!'

Lambert attacks the knotted cloth again, but nothing gives – maybe he can just cut through this convolution – he tries to remember where in his work desk he has put the big scissors – no, that's too far, she'll scarper while he gets dressed and goes to get them. He looks at the muri-walla just standing there and finds himself losing his temper. Why the hell is this man still in his room when he – he turns to the woman and says, 'All right, tell me the Bengali word for scissors!' The woman screams with laughter. 'No! I'm not telling you! You can't cut my sari!' Then she seems to change her mind. 'All right, look, come here, I'll tell you.' When he leans forward, she kisses his ear, whispering something he can't make out.

The December air outside the hotel windows is definitely cold now, but on the bed, Lambert is beginning to perspire. He reaches into the woman's thick black hair and grabs a fistful, yanking back her head. He can see she is excited by this, and she releases rapid breaths on his face. Suddenly, she calls out a word he can't understand, and repeats it. The muri-walla looks up, nods in assent and goes off, leaving behind his paraphernalia. The woman grabs Lambert's hair and brings his mouth to hers. Outside the door, the muri-walla has returned. Lambert can hear him knocking, trying to get in. Lambert's rage mounts – he's back too quickly for him to have found the scissors.

Lambert turns to the woman, trying to find her mouth again but the knocking grows too loud to ignore. He opens his eyes and gets out of bed, all in one motion. He can hear the air-raid sirens now and they are not in his dream. He reaches the door and opens it to find Deyton standing there. 'Raid, sir. Not big. They're reporting about four aircraft, but might be six. The observation post at Canning reported four Randys overhead, but Dum Dum tower is saying to keep in mind this may just be a diversion.'

'Right. Targets?'

'They've dropped a couple just up the road, sir, just north of Dalhousie Square. I'm amazed you slept through them.'

SEVEN

Rice Blood

24 DECEMBER 1942

I

AN AUSPICIOUS DAY

The island is alive, like some very large animal, with boats nibbling at it from all sides.

The river is good today, which is a relief. Even though the boats are moored in a small lagoon at the edge of the island, and more or less protected from the main water, the big river has dangerous moods. When it feels like it, the wide swathe of grey-green can reach in with frightening ease to toss the boats about like so many wooden leaves, like eye-shaped dice.

Today would not be a good day to have the boats rocking, spilling their load. Even before Gopal quite reaches them, his nose starts sending him little alarms of pleasure. As he comes up to the lagoon, he recognizes that each group of boats has its different fragrance. Steam rises from the insides of five boats in the first cluster, unmistakable, the dizzy smell of freshly cooked rice. Coming closer, he can see the fat grains glistening. The green of the water, the curving, dark brown frame of the boat, and inside, full from pointed prow to pointed stern, undulations of rice, little hillocks of five parallel rice worlds.

The next bunch of boats hold the dal. Green water, black-brown boat wood, and inside each vessel, a long, pupil-less eye of golden liquid. Mung dal, flecked with black spices, pungent with coconut and chilli, an occasional fish head dancing up to the surface, as if the whole fish was still attached to it, tantalizing, the river water very still outside, but the liquid filling the boats circling in its own currents, still swirling from the moment one of the cooks has poured in yet another boiling hot bucket.

Five boats filled to the brim with dal, five with rice, three more with alu-patal dalna cooked in ghee, or maybe just oil, because who could afford so much ghee? Certainly not his parents. Maybe the girl's side. 'They have more money than us', as he has been told many times now. Three boats with kalia of rui fish, the gravy thinner than the viscous dalna, and then the last three boats filled with his favourite maangsho, the dark brown meat curry almost seamlessly melding into the grey-brown of the boat, solid wood, liquid gravy, solid pieces of meat, the occasional glisten of light yellow bone.

Six or seven young boys, naked question marks, a darker brown than the boats, standing in the water, using straw fans to ward off the flies.

The island is small, narrow, slightly curved by the river that carves away from it in one season and adds to it in the other. Even though he has never been here before, somehow he knows the village has about twenty huts and a small Kali temple. The rest of the ground is covered with paddy. Just like around his own village, in some years some families lose their plots, in other years others. When the monsoon comes full strength, there are days, weeks, when you can't see either riverbank, and the island feels like a slippery boat on a dense, limitless ocean. Again, somehow he knows this. Winter fog, too, creates a similar effect, only that's when the ghosts abound, having returned, naturally, in the most pleasant season.

Today's auspicious date has fallen in the month of Sarath. The festival of lurid clouds above the water indicate that monsoon has finally gone, that it's too early for winter. Even in his village they sometimes use boats to keep cooked food before the big feasts, and he, Gopal, is good at keeping the flies away. The people in the village also know him not to be greedy about eating. They know he can also be trusted to keep the other boys from sampling too much of the floating food. 'So tough and strict! You could grow up to be a police havaldar! But an honest one!'

He can't be on boat duty today, though he can't quite place why. Maybe because it's not his village, but there is something else as well – some other reason that he can't catch. The other polas call out to him, insults, taunts, encouragement, all mixed up in their high-pitched boy-voices. 'Hey! Shit eater! How big is yours? Show us?', 'You're such a tiny baby yourself, how in hell will you make other babies?' 'How long before you can get her pregnant? At your size, you'll need to be twenty before it's big enough to go into an ant's cunt.' 'Should we come and help you? After all, she's our girl!' 'Our girl!' 'Our girl! Too good for an ugly little mouse like you!'

They see something behind him, and their faces turn pale with terror. They leave the boats and run. One or two who are on the river end of the boats slide into the water and swim away, slapping the water for dear life, leaving the boats knocking into each other, the fish slopping into the meat.

As always, she comes to him from behind, where he can't see her or meet her eyes. Gopal is too scared to turn around, but he can smell her. She smells of warm ash, of newly burnt human bones and flesh, and of raw mango. Her voice is low, but he can hear it clearly over all the other noises, the boys pelting away through the underbrush, the panicked splashing in the water, birds squawking, the knocking of wet wood on wet wood, the screech of the holding ropes.

'Boy. You know you don't need to be scared. Of anything. You know that, don't you?'

He feels her hands on his trembling shoulders, steadying them. He feels her other two hands cup his head and begin to stroke his hair.

'You know I'm with you, wherever you go, don't you?'

He nods, unable to open his mouth. He can feel her necklaces against the back of his neck, the sharp edges of the skull-holes poking slightly.

Today, she lets go of him quickly, with a very gentle push, a mother sending off her son to do a job that must be done. Her voice doesn't rise. 'Remember to carry your own weapon. One that belongs to you.'

He feels her recede and he looks up from the churned mud at his feet. The boats have loosened from their moorings and the river has already pulled some of them out to itself. He can see two of the dal boats bobbing and spinning as the current takes them away. The boats filled with fish and meat have gone in another direction, he can see the last of them rounding a bend around a clump of low-hanging trees. A mist has come down to his left, a winter mist that has lost its way into Sarath, and he can hear voices calling for him. 'Gopal! Gopal! Where did that rascal disappear now!', 'Gopal, this is not a day for jokes! The time has come! Where are you?' The rice boats are the heaviest and taking their time to move, two of them have disappeared and two of them are already sliding slowly away, their mooring ropes chasing them like snakes on the surface of the water, the one that's still within reach is starting to move, as if an invisible hand is tugging at it. The voices sound closer, the beseeching now turning into threatening shouts and wails. Gopal knows he has to decide now. He lifts up the awkward crisp new dhuti and wades into the water, not caring that his new kurta is about to become soaking wet. As he starts to climb into the boat, he realizes he's still clutching his delicately carved pith crown in his left hand. He throws the cone into the water and watches it float away. He hopes they'll see it and think he's drowned. As his leg goes over the edge, he feels as if he's stepped into a bucket of fire. But, with the voices coming closer and closer, he doesn't stop until he has hauled the rest of himself on to the boat. The rice is still piping hot as he sits down in it, but gradually his body adjusts to the heat. As the boat glides away from the island, there is a delicious moment where the top half of him is shivering in the chilly river air while the bottom half is being toasted by the bath of rice.

'Ei, Gogai!' Gopal's elbow hits the wall at the same moment Chuni's Ma bangs on the door of his room. 'Ei, Gogai, ei!' You told me to wake you up when I left for work! Othh! Wake up!' Opening his eyes, Gopal sees his quilt has slid down to his waist and bunched up around his legs, leaving his torso in its thin sweater exposed to the bite of the winter cold.

ALL HERE IS RIVER

This is what a river becomes, she thinks. This is what it suddenly deposits just before the end of its long journey. Along with all the silt, this strange detritus of buildings, roads, bridges, people. Her history professor's voice starts up in her head: 'Bengal is all river. Eikhaaney shob kichhu kintu nodi. All here is river. Or rather, to use a geographical term to describe it, river*ine*! This city, this history, the linked rivulets forming the network of politics! Nothing is ever direct here, things surreptitiously flow sideways, flood in strange directions, form new waterways, go underground to make invisible linkages. As a historian, you have to learn to perceive this. Just as a surveyor doesn't need to see the actual river – he observes what has sprouted around it and he can map the flow.'

She peers at the city, trying to prise apart the mist and the pall from the morning chulhas to locate any smoke still rising from the bombing raids. Coming here on the tram yesterday, she has overheard someone waxing knowledgeable about different kinds of plumes – chulha smoke is greyish-white, bombing smoke is black or deep grey, unless they have hit an ammunition depot, in which case it will be more reddish – she has no idea whether the man was talking through his hat, but the codifications have lodged in her mind. She tries to locate black smoke from around Hare Street and Esplanade, two of the places the Japani have bombed, but she can see nothing unusual. The docks and other bombed areas are too far away and out of sight. In any case, by now the fire brigade would have put out any fires and the ambulances carried away the casualties. She feels vaguely guilty for coming up here to gawk like some bystander enjoying a disaster, and she's glad everything seems normal about the winter morning vista.

'Earlier... earlier it took some time to wipe out a great city, to bring about the ruin of say Mohenjo-daro, or of Athens or Rome.' Bakul-babu a few months ago, tapping his pipe on the lectern, taking a detour from economics into history. 'In the past, it might even have taken more than a few days for a dedicated army to raze a city to the ground. But now, of course, this can be achieved much quicker through aerial bombing. We can perhaps argue that all these vayu sena, all these air forces, have arrived to speed up history!'

In the endeavour to burn Calcutta to the ground – if that is indeed their intention – the Japani bombers have failed so far. Standing on the terrace of the Shyambajar house, she can see nothing different from what she would have seen five years ago. Except, of course, for the bridge.

The thing seems almost complete. From her point of view, she can now barely make out the two closer pillars, now knitted together by a criss-cross of girders to form a crest. The two further pillars, the ones on the Howrah side, have disappeared into an accompanying pinnacle, the gap between the two high points now filled with a dipping, curving nest of grey steel. While river mist further smudges the construction, the morning sun catches the tops, turning them into odd peaks, as though someone had peeled away the skin of the high Himalayas to reveal the scaffolding underneath.

'Niru, ma? Can you see anything?' Her father calls out the question coming up the stairs.

'Yes. I can see everything and I can see nothing.' Niru doesn't turn around. 'Maaney? Meaning?' Her father adjusts his spectacles before stepping carefully over the threshold.

'There's nothing to see, Baba, not from here. Your city still seems to be there. I don't think the Japani have inflicted much damage. Not yet.'

'So they're saying, so they're saying.' He comes and puts the folded newspaper on the parapet. 'This is *Amrita Bazar*. I haven't seen *The Statesman* yet, but someone also heard it on the radio. Only minor damage. Once again, the fighter planes didn't allow them much time over the city. Or so the authorities are claiming.'

The first bombing raid was five days ago, on the 20th of December. Then they've come again, on the 21st and the 22nd. Yesterday has been quiet, allowing Niru to make her way from Dover Road to Shyambajar.

'Meanwhile, around the Volga in your Stalingrad, the game has changed!'

'So it seems. I wish I could see that Sir Naren fellow's face as he reads his morning newspaper!'

'Yes... and the Ingrej and our soldiers have pushed them back from Cairo as well.' Her father pulls out another large piece of paper from under the newspapers. 'By the way, I saw this. Did you bring it in?'

'Oh, yes, I got that on my way here yesterday. I saw dozens of them floating about on the pavement near College Street, so I jumped off the tram and picked one up.'

The texture of the paper is alien – thin, cheap rag which is also strangely oily and smooth. The image is printed in colour that seems to barely hang on to the paper, and yet the definition of the picture and words is clear. A globe tilts among clouds. On a bench coming out of the Bay of Bengal sit five figures, their feet dangling, all triumphantly raising glasses of beer. Below them a round, upside-down Humpty

Dumpty figure falls away, a quasi-Churchill in a Union Jack waistcoat and riding boots, grimacing as he drops, a small sack marked with the sterling sign, dropping with him. On top of the pamphlet there is amateurishly penned lettering in Hindi and Bangla: 'This is the opportunity for the peoples of Asia to drive the British away from Asia!'

Niru's father starts to chuckle. 'All right, so what do we have here? These two on the left are wearing lungis and caps so they're clearly Muslim, so one is a Malay and the other from the East Indies...'

'Indonesian, as he might call himself...'

'Yes, and this one on the far right, judging by his costume, is a Chinaman. Next to him, unmistakably, we have our friendly Japanese soldier. And in the middle...'

'We have our Shordarji in his turban and panjabi-pajama!'

'Yes, he's wearing a kurta-pajama definitely, but he doesn't have a moustache or beard so clearly he is a generic Indian.' Niru's father wipes his glasses, still chuckling away. 'I hope they are not dropping these in Malaya or in Java and Sumatra. Perhaps someone should tell General Nippon that Muslims don't celebrate by drinking beer and neither do most Sikhs.'

'Baba, they don't need to drop flyers in Malaya and Java-Sumatra, they are already occupying them.'

'True, true, so this work of art is clearly only for us, which is why this North Indian gentleman is in the centre.'

'The handwriting is like a child's, in both the languages.'

'Yes, like a ten-year-old's. And someone should tell Subhas that the spelling for koriya dibaar is—'

'Ma! You should have called, I could have brought the tea up!'

'Why? Am I a cripple? Am I walking wounded, still carrying scars from riots? Or am I pretending to be already old and infirm, like some people here?'

Niru's mother pokes Niru's father with her elbow – quite gently. 'Ei, shoro! Give me space to put this down!'

'You know, Saki, when I see married people nowadays? So often there is such real and extreme bite to their exchanges, I remain glad I never got married. But between Ma and Baba there has never been – there *was* never, I should say – any rancour...'

'At least you don't remember any, let's say.'

'Well, I was twenty-four at the time I'm talking about, December '42, and forty when Baba died, so I think I would know. But you tell me – did you ever see either of them get vicious with each other?'

'Dadu would make mild jokes, but Dida could be acerbic. But she was like that with all of us.'

'Well, that's a normal Bangali Ma for you. But she would always cover any verbal wound she made with antiseptic cream. Immediately.'

'Yes, and so can we agree that *you* are not a normal Bangali mother? That you've never even heard of Boroline? Verbal or otherwise?' I say it as a joke, immediately wishing I hadn't.

'I only punished you when you deserved it. Whatever bokuni you got from me, you deserved.' For a beat, I think she's going into one of her moods, but then she smiles. 'But this omelette you've made is nice, with your fancy French cheese.'

We both burst into laughter.

'See?' she says. 'I'm learning to put Boroline in my speech.'

'Well, you're better than Keda-mama and Imo-mashi. You should have seen them fighting. It was like Ali and Frazier.'

'It was also a lot of alcohol, no?'

She comes back to the painting I was asking about, the cityscape he'd made of the view from the Shyambajar terrace she'd described to him.

'It's a pity it's lost. I would've liked to have seen it...' She clears the table and I follow her into the kitchen. Running the tap over the plates, she suddenly starts laughing to herself.

'Ma? What's the matter with you? Laughing *twice* in one morning? Are you feeling all right?'

'No, you know how you sometimes remember quite ordinary moments quite indelibly, in great detail? That morning was one of them, that one exchange with your Dida keeps coming back to bite me from time to time.'

Niru looks at the bridge one last time and puts the empty teacups in the tray. Her father has already gone down, and her mother is doing something to the flowerpots.

'I'll go get ready after Baba's finished.'

Her mother straightens up. 'Must you go out today?'

'Yes, Ma, I have Party work with Keya, and then we're meeting the other two girls at Dover Road. I'll see you in a few days.'

'God knows where you'll all end up.'

'Don't worry, Ma. No one knows. Even history doesn't know. So no point worrying.'

'Yes, whatever, you're lucky, you know this mother of yours will be there for you, no matter what you need or when you need.'

'I know, Ma. But also... not that that their mothers are uncaring or anything, but none of the other girls can actually say that.' Nor can Imogen, she thinks to herself.

'Take these down and put them in the pink vase, I'll be down shortly.' Her mother puts a bunch of plucked flowers on the tray. 'I used to wonder what it would feel like, once you got married and left the house. Now I feel as though I know. Except, what you're married to is a political party.'

'Well, Ma, at least we know you won't have to deal with any grandchildren!'

'Yes, that's at least one small mercy in the middle of all this.' Her mother turns back to the flowers. 'Anyway, there's some panta bhaat and alu, so make sure you eat before leaving.'

NO GUNS AND NO BLOOD

'I don't know how to describe it to you. When you first look, you are reminded of some photograph of a war massacre where people have been machine-gunned from all sides. But since there are no guns and no blood, it feels as though god himself has littered the streets with human bodies. God – or whatever, I don't know – as if some power has just picked up fistfuls of people

and strewn them in heaps all over the pavements, in every nook and cranny that is shielded from the sun. In fact, some of them are so far gone that they can't even search for shade. They just lie there on the pavements, on the grass, even on policemen's traffic platforms, everywhere, randomly flung, like abandoned human chaff.

'If I half close my eyes, these actual humans, my fellow countrymen, my supposed brothers and sisters, are reduced to black and dirty white dashes, black = skin, white = whatever few clothes they are wearing, all faded in the sun to a kind of white–off-white. Since when did Bengali peasants have such dark skin? Maybe they don't – at least, not all of them – maybe, just as some of the dirty cloth has faded to a light shade, the skin has darkened in the sun to a kind of dark brown–almost black. I can't really look at any one of them properly. Something forces my eyes to always stop between the bodies lying there – me: my eyes attached, always, to my full stomach, my own body always attached to a proper covering of nice clothes.'

Though the date is half chopped off in the photocopy, the letter looks like it's from some point in 1944. Eva Margenik, née Attali, has been very kind in the few phone conversations I've now had with her. She has gone through her correspondence with 'Lahiri' and copied certain portions that she thinks would throw light on his life and particularly his early career. On the line from California, her voice is careful. 'I won't, you will understand, send you entire letters, yes? When people are young, they are… they write all sorts of things that are, that are best kept between those young people who no longer exist, even if their older versions are still alive, you understand me?'

Of course I understood, and I was very grateful, ma'am. Anything she thought appropriate to send my way would be happily received.

The first packet arrived: one of those lovely, thick American manila envelopes, with my name neatly typed on a label: *To Mr Robi N. Jones-Majumdar*. Inside was a stack of A4 sheets on which sections of the letters had been photocopied, many of them with bits carefully redacted by pieces of blank paper taped over them before they were copied, the edges of which created a kind of minimalist collage of white shapes on white. Most of them were in a younger version of Elko's typical handwriting, what I call 'impeccable Calcutta copperplate', a kind of beautiful, bravura rendering of handwritten English, heavily influenced by the swirls and points of Bangla script, that an entire elite class of Bengali boys and girls of that time seem to generate effortlessly. Some sheets had passages transcribed by typewriter, with the date of each passage carefully noted on top. Occasionally there were slip-ups, either where Eva's or perhaps an assistant's eyes had missed something, or where they could not have known what Elko had told me, nor what I might be able to deduce from what I had read in Eva's letters, entire ones that I had in my possession, to Elko.

Elko's letter from 1944 continues: '*When I try and draw them, draw this reality, I find myself cheating. I find my body becoming slightly tense, as during those rare occasions when I tried to cheat in school exams. I make dots and dashes, as though trying to find a Morse code or a shorthand to convey these impossible sights attacking my cowardly eyes. Everything, all the little bits I know about drawing the human body, the well-fed, healthy human body (your body, for instance) all that just fails. My pencil falls off their bones, my pen won't follow the contours of these faces – I'm not enough of an artist, not brave enough or strong enough to put aside my shame and guilt.*' Someone has tried to redact the parentheses about Eva's body, but it is shoddily done – one of the few instances in this batch of copies – and I can make out the words under the tape or whatever they used. A sentence in the letter stands out, separated from the body of the writing by a piece of paper laid over the preceding words: '*... can I possibly touch someone again? How do I paint the smell? How do I paint the horror the stink sets off inside me? Bad drawing, wrong drawing!*'

Though he has recorded that he started to draw people sheltering on the street towards the end of 1942, Elko seriously attempts to make drawings and paintings about the famine only around the middle of 1943. By that time, the city is filled with the victims of the famine, thousands upon thousands of destitute villagers who have taken over the pavements everywhere except in the white neighbourhoods. The dead lie completely still among the ones who are barely able to move, the stench of decomposing bodies mingling with that of shit and vomit, and mixing yet again with the occasional smell of rice being boiled in the langarkhanas set up in parks and on street corners.

For so many of the painters working in Bengal, portraying the reality of these hunger-bombed peasants pushes aside all other subjects and, for a while, Elko is no exception.

'Take, eat.' The volunteer woman slaps a greyish-white dollop into the man's tin bowl. The man stands there, not moving, his body vibrating like a twig in a light breeze.

'Ki holo? Geye boshey khaao!' What happened, asks the volunteer, go sit and eat! The man makes a gesture, raising his hand as if holding food, and points towards where some children and women are sitting under a tree. Can I have some more? The volunteer now loses her patience and snaps. 'Now, Dadu, don't try all that with me! I've given them their share before you. They were here at the very start of the queue, don't think I don't know who I've fed today!'

Standing a few feet away with his sketchbook, Kedar tries to capture the peculiar quality of the watery rice in the bowl. The thinly cooked rice has turned mushy, but the pencil lines have too much definition and the collapsing wet mound looks like an octopus with water-tentacles. In frustration he puts the pencil back into his box and reaches for the fountain pen – even though the nib is much finer than the soft tip of the pencil, it somehow gives him more control in capturing the gloop.

'Meye ta ke toh shudhu phyan diyechho!' You gave only rice water to my daughter! The man still refuses to move. The woman clangs the ladle at the edge of the rice bucket – a warrior brandishing her sword. Before she can speak, an older volunteer puts a hand on her shoulder and begins to address the crowd.

'Listen! All of you listen! We've explained this many times but let me explain again. We are not saving the rice for anybody, everything that's here is for you. And it's good rice, exactly the same as we are eating at home. But those of you in a really bad state *cannot* eat rice just yet, not solid rice! If you do, you will die! Your stomach will burst inside you! We now know this from other langarkhanas where many people have died. That's why Doctor Moshai is also here, to tell us who is well enough to eat solid rice and who is not!' She points to the man with a stethoscope hanging from his neck. 'So, again, if you haven't eaten for a long time, you need to have only rice water for a few days. Once your body becomes stronger, you will certainly get rice! Understood?'

Some people in the queue nod. A couple of them shout at the old man, telling him to move on. The nib maps out the mass of shrunken bodies pressed up against each other but, try as he does, Kedar can't bring himself to detail any faces. He can't recognize these eyes as human eyes, the mouths he sees are not mouths like his own but from some other species, small gateways to some abyss that each person seems to be carrying within herself, himself. As his pen moves faster and faster, almost tearing the paper, Kedar realizes there is something lurking behind the pity he sees himself feeling for these villagers: fear, a terror that if another human being could be reduced to this, he too could one day find himself pasted against others, waiting desperately for a bowl of rice water. It is this fear that's making his pen move faster.

'You know, old boy, I now understand why there are no great still lifes of Indian food, especially our Bangla food. I mean, what can you do with a mass of bhaat in a bowl, how much… what's that quaint old phrase? Oh yes, how much *pictorial interest* can you squeeze out of a characterless lump of greyish white? And what is rice anyway, without the contrast of dal, or fish, or shobji-torkaari?'

The label on the cassette says May 1974. I was recording our conversation and I'd meant to stop before the meal. As it happens, I forgot and left the recorder on.

Missus is away. Elko's been craving shukto and I've tried my best to approximate it from what I can find locally. Aubergine, potato, sweet potato, haricots vert, fresh ginger and milk have been no problem; I keep a stock of Indian condiments in the kitchen, so we have turmeric and other spices, including radhuni and mustard seeds, for the two pastes, and mustard oil; I've just visited Marseilles where I've scored plantain and something that looks vaguely like karela from one of the

African stores; I've used unsalted butter instead of ghee; there's nothing to be done about the members missing from the shukto team, so no drumsticks, sheem beans or dal-bori. The nearest thing to Bengali rice is the stuff from an Italian shop in the city, something the man calls Arborio, but it's not very close.

'Well,' says Elko, 'you can't have everything, can you?' He picks up his fork and puts a bit of the shukto on the rice. 'I have to say though – this almost looks like the real thing.'

'Don't you feel like eating with your hand?'

'Saki...' He looks up like a kid caught doing mischief. '... one of the worst tyaansh things about your old Keda-mama is I always used to eat bhaat with cutlery, even as a child. Knife and fork when Ma or Baba or the Bulldog were watching, especially Ma, knife and spoon when she was wasn't. I love rice, but I can't stand the feel of it on my fingers.'

I already know this from previous conversations, what I meant is doesn't he want to touch cooked rice a few times before he... but I refrain from explicating.

He takes a forkful of shukto and Italian bhaat and slowly inserts it into his mouth. I have a hand towel at the ready, but most of it goes in and stays in as he begins chewing. He wipes the small dribble on his chin with his own napkin. I stop holding my breath and put down the towel.

'Dear boy!' He grins at me, a couple of rice grains flecking his teeth. 'It's not *bad* you know! Not bad at all!' He organizes another forkful on his plate. 'You can start eating, I don't think I'll bring it up today. It tastes too good to waste!'

I wait for the second forkful to go down before starting on my own plate. The rice with the butter almost feels like it could be home bhaat and ghee, especially once you add the vegetables with their spices. Thankfully, this is not the long-grained basmati you get in Indian restaurants here in the West, but neither is it quite like the rice at home, the grains are too fat and almost bouncy against my fingers. 'Umm, this African gourd I found is okay, but it's not properly teto like karela, I'm really missing the bitter from the karela.'

'Yes, true, the teto is absent. Maybe if there's an after, they'll have teto.'

I glare at him for breaking Missus's rule of no morbid talk at meals. 'You'd better hope it's not only teto.'

I watch, unable to eat until he manages a few more forkfuls. After a bit, he retches, brings the napkin to his mouth and pushes away the plate. 'Thank you, dear boy, that was really smashing.'

As I eat, he reaches with his fork and absently toys with the remaining food on his plate. 'Now that I can't really put much in my mouth, I suppose I can sort of understand what those poor bastards were going through. Only sort of, mind you!'

For a while, the tape has nothing but the irregular click of fork on plate, but then he starts up again. 'You know, the thing is, very little of it has any shape, our food! Rice is amorphousness incarnate, a ruti is bloody flat, or a pile of soft disks, vegetables are gloopy mounds, each with its own mess of colours, yes, but visually very hard to define! But a loaf of bread now, or a whole roasted chicken, d'you see what I'm getting at?'

He goes silent again, his mind on some trip, and then he comes back into himself. 'Not that, not that that was the reason I couldn't do anything with... with what was going on. I tried, you know, from those first days when they started to fill up the footpaths in late '42, from when the first langarkhanas started, I tried then and again later, but I have to accept that Kedar Nath Lahiri, aspiring to great painting, chickened out, as the Yanks like to say. Chickened. Bloody. Out.'

'Well, don't be so hard on yourself. Others were already painting those things. You were looking for something different and sometimes that takes time. You were a painter, not a reporter, right?'

'Yes, well, that's the excuse, that *is* my excuse and you put it better than I can. Try and remember it, will you, if ever...'

Kedar puts the pen and sketchbook into his jhola and forces himself to walk away from the langarkhana. In his mind, he starts composing a letter to Eva where he will tell her how much he misses her, she who has now been gone for just over a year. He will be funny and tell her that it was hilarious how people carried out this mass exodus last January, terrified the city would be bombed, only for the Japanese to disappoint them, and how, after they've all now come back, the bombs have finally begun to fall. The sentences begin to form in his head as he walks back from Triangular Park to Palm Avenue. *The decorations for this Christmas of 1942 are up in Park Street. The Europeans, Indian Christians and all those others who like to celebrate the white man's Big Day have all purchased their Christmas trees, big and small. The Japanese decided to join the celebrations with five days to go. The first bombs fell on the 20th, just a few small explosions in north Calcutta, near my college. On the 22nd, our friends visited again, in greater force, but again, just a few scattered bombs, apparently around the port and near the new bridge before the fighter planes chased them off. Today is, of course, Christmas Eve and a perfect day to disrupt the festivities. If a bomb falls on me and I am killed, remember that I always loved you.* He wonders yet again if he should mention Keya, and then decides yet again it would be best not to – this little room he shares with Eva exists only in the letters, whereas his room with Keya is located in an entirely different wing of the hotel of his being.

Walking down Rashbehari Avenue, he tries to remember the time when the pavements were empty of desperate villagers. Was it only three months ago? Six? The peasants had started to trickle in about two months ago, but now it feels as though they've always been here, and their number seems to be growing every day. He has heard that they've been ruthlessly driven away from the shaheb neighbourhoods like Alipur and Minto Park, and neither are they too visible in the lanes around his own house in Palm Avenue. It's no surprise that the goras don't want to see these wretches outside their gates, but another reason, clearly, is that people with walls and gates around their mansions were much less likely to part with food, whereas in a Bangali area, with houses opening right on to the street, the hungry stood a much better chance.

Even as he thinks this, Kedar finds himself walking past one of the big houses on Rashbehari, complete with a gate and driveway. He knows this house because he has come here once with a schoolmate to enviously admire the Mercedes the family had just bought – if he remembers correctly, the only supercharged 380K in Calcutta, probably in 1934. The gate is open, and Kedar looks in to see if he can spot the old monster. There are recently built baffle walls in front of the portico and the garage, but from where he's standing, he can just about see the typical Teutonic snout of, yes, the 380. He notes with satisfaction that they've taken off the Mercedes star and put some kind of metal cap to cover the smaller decal on the radiator.

Back home, Kedar settles down at his desk on the veranda and begins to transfer some of the morning's sketches, copying them into a larger drawing book and elaborating on the originals. Rasko has offered to bring him breakfast, but Kedar isn't hungry. 'Just bring me some tea. And change this ashtray.'

By the time Rasko comes back, Kedar is struggling with the old man at the rice station, trying to coax the bones showing through the skin into the exact supplicant stoop that he remembers. He hates what appears on the paper and rubs it out. He starts again, this time trying to improve upon the rough ink sketch of the people pressed up in the queue. Again, he botches it up, the lines are correct but they come nowhere near conveying the barely supressed desperation he has witnessed. He starts to erase and then stops. His pencil moves to another part of the page and, almost with a will of its own, starts to draw the nose of the Mercedes poking out from behind the baffle wall. He goes back to the queue drawing but stops again. This time, his pencil starts looking at the teapot and cup on the teapoy to his left, making it appear on the page, not exactly as it is but in another location, maybe Flurys, a woman's hand with a lit cigarette resting next to it. After a while, he goes back to the small mass of bodies, but whatever he adds just makes the failed drawing worse. Fury rising, he takes the eraser and slashes across the half-formed faces and torsos, reducing them to stripes and smudges.

'Yes, leave it Dada-babu, you will never understand that kind of life. It's not your reality and for this you should thank god. Best is if you stay with your land-escapes. I can see those make you the happiest.'

Rasko has been very quiet, standing behind Kedar. Kedar turns around, his anger shifting from himself to Rasko. He stops himself just in time. Rasko has come back from leave only yesterday and Kedar hasn't yet spoken to him properly.

'How are things back home?'

'*My* home, Dada-babu?'

'What else? Who else is standing here?'

'No, things are bad, not just in my village, things in all of Mednipur are really bad.' Rasko pauses to take a breath. When he opens his mouth again, the keening of an air-raid siren comes out of it, taking over the surrounding air.

THE BIG MAN

I jumped in my chair as a deep wail suddenly started up somewhere very close by. The sound rose until it took over the whole room, almost making the windows vibrate. Instinctively, I held on to my teacup to stop it from clittering off the saucer but then forced my hand away – I saw the Big Man had left his cup and saucer on the desk and nothing was happening to the china. The Big Man caught my gesture, just as he caught everything, and gave me a smile.

'Don't be scared, Saki-babu, don't be scared, it will stop in a minute!' His Bangla took on a village mother's tone – bhoy korte naai!

The sound rose a bit more – now joined in my ear by the sound of birds flapping out of trees – and then it subsided.

'You have never heard a siren?' The look of wonder on his face was almost comical. 'Surely they have factories near Jodhpur Park?'

'No, I mean, yes, yes, I have heard sirens but not from this close. I just got a bit startled.'

'We have them twice a day. Nine o'clock and five o'clock. This one was the signal for the start of the morning shift in the factory next door. Not that the labour pays any attention to them any more. These days, the workers more or less come and go as they please – communism, you see.'

I nodded, pretending some knowledge. 'But I thought this Emergency meant—'

'Yes, well, at the beginning, when she imposed it suddenly, there was great punctuality. For a few months. But you can't tether a Bangali to a clock for very long, doesn't matter whether you are Indira Gandhi or Siddhartha Shankar Ray. And Kolkata's non-Bangali workers, the Biharis and the UP-walla labour have also become Bangali in this, so gradually things went back to almost normal. And now, with these elections called, people sense she's losing power, so they are making up for all that awful schedule-keeping she had imposed on them. God knows how anyone will get them back on the floor if she loses, which she very well could.'

He paused and looked around his domain. 'But I'll tell you, since you are asking about that time, *that* was when this siren sound caused real fear, when the Japanese actually began to bomb Kolkata. What was it, hyan, yes, December 1942, late December, when they first came with their planes. At first, people thought it was another air-raid drill and everybody ignored the sirens. But then, the first bomb fell, I think near Tiretti Bajar or somewhere, followed by more real bombs, and that was it. Everybody's shit came out, everybody began to take cover at the slightest loud noise, cowering behind baffle walls and scurrying into the air-raid shelters. It was funny to watch – like one of those Markin movies, ki boley jyaano, slap—like those slapstick comedies.'

'Was it bad for you?'

'Me? Personally? No.' The Big Man half pulled out a Dunhill and offered me the pack. I gestured at my own cigarette still going in the ashtray. 'I mean, yes, the first time was a bit of a shock. The second day of the raids, I was out making deliveries when these planes went over, really low and loud – fast, you know – and then there were these explosions somewhere not far, close enough for the ground to shake under the tyres, and my driver almost drove into a ricksha-walla, nearly killing the poor fellow. But then you figure it out – it's like a reverse lottery – if your name's written on a bomb then you won't escape it. So, no recklessness of course, but you have to go about your business as per normal. But you know, Saki-babu...'

'Ganesh-babu, please just call me Saki, and tumi, not aapni.' This was the third time I'd asked him.

'Yes, yes, after a while, I'll get around to it. I don't meet that many foreigners, you see, so the formality comes automatically. I feel like I should be speaking to you in English.' He raised his hand before I could object. 'Yes, I know, you are not exactly a foreigner, I know, but when one first looks at you... Anyway, so the thing is, first of all, it was never a rain of bombs like people experienced in Rangoon and Penang, you know, or like in London and places. Some of us – those of us who understood the logic – we quickly sensed that these were khujro, small-change raids done to create panic in the population. Because, if the Japani actually had the capability, they would have come in force and flattened the port, or Howrah Station and the new bridge, or all the huge army camps around the city. But they were running in and out like street dogs, barking a lot but unable to bite. After a while, we saw they were dropping leaflets more than bombs.'

'Didn't they did bomb Kidderpore heavily?'

'Yes, but that was almost a year later, one day they came in force and attacked the port. That was the worst raid, as I heard. You know, I missed most of all this bombing-shombing because I wasn't in Kolkata in those days. I was here for those first few raids, but by early January 1943 I'd left the city. I would come and go as and when work required, but I was mostly away for about two years.' He played with his empty teacup. 'By the time I returned properly, the Japani were gone. They were no longer the problem, if they'd ever really been. When I came back, the big thing was the famine, and then soon after that the Hindu–Muslim thing. When I came back, some neighbourhoods were almost carpeted with dead bodies, as I'm sure your mother has described to you. Then, a couple of years after the famine eased up, there was a different carpet of bodies, this time from all the killings.'

'Why did you have to leave Kolkata?'

The Big Man took off his glasses and looked at me. The room became a different place. It wasn't exactly a threatening look – he was almost smiling – but it was clear I'd inadvertently crossed a line. I felt a sharp jab of fear. Then his face broke into a full smile.

'Saki. You said you had time, no?' He had shifted to the familiar tumi.

I nodded vigorously.

'So, let's take things as they come. Maybe a bit slowly. And as I told you at the beginning, I may not be able to answer all your questions, or not all your questions might be answered. But I will do whatever to help you with information about Kedar-babu and his paintings, also with whatever Niru-di says I can tell you, say about her work and the Kolkata of that time. I saw it from a very different place than she did, or Kedar-babu did.'

'Yes, of course.'

'So, perhaps, the first thing is, you should go and meet these two ladies in Dharmatolla. They will enjoy meeting a tall-body, handsome young man like you. You'll have to be careful they don't enjoy it too much.'

My notes remind me it took me a month of trying before I got to see the Big Man. During this time, I understood that he was referred to by different names by different people: Bodo Babu, i.e., the Big Man, then Poitallish, i.e., Forty-five, though he was certainly not born in the same year as me, and then, when he finally responded to messages and telephoned Ma, I heard her trip over the first syllable of his name before calling him Ganesh, with his tinny voice over the receiver calling her Niru-di.

They hadn't met for a while, but both greeted each other warmly. 'Your son, Niru-di? Oh, of course, he must be all grown up now. Back from abroad? America and then France? Wah, very good.'

Ma explained that I was cataloguing Kedar Lahiri's paintings and researching his life for a possible book to go with an exhibition. Could Ganesh possibly help? Also perhaps put me in touch with those girls – those women – at the Dharmatolla house?

'Let him come and meet me. I'll see what I can do.'

So, early one morning in March 1977, I took a taxi to an address in Fairlie Place, just behind the Reserve Bank at Dalhousie Square. The building was one of those completely geriatric, miraculously still standing late nineteenth-century commercial piles that populate the Dalhousie area. I went into the dimly lit entrance and began to look at the board which listed all the company offices housed there. A man came in behind me. 'Are you looking for Shyama Export-Import?' I nodded. 'Saki-babu, toh? The car is over there.' As I followed the man, I noted that he was a well-built, muscular type with a certain no-nonsense way about him, nothing like the normal peons and office gofers you found in this district. He got in the front of the Ambassador next to a similarly chunky driver, and we made our way on to Strand Road. The man turned and pointed to the little fan suspended between the front and rear doors – 'Do you need it on?' 'No, I'm fine.'

We crossed Howrah Bridge, bore right and made our way through the network of narrow roads along the river, heading north into the hinterland of factory clusters and small satellite neighbourhoods. After about forty minutes, the car turned into a compound gate with a metal sign curving across it. All I could read of the weather-effaced letters was 'ute Mills Pvt. Ltd.' Inside, we drove past sheds and warehouses around which a jungle was fighting to establish itself – branches and bushes sat in ambush between the rusted tin roofs, while whole tree trunks had wrestled their way out from the cracks in the masonry. Closer to the river, the old main building was in better repair, as were two or three large sheds to the sides. The car went around and stopped under a row of Gulmohar trees between the building and the river.

At the centre of the facade facing the river was a cavernous opening. In front of this was a big, rusting metal disk in the ground, bifurcated with an equally rusted segment of what looked like narrow-gauge rail tracks. A jetty began where the disk ended and ran out about a hundred feet into the water. I could see no trace of them, but clearly there would have been tracks on the big jetty that could be aligned with the section on the disk. My escort saw me looking and nodded. 'Yes, in the old times there was an entire mini-railway system here, with cranes and small wagons to move the raw jute from the barges to the factory sheds and the finished bales out again. All gone now.'

Inside the building, we entered a dark hallway and went past a big room piled with wooden crates and jute-covered packages. A grand wooden stairway appeared from the gloom, and we went up to the first floor. A long balcony ran along the side facing the river, the old pillars and ceiling with wooden beams both freshly painted. The man led me into a room where two secretaries sat at desks typing away. He took me past them into what was clearly a reception room of some sort, with chairs and old sofas arranged roughly to seat an audience facing a chair and a desk.

'Please have a seat. He will call you as soon as he's free.' The man switched on a ceiling fan and went away.

I looked around, marvelling at the grace of the high ceilings and generous French windows the Ingrej had managed for themselves even as they bled the local countryside dry of all its bounty. Now, other than the unmistakable colonial architecture, the only trace of anything English was in the photographs of the First Division and FA Cup matches on the walls. In fact, almost all the available wall space here was covered with large photos of sportsmen in action. The Brazil team of 1970, the Dutch hero Johan Cruyff, then the Germans from 1974. Besides the football, there were several pictures of Mark Spitz, the Olympic swimming champion, and a few tennis players. A few of the framed images were colour posters from abroad, but most of them were enlargements of photographs shot from the pages of magazines. At one side, there was a glass fronted cupboard with cups and medals, next to which hung smaller, more expensively framed black-and-white photos of a local football team lifting trophies or lined up for celebratory functions.

Going closer for a look, I saw that these were all pictures of Hitoishi Athletic's triumphs, 'Hitosh' being one of Calcutta's big four football clubs.

'That was taken when we won the Durand Cup in 1970. That may have been all-India, but my favourite cup is still this one, Calcutta League 1966, when, in a crucial game, we beat Mohun Bagan 5-4 with only ten men. Eleven years have passed, but Chuni Goswami and that Bagan lot *still* can't look me in the eye when I bring it up!'

I turned around and did a nomoshkar even before I focused on him properly.

'Thank you for finding the time to meet me.'

'Do you follow football, Saki-babu? Ever played?'

'Uh, no, not really. I've always had these glasses, so a bit of cricket was okay while wearing them, but football, no chance!'

'I see, I see. Achcha, sorry to drag you out of the city and that too so early.'

'Not at all! It's a very pleasant drive. I was happy to get away.'

He led me through a door to his office, offered me a seat and went around the desk to his chair.

'You'll have tea, of course? I'll ask for breakfast in a little while, but first let them bring tea.' He smacked the little bell on his desk twice just as the phone rang. 'Just give me a minute, this shouldn't take long.' He picked up the receiver and began to breathe a series of monosyllabic noises into the mouthpiece. Shortly, a man appeared with a large tray laden with a full, Western tea service and some biscuits. As the man poured, I noticed the tea set was neither old English china nor Bengal Potteries, the two usual suspects in Calcutta, but newish, imported – possibly Japanese. Good Darjeeling tea, milk and sugar for me, less milk and one tiny tablet for Ganesh-babu. As he continued on the phone, he ripped open a packet and lit a cigarette, offering me one. I raised my hand in thanks and pulled out my own fags.

Sipping my tea, I sneaked a couple of looks at the man, still unable to get over the sense of disbelief that I was actually here, finally meeting him.

By now, I had a whole stack of imaginary pictures of the Big Man in my head, but none of them came close to matching the man I was looking at. First of all, I'd always understood that 'Big Man' didn't mean actually, physically big, but I hadn't expected to see someone so short, even shorter than Elko, so no more than about five foot five inches. I hadn't exactly imagined a lithely muscular man, but perhaps someone who had a memory of once having been quite athletic – while Ganesh-babu was nowhere near fat, the crisply ironed cream safari suit, the not particularly muscular arms, the heavy expensive watch and two glinting rings on the left hand tended to bring up thoughts of wealthy Marwari businessmen rather than someone capable of moving quickly and forcefully. Most of all, what I found wrong-footing me was the face: he wasn't bald yet, but it was only a matter of time; the slightly wavy receding hair was cropped quite short, dyed jet black and slicked down; the sideburns were contained and manicured straight, coming down just below the line of his earlobes; the moustache, also jet black, was unexpected – quite full, restricted to his mouth; the face had once been lean, but now age had rounded it a bit, added a small double chin; the spectacles were the most surprising thing, bifocals of a low power, but thick enough to obscure his eyes from some angles. The main thing, I only realized later, was not the individual parts, the ageing, the small indications of vanity, but the unspoken, immutable power conveyed by the whole, the confidence and—

'I also imagined you differently, Saki-babu.' He'd got off the phone without my noticing. I found his eyes boring into me as he polished his glasses. 'I didn't think you would be so tall, almost like our Ray-babu. Without the glasses, you would have made a good centre back.'

'Satyajit Ray is six feet four, I think. I'm only about six-one. And probably always too thin for a centre back.'

'So, tell me, how can I help you?'

I told him about Elko in his last days, about the paintings, about how he died. I told him about trying to locate all the paintings and putting together an exhibition and a catalogue. Yes, he'd heard that Kedar-babu had passed away in France. What a thing of sadness, what a talented, special man. I began reaching in my bag for my tape recorder.

'Would it be all right if I recorded you?'

'Recorded, meaning?'

I showed him the tape machine. 'May I tape record our conversation?'

He smiled and shook his head in way that killed any negotiation. 'Oita chhedey dao. Let's leave that. Who knows what I might say that I might regret later. A man in my lines of business has to be careful. You can take notes and use things pertaining to what you need. But at no point must you attribute anything to me. Are we agreed? Then I can talk freely. Without worrying.'

'Sure, certainly, forgive me.'

'Nothing to apologize for. You are rigorous in your work, which is a good thing. I have to be equally rigorous in mine.' He rang the bell again and the man came in. 'You have a notebook and pen?' I did, and

I took them out. He nodded to the man. 'Take babu's bag and keep it outside carefully. Make sure he takes it when he leaves.' The man took away my bag with the recorder inside. 'You see, when remembering things, the mind can wander, I may say extra things which would create complications for you if they were... you know...'

'I understand.'

'You're a very sharp young man. Not surprising in a son of Niru-di's.'

My notes indicate that this is where Poitallish laid out that he would speak freely about Kedar-babu and about whatever to do with Calcutta in the war years that was relevant to Kedar, but repeated that not everything I asked might be answered. There was also a reiteration about attribution which I have down in a scrawl as *Agreed – no quotes, no direct quotes!* At some early point, I remember I went back to what I thought then was safe ground.

'So, can I ask, where did you first meet Kedar-babu?'

'The first time...' He turned his head away, and whatever he remembered made him break into a smile. 'The first time – well, as many people have said, Kolkata is actually a small town in the body of a big city, yes? So, I'd seen him around, I sort of knew who he was, this boy who was around my age, maybe a couple of years older, but the son of a big family, from a class and a world that I couldn't even imagine at that time. I'd be standing on the street, and I would see him go by in his sports car, open-top green car. This used to happen around the Great Eastern Hotel, he liked to go there... But oddly enough, the first time we were formally introduced was in Paris.'

'Oh! Which year was that?'

'It would have to be... 1952. I've only been to France three times, and that was the first trip. So 1952, yes. I'm saying "the first time", but to tell the truth, that was the only time we met properly. After that one time, I never had the good fortune to meet him again.'

OPENING

'Oh god, yes, I do remember that, and he's right, that *is* the only time they met properly! How could I forget? If you wanted to be melodramatic, you could say those were the three or four hours that changed my life.'

'And if you didn't want to be melodramatic?'

'Well, several things led up to that moment, didn't they, darling? And, stemming from that moment, pennies take their time to drop... and from the moment they start to drop, they sometimes take an inordinate amount of time to hit the ground.' She starts fidgeting and looking around. 'Why don't we...'

'No, Imo-mashi. It's only four o'clock. We agreed you can't have the first one before six. Tell me this story and it'll be six in no time. Come on.'

She stared at me with something like low-voltage hatred. I stared back. I'd already lost Elko, I wasn't going to lose her in quick succession, not if I could help it.

So, if I remembered, Kedar Lahiri had travelled to London soon after the war, in early 1946. Cold and miserable, he had returned to Calcutta by the end of the year with – in his own words – his tail between his legs. In 1952, having met 'the Bombay mob', he decided to invade Europe again, this time Paris firmly included in his plans. After a few desultory months in London, including the infamous encounter with Souza, Kedar moved to Paris.

'The first time he'd come to London, I was with the Albatrosses, first in Malaya and Singapore, and then in Egypt. Mummy and I cleaved to Papa as he attempted to execute bits of housekeeping for King and Empire, *dire* stuff involving everything from repatriating refugees to rebuilding bombed sewage systems. I loved Calcutta, but obviously couldn't stay there on my own. Equally obviously, I couldn't be allowed to go back to England, not after "what had happened" with Andrew. So, with the people they met, Mummy and Papa put it about that I was a war widow of sorts. The fact that there had been no marriage, or that the chap in question might not even be dead were unnecessary details. As for me, I couldn't stand the thought of returning to England, but I did, just as Kedar was about to leave and we met once, briefly. He escaped back to India, and sure enough, I couldn't *fucking* bear bloody London. It was a foreign country, cold and shuttered, and not only because of the war – *I* had turned inside out like a sock in the years away. I suppose you could say the new skin that was suddenly exposed to old Britain wasn't thick enough, not tough enough to take the constant assault of Englishness. Suddenly, I was allergic. Who *were* these people? In what way were they *my* people?'

Luckily for Imogen, there was a grandmother – her mother's mother – who had a small house in Provence, about forty minutes' drive from Aix and not far from Cézanne's blessed Mont Sainte Vic, and Missus began to spend more and more time there, getting away from 'ghastly grey Blighty' as often as she could.

'Granny had always promised it to me, but I suppose I took possession a little early. Granny, poor darling, took the cue – having brought Great Britain safely through the war, she took her leave of us in 1951, officially making me, Imogen Snell, the owner of the property, a petite zamindaresse of rural Provence.

'So, Kedar's first letter arrived here at some point in late spring '52, forwarded from London, him trying to be cheerful – *Hello! I'm in London! Are you here or nearabouts perchance? I'm really enjoying myself this time around!* – Clearly bollocks. I could *see,* see just from the handwriting that the poor sod was miserable, all heavy impression scribbling, sentences scratched out into black bands, the immaculate handwriting just falling apart, *Yours, Larry Lahiri* indeed... I ignored it for a while and then sent him a brief postcard saying I was in Cézanne country and how nice it would be if he could visit. I wasn't completely insincere, but nor did I specify quite when he might come. I was quite happy on my own and didn't particularly want company. I didn't include a return address. I may've also said I'd be back in London shortly.'

Kedar moves to Paris at the peak of summer and immediately regrets it – Paris in August is worse than Calcutta in April. Roasting, no fans, hardly anybody around, the whole city bleached of people, ugly light, and the eternal questions plaguing him like twin nemeses – What to paint? Why to paint? All this he puts into another letter to Imogen.

'There was one bit that stayed with me: *I can't bear to see another painting of the bloody Seine. It's not a river, it's a dried up nallah. Why would I paint a "river" that's not even deep enough for someone to drown themselves in? At least, no self-respecting Bengali would consider it.*'

Reading this, Imogen is unclear whether he meant painting or drowning. By now she has returned to London, and writes back saying she'll be returning to France in the autumn and they must meet then – by which time the Seine should be deep enough to accommodate both of them.

'He was living in some cheap digs around Pigalle that Raza has found him, Raza being much kinder than Souza. So Zemindear was paying not very much in rent, but he still needed to eat and buy materials. The family at home kept turning off the money tap, insisting he come home, get a degree in law and take over his father's practice. Old man Lahiri was ailing by then and Uncle Bulldog, bless his sensitive artistic soul, wanted to whip the young wastrel into shape.'

Imogen returns to Provence in the autumn, stopping in Paris only to change trains. 'You know, Saki, I kept looking out of the cab between stations, ready to duck in case I spotted Kedar. I realized this only later, how much I wanted to avoid meeting him, and I felt ashamed.'

'Why did you want to avoid him?'

'Because... I suppose because I knew he would revivify Calcutta for me. The whole mess, you know? Andrew, Niru, the happiness that I could only connect with Calcutta and also the misery that belonged nowhere else... Fear of re-opening old wounds, you know, that sort of thing... except...'

'Except?'

'Ah, *here they are*, you little bastard! Hidden them in plain sight, had you?' I'd taken my eye off her for a moment, not clocking that even as she told me the story a little spotter aircraft inside her was circling, hunting for the booze. She'd removed the stack of blank canvases and torn away the blanket covering the case underneath. Luckily, this was just the wine. The gin and other hard stuff were still secure elsewhere.

We clinked glasses. 'Except, the truth is, I was also desperate to reconnect with the mess. I just didn't want it to be *my* choice, that's all.

'In early October, I got another letter from him: *I'm still in Paris, participating in a group show of mostly Indian artists. Five of my oils have been selected. Galerie Pillet, small gallery, but in the Rue de la Boetie.* A date for the vernissage in the first week of November. *Do come?*

'Against my better judgement, I took the train up to Paris. So, it was my choice after all, d'you see? Everything that followed was also, in a sense, my choice.'

Imogen checks into her usual hotel and takes a cab to the gallery. She hasn't brought her heavy winter coat, and the November wind punishes her ruthlessly, just between hotel doorway and taxi, taxi and gallery entrance. As soon as she sidles in through the door, there is a different tithe to be paid: the small gallery is stiflingly hot, her coat now unbearably warm, the press of the crowd making it almost impossible to take it off.

There is something odd about the milling crowd, and it takes her a while to realize what it is – she hasn't seen these many non-Europeans in one place since returning from the East. Most of them seem to be Indian-ish, but there are also some others, possibly Siamese, Malays, Vietnamese, even a couple of individuals who could well be Burmese. In fact, she has to search to find the whites scattered among the small sea of brown faces. Through gaps, she can see the pictures on the walls. A thick fug of cigarette smoke softens the shapes on the hanging canvases.

She sifts through the heads, looking for Kedar. It's he who spots her first, poking up above the crowd. 'Miss Sn—Imogen! Over here!' She makes sure it's him, waves and makes her way to his group.

'There you are, Kedar!'

'Hello! I'm so glad you could come!'

They haven't met in six years, not since London in 1946. A brief but vigorous handshake, his hand warm through her glove. 'You haven't changed a bit!' they both exclaim, simultaneously and more or less truthfully.

'I'd imagined it would be awkward and it was, but only briefly. I was introduced to his crowd. There was Paritosh, of course, and there was Raza and a friend of his from Delhi, a chap called Ram Kumar, and there was an ebullient little fellow, another Muslim name, Akbar something? For whom everything was a joke. I could see his eyes immediately pairing us up, short Lahiri and his giraffe Englishwoman.'

Kedar is dressed dapperly enough: smart corduroy jacket, brightly striped tie, argyle jumper, but Imogen can't help noticing small details: the collar of the shirt is slightly frayed, the tie is askew, not knotted carefully, there's a woollen scarf poking out of a jacket pocket, he hasn't polished his shoes properly and one is scuffed on the outside, all most unlike Larry Lahiri. Most worryingly, his face is quite gaunt around those lovely cheekbones, and he has a slight pallor she would never have associated with his complexion, as though he's running a low fever of some sort.

Their group is loud and cheerful, the wine circulating just about acceptable, the jokes and conversation knocking about between English, Hindi and French, but no Bengali as far Imogen can make out. There are three other women – if she remembers correctly – two French, one Ceylonese, all of them clearly upper-class, each attached to one or the other of the painters, but not to Kedar. Raza, Paritosh, Kumar and Akbar are very relaxed, and Imogen quickly understands that's because they are not involved in the show. Kedar and two others with paintings in the fray are making a good fist of joviality, but she can see their eyes anxiously raking the crowd from time to time.

A Frenchman comes over wearing evening suit, bow tie and quiet authority. The deference some of the artists show him indicates to Imogen that he's Monsieur Pillet, the eponymous gallerist. Grave as a priest, Pillet gently grips one or the other of the exhibiting artists by the elbow and leads him away like a prize horse. After a few minutes, the artist returns, smiling, having been introduced to the person who's bought his work. Everybody clinks glasses to celebrate what Imogen understands is a sale, though no one actually utters the word. Pillet does this a few times across the evening, but never with Kedar.

At one point, Akbar makes some joke about how Bengali artist-types are hard put to decide whether they are the Irish of India or the French of India. Everyone laughs. 'Well, no, that's not true, we're actually quite clear,' says Paritosh. 'If you're a Bengali writer, you get to choose between being Irish, French or Russian. But as Bengali painters, we have no such choice – obviously we can only be French!' Kedar joins in. 'Well, that's currently! The previous generation could also be a bit Chinese or Japanese, but now alas...' One of the other painters laughs and shakes his finger at Kedar. 'No, Lahiri, you yourself are definitely French and here's the proof.' He pulls out a beret and puts it on Kedar's head.

'You know, Saki, I'd never actually seen Zemindear's dark side before that. He yanked the beret off his head and flung it into the crowd. For a moment, we all thought he was going to hit the chap, but then someone defused the situation with another joke.'

Imogen can see that Kedar's joviality is fraying – the absence of a sale is cutting into him in all sorts of ways.

By and by, as the wine runs out, the crowd starts to thin a bit, allowing Imogen to wander and get a better look at the paintings. The exhibition presents four painters – five canvases each – and there is also a sculptor, his work on plinths distributed around the gallery.

'To my eye, most of the paintings were what I thought of as the usual suspects, you know? Figures, landscapes, still lifes, all somewhat "cubistified" or "cubastardized" as Zemindear liked to say later, in other words all owing something to that old firm of Pablo P and G Braque, the kind of well-behaved cubism you saw all over Paris in those days. I obviously can't remember any of the names, but two fellows, one each from Bombay and Madras and one other Bengali. The sculptures weren't bad, small heads in bronze and fired clay by some chap from somewhere Caribbean, British Guyana or Trinidad or somewhere, but Zemindear's work was what stood out for me. It was old-fashioned at first glance but then it wasn't, if you know what I mean? I'd never actually seen any of his paintings until then, and these were different from what I'd imagined. I think I was quite taken aback that Kedar Lahiri's paintings were more than just products of a rich boy's hobby.'

There is a portrait of a woman in a sari leaning against a sunlit doorway, looking into some trees and smoking a cigarette; Imogen can clearly recognize Keya. There is one of a Calcutta house garden full of flowers with the neighbouring house in the background. This is a scene that Imogen can immediately place somewhere in Ballygunge or Alipore, except the beautifully manicured lawn is scarred by something that looks like an elongated open grave or a trench of some sort. A view of Calcutta from a rooftop, the unfinished bridge on the horizon, air-defence blimps hanging above, plumes of smoke rising from different parts of the city. Imogen knows this one too, from the time Nirupama had described her terrace after the first bombings. There is a small still life of those awful spiky things that look like snuffed-out green baby dragons, what are they called now? Oh yes, karela. Then there is one of the chappal series, hundreds of bits of orphaned footwear stretching away on a dark background, dotted with dirty yellow balls of flowers and the odd banana leaf. This one brings back that day from ten years ago. The two kids playing in the dunes of slippers, and later Andrew driving her to the club.

The KL paintings also stand out from the others in that they are the only ones without a red dot indicating a sale. Imogen turns around, looking for the gallerist and sees he is with the cluster of artists. As she gets closer, she sees he is introducing someone to the circle.

'*Mesdames et messieurs*, may I present to you one of the greatest maestros creating in France today?'

The large man carries a sense of genial, almost florid self-importance, and he smiles and dips his chin with the most parsimonious modesty. Imogen mentally sifts through images of currently famous French painters but comes up with nothing. And then she recognizes him – that chef from the Great Eastern... Pillet announces the name just as she remembers.

'Chef Paul Bonnemaison! Celebrated as one of the premier culinary artists now pulling our great French cuisine out of the abyss of the dreadful Occupation. The maestro spent the war in Calcutta, as chef at the Grand Hotel—'

'Actually, the Great Eastern Hotel. The Grand was only the second-best hotel in Calcutta…'

'Knock me over with a feather and all that, Saki, but I suddenly remembered His Frogness in his chef's togs at the Christmas Eve do in Great Eastern, in '41, I think it was, and how he was all over Zemindear, fawning and addressing him as Prince and so on, *l'envie de faire la bête à deux dos qui lui dégoulinait des mirettes* as the French might say. This time, when they were introduced, he was cool as a cucumber sorbet. Neither he nor Kedar showed any sign of having met, though I could swear the Frogman's pig-eyes widened a tiny bit, for a tiny second. So, don't be too proud, Saki, when you look in the mirror today – remember the most fulsome beauty is but fleeting!'

'Imo-mashi. It's not a weight I carry.'

'So modest, darling, so lacking in vanity! Your mother would approve.'

Bonnemaison is accompanied by another Indian, a little chap who, to Imogen's eyes, can't be anything but Bengali. Sure enough, he is introduced as Ganesh Mondal. He does a nomoshkar to everyone and mostly stays quiet. Hair stiffly combed with pomade, good clothes, new, but clearly not fully at ease in jacket and tie, with which he keeps fiddling. From the way Mondal nods and smiles at some of the jokes, you can see he understands a bit of English, but he only speaks in Bangla to Kedar and Paritosh, and a few basic Hindi words to the others. 'The label "toy boy" entered my mind but didn't quite sit – the chap's demeanour suggested too much independence. This Mondal was obviously associated with Bonnemaison, and clearly dependent on him for social navigation, but… their relationship was… devoid of the inequality required for concubinage, catamitic or otherwise, if you see what I mean.'

After a few minutes, Pillet guides the two men away to look at the work, and the painters go back to ribbing each other. To Imogen's relief, Kedar seems much more relaxed now, seemingly resigned to being the one without any sales. Looking over the shoulders of the boisterous young men, Imogen keeps an eye on the gallery owner giving his tour.

At one point, Pillet turns away to speak to someone and Mondal takes Bonnemaison aside for a short discussion. They rejoin the gallerist, and the two Frenchmen have a conversation. Bonnemaison relays something to the Bengali. Mondal nods. He and Pillet shake hands.

Someone says something to Kedar and he bursts out laughing, slapping the speaker on the back as he does. A sliver of glass flies across Imogen's memory and comes to rest, teetering on the large leaf of a tropical house plant. She walks away from the group and waits for Pillet to be on his own before approaching him.

'Excuse me, M'sieu, but I have a question?'

'Of course, madame, how can I be of help?'

'I wanted to enquire about the price of two of the canvases.'

'Of course, madame. Which ones?'

Imogen walks over to Kedar's paintings and indicates the river of slippers and the view of the city.

'*Ah, madame, je suis desolé,* but this one, *Mort de Tagore,* is already sold, for 220 francs. The Indian gentleman over there just confirmed his purchase. But this one is still available, this very startling and original view of the city of Calcutta. The price is 200 francs, payable by tomorrow, since one is, unfortunately, unable to reserve the work beyond a day.'

'Oh, I really wanted the chappals… but yes, all right, I'll take the city view.'

'Madame, please allow me to confirm again that Monsieur Mondial is taking *Mort de Tagore*. And I will treat the Calcutta *toile* as bought by you?'

Kedar has spotted Imogen speaking to Pillet and immediately understood what she's doing. He is already walking up to her as the Frenchman goes over to Mondal.

'Imogen. I heard that!' Kedar says in a low voice. 'You're *not* to pay any money for my paintings! I can't have that! I'll give you the rooftop one, for god's sake, and I have a couple of other versions of *Ocean of Pea* – of the slippers, even better than this one, so please—'

'Larry, do be quiet! I'd have bought them even if I didn't know you. And it's good for the gallery to see that your work can sell, don't you see? Two out of five is not bad. Only one of the others has three sold.'

'Well, I can always pay you back later, I suppose, whatever the fellow hands over after deducting his commission.'

'I won't hear of it, but just out of interest, how much will he take, say from 400 francs?'

'Oh, he'll deduct costs for framing, and then he does some calculations for the gallery and his commission, so maybe a little less than half, say 170? But why did you waste your money? I can't possibly take money from you!'

'That is absolutely the wrong way of looking at it. Think of it as a small but necessary investment towards turning you into a commercially successful painter!'

'Ha. That'll be the day!'

'Don't scoff, Larry. If you don't have confidence in yourself, nobody else will.'

Outside the gallery, the group breaks up. Raza and his friends peel off, taking the Guyanese man with them, leaving the other exhibiting artists, Paritosh and Imogen. After a brief word with Mondal, Bonnemaison nods goodbye to the group, hails a taxi and disappears. Mondal turns to them and asks in Bengali whether they are planning to eat dinner somewhere. Imogen gathers that all the men are sick of eating bad French food; at Paritosh's recommendation, they take the metro to an Algerian place.

'Speaking of poor neighbourhoods, Saki, this quartier where the Arabs lived was the worst of a Paris that was already rundown because of the war. Coming out of the metro, I thought we were back in the blackout, with an extreme version of that particular garbage stink only Paris can produce. But the restau—the eatery was warm enough, the owner and waiters didn't look askance at a group of coloured people, nor bat an eyelid at the one white woman with them. And the fare was cheap enough not to test anyone's pocket. I'd eaten all over Paris, but I'd never had couscous until then. While obviously nothing could compare with their home food, it was Paritosh's contention that couscous and lamb sort of replicated Bengali rice and meat curry.'

The conversation is mostly in Bengali, with Kedar and Paritosh translating occasionally for Imogen. When the food comes, the other Bengali painter wants to eat with his hands. Paritosh looks around and gives him the go-ahead. The man puts his fingers into the couscous to mix in the meat and gravy. Everyone eats while keeping a lookout. Whenever a waiter approaches, the man quickly shifts to knife and fork. Imogen notices that Mondal is adept enough at handling cutlery, though he eats carefully and slowly. As with the clothes, he's not at ease but he's managing.

After a while, one of the waiters comes and says something to Paritosh, causing both of them to laugh. The waiter leans in past the man using his hands, removes his knife and fork and puts them firmly next to his plate. He says something to the man, squeezes his shoulder, laughs again and leaves. Imogen can hardly understand the Maghreb accent, but she thinks he says: This is Barbès, not the Champs-Élysée, eat in a way that fills your heart.

At the end of the meal, Paritosh and the waiter have a quick conference, counting up the plates of food and the carafes of wine. The waiter scribbles something on a small square of paper and hands it to Paritosh, who looks up to convey the amount to everybody. Mondal, who is sitting next to Paritosh, asks to take a look at the bill. Then he gestures to indicate that he will pay for everyone.

'I was going to offer myself, but the little man beat me to it. It wasn't expensive, the place, but as Zemindear liked to say, there is nothing more penurious than a penurious Bengali painter. KL and Paritosh protested a bit, as did I, but the sense of relief among the other three was clear to see. The man pulled out his wallet and counted out the unfamiliar currency, checking with Paritosh the correct amount to leave.

'I suddenly felt Kedar stiffen next to me. I wasn't looking at him but, Saki, I tell you it was palpable. I thought it might be that he was feeling insulted that this nouveau riche upstart was treating us, but that didn't make sense, Kedar had never struck me as a snob. I turned to him and saw he was staring at Mondal, or rather at Mondal's hands as he forked out the dosh. I wanted to ask, but obviously I couldn't, not then. Mondal, sharp fellow, also noticed, and he smiled at Kedar as we all stood up.'

On the street, the party starts to head for the metro station, but Mondal takes Paritosh aside and shows him a slip of paper. Paritosh nods and the two of them step off on to the street to look for a taxi. The other Bengali is quite drunk, and he keeps calling out to Mondal in a mix of languages. All Imogen can make out in the jumble of Bengali and mispronounced French is the repeated 'Thank you!'. Mondal cheerfully replies once and then ignores the man, keeping his eye on the sparse oncoming traffic. Imogen can see that Kedar has also gone towards the street and that he's hesitating, wanting to say something.

The men wave down a taxi. Paritosh leans into the window and explains where Mondal needs to be taken. Mondal turns around and folds his hands in goodbye to the group. Kedar makes up his mind and goes towards Mondal as he's getting into the cab. He says something, to which Mondal replies with a laugh. Then Mondal calls out something to the drunken painter. And then he's gone.

'You know, it took me *years* to get it out of him, what that exchange was about.'

'Yes?'

'You see, Zemindear had had his pocket picked when he went to see Tagore being taken to his cremation. He lost a wallet that day, and he was convinced the wallet this Mondal fellow pulled out was the very same one he'd lost all those years ago. So, he asked. And the cheeky bugger gave him a reply.'

'Which was?'

'"Kedar-babu, are you more interested in my wallet or what's inside my wallet? Because the inside of my wallet looks forward to buying more of your beautiful work!"'

'Oh! And what did he say to the drunken painter?'

'Oh, that Zemindear translated immediately. The painter kept saying the couscous was nice but it wasn't rice. And in any case, there's no rice like home rice... dyesher bhaat, is it? It's one of the few Bengali phrases I remember.'

'Yes, dyesher bhaat, I suppose you could translate it as one's native rice, but home rice is fine.'

'Yes, so Mondal's parting comment was "You're so right! Home rice is home rice!"'

2

A LOT OF RICE

'Five thousand rupees! That's a lot of rice, Ustad!' As he washes his face and arms in the freezing water from the tubewell, Gopal remembers the words bursting out of him, part real surprise, partly strategy – exactly what he was supposed to say, but also with the exact surprise he was supposed to display.

Ustad had turned and stared at him and then at the other two, the half smile on his lips they had all learnt to fear, that slight grimace that stayed far away from the old man's eyes. 'Yes, think! And remember, it's not at today's prices that we delivered it. All two hundred mawns were sent to this sisterfucker Jhunjhunwalla at twenty-five rupees a mawn in November. Today the official price is forty-two rupees, in the black market it's even more. So, imagine! If he's selling it today, he's making—'

Aurangzeb tapped the pen on his closed notebook. 'Between 8,500 and 10,000 rupees.'

'Exactly. That mother-pimping Marwari is making nearly double, maybe more if he manages to keep it free of insects and sells a bit later.' The old man leaned to the little window next to him and spat his paan into the river. 'Now, I don't have a problem if the motherfucker makes his money. That's the market – you gamble, you lose, you lose, you win, you win. Pay me, take your stuff, sell it for whatever profit, it's not my concern who you are buggering for your profit as long as it's not me. But here I am, bleating for my payment, bleating like a goat going to the butcher, while you're making your money like King Kuber. What am I? A chutiya? A fool?'

'When was he supposed to pay?' Gopal asked.

'And so I wait, and what happens? This cockfucker tells his friends over samosas and laddu, "That Ustad is soft, you can take delivery and then yank him about a bit for payment. He won't do anything"... Within two weeks. He was supposed to pay within two weeks, excuse was the police pressure was very heavy, he had to be extra careful how he got rid of the sacks. Within two weeks, at the price we agreed. He paid two thousand on delivery, so that leaves three thousand. But if he doesn't pay the full amount tomorrow, tell him the bill will go up. From day after, I'm going to add hundred rupees a day to whatever he still owes. For one week. And then that's it. I can't afford to ruin my name in the market.'

Aurangzeb turned to Gopal. 'You understand neither Gourango nor I can go see this bastard?' Gopal nodded. 'Yet he needs to be spoken to.' Gopal nodded again.

'What about this Jhunjhunwalla's people?'

Gourangzeb shook his head. 'He doesn't have any people as such, besides the usual godown guards. And they should not be any problem. As to Jalal Sheikh's boys, I've heard they've been moving around in that neighbourhood. But they mostly deal with the factories selling extra war material from the back door, stuff like boots and tent material, offering them protection. Our business they shouldn't interfere with. Not if they want to sleep at night.'

'Anyway, Chhoto Madhai will come with you, and he will have Gourangzeb's pistol. Not that you should need it.' Ustad turned to open another ledger, indicating the matter was now dealt with.

'Is that necessary, Ustad? I mean, all I'm going to do is talk to Jhunjhunwalla. So even if anyone acts tough, all I will do is lower my head and say I'm only delivering a message, right?'

Ustad had looked up and looked at Gopal.

'Ey. You. Yesterday's newborn. Since when did you find the courage to question your Ustad? Hain?' The old man's stare had made both Aurangzeb and Gourangzeb straighten their backs, but the sudden absence of abuse was the real sign they had all learnt to recognize and fear. The two older men stepped back slightly, away from Gopal.

Over the last year or so, Gopal had managed to control and put aside his deep fear of Ustad. That tightly bound sack was now ripped open. His pounding heart made it difficult for him to form his words and he barely managed to get them out, slurring them.

'No, Ustad, please forgive me, I was just... please forgive me.'

'Just because I sometimes treat you like an addled son, you think you know everything, know more than me? Hain?'

Gopal bowed his head and said nothing. In his mouth, his teeth clamped around his tongue in fear, trying to stop it from coming out.

'There's a reason Gourangzeb has been training Chhoto Madhai to shoot that revolvaar. It's not a shaukh, it's not a hobby or a sport.' Ustad's tone was no softer, but the fact that he was offering an explanation made Gopal ease up. 'Other outfits already have guns, some of them more than one, proper pistols, and also now some home-made ones from UP which fire just one shot. And one shot up your backhole is all it will take to send you into the lap of your Ma Kali. And I would laugh if that happens, all of us would laugh, except that I've invested too much in you to lose you now. And you know too much about our business to have you singing when someone puts a gun to your temple.'

'I would never talk, Ustad.' Gopal said this in the barest whisper.

'Maybe you wouldn't. Who knows? But it shouldn't come to that. Which is why you are taking your own bodyguard, like the ass-fucked nawabzada that you are.'

Her hands on his shoulders. He puts on a vest, tucks his shirt into his trousers, puts his head through a sweater and finally pulls on a woollen jacket. Her hands stay on him through each layer of material. He folds his palms and ducks his head in a quick prayer to the gods before turning to the door. She gently tugs him back. What did she say in the dream? Carry your own weapon.

Gopal moves the pictures and statues and lays them on the bed before removing the red cloth on the wall. He pulls out the bricks and looks at what's inside the hole. The pile of fruit stares at him from the painting, the light catching bits shining even in the shadow. The wallet sits where he has left it, one strand of cobweb curving from a corner into a crevice between bricks. He pulls out the dirty white cloth bag and lays out the contents on the bed next to the pictures of Krishna, Shiva, Durga, and the statue of Kali-ma. The gun is now accompanied by an extra magazine and a box of .45 bullets. He clicks free the magazine from the pistol and replaces it with the heavier, fully loaded one. Eight bullets should be enough. If they are not, then the trouble would be too big for a single handgun. He points the gun away from himself, releases the safety lever and slots a round in the chamber. Then he flicks on the safety catch and slides the gun into a specially made pocket on the inside of the left leg of his trousers.

ONION

'So, Ma, how did you learn to shoot a rifle?'

'That damned tape machine of yours? It's not around, is it?'

'It's in my room, Ma. No, I just want to know. You know, for myself. I won't report you to the authorities, don't worry.'

I've bought her a new fridge to replace the old one Roma had given her. She fiddles around inside it as though she's ignoring my question. After a while, she starts taking out the food for lunch and starts speaking to the steel containers.

'Well, at one point in the struggle, it became clear that the police weren't hesitating to use weapons. At the beginning of Tebhaga, they would fire in the air, such as when they felt threatened by a crowd of people or something, but now it was no longer like that. They were shooting at the villagers and Party workers regularly. So, there was a decision by the Party command that we too needed to move to armed resistance. Of course, we were in no position for all-out warfare, but we needed to let them know that guns could be used by both sides. So, at first, it was a few rifles and pistols, only for the boys, naturally, and only for a few chosen ones who could be trusted with firearms.

'The farmers and tribals were not consulted about this and they were unhappy. Their bamboos and sickles they were comfortable with, and the tribals with their bows and arrows, but these rifle-bondook were a different thing and they generally kept away from them.'

'And what did you think of this?'

'Oh, many of the girls were completely horrified. Keya was especially vocal at Party meetings – this was a mistake and one that we all would pay for, the villagers and us other comrades. I myself wasn't sure – I could see both sides of the argument.'

'So then?'

'So then.' She lights the gas to heat the food.

At first, we women would only be involved to the extent of being couriers. We were less likely to be searched at checkpoints, and we were already couriering posters and pamphlets and such. Now we also began to move ammunition from place to place. Nothing much, mind you, just a few .303 clips at a time, one or two boxes of .38 bullets, that sort of thing. But after a few months of this, I'd had enough. I had an anger growing inside me – everything was for the male comrades, the top posts, the decisions always made by them, orders that we had to follow, even though some of those boys were *so* stupid! And now they had the guns and the choice when to use them. There were many instances when we were alone, meaning only us women in a village or an area, where the men had to be elsewhere, or had been chased into hiding, and then where was our armed defence?'

'So you had a fight about this, naturally.'

'Well, I was insistent, and I wasn't the only one. Finally, reluctantly, they agreed to train some of us. Me, Swaroopa, a couple of other girls from the Party, this Santhal girl, Savitri. They trained us, how to dismantle the .303, how to clean and maintain, how to load and cock. Then we practised firing, at first stationary scarecrow targets, coconuts on bamboos, bottles. Then we graduated to a target hanging on a clothesline, a man-sized cut out that one could see through a thicket of trees. Someone would pull it by a string, slower, faster, forwards and backwards, and you had to try and hit it.'

'Did your shooting come in any use?'

'Well, yes, a few times when we were moving rice from one place to another and the jotedar thugs came for us. We fired above their heads and they ran away. But otherwise, no, not really.'

'Except...'

'Except for that one time, yes.'

I'd been curious about Ma and her rifle since I first saw the photograph of her and Keya when I was a child, but every time I'd ask her, she'd say she was just posing with it for the photograph. One day, when I was about sixteen, I heard her and Roma-mashi talking in the next room, and Mashi let slip something about the time Ma had 'shot those men'. After that, whenever I'd confronted Ma, she'd never given me a straight answer – oh, we were shooting at each other, the police and us, but I don't know if my bullets ever hit anyone, Roma-mashi was just exaggerating – oh, it was a long time ago, nothing to get excited about – oh, I maybe fired a rifle twice or thrice in a real situation, just to scare people off. She finally told me the truth only when I was visiting from Paris, after she knew I'd been talking to Missus and Elko about that time. – I didn't tell you when you were younger because you were so deeply into those war comics and spy novels I didn't want to give you further ideas.

By that time, I had developed the courage to repeat some other questions as well, and the growing heft of my years meant she could no longer avoid answering at least some of them.

This was the time when I also asked her what kept her going in Tebhaga for so many years.

'I'm not sure, I'm really no longer sure... you know, when the famine was at its peak, in 1944 I think it was, I got to know a family that would come to the langarkhana we were running near Kasba. Family means there were three women – a mother, must have been about thirty-five but looked like she was much older, like fifty or so, and two daughters, one just around eighteen and the younger one about sixteen. They never came together. It would be one of the girls first, then the other, and then the mother last. I knew they were a family because they looked so alike – it was like watching the same person age before you, from a really thin girl to an emaciated older woman, like in one of those cartoon animation films. Taking their food, they would even say, my older sister will be along in a while, or my Ma will come soon, just to make sure we didn't think they were coming twice.

'One day, I decided to follow one of the girls back to where they lived, which was in a cluster of ramshackle tents in a park near Mandeville Gardens. I saw the girl go into a tent, so I went up to the opening and called inside. Of course the girl was unhappy to see me, but she let me in. The other two were sitting on some jute sacking, cowering under a thin sheet. It took me a few moments to realize they were both, you know, that they didn't have any clothes on. You know, Saki, the reason for only coming out one by one was they had just one single sari between the three of them. Even more than the lack of food, that left a mark on me.' Ma started to shiver and put her arms around herself. 'At first it was that, then it was Keya.

'At one point, I was about to come back to Kolkata, thinking you were no longer a baby and I should start looking after you.' She was still avoided looking at me as she transferred the warmed dal, rice and chicken to the serving bowls. 'But then the thing happened with Keya. I saw her body and I couldn't leave, not just then, so I stayed in the fight for another few months. I came back right after we did the... the action with the jeep. After we did that, I expected some sort of punishment but, no, the senior comrades ordered me to disappear, saying they would be better able to handle the police reprisals if Savitri, I and the other two girls were not around.'

'You came back. Where did the other girls go?'

'Three of us were city girls and we were just sent back to Kolkata, one of us went on to Poona, two of us went back to out 'normal' lives. But Savitri was a Santhal and somehow she was the only one the police identified immediately. She nearly got caught when the police raided her village, looking specifically for her. But she was made from some other substance, that one! The village was on a river, and she went under the water and stayed there, breathing through reeds. Later I heard she escaped to Chota Nagpur or somewhere. I never saw her again after the action.'

'And how did you city girls get away with it? Surely the police must have kept searching?'

Com. Niru paused her eating, looked at me and smiled for the first time. 'Oh that was simple, in retrospect, that is. Two other comrades, two boys, died in the battle with the police a few days later, The Party made sure to give them the credit for Dasgupta's killing. The police suspected otherwise but neither the Party nor the police wanted to admit that some *girls* had ambushed and killed four cops in a gun battle.'

I want to ask, but I know I never will. While you were there, fighting, did you not think of me? How could you blank me from your mind? I want to hear her answer, but I know it would be a punishment for something she chose long ago, when she was roughly the age I am now. Anyway, I know the answer already. I was an inconvenience, a biped memory of the man who had left and never written, a responsibility, yes, but only a personal one, one that her parents could handle for her, and therefore lower priority than the responsibility to the revolution that was about to come, that was surely just around the corner of the next month, the next year. Which also explains why Nirupama, even after she had left Tebhaga, brought me up like a loving but strict aunt rather than a mother whose love could occasionally overflow, like I saw with my friends' mothers, like I got from my Dida.

As a child, the only time I really felt her affection was when she would give me her history lessons.

'So tell me again, Saki, who didn't want to give the farmers their fair share?'

'The zamindar, the jotedar, the police, the military and the politicians.'

'Very good, but you forgot the priests and mullahs.'

'Oh, yes, sorry, also all the religious leaders, they are also against the poor peasants even though they pretend they are not.'

'Well, not all of them but most of them, but we'll keep that for later. But how *do* these god-sellers manage to get a hold on so many people?'

'By using people's fear of death. They promise them some kind life after death, which is a lie – there is nothing after death, when you die you die, just like a bird or a fish... or even a tiger!'

Whenever I talked to Dida about death, I got a different viewpoint.

'You know, shona, no one can say for sure what happens after death. Your Ma can say there is nothing, but that is the theory *she* believes in. Everyone can believe in the theory they like best. The only thing to remember is that no one has the right to force anybody else to believe in their theory, not even their own child. Let each person make up his own mind once they are grown up.'

'What do *you* believe in, Dida?'

'I suspect that each of us, we do have an atma, a soul, as they say in Ingreji. And I like this idea we have in our culture, that the soul moves from body to body.'

'Are you scared of death, Dida?'

'Sometimes, but mostly when I think of what all of you will do without me. Otherwise, no, death is nothing. Just a bird moving from the branch of one tree to another, as casual, as ordinary as that.'

I thought Ma would be angry when I told her this, but Ma tried to avoid contradicting Dida, especially over me. 'Yes, well, Dida is right in a sense – the cluster of molecules that makes you moves from one branch of the physical realm to another. This happens gradually if you're buried or rapidly if you are cremated.'

'Oh, so you're saying your consciousness then disappears, like the poop dropped by the bird as it hops, yes? Is that why people say it's lucky if you get hit by bird droppings? Is it someone's consciousness dropping on you?'

Some Bengali boys can be annoyingly precocious through the sin of over-reading at a young age. I was one of those boys. Ma knew I understood the basics about things like molecules and consciousness, so I wasn't sure why she was laughing so hard.

'Ma, I think you remember a lot about the past, but you only tell me little bits.'

'Why do you think that, Saki?'

'Well, I don't believe you when I ask you something and you say you can't remember. You have a very good memory, and you remember what happened a year ago absolutely exactly.'

'Not always, shona, not always. And last year is closer than ten or twelve years ago, isn't it?'

'So... memory is part of consciousness, no, Ma?'

'Yes, of course it is.'

'So when you die, if you haven't told me something, I'll never know, yes?'

Ma was a master at deflecting questions and sending the conversation in some other direction.

'You know, Saki, memory is a funny thing. Some people say it's like the rings in a tree trunk. So each year brings a new layer of memory that wraps around the earlier ones. But I think memory is more like an onion. Like a tree, there are succeeding layers, yes, but if you cut off the top and bottom of the onion, the different layers all scatter. Some layers stick together while others just drop off. Time is one kind of knife that can cut the onion, but also something big that traumatizes you, that can also scatter the onion petals of your memory.'

PANCHPUKUR

'Tumi pyaaj, roshun khaao toh, baba?' You do eat onions and garlic, son?

'Hyan, hyan!' Of course.

I wave away the flies and lean back against one of the bamboo supports of the thatched roof that slopes down over the porch, thankful to be out of the sun. I watch the old man as he squats down and lays out four onions, some cloves of garlic, a knob of ginger and a pile of green chillies on an aluminium thhala. I can see him carefully considering each item before adding it to the plate. He picks up an onion in one hand and a small, dented knife in the other. He starts dicing the onion, pulling the blade through it and into his thumb, letting the slices drop on to the plate until he's left with just the root and a little disc of purple around it. I wait for him to pick up the next onion. Instead, he presses the disc down on the plate and cuts around the root, making sure to capture every tiny edible bit. He repeats the process with the other onions and then chops the heap of rings into a mass of tiny cubes. I think of how I cut onions back home in Paris and I feel uneasy.

Behind the old man, at one end of the porch there's a double clay unoon on which two handis are already bubbling. He turns around, still squatting, to fiddle with the pots. Then he turns back and starts on the garlic. He is equally meticulous with dicing each clove, making sure every sliver is captured. Next, he peels the ginger with great dexterity, sending the point of the knife into every nook and cranny. A few mini-knobs end up on the thhala, their skin still on. Just as I'm thinking even he can't use those, he picks up each little sphere and takes off the skin.

He catches me looking as he starts reducing the ginger to a mound. 'Ah, you are marking how carefully I'm cutting these? It's a habit, baba, I can't waste anything.' He does some mental accounting and pushes the three separate piles to one side of the plate. 'I didn't cook a lot in Palm Avenue, that was the cook's job, but whenever I helped out, I used to waste a little bit. "You cut like a millionaire!" the cook always said, but neither of us cared – there was never any shortage of food in the Lahiri house. Here in the villages, it's always been a different story, even before the famine. Even after it ended, you never knew when you might be eating an onion again, or when you'd next be able to afford this or that food.'

'Rasko-da, the famine was thirty-three, thirty-four years ago. Do people here still not get enough to eat?'

'We get enough, just about enough rice and dal, most of us. Only a few people starving now, here and there, only the ones with real bad-luck foreheads. And those of us who have a little patch of land, we grow our own vegetables. With god's mercy, everything sprouts easily in this soil. And if you have a pond or a river nearby, you can get some fish and other things. But, still, you still never waste anything – your own hand won't allow it, the memory of that hunger still sits in your fingertips.'

I'm sitting cross-legged on the mud porch that curves up into the front wall of the small house and I catch myself rubbing my palm over the packed earth next to my knee. The light brown surface is somehow both gritty and smooth, almost like extremely fine sandpaper, the bits baked by the morning sun still warm to the touch. The thatch slopes down from the house, extending over the porch to give us shade from the noon heat, but the respite is minimal – I can see the slight shine between Rasko's nose and eyes, and feel my own sweat etching into my face.

I've seen a couple of photos of Rasko and Kedar, but they haven't prepared me for the old man who's greeted me. By all calculations, Rasko is only about sixty or sixty-one but he looks much older. The thinning hair is spiky and white, the cheekbones now really prominent in the age-whittled face, but the eyes are still bright under eyebrows which are still almost black. When he smiles, a decent array of teeth break through the deep lines around the lips. He seems in reasonable health – for a man who looks nearly eighty. Leading me through the village, his walk has been steady but there's something in the voice, a kind of scarcity sewn into the breathing, a parsimony in his choice of words, in the way he looks around, constantly alert for any kind of potential damage and loss. 'I am one of the lucky ones, baba,' he says, ushering me in through the little opening in the wall. 'In fact, my whole family was, because I had that job in the city, but even now we never feel secure. The memory of misery is something that's passed on in the mother's milk, do you understand? The days of wretchedness so many of us have seen, they will take time to fade from the soul.'

The house and the small, walled courtyard are made from the same raw sienna-coloured mud. There is a bit of open ground in front of the low porch platform and it is ringed by the criss-crossing green of banana trees and other vegetation. When he shuts the door in the wall I notice it's constructed from assorted wooden planks, more a gesture than a door, just something to dissuade the village dogs and nosy cows.

When Niru told me she had Rasko's address and that, yes, he was literate, I'd written to him. We've exchanged a couple of postcards and I took a train yesterday to Midnapore town, spent the night in a cheap hotel and caught a bus to a stop near the village. Rasko has met me there – You reached here without problem? I hope the address was clear enough? Village Panchpukur, Jila Pingla, District Mednipur?

Back in the city, it's been so hot people have given the weather a name – they're are calling it Indira's Revenge – and in the peak heat of some afternoons you can easily believe that the evil old woman has convinced the weather gods to wreak hell upon all the millions who've just voted against her. Here in the village, the heat is somehow different – still like the inside of a steaming oven but somehow roughly kind, as though you're sitting in the lap of a difficult mother, uncomfortably warm at first but when you give in to it, not not benign. Here you sweat differently, no fumes from diesel engines imploding in the heat, no hot blast bouncing off concrete buildings. There's the heat, there are the smells, things rotting, things ripening, the waft from the innards of different kinds of water-bodies, someone frying radhuni seeds, someone else cooking fish, somewhere close by fresh cowpats drying on walls. There's the heat, the constant conversation of flies and there's your body in its wrapping of sweat-sodden city clothes – my kurta was okay for the trip but the jeans were a bad mistake. Rasko has hesitatingly offered me a big gamchha as a lungi, and I've changed into that and a spare t-shirt I've carried.

'Baah, kichhu mone korbe na, kintu tumi praay amader moton shyamborno.' Don't mind me saying so, but you are dark enough to be one of us. 'Though such a tall-body boy like you could never be from these parts.' Rasko chops the green chillies quite coarsely, releasing their pungent sting. 'Thiik-thaak jhaal khetey paro toh?' You can eat properly hot food, right? He pauses for a beat, looking into nothing and swallowing hard. 'Dada-babu liked his food properly hot. He'd shout at the cook if there weren't enough chillies –"Have you made this for some gora or what?"' Rasko reaches into the market bag to pull out two more chillies. Then he opens a tin and pulls out some dried red ones, putting them to one side, like a reminder. 'Over there... in France... can you get proper chillies?' He wipes his face with the edge of his dhoti, dealing with both sudden tears and the sweat. 'Would Dada-babu get to eat any decently hot food?'

He's warned me the village doesn't have electricity yet and I've made sure to bring a box of fresh batteries for the tape recorder. The Phillips works fine at first, but then I can feel it really heating up. Every forty-five minutes or so I find it wise to give it a rest and I try and do it as unobtrusively as possible so as to not break the old man's flow.

Later, when I transcribe the tapes and piece it all together for clarity, I try my best to remember what he was saying when the machine was off. I translate the whole thing into English, quite roughly, so that Missus can also read it, but even there I retain some of the Bangla phrases for myself. While transcribing, I work around the sounds of spices frying, of food being stirred in the handis, lids being moved, the hiss of rice boiling softly.

> You know, when they kicked me out from the Palm Avenue house, I'd worked there for over twenty-five years. I started when I was about thirteen, I think it must have been 1930 or thereabouts, and when Boudi died it was 1955, so I was about thirty-eight, Dada-babu would have been thirty-four.

That Bulldog-kaku was always hard-hearted – that Colonel Shaheb – but Borun-babu was the real shock for me – I made the mistake of thinking we were actually a bit like friends, as much as a malik and servant can be, like me and Dada-babu. But all that teaching me English and Robi Thakur's poetry and all that 'Rasko is a man of many parts', oi shob, all that went out of the window. While Boudi was alive, both younger brothers were scared of her and I was safe. After she went, that Borun was scared of the Colonel brother, so he also chimed in... 'we will need you to clear out of your quarters and leave by the end of the month. Obviously we will give you a good recommendation for other employers.'

You know that song, don't you? *'Jey raatey mor duar guli...'*? Well, that's actually supposed to be about love and passion, but that day I realized *'koto rokomer jhor hoy, koto rokomey duar thaakey...'* how many different storms there are, how many different doors you have, that can be smashed open.

Dada-babu protested, of course, but that Colonel Shaheb and Borun-kaku told him 'You aren't living here any more. If you want, you can employ him, take him wherever you want, to France if you want, but we don't need him.' Then they gave me this letter and three hundred rupees, twelve rupees for each year I'd worked, and that was it – go!

On the day I was leaving, Dada-babu called me aside and quietly slipped me a sealed envelope. A whole eight hundred rupees! Which was a lot in those days, you understand? He had somehow got money out of the family's joint bank account before they closed it and stole all of Dada-babu's share. From that money, I added to the tiny patch of land we had – bought a larger bit of farmland, got rid of our old hut and bought the land for this house.

I think Dada-babu also left for abroad a few days after that and, as you know, he never came back. In Kolkata, I found work in other houses but it was never like the times in the Lahiri house. It should have been Dada-babu's house, or at least one-third of it! I hope those two uncles are rotting there in the cess-pit of their stolen wealth.

I came back here permanently about twelve years ago and it was good that I did. The times in Kolkata started getting bad soon after, and things here weren't so good either. It was not a good time to be away from your land. All sorts of people have all sorts of eyes on other people's property, you know.

Wife died eight years ago, bless her soul. Luckily, the children were all grown up and settled by then. My older daughter is married in Kharagpur, the younger one is in Asansol, and my son has a good job in Gauhati, of all places. They are all good children, can't complain, they come and visit when they can, but basically I am on my own here. Though my niece and her husband live just three houses away, and together we manage what we have.

The first thing he serves me is rice straight from the handi. Two big dollops in the centre of the brass thhala he's pulled out for the occasion.. 'This is from my own field, it's our fat local rice, hope you can eat it?' He opens a little jar and spoons some dark yellow stuff over the almost round, off-white brown-flecked grains. 'Just eat a little bit by itself first, just with some salt and this ghee. Careful you don't burn yourself, it's hot.' I wait a bit before mixing in the ghee but my fingertips still tingle slightly. The ghee momentarily turns the rice a light golden colour. Once I'm sure I won't burn my tongue, I wave away the flies and pick up a mouthful. The ghee and grains create an argument in my mouth and I find myself shaking my head – I've tasted ghee-bhaat many times but never like this.

I notice Rasko hasn't taken any food for himself. He explains before I can ask: 'I can't serve you and eat at the same time. One only serves with the right hand, as you know, and that's also the hand you eat with! And you only have one right hand, isn't it? You eat properly, I'll eat right after!' I think of arguing but I don't.

As a second step, Rasko puts some karela on my thhala, the green darkened, almost crisp. 'Now, try the teto. The bitterness opens up the tongue to all the other food.' The rinds break into small bits as I work them into the rice; the taste in my mouth is transformed yet again, the flinty sweetness of the karela sidling past the first kick of bitter to mix with the rice and ghee.

My thhala keeps transforming as the meal proceeds, the rice a sort of animated canvas into which different smells and tastes paint themselves: the karela is followed by a light summer-yellow mung dal, the thin liquid disguising a heft of flavour, the turmeric, ginger and Elko's much loved chillies climbing straight through my head to knock on the skull; the leafy green mash of notey shaak adds a different green heat, before the chicken and its gravy take over a fresh pile of rice. Rasko keeps filling my brass glass with water and, as I eat, I keep waving away the flies, dabbing myself with a smaller gamchha he has given me, trying to make sure the sweat from my face doesn't drop into the food.

'Have a bit more, baba?' He ladles some more chicken past my protesting hand. 'When I told them you were coming, my niece said to cook some jackfruit, it tastes just like meat, we call it gachh-paantha, tree-goat, the jackfruit is fully in season now and we have some good trees, but I said no, the son of Dada-babu's friend is taking the trouble to come all this way and I will give him actual murgi. I bought this one from my neighbour, he keeps good local chickens.'

By now, I've had several different combinations across the seemingly simple meal, rice and ghee, rice and karela, karela and dal, shaak-mash and rice, chicken and rice, a bit more dal and shaak, with a bit of chicken gravy accidentally mixing in. About halfway through, Rasko has put a chutney of raw mango at one side of my thhala, adding a sweet and tangy contrast to the party of savoury flavours. It's only as I'm about to finish that I notice the untouched slice of lime and raw green chillies sitting patiently at one side.

Once he's sure I'm close to finishing, Rasko finally serves himself. I notice he takes much smaller portions, quaffing them quickly and without attention, as if his stomach is full from watching me eat.

'Don't mind, I didn't make any fish and there is no sweet. The man who runs the mishti shop is away and the other fellow in the next village makes rubbish. Dada-babu wouldn't often have sweets, but when he did he was very particular about which shondesh and which doi he ate. He got that pickiness from his mother.'

'Not to worry, Rasko-da, I couldn't eat any more.'

'What was that Robi Thakur thing...' Rasko looks upwards, mouthing some words, trying to remember something. 'Oh, hyan! Aamshotto dudhe feli...' He uses his finger to mark Tagore's line breaks.

'Put dried mango-paste in the milk.
Into that mash banana,
Then sandesh mix in...'

I join in and we finish the verse together:

'Hapush-hupush sound,
Then silence all around,
Ants pass the plate, weeping.'

Who would have thought I'd live longer than Dada-babu? He was so active, so dedicated to his tennis and exercise.

You know, on the day Robi Thakur died, Dada-babu went to the funeral. You know there were lakhs and lakhs of people on the street, the whole city had come to a stop. He came back in the late afternoon, his kurta torn, his pajamas filthy, no chappals, his feet bleeding from walking barefoot for all that distance from Barabajar. Why did he walk? His wallet was picked by some pocket-maar! He could have taken a taxi, of course, and paid when he got home, but there were no taxis that day, not a single one.

So he came back and sat there on the garden veranda, his feet in a bucket of hot water I brought for him, and ordered me to make him a ham samwhich. Now, anybody else would have called it a day and rested at home, but not him. He had his tea, had a bath, got into his evening suit and shoes, limped to his car and drove off to a party! That Palm Avenue house was so big, no one except me knew he had gone out. And you know when he came back? Only early next morning, looking as though he had visited heaven, still limping but limping happily. Clearly hadn't slept all night. No one was up except the darwaan and me, so I made him some breakfast and he went to bed!

That was the time of Eva, that bideshini girl. I knew because he would keep making drawings of her. Drawings, but never a painting. No one else saw them, of course, but me he trusted, so he didn't care if I saw what he was drawing. Then, after a couple of months, this Eva left and he was heartbroken. Young fellow, first love, you can understand, obviously. He couldn't show his sadness to anyone in the family, no one even knew! Gora girl, there would have been such a scandal! But with me, he was unguarded. He didn't say anything to me, of course, but he tore up some of the drawings of her right in front of me, and he burnt some of her notes or letters. He could shout at me and he knew I wouldn't mind, so for a few weeks he snapped at me about everything. Then, one day in December, as if by some magic, he stopped. I soon understood – that was when the time of Keya began.

He would still remember Eva from time to time. A letter would come, he would paint something from the hotel room, you know how, long after you've eaten something, the taste keeps coming back on your tongue? It was like that, something like that.

I thought for sure he would marry that Keya, even though Boudi – his mother – hated the girl, but then Keya died and he was never the same again, until he left for good.

Tell me something, Saki baba. This Imozen Memshaheb... was there nothing between them, then?

– No, Rasko-da, nothing like that between them.

They were like brother and sister then?

– No, not exactly. They were like a married couple, but with no... physical relationship and no romance. But they cared about each other deeply. In their own way, each looked after the other one more than they looked after anyone else in their life.

– And, Rasko-da, it wasn't that he didn't have any, you know, bhaalo-basha, love, during his time in France. He had... other women friends in nearby towns.

Oh, that's good. I can't imagine Dada-babu living without any romance!

Along with the money, he also gave me his address in France, in big English letters – *Keep this carefully, you can write to me here. Remember it takes about ten days for a letter to reach there and another ten for one to come back.* Then, in Bangla, he wrote down your Ma's address in Shyambajar. That was in case there was any emergency or if I needed any small help. A cousin of mine was working at a house nearby, in Mayfair Road, and we agreed that he could write to me there.

Initially, I wrote to him once in every two or three months, and every now and then I would get a reply. But, you know, what was I going to write and tell him? About how I was serving this family or that? About how things were good or bad, here in the village? And what was he going to write to me and say? What would I even understand about that life he was leading, about that world which I would never see? And once I came back here, it became even more difficult. The local post office doesn't even stock those international aerogrammes, and even the Mednipur P.O. often doesn't have them, so it was difficult to reply. So, in the last ten-twelve years, I've just stayed in touch with your Ma, and Niru-di has been very kind, sending me Dada-babu's greetings from time to time and keeping me informed. Once Imozen Memshaheb was visiting, and they said they would pay for me to come to Kolkata to see her, but the harvest was on and I couldn't go then... I went later and he had sent me a nice bideshi sweater, made of thick wool. It's a bit moth-eaten now, but I still wear it in winter. Can't bear to throw it away.

I offer to help him wash up after the meal, but he won't hear of it. He lays out a chatai and pillow at one end of the porch for me to lie down, and hands me a hand-fan made from bamboo strips. 'Inside is too hot right now. As you know, we have don't have a fan or anything. But there's usually some breeze at this end of the porch.'

He lies down a few feet away, and I realize he's probably given me his sleeping spot. I think of protesting, but the early morning start and the heavy meal engulf me and I fall into a sweat-riddled sleep for forty minutes. When I wake up, he has tea ready for me.

'Nao, Baba, chaa. It's four o'clock. The bus for Mednipur only leaves at seven, but we should look at those paintings and the stuff on paper while there's still light.'

As I've explained to Rasko in my letters, the chief reason for my coming here is to look at the few of Elko's early paintings and drawings he says he has. I've hesitated to bring them up, in case he was exaggerating – talking to him has been worthwhile enough. The feeling that he may not actually have much has been reinforced when he himself hasn't mentioned them. Until now.

He leads the way into the one room of his house. The first thing that hits me is the smell of stale dhoop smoke, and then the whiff of slightly musty clothes and bedding. As my eyes adjust to the gloom, I can see the high bed with its halo ring of a rolled-up mosquito net, a barred window looking on to dense foliage at the back of the house. A cupboard and an old, heavily discoloured mirror. He reaches for something on the wall on the other side of the cupboard and comes away holding a frame. 'Can you take this, baba? I'll bring out the other ones.' I take the painting out to the porch and lean it against the wall. After a couple of minutes, he comes out with another smaller painting, also framed. Then he goes in and brings out a large envelope, smacking the dust from it as he comes out.

The paintings are in frames that Kedar had put them in originally, the old wood and glass managing to preserve the colours over the forty-odd years of heat and humidity.

'He made this one of me after he came back from his first trip to London. "Rasko! Why haven't I painted you before! Stand there for fifteen minutes!" I told him I had work to do, but he said I had to come and stand there next to the window for ten minutes, at the same time every day, around 11.30 in the morning. It took seven days of this standing, Didimoni shouting at me later, the cook growling that I was skiving off work, but Dada-babu would only paint this when I was standing there. Look, he's even put my name there in Bangla and English. I begged him to put my real name, Radharomon, but nothing doing. "You will be famous in history as Rasko!" he would laugh.'

The portrait of Rasko clearly goes alongside the one of Sheyali and Radhuni, the same expressionistic style, lots of thick paint applied with palette knife, except, instead of a corridor in the background, here there is only the room wall with patches of sunlight. What is different from the bride-light portrait of Keya is that the brush and knife work is much more confident and there is no attempt at smoothing down the contours of the face and torso. A man, perhaps in his early thirties, clearly working-class from his clothes and the slightly stiff way he holds his body with his hands behind his back, under shiny combed-down black hair, the eyes bright, with a certain intelligence and defiance.

'And this one?'

'Oh, this one I asked him for, after Didimoni died, just before they told me to leave. It was one of her favourites. Actually, he'd done another similar one of the garden from one of the upstairs balconies, you know, wintertime, the palm trees like ghosts in the morning mist, but he'd given that to Keya. His mother got very angry about him giving it away, so he somehow got it back. But by then he'd done four or five of these. The original one got lost when the rooms were being painted, so this was what Didimoni had on her wall. He used to call it – ki jey bolto? – yes, the runner-up, that's what he called it, meaning the one that came second in the race.'

In the envelope are a few drawings, some on whole sheets, some on scraps of paper, done with pencil, pen and ink, some drawn with his fountain pen and rust-coloured ink. Some of these are clearly from the time of the famine, people in queues, sunken faces, concave torsos and stomachs. Then, on another kind of paper, thicker, cream-coloured, there are sketches of a naked woman lying on a bed, mostly just the body with the face only roughly outlined, except in one drawing of the woman's back she's turning around and you can see she's wearing glasses.

'You know, Saki baba, I shouldn't really have these. This was when he got the news that Keya had died in the villages, caught in some fire, though I don't fully know that story, actually. So one night, he was very drunk and he went out into the back garden behind the kitchen, poured some whisky on these and set them alight. A few of them got burnt, but it was a wet night and the fire went out. I saved these and put them away, I don't know why, but I never told him. If he's watching us now, I hope he won't be angry.'

'No, I don't think so, Rasko-da. It's good you saved them.'

'You said you wanted to take all these to...'

'To Calcutta and then possibly abroad, to France, where we will try and have a show of his work. Not all of it, just a few of the best ones.'

'That would be good, if the world could recognize his gift.'

'Well, let's see. We are also thinking of putting together a book of his work.'

'With all of his drawings and paintings?'

'No... that's a different kind of catalogue, they do that for really famous artists whose every line is regarded as precious. In French they call it a Catalogue Raissoné. I don't think we'll do that for Keda-mama.'

'Kat-a-logg Radhuni, no... cat-a-logg Roshun-i... Well, he did like to look at books with photos of other people's paintings. There was one time, one morning he came home from a famine langarkhana and tried to make some drawings. Then there was a siren and the Japani bombers came for a raid. Everybody ran inside to shelter, but Dada-babu kept sitting there in the veranda, looking at this book of paintings by someone – Ṣi—yes, Si-jhaan! This one, same mountain he painted over and over again, as Dada-babu explained to me, it was about the changing light and the changing seasons and the geometry shapes... He later wrote to me that the house where he was living was near there, near Sijhaan's mountain, but that he, Dada-babu, was no longer interested in painting the scenery.'

SAINT ANT

'I didn't quite understand that bit! How exactly did you explain Zemindear and me to old Rasko? '

The tape has an orange sticker for the Missus cassettes, with 'IVS, June 1977, St A' written in black marker. Her voice is clear because it's mid-morning and she's not too hungover from the night before.

She's been waiting in the Provence house when I get back from Calcutta, and now she's gone through the Rasko transcripts.

'Darling, I don't know if you'll ever be able to explain this to Rasko or, indeed, if it matters at all... but as I've told you, that first time, I thought I was only inviting Larry Lahiri, as I called him then, to come and stay for *a couple of bloody weeks*! And, let me hasten to add, Zemindear too had the same idea – he was clear he was only coming for a painting trip!

'Don't quite know what got into me, but these tiny instances alter the course of your life. For example, when I first met your mother, I thought I'd just stopped to take an interesting photograph! Similarly, by the time I met Kedar again, a couple of days after the opening at Pillet, I'd decided the good chap deserved to fulfil his dream and see Mont Sainte-Victoire and Cézanne country at least once.

'We met at some ghastly cafe near his digs in Pigalle, the coffee still the post-war bilge you got in the cheaper places. "Would you like to come down?" I asked. "Of course I would! What a question! But look, I don't want to put you out in any way... " "Oh, I wouldn't ask if I wasn't sure! You can stop being so polite, Larry!" Bad mistake, after which he consistently reduced politeness towards me over the next twenty years...'

She picks him up at the train station at Avignon. He's stumbling along the platform with his painting stuff, all bundled up, still dressed for the Paris winter, when she greets him. They pile his luggage into her grandma's old Citroen 12 and he spends the drive divesting himself of his warm clothes.

'You know, I've often thought of that drive, Saki, and Zemindear stripping himself off. Now I can only see it as him getting rid of all the bits of his past life. He'd never before sat in a car driven by a woman, and that too pelting along the right side of the road! So I want you to imagine a Jacques Tati film, a much shorter Tati type fighting with his woollen scarf, his jacket, with his jumper, and each time he wrestles free of an item some new terror presents itself on the road – A farmer's truck! A man on a bicycle carrying a tower of fresh baguettes! Rows of poplars on both sides! A pair of motorcycles weaving in a dance – idiots from the city! Even a tank and some soldiers on a march, as I remember… The intention was for him to take in the landscape, that was the idea, but he spent the whole drive gawking ahead, petrified, making calculations and pressing his braking foot through the floor!'

'Well, with your driving, I don't blame him.'

'Yes, well, you can go bugger yourself, darling. I was quite fine with my driving in those days!'

Reaching the house, Imogen shows Kedar his room.

'Oh, it's lovely! Just like Van Gogh's room!'

'I suspect this is a bit bigger, actually. Arles is not too far. We can go see the actual one and you can compare.'

He doesn't know it yet and neither does she, but this will become the bedroom he occupies for almost the rest of his life.

She teaches him how to pronounce the name of the nearest village, Saint-Antoine-la-Fontaine – Santantwaan-la-Fon-ten – 'In the family we just call it Saint Ant, but that's typically English, must maul any foreign name you come across!'

The next day, they drive out to see Mont Sainte-Victoire (Saint Vic, obviously), him dutifully carrying a small sketchbook and pencil case. They reach a good viewpoint at about 10 a.m. on a sunny winter's morning. They walk around for about an hour. He keeps looking at the mountain almost worshipfully, but he doesn't touch his sketchbook. She then takes him around the other local sights, the old Roman aqueduct, two ancient dolmen sites from the Neolithic period, a couple of local chateaus, and then some vineyards which she informs him make mediocre wine. They end the tour at the village church and the Roman fountain after which the village is named.

On the third day, she introduces him to Agathe, who comes in to clean twice a week and occasionally to cook. She sets him up in the unused room flooded with light from large windows. There is a beautiful view of one part of the garden, the gate and driveway, and the fold of low hills beyond. 'I think Granny added this extension intending it to be a kind of breakfast-cum-lounging room for the rainy days, complete with a pantry, but we never used it. It's unbearable in the summer.' She spreads her arms dramatically. 'Well, maestro, it's all yours for the next few days!' They both laugh. He thanks her profusely and begins to unpack his paraphernalia.

'I soon heard the sound of soft knocking, and when I looked in he was already at it, hammering together the frames for the rolled-up bits of canvas he'd brought. He didn't notice me, and I watched him for a while thinking how odd it was watching Larry Lahiri doing something physical, actually working with his hands.

'I then left him alone for a few days. Meaning, we'd meet at breakfast, neither of us much for eating in the mornings, so mostly coffee and cigarettes, and then I'd go into the garden or take the car and go do my errands. I'd come back around lunch and call out to him, resisting any urge to peek into the "studio", as I'd now begun to think of it. On some days, we'd go for walks and so forth. At other lunchtimes, I could see he was dying to get back to work, so again, I'd make myself scarce. In the evenings, we would... drink and talk. This went on for a few days...'

'And then...?'

After about a week, one morning she knocks on the door and looks in. 'I'm just driving to Aix, do you want to come along?'

He's brought along a small portable easel, and perched on it is a canvas, about two feet by one a half feet. Leaning against chairs and the wall there are three smaller canvases. On the small table covered with an old tablecloth are his paints, brushes, pencil boxes and two open sketchbooks.

The big canvas has been worked on the most, a view of Saint Vic through winter branches, the sunlight on the mountain caught quite nicely with choppy, squarish brushstrokes, '... all in all a very competent advanced student's homage to old Oncle Cézanne, you understand? What startled me was the black scrawl of some Bengali words slashing right through the middle of the picture. I looked at the smaller canvases and they all had some landscapey drawing and underpainting, but each also had a violently made X right across the surface. The chap was bent over a third sketchbook, cigarette dangling from his mouth, drawing furiously. I've always wished I'd taken a photo at that moment.'

Kedar jumps when he notices her. He catches the cigarette just as it falls from his mouth, burning his fingers. 'Aaah, *fu—damn* it!' He finds an ashtray. 'So sorry, I do apologize, I didn't see you come in!'

She repeats her question, and he's more than eager to join her on the car journey. 'He didn't exactly usher me out – my own house after all – but he moved quite briskly to gather his things and come away from the room. There was no move towards showing me what he'd been up to, or discussing it or anything. Outside, he began talking about something we'd heard on the BBC World Service. I seem to remember we had quite a nice outing to Aix. Across the day, I made no mention of the "paintings" and neither did he.'

Two days later, Imogen takes the liberty of sneaking into the studio while he's having his bath. The big painting has been repaired, the scrawled words absorbed under new brushwork. Somehow, this had made the image more interesting and altogether less Cézanne-ish. As to the smaller paintings, two have been hidden away somewhere and one has been turned into a beautiful sketchy still life of a coffee cup, an ashtray with a smoking cigarette, and a couple of tubes of paint.

'I always wondered what the Bengali words said. Always wondered, but he never told me.'

'I can tell you. He spoke about scratching over his early paintings here, so it would have been something like Eita aagey hoyegechhey! This has already been done! Or something ruder, maybe, Tumi ki baal Cezanne!?! Are you – rude word – Cézanne!?!'

'What rude word, darling? I know quite a few Bengali ones by now, you know.'

'Probably baal, as in pubic hair, so – Are you, pubic hair, Cézanne?'

'Ah, yes, baal, as opposed to baanra.'

'Yes, Imo-mashi, quite.'

The time is approaching for him to go back to Paris. She takes him out to dinner, to a nice auberge near Durance.

'Colette's place?'

'Yes, then her father's place, old man Georges, you never met him, lucky you.'

'Oooh, what did you eat?'

'For the life of me, I can't remember. But you know, their type of food, nice winter grub. That might've been the first time he had their daube.'

Georges, the patron, was clearly a bit of a racist, and he made his distaste for Kedar obvious through being obsequious to the point of parody. Kedar, not one to let things pass, put on his best snobbish air, calling Georges 'my good man' and 'my good fellow'. Whatever the food, it was the wine that took control of proceedings. They started with a bottle of white but rapidly moved on to the red, working through one bottle then another and actually moving on to a third.

'So, Larry, if you don't mind me asking, why do you keep crossing out your canvases?'

'Oh, you noticed those, did you?'

'Hard not to, those big black crosses across the pictures. And then, what does the writing say? When you use words to cross out what you've done?'

'Oh, nothing, not important, just me letting off steam. Nothing to do with your lovely house, but I've really not been happy with anything I've made here. On some days I just feel like packing it in, this whole bloody painting business.'

'Throwing in the towel?' She takes a swig of wine and reaches for her pack of cigarettes. 'Well, perhaps you should, you know?'

'What? So you also think my work's rubbish?'

'It doesn't matter what I think, does it? I mean, if something doesn't come easily, why bother doing it?'

'What do you mean? I'm not sure I follow.'

'What *do* I mean? I mean why should a well-to-do, self-indulgent chap such as yourself have to actually *work* at anything? You expect brilliance to drop into your lap, don't you? Just as everything else has in your privileged little life.'

'Privilege! I can't believe you of all people have the nerve to call me privileged! I mean, look at you! Sitting in your inherited houses, living off your inherited money, no need to put in a day's work ever again in your life! Forgive the pun, but that's pretty rich coming from you!'

It escalates from there, their voices rising, other customers turning around to look, the last dregs of the wine flying from Imogen's glass into Kedar's face, Patron Georges leaning over the table asking them to leave, saying something in French to Imogen who responds furiously, also in French, none of which Kedar can catch, Kedar reaching for his wallet, cursing inwardly that he might not have enough money, Imogen flinging a cluster of notes on the table before staggering to her feet and swaying to the door, a five-hundred franc note with its picture of Victor Hugo flying up in the air and then side-slipping down to be trapped by a curl of cream atop a half-finished dessert. Georges silhouetted, yelling something at them before slamming the door, Imogen slipping and coming down hard on the gravel, badly grazing her knees and hands, Kedar trying to help her up, her fighting him off, standing up and falling down again, both of them at the car, trying to open the same door, her blood smearing the door handle slightly.

'I tried to argue, but then even I realized I was too far gone to drive. Not a glorious moment for Imogen Snell. So, adding humiliation to insult and injury, the little bastard Larry had to drive us back, poking me awake every now and then to check the route.'

'And stop fucking calling me Larry! All these years and you can't even pronounce my name! Privilege indeed!'

'Shall I call you... shall I call you... now, what did the love of your life call you, not the Polish one, the Bengali one... *chemin de fer*... no... zemi something...' She slumps into her seat and lets the cold air hit her from the half-open window. '... though I wouldn't want you to get the wrong idea... not that a chap like you would ever find me attractive!'

Kedar looks at her, slightly alarmed. 'You don't really want to... do you?'

'No, but it's the idea that someone like you would never find someone like me... that's what I can't stand!'

'Yes, I do see, but my dear girl, the same applies vice versa, don't you see?'

'Well... yes... true... but... WATCH OUT!'

Turning on to a bigger road, Kedar has automatically begun to drive on the left. The headlights bear down from less than fifty yards away, having just rounded a bend. Kedar yanks the wheel hard right and stamps on the accelerator. They feel the air-slap as the other car passes within a couple of feet. The driver slows down to deliver an outraged shout before pulling away. Kedar shakes his head, makes himself more erect in the seat and continues driving.

Imogen puts a hand on his arm. 'Are you all right?'

'Yes, fine, and you? Thanks for the warning. Bloody close shave. How utterly stupid of me. I'm so sorry.'

'Well, good thing you're driving, I'd probably have ploughed right into him.'

They light cigarettes at almost the same time, both of them suddenly much more sober.

'Look, Imogen, I'm really sorry about the earlier...'

'So am I, so am I. I started it, so the whole row is my fault really.'

The next morning, he wakes up still full of regrets and offers to leave immediately.

'What? Just when we've found you're actually useful at something? You're not going anywhere, dear benighted Zemindear, at least not until day after tomorrow as per plan!'

She drives him to Avignon, and they say goodbye on the platform.

'Listen, Kedar, you know you're welcome here, don't you? You can come back jolly well any time you want to. If I'm back in London, I'll let Agathe know – she always has a set of keys.'

'Thanks, that's so very kind and, well, yes, I would like to come back soon. I'm going back home next month but, if I can afford the damn return boat, how would April suit?'

'Don't worry whether it bloody suits, just come!'

Missus adds another stack to the pile of old clothes she's going to take down to a charity shop in Marseilles. She picks up the corner of a folded dress and wipes her eyes, almost as if they are someone else's tears.

'And so it begins, Saki, the time of Imogen. I did ask for it, I suppose, with all the ups and downs.'

'It seems you did, yes. Did you regret it sometimes?'

'Oh, many times! But only when we'd fight! Which wasn't all the time, you agree?'

'Only about half the time, the other half the two of you spent laughing at the world.'

'Quite. Yes, quite, I never saw it that way but now that you say it...'

He goes, leaving behind most of the canvases since they are not fully dry. She misses him and is happy to see the accidental little exhibition in the studio when she wakes up in the morning. He returns three times that year, first coming back for three weeks in April, when Imogen is back in London, and manages to live in the house with Agathe's help. He only goes back to Calcutta in May to deal with the death of his father, and returns in August, declaring he doesn't mind if he never sees another bloody Calcutta monsoon again. He gets his wish. He makes one last visit to Calcutta when his mother dies unexpectedly in March 1955 and the uncles execute their inheritance skullduggery, and that's that.

'You know, one prays to Saint Antoine after losing something. He's supposed to be the patron of thieves. You promise to light him a candle after your things, keys, jewels, money, whatever, are retrieved. People say it works every time. Elko never prayed to Saint Ant, but I suppose once could say what he lost in Calcutta, his home, family, a place to work, he found here.

'The last time, in 1955, he took a plane and not a ship, "Travelling light!" as he put it, Air India, I think Bombay–Tehran–Athens to Zurich, from where I picked him up. By then, I was already working with the women's peace league in Geneva part of the time, so it was easy enough. I'd made it clear to him that he could stay here as long as he wanted and we'd manage somehow. I would come and go, I had work in Geneva and London and some vague family attachments in England, but this was more or less becoming home, I suppose.

'And it wasn't as though he was isolated. By that time, Raza had also started coming down, getting away from Paris to work here quietly in the summers, usually around Menton and Gorbio, where he and Janine later moved, and then there were others, you know, European friends, writers and suchlike. So he would be all right.

'But the day I really knew he was here for good was a few months later, when the money order arrived. Paul Bonnemaison had sent M. Lahiri a relatively large amount. The accompanying message simply said *Greetings from Monsieur Ganesh Mondal.*'

MONSIEUR MONDIAL

I remember coming away from my first meeting with the Big Man with a mess of questions short-circuiting in my head, many more questions than I'd had at the start of our meeting. Again, the man seemed to read my mind as he saw me off at the door of what I thought of as his little sports museum.

'Listen, Saki, don't worry. We will talk some more in a few days. All the important things you need to know, I will make sure you find out. Either I will tell you or, as they say in Ingreji, "I will point you in the right direction."' Every time he switched to English, I was startled as to how clean his diction was, despite the heavy Bangali accent.

He'd put his hand on my shoulder. 'Please tell Niru-di Ganesh sends her a younger brother's pronaams, all right?'

On the return trip, there was only the driver and me in the car. The route between the jute mill and Calcutta was bumpy, but this didn't stop me from scribbling madly in my notebook, trying to put down everything before I forgot details. Only some of the notes had to do with Elko or his work, because now I wanted to know about other things, things about Ma, other things that were absolutely not my business, things about this man I'd just met.

One of the notes is just a list:

Bodo Babu (Big Man)
Poittallish (Forty-five)
Ganesh Mondal
What about the other G?

The notes remind me that, at our second meeting, I'd summoned up the courage to ask about Gopal.

'Ganesh-babu, when I was young, Ma used to talk about a fellow called Gopal. Do you know this man?'

'Oh yes, I used to know him.' There is no hesitation in his answer, in fact, it's as though he has supplied this reply many times. 'Gopal... Kundu. He was also known as Pocket Gogai or Chhoto Gogai. He died, I think, just as the famine was becoming apparent. He used to work for Shahabuddin, the same man I briefly worked for, but this Gopal was a minor pawn involved in the criminal side of Shahabuddin's operation, you know, pickpocketing, smuggling, extortion, breaking into goods trains, that sort of thing. I myself used to do some basic stocktaking and bookkeeping for Shahabuddin's legitimate wholesale business in pharmaceuticals and dry condiments, and I mostly kept away from people like this Gopal. Perhaps Niru-di remembers him because, in the early days of the famine when I would send sacks of rice and dal to Niru-di for their langarkhanas, it is this fellow who would have made the deliveries.'

'So... how did he die?'

Ganesh-babu frowned, trying to remember. 'I'm not exactly sure... I think he got involved in some bad business, I believe some gang war between Shahabuddin and Jalal Sheikh of Howrah, where they had some quite bloody falling out over black-market rice.'

3

EVERY MARKET HAS A GAIT

'So what does your Ustad think? Does he think he can trample over the market? Hain? Does the old man think everybody else will stop in mid-meal, push their plates towards him and sit there watching him eat?'

Something is very wrong with the tune and Gopal can't quite put his finger on it. It's not unusual for people to protest when he goes to collect overdue payment, and sometimes these traders can protest quite vehemently. Today, there are two things that are off-key: whereas desperate people shout begging for more time, Jhunjhunwalla's tone is polite, his voice absolutely even. The second thing is the choice of words which is rude and brazen – 'old man' – impossible to imagine anyone who has dealt with Ustad using that kind of disrespectful term, and even the way the Marwari pronounces 'Ustad' and 'he' are completely new to Gopal, new and wrong. Something in his demeanour also sends an odd signal. Even the clerk sitting at a small desk against the wall seems to be too confident, too free of fear.

Chhoto Madhai also senses something amiss, but his reaction is to start bristling. 'Others are paying on time. We have waited a long time for your payment. Are you saying you aren't paying?'

Jhunjhunwalla wipes the cheeks under his glasses with a handkerchief. 'What I'm saying is the market has its gait, and we all have to bow to that, understood?' Jhunjhunwalla wipes his moustache and the creases around his mouth. 'No one is going to starve themselves while your Ustad gets fat on the sweets, not any longer.'

The godown has an all-pervading smell of rice-dust and jute. In a small, caged-off area behind the Marwari's desk, there is an old safe, and next to it a small shrine where sharp incense is burning before a statue of Ganesh. Gopal can also smell the hair oil from the Marwari's scalp. It's winter, and this godown next to the river is quite cool, so why is Jhunjhunwalla sweating? Outside, somewhere, the peculiar whiff of adulterated wartime petrol coming off a warm engine. Clearly, a car has pulled up and Gopal hasn't heard it. Clearly, someone has switched off the engine and coasted down the slight slope leading to the godown.

His eyes flaring, Madhai opens his mouth to reply. Gopal is already turning to look at the door when the two big men walk in. He recognizes one of them as Miraj, one of Jalal Sheikh's senior heavies, and he has just enough time to register that the second man is reaching for something in his waistband when Miraj's open hand grabs the side of his head and sends him flying into a wall.

Madhai has more time to react. His head spinning, Gopal looks up from the floor to see that his partner has jumped back, his revolver out, pointing straight at Miraj.

'You sisterfucker, I'm going to shove your body up your Sheikh's asshole.'

Either Miraj doesn't register the gun, or he doesn't care. As he advances, his body ducks while his arm scythes up towards Madhai's gun. Gopal sees the finger pull the trigger, hears the report, and then Miraj's hand clamped around Madhai's wrist, forcing the gun upwards. Two more shots go off as Madhai is twisted around by the hand, a shot ricochets off a girder, the other is pillowed by one of the piled sacks of rice. Suddenly, there is a waterfall of dirty white on the brown jute, the grain drumming on the hard floor, but to Gopal it feels as if the sharp sound is being made by the knife that has cut open Madhai's stomach.

As Miraj holds Madhai tight, the second man stabs him again and again, in the throat and then in the chest and then a second time in the throat. Madhai's body starts to jerk and his revolver clatters to the ground. The throbbing in his head seems to help Gopal think more clearly. Before he goes into a squat against the wall, he manages to pull his trousers to his knees, just in time so that he doesn't soil them too much. He crouches there, his breath steadying, as the shit splatters out.

The sudden stink reminds the men that he's still there. Miraj looks at him and starts to laugh, holding his nose as he does. In his peripheral vision, Gopal senses Jhunjhunwalla and the clerk getting up off the floor where they had ducked. He can feel himself shivering and he exaggerates the shaking. The second man starts to drag Madhai's body somewhere, and then thinks the better of it and straightens up. Miraj is still standing there, pointing at Gopal with one hand while holding his nose with the other. Gopal can almost see himself in the man's eyes, a thin, dark, creature, petrified, naked, hands shaking inside the opening of his half-dropped trousers. He can hear the Marwari and his clerk joining in, their laughter loud and high-pitched, trying to control their terror.

The big man raises his head to the ceiling, taking his eyes off Gopal for a moment, another wave of laughter convulsing his stomach just before the bullets convulse his chest. Gopal is not conscious of having waited for the knife man to be right behind Miraj nor of firing two shots, perhaps it is luck, perhaps instinct, but as Miraj drops, he can see the other fellow stumbling away as if hit by a hammer. Gopal has used two hands to fire. Now he gets to his feet, yanking up his trousers with his left hand as he does. Steadying himself, he returns the hand to the Colt. The second man is on his knees, his back to Gopal, confused about what is going on. Gopal takes a couple of steps forward, just to make sure, and fires another shot from about five feet away, aiming for the middle of the man's back. This time the recoil hurts a bit, but Gopal doesn't mind – the satisfaction is in seeing a hole appear near the shoulder blade, just before the man topples over.

Gopal finds himself standing almost on top of Miraj. The man is blinking desperately, his body writhing, and he's clearly no longer a threat. Gopal points the gun down and shoots him again anyway, closing his eyes as he squeezes the trigger. There is a hard sound as the bullet goes through to the floor. When he looks again, there is a circular mess of blood and bone in the middle of Miraj's face. Walking over to the knife man with the gun still pointing, Gopal keeps his distance, checking for signs of life. The bastard is now lying face down, twitching in a small lake of blood and rice, and Gopal can see that one of the first two bullets has gone right through Miraj to hit the man in the centre of his back, not far from the second, slightly to the left of the spine. He understands that three out of his four shots have been lucky hits. Or, maybe, it was She who was doing the firing.

Gopal waits for the second man to become completely still before he engages the safety catch on the Colt. Still holding the gun, he pulls up his trousers and secures them with the belt, ignoring the smell and stickiness. Then he wipes the sweat from the gun handle with his shirt, releases the safety, and goes out to take a look. An old Austin sits just outside, empty, its doors still open. There is no one around and no one seems to have heard the shots. He comes back, looking for Jhunjhunwalla and the clerk, and it takes him a moment to locate them hiding behind the desk. Four bullets gone, four left. He walks around the desk.

'Now, you. Motherfucker. Open that safe.'

COUNTER

'Yes, it was quite bad, that little war between Shahabuddin and Jalal Sheikh. I mean, Calcutta's four or five big gangs had always had conflicts, it's the nature of the business, but there was an important difference this time – for the first time, guns were used.

'At that time, the only people to have revolvers were the gang bosses or the main bodyguard protecting the boss, and only to be used in extreme emergencies, because the use of pistols brought extra attention not only from the police but also the Intelligence Bureau. The IB was always worried about firearms spreading from the criminals to the political groups. So, every time someone used a pistol lethally, you heard about it, and it wasn't that often, maybe once every two or three years, one shooting somewhere, and usually only one party doing the shooting, usually over a woman or gambling or something and not over business, certainly no gunfights like in the American movies.

'This time though, something went wrong in Howrah, in some godown there. What the police found were dead bodies, five of them, but only one of them killed by knife, the other four killed by a handgun. They also found a revolver that had been fired, but only three chambers empty, and the bullets from that didn't match the ones that had done the killing. Those were from another, heavier pistol.

'The one killed by stabbing was a known member of Shahabuddin's gang, two of those shot dead were a Marwari black marketeer and his clerk, the other two were senior mastans working for Jalal, two really nasty men who were feared in the Calcutta underworld. The whole thing was quickly covered up, no newspaper was allowed to report it, in case it added to the public's war panic which was already high. Nobody was supposed to know the details apart from the police, but of course, those who knew, knew. By which I mean Jalal Sheikh had his informants in Lalbazar Headquarters as did Shahabuddin, and this escalated their fight.'

'You seem to know a lot about it.'

Ganesh smiled and nodded. 'I found out much later, once I had the means to access certain police files in Lalbazar I was curious about the case.'

'So, then, Gopal? Was he the one who was... stabbed?'

'No, no, I don't know how they came to the conclusion, but the police figured out that Pocket Gogai – this Gopal – had also been present at the godown, obviously along with whoever did the shooting. So then the authorities started looking for the gunman and him, both. I think he tried to escape into East Bengal, but they caught him somewhere over there, in Khulna or Mymensingh somewhere. He was a petty criminal, not important, there was a war on, so the story went that the mamas just got rid of him.'

'Meaning?'

'Meaning what we now call "encounter". You know what an encounter is, yes?'

I knew, but I wanted to see how he would explain it. 'I'm not sure, as you know I've mostly been abroad since '66, so all these new terms...'

'Hardly a new term, Saki-babu!' The Big Man smiled, clearly seeing right through me. 'So, you should know that about seven–eight years ago, when the police began executing these Naxalites they'd arrested – these boys just a bit younger than you, come to think of it – the mamas always said "so-and-so Maoist was killed during an encounter with our force", basically implying that this was some sort of equal gunfight or something. Actually, everybody knew they'd just tied the poor goatfucker's hands and shot him in a field somewhere. Everyone also knew the cops had unofficial permission direct from Indira and Siddhartha Shankar Ray. So, encounter. It's now a common word in the villages, shortened to "counter", where they'll tell you "oh, pulish oke counter korechhey" – the cops have countered him.'

I suddenly had a vision of Gopal Kundu lying dead in a paddy field, his back riddled with bullet holes. For a moment, I almost believed Ganesh-babu. But then, as he reached out to pour me some more beer, I understood that this was the story we were both supposed to agree upon and follow.

For this second meeting, I'd been invited for lunch. 'Come and see me. If you are not too busy, of course.' His voice on the phone was full of humour and warmth. 'I'd like to know what all you've found out about Kedar-babu. Also, what stories those two Dharmatolla ladies have been telling you. Let's get to know each other a little bit.'

A month had passed since we'd last met. The elections had taken place, and Indira Gandhi and her Emergency were suddenly gone. I realized things were different from Fairlie Place itself. The same burly man was waiting for me at the Shyama Export-Import office, but the transport and driver were different. The car was a Mercedes, not that old, probably an early '70s model with some sort of air conditioning, so, despite the May heat, the trip was much more comfortable. 'Car was being repaired!' the man told me without my asking.

When I reached the jute mill, the Big Man greeted me on the balcony overlooking the river.

'Come, come, Saki, good to see you!'

'Likewise, Ganesh-babu. How have you been?'

'You can call me Ganesh-da.'

'Yes, Ganesh-da.'

He led me into his office, chatting away about the great upset of the national election results and the communists coming to local power in West Bengal. We sat across the desk again, and this time, instead of tea he offered me a choice between gin or vodka with lime juice and soda, or beer.

The beer came in an ice bucket accompanied by two pewter tankards of the kind you only saw in the city's clubs and top restaurants. He saw me examining the one in my hand.

'Yes, I know, they seem a bit pretentious perhaps, but occasionally I like drinking from them. There is no chance that any of these clubs will ever accept me as a member – I'm too "native", me and my poor Ingreji, for these Company Limited Bengalis who actually think of themselves as white Englishmen – so I do what I can to recreate the atmosphere sometimes, just to laugh at them. Mostly, I drink my beer from a glass, but today, I thought, why not?'

I couldn't quite figure it out, but something had shifted with Ganesh Mondal since I'd last met him. At first I wondered if it was the unexpected ejection of Indira, but as we spoke it became clear it wasn't that. We went through everything I'd talked about with Sheyali and Radhuni, and I got the feeling that he already knew most of it, but it wasn't that either. It seemed he had arrived at some sort of a decision. In my mind, I saw Ganesh-babu as a man who lived within a set of protective concentric rings – if at our first meeting I had been allowed into the outermost circle, it now felt like I'd been invited perhaps two rings further inside. We talked about Elko, of course, but when I asked him about Gopal, I felt he almost welcomed the question, that it was something he too wanted to talk about.

As our conversation progressed, I realized he was playing a game, as much with himself as with me, throwing out titbits about Gopal as though he was conjecturing and then doubling back and contradicting himself, half erasing what he had just said.

'I mean, there was no real proof that this Pocket Gogai was actually there when the massacre took place. And, even if he had been there, there was no way Gogai-Gopal could have done the killing. It was absurd! Why would Shahabuddin, also known as Ustad, entrust him with a gun when there were so many other better men available? From where would he have got the gun? How would he know how to shoot? It seems all this didn't matter to the cops who maybe wanted to just close the file. So, they hunted him down somewhere and closed the file.'

'When you say file, Ganesh-da, do you mean you saw in an actual file that the police had, er, encountered him?'

'No. No. They would never write it down. The file said something like *Gopal Kundu, absconding, yet to be apprehended.* Then there was a handwritten query in the margins by some IB officer, *Possibly deceased?* Nothing more than that in writing. From what I understand, it would have just been a private conversation between an officer and his superior. "Sir, we met with armed resistance from an individual and were forced to shoot him. Unfortunately, the body fell off the ferryboat into the river and we could not recover it. But circumstantial evidence points to the man being the criminal we were looking for." And something like that would be the end of the story.'

The questions started to flood into my head and I had to make an effort not to spew them out. I wasn't foolish enough to think I could tease anything out of Ganesh-babu, nevertheless I found myself being careful to let him proceed at his own pace.

Over the actual lunch, we went back to talking of Elko and I went over the broad graph of his life.

'So, when would you say Kedar Lahiri's story begins? By which I mean, when do you think he becomes a proper painter?'

'I would say the painting he makes of the chappals he sees on the day of Rabindranath's death is the first sign of something original. Until then, and even after that for a while, he keeps trying to emulate the nineteenth-century European greats, you know, portraits, landscapes, still lifes. But here is the beginning of his own visual expression. And then, a few years later, when he builds on that chappal series and starts to try and tell the stories of what he has seen or heard, those paintings become really different from what most people are doing and suddenly you can see him in the work.'

Ganesh-babu looked down and nodded, almost to himself. 'I'm glad you mentioned that series. I actually have two of those chappal paintings.'

'Oh, yes, I meant to ask, can I see the paintings of his that you have? Where do you keep them?'

'Oh, I have a little private space in the city. Next time we can meet there.'

I couldn't resist the opening he'd provided me. I sensed I had the permission to move away from Elko and ask other questions.

'So, Ganesh-da, where does this Gopal Kundu's story actually begin, would you know anything about that?'

'Well, there are many stories, but funnily enough, one of them puts his elevation from pickpocket to full-time gangster on the day of Tagore's funeral. You could say it was a promotion of sorts. The night of Rabindranath's death, Ustad apparently sent this boy on a job with two of his most trusted men – Gaurango and Aurangzeb – I remember seeing them, occasionally they would come around Shahabuddin's main depot where I worked. Each was scary in his own right, quiet, not saying much, but if you looked at them you could see it, you didn't want to go near either of them. Aurangzeb, big and broad like an elephant, Gaurango almost as tall but very thin.

'So, the rumour was that they went to the docks to take a delivery of some smuggled goods and there was a problem. Gopal couldn't have been much more than a bystander, he was a thin little fellow, not capable of any feats of violence, but as the sadhus will tell you, Ma Kali puts her devotees into all sorts of situations, just to test them. Ustad got his goods, but the people handing them over, some foreign sailors and a Madrasi, those fellows never made it back to their ship. Gopal would have witnessed whatever happened, but he would have been a bystander, a coolie, nothing more.'

'So then, no one ever talked about the details of what happened?'

'Well, what I can tell you – from what I heard – is that Pocket Gogai's last day of working the streets was perhaps his most successful one as a pickpocket.'

'So, what happened at the docks?'

'Well, when we see a movie or read a thriller novel, what we most enjoy is the detailed action, I know!' He picked up a tube of bone from his mutton curry. 'But, see, when you have a meal with someone and you recall him eating, you can say he ate a piece like this.' He takes the bone in both hands and sucks out the marrow, tapping the opening on his plate to release the last of it. 'Now, logic and memory would suggest that this nalli piece was best eaten with two hands, like this, but in the heat of gluttony he could have eaten it with one hand as well.'

He wiped his hands on a paper napkin and took a swig of his beer. 'Saki, there is a simple test. What I've learnt from people telling these stories about some "action" is that the more detailed the story, the more likely it is to be made up. From what I understand, all second-hand of course, is that when you are involved in something like this, some quick and extreme physical thing, your memory smudges things, things get erased or twisted. So never fully trust anyone who says this is exactly what happened and describes the minute details the same way each time. That only belongs in your thriller novels.'

NOT YOUR WORK

'We were just the scouting team. As the superintendent's jeep passed through the village, we quickly pulled a flag up a bamboo pole so that comrades waiting by the nallah could see it. They were looking out for it, and the flag meant that the police team were coming. The other comrades then carried out the ambush.'

That was one version, from when I was around sixteen. This one came a bit later:

'Oh, there was a situation when we suddenly found ourselves being fired upon by a police patrol. We girls immediately lay down flat among the bushes, and when we could, we began to fire back. We were above them on a hill and they were firing and running up the slope, they weren't really expecting return fire, so they were surprised. We fired two or three rounds and then we ran. I got hit, yes, but I have no way of knowing whether we hit anyone. Then some of those policemen got killed later in the day, elsewhere, and they said our group had done it. At the time, we were happy to take the credit, only within the Party of course, but now I realize that a murder charge means hanging. You would have lost your mother at a young age.'

'Ma. Comrade Nirupama. Don't lie, now. You're forgetting what you've told me: you knew could die and you were fine with that. Me, i.e.

the baby, hardly knew you. Between Dida, Dadu and Roma-mashi, they would have brought me up.'

That brought silence about this for a few more years.

She finally told me the truth when I came back briefly in the winter of 1973. I'd told her that Elko had just talked to me about Keya. I was trying to get her to come and visit all of us in France, and she didn't want to go through the standard police check required to get a passport, 'just in case I come to their attention again for some old thing'.

'Com. Neem, that old thing is a very old thing now. What you did or did not do twenty-two years ago, for which they have never ever pursued you, is unlikely to come up.'

'I don't know, I'm told they keep all sorts of files for decades. Anyway, I can't come this year because of my work, so let's talk about it later, all right?'

'Hm. Listen, are you ever going to tell me about the...'

'Why do you want to know? What do you want to know? Why?'

'I am your son. I need to know the truth. It's not like I'm going to never speak to you again. Or go tell the police.'

'That damned tape machine of yours? It's not around, is it?'

She stops dusting the bookshelf, raises her head and closes her eyes behind her spectacles. As though she's trying to remember a melody.

There are four of them. Two magazines each, one on the rifle and one spare, so a total of twenty bullets each, eighty in total, which is a lot for any operation. 'Your first volleys will be the most crucial, so really try and aim calmly. Remember, slow and steady is better than fast. Remember, you are only targeting the officer, as for the rest, you are trying get them to keep their heads down. You'll be only about fifty–sixty feet away, and once they start shooting back, your job will become more difficult. So try and get away after the first ten rounds each. If you can't run, try not to be changing magazines all at the same time.' Lying there on the hard earth in the mess of trees and bushes, each girl understands that she will most likely be dead before she can use up all her bullets.

There is indeed a scouting team in the village, and all four of them are looking at the bare bamboo pole sticking out above the thatched roofs.

There is a faint noise that sounds like a motor engine, but they can't be sure it's the police jeep they are waiting for. The flag struggles up into view and then drops back, as though someone's made a mistake. After a long moment, it comes back into view, hopping up the pole in quick desperate tugs, the triangle of red fluttering in the wind as it reaches the top of the pole.

The engine grows louder as it approaches, and then the jeep bumps into sight around the clump of palms. The driver slows down as he sees the ground sloping into the shallow rivulet. Left-hand drive vehicle, American war surplus, Dasgupta to the right of the driver, two men in the back, total of four, and not the five or six they sometimes carried, which was good.

She remembers the nose of the jeep dipping as it moved to cross the small stream. Dasgupta's arms spread, braced, holding the hinge of the flattened windscreen, the man half standing to avoid the bumps as the jeep nosed into the water, offering her the clearest of targets. The third shot had missed completely as Niru became conscious of what she was doing, the fourth was even worse as a fly angrily attacked her shooting eye, but by then the superintendent was splayed back across his seat and the other girls had also opened fire.

'Someone told me later that the police report said Binayak Dasgupta was hit with five bullets but the ones that killed him were two in the chest. I know those were mine. I know only that my first two bullets found their mark and then, before I knew it, my magazine was empty and I was struggling to change it because my hands had suddenly gone slippery. There was this horrible chattering noise and bullets were chopping into the branches above us. The two men at the back had Sten guns, which we didn't expect at all, but they were shooting in panic, the bullets going high. Most of them. I was getting angry with myself because my hands were slippery, and then I realized they were slippery with someone's blood and my left arm was not behaving properly. I managed to load the magazine but couldn't raise the rifle. Just then, something exploded in the jeep, not the petrol tank, maybe they were carrying a tin of kerosene or something. The whole jeep was on fire and I wanted to shoot whoever came out of the blaze but Savitri and the others were dragging me away. Someone had snatched my rifle while another one was supporting me, saying, "Let's go! Let's go! They are finished!"

'Two of the others had scratches and cuts from stone chips and wood slivers, but I was the only one who took a bullet. The pain was bad for the next few days, but I felt nothing inside, just strangely numb, like in Ingreji you would say "anti-climax". I kept wishing the bullet had killed me and – irrationally – taken me to Keya. I couldn't sleep for the next few days, and in my mind I my kept recounting the whole thing to Keya, who kept consoling me, "Korechhish toh korechhish, ebaar chhede dey. Abar kortey hobey na. Eita tor kaaj noy. Chhede dey." Keya, sitting there smoking calmly, wiping my face with her pallu, "You've done it, you've done it, now let it go. You don't have to do this again. This is not your work. Leave it."

'Later, when I would dream of this, sometimes I was shooting that superintendent and sometimes those Markin soldiers. Not the ones who were going for the girls, not the man with his pants open, but those big men with the white armbands... the MPs... I was shooting those MPs one by one.'

'Com. Neem. You know, that's another story you haven't ever told me properly. Imo-mashi told me.'

She hears me but doesn't. 'I was shooting the Americans, and also the men in the jeep near Koyra, and running out of bullets, and Keya would be patting me on the shoulder saying "Enough, now, enough. Stop. This is not what you're meant to do. This is not your work."'

LAND-ESCAPES

'Oh, that horrible Southern Avenue business. I made a couple of small ones around that, if you remember. I wanted to make a really big one but I stopped.'

I'd just returned from Calcutta, where Ma had finally told me about the jeep ambush. After a couple of days in Paris, I'd made my way down to Saint Ant. Elko was alone in the house, Agathe coming in to cook and clean, and Missus was away. 'Gone back to Blighty for one of her infestations – beg your pardon, I mean manifestations! Actually, it's not a demonstration she's gone for... You know, your Missus-mashi and her lot have actually set up a women's centre now, in Hampstead somewhere? I'm laughing, but in seriousness – good for those women!'

I looked at him to make sure he was feeling all right. He stared back at me from his easel. And then fired both barrels of grin. 'Now don't you dare tell her I said that, you!'

'That she was participating in an infestation?'

'No, no, that I was in any way cheering Her Ladyship and her, um, what's the new jargon, her... *feminist* group!'

'You do realize it's not that new any more? Been around for a while for those of us who don't live in a bubble.'

'Yes, yes, and I'm a male chauvinist pig, I know!'

'Now that's old, almost archaic.'

'I know, but so am I.' He got up from his stool and poured me a glass of pastis. 'Speaking of women and revolution, how's your Ma?'

'Comrade Mother sends warm greetings. She's fine, I suppose... No, she's all right, quite happy inasmuch as you can use that word for her. I was trying to convince her to get a passport and come for a visit. I said you'd be so happy to see her after all these years.'

'And?''

'She was reluctant to get a passport.'

'She's not scared of flying, is she? Surely not?'

'No, no, she's taken a couple of flights inside the country for her work, it's not that. She's scared the mamas might open old files.'

'Bengal Police. Those buggers are too busy killing Naxalites. In any case, I'm sure the rats in Lalbazar have eaten the files by now.'

I told him how she'd finally recounted the whole story, and then how she'd half mentioned the GIs and the girls and the Military Police.

'So Missus and I were talking about that at one point, and I did make the two small ones. Rosenzweig took the one that survived and I was beginning to think of a bigger canvas...'

'Why did you stop?'

'Having painted two, I felt it wasn't my story to tell. God knows there were so many others that weren't mine to tell, perhaps none of them were, or most of them, but this one, with this one I really felt I was crossing some line...I mean, as you well know I've never escaped those twin questions. What to paint? Why to paint? They've always stalked me, like bloody Thompson and Thomson from *Tintin*, but I really felt this was a moment that should stay between Nirupama and Imogen... meaning they both have a right to speak about it, but I don't.'

'But you said you'd done some work around the jeep thing, hadn't you? So that was all right for you to...'

'Well, again, not directly. Once she came away from the villages and her wound healed enough not to be conspicuous, Niru met me. She told me how they got that bastard and how the whole thing unfolded. We both agreed it didn't lessen Keya's absence by an iota.'

'She said that to me as well.'

'I never felt like painting the actual thing. It was like our private secret. And it was precious how that... retribution... kept changing in my imagination. I didn't want to make it concrete, and I knew that your Ma didn't either, for her own reasons. But then there was the aftermath, did she tell you about that? Did she tell you about this tribal girl Savitri?

'She told me a bit, yes, about her going under—'

'This Savitri was apparently quite striking looking, tall and big for a Santhal, huge eyes. Niru told you she escaped by diving into the river and staying under water, breathing through reeds?'

I nodded.

'Yes, well, the painting of Savitri is one of the few I do regret destroying. So this was the painting, the police on top, villagers lined up at gunpoint – I may have stolen something from Goya there – and then Savitri, her body stretched out under the water, floating, a reed in her mouth, bubbles floating up. When it was done, I thought it was a khichuri, Goya, and Benode Behari and bits of patua-style outlines. I should have let it rest, but again, was it mine to tell? In any case, it went.'

'No photographs? No surviving drawings?'

'No, afraid not. It was a while back, about ten years ago, I think.'

'And what about the other thing...?'

'Southern Avenue? As I said, I started and then stopped. I had a mixed group of soldiers, white GIs and Neg—beg pardon, and black GIs, but then Missus corrected me. Anyway, all gone, trashed.'

SPECIAL LOVE

Today, they've decided to walk around the Tollygunge area. Niru has taken her for a walk past the film studios where the war hasn't quite managed to impede the filming of the apparently very popular Bengali films. At one studio, a man has recognized Niru. He's an occasional assistant to Niru's father, who mainly works in the theatres in north Calcutta but sometimes makes the journey to the far south of the city to work on these film sets. At the man's insistence, they've gone in and peered through one of the big studio doors at the shooting going on inside. There is a sphere of hot illumination in the middle of a cosmic darkness where people seem very busy shouting at each other. Poking her nose in, it's the smell that assaults Imogen, a wave perfumed with alien chemicals, the dangerous warming of all sorts of things that feel as though they shouldn't be heating up.

They don't stay long, refusing the insistent offers of tea, Niru having a short, serious conversation with the assistant chap, and then they are out, walking along the tram tracks.

'The film work must pay your father more money than the theatre, surely?'

'It should! But my father is a true innocent when it comes to money. He regards cinema as something far lesser than theatre, so what he charges these film-wallas is almost a joke. As Ma and I keep telling him, lesser art doesn't mean less money! On the contrary, it should mean more! But he isn't adept – isn't good – at listening to women about work. He smiles at us as if he is indulging children, whereas it is actually we who are indulging him. I think he really enjoys it when they send a car to bring him here and take him back.'

'I say... isn't that the Tolly?' Imogen points to a gate that interrupts a long stretch of green metal fencing.

'Yes, Imogen, look, Tollygunge Club. It says on the board.' Niru points to the sign curving over the gate. Just inside the gate there is a notice-board announcing the programme of festivities for bringing in the approaching 1944.

'Yes, I can see. It's just that I've always driven through here, never actually walked past it, you see, and it looks very different.'

'Yes.' Niru smiles.

They keep walking north in the quickly falling winter dusk. Imogen can see little pinpoints of light appearing in the blackout darkness as the hutments at the side of the road light up chulhas for the evening meal. After a while, she puts her scarf over her mouth to ward off the coal smoke. By the time they've walked through the brick arches of the railway bridge of the suburban line, her nose is singing with the smell of spices thrown into fresh combat with hot mustard oil.

The hutments fall behind and low buildings take over the pavement. They come to where the curve of Southern Avenue joins the big boulevard from the right. Having walked down it several times, Imogen knows Southern Avenue is lined with small houses with gardens, small apartment buildings, and a series of grass dividers in the middle. Imogen sees some soldiers milling about on the far pavement and thinks nothing of it. Then she notices that Niru's pace has slowed because she's peering hard at the group of men. Imogen starts to ask a question, but Niru has already changed course, glancing right and left for traffic before striding across the road. Imogen follows, suddenly struggling to keep pace. Niru's fast walk changes into a run as she crosses Southern Avenue, cutting diagonally across the patch of grass in the middle.

Imogen can now see what has pulled Niru away. The five soldiers, Yanks by the looks of it, are loosely circled around two local women. The women – girls, really – look terrified, stuck to each other, eyes wide, mouths pursed, hands clutching their saris to stretch them across their chests, the other hand lifting up the sari bottoms as you do when you need to run.

As they get closer, she can hear a nasal voice rising above the others. 'Can I give you something special from Milwaukee, baby? Let me give you some special love!' Imogen identifies the speaker as the thin, gangly, ginger fellow standing closest to the girls, the one who is gesturing and repeatedly looking down at something. Imogen follows the man's eyes and sees the silvery glint of something in his hand. She opens her mouth to warn Niru about the knife and then realizes the man is holding a half-peeled chocolate bar near his crotch and waving it up and down. 'You want to taste some of this, don't you, honey? Some chocolate with some Milwaukee cream, huh?' The man reaches across with his free hand and strokes one of the girls on the cheek. The girl flinches and shrinks further back into her companion. In the ensuing tittering, one of the other men, the one wearing a Christmas cap, reaches down and fiddles with his trousers. 'Don't pay him no mind! Look! He ain't got what I have here!' The girls recoil as if hit. The men are taken over by an explosion of laughter as they point at the penis Christmas Cap is holding in his hand. Their screaming laughter is joined by another scream as Niru launches herself at the man, her fingers clawing for his eyes.

Imo finds herself somehow plucked from outside the circle and wrestling with two of the bastards, their alcohol breath slamming into her face, making her gag as she struggles to get a grip on something, an arm, a face, hair. A fist hammers into her ribs, knocking her into the struggling mess of Niru and the penis man. Another punch, in the stomach this time, cannons the breath out of her, but even then she is aware of the two girls already in the distance, pelting away for all they are worth.

Two men are on Niru, one of them clutching a scrap of cloth torn from her blouse. Somebody has a lock on Imogen's neck from behind, making it difficult for her to breathe. Through the pumping in her ears, she hears a shout.

'Fuck! This one's white! She's goddam white! Stop!'

'Fuck, what? Fuck! Let's get out of here boys! Now!'

The arm loosens from around her throat. The men push themselves off Niru. From a nearby window comes the smell of evening dhoop.

The smell seems to have a wailing sound. As Imogen takes in gasps of air, her lungs fill with incense sound and siren smell.

'MP patrol! Run!'

They are breaking traffic rules, she thinks, as she watches the jeeps speeding up the avenue, driving on the side that's supposed to be going down. Barely able to move, she reaches for Niru, who is doubled over on the pavement. The men have gone, or have they? The jeeps screech to a stop. A man in a white helmet raises his arm and fire shoots out of it skywards with a report that hurts her ears.

'*Stay where you are!* Stay where you are, goddam it, or I *will* shoot you!'

Imogen looks around and sees the Yank soldiers – all five of them, she counts, at various points of dispersal – freeze into statues.

She hears a growl and thinks there is a wild dog about. Niru raises her head slowly, the rage still coming out of her throat. Imogen quickly puts her arms around her friend, covering her from the gaze of the new bunch of soldiers as if protecting her from bullets. Holding her tight, Imogen feels collisions inside herself – she needs to hold Niru tight, and yet she feels deeply soiled by the touch of these swine, feels that she should not touch anyone – most of all Niru – until she's had a bath and scrubbed away the filth.

'You sons of bitches.' The sergeant's voice is carrying but matter of fact. 'Come to me, walking slowly. This pistol ain't shot anybody in a long while and it's hungry. So don't tempt me, you hear?'

The men emit grunts of acquiescence and walk slowly to the jeeps.

One of the MPs from the second jeep, a large man, comes up to Imogen and Niru. He squats down, careful not to be too close.

'Ma'am? Are you okay over there?'

Imogen can't find her voice.

'And is your maid okay?'

Imogen and Niru both snap up their necks to look at the man. The MP tilts back and falls on his posterior.

'*Okay??? No, we are not bloody okay! And she's not my bloody maid!*'

The man gets up off the ground and dusts himself down before walking back to his jeep. Imogen can hear him call out, 'She seems fine. The other one too. Let's go.'

As Imogen stumbles towards the jeeps, she can see the five soldiers climbing into the two vehicles, one of them holding his eye, blood coming out from under his hand. She sees one of the MPs cuff another man on the head, a hard smack, bringing a yelp from the soldier. One MP stands on the street to block oncoming traffic while the jeeps manoeuvre to turn around. She and Niru are clearly no longer of interest. Imogen starts to shout. 'I want their names! I want the *names* of these men! They were outraging two young girls! The girls have escaped! But we are witnesses...! And then there's the assault!'

The MP on the road looks at her with bored contempt. 'It's okay, lady, you ain't hurt, are you? Not really, are you? You can get home, can't you? So head on now!'

Another MP sitting in the jeep joins in. 'Hey, Miss? Know something? You're lucky the coons didn't get ya! Now *they* can be real animals!'

'Animals?' Imogen feels the word regurgitating up through her body, again and again like vomit, shaking her bones. '*Animals? You're the animals! You're the bloody animals! It's you!*' As the jeeps start to pull away, she feels Niru's hands grip her arms from behind. Her voice in her ear.

'Imogen. Imogen. Imogen. Let them go. We have saved those girls.'

'You little sons of bitches are going to wish you were dead!' The voice comes from the departing jeeps, clearly projected for the women's benefit.

Imogen starts shaking. No matter how hard she tries, she can't stop herself. Each word that comes out of her is a sob.

'Those girls got away, didn't they?'

'Yes. Look there, they lost their chappals, but they got away...'

Imogen turns to see four slippers on the pavement, scattered as if unrelated to each other.

'They got away with everything else, Niru, thank god, they got away with everything else!'

EIGHT

Strange Fruit

2–3 JANUARY 1943

I have a lot, but I keep feeling I don't have enough.

As far as Elko is concerned – or when Missus and I refer to it formally, the *Kedar Lahiri Posthumous Retrospective* – I now have more than enough material. I have many of the important surviving paintings and drawings, and the best possible reproductions of the ones that are inaccessible or were destroyed. I have the armature for the long overview essay I want to write for the catalogue. I've also asked a few people – critics, his painter friends Paritosh Sen and S.H. Raza, and a couple of others – to contribute essays, short notes, memoirs. I work at the project whenever my job allows me, but the real delay now is from Eva Margenik in California and from Missus who is somewhere in England.

The Margenik Foundation has offered to fund the whole project, but it seems Mr Margenik has developed some sort of serious illness, so communication with Eva is intermittent and has to be sensitively conducted. As for Missus, she spent some time with me at the Provence house after I returned from my trip last year, but I haven't seen her since she left Saint Ant in September, which now makes it over a year. She's been in and out of contact quite erratically – a postcard here, a phone call there, disappearing into radio silence for months – and has remained shifty about why that is so. Here too, I'm smelling that something's not quite right with her health.

On the other hand, Ganesh-babu has stayed in regular touch. I'd given him both the Provence and Paris phone numbers when we parted after our meetings in 1977; I'd done this just as a formality, not really expecting him to call. Nevertheless, the Big Man began to telephone me once every few weeks, usually on a Saturday or Sunday. One weekday, the phone rang and a French secretarial voice said she was calling with a query from Shyama Exports, Calcutta. Would I be able to receive a phone call from M Mondal this weekend, and if yes, could we discuss the most convenient times?

And thus it began, this unexpected communication. The phone would ring at the mutually agreed time, the operators would put the Big Man through, and we would chat for ten or fifteen minutes. Ganesh-babu never seemed to have any pressing reason for calling, though he quickly made it clear, without actually saying so, that I was to avoid any talk about his past or his current business. In fact, it was always he who set the agenda for the conversation: he wanted to know how I was doing; how was the work on Kedar-babu going; what did I think of the current political situation in France; he had just remembered some amusing detail of the war years and thought he'd tell me before he forgot – did I know that this new Janata government had just banned Coca-Cola from India and that shortly it would be gone?

'I remember in those days Coca-Cola coming in concentrate form for the Markin soldiers. Tons and tons of drums being winched down from ships in Kidderpore... There were about 1,50,000 Markin here in India so imagine, Saki, how much Coca-Cola they needed! The concentrated liquid would be taken to their garrisons and then local soda would be added, same as they do in the bottling plants now.'

'Local soda!' A bulb lit up in my head. 'That's it! Now I understand why Coke tasted so different when I got to America! It didn't taste like it did at home! And this "Coca" in France, it's different yet again!'

'Yes... I suppose there is nothing like the taste of one's home Coca-Cola, eh? Anyway, we must meet and talk properly when you are next in Kolkata.'

Between last June and this July, there must have been about eight or nine phone calls, during which I asked only the most general questions and Ganesh-babu revealed nothing important about himself. The decision to make the phone calls was each time his, though I also began to look forward to the regular, static-filled conversations that were far less stressful than the infrequent calls I made to Ma. On the flight back to Calcutta for my annual visit this time, I realized that Ganesh Mondal had very casually teased out a lot of information about me, but I had to admit I didn't particularly mind this. I also had to admit that, putting the usual time with Com. Niru to one side, what I was most looking forward to was seeing the Big Man again.

'Saki! Esho, esho, esho!'

A couple of days after getting to Calcutta, I called Ganesh-babu and he sounded very happy to hear from me: So, when did we want to meet? There was an invitation to lunch on a Saturday. He knew Niru-di's address, of course, and he'd send a car for me. His apologies to Niru-di for not including her, but this would be a work meeting of a sort, and definitely, soon, we must all meet together.

This time, a nondescript, newish Ambassador brought me to a large, five-storey colonial block of flats on Chowringhee Road. The letters stood out in relief over the portico – 'Queen Alexandra Mansions 1905'. The driver escorted me to the lift where the liftman worked the lever to take the rattling old cage all the way up to the top floor. I'd been to other buildings such as these, massive apartments built in the first decades of the century for Raj boxwallahs, and I expected to see a number of doors for the different flats. By my reckoning, each floor would have had at least four, one for each corner, but here the only thing interrupting the walls of the large hallway was a pair of beautifully polished, large, old-fashioned wooden doors. There was a new bell, but no nameplate. The liftman rang the bell and waited. A uniformed bearer opened the door, saluted and led me inside.

We walked through a small reception hall, a large, modern conference room with a long table and an imported rolled-up screen for projecting slides or films, and then an empty office space with desks and chairs. The third room was a pantry with a small fridge humming its presence, stacks of dishes and serving vessels ready to be filled with food that would clearly have to come from elsewhere. At one end of the pantry, there was an open door that looked out on to the back of the building and the top landing of one of the circular wrought-iron fire escapes you always found in these colonial piles. At the other end was a small, solid-looking door. The bearer knocked on it and a voice responded from within. The man twisted the heavy brass door handle, showed me in and shut the door behind me.

'... Esho, come in!' Ganesh-babu clapped me on the upper arm and led me into the room. We had parted warmly enough a year ago, but there had been no such familiarity or physical contact. It suddenly felt as though a year's absence and the chatty phone calls had somehow brought us much closer than was logical.

Following him in, I noticed the Big Man wasn't wearing one of his usual safari suits – the shirt was imported, made from some slightly shiny silk-type material, a bright zigzag print of dark blue on canary yellow, with the big Pierre Cardin collars that had been fashionable a few years ago. The trousers were dark blue, almost the same shade as the print on the shirt. There was an expensive new watch on his wrist. As he led me by the elbow to a chair, I caught a slight hint of some musky cologne on the shirt, but from last night, not today.

'So! What would you like to drink? Unlike at the factory, I have a wide choice here. I even have that pastis you French love so much!'

'Could I start with a soft drink perhaps?'

'Of course! How about some Coca-Cola? I still have a supply of the last few bottles!'

We both laughed. The Big Man handed me a freezing bottle of Coke and a glass full of ice before pouring himself a beer. Then he settled himself into a sofa. 'So, my boy, let's look at you!' He lit a cigarette and took his time examining my face. Then he nodded as though confirming something to himself. 'You know, it's funny, but this happens. Until last year... how old were you then?'

'Almost thirty-five when you met me.'

'Yes, this happens, especially with our Bangali boys, until last year there was a still a trace of the boy on your face, but now that's gone, you're completely a man!'

'Some would say that happens a bit earlier, no? Between eighteen and the early twenties?'

'Yes, but often with our ancestry, I don't know if it's the fish or the water or the air, we Bangalis stay looking much younger than we are. With women it's a different story, of course it depends whether a girl has children, and when and how many, but a Bangali girl's face can change any time between fifteen and twenty-seven. Boys, as usual, are privileged. But if you were a gora boy, your face would be approaching forty by now.' He took a swig of his beer, and his eyes went far away. 'There is a moment, like a hinge in a door. It takes a few months to a year, during which you shed your childhood completely, like, like those butterflies coming out of their – ki boley? – chrysalis. I saw it happen in the mirror with myself, though I was a bit younger.'

I looked around. 'What a place, Ganesh-da!'

'Yes, I was lucky. This was the residence of the boro babu of McKenzie-Douglas, the last of the Ingrej engineering firms. They finally decided to sell and leave once all the Naxal stuff started. I negotiated for two years and finally got the place in 1971.'

We were in a large space that people would now call a 'living-cum-dining room', except the size of it came from perhaps two of the big Edwardian rooms being knocked together. On the north side of the space, there were sets of windows with a view of the Tata building just down the road. On the western side, there were more windows and two sets of doors opening on a long veranda that looked out on to the rear of St Paul's Cathedral just across the road. Beyond the church, rising above the trees, you could also see the dome of Victoria Memorial.

'They owned the top two floors actually, so that's what I bought – better for privacy, isn't it? And then I spent some time and money doing it up. The floor below is rented out. Parts of this floor I hire out to companies for conferences or when people need to have a negotiation in some neutral space, but this is for myself, this big room and then three bedrooms. I rarely invite other people here. For socializing, I have other places, Ma Kali has been kind.'

I nodded to acknowledge the honour. 'So, is this what you call home?'

'Saki... I don't quite know how to explain this... but I have no home, as such. I have this, I have the Dalhousie office and the factory and a couple of other places. Except for the office, I can spend the night at any one of these. It just depends on work and circumstances. I can also stay in the nicer hotels, if that's what the mood demands.'

Looking around, I could see this place was furnished quite differently from the jute mill. Old carpets, chandeliers, some spot lamps and quite a few paintings. The furniture was a mixture of high-quality colonial antique, art deco pieces, and a few chairs and side tables of '50s Scandinavian design that were probably knocked off locally. A part of the wall facing the balcony was lined with bookshelves, a lot of big coffee-table books on the lower shelves, and novels, mostly Bangla, on the ones above. The only contemporary thing that stood out was a bit of specially made metal shelving that sat among the bookshelves – a kind of a music tower, on top, a shelf each for records and cassettes, then a much taller shelf for a Sony 1/4" reel-to-reel, a Pioneer amp on the shelf below, and below that a Panasonic twin-cassette deck and some fancy turntable. Flanking the tower and bookshelves were two large floor speakers of some obviously expensive foreign make.

I could see this was not a space that was used on any daily basis, but neither did it feel like the show-off living room of some rich parvenu. Everything, the paintings, the few small antique statues taken from various temples all over the country, the beautiful Kalighat woodcut of Kali surrounded by more kitschy images of the goddess, it did seem as though all of this was primarily meant to be enjoyed by just the Big Man himself.

'You don't feel the need to have a fixed home, then?'

'Quite the opposite! I feel tied down by the idea of one house. You know, last time I mentioned Shahabuddin, the Ustad? I think I learnt that from him, though he had two or three different households plus many other places where he slept at night. As he was fond of saying, "This whole sisterfucking city is my hotel!" Yes, sure, for him sometimes it was an issue of safety as well, which, with Ma's blessings is not a problem I have. I won't claim to be a gaachh-tolar Baul, no, but I do like different beds.'

'A gaachh-tolar Baul?'

'You know the Bauls, yes, our singers from the villages?'

Every Bengali knew about the Bauls, Bengal's 'traditional wandering troubadours' who had so inspired Tagore.

Ganesh nodded and continued. 'So, the Bauls are supposed to be ascetics and mendicants, with no home or possessions except for their musical instruments and a few clothes. *Supposed* to be, you understand, though almost none of them are! One of the things they say to claim simplicity is that aami toh gaachh-tolar Baul, a Baul whose only dwelling is under a tree, as in a tree-shelter Baul.'

'Ganesh-da, were you yourself... ever... in a position like that? With only a tree above your head?'

The Big Man released a wide grin. 'See, this is why I like you. The Bauls have another favourite word to describe themselves, again more in intention than reality, and it is nikhaalosh, meaning totally open and without subterfuge. Now that I know you a little bit, I can say our Saki is nikhaalosh!' He got up and patted my shoulder. 'Come, another drink? Now, beer? Vodka and lime? Since you are so interested in stories, let's take a look at some of the stuff this old man has gathered in his vanity.'

'As you can see, all these are normal pictures for a bhadra home in Kolkata.' Ganesh quickly took me past a set of paintings by Jamini Roy, two beautiful landscapes by Gopal Ghose, a tiny, strangely haunting tempera of a boy and toy boats by someone called Ganesh Pyne 'who lives in a hole in north Kolkata'. Above a large sofa, there was one of Husain's long rectangles of prancing horses. As soon as I saw it, Elko's voice started sneering in my ear: 'You know how some poisonous insects bury their eggs in different hiding places? The insect dies but the eggs sprout independently, carrying on the foul work... A good description of Picpisso, don't you...'

'These, I think will interest you most.' He ceremoniously pointed to two of Elko's chappal canvases hung between antique, glass-fronted cupboards of dark, polished wood.

The painting on the left was probably among the last he made of this series, and in it you could see the cascade of footwear as though you were directly above it. The slippers and some shoes were small in the frame, a melee of strange, lost punctuation marks, all about the same size, except for a few tiny ones breaking the pattern here and there. Painted in shades of yellow ochre, brown and bright yellow, all these stood out against a background of flat, bright vermilion.

The painting on the right was signed in his earlier style – *KL '52* – and here Elko was still trying to deal with the same subject but realistically, almost like a too-alive still life. Here, the chappals receded away from the bottom of the image, fighting with each other, their size diminishing in perspective, sometimes forming small mounds of indistinguishable leather. The rendering was violent, drawn more than painted in rough black strokes, the road below the footwear a damaged grey-brown, interrupted by implosions of marigold flowers. Two very different paintings but clearly made by the same hand, by the same pair of eyes looking at the same thing, but in very different frames of mind.

'You know, I bought the one on the right from that early exhibition in Paris, and the other one he sent me a few years later, when I asked through Niru-di if there were any more on the same theme. I think your Miss Imogen brought it on one of her trips. But since I hung them together, I haven't been able to part them. I couldn't ever look at just one of them on its own. It felt like sundering a pair of long-lost siblings.'

I thought of the two or three hours he spent following Rabindranath's cortège being distilled over the years in Elko's mind. The first drawings were made in 1941 itself, the last paintings of the series between '57 and '58, the image almost like a metronome in his mind, constant yet shifting, even as he produced very different sorts of work.

'Ganesh-da, I would agree these are siblings, but they are not twins, not even unidentical ones, if you see what I mean?'

'Of course, yes, exactly!' Ganesh nodded as though we were keeping time to the same bit of music. 'He was clearly thinking of some things while painting the first, and maybe connected but very different things when making the later one.'

There was a soft clatter of plates and serving vessels where the bearer was laying out lunch. Ganesh sat at the head of the table, with me just to his right.

'I hope you like Chinese? This is nothing fancy, I just got the driver to pick it up from Jimmy's Kitchen at the other end of Theatre Road. Have you ever eaten there? They know exactly what I like, so no extra jhaal except in the specified dishes, and they avoid that wartime ajino powder the Chinese places put in everything.'

Ganesh-babu served me before helping himself. He brought the first forkful to his mouth, stopped and put it back on his plate. When I met his eyes, the genial mask was gone. There was no threat, I felt no sense of fear, but suddenly there was nothing between us except what he was about to say.

'Saki. This project of yours. This... what one can call *labour of love*,' he pronounced the words carefully in English. 'It's not only about analysis by scholars, is it? From what I can tell, what's equally important is that you are also putting together stories, isn't it? At least for yourself? The stories Kedar Lahiri was trying to tell in his paintings, yes?'

'Well, as they say in English, I'm just trying to join the dots.'

'Meaning?'

'You know, like in those children's puzzles where you have the numbered dots? And you have to draw lines in a sequence that follows the numbers, and a shape emerges?'

'Ah, yes, understood!' Ganesh-babu began to eat without looking at his plate. I could see his eyes were trained at the middle of the table, beyond the serving bowls, as though he was trying to work something out. 'But... actually what you are doing, while you are finding out facts about Kedar-babu, you are also using your imagination to connect the lines, because not all the dots have numbers, yes?'

This was undeniably true, yes.

'And, in this process, you are also joining *other* sets of dots, about the other people you've come across in the story. And the shapes that emerge sometimes overlap, don't they?'

As I nodded, I found myself thinking of Elko in the field near Saint Ant, desperately trying to coax petrol out of a tin to burn some of the overlaps. Outside the air-conditioned fortress, the monsoon rain began to parade across the windows.

Waving his fork, Ganesh-babu urged me eat. 'For instance, it's completely natural that you're also curious about your mother's younger days, when she was with the Party? I'm sure she can't have told you everything?'

'No, and she probably never will.'

'And similarly, the last time we met, you asked me a lot about this Gopal Kundu. It seems you want to know the story of this Gopal fellow, isn't it? Even if you can't know everything, you are curious to know some of the elements, am I right?'

'Yes, that would not be—'

'Not be incorrect, yes? So many stories. Some I can tell you, others I can't. Others will no doubt give you other narratives. But what occurs to me is that perhaps you can write a golpo, a story. Perhaps, after you finish this project about Kedar-babu, you could even write some sort of a novel.'

I put aside my cutlery and found my proper voice. 'Ganesh-da, I'm not a novelist. I'm an architecture historian, with a specialization in modern, twentieth-century architecture.'

'No, it's very understandable you would say that. However, just as with Kedar Lahiri, and maybe also with Niru-di, maybe you can imagine some things about this Gogai-Gopal, maybe... *join the dots*, or maybe we can...meaning with my help maybe you can put together a *story*,' he says, using the English word. 'Though I prefer the Bangla word *upanya*s to your English *novel*.'

I couldn't help laughing as I pointed to the bookshelves filled with Bangla novels. 'Ganesh-da, our writers have written so many novels about that time, about the famine, the Hindu–Muslim riots in Calcutta, about Partition and what came after. I can see you've also read them. So what new stuff can one add?' I immediately regretted the vehemence in my voice, but I saw the Big Man was amused. He shook his head like a naughty boy who'd been caught out.

'Actually, Saki, I only read for my work. The novels, I actually get people to come in and read to me, young actors who need some money, people like that, and I just sit in my chair, close my eyes and listen.'

'Oh, I see. But in any case, you've absorbed most of them, am I right?'

'Yes, yes, of course. Not as many as I would have liked, but enough. So, yes, we know those stories about that time in detail, but now I need something new, something that's outside and around that famine and Partition, onek kichu achhey jaar kono noksha nei, there are many unmapped corners of that time, something that fills in some other gaps, I don't know...'

I felt I had no choice but to ask the question directly. 'You mean you don't see your story in there, in any of those books? Or, say, Gopal Kundu's story?'

The Big Man added some more pork to the noodles on his plate. 'I don't see Gopal, I don't see me, Ganesh, I don't see your mother, I don't see Kedar Lahiri, I don't see goras like Imogen... Maybe we were not important to the main story, but maybe as a side thing... what do you call it?'

'A frame? Like these paintings have frames?'

'More like *side plate*, no, I mean *side dish*,' again he inserts the English words, 'I was going to say *main dish* of famine and *side dish* of connected stories.'

The words slipped out before I could stop myself. 'I would say... only Gopal is worthy of a novel, perhaps. Or Gopal and Ganesh together.'

The Big Man shook his head firmly. 'No... no, I don't agree at all.'

I thought it spooky that he'd sensed there were so many half-written scraps sitting in my flat in Paris. 'Anyway, so how would a novel about Gopal begin, then? Or, no, let's say a novel that *begins with* Gopal? Where would it start?'

Ganesh-babu looked down at his plate. Then a strange little smile pushed his head up.

'Perhaps it could begin at the railway station.'

'So, Howrah?'

'No, Sealdah Station. At the very beginning of 1943.'

VIA SEALDAH

It's strange to feel the air between his legs. As he gets off the tram, a cold draft lifts his lungi more than he has calculated, briefly exposing his knees and thighs. Surely anyone can tell from his legs that he's not a nedey? As he jabs down on his lungi, he understands there is no sense to that thought at all, just his fear whispering nonsense in his ear, there is no difference between Muslim legs and Hindu legs or between the legs of Bengali boys of different religions, it's not as if he's trying to impersonate a Markin, a gora or a hobshi, with their pillar-like limbs. As he moves away from the jangle of trams, he finds his left hand still right between his legs, holding down the lungi as he walks. Surely this will give him away to some experienced cockroach who can tell cutpricks who are at home in their checked lungis from some Hindu idiot pretending to be a Mohammedan?

'We should have got you snipped when you first came as a boy!' Ustad reaching for Gopal's cock, a cloth in his hand. 'A sisterfucking day like this was bound to sisterfucking come with a brain-diseased goatfucker like you, and it would have saved us so much trouble!' The fingers grip him through the cloth. 'Now *hold* it while I do this, you assfucked motherfucker! You're not with one of your assfucking cockheads, so hold it yourself before it disappears up your belly and becomes a cunt! We don't have all day!'

As Gopal traps his fast-shrinking crotch-comma, Ustad also grips the diminishing tumescence through the cloth and expertly flips back Gopal's foreskin, right back, as far as it will go, causing, not undeliberately, a lot of pain. 'Now give it to me.' Ustad holds out a hand and Aurangzeb smears a gob of dark, sticky liquid into his palm. The old man deftly transfers the gluey stuff to the cloth and rolls it around the upturned flesh until the exposed pink of the underskin is covered and the shaft is a dark, even colour and the glans standing out bright pink – to all appearances the small, flaccid, circumcised member of a diminutive Muslim peasant from Khulna or Mymensingh.

'Allah is also great in his wisdom. You Hindu assfuckers can disguise yourself in these bad times, but what is a poor, devout Mussulman to do? It's not as if we can stitch on some extra skin, is it?' Ustad works on the penis for a while longer, making sure the foreskin is now pasted down. Then, three different kinds of disgust still fighting for his face, with Aurangzeb pouring the water, he soaps and washes his hands over the side of the boat. 'Listen, Gogai. This will only be enough for a cursory look, you understand, and not if some chief superintendent wants to personally give you some hand-joy. So, no fiddling with it in excitement if you see someone's pretty cock, and no sticking it into some chicken or baby goat, yes? And avoid putting any water on it. For the next four days, until you get to the place, this is what you piss with and that's all, and that also, not too often!'

Gopal feels for the jhola holding a few extra clothes and adjusts it to make sure it crosses comfortably across his shawl. Putting his hands under the shawl, he feels the two pockets of his kurta, checking against a mental list that he has everything. Three little bundles of money, distributed between kurta pockets and the waist-roll of his lungi. In his right pocket, a small cloth pouch with a little cardboard rectangle – the train ticket that someone has already bought for him earlier that day. In his left pocket, money knot and a packet of bidis and a matchbox. He desperately wants a proper cigarette, but the Charminars are gone, as is the lighter the American gave him, taken away and replaced by a stinging slap. 'Bullets, lighters, what *else* have you had shoved up your backside by these Markin pimps?' More than not having a weapon, he misses the voluminous pockets of his trousers – it's as if he's been cut off from below the waist except for the pain around his genitals, a burning that seems increased by the absence of underpants. 'You're not sisterfucking Laad Linlithgow that you would wear kachchas! You're not Gopal or Gogai any more, remember *Gogai is dead*! You're a chutiya cutprick going home to his fields where he's used to watching out for snakes trying to bite off his nunu.' The one concession Ustad has allowed are the old leather chappals. 'You could have bought them on your last trip to the city, I suppose.' No longer used to being barefoot, this has been the one relief. Jostling through the crowd, his left shoulder and upper arm hurt far more than his cock. That bastard Miraj was strong and the shoulder was badly bruised where it had been slammed against the godown wall, but Ustad's spy in Lalbazar has said there is no way the police would know this.

According to the spy, Gopal's police file says they are looking for a *short, dark, stockily built Bengali (Hindu) of about twenty-eight... treat as highly dangerous, expert with knife, knows how to shoot, speaks Bangla and Hindustani, with some small fluency in English*. The file also describes a small scar on the right temple, a fiction that has been woven in by the spy manipulating various informers. The name on the file is not Gopal Kundu but Gogai Sheel, with two additions in brackets below: *[a.k.a Pocket Gogai] [NB: not same as Gopal Pantha?]*

As Ustad had recounted this, a rare thing had occurred. At the mention of 'expert with knife', Aurangzeb began to shake, silently and uncontrollably, eyes screwed shut, his teeth in a rictus. Seeing the alarm on Gopal's face, Ustad grinned. 'Watch this while you can, not many people have seen it. Aurangzeb only laughs once in every ten years.' Ustad then slapped Gopal on the shoulder of the uninjured arm. 'It's good, Gogai! The bad thing is the gun, Madhai and the four fuckers dead, and the stored rice they found means the case has gone to the CID and maybe even army intelligence people. The good thing is they've got things half right, and therefore worse than fully wrong! Fully wrong, they would have understood quickly and started again. But now they may just confuse themselves. The name Gopal is correct but they're confusing you with that Bowbajar butcher Gopal Pantha who is built like an ox! *Pocket* Gogai! Must be what some of the boys call you! What you and the boys don't know is one of the most dangerous ships in the navy is a pocket battelsheep, which, for all your assfuckery, is what you are! Pocket Gogai, my pocket battelsheep!' The old man then put an amulet around Gopal's neck. 'This is all the way from Ajmer! Maybe if you show some faith, then Salim Chishti will see you through to the other side!'

Gopal looks up and sees the clear winter sky above the station pockmarked with barrage balloons. Ustad had described ports where each warship has its own cluster of barrage balloons to make it difficult for the enemy hawai jahaj to come in and bomb it. Looking at these odd, white, swollen breasts that yield no milk, Gopal feels no sense of a protective umbrella. Looking right, he sees the two taller, five-storey buildings on the road, each with an anti-aircraft gun on the roof. Since the raids over the last few days, everyone has developed a habit of glancing up at the sky every now and then to make sure that all is clear before embarking on journeys. Even though they are supposed to trust the sirens, no one does.

The large sign across the front of the big, slanting tin roofs says 'Sealdah Main Station'. Gopal finds himself checking it and checking again, he who would normally know Howrah or Sealdah blindfolded, just from the sound of how the jhurrie-garries were differently ranged at each station. With a small jolt, he realizes he's reading English, fluently, without thought, and not just the big English of the sign but also the smaller notices and advertising billboards. When he'd first arrived into the Everything about eight years ago, arrived at this very same Sealdah, these signs had frightened him. Pictures he could sort of understand, but could he? Did they mean what he thought they meant, or was the code something laid down by the words, the impenetrable march of bafflingly different letters and bunched up words? As he approaches the steps to the main entrance, he reminds himself he's an illiterate farmer boy from Mymensingh. Ustad, he of unending cunning, mindful of even this – Gogai, don't make the mistake, even in your eyes, of being able to read anything at all.

He rakes the crowd at the entrance for police, both uniformed cockroaches and plainclothes mamas. He checks for plainclothes goras too, seguriti goras, this new species of danger, because of the war, now hanging around where you would never previously find a white man. Two normal policemen at the bottom of the steps, busy keeping the horse carriages moving, one more, whistle in mouth, deployed for the civilian cars and taxis. On top of the stairs, three slashes of khaki, military officer goras looking at an open file and gesturing at the station. Those porters, red tunics squatting near the side-gate, were they… no, all normal, genuine. That man selling roasted sweet potatoes, standing under the Army Recruitment poster? No, Gopal remembers him, he has been here for years, always here, every winter. Just inside the station, to one side, another thick squiggle of khaki against the grey station floor, soldiers, Indian, sitting on a rolled-out jute mat, fresh-looking Kumaoni mountain boys, stupid as the day they were born, no danger. A ticket collector in his almost-clean white uniform, no problem, not him.

Away from the sunlight, it's chilly inside the main hall. As his sight dims, Gopal's nose takes over. The pervading smell is of steam-engine metal cooking in coal heat, at the sides of it a faint intertwining of piss and phenol, then somewhere out of sight a pile of rotting flowers and puja leaves like at the cremation ghats but muted in the cool winter air, then strong fresh paint where some railings near the platforms have been repaired, followed by a whiff of hot ginger-spiced tea. As his eyes adjust, he can see blast walls of sandbags, strategically placed to protect important station offices and the first-class waiting room. He waits for a minute or two before wandering up to the board where the daily departures are listed. Having learnt to look at maps, he knows that the routes on this side of the Hooghly all fan out eastwards from Sealdah, a man-made spiderweb laid over the god-made one of rivers, all the way to Assam.

Black Ingreji letters against the ivory white of the board: Khulna 4.30, Krishnapur, Chittagong Exp., Siliguri, Surma Mail, the one he needs – Goalundo 11.15, leaving in half an hour from platform 5 – then Assam Mail, Barisal Exp., Lalgola Ghat, Amnura, and again, his heart tugging as he reads the name, Khulna 19.30. He makes himself gawp at the board, scratches his head once, turns to a clerk-type babu and asks about a different train in his best Khulna village accent, 'Babu, mui Borishaal zaabu, gaadi kawtaay ektu bolen?' Babu, I'd like to go to Barisal, can you tell me when the train is? 'Half past one,' the clerk reassures him kindly, 'you've got some time yet.'

Gopal finds himself surreptitiously looking over the clerk, as he would a mark in the old days. Oiled-down black hair, neatly parted, spectacles with thick black frames, cheap woollen jacket, around his neck a muffler, sweater, under the sweater a kurta, below the kurta a dhuti. A man trying to look older than he is, as all these file-shuffling babus do. A cheap watch on his left wrist. The wallet probably in the inside pocket of his jacket. But clearly carrying whatever is valuable to him in the little attaché case gripped in his left hand, maybe jewels for his daughter's wedding, or something precious like that. On his feet, thick socks, shoes, not new, but in which the man is not fully comfortable, something that could come in useful were he to… '*For army personnel, for army personnel! Special train number ASM 26 will depart from platform 8 at 11.45 hours! Train number ASM26, platform 8 at 11.45 hours!*' Gopal pulls himself back from the thinking that would seamlessly slide into the old physical process and moves away from the clerk babu.

Promoshun. Promotion, as he now knows it's spelt. There is an opposite word, Gopal can't remember it, dim-something, but that's how he now feels. As if he's been kicked in the direction opposite from promotion. He tries to pull back from this line of thought as well – Aurangzeb seeing him off, a street away from where he caught the tram: 'I don't understand why Ustad didn't kill you.' The Pathan's tone almost friendly. 'I would have killed you. You're lucky, but now don't do anything stupid, keep your luck close to you. Khudaw hawfiz.'

There's a monkey-man rattling his little drum, walking along the station hall, three monkeys in filthy little frocks and tunics following him, leashed by thin rope. There's a baby monkey on the man's shoulder, no leash. What chance would the baby have if the bandar-walla dressed him in some costume and sent him on his way into the station rafters? How long before some wild monkey got it, or a kite or a dog?

He forces himself to look around, just as a peasant would. There are far fewer goras at this station than at Howrah, he notes. His eyes drift over the snack sellers, the newspaper kiosk, the recruitment pimps standing around with their placards in Bangla urging young men to join the army to fight for the nation. Scattered around the station, he sees some strange-looking cops in a different uniform. Most of the men much darker than the Calcutta cockroaches, but Indians, not African-hobshi or anything, a red topi instead of the usual blue one, khaki shorts and not blue as in Calcutta. He wonders briefly why they are here, calculates it has something to do with this crazy war and nothing at all to do with him, and carries on his survey as he meanders in the direction of platform 5.

The scale of Sealdah is much smaller than Howrah, the fluted iron pillars in the main hall thinner, from another time, and there are fewer, far more temporary-looking tin roofs over only some of the platforms. But he can also see construction going on to the right, on the southern side, as if someone is planning a bigger wedding for this station. A few platforms roped off, no trains there, new stuff being put in place. He can see coal fires burning in the open hatches of the round black cylinders that look like baby steam engines, workers huddled around the hatches for warmth.

He hasn't been to Sealdah for a while, and there is something odd about the people at the station today. It takes him a while to put his finger on it. It's almost eleven o'clock, and by now the usual morning rush into the city should be over. This is the point when the volume of the arriving crowd and the leaving crowd should start to even out, the overall press easing sharply. As a young pickpocket first starting at this station, the seniors in the gang would always take the first morning rush and he had to learn to use the clash of bodies in the counterflow of passengers between 10.30 and 12.30.

Today is different. After the bombing raids, he has heard that people are once again swarming Howrah Station, trying to head west out of the city. But here, it's different. There seem to be hardly any passengers leaving, but the flow of people coming in is regular, unabated, wrong. He realizes the influx is being thickened by many villagers among the normal passengers, sometimes just groups of men, sometimes whole families carrying everything they own, a slightly hunted look in all their eyes, as if there is something far more fearsome than Japanese bombers chasing after them.

For a moment, he has a vision of a crazy drainage system, where a stream of the goras and the wealthy are flowing away, siphoning themselves away through Howrah, while, just behind them, another darker flood fills into the city from the east, via Sealdah.

Every now and then, without being obvious, Gopal contrives to turn his head to look behind him. It's a technique he's perfected over his years on the street, but hasn't had to use of late – an invisible fly buzzing in his ear, which he brushes away while flicking his head almost around, a crick in his shoulder which he grips with the opposite hand while snapping his head to release the pain, a push from the oncoming crowd, or negotiating a group that won't budge from their path, that spins him around almost 180 degrees, but completely naturally. Even during these manoeuvres, he never quite looks back fully, his flicked glances don't focus on the people behind him, he's actually looking for patterns, for something – a face, a shirt or a pair of feet – that stays oddly constant in the shifting picture. Each glance though, is like an added piece in a jigsaw puzzle, building up semi-complete pictures of possible chasers or quarry. As he reaches platform 5, Gopal has picked up two crinkles of worry at two different points of the compass behind him.

Behind him to his right, a tall porter who doesn't seem to know exactly where he's going, changing course all the time, making a meal of balancing a suitcase on his head that doesn't seem heavy enough, his face somehow too healthy for his profession, not dried-up enough by regular labour in the relentless cold weather of the last few days. Well wide of the porter, in the left quadrant, a short, bald, fat man in coat-pant, a man who seems engrossed in making notes in a little notebook, but who nevertheless seems to have no problem maintaining a constant distance behind Gopal.

Observations start to coalesce. His feet tell him to pick up speed, but Gopal fights the instinct. Don't run before you're chased. Don't invite the chase. If they've got you, they've got you, but they may not be sure of you yet. They may yet lose interest, there are many idiots among them, give them the chance. Whatever you do, in these situations it's always good to be ready early and move late.

A simple test. Stay still for a few moments and see how the water goes around you. Then see where the water around you goes.

He changes direction away from platform 5, where he's been heading. There are no trains on the adjacent tracks of platforms 4 and 3, and he makes his way to platform 3, which is just crowded enough to be useful but not with so many people that they would get in the way if he needed to run. There is a water stand with several clay pots, and he chooses a space between that and a group of passengers waiting with their luggage – from there he will still see what's coming but the route to him won't be straightforward. Looking around casually, he forces himself to squat down, tucking a bit of his lungi between his legs, nervous about his exposed glans touching the floor. He pretends to go into a fully relaxed squat, but under his lungi he is balanced on the balls of his feet, ready to spring up and go.

On the other side of the tracks, across the next platform, he can see his train chugging in from the sidings, its empty carriages cleaned and ready. Relief mixed with anxiety, he notes there don't seem to be too many passengers for the Goalundo Express. His heart thumping, he reaches into his pocket for a bidi. As he strikes the match, he sees the tall porter walking away, suitcase still on head, looking straight ahead but arguing now – red porter tunic vs bright blue sweater – having words with a passenger that Gopal hasn't spotted. The fat notebook man, Gopal sees, has turned and is hurrying away from his platform, waving at someone in the shadows of the main hall. Gopal's heels come down, and he's thankful even for the acrid taste of the bidi. He has eaten well before leaving, but now he feels sharply hungry, a specific hunger, for Khulna wedding food... A boy's hand giving him half of a scoured coconut shell, 'Ney!' Take! He dips the shell into the undulating boat, into the meat gravy, and brings it to his mouth, succulent bits of meat, bone-shards sharp against his gums, the deep black-brown alchemy of spices, marrow, liver, innards and almost-melted hooves. The faint smell of monsoon rot at the edge of the river lagoon.

He shakes his head, trying to clear it. A pair of winter birds, he doesn't know the name, swoop by low, almost across his face, before climbing to land on the thin iron girders supporting the sloping roof of the main hall. The birds are silhouetted against a brightness he hasn't noticed previously, a hatch in the high roof, open now to the winter sky. Also silhouetted against the light blue is a figure, obviously crouching on a landing outside, a man looking down into the station with a pair of binoculars, looking, Gopal is suddenly sure, directly at himself.

The hair on his spine finally tickles. It's a sign he's learnt to trust, Ma Kali warning him of danger.

Making sure he doesn't at all look as though he's hurrying, Gopal gets up and begins to move, using a passing porters' cart piled high with jute sacks to efface himself. As he walks along the platform, he tries to keep an eye on the figure in the hatch. To look at the man again, he has to allow himself to be seen as well, which he does briefly. The square of sky is empty, the binocular man is gone. As Gopal moves down the platform, the questions assault him, creating panic. How long before the man gets down from the roof? What's the distance to the end of the platforms and the maze of tracks and sidings beyond? Too far, and besides, he knows there are now guards at the end of each platform. Where to go? He looks over at the mess of construction work on the southern platforms, again too far, but probably his best chance. Should he run or wait? As if in reply to his question, the curtain of normal station noise is pierced by two sharp whistles, then two shouts, one command, one answer. The creatures erupt from nowhere. Cops in normal uniforms, plainclothes mamas in all costumes, other types that he can't quite place, all pelting towards him. With a sinking confirmation, he sees the tall porter and blue sweater coming straight towards him, suitcase clearly abandoned, the fat man he can't see yet. Gopal looks around and understands there is actually nowhere to run. He's at the edge of the platform, no helpful train docked, and there are now uniform cockroaches jumping down on to the empty tracks from the other side. Briefly, he loses his mind. No Khulna, no Tangail, but the bed of an ice block at Lalbazar. He wonders if he'll betray Ustad. He wonders if the noose will scratch his throat. He wonders if it will hurt when the trapdoor opens under his feet.

It's the same panic he felt on the day that Robi Thakur died last year, when skipping from boat to boat he saw Aurangzeb and Gaurangzeb on Ustad's launch, when he almost turned and ran, but didn't. As he moves to slide his feet out of his slippers, from the corner of his eye he sees something besur, something that doesn't fit the tune. He realizes that the clerk-babu from the departure board is not far from him, that, for some reason, the man is doing the same thing as himself but a couple of beats ahead. Gopal sees the clerk's feet slide out of his shoes. He sees the man's hand hike up his carefully ironed dhuti.

As the clerk begins to sprint, his glasses bounce awkwardly on his nose and his suitcase makes a funny knocking noise. His own feet now fused to the platform, Gopal sees the man streaking towards the jumble of new construction while fiddling desperately with the clasps of his attaché case. Three mamas pound past, going around Gopal as if he's a pillar. The clerk's glasses fly off, land in the path of running boots, and are crushed. The man jumps over the low rope demarcating the construction area and barges through the huddled workers to reach the hatch of an open cauldron. His suitcase is open now, and there is a bundle in his hand that he flings into the fire just before his hunters reach him. Then he turns and spreads his arms to protect the hatch. It is so pitifully futile, Gopal almost wants to laugh. The big porter reaches the clerk first, and just lifts him up and away from the cauldron. As the men swarm around the clerk, he goes down, disappearing from sight. Gopal can see a gora in a planter's outfit, he can't be sure if it's the same man from the roof, yelling instructions as two men run up with sticks they have procured. As the gora shouts, the men jab their sticks into the fire, trying to fish out what the clerk has thrown in.

There's a hubbub around the station, people staring, a few running forward to see what's going on. Gopal begins to feel cold relief wash over him and, at the same time, something blocking that relaxation. He feels something that he can't believe he's feeling. The left pocket of his villager's kurta is getting gradually lighter, the pocket in which he has his bidis and one of his small bundles of money. Could one of the passing cockroaches have torn open his kurta pocket? Before he can stop himself, he has grabbed the little hand just under his pocket, and he's twisting it to cause maximum pain. As the kid cries out, Gopal whirls around and slaps the little fucker hard, twice, on the same side of the face, catching the nose, drawing blood.

'Bokkkachhodaa! Khankir bachha!' Goatfucking son-of-a-whore, pick my pocket will you, you bastard? 'Amar pocket marbi, haramzada?'

The bundle of money, the bidis and the matchbox fall to the ground, and Gopal accidentally steps on the matchbox, scattering the sticks. This sends him into further fury, and he slams his hand into the top of the boy's head, his open palm meeting hard skull through the dirty, matted hair.

Gopal allows the boy to stumble away, spitting red snot. He bends down to pick up his things and find his slippers. 'Khankir goo tui!' Whoreturd, you! The boy is screaming at him from what he thinks is a safe distance. 'Tor putki maari!' I'll fuck your ass, he screams through his tears, his voice muffled by the arm he's using to wipe his nose. 'Tui baanda ke bey, nedey?' Who the fuck are, you cutprick? 'Katua shala, pulish ke daakbi? Daakbi toh daak! Eikhaane aajke mamara shob Hindu!' Fucking cutprick, are you going to call the cops? Call them! Try it! Today the cops here are all Hindu!'

Gopal turns and begins walking quickly to reach platform 5. As he looks behind him, he can see the boy has been joined by a little girl. Both boy and girl are chanting 'Nedey, nedey, nedey!' Cutprick, cutprick, cutprick! As the girl jumps up and down, she has her hands cupped around her eyes, as if she's looking through a pair of binoculars.

DINNER AT FIRPO'S

'Sheyaldar! That was Lalbazar on the line! They've got him finally! They've got Tiger! At Sheyaldar Station!'

'Oh, good show!'

'Tiger?'

'Yes, Tiger! Finally!'

'I thought Tiger was that Joetee Basu chap, that commie bugger, committee member? Surely the Reds aren't—'

'No, no, no, man, do keep up! This is the *Congress* Tiger! They're not very inventive with their code names, our Indian friends.'

'Oh, oh yes, sorry.'

'Yes, this one's a bit younger than Basu, actual name Shoodip Butt-a-chariot, underground since '41. We've been chasing him since May that year. He is – *was* – the kingpin of their East Bengal courier network, also handled some of the safe houses in Dacca and Chittagong. Slippery as hell, made us look like fools, but now we've got him!'

Lambert has heard Farquhar in the next room smacking down the phone receiver and crying out in triumph. The Domestic Section chaps have been highly strung for days now, chasing all sorts, and he tries not to pay attention to the self-congratulatory shouting.

The latest photos show that the rail tracks west of Arrah are a mess, and this despite Gloucester patrols having strafed and chased off three separate teams of saboteurs in the last ten days.

'The buggers just don't give up, do they?' Deyton has laid the pictures on Lambert's desk as though showing him a plate of poisoned food. 'They're managing to get through at night now, clearly.'

'Clearly. Damn them.'

There's a chuckle from Todd-Cartwright as he looks up from his desk. 'You do know there are memos circulating, Jeremy, suggesting that the Gloucesters might be better deployed for the air defence of the city rather than ineffectively strafing our own subjects? Insurrectionary though the bastards may be?'

'Really? Yes... I can just see our doughty biplanes bringing down the Sallys as they whizz past, leaping upon 'em as the Hurris pant behind.'

'You can sneer, but that's a serious question heading in our direction, so be prepared.'

Now that some semblance of war seems to have arrived at the aerial gates of the city, the mood in the Ochterlony Suite has, bizarrely, shifted to almost celebratory. The new spring in Currie's step is almost unbearable, the turgid snap of his instructions painful in Lambert's ears. January's gift of the best weather of the year rules coolly paramount over all the contradictory news from the front. For Todd-C, Lambert and Deyton, these are again days of unspoken vindication and quiet triumph. Their continuing assessment has been that, from their current airfields, the Japanese will not be able to inflict any serious damage on Calcutta. Exactly as they've predicted, these first few raids have shown that the enemy's light bombers are at the very limit of their range by the time they arrive above the city, forcing them to drop their loads quickly and haphazardly while running the gauntlet of Hurricanes and anti-aircraft fire.

Like the gradual shift of an invisible tectonic plate, the thinking in Eastern Command's intelligence circles has changed over the last month or so, the collective transformation becoming apparent only now. Lambert and his recce team have had an important contribution to this. The four new Harvard reconnaissance aircraft promised by Goodsugar have arrived in November. Most of Lambert's days now go in dealing with the 'morning post': the Harvards head for Burma just before dawn, returning around 11 a.m., bringing back drums of film shot with far better aerial cameras than Lambert has ever used before.

These startlingly sharp new pictures clearly show that the supplies to Jap forces in Burma are just enough for holding the territory, and General Yamashita is in no position to launch any kind of an assault on

Assam and the north-east in the near future. As for the landings feared for further down the eastern coast of the peninsula, it has become clear through other intelligence sources that the Imperial forces have their work cut out grappling with the Americans in the Pacific. Across 1942, invasion fear in the locals and panic in the British administration had emptied the populations of Madras, Vizag and several southern coastal towns. Now that the probability of attack has reduced, these people are slowly trickling back. In any case, East Bengal has been made as safe from invasion as is possible: the defensive lines are in place in Assam and Imphal, the province has been denuded of all usable rivercraft, boats and even bicycles, and there are even operations planned behind enemy lines in Burma itself.

Over December, Lambert's dreams of assault, debacle and imminent death have decreased in both vividness and frequency, now appearing only once in a while, like the squeak of perverse chalk on the blackboard of his sleeping psyche. On 28 December, when the wail of the air-raid sirens starts again, Lambert realizes something. The damn dumb waiter has been silent for many weeks now. It's almost as though that semi-human wailing was a sort of precursor to this very real howling that warns of actual bombs about to come down.

As far as the relieving of other tensions goes, since the monsoon Lambert has now actually visited Madame Toussaint's a few times. The results have been mixed. On the one hand, the immediate backlog of pent-up desire has found efficient dispatch; on the other hand, his obsession with the Bengali beauty from Firpo's and New Empire has grown almost unbearable, to the point where he now keeps looking out for her in every, cinema, bar and restaurant he visits. Side by side with this fixation, his craving for local food has also grown rampant. Though Deyton, sharp as a razor blade, has picked up some of this, Todd-Cartwright is obviously the only one in whom Lambert has been able to confide.

The winter season has brought with it its own local culinary seductions, either things that are simply not available in the hot months, or food that is best enjoyed when it's not sweltering. At some point around the local Goddess celebrations – what they call Durga

Puja – Lambert has begun to keep a secret journal of the different kinds of food he's been coming across. Puja food. Puris with pea-mash inside. Paya – hooves cooked in a broth. Nihari – another kind of bone broth. Biryani – this infernally delicious rice and meat. A bewildering variety of local fish dishes. Nolen gur sandesh – these moulds of soft cottage cheese sweetened with fresh date-palm jaggery. In the Chinese quarter, chicken feet, chilli pork and the irresistible crispy duck in unctuous sweet-and-sour sauce. The strong awareness that all this was being produced and consumed despite the huge shortages all around. That only those with extra money could partake of this ever-changing feast.

Todd-C waits for Deyton to leave his desk before coming over to Lambert.

'Jeremy? Do you fancy dinner at Firpo's tonight, just us, obviously? My treat.'

Lambert hasn't been to Firpo's in a long while and he can't help looking up eagerly. 'What's the occasion, Alan?'

'Nothing in particular! I found myself thinking of their dollar steaks, and I've heard they've got some new cocktails. Just thought we ought to celebrate the New Year before the Nips manage to bomb the place. Unless, of course, you're too stuffed with your local nosh.'

Lambert's mood is buffeted upwards by this happy turbulence. 'Well, that's jolly kind of you, Alan! I won't say no!'

'Just as long as it doesn't bother you to go through the entrance.'

'What's happened to the entrance? I haven't been that way for some time.'

'Nothing, it's just that the last time I went, the Yank in front of me had to drag aside, you know, one of these poor devils. There are rather a lot of them on the pavement outside, and this poor bastard had just, you know, just given up the ghost. Everyone was stepping over him to get to the stairs and the bloody doorman wouldn't touch him. All rather distressing.'

ONE END OF THE WORLD

Sometimes, I just want to close my eyes and listen to whatever life happens to be reading out loud.

Here in Saint Ant, the birdcalls change in early autumn, or so Elko always said. 'They come past in April heading north, and they like the trees around here as a resting point. And the same again going the other way, in September. The little bastards start early in the morning, louder than Bangalis, and sometimes the noise is unbearable. And then, one morning, they're gone, disappeared like inspiration, and you almost miss the buggers.'

On this September day, the birds have checked into the trees, but I can also hear the sound of another itinerant visitor inside the house. Missus is back after more than a year and she walks through the place like someone visiting for the first time, a guest here for a few days, as though she doesn't know where everything is. I can hear her moving through the house without her usual clatter, using a stranger's cautious footsteps. She's sober – we haven't begun the day's drinking yet – so it's not the befuddled late-night stumbling where I'm always afraid she'll break her neck falling on something.

I got here a couple of days earlier to start up the house, and she arrived a couple of hours ago. I find her oddly shrunken, and yet the skin is somehow tighter across her face and neck, the shrinkage more to do with what she emanates than her physical appearance. I find nothing when I search for signs of illness, but then, I'm not a doctor. There's nothing she's willing to admit to, even under the most direct interrogation.

'No, Saki darling, stop. You're not cut out to be a worrywart! I'm fine, really!'

Sitting in the big room downstairs I can hear her above my head, slowly opening and shutting things in her room. After a while, I can hear her cursing softly as she starts to drag something heavy down the stairs, step by step. I go to help and find her quietly fighting an old suitcase that usually sits under her bed.

'Imo-mashi! What's wrong with you!' I fail to keep the irritation out of my voice.

'It's all right, darling, I can manage. Not quite dead yet...'

I take the case from her and bring it to the main room. "What's *in* this bloody thing? Gold ingots? Where do you want it?'

'Oh, most of it is going in the rubbish... I don't imagine you'll want my useless stuff cluttering up the place.' She finds an armchair, sitting down a touch quicker than she wants to.

'Me?' I shake my head to clear it. 'It's *your* house, in case you'd forgotten?'

'Well, yes, about that... I've missed you, of course, but I've partly come to discuss things.'

'Discuss what, exactly?'

She holds a lighter in her hand as she looks for her cigarettes. 'I suppose you'll say it's too early for a drink?'

'It is, and you know it.' I get her fags from the dining table. 'You know you can actually talk to me without a drink?'

'Now, now, don't you get cross with your old Mashima now.'

'Well, stop with all this old Mashima nonsense for starters. That'll help!' I light my own cigarette. 'I'll make us a G&T before lunch. One.'

'One!'

'Go on then, discuss what?'

She raises her shoulders and drops them, gathering herself before she starts: to state the obvious, she's getting on now – almost sixty-three – there's a lot of stuff taking up her time back in England. Who knows how long she has and she'd like to arrange everything well in time so she can live the rest of her life peacefully. She's always loved this house, as I know, but it just hasn't felt the same since whatshisname took himself off. It's not that she won't ever visit, not that, perhaps just not that often and, obviously, she'll continue to pay for the upkeep while she's around, god knows the maintenance is not cheap. But, basically, all said and done, as she's mentioned before she'd now really like to turn it over to me – if I wanted it, that is.

'You're not going to tell me what's actually going on, are you? Your grandmother lived into her nineties, your mother well into her eighties, what's *your* particular hurry with all this wrapping up?'

She searches for a reassuring smile, fails to find it, and continues with the lying. There's nothing to tell, darling. The usual, boring botherations of ageing, nothing out of the ordinary, but she'd like to travel to places she's never been – Africa, South America. Also, she'd love to see Niru again regularly but other than that she's done with India, she feels. She's convinced my mother to finally come to Britain next summer, has Niru told me? And I haven't answered about the house. She'd be loathe to sell it but if I really didn't want it she could put it on the market and give me the money instead. She has more than enough in England, and she's leaving the Hampstead place to the women's group and the Shelter, she hopes I won't mind...

'For god's sake! You're *not* bloody selling this place! You know I love coming here and I'm happy to keep looking after it. I'm extremely touched and all that, but I'm really not expecting... you know... Anyway Imo-mashi, look, you can decide what to do with it in ten or fifteen years when you're closer to...'

'Popping my cork?'

'Exactly.'

'Speaking of corks, where's that G&T you promised? Don't stint on the gin, there's a good chap.'

I go to the sideboard and start making our drinks. Suddenly, the touch of things, the glasses, the fridge door when I open it for the tonic and ice, the knife as I cut the lemon, the wood under the bottle of Gordon's, all of it feels foreign, as though I've lost the home I had at Missus and Elko's.

We talk, we drink, I make sure we eat, and then we go into our separate confabulations with the house.

One early morning, while photographing a bookshelf near the stairs, I move the camera right to include the mirror next to it. I'm still focusing, my hand away from the button, when I hear the sound of the shutter. There's a ghost in the mirror photographing me.

'*Fuuuck!*'

'Sorry, darling! Did I give you a fright? Sorry, sorry, sorry!' She comes and hugs me from behind, trying to stop me shaking.

'What the hell are you doing, up so early?' I remove the poke of her lens from the small of my back. 'I didn't even hear you.'

'I couldn't sleep. I just thought I'd get a few pictures of the garden in the early light. I haven't seen that for years.'

Another time, she comes in from her garden, secateurs poised, and sees me going through a file of Eva's photocopies. 'Are those Zemindear's letters to his lady love?'

'Yes. From 1944.'

'Read one or two bits out loud, won't you?'

'Why? Do we Bengalis all sound the same?'

'Not always. But yes, I sometimes hear his voice in yours, though they are very different, of course.'

I find a variation of a recurring theme:

'I had this notebook of sketches I had made on the street, and based on that the beginning of a small canvas of two little waifs with bloated stomachs whom I had sketched on Hazra Road. A couple of days later, I took the sketchbook into the garden and lit a match to it (meaning I set fire to it). As for the painting, I must confess canvases are hard come by, so I scraped off as much fresh paint from it as I could (which was not much, but the under-drawing in sepia had hardened) and painted over it a grey background for a still-life of a vase of flowers. Even when I was painting the flowers, I could still feel the bumps of the terrible drawing of the kids under my brush.'

'I used to laugh at him about this, sometimes' – she squeezes the secateurs rhythmically, snipping air – 'about him, you know, twisting himself into a rope for not being able to... I can't find that laughter now.'

'Copies of copies, or even worse than that! I've seen what others are doing, and some of them are making remarkable work, images that will become the stamp of this time long after we are gone, like Goya's 3rd of May 1808. *I happened to chance upon a communist paper at a friend's place, and there was an article, with both photographs and drawings, of the famine in the villages. The drawings are by a fellow called Chittoprasad – Paritosh knows him – about my age. They are rendered in plain black lines, no tones, presumably so that they can be reproduced better by a simple letterpress, but those black lines sear into you. And then there are the photos by this boy Janah, a lesser medium they call it, and perhaps yes, in terms of art it*

is, but in terms of what the images need to convey, there is nothing like a photograph to capture certain kinds of truth, certain kinds of reality. I see no point in merely being a background chorus to what this Chitto has achieved and it's equally stupid trying to mimic what Janah has captured. I have to find something else, and it will take time.'

'And you did, Cheddar Zemindear, you did!'

'I can just hear you saying, "Prince! You are being over-drama!" and yes, maybe you are right – or would be, if you were indeed saying this – and yet, and yet, and yet, what else can a man paint at this moment? I can admire Van Gogh all I want, but if he was here, I can tell you there would be no bloody sunflowers, no beautiful trees in orchards, no stars in the sky, no studies of the chair in his room...'

Her hands are now kneading her eyes. I can see her dress heaving under the cardigan, but she refuses to release any sound of crying. I go and put my arms around her, her head against my chest. 'Just let it out, Imo-mashi, for fuck's sake, cry properly and just let it out.'

'Properly like an Indian, you mean?' Somewhere from the mess of hair and sniffles and wool she digs out a laugh. After a while she pats me on my arm, and I go back to my chair.

'It's four years now, since he went and it's the bloody small things that set me off, not the big ones.' She lights up and straightens her hair. 'I suppose I come here for the crying. When I've got too much of it stored up in the bank, you know? But now – maybe – I hope – I'm done with the immediate grieving.' She points to the open file of letters. 'Do go on, any other bits? Has she really blanked out all the dirty bits?'

I flip back to nearest likely snippet in the file. 'There's a bit here where he mentions attending poetry sessions near Lake Market somewhere with literary-minded American soldiers and local poets, and also art discussion groups with some American fellows where they discuss Kandinsky, Picasso and Dali. *I suppose I did learn some things – it was interesting to see how differently these Yanks view the whole business of art, their knowledge mostly stopping in Europe, hardly any China or Japan and almost no knowledge of Indian art. Some of them were nice chaps, no doubt, but after I came away, I thought all this talk was useless, self-indulgent, masturbatory.* Then there's this sentence which the Attali people thought they'd covered but it shows through faintly. *It's better and far more honest that I pleasure myself thinking of you. The way you make art with your mouth and fingers on my body.'*

'Oh dear, oh dear!' Imogen is grinning now, and pretending to shudder and cover her ears. 'Is that what Americans would call hokey, or am I looking for another word?'

'Cheesy, perhaps? But look, Imo-mashi, he is only twenty... what at this point?'

'Born in 1919, so twenty-four in 1944, or not quite twenty-five... Yes, I suppose one must make allowances...' She goes into a silence for a moment. 'And who am I to be snide? I did fancy him at first myself, didn't I? For about five minutes? He was beautiful then! Luckily, that evaporated quite quickly, from both sides, I think. For which, thank god, or all your goddesses actually, they were looking after us both!'

'There's another interesting bit I found yesterday. No smut, mind you...'

'Yes, go on, we've had enough of that for today, go on.'

'So this is in 1950, well after the war, so it's quite clear what's happened to most of her family in the camps.'

'Ausch—no... where were they, er...'

'I think she writes somewhere that many were killed in Riga itself, and then a few of them were taken to a camp Kaiser-something and died while doing forced labour. So, this is Elko describing the Calcutta killings: *I don't know what you will think of this after what you've been through, what you're suffering, but I've been meaning to tell you this story for some time. A friend who was there during the '46 bloodbath in Calcutta told me that one of the strange sights around Park Circus and Wellesley Street was that the Hindus and Muslims would stop the killing at 9 a.m. sharp in the morning and retreat to their respective areas. This was to allow their Christian and Jewish neighbours to go do their morning market. So these non-combatant Jews and Christians would walk through the no man's land, buy their food and get back home by 11 a.m. or so, after which the killing would begin again. I can see you're now happy in Oakland, but if you were ever to consider it, there are other places on this earth, like Calcutta, where there's no history of hatred towards your people.'*

'Good lord, he's not proposing to her, is he?'

'Well sort of, perhaps. Keya is gone by this time.'

'But Eva is also married by now.'

'Yes... the futilitacious hoping invites extreme astoundation.'

She catches me in the kitchen one evening, the last of the day's sunlight painting a wall. I'm roasting a chicken and some vegetables for dinner, and she insists on taking several photographs. 'I'll send them to Calcutta! Let Comrade Mother see what a brilliant cook her Nagasaki has become!'

'How will you show the brilliance when it's all in the oven?'

'Oh, phsaw! Details! It's the light, it's the apron, it's the hair that belongs to Beethoven composing the Ninth!'

Later, eating the food, she's candid, as candid as three-fourths of a bottle of red can make her. 'Saki, darling? Can I say that Niru, bless her heart, is not the world's best cook?'

'You could say that, yes, and she'd agree. So would Dida.'

'And, let me hasten to add, I'm pretty terrible myself.'

'Well... not terrible, but—'

'Terrible! No need to be polite among friends – family – is there?' She eats some more of the chicken, her eyes closed, her head shaking in ecstasy. 'And Old Elko was the worst of the lot, no need for any debate there!'

'No debate at all. He was a menace in the kitchen. Most Indian men of his class tend to be.'

'Your grandma, may her soul rest in peace, and Agathe are exceptions, but otherwise you've been surrounded by...' She pops a couple of baby carrots into her mouth, and I realize I'm relieved to see her healthy appetite. She's a bit drunk already, but that doesn't stop her from eating.

'You know, good cook or not, that girl... that girl turned out to be quite something...'

'Which girl?'

'Your Ma, of course! Niru! At first, since I was older, I thought I was the, the whatchamacallit, older sister, the *didi!* But then, you know, she raced past!'

'It's not logical, but I think of both of you as being each other's didi.'

'Well, I'll tell you this much – Nirupama loves me but she's never needed me! In the sense, she has never been dependent on me! For anything, at all! Or, hardly! Whereas Zemindear and I *did* need each other, like two refugees in exile from two different countries, like... memory refugees, can one say that? Or refugees from memory, running from what we couldn't forget.'

On another day, I'm driving her to Aix where she needs to buy something and she's looking at the passing landscape. Suddenly, she starts laughing, breaking the silence.

'What?'

'Nothing, darling, nothing. No, I just remembered something... You know the first time he gave me a lift, dropped me home to Alipore, he said, "You're hardly taking me to the end of the world," but I did, didn't I, silly Larry Zemindear? I did manage to pull you to one end of the world, without meaning to, didn't I?'

A bit later in the drive, she's clearly still communing with him but remembers me. 'On his early visits, I'd drive and he'd look out at all this – once he'd got over the terror of my driving, that is. One day, he smacked the dashboard and shouted, "My landscape is here! I don't need to paint it! It frees me to paint other things!" He'd realized much earlier, of course, but he was putting it in words like a declaration... It's funny that someone like Raza comes here and gets deeper into Cézanne, while our Elko ejects him like one of these cassettes that he's done listening to.'

'Not quite ejects, I wouldn't say...'

'Well, no, but he regularly starts listening to the music of other painters.'

'It's funny you should say that, he always said Mallikarjun Mansur, the Hyderabad vocalist, was like the Bonnard of Indian classical music.'

'Yes... it was strange when he started playing that khayal stuff. On his first few visits, I think he used to wait for me to be away, but one day I came back unexpectedly, and he was singing along loudly and painting.

Caught in the act!' There's no sunlight on her side of the car, but she quickly puts on her dark glasses. 'I suppose, I suppose I liked having him here, growling at his paints, singing that strange noise of his, and I realized I missed him when he wasn't here.'

Like a child, she makes a bed with her hands on the rim of the car window and puts her neck on her hands, her head sticking out to catch the wind in her hair.

NEW MOUNTAINS

The speeding train sharpens the cold air hitting his face. Despite the sandpapering of engine-soot, it feels fresh in a way that Gopal hasn't smelled in a long time.

Outside the window, two small rivulets criss-crossing, like children running across each other's paths. A triangle of pure yellow, a mustard field, rudely bright, pulling all the sunlight from the muted winter greens of the surrounding farmland. Then the walls of a PWD compound, as if a nasty child has scratched straight, cream-coloured lines into the patchwork of fields and ponds. Inside the compound walls, sheaves of an odd colour. A strange mix of silver and black, layered like greying metal hair. Small pipes? Scrap metal? No. Gopal has to look, and look a second time, before he understands it.

Enclosed by the walls is a small lake of piled up bicycles, the dirty silver of the handlebars and wheel-spokes shining through the tangle of black frames, the whole mass dotted by the browns and reds of leather seats, like some strange lice spreading through the hair. As Gopal stares, he can see that each bicycle has a strip of cloth tied to the rear wheel, with black smudges on the cloth that look like numbers.

'You haven't been back here for a while, have you, boy?' the old man sitting across from him grins, opening an errant set of teeth into his pointed beard.

'No, I...'

'No, mian, you haven't been here for at least two months and no one from home has told you anything, am I right?'

Gopal nods, eyes flicking around to see if anyone else is listening.

'The haramzadas have taken all the cycles, each and every one of them, and bent the wheel-rings so they're useless. They've given every one receipts, promised to give them back "at a time the District Commissioner deems appropriate", but now if you're caught riding one they take it away for good! And fine you three whole rupees on top! Bastards!'

'Why?' Gopal asks, even though he suspects he knows the answer.

'Why? Why because the shahebs think the Japani are going to drop from the sky. Because the shahebs' shit is spreading loose imagining the yellow rakkhosh will come down like rain, snatch the bikes and ride them all the way to Calcutta!'

'Ride them across the rivers?'

'Rivers!' The old man starts to laugh. The sound reminds Gopal of the dumb waiter in Bonnemaison's kitchen, the one which houses the ghost. 'Wait, wait, you little know-nothing! You haven't seen anything yet! Wait until you see what else they've done!'

'What have they done?'

The old man's mouth continues to laugh in tandem with his shaking body, but his eyes have developed a glisten. Tears, but not tears of laughter. 'Let me not tell you. I'll let you see for yourself. I want to see your face when you see them.' The man wipes his eyes with the end of his lungi and hugs himself to stop the shivering. 'Allah won't forgive them... one day, one day He will make them pay. Maybe the Japani will come and make them pay.'

'Why don't you tell me?'

The old man shakes his head and looks away. 'Wait until we reach one of the big ghats, or even one of the smaller rivers. I won't have to tell you anything.'

The fields jerk past, green and brown interrupted by slabs of mustard yellow, the eye occasionally slashed by the vertical of a palm or a telegraph pole. Gopal realizes it's been a while since he's seen a human figure in the landscape. No one tilling the land, no bullock carts, no one fishing at the ponds, no women sitting outside huts, catching the winter sun as they thresh paddy, no children running alongside, racing the train.

At Sealdah, he has jumped on to the Goalundo Express at the last possible moment, just as it's begun to leave the platform. This has been more out of accident than design, but thinking back, he realizes it's what he should have done anyway, to cut down chances of being followed. In the carriage, his first instinct has been to find the darkest corner of a top berth and curl up, to efface himself as far as possible, but again Ustad's voice repeating the basics that are second nature to him anyway: 'Don't hide, don't show fear, the last person someone notices is the one standing right in front of him.' Gopal knows there's every chance there are already cops on the train, searching for him, or that they will get on at one of the stations down the line. Pocket Gogai, stocky, Hindu, scar on forehead, knife and pistol expert, not him at all, 'My name, sir? Razzak Mian, Ghiasuddin Razzak, taanti, weaver family, from Tangail. Why Kolkata, sir? To deliver some saris for an order, sir, here is the challan-bill. Taking the payment back to my Abba, sir, which is why so much money...' Ustad lands an invisible slap – 'Don't practise being Razzak Mian, if the time comes, pray to Allah for mercy and *be* this shit-eater peasant weaver Razzak with all your being!'

The extreme alternative to hiding on a top berth is to squat right next to one of the open carriage doors, but it's winter, when normal people avoid the cold air, and the train isn't crowded enough anyway. Gopal has found a seat next to a window, all the early passengers huddling away from the openings. He has wrapped his shawl tight around him, lit a bidi, and settled down for the five-hour journey to Goalundo. The train will arrive, Gopal knows, just before the evening steamers leave Goalundo's ghats in different directions, south towards Dhaka, east towards Sylhet and Assam, and north and back west through the top of Bengal towards Bihar. About this, Ustad has been grudgingly reassuring. 'It's unlikely they will expect you to head east from Calcutta. It's a real mess over there, on that side. Everybody thinking the sisterfucking Japanese are coming tomorrow. No food, people rioting for rice, all chaos, everybody heading this way.'

Leaving Sealdah, they've wound their way out of the yards past the camouflage netting and the anti-aircraft guns. Within ten minutes, Calcutta is almost behind them and they are passing through the small suburban stations just outside the city. Between the stations there are square ponds, more and more mud houses and small, newly assembled war-supply factories, their corrugated roofs yet to catch any rust. Then, abruptly, they are in the vast flat fields, heading towards Jessore and beyond.

It's only when they've slipped the last hook of the Everything that Gopal realizes he hasn't really left Calcutta since he arrived as a stowaway little boy nine years ago. There has been the occasional job in the hinterland, usually westward, beyond Howrah, but never so far out east, never so dangerously close to Khulna. As the last tin and concrete clusters fall away and the fields engulf the train, Gopal feels an old fear rising inside – his desperate mother and father finding him in Calcutta, kidnapping him and taking him home, each twisting one of his ears, with no chance of either letting go. He fights down the idiotic panic and pays attention to the real anxiety, to the Railway Police and other cops walking through the carriage at regular intervals.

Now, when they're actually cutting across the northern edge of Khulna district, Gopal finds that the box of his ancient panic is empty – there is no possibility that even his mother would recognize this twenty-two-year-old Muslim peasant boy, and even less likely she would have recognized him in his real avatar in the city, this man who now wears full pants with his shirt tucked in and a watch on his wrist, this fellow who on occasion wears Brylcreem and cologne, who understands Ingreji and bits of Phorashi.

As they move deeper towards the centre of Bengal, Gopal finds himself struggling to remember a particular phrase. In Ingreji. Something someone had said around Bonnemaison, which the chef had then translated into Phorashi. Something about 'fire'. One comes to him – now-tha-phatt-ijh-inn-tha-phaayer, now the fat is in the fire – but it's not the right one, something else, Bonnemaison mumbling about something, shaaribda-on-skeela-tome-bey something.

At some point, he dares to sleep – lightly, as he's trained himself to do when necessary. Coming awake, just before he opens his eyes he senses the train has stopped at a small platform somewhere. Close over his head he can hear an officially arrogant voice demanding names from other passengers. A litany of voices answering, mostly Muslim names but two Hindu ones: Ramaprosad Sen, Brojogopal Banik.

'You two, let's go!'

'Go where, sir?'

'Don't ask questions, get up!'

'But what is my fau—' There is the crack of a hard slap through which no one could sleep. Gopal-Razzak opens his eyes and looks. Towering over him, their backsides almost in his face, are two men. The slap has been delivered by the one in khaki police uniform, the man who is yanking up the unfortunate passenger by the hair. The other man is in plainclothes and clearly senior. Quickly, they grab the two passengers and frogmarch them to the exit. Gopal gives it a few moments before joining others who have come to their side of the carriage to crane their necks out of the open windows.

'What's happening?' someone asks.

Pushed by others' shoulders, Gopal can see the men being led to join a queue of about ten, all of them wearing either shirt-pant or dhuti-kurta, no checked lungis. Several uniformed mamas stand around the men with batons and bamboo rods. At one side of the platform is a makeshift bamboo booth, curtained by jute cloth on the front and sides, with a slit through the front at eye level. One by one, the men are made to walk past the booth, two constables holding each man but staying a bit behind so that the man's face is clear. Gopal can't hear anything, but clearly there's some signal after which each man is released into a looser group. Twice a man is paraded a third or fourth time and made to stand facing the dark slit before being released. Gopal notices those men are about same height and build as himself. He notes that there seems to be no interest in any scar on anybody's right temple.

After a while, all the men are released, the constables shouting, making ghost blows with their sticks to hurry them back to their carriages. The train starts to move even before all the men have got on. Their two suspects return to the carriage, the slapped one indignantly trying to retrieve his dignity.

'Arre, I'm afraid of no one! Dare touch my hair! I would have sent him to his great-grandmother, except that there were so many of them!'

The other man is more realistic. 'Don't talk nonsense! There were armed police there as well. It's clearly something serious. We were lucky they didn't take us all to some overnight lock-up.'

'What happened, brother? What was that jute booth?'

'They are looking for people and there's someone behind that jute curtain who knows them by face. I think they are looking for maybe just one person, because I heard an officer say in English "not him" several times, which means "not this man". Then twice, the man inside tapped the bamboo and they made those men walk past again.'

'They kept asking me if I had other names besides Brojogopal. I told them my mother calls me Biju, but the whoresons weren't impressed.'

'Are they still on the train?'

'I think just the normal railway mamas. I'm not sure, but I think all the special ones got off to wait for the next train.'

Gopal comes back into Ghiasuddin Razzak, and he unfolds his legs and stretches them to loosen his tensed muscles. His stomach relaxes and suddenly he's hungry, but hungry for one of Bonnemaison's unreachable hot soups, for that chicken he makes with white wine and butter. And then, fleetingly, his hand is hungry for the gun again, for what it sent back through him as he fired it at that fat Marwari. There is a slender crack in the floor of the carriage through which Gopal can almost see something flickering, probably the tracks, and he forces himself to imagine pushing the chicken through the crack, and then, equally impossibly, the gun. He can almost hear its metal striking the wood of the sleepers, see it bouncing, hear it being slapped away by the blurring steel wheels. All that's gone. If they catch him, they mustn't find any of it, even in his mind. All that's gone. What remains is the slight gurgling of his empty stomach, no food having entered it since that morning. He is where he is and he'll now take whatever he gets, filluries, fried fish, some hot rice and good dal, his mother's chorchori, some peanuts, some chirey of dried puffed rice.

The train rounds a bend through some small hillocks and suddenly they are surrounded by a patchwork of water. Ponds, rivulets, little pools breaking up the fields, their connections increasing as they lead up to the thick line of water that now stretches across the horizon. They pass a junction house and then, set a little further away from the tracks, another pucca concrete building. The police station is dwarfed on one side by debris, and among the broken trucks and wrecks of automobiles, Gopal sees more stacks of bicycles. Past the police thana, a field has grown hundreds of them, more rotted and mangled than the previous stack he's seen, a strange harvest of tube, wire, rubber and rust. As they draw closer to the river, odd, solitary mountains become clearer, dark peaks made up of some odd regularity. As they approach the first one, he recognizes what it is, and the shock takes his breath away.

Boats. Piled viciously on top of each other by some giant, vindictive hand. Big noukos on the bottom, smaller ones on top, making pyramids that should be teetering but seem fixed by the mortar of dust and mud and cobwebs. As the train jerks by a few yards from one pile, Gopal notices the holes in the hulls, each curve of wood smashed, irreparable, huge splinters stabbing into each other, each and every boat made completely unusable.

He feels a small creature crawling just above his knee and he starts, ready to swat it away. The old man's hand grips his leg harder, the fingertips trembling. There are no tears in his eyes, his eyebrows arch as high as they can go, and his grimace stretches from ear to ear.

'Look at you, boy. Just look at your face. This is what I was waiting for, this one moment when you first saw them, these new mountains of ours.'

GANGA, JAMUNA, SARASWATI

Ganesh looks at the photos of some of Elko's paintings that I've brought along. He starts tapping one and shaking his head in wonder.

'Saki-babu... it's so funny how stories travel, isn't it? Like rivers, actually! But whereas Ganga and Jamuna are rivers we have all seen, where exactly is this river called Saraswati that is named after the Goddess? In some people's spiritual universe, it's a river of knowledge and devotion, and rationally you could say it is a mythical river. But for devotees it's a very real river that runs underground, rising to the surface in surprising places.'

'Not surprising to find that image in Bengal, I suppose.'

'Exactly, we have many rivers and streams that go underground and come up somewhere else, so also stories, clearly!'

I gesture to the photograph without asking the question – what has brought on this line of thought?

'So, see. Someone – Gopal or, say, me, Ganesh – meets Niru-di from time to time once he is properly back in Kolkata in 1946. He likes to meet her because... she provides a relief from the harsh world he inhabits... she is not tempted by money or power, it's not even her stubbornness, that is there, separate, but this business of greed is just missing from her being. She likes to meet him because he gives her a different insight into the, what's the Ingreji word, oh yes, the "pro-le-tariat", and also because occasionally he can help out with things she needs for her work in the refugee colonies.'

I nod without interrupting – this much I've figured out myself.

'Now, this boy – this man – tells her stories from his life. Some stories only, others he can't involve her in, and she never asks prying questions. He tells these stories and she, in turn, tells some of them to someone else without mentioning who they've come from. Here we can see she has clearly told some to Kedar-babu, and like a river, the story has changed shape to emerge as a painting!'

'What story do you mean?'

Ganesh points at the photo of an Elko landscape – a cluster of trees next to a river, some big fruit hanging from the branches, some of the fruit clearly rotting, dripping stuff to the ground.

'Can you recognize this fruit tree?'

'No, Ganesh-da, I can't.'

'This is gaub fruit hanging from the trees. And in those days, this was a strange, almost shocking sight. Why?'

'Why?' I oblige.

'Because gaub, while it *was* eaten here and there, primarily served a different purpose. All over Bengal, and especially in what we now must call Bangladesh, the fruit was plucked when still unripe, crushed and soaked in water for a few days. Then you would make a paste of this gaub, and it would be used to seal the boats and coat sails and fishing nets. It was a wonderful kind of natural waterproofing, you see?'

'So... far more useful than as something to eat?'

'Exactly. And when someone returning to the villages after many years saw these trees heavy with fruit, it was almost like seeing a disease sprouting. Why hadn't the gaub paste been made this year? How were they sealing the boat-wood?'

'Ah, I see!'

He picks up photos of two other paintings. 'And these answer the question.' He points to an Elko landscape with stacks of broken boats, and another one of a police thana as seen from a passing train, a squat yellow PWD building surrounded on three sides by piles of rusting bicycles that are almost higher than the building itself.

This is my second visit to Alexandra Mansions, and this time I've been offered Fino sherry, Ganesh-babu's favourite alcohol. For snacks, we have home-made paneer pakodas, onion filluries and kashundi, with a promise of a good dinner to follow.

Ganesh stays silent for a while, sifting through the photos. Then he quickly gets to his feet, some decision made.

'Come, Saki, let me show you a different painting of fruit. And some other things.'

He walks to a door between two glass cupboards, unlocks it and goes inside, gesturing at me to follow. Inside the dark room, he taps on a few switches, turning on lights. I see that I am in a small museum or, rather, a smaller secret museum inside the more public one outside. As with the space outside, Ganesh-babu has clearly spent money here: there are proper spotlamps angled down from the ceiling, focused on a few plinths, and some discreet lighting to illuminate the objects inside the glass cupboards lined against the wall. There are not too many things here, but each one has been given its proper place. On one wall there is a small, almost square painting of peaches and lemons with a white jug in a style that is unmistakable – someone has made a superb copy of a still life by the great man.

'Wah, Ganesh-da, who made this? It's a beautiful copy.'

Ganesh releases a low, satisfied sound. 'That's what I also thought, Saki, that's what I also thought! But then I spent some money. When I was in France, I made some quiet inquiries. Thanks to my friend M'syu Paul, who was a very famous cook, I managed to find a man who was... let's say, a scholar of art... who had a side business in authenticating works that people didn't want in the public eye, works that these collectors may have come across accidentally but which they didn't want the authorities to know about.'

My mouth opens on its own. 'No, Ganesh-da, you're not saying...'

'Arre, listen first, na! So, for a reasonable fee this man was willing to travel to different parts of the world to inspect whatever someone might want to show him. I should say that this fellow was very clear that he wouldn't comment on any non-European art, so no Chinese, Japanese, Indian, African, et cetera. Only European art of the last six–seven hundred years, though he may have considered looking at old Greek and Roman stuff depending on the context.'

'I see. So you...'

'So, this gentleman flew to Kolkata. His official reason for coming was that he wanted to look at some of the old paintings in the zamindar collections, you know, in the rajbaris in north Kolkata?'

'Like the one Rubens that those people have? What's their name?'

'Yes, exactly, the Rubens and a few other old paintings, Italian, English, that kind of thing. He had corresponded and made appointments with some of these old families. One day, during his visit, my car picked him up and he was blindfolded. He was brought to one of my godowns where he couldn't see anything but trees outside the window. There were also plenty of lamps, plus he brought his own equipment, some lights and whatnot. I even disguised myself like a cheap theatre actor, can you believe, so that there could be no identification later.'

'No...'

'Yes. After about two hours of slowly examining this thing, he confirmed that it was not a copy. Inasmuch as he could without examining it in his own laboratory back home, he said he was ninety-nine per cent sure this was painted by Paul Cézanne himself.'

I go up to the painting to look at the brushstrokes from up close.

'Saki, don't get caught up with that. You can come back for a proper look later. Let me introduce you to some of my other friends here.'

In a cupboard, visible through the glass, are three objects. An old leather wallet, open, with a small picture poking out from one of the pockets, a black-and-white reproduction of a Cézanne still life not dissimilar to the painting on the wall. Next to it is an empty lidless tin, about three inches high and four inches wide, the label with typical early twentieth-century French typography identifying a brand of foie gras. A few inches to the right of the tin is a small box made of some sort of clear glass. In it, tied by a string in the middle, is what looks like a sheaf of wispy white hair.

The wallet I placed immediately. 'Is that... hair from... the day he died?'

'Yes, that's what I believe. Everything on this shelf is connected to the day he died.'

'Why the empty tin?'

Ganesh drew on his cigarette and waved it at me. 'I don't normally bring anybody in here. I've decided to show these to you because I want to tell you stories about some of the things you're looking at. But this will take time. You'll have to be patient.'

Even as I'm nodding, my eye catches on a plinth standing not far from the cupboard. In the glass case, I can see an automatic pistol with two empty magazines next to it. Ganesh follows my eye.

'Now that is not the original gun, but another one that is almost exactly like the original.'

'What happened to the original one?'

'Oh, broken up and distributed at different points of the river.'

'And what day does that belong to?'

'Good question. Difficult to answer. It belongs to the day Robi Thakur died, but it also belongs to the day Gopal Kundu ceased to exist.'

TWO BAULS

As he squats in the toilet enclosure, the ferry starts to judder to life, the throbbing engines, the shaking metal, all encouraging the piss to jet out of him, the turned foreskin somehow not unpeeling, hanging on. His urine slams straight into the large hole at the join of the deck and metal wall, and he can hear it drumming down the tin chute. He gingerly shakes his cock and stands up, his knees trembling. The boat tilts under him and the low wall of the toilet dips to reveal the vast spread of water beyond. For a dizzy moment, he feels as if he has pissed the entire river into existence.

As they heave into midstream, Gopal can feel the massive palm of the river cup the steamer and lift it, drop it and lift it again. Suddenly, he feels emptied of everything, water, food, Kolkata, everything. His head still spinning, he realizes he hadn't passed water since he left for Sealdah in the morning, not even in the train where caution had kept him more or less stuck to his seat. Moving away from the stink of the toilet, he works to steady his legs but realizes he doesn't need to – the vessel has found its perch in the current.

The top deck of the ferry, open on the sides, is packed with people, but Gopal has found himself a little space towards the front of the boat, right against the steel side, next to a young couple who have promised to keep his place while he goes to the toilet. From the marks on their foreheads and their patchwork clothes of saffron, yellow and red, he has guessed they are holy mendicants of some sort. As he returns, they make room for him, lifting up their side-satchels and four cloth bags shaped around some objects. He squeezes in next to them and smiles his gratitude.

'What's in those sacks?' he asks.

The man smiles. 'What would a poor Baul carry in a sack, bhai? These are our instruments.'

'Oh, you are Bauls, then?'

The woman leans forward and engages his eyes, also smiling. 'Can't you tell? Who else dresses like this?'

'Oh, I don't know, Bengal is full of all sorts of sadhu-babas, who can keep track? Bauls, fakirs, tantriks, kirtoniyas... I get confused.'

'Mian, you've spent too long in the city, I can see!' The woman lets out a small snort, but her smile robs it of sting.

The man points to the different cloth-covered shapes. 'That's my khepi's ektara. You've seen an ektara, right?' His tone is as if speaking to a child, his pupils are jet black and glinting, his cheek-lines full of mischief. Gopal nods. 'And then this is my khamak, what we also call a gabgubi.' Gopal nods again, unable to take his eyes off the man. 'And then this potla has a dubki and this one has kartals. Now tell me. What do you want to steal?'

'What did you say? Steal? Steal what?' Gopal starts to stiffen with irritation but fights the urge. His arm and leg are pasted to the Baul's, and there is no other space on the deck.

The man reaches across with his free arm and caresses Gopal's face. 'I was just joking, Kaliya. You look like a beautiful black Krishna, so I had a vision of you as a baby thief, stealing butter. Except, the only things Noni Khepa and Chintamoni Dasi have are these poor instruments. And the only butter I can give you is from the pot of my heart!'

'Oooh! That's not the only receptacle you have, why don't you say?' The woman's voice is clear as a pealing bell, as is her laugh, but in the hubbub of people settling down, no one else seems to have heard her. Under his beard, the man's thick lips widen into a grin. With a rise of the vessel, the pain returns to Gopal's shoulder. There's also an ache between his legs. He smiles back.

'My name is Razzak. I don't like butter.'

'Oh? Have you tasted all the different kinds of butter there are in the universe, then?' The man buries his face in the woman's neck to stifle his laughter, while the woman pulls an end of her shawl to her mouth and bites it. Gopal finds himself smiling at them, but he finally looks away.

He can smell coals being lit somewhere, and he suddenly feels painfully hungry. Below the deck, there are cabins for the wealthy, the military and government officials, and berths for the next class of passengers. From hearsay, Gopal knows there are quite elaborate arrangements for feeding all these worthies. This open deck above is for everyone else, all the people who've managed to scramble on with their six- or eight-anna tickets, many now being sold by touts for as high as three rupees.

Automatically, Gopal scans the deck for plainclothes mamas. The crowd that rushed on to the ferry has now woven itself into different clusters. Up here, in clear sight of the water, people have set up small camps between the benches, small households without walls. Gopal can see people making ready to deal with the different kinds of scarcity that the oncoming winter night will sharpen. Families make furtive huddles, already deploying whatever few warm clothes and coverings they have. Mothers quickly open their little cloth bundles and dole out whatever food they have to the children. From what Gopal can see, it's mostly little fistfuls of dry puffed rice and khoi that are changing hands, a tight slap for a child that spills anything, short shrill words for anyone who asks for more. Here and there, somebody pulls out one or two precious onions from the knot of a dhuti, four or five carefully secreted boiled potatoes from the folds of a sari, or some dry rotis and a handful of green chillies from a jhola. All of these have been stored separately, brought out as carefully and reluctantly as family jewellery. These are rare items and passed around almost surreptitiously in order not to invite envious stares from other groups. Many groups don't seem to have any food at all, and they are busy making themselves ready for the freezing cold with which the river is bound to envelope them. Almost without realizing it, families are forming little circles, ringing themselves in with rough cloth and thin kantha coverings, arranging as far as possible for the smallest children to be in the middle, the bigger ones in the next circle, and then the adults outside.

'Everyone, remember! No lighting fires of any sort! No fires at all! If I see an unoon or something being lit, I will throw it into the river, and you after it!' The ferry stewards swagger about, stepping through the huddled groups, flicking up their lungis and peering into what various people are doing. 'Blyaakaut means blyakaaut! Means after darkness, no lights! It's not a joke, being bombed by the Japani planes! Ask the poor fools in Chittagong! Ask the benighted souls in Assam! Eat your dry food! Don't dream of hot gravy! One bomb on your head and all the gravy will come out of the other end!'

'What are these sons of dogs saying to us?' Noni Khepa covers his mouth and growls. 'No one has any food here! While them, these whoresons, have their hot fish jhol and rice waiting downstairs.' Under their shawls, Chintamoni pokes Noni to shut up and he pushes into Gopal. Suddenly the couple's laughter has gone, carried off by the river wind.

As darkness drops, sight is replaced by smell: winter sweat, matted hair, smell of old coconut oil mixing with the diesel and coal, a certain tiredness in the crowd, a conserving of energy, even discouraging the children from being overactive, saving their energy for something that lies ahead, whatever is forcing these people to go against the current of humanity that seems headed only in one direction – towards Kolkata.

Reaching Goalundo Station, Gopal had felt it almost immediately. There was a smell of fear in the air, a sense of some slow-moving panic at the station itself. As the Sealdah train pulled into the platform overlooking the river, crowds were already waiting. People began to jump on to the train even before it had stopped. Gopal and the old man had to struggle to get out of the carriage, pushing against the mass trying to climb in. The old man had clutched Gopal's hand tightly and held on as the younger man shoved and jabbed a way through the heave of bodies. If the old man was happy for the support, Gopal-Razzak was doubly grateful to be stepping out of the train as a unit of two, an old mian travelling with his son or nephew – not what the mamas were looking for.

Gopal had been warned – 'The other dangerous point will be where you get off the train, there will be a lot of them around the ferry ghat waiting to catch whoever's slipped through the net earlier.' Sure enough, Gopal immediately spotted two of them, standing near a hand rake on the other track, wearing railway engineers' garb but not a stain on their hands or uniforms. Outside, trying to mingle with the stream of people heading to the ghat, there were two more plainclothes cockroaches, these ones pretending to be boatmen. Instinctively, Gopal took the end of his kurta and wiped the old man's face as they approached the cops. As he passed, he fancied he could smell Kolkata on them.

Near the ghats, the famous pice hotels were all shut, their signs – 'Belly Contract! 6 Annas – All the Rice and Dal you can Eat!' – now looking absurd. Gopal had heard of these eateries and their well-known trick. The hotels would draw you in with the cheap prices, take your money in advance, and then delay serving the food, bringing it out just as your ferry was about to leave; the customer would quaff a few mouthfuls and run, and the rice and dal would return to the kitchen to be reheated and brought out again for the next mark. Thinking about a thhala loaded with hot dal-rice churned the acid in Gopal's empty stomach.

'Oh, it would have been nice to eat something, wouldn't it, mian?' The old man seemed to have read his mind. 'But there's no food now, hardly any food anywhere! They shut these places after a crowd attacked them, looking for food. Even the haramzada police couldn't do anything, the havaldars all ran away.'

'Chacha, where did you say you were going?'

'Dhaka, my boy, I'm going to Dhaka, but first I have to get a ticket!'

Gopal fought his way through the milling crowd, found a tout and bought two tickets, one for Dhaka and his own for Tangail, paying well above the normal price. For himself, he was very tempted to buy a berth below deck, but that would be a giveaway – a poor weaver like Razzak would not waste that kind of money. Near the jetties, he kept the old man close to him for as long as possible, sending him towards the Dhaka ferry at the last possible minute before boarding his own steamer.

'Chacha, here's your ticket! You know where you have to go?'

'Yes, I do, but what about the money for the ticket?'

'Don't worry about that, chacha! Just go!'

The old man's eyes opened wide. He tried to find some expression of thanks, but the thin, dark boy was already four people away in the press of bodies pushing up the gangway.

'Khuda hafiz, my boy! Allah keep you well!'

'Khuda hafiz, chacha!'

Gopal moved up the sloping planks as quickly as he could, using all the pushing and jostling, hoping it would be a while before the old man discovered the five-rupee note Gopal had slipped into his pocket – it wouldn't do to have the old fellow loudly thanking him for the huge amount of money he'd been gifted. At the top of the gangway, there were two uniformed mamas and a gora officer standing a little behind them, but they paid no attention as the steward punched his ticket and let him pass.

Now, he's glad he's wedged between the Baul and a huge metal box jutting out from the sides near the prow of the boat. Even if someone was searching the crowd, he's more or less hidden from two sides, fused into the subgroup of three by overlapping shawls, this Khepa's head now resting on his shoulder, while the woman's head is cradled by the crook of her husband's other elbow.

Gopal has never been in an airplane, but a few months ago he had seen a photo of a damaged warship taken from the sky. Sitting here, squeezed in one corner, he finds himself imagining how this ferry might look from above – no smells, a black-and-white lozenge in a wide corridor of flat green, the water turning dark as the early sunset closes the day on Bengal, mist rolling in from the banks obscuring the vessel every now and then, the steamer cutting a wake not only of water but also, a bit like that turning warship, of smoke, not only the smoke from its funnels but also trailing the cape of smoke from the cooking fires on the lower deck. For sure he wouldn't be able to smell it from an aeroplane high above, but here the aroma of food being cooked is sharp and painful.

Just as the shuttered pice hotels on shore are famous for the ilish fish they serve in the monsoon, at an extra cost on top of the dal and rice, the chicken jhol they make on these ferries is also legendary. A long time ago, Ustad had described it to him. 'Gogai, I don't like much of you Bengali people's food, but there is no doubt that murgi is made with Allah's help. Nothing too complicated goes into it, just some mustard oil, onions, green and red chillies, then the chicken, and then, as you add water, you also add an amount of finely chopped prawns which disappear into the gravy as it cooks. Ah, but the taste! You're supposed to have it with rice and never with roti or paratha, just this chicken jhol on fresh hot rice...'

Gopal's stomach sends a rush of bile up into his food pipe. He suddenly remembers the bits of brain matter and blood spreading on the piles of spilled rice in the Marwari's godown and he starts retching violently. Noni is up and alert as though he's never been asleep. Chintamoni also wakes up quickly. She taps Noni on the shoulder.

'Should I...?'

'Yes, but not too much, I'll just give it to him in small sips.'

Chintamoni reaches into her jhola, pulls out an old glass bottle, unscrews the cap and hands it to Noni.

'Here, Kaliya, have some water, don't gulp, just wet your mouth.'

Shivering now, Gopal does as he is told. The water is cool, and it helps push down the acid in his throat. Noni feels Gopal's forehead and throat, reaches into his kurta and puts a hand on his heaving chest.

'He's got a bit of fever, this boy.'

'Looks it.' Chintamoni nods.

'Listen, you! You need to be away from that cold metal. Come between us.'

Noni manages to cross over and push Gopal between himself and Chintamoni. The two of them wrap themselves and their shawls around Gopal and hold him until the shivering subsides.

'You haven't eaten for a while have you, little mian?' Noni strokes Gopal's hair and takes his head on his shoulder. 'Sleep now. At dawn this isteamaar will stop at Nobighat. We'll find some food then.'

BELLY CONTRACT

'This stupid fridge! There's too much food! Babu, just show me the top shelf again?' I move the torch beam to where she wants it.

'Are you complaining that I got you this fridge? Just the other day you were telling, who was it, that it had completely transformed your life.'

'No, no, I tell everyone how grateful I am that my son has been able to afford this for his mother... A little to the right, yes, just keep it there... It's just that, whenever you come home, I buy too much food and with this constant load-shedding it becomes a nightmare to see what's what at night! When I'm on my own, I have maybe three small bartans, and bread, milk and eggs, that's all. I don't even drink fridge water like you young people.' She opens a container, smells it and puts it on the dining table. 'You know, it's obscene how much... no, not obscene exactly, but this was not imaginable when we were fighting for...'

'... Two handfuls of rice per person. I know, Ma, I know, but you cannot put history on a pause button forever. Things change! And they change unevenly for different people.'

She pulls out two more things and my torch follows her like a spotlight tracking a performer. 'It's not just that there's too much food, it's also a problem because of this electricity going off all the time! The freezer starts dripping into the main compartment, you don't know which food is fresh and what's gone bad. In the old days with the kitchen cage, you knew exactly how long something could keep.'

'Yes, yes... It's as though the Party knows Comrade Niru has become bourgeois and bought a fridge, so they deliberately target Jodhpur Park for the load-shedding.' I help her move the food to the gas.

'Are you suggesting there was no load-shedding in Siddhartha's time? Are you forgetting the Congress years?' I can't see her face, but from her snapping I can tell I've hit my mark. 'In any case, Saki, many of them have fridges now, and not just the politburo people. And a few of them live around here, so...'

'Yeh azadi jhoothi hai!' This independence is a false one! I supply the Hindi slogan of the Communist Party around 1947.

'You can joke about it, Saki, your generation can, because we fought to make it less of a lie. And just because I left the Party doesn't mean I've given up all the ideals, you know that.'

She has found two candles and lit them.

'I know that, Ma. You know I know that. And you know that central to independence is the freedom to be able to joke about it. Same goes for your revolution.'

'Yes, all right, but I can't laugh when I look at our Bengal right now, and I can't laugh when I look at what's happening in Bangladesh. It's what? Seven years since the country was formed? It was terrible to see a kind of repeat of '46–'47 in 1971... then his own military slaughters Mujib, and then, if things aren't bad enough, the Burma generals push these refugees into the country, these, ki naam, Rohingyas... *two hundred thousand* of those terrified people in Cox's Bazar! When does this end?'

She goes silent, concentrating on warming the food in the flickering light. Across my years away, I realize I've become a foreigner, I now find the heat and the mosquitoes unbearable. But then I can hear my cassette player in the next room, running on battery, double bass being plucked softly, Mingus, hanging points of sound in the air and then stretching the occasional note to join the points, creating a spider's web that appears and disappears against the other instruments.

I remember me at fourteen. 'So, Comrade Niru, all of you stopped the peasant struggle and accepted the new nation, didn't you?'

'No, not quite, shona. We just changed our movement after recognizing the ground reality.'

As a kid, I'd always had a problem understanding how it all ended with Tebhaga. 'Yes, but the ground reality was you could not overthrow the state like you wanted, right?'

'Yes, but the problem was that we were suddenly fighting two states who were also hostile to each other. It was after Partition that our leaders decided to pick up the gun. Then things were awful enough on this side, but on the East Pakistan side they were worse. Santhals were burnt out of their villages, our police may not have had time to rape women, but over there the police and the army, *their* Bengal police and *their* Pakistan Army but the same people who were Indian a few months previously, do not forget, had plenty of time to torture women in the worst possible ways. So many thousand Santhals were forced over the border to Malda on our side. They also captured leaders like Ila-di and other women, and I cannot tell a child like you what they did to them...'

At sixteen or seventeen, my questions began to centre around me. 'Comrade Neem. Tell me, do you wish you had stayed with the gun? Was it me who got in the way?'

'No, Saki, it wasn't. I just instinctively realized that violence would only add to the mess, not improve it, and in a few months that was proved right.'

Over the last few days, she has given me a long, taped interview about everything except the ambush business:

'I did things in my life, I did things because they felt right at the time, now I'm not sure my decisions were correct decisions, I think I was wrong. We thought we were right and these kids, these Naxals, these PLO and Red this and that, Red Army Faction, Red Brigades, Japan Red Army and others think they are right to kill and bomb, but they are not. You know, people always justify their own violence: "there was no choice", "we had to resist the violence being inflicted on us", "the cost of non-violence was too high". I don't believe all that now.' She says the last words in English: 'We were wrong, and they are wrong. You cannot exit from that exit.'

In another bit, speaking about the encounter executions of young Naxals, she says: 'I would have hated it if you had chosen this path. If you hadn't gone abroad, I don't know, I've often imagined going to a police morgue to identify your body, or preparing it for cremation like I did Keya.'

This evening, the lights come on just as we are finishing dinner. I quickly go and take out the batteries from the Phillips. Then I plug it in and restart the tape. Almost on cue, a new track begins on the cassette player, *Haitian Fight Song*, with the horn section pumping forward everything else.

'Saki?'

'Yes, Ma?'

'See if there's still some ice in the freezer?'

'Yes, Comrade Commissar, at once!'

It had started one winter a couple of years ago, when Niru had a bad cough. 'Eijey, can you give me some of your precious duty-free whisky? Just as medicine, you understand?' I knew she had sworn off all drinking after Jones left. Communist Party morals and witnessing Imogen and Kedar becoming enslaved had only strengthened her resolve, and she would watch me drink while tamping down her disapproval. The tot of whisky and hot water was the first time she'd touched booze in thirty-odd years. Now, we had this ritual, always post-dinner, American style, where we'd have a drink together once or twice a week – whisky in winter and pastis in the hot seasons.

The small balcony accommodates two chairs and a pedestal fan to keep the mosquitoes away. Luckily for Niru, the balcony overlooks one of the few plots in Jodhpur Park that are still empty, which means none of the neighbours can see her drinking. At times, I'd rib her about this. 'Com. Niru? Why do you feel so guilty about drinking? You've never been a Gandhi follower!'

'Well, at some moments I find I can't dismiss him like I used to. Or not everything about him.'

'Oh my god, are you becoming a patriot now?'

'Well, I'm only loyal to the people, not to the... what was that Kedar used to say?'

'My be-hated country that I now miss so much!'

Today, she's in an oddly relaxed mood. We sit without talking for a bit, the jazz barely audible over the whirr of the fan at full speed, its blind cyclops swivelling metronomically from one side to the other. Adding to this, the early night sounds of the colony come and go. The wooden clatter of a lone ricksha passing, the ricksha-puller using his handbell only at long intervals, dogs waking up for their night patrols, Uttam Kumar dancing soundlessly on the TV in the ground-floor flat across the road, the traffic on the main road, the local trains between Sealdah and Budge-Budge passing every now and then, letting off long horns to warn the slums abutting the track.

On her second drink, Niru waves away my cigarette smoke. 'I can't escape the fact that, once I decided to be there for you, once I accepted that you were mine to look after, I became a predictable Bangali mother. I not only had to move away from engaging in violence, I also had to protect you from it, do whatever was required to protect you. I suppose to that extent I betrayed the struggle.'

'Funny you should suddenly say that right now. I was just thinking, what about the other kind of violence, you know, someone who's poor who gets into criminal violence? I was just asking Ganesh-da—'

'Well, about that Ganesh knows better than me, he can tell you if he wants.'

'But, Ma, haven't you let Ganesh support your work from time to time? And surely you know his business isn't all legiti—'

'When one is desperate, one makes some uncomfortable decisions. And why only for my work? I even accepted his help to send you abroad.'

'What?'

'Well, what I told you was I'd discovered some savings Ma-Baba had left for you, but there were no such big savings. It was Ganesh who arranged the money you needed beyond your scholarship, your... tuition waiver... you know, your living money. Imogen also offered, but I knew at the time she was not particularly...'

'Why didn't you tell me this earlier?'

She ignores my question. 'Ganesh once told me about these food places near the ferry ghats in East Bengal. In those days, they used to have this thing called *peyt chukti*, belly contract... I suppose this was my different belly contract with the child I'd produced.'

PROFILE

'Arre bhai, Saki, why are you asking about that now? It was a long time ago. Why did Niru-di even tell you? She should have forgotten it, just as I have!' I have never seen Ganesh look pained and embarrassed. 'You see, Niru-di had never ever asked me for any help for herself, always only for the work she was doing. But then you got this scholarship, and as you know, it wasn't enough. So, she was just telling me about it, and not in that roundabout way when people want something but don't want to ask. I don't think it occurred to her that I could, you know... but I offered. At first, she said no, but then she changed her mind. That made me happy.

'No, look, I can understand that you may feel the pressure of being the only child for many people, and not just your Ma and grandparents. Kedar-babu, Imogen, Niru-di's other friends, who weren't able, or perhaps didn't want to bring children into the world they were witnessing. But it's nothing like that with me, don't worry! If you were someone I couldn't talk to, I would just have thought I helped out a didi of mine, that's all. There is of course no guarantee with these things, but you turned out all right.'

Across my visits to Alexandra Mansions, it's become clear to me that Ganesh has always wanted to tell his story to someone, and until he met me there was no one he could tell it to. Even with me, the vetting process has taken a while.

'You're very methodical in your notes, Saki, and that is pleasing to see.' Ganesh asks to look at my notebook from time to time and I have no choice but to let him. At first, I thought he was just making sure nothing was being put down that he didn't want recorded, but now I feel he is also interested in the process. Today, he goes through the list I've made of the objects in his museum. 'Hmm, you know, this is all very good, but how will you... You know you can't tell a story like an accountant recounts debit and credit.'

'I know, Ganesh-da. All this is just for making the connections, or maybe like seeds from which some story can grow, but I'll have to work out how to tell it.'

'Well, as I've said, I can't tell you every detail, not everything. I'll tell you some of it and the rest you have to imagine.'

We've had variations of this argument before.

'But, Ganesh-da, whatever story I tell, doesn't it have to be accurate? I was reading a history of a Second World War battle in Russia, and someone said of the writer, "If he says the tank barrels glinted in the sun as they advanced, you can be sure that day would have been sunny."'

'Accurate? An upanyas is a work of fiction, yes? As in, a mixture of true facts and false facts, yes? There's a difference between your Ingreji *accurate* and *true*, no?' He uses the English words to emphasize his point. 'They are not always the same thing. And you, with Kedar Lahiri you're working on a man who never painted reality accurately! But you are saying he reached some truth, maybe the profile of the truth and not the front face!'

True facts and false facts. I find myself laughing. 'But somewhere the profile has to be a likeness, doesn't it?'

'Hyan, Saki, but what about those paintings where you can't make out all the features of a face and yet the presence of a particular person is unmistakable?' We are in the inner room, and he points to a painting I haven't noticed before. At first I think it's a print, like on a calendar Niru has at home. When I look closely, I realize it's another original.

Ganesh watches me gape. Then he pats me on the back. 'Yes, yes, old Ganesh-da has done well, hasn't he?'

Rabindranath Tagore began to paint seriously only when he was about seventy. By now, almost all of the paintings are accounted for, many of them reproduced in books and calendars and such. This is unmistakably by the old man, and not one I've seen before. The profile of a woman's head emerges and disappears out of a forest of dark strokes done in ink and watercolour, the features unclear except for the eyes and mouth but, by some trick of brushwork, the person and their sorrow fully present.

Another day, Ganesh is standing next to a plinth when he points out that I haven't listed some objects. On the plinth is a glass case with a pair of slightly soiled football boots inside, some faint red stains in the dried brown. 'They say these are the boots worn by Pelé during his first game against Bulgaria in the 1966 World Cup. They fouled him so much, the Bulgarians, that there is even blood on them! There was no way to get proof of this and I'm not sure I believe the seller, but I bought them anyway, sight unseen. Sometimes the pleasure comes from what you choose to believe.'

I've been meaning to ask about something else. I point to the vitrine next to the plinth with the boots. 'What about these, Ganesh-da?'

We both examine the four knives laid out according to size, the biggest with a six-inch blade, the smallest about three inches where the hooked blade is almost an afterthought poking out of the handle. None of the knives have a bolster. The blades of each of the three longer ones are the same length as the dark brown handles with which they form straight lines, with no heel flaring out and no bulge at the bottom of the worn handles.

'These knives belonged to Gaurango, also called Gaurangzeb by the Ustad.' Ganesh looks at me. 'Ah, you should have seen him throw these. Not the two small ones, those were always used in the hand, but the longer ones could kill a man at twenty feet. One minute you were standing there, the next moment you were clutching at your windpipe or the back of your neck, wondering how this thing got there. The story was that when Gaurango was a boy, he had apprenticed with a circus and learnt the art there.'

'You saw him actually kill people like that?'

Ganesh quickly shakes his head and grins. 'No. But Gopal Kundu did.'

We go out to the main room and sit down.

'So... what happened to this Gaurango?'

Ganesh ignores my question and starts somewhere else.

Ganesh is away from Kolkata between early 1943 and late 1946, only coming in occasionally when the Ustad needs some particular help. By the time Ganesh comes back to the city, the only Gopal in the Kolkata underworld is the dreaded Gopal Pantha, the butcher reputed to have killed many Muslims in the riots. The Ustad is clearly not well when Ganesh meets him on the boat.

'When I asked about him about Aurangzeb and Gaurangzeb, he just said, "I don't think you should worry about them any more. Just concentrate on what we need to do now." Which told me everything and nothing. One the one hand, it was clear the two big fellows were out of the picture as far as Ustad was concerned. On the other hand, there was no indication of how this had come to pass. I had been away for about six months at that time, in Tangail, and I hadn't heard anything until the instructions came from Ustad to return.

'It was only when I spoke to Ustad that I realized I didn't need to go back east, that I was back for good. A couple of days later, Ustad opened up a bit more. He told me that Gaurango was dead, killed by Jalal Sheikh's people. His body was found riddled with bullets on a mountain of tarpaulin-covered rice sacks in the Botanical Gardens. He hadn't had time to reach for his knives and they were all still there inside his jama.

'Aurangzeb had exacted revenge almost immediately, but he had gone too far. There was a big fire in Howrah, where Sheikh and his main people died, but there were also several dead women and children, all part of Sheikh's family who had gathered for a wedding. Aurangzeb disappeared back to Peshawar where he was from, and after Partition, Calcutta Police gave up the chase and closed the case.'

'So you never saw him again, this Aurangzeb?'

'No. And obviously, his real name was something else. Only Ustad knew, but he never ever told me.' Ganesh leans on the balcony parapet and blows smoke in the direction of the church and the Memorial. 'It was quite quick after that, surprisingly so. Without those two, Ustad was completely dependent on me. I was the one who went and made peace with Sheikh's remaining people. There were two police officers, quite high up, who were also in attendance, to make sure this unprofitable bloodshed in the middle of the larger bloodshed ended as quickly as possible. The Sheikh's people were satisfied that Gaurango, and before him Gopal Kundu, whom they'd never seen, were both dead and that the big Pathan was gone. They also needed to get on with repairing their business.

'The old man's body had suddenly begun to fall apart. It was odd to see his power seep away with his health. During those years, I became his shield, conveying his orders or, with his permission, my own orders as though they were his. Looking back, I now realize that maybe he had already been shaky for a few years but just hidden it well. Also that those two, Aurangzeb and Gaurango, were obviously expecting to inherit control, but I was the little spoiler that Ustad promoted as a kind of counterweight. Till the godown business ruined all his balancing and everything went wrong with everyone's plans. By 1949, Shahabuddin was gone, and I'd become the karta, the main man, of the whole enterprise. It was tricky in those first few years of Independence, it took a lot of work to keep control, to change the business... There are many stories, I will tell you some the next time you're back in Kolkata.'

He says all this quickly, without his usual detours into detail. Listening to him, I feel it's a kind of test run, a rehearsal, just to see to see how it sounds when spoken aloud.

One afternoon, when I'm there to say goodbye before leaving for Paris, Ganesh asks me: 'So, Saki, what would you say is the difference between writing a golpo and mounting a painting exhibition?'

The question surprises me and I have to think before answering.

'Well... I would say both are about telling small stories within a larger story. A novel, or at least an old-fashioned upanyas, would have a narrative leading up to some sort of a neat, satisfying ending – that is what we have come to expect of novels. If told well, the golpo unfolds like a piece of music, like in a raag., new things reveal themselves while reminding us of what we have already heard. But the direction is usually one way, like the listener, the reader is taken from the beginning to the end.'

'Hm. And in an exhibition?'

'Well, a normal old-fashioned exhibition is always within a space, usually situated within a building. So architecture and an exhibition both work similarly – a person can move forward and back and circle around in that space. Now, in that kind of exhibition, what pictures do I want? Which pictures in which section of the show? Then, in each section, which paintings go next to each other? Because we already know "what happens to whom". It's not about that. It's about the new understandings that form when we mix up stories we already know.'

A few minutes later, he's seeing me off at the door.

'Have a safe journey back, Saki. I hope you don't mind that I call you from time to time?'

'Not at all, Ganesh-da. I look forward to our phone calls.'

'I'm happy to hear that.' He reaches up and gives me a pat on the cheek, and then a half hug with one arm across my back. 'It's still strange for me, to be sitting here, to be able to talk to you halfway across the world just by dialling an instrument. Sometimes I think I have no right to be here. There are many times when I should have died, but Kali-ma had other ideas, so here I am. I envy atheists like Niru-di, and I suppose you also, your freedom. I can't share that clear belief that, you know, that we all blow out like light bulbs at the end. Too much has happened in my life, things that have no logical explanation, and too often for it to be mere chance.'

THREE BAULS

As he awakes, just before he opens his eyes, he understands that his hands are tied and there is also something tightly wrapped around his mouth. Cloth. Cloth tied across his mouth, but his nose is free and he can breathe. Some kind of thin rope, not around both feet, just his right ankle, the other end of the rope attached to something outside his body. His hands can move a bit, but his whole body is still bound by something. The ground lurches slightly under him, and he understands that he's still sitting on a blanket, with the wood of the deck underneath, that he's still on the boat, that whoever has arrested him has not yet been able to move him off the ferry. Fully awake now, he keeps his eyes shut – let them think he's still asleep while he works out as much as he can.

People speaking, a group of men, new voices who weren't there yesterday. In fact, from what they are saying, two groups of men who've just met on the shore and boarded the ferry at Nobighat. Clearly there has been a stop there just around dawn, exactly as the Baul had mentioned. Clearly most other people on the deck are still asleep, because he can hear these new men despite their voices being quite low.

'I'm telling you! My cousin knows the fellow who handles the telegraph at Jessore Main Post Office, and he got it from him directly!' Not peasants, educated men, men who work with writing and reading of some sort. But not police. Men who don't seem to have noticed him in his condition. The man speaking is clearly used to deploying his authority in some circle. 'I'm telling you! They're not announcing it yet, but Delhi has fallen! Wavell has been captured and killed! The Japani and Germans together, the Japani flying in from the sea near Karachi with those troops that fall from the air, and Germans through Afghanistan where they had hidden a secret army!'

Another man starts to laugh. 'Arre, bhai, you are too much! These fairy stories are exactly what the Japani want us to believe! It is these rumours that will finally sink us! Don't spread them! Let me tell you what is actually happening, and you should think accordingly as to what you want to do!'

'Oho. So, sarvagyani, know-it-all, tell us! What is actually happening?'

'The attack has happened, that is true. British India is under attack, that much is true.'

'But...?'

'But they are nowhere near Delhi, it's not that easy to get to Delhi. And it's only the Japani, no Germans. The Japani have landed from the sea and actually captured Madras! In the far south! As a direct result of this, the man who has been killed is the Nizam of Hyderabad, killed by his own people, a crowd stormed the palace three days ago and slaughtered the whole family, the Nizam, all his seventy wives, all the children, understood?'

'Oh..!'

'Yes. I know people in the royal family of Cooch Behar, and someone there related to the Hyderabad royalty received a last trunk call from the Nizam's palace, even as the mob was pouring in!'

'Oh, but...'

'Yes. Now listen, that's not all. The latest reports I have say that the Nizam's army has now joined up with the Japani troops and they are advancing on Poona and Bombay, and from there they are sure to move towards Delhi.'

'And what about us here?'

One of the men strikes a match and Gopal can smell tobacco – not a bidi, but proper cigarette tobacco.

'What about us? We are in the far armpit of the country and the attackers are happy that the main Ingrej and Markin army is here, looking east every day for the Japani to rise like the sun. These Ingrej have taken our boats and our cycles and everything, destroyed us, basically, while the sisterfucking Japani have gone around them and put a bamboo up their backside!'

A hand strokes Gopal's cheek, and he can't help but open his eyes.

'Orey, Kaliya. Wake up. It's morning. We've got some tea.' As he opens his eyes, he realizes that the Baul and his wife have been holding him tight. Noni quickly unties the cloth around Gopal's mouth and gives his face a quick, light massage. Then, as Chintamoni holds out a battered metal cup, Noni unties the rope from Gopal's hands and foot, taking out the other end from an iron hoop sticking out of the ferry wall. The tea is still warm, just brown-red liquid, no milk or sugar, but it still tastes good.

'They only had red tea on the dingy at Nobighat.' Chintamoni pours him some more from the old thermos.

'What a night you had, babu, what a night! What a fright you gave us!' Noni takes the cup from Gopal's hand and has a sip.

'What happened?' Gopal is still not sure this is not a trap.

'What happened?' Noni starts to laugh as he wipes his beard with the back of his hand. 'What happened was first you fell asleep like a piece of stone, like you hadn't slept for several nights.'

'But then, ooorey baba!' Chintamoni flings up her arms at the sky. 'Suddenly you were talking in your sleep, then shouting, ki – what – all sorts of things—'

'Then you leapt up! Like a tiger on hind legs! And headed straight for the edge of the boat over there! Saying what—'

'*Won't get married, I won't get married, you won't get me married!* And if Khepa here hadn't grabbed you, you would've jumped into the water.'

'What? No! I couldn't have done—'

'Arre, bokachoda! You were a handful! Hardly any meat on your bones, who would have thought you had such strength? We both had to drag you back, other people waking up and saying, "He's gone mad!

He's gone mad!" We sat you down and you stayed quiet for a while, but then – again you did it! Shouting and trying to jump off! Which is why Khepa finally tied your leg, and we also put that cloth around your mouth.'

'Yes... you were also shouting something about some Madhai... *Madhai, Madhai, forgive me, I couldn't save you!* And something about bullets, ki? *I have to count the bullets, I have to count the bullets...'*

Gopal forces a smile. 'Oh, that's me playing marbles with my friend Madhai when we were kids. We used to call them bullets – same word, no? Do forgive me, I gave you a lot of trouble!' He shakes his head as if to clear it, but uses the movement to check if anyone else on the deck is paying attention. No one seems interested. People are waking up, going about the business of winding up bedding and feeding their children. The four men talking about the Japani attack have now moved over to the other side of the deck, pointing to something out on the river. As he had guessed, educated, more money, two of them in shirt-pant and sweaters, woollen monkey-caps, two in dhuti-panjabi but also with sweaters, same monkey-caps and shawls. All of them wearing socks and shoes, but no danger to him.

Gopal stands up, stretches and looks around again. A few new faces from Nobighat, but no one that rings any alarm bells. He makes his way to the toilet enclosure, recoiling for a moment as he enters it. On his way back, he stops and looks around. He suddenly feels the huge separation between the cauldron of Kolkata and this land, this water. To his right, the sun is now semi-solid in the winter sky, and far away he can see the line of the riverbank forming the horizon. To his left is an equally daunting stretch of water, and a line of mist through which he can just about make out the soft green and brown of the western bank catching the first rays of the sun. He looks at the vast river, placid on the surface, flowing in the opposite direction from the boat. He knows that just below the well-behaved waves is a maze of shallow silt banks and troughs almost as deep as the sea towards which the water is headed. For a few minutes, the light green-brown, opaque waves close to the ferry hypnotize him. He breaks off with a small shudder, remembering yet again that he is not a good swimmer, and certainly no match for this massive flow.

There's something not right with the view, and he only places it as he sits down next to Noni.

'It's strange not to see any other nouko on the river.'

'Yes. It's been like this since just after the rains, since Bhadro, and whatever was left, the few they allowed, were all gone after the storm in Kartik, many destroyed by the cyclone, and the remaining ones the officials snatched in some new wave of panic. Now there's only the few ferries and official boats. They've taken all the rest.'

'So how do people...?'

'Arre, Kaliya, if someone cuts off your legs but leaves you alive, will you give up and die? No! Like any other creature in god's factory, you will try and live as long as you can, crawling, climbing, biting... They snatched our boats because they were afraid of the Japani attacking... There are still no sons of pigs Japani and still no boats, so we are all dying slowly.'

Noni turns to Chintamoni and grunts. She hands him one of the cloth bags and begins to untie one herself. Noni takes out what looks like an open-ended drum from the bag and puts the strap around his shoulder. He reaches inside the opening of the drum and pulls out the two gut strings attached to a brass knob, the other end of the parallel gut fixed to the skin of the drum. He then holds the brass knob in his left hand, moves his wrist to make the strings taut, and plucks them with his right hand to check the tone. Rummaging in the bag, he pulls out a small eye-shaped piece of wood with a hole in the middle. He hooks his index finger into the hole, tightens the strings again and flicks them with this plectrum, sending a whiplash of sound across the hubbub on the deck. Gopal has seen Bauls and others play this thing before, but he didn't know what it was called until Noni Khepa told him yesterday. He does, however, know the name of the instrument Chintamoni is tuning. A single wire rising from a gourd bowl, with two curving strips of bamboo creating a parenthesis, all joining at the tuning knob at the top. The name comes from the single wire – *ek taar* – so ektara.

There is now a bit of space around them and Gopal pushes himself back, a bit away from the couple, in order to see them properly. For a minute or so, Chintamoni and Noni Khepa exchange single notes, matching the tuning, and then, having got the attention of some of the passengers nearby, Noni calls out:

'Horeyyy Krishno, Horey Krishno, Hori Bol, Hori Bol!'

Some people respond to the incantation, answering back, 'Horey Krishno!', 'Hori Bol!'

Noni Khepa twangs his khamak again and just speaks out the first words:

'Ei... dil darya'r maajhey tey, bhai,
Achhey mojaar karkhana,
Ei dil darya'r maajhey!'

A series of note-beats trip out of Khepa's khamak and then his voice climbs into the tune:

'In the ocean of the heart,
There is a curious machine...'

Chintamoni's ektara creates a repeating high drone under which Noni's khamak can play. At times, Gopal thinks, the sound is like a round pot being dunked in water, the liquid hitting the sides as the vessel fills up, and when Noni picks up speed, his wrist blurring the plectrum and disappearing the twin strings, the thing sounds like some twisted industrial machine, its parts exploding and falling off, even as it continues to operate with electrical abandon.

There is a house in the body,
There is a house in the body,
Thieves in the house,
Six of them broke through,
One got away with the goods!
In the Ocean of the Heart...

Chintamoni's face is turned upwards, her eyes half closed. Both she and Noni are working themselves into a trance. Gopal finds himself mirroring Chintamoni, his body swaying, eyes closed, moving his head to the beat. Something soft hits his face, hits at the precise point of a beat, and briefly envelopes his head. Chintamoni is looking at him and smiling. 'Wear your alkhalla!' She mouths the words and gestures with her free hand. He looks down at the crumpled alkhalla lying in his lap, the bright patchwork colours fighting each other. He finds the opening for the head and slips it on, straightening the cape around his body and spreading it over his crossed legs. Chintamoni then catches his eye again and gently tosses a pair of kartals towards him. Gopal nearly misses, but then his fingers trap the thick red string connecting the two ears of brass just before they hit the ground. He gathers the kartals and keeps them in his lap, no wish to interfere with this music.

In the ocean of the heart,
There is a strange factory,
In the Ocean of the Heart,
There is a curious factory,
A river flows in the body,
A flood bursts its banks,
Six pull the boat-rope,
But one holds the helm.

In the cold morning river breeze, Noni sits cross-legged, his back sometimes absolutely straight, as if there is a single wire running through him as well, a wire that someone is pulling upwards, and then, suddenly, he curves over the khamak and rotates his whole torso, body and instrument together producing vortexes of sound. Something inside Gopal starts to release, the big Everything unhooking itself from his navel, from the small of his back. There are no boats dotting the horizon today, but now he vividly remembers the big noukos of his childhood, their cascading sails bright against the tall, winter-blue sky.

A small circle of listeners has formed around the three of them. Old farmer mians, eyes closed, fingers running through beards, young mothers, one or two breastfeeding their babies under the pallu of their saris, children sitting in parents' laps, eyes locked on the magician with the thick, black beard who is producing such scary, other-worldly sounds. Beyond the circle, travellers are going about their business, some sorting their belongings, others playing cards, many others having gone back to sleep, the rows of bodies forming lines through the benches and ferry apparatus, head near feet, feet near head, like the mound-lines of earth that divide the fields.

In the Ocean of the heart
There is a strange contraption,
In the Ocean of the Heart – Ooorrrey, Khep-ppaaaaaaaaa!

Noni jerks his khamak away from his stomach and bends forward, going low over the ground, plectrum hand pointing up, his voice releasing a long taan that seems to leap off the boat and go bouncing across the water. Before it fully dies out, there is a call in reply. Not a human voice but a machine honk from something Gopal can't see. There is a second honk. Clearly from outside the ferry. The people standing on the far side of the deck start leaning over the side and pointing. 'Look! A launch!' 'Look, look, police on it!' 'Gora police also! All carrying rifles, look!'

The children jump up from their mothers' laps and go running to the other side. Noni and Chintamoni stop. Gopal's right side stiffens where the recoil from the automatic had twisted his shoulder and upper arm. The cold air suddenly develops teeth, and despite the alkhalla and the shawl, Gopal finds himself shivering slightly. There's a loud hailer exchange between the launch and the ferry, but he can't make out what they are saying except that it's in Bangla, not English. The ferry slows and then stops.

Noni Khepa takes the khamak off, reaches into his kurta pocket for a bidi and lights it carefully. Their audience has now completely scattered, and people are no longer paying them any attention. Noni looks at Gopal, his face expressionless. 'You're not wearing anything on your head.' Noni's black eyes stay on Gopal while Chintamoni starts rummaging inside one of her jholas. She pulls out a long strip of cloth, bright saffron, the same colour as Noni's pagdi, and hands it over.

'Come a bit closer, Kaliya. And keep your head still.' Bidi still in mouth, Noni takes the cloth and begins to tie it around Gopal's head.

The police launch seems to have come alongside, and there's a clanging of metal and wood. Moving his eyes to the right, Gopal sees that everybody has turned towards the other side of the deck. The hatch has been removed from the gangway opening, and through the crowd of people, he can see one of the stewards throwing down a rope ladder.

'Kaliya, what did you say your actual name was again?' Noni's voice is low, his tone casual.

'Razzak Mian. Ghiasuddin Razzak.'

'Razzak... hmm... listen, forget Razzak. Razzak is dead.' Noni finishes tying a topknot in Gopal's turban that presses the ball of cloth down into the centre of his skull. 'Now remember, your name is Robi Pagla. Robi. Pagla. Got it? It's the name of my dhol player who stayed behind in Birbhum. But the three of us went together to the Paush Mela, and I have a letter with his name also in it, inviting the three of us for another festival right afterwards, you hear what I'm saying? We are returning to Kushtia, but first we have an invitation to perform in Tangail. And you are Robi Pagla, understood?'

'Robi Pagla.' Gopal nods after repeating the name. He doesn't ask any other questions. Looking over, he sees the cops coming aboard one by one. Four havaldars with bamboo rods, local cockroaches, two mamas clearly from Calcutta, armed with rifles, one deshi police officer, dark, big built, revolver with lanyard in holster, and then one gora, not tall, not short, shola tupee, crisp khaki uniform, tunic and half pants, even in this cold, could be police, could be military, difficult to say, also revolver in holster, no rope attached to pistol, but fingers opening the holster flap as he climbs on to the deck. In total, eight of them. As soon as the English officer joins them, six of them troop down to the cabins below, leaving two havaldars at the ladder. Gopal can hear the boots clattering on the metal staircase. A reverse of the black tea climbs up his throat, reminding him he hasn't eaten for many hours now.

The stewards start moving through the passengers, calling out loudly. 'Everybody stay where you are! Police check! Police check! Police are checking the jahaj! Stay sitting where you are, don't anybody move about!' People go silent for a while. Then the hubbub starts again, but at a much lower volume. After a few minutes, Noni picks up his khamak again. He puts the strap around his neck and nods to his wife and Gopal. Then he smacks the plectrum across the strings.

In the ocean of the heart!
In this... ocean of the heart...

Gopal can't believe the crazy Baul is actually attracting attention to them. For a moment he wonders if the man is about to betray him for some imagined reward, but that thought flies away with a series of khamak beats. Looking down, Gopal finds his hands moving, chiming the hand cymbals more or less to the beat set up by the khamak and ektara and, because of the huge skill of the two, his kartals, the simplest of local instruments, sound practised and sure, at least to his own ears. Around them, people start turning around again to listen to the singing.

In the ocean of the eart,
There is a curious machine.

In one part of Gopal's hearing, the police have come back up the stairs and are now moving around among the deck passengers at the rear of the ferry. From the corner of his eye, he can see two stewards standing a few feet away, watching everyone nervously, both clutching their lungis at the crotch. Gopal can smell the water flowing around the stationary ferry, and the sandalwood paste that Noni has used this morning to mark his forehead. He can smell the sweat on his own body, unwashed for a day now, the odour carrying traces of the train and the night on the ferry, but mostly, to Gopal, carrying the loud smell of fear.

There is a garden in the body,
A flower opens in the garden,
The fragrance drives the body wild,
Oooorrrey pppaaagol! The fragrance drives the body wild...

One of the stewards can see around the central stair block to the front of the ship, and he begins to look agitated. He says something to the other steward and they both start gesturing violently at Noni and his group. Noni ignores them, churning up another flurry on his khamak. One of the men shouts, furious. 'Ei! Chup koro tomra! Bas chup koro!' Hey, shut it, you lot, just shut up! Noni does the opposite, going impossibly high with his voice, taking one word and stretching it – *saurav* – fragrance – while Chintamoni also raises her ektara and twangs the string harder in response, squeezing the bamboo strips to yaw the sound further. Gopal feels his own back straightening, his eyes focused on the slats of the deck three feet beyond his crossed legs, the kartals now playing his hands rather than the other way around, creating a shimmering sound that seems to have nothing to do with him.

There is a garden in the body,
A flower opens in the garden,
The fragrance drives the body wild,
But Lalon is not moved,
But Lalon, Lalon he's not moved.

By the time Noni finishes, the two officers are standing right over them. Gopal glances up but doesn't really see them, his eyes sliding down the slope of panic. He keeps his eyes on Noni who is bent forward, hands folded in a deep pronaam. After a long moment, Noni straightens and smiles welcomingly at the cops. 'Syer! Please forgive this poor Baul if I've done something to offend! We were just starting the morning by taking the name of the Almighty, that's all!'

One of the rifle mamas from Calcutta starts to translate for the two officers. The Indian officer, angry, seems to be listening, but the gora officer raises his hand. 'Thiik achhey. Aami bujhtey paarchhi! Tomar naam ki?' It's all right. I can understand. What's your name? Noni keeps smiling back, warm, gentle love overflowing from his face. His Bangla becomes formal and obsequious. 'Myself, sir, am your humble slave, people call me Noni Khepa and, when the Almighty allows, I live in Kushtia. This is my sadhavi, Chintamoni Dasi, and this is my accompanist, Robi Pagla.'

'Robi... Pagla? What do you do, Robi Pagla?' The Englishman's accent is hard to follow, but not so bad that Gopal can pretend not to understand. He looks at Noni, who is smiling, laughter about to burst out of him.

'What do you do, Robi? Tell the shaheb! Go on!'

The boots are in good shape, not new, but polished, the thick leather clearly supple. The woollen khaki socks are of top quality, and they stretch all the way up, spreading over solid calves to just under the Englishman's knees. The knees are encased in muscle, indicating strong legs, legs that quickly disappear into crisply ironed shorts that stick out like the upside down noses of sea ships.

Suddenly the Ingrej officer's face is right there, looking at Gopal. His skin is pale under his tupee, and there is an insect rash of some sort on his lower cheek, just to the right of his yellowish-brown moustache. Despite being blue, his eyes are kind and intelligent, and Gopal doesn't like that at all. This man seems to be able to laugh at himself, and this puts Gopal into extreme unease, because in his experience these are the people who are the hardest to fool, the ones who don't let their own status or uniform get in the way of remembering they could be missing something. What would Ustad do here? What would he want him to do? And what is She saying, his Ma Kali? He waits to feel Her hands on his shoulders, but he's not sure... and then She's there, just behind him, invisible, but he can feel the front of her legs straightening his spine. Be afraid of nothing. Gopal forces himself to meet the man's eyes, briefly, shyly, but not too shyly. Gopal folds his hands, does a nomoshkar and smiles back weakly. 'Shaheb, I just follow my Khepa. I go where he goes. We make joy with the music and then sometimes we get to eat two or three bits of food. Gaur, Premananda, Hori Bol!'

'Du-tiin-te ruti, tai?' Two or three bits of roti, is it?

'Aggey, hyan, shaheb.' If you will, sir, yes. Gopal takes his eyes back to the man's briefly, before looking away at Noni.

'Mathews? What about this one? He looks about the right size and shape, if a bit young.' The gora turns to the Indian officer, speaking in English.

Gopal thinks of the river just beyond the curve of steel wall to his left. No. The current would take him under in seconds, and if it doesn't, the police boat would catch him. Ma? Where are you, Ma? Maybe he can escape while they are taking him back to Calcutta, maybe even when the police launch—

'No, sir, I wouldn't say so... too thin. Our man is a strong fellow. Short but bulky, it says.'

Gopal looks up again to find the Englishman smiling at him like a long-lost friend. 'I don't know, I don't know...' The officer rakes three fingers across his right cheek. From the corner of his vision, Gopal can see the other mamas suddenly start looking in different directions into the crowd, searching for something.

'Mathews?' The gora's voice is conversational. 'Take this singer of ours to the side over there, will you?'

'Yes, sir.' Mathews also seems to be chatting.

'Take the cheeky bugger to the side and shoot him. One shot to the head, then throw him into the river.'

'Yes, sir.'

As if he's still keeping to some silent beat, Gopal's eyes are down, locked on his kartals, the conversation opaque, nothing to do with him. Ustad's voice growling in his ear – *If you hear Ingreji, remember you don't understand a word!*

He has no idea what Chintamoni will do after they shoot her man. He can only hope she won't give him away. If Noni Khepa senses any danger, he shows no sign of it. He has taken out a brown clay chillum which he is cleaning with a small sharp scoop of metal, releasing a clear smell of stale ganja. Gopal tries to interest himself in the chillum, while walking the tightrope of not looking up and not looking too far away either. The scratch of Noni's metal tool is answered by the scrape of the gora's boots as they turn his legs around.

'Right. Let's not waste more time here. We still have the Bihar ferry to catch.'

The boots walk away, pause, turn around again. Gopal feels a hand on his shoulder, exactly where the Colt's recoil had wrenched his muscle. He looks up. The blue eyes are very close to his. There's a small insect crawling on the front edge of the tupee, but he's too close to see what it is. He can smell tea on the gora's breath.

'Robi Pagla, you need some food and some medicine.' The gora's Bangla is just about understandable. 'Tell your guru to take better care of you, all right?' The eyes shift to Noni, who nods sheepishly. Then the hand lifts and is gone.

The gangway hatch clangs shut, the bolt is driven home. The police launch hoots as it goes, the sound diminishing with distance. Slowly, the ferry engines come to life and Gopal can feel the vessel engaging again with the river. As they start moving, he closes his eyes and puts his head in his hands. He feels Chintamoni's hands stroking his back in firm, long strokes, her fingers pausing every now and then to massage his neck and shoulders.

'If you ever meet Robi, you should thank him.' Noni's voice has bits of laugher in it. 'Because Robi's Ma-Baba took him to Shantiniketan when he was a baby and he was blessed by Robi Thakur himself. That was lucky, to have such a close darshan of the great Rabindranath himself, and those blessings have clearly transferred to you!'

'But, Khepa, how did you...?'

'First of all, you don't look like any taanti I have met. Just look at your hands, there are no marks! Have you ever seen a weaver's hands? You're no weaver, and I would bet you're not even a Mussalman, that back of yours has never done namaz, forget about five times a day! Just the way you walk, the way you hold your body, it's entirely from the city. You're a shirt-pant wearer. I'm surprised the mamas didn't spot that, but then, they're not very bright and you were sitting all the time anyway.'

Gopal looks up like a child caught doing mischief. Looking at his expression, Khepa and Chintamoni start laughing quietly. After a while, Chintamoni gets up and goes off. Noni then leans forward.

'Also, you goatfucker, when talking in your sleep, you mentioned not just bullets but also something about a gun, bullets and a gun?'

Gopal opens his mouth, but no words come out.

'It's all right. Nobody else heard you, just me. And, listen, I don't care what you've done. When Chintamoni and I meet someone, we don't look at the outside, we try and look at the inside of a person. Sometimes one can make a mistake, but if your heart is clean, you don't get it wrong that often, you understand? So once, I, Noni Khepa have taken to you, I've taken to you, that's all! And it doesn't matter if our time together is for years, across several lifetimes, or for a few hours on a boat, you understand? I don't want to know what you've done, what your real name is, or where you are going, nothing! Ultimately, we are all going to the same place, Joy Guru, Hori Bol!'

Gopal's head drops for a moment, and then he looks up and nods in acknowledgement. He struggles to his feet, his knees protesting, and he goes over to the other side to make sure the police boat is actually gone. As he leans over the railing, he can see the launch is now a small dot way down the river. After a while, he turns around and stops, his heart thudding again.

The prow of the ferry is nosing towards a wall of mist, like he imagines an airplane might fly into clouds in mid-air. The soft silver wall stretches away unevenly, extending in a line across the flat river as far as the eye can see on both sides of the deck. It's as if god has removed everything from the world except the soft sunlight falling on the water, the cliff of mist and the boat.

Soon, they are inside it, surrounded by the scud of white and dark grey. At its thickest point, Gopal, sitting next to Noni and Chintamoni, can't actually see the people at the far end of the deck. Noni Khepa goes into a squat, takes out a chillum and loads it. The pipe to his lips, he bends his head towards his wife. Chintamoni strikes a match, and Noni takes a big pull, leaping slightly off the balls of his feet, sending up a plume of smoke. 'Diiiih!' he calls out. 'Joy guru, joy guru, joy guru!' The air becomes pungent with the musk of the ganja. After Chintamoni has taken a toke, Noni holds the chillum in the fingers of both hands and passes it to Gopal. 'Here, Robi Pagla! Serve yourself a little bit!' Gopal puts his mouth to the opening and sucks hard. The smoke curls straight down into his chest, ripping it apart with a series of coughs. As he gasps for air, trying with the back of his hands to keep his eyes in their sockets, Noni Khepa and Chintamoni throw back their heads and howl with laughter. The smoke from the chillum starts to play with the rolls of mist dancing just above their heads.

EPILOGUE

PARIS, 1979

There is a garden in the body,
A flower opens in the garden,
The fragrance drives the body wild,
But Lalon is not moved,
But Lalon, Lalon he's not—

I hate to cut in before a song is over, but I turn the lever to stop because the taxi is waiting and the train will not wait. I wait a beat, and then switch it to rewind. The ribbon of tape vibrates and blurs as the left spool takes back what belongs to it, ending in a thin, plastic whip of sound as the reel whimpers to a stop. I return the spool to the box and flip the lid shut. The label on it is in Elko's neat handwriting, in thin orange marker: *Noni Khepa / Night performance / Tarapith / Jan 1966 / Deben Bh.* And then in pencil underneath, in a smaller scrawl: *'Acc'ding DB probably NK's last performance before fatal car crash...'*

I love this particular recording, and I wonder whether to take the tape with me. I decide against it. I will be back sooner or later, and I will need some of this music to be here. I take a last look around at the house, making sure all the windows and doors are shut, not that there's anything valuable to steal, except maybe the Marantz reel-to-reel. I've gutted the place of Elko's stuff, meaning of all his work, though I haven't touched the books or posters or any of the kitchen things.

Just yesterday, the movers have taken the last canvas and packed it, right after I've shot some slides of it on my Minolta, but it's as if the thing is still lowering at me from the easel on which it stood for so many years. God knows what it will look like in a gallery, what meaning it will take on or not, how it will behave with other paintings, Elko's or other people's, but for now I've put it down in my notebook as the last of his works to leave the house in Provence. The paintings are all gone, but his stuff is still there, the paints, the brushes, the long-dead knobs of unused colour on the makeshift palettes he had balanced on different tables and stools. I've photographed the studio, both wide and in detail, but perhaps I'm getting ahead of myself – there may be no interest in the paraphernalia of a minor painter.

We'll see. But for now, I'm done with the house.

Done with it at least until spring, if not later. Missus says she doesn't know if she'll ever come back to this place, but who knows? The report from her doctors in London is positive: amazingly, there is no obvious sign of cirrhosis or any alcohol-related disease. She is a little older than Nirupama, pushing sixty-four now, but hopefully there's still some life-juice left in her batteries.

Gaston is waiting for me in his taxi, which is actually a van. I take one last look around and switch off everything before I lock the door. As we bump our way down, I look back at the property in the late January light. I tap Gaston on the shoulder and ask him to stop. I walk back up the track to the gate. I've just noticed that the little wooden sign Elko and Missus had put up is hanging vertically against the stone wall, one screw gone from the two that were holding it up. I tug at the sign and pull it off. If I do inherit the place – as Missus keeps threatening – this is not what I would want to call it. I find a place for it in one of my suitcases.

The train back from Avignon to Paris is uneventful. I don't have too much luggage this time, thank god, and taking the metro back from Gare de Lyon is easy enough. As D&D would put it, I ate Paris and I ate Calcutta. Currently, I ate Provence too. At the moment, I ate Paris the least, and that's good because that's where I have to be.

I come into the apartment and find space for the wooden sign on the big mantelpiece of the dead fireplace where, I have to say, it goes quite well with all the other stuff that's there; all the other objects on what I think of as my altar. Just as I don't want that house name next to the gate in Provence, I avoid putting the sign anywhere near the centre of the mantlepiece, but it looks just fine on the left, at the very end of the array.

I look around the apartment and, yet again, realize to what extent these characters have taken me over. The timeline stretches on the windows, the tape coming off at points, making the acetate sag. There are two spiderwebs, a small one at the very start of the timeline where it says *RT Dies* and then a larger one crossing over *January 1943* and the first place where I've written in Bangla: *mannantar – aakaal*. The spiders have found no purchase on the acetate itself, but somehow they've managed to make complex bridges of web over and across the material from glass to glass, putting those particular dates and words in silver cages, as if they too know the history and the importance of those two dates.

On the big dining table that I never use for eating are spread my notes and stacks of photographs. Here too, some of the paper has already yellowed a bit. Typically, it's the paper that I've picked up in India that has aged while the local stuff looks untouched by time. Sticking out of a file is something I'd typed on a trip back to Calcutta in 1972, just after the Bangladesh War. The paper I was using was exceptionally cheap newsprint from a stack of pads that a friend had stolen from his job at *The Statesman*. The paper is a dirty brown and, for some reason, the ink ribbon was a red-blue one on the little Olivetti portable that I had then. The first part of the typing is in blue and the second bit in red.

Calcutta, 1944 – ~~Kyd Street~~/New Market

So, yes, let's do this to jazz: the percussion sound of bone-crack, not full crack, just the light crunch of skeleton upon skeleton, the long trombone of the 9 o'clock siren, the long whimper of the truck engine dying down, good old Bedford 4-stroke bass, the bone-beat still going, the scat of morning dogs about to be left hungry, their food being trucked away like a tune being pulled on them, but, but, but, just before the half-number ends the horn yowl of 'maaaaago, O! maaaaago', some poor dame's voice shiny as if through brass rubbed paper-thin, but still full, all the timbre of life, not clear if she's going high for some husbandman's face she's seen on a body drumming into the morning transport, or if it's just her own face she sees there tomorrow, or her third or fifth's baby's, or her old mama she's just seen going down.

In grand and meaningless memory, hey man, let's put the sharpest cook-knife into the carcass of jazz, between the luscious dead meat and the marrow-rich bone, between the smooth score and the maverick high-hat, between the slothful, slumberous, deep sax – bar-y-tone sax, since you akse – and the hopped-up guitar strangling its own strings, between the LieutCol's white-ass double-

bass, who does the motherfucking-motherfucker fucking think he is, Motzart? and the mewling of the rear-gunner's clarinet, hope for his crew's sake he shoot sharper than he blow, hope for all of them a quick and early death, a clean wipe-out, unlike the bone-bags being shuffled here in front of my sad and sorry eyes, a clean go a mile above the whitest mountains on earth, maybe as many as five seconds, ten, maximum fifteen, of knowing that this is your end, your big hello to Hell-heaven, and then you'se goooooone, either the record-finish scratch of nothing-type eternity or, or, or, or floating in that ocean of air like one of these statues these people love to float into the river after their carnival, floating and knowing you managed to take a few slant-eyes with you, who knows whether foe or friend, Jap or Chink, but knowing for sure the flak can't touch you no more, knowing the shell-puffs is now like some sort of celebrationary send-off to you, your life, who you used to be.

But not like this, not like this, not like this card-pack shuffle of bodies, filthy with the ghost of a shit they managed to pass before their passing, their stomachs still craving, empty as a beer-barrel on Monday morning. Even after death, their eyes looking for food, their mouths looking for a taste they was unlucky enough to have when they was kids. Sound of an ungrown kid, all of this rattling, sound of a mass kid that never grew up, sound of something that learnt to dream too damn early for its own good, like a bunch of mosquitoes trying to write poetry, like a band of cockroach trying to follow a tune-sheet.

It's like someone drop a big slow bomb on these fuckers, a bomb bigger than god, that spreads and spreads and spreads, something like the Universe, big four, eight, twelve-engine silver bird dropping a big piece of resonance, and you know what? It's gonna come down the old Mississippi one day, just like it come down this here delta wearin the face of hell. But what hell, where in hell is hell except right here, right in front of my burning eyes, and maybe I shouldn't feel so bad for them, at least not for them that's dead because they done got away, the whole daily stack of them. Hell maybe gets carried away to the river every morning, in three camouflage-green trucks, the backs filled to the top, and baby there's nothing you did-could give me, nothing you can take away, that plays any tune with this. So, let's do this to sound, let's do this to jazz, let's just do it.

Something stands firm behind Byron's head, doesn't swim and slide like everything else around him, and he realizes it's the wall he's been leaning on. As he stares, trying hard to stop his eyes from prancing, the men pull down the tarpaulins, curtaining the packed corpses. One by one, the Bedfords growl to life, their exhaust pipes blasting out in sequence, first one, then the other, then two together, then all three going at once in smoky agreement. The scraping of the horn rim against the wall comes to Byron much after he finds himself tottering in the middle of the lane, much after he has pushed himself away from the support and walked right into the exhaust fumes. As the first weary lorry creaks away from the narrow pavement, he looks down and sees: without any permission from him, his feet have spread themselves into playing position. That's right, he thinks, let's do this.

As the trucks nudge themselves into line and head towards New Market, Byron brings up his cornet and presses the mouthpiece to his lips, not too hard, just so. He breathes in everything, the smoke, the morning air on Kyd Street, the whole dirty blue sky above him. Then he narrows it down to his instrument and lets go of it all.

I've had no choice but to imagine him, imagine him the best I could, and now I realize I have no need to imagine any more of him. Byron Jones is finally a ghost that the missile of time has shot off my radar; I have other ghosts, the ones I actually knew when they were alive, who've taken over my airspace. The ones I knew when they were alive and the ones who are still alive; the elusive ones like Gopal/Ganesh/Big Man/Chaar-Paanch Ustad, the I-hate-to-talk ones like Nirupama, the drunken ones like Missus.

Looking back at all the material, I now realize there was no way there was a novel in this, or no way that I, at least, could have forged a proper narrative, but it was useful to try, I guess, because it helped to illuminate things. Trying to arrange the stories into a unified narrative helped clarify the fact that history, or life, can't always fit into a suit of plot. Once I finished putting most of the stories together, the completed jigsaw looked more like an Escher print with Bosch and Kalighat elements than a straightforward fictional text that could be bound within the covers of a book.

There's other stuff, photographs, the tapes I recorded with Elko and Missus, though I was always careful to label them with their proper names or initials, always Kedar Lahiri or KL and Imogen Snell or IVS for Imogen Valerie Snell, and then the date of the conversation.

Tacked up a little bit away from the photos of Imo and Niru at Flurys and Niru and Keya with the rifles, there is a picture of Kedar with Eva at some afternoon party, probably at the Royal Golf Club taken by Imogen. A young couple, both beautiful, looking at each other, laughing, possibly in love; both in Western dress, the man just a bit darker in complexion, but the hair equally rich and black on both heads. Then there is a blurred photo – another Jodhpur Park find – of a peasant family carrying all their belongings crossing the tramlines, on the reverse a note in Imogen's hand which says *Near Hazra Road, 24/11/41 – snapped on the day we met! Ixx*. There are other bits of paper, some throwaway sketches by Elko and his notes, which I will never make public – *Husain is a hustler! Souza is a Peon!* – Husain would probably ignore this, but Souza might take fresh offence and Elko doesn't need rewarmed enmity, even posthumously.

Besides the small photos on the acetate timeline, there is also another wall where I've pinned or taped larger photos of Elko's work, mostly black-and-white but some colour prints too, made from slides. Of the three or four paintings he was working on when he died, the *Victoria Iceberg* works fine in black-and-white, but the other really large one, the last painting the transporters packed from the house, definitely needs a colour print.

In the painting, the river is flat, seen straight from above at the centre of the canvas, the grey-green liquid rug roiling gently under smudges of mist. The Goalundo ferry seems to be going down a slope of water, its funnels tugging smoke, heading to the north of the frame and a bank of opaque silver fog that forms the top border of the image. The much smaller police launch chugs away down a mirroring slope, heading south and, it seems, almost under the planet of the canvas. In the flat, central bit, you have the faint whitish wake of the ferry going straight up, with a sharper scar curving away from the straight line, going down and slightly to the left until it meets up with the launch, together the two marks looking like the tantric markings you find in Bankura and Birbhum.

I must make colour prints from the transparencies and send them to Ganesh, along with the prints I promised him of the photos I took of the hotel when he arranged for me to visit the dilapidated old monster.

It's late afternoon and I debate between having an early aperitif or a late coffee. I choose the coffee and put the kettle on to boil. Unlike the orderly displays at Alexandra Mansions, my museum spreads its tentacles all over the apartment, objects ambushing me from strange places. For instance, the Kepi from Saint Ant hangs next to the pots and pans over the kitchen counter, and when I go to the turntable, I see the flat, thin tin box next to the records, the Caran D'Ache colour pencils that I've brought back from my last visit, the pencils still untouched, the shine of the box somewhat dulled after twenty years. I pick out Miles from the stack of albums; *Kind of Blue,* because I'm in a mood for a classic. Just as the second track starts, the peal of the phone interrupts the sax solo. Who can it be now? I push back the lever to lift the arm off the record.

'*Oui? Ici Madjumdar.*'

The first operator is French, the second one seems to be in Delhi, and the third one, finally, has a proper Bengali accent to her English. 'Mr Mojumdar? Please hold! Trunk call from Cyalkata!'

'Hello, Ma? What's happened?'

'Saki, can you hear me? This is Ma speaking.'

I can hear her voice, and it sounds strong. I've last seen her about a month ago in Calcutta and she was fine. We speak on the phone about once every two months, me usually pre-arranging a call on her neighbour's phone via aerogramme. For her to call me, she would have had to ask for a major favour from the neighbour or some friend.

'I can hear you clearly, Ma, what's happened?'

'No, I just thought I'd let you know.'

'Yes? Let me know what?' Nirupama is usually direct and clear on the phone, so when she answers at an angle, my anxiety begins to shoot up. 'Ma! Will you kindly tell me what's happened!'

'No, you see, we are hearing these people have just killed a lot of folks... and just dumped them into the delta waters.'

'Who has killed who, Ma? There's nothing in the news here!'

'Killed women and children also, my sources are telling me. If it's true, it's a massacre, in English you could definitely call it massacre. But we don't know if it's true. So I'm going there. Some of us are going there tomorrow to investigate, so I thought I'd let you know.'

The operator's voice cuts in sharply. 'Three minutes is ovar! Do you want to continue?'

'Please continue!' I snap.

'*You* cannot continue. Only calling party can continue. Madam, three minutes over, do you want to continue?'

'Yes, please continue.'

'Okay. Three more minutes only. I have to connect another call after that.'

The operator crackle recedes.

'Ma. I'm not understanding. Who has killed women and children?'

'The CPI-M, who else? They are trying to evict people from an island in Sunderban. They may have killed some people. Dozens of refugees in Marichjhapi. Police, apparently helped by local gangsters, people are alleging these were direct orders from the chief minister. Reports say the women were raped before being killed. So I'm going to find out what really happened.'

'How many of you are going, Ma? Who all?'

'I don't know yet, but Mango-mashi for sure, and three or four other women. But it may be... not safe, so I'm telling you, just in case.'

'Thiik achhey, all right, I've understood. Be careful. And try not to rush into situations on your own. I'll wait to hear from you, so once you are back call me from Mango-mashi's or whoever's phone. I'll call you back after three minutes.'

'I'll try. Or I may just send an international telegram. I hope you're well?'

'I'm well, Ma. Everything is fine here, don't worry. The weather's turning nice. Work is going well.' It's the nature of these international calls and what they do to you – my mother was talking about heading to investigate possible killings by the government and I was babbling about the weather.

'Okay, babu. Lal salaam, inquilab zindabad.' Red salute, long live the revolution. She almost never says that to me.

'Inquilab zindabad, Ma.'

She puts the phone down and the rough static of absence snakes all the way from Calcutta into my ear.

I stop the turntable and garage the needle arm. Suddenly, I want silence. But after a while, as I pour more coffee, I find myself humming something not quite out of tune. I can't place it at first. I sift through a few rock 'n' roll and jazz suspects before I realize that old man Rabindranath has bushwhacked me yet again – the tune I'm humming is Nirupama's war song:

If no one heeds your call,
Walk alone, walk alone, then walk alone, my friend.
Tawbey ekla cholo, ekla cholo, ekla cholo, ekla cholo rey…

I remember in school, in class 7, I'd tried to play it on the trumpet and D'Mello, our Western music teacher, had smacked my ears. 'That instrument is not for local music!' he'd snarled. I hope that old bastard is still alive and someone is forcing him to listen to Don Cherry blowing Raag Malkauns and McLaughlin playing quasi-Carnatic on his guitar. He was a fool, D'Mello, but he'd inadvertently put his finger on a problem that's alive and well.

Elko's paintings also fall between the stools. They don't obey the rules set for modern paintings by Indians, nor do they fit into any properly understood vernacular of Western art. As he always complained, not without some satisfaction, 'Both sides hate my work because neither understands it. The goras scratch the left side of their heads and the deshis scratch the right side. Between them, my work turns into dandruff!'

Well, thanks to Eva Margenik, née Attali, the mass of the precious dandruff is now safely stored in an art warehouse near Aubervilliers, paid for by the Attali-Margenik Foundation of Oakland, CA. We will now look for a first posthumous retrospective somewhere in France and then in Calcutta, and also money for the catalogue. All this I will do later, right now I'm exhausted with the long exhumation of the work and I need to take a break. Right now, I need to do something else, to get back to my real work and the book about Chandigarh and Ahmedabad and Corbu and Kahn.

I remember Kahn's observation about ruined buildings actually being the most complete. Mixing metaphors, I wonder if a period of time can be seen as a building, and the remnants of that history examined as you would a ruin. My eye falls on the sign that I've just rescued from the house in Provence. The board is in weather-damaged white, and the scarred letters were once in deep blue, painted not by Elko but by one of the local sign painters. Given the curve of the brush, at first you automatically read for French, but then you realize this is in English and it says:

Great Eastern Hotel.

This was Elko and Missus's little joke, their little nod not just to the hotel but also to Calcutta, the much greater Great Eastern Hotel. As I look at the sign, it occurs to me that this Great Eastern Hotel is not a ruin, not dead, it's alive and constantly moving across the planet, sliding from Bengal to Biafra to Cambodia and then back to Bengal, and then going god knows where else.

To the right of the sign, not exactly in the middle of the array on the mantelpiece, is the cornet Ma bought me when I was seven or so. I still remember the smells of aircraft fuel and brass polish mingling in that hangar at Dum-Dum. I still remember the feel of the foreign paper when I touched the cover of a *Life* magazine some Markin had left on a chair and the sting of Ma's hand as she slapped mine, telling me not to touch what didn't belong to me. There are times when I've wondered if these stories were mine at all to tell, if I had any right to excavate them. There are times I've felt that sting of Ma's slap – *Don't touch what's not yours!* – times when I've come close to abandoning the whole mess, when I've been close to walking away from all the chipped tiling of memory. When I came back today, I found myself wondering again. After the phone call I realize that these stories haven't really ended. I have a lot, but I don't have enough. I realize that I'll need to get back to them.

All I need is a break.

ACKNOWLEDGEMENTS

The writing of these acknowledgements has been imagined and reimagined many times. To say that this book took far longer to write than anticipated is to insult the noble art of understatement by pushing it to absurdity; but it is, without undue elaboration, perhaps the best way to put it.

My deepest thanks, then:

To David Godwin, agent, friend, agent again, and, across this very testing haul, the one with the almost magical ability to conjure up stamina and optimism. A writer can have no one better to fight in their corner – as they say (or should be saying), 'Speak softly and carry a David Godwin.'

Philip Gwyn Jones, for the initial commissioning of the book, for his ebullient and unwavering faith, for his constant encouragement along the way.

Karthika V.K., for the longest, most granular and generous support a writer could have hoped for, editorial, emotional and pecuniary. To bring in our shared passion for cricket, for being the one who got us through the challenging middle overs and brought the book within striking distance of the target.

Nick Pearson – what are writers for but to shuffle metaphors – for standing by the large alien ship once it arrived, and for helping it dock.

Finally, Rahul Soni, for being calm and undaunted in taking on the manuscript, for his perspicacious reading and editing, for the soft-spoken yet acutely sharp-eyed support that saw this text finally checking out of the hotel of writerly chaos and indecision, ready to travel into the world.

Gratitude beyond measure to Heather Godwin, and to the team at DGA.

Thanks also to the teams at 4th Estate/HarperCollins in Delhi and in London.

Several institutions offered residencies at critical junctures of the writing. My gratitude to the Charles Wallace India Trust, Pro Helvetia New Delhi and Christoph Merian Stiftung, Basel. The time spent respectively in Canterbury and in Basel has stayed with me well beyond the confines of writing this book.

Of the several small armies of people that helped with the research and the writing, my first salaams go to the Calcutta division:

Ananda Lal, oldest friend, for his acerbic yet patient generosity in helping me grapple with the phenomenon of Rabindranath Tagore.

Ian Zachariah, for sharing his knowledge of Calcutta history, and for introducing me to the late Sam Sadka and Lance D'Cruz, both of whom gifted me invaluable stories and insight about Calcutta in the 1940s.

The late jazz musician Anto Menezes, for taking me into the fascinating world of Calcutta jazz, post-war horse racing and piano rentals.

Dr Ranjan Ray Chaudhuri and Suchismita Dasgupta for sharing expertise from their respective fields, medicine and Bengali clothes, and for rock-like friendship.

Pritha Sen, master chef and savante food historian, for being the most knowledgeable and generous source of all things to do with Bangla food and food history.

V. Ramaswamy – Ramas to me – long-suffering companion in un-Bangali-ness, in the twisting joys of engaging with literature, with our mothership Kolkata-Calcutta, and Bengal; comradc in fatherhood, in darkest despair and in raucous laughter.

Kavita Panjabi, cactus-sibling, closest of friends, great engine of stern encouragement, and the most open-hearted scholar in explaining to me her brilliant work on the women's movement in mid-century Bengal and the Tebhaga Andolan.

Nilanjan Bhattacharya, partner in crime, staunchly alongside from the beginning of this project, opening windows into Calcutta, Bengal and Bangla culture, helping me find the stories and the ways required for telling them.

Surajit Sen, for constantly bringing me all sorts of material that helped us to happily delve into Calcutta's past.

Shreevatsa Nevatia, word-warrior, fellow prose-mendicant, ace editor, for being the one-man cavalry brigade that comes in at the end to help save the day and, indeed, to propel it into a possibility of tomorrows. For the sympathetic yet forensic readings, for the many discussions, for the whisky, the whimsy and the sharp analyses.

Malini Panjabi, for being there, as ever, to give me masterful help with all things graphic.

Inexpressible thanks to the late Hari Vasudevan, for imparting invaluable lessons from his great scholarship in history, for his large-hearted, laugh-ridden friendship. You left our gulag too soon, my friend.

In Delhi, where a large part of this book was written, my gratitude goes to:

Historians Neeladri Bhattacharya and Indivar Kamtekar, Neel for the comprehensive bibliographies and Indivar for sharing insights and his brilliant essay 'The Shiver of 1942'.

Rana Behl, for putting me in touch with the late Professor Sabya Sachi Bhattacharya and Mala Bhattacharya who gave me so much of their time to recount stories about early and mid-twentieth-century Bengal.

Amita Baviskar, for her ferociously acute readings as the manuscript grew, for her insights and critiques which changed the story so much for the better.

Sheba Chhachhi, for the all the love and constant support, spiritual and material.

Anand Vivek Taneja, for his readings, comments and encouragement.

Nirmalya Dey, for his wonderfully detailed expositions about dhrupad and khayal.

Arundhati Das and Mukul Kesavan, for being the cornerstones they are in my life, for their huge love and patience.

Kai Friese, for sharing his amazing research into the whole business of 'flying the Hump', for being a one-man logistics, ordinance and intelligence corps, for the precise warfare-nerdery and the constant supply of loving, ego-deflating humour. There are no mud vials on this mission.

Nilanjana Roy, Empress of Erudition, fellow prose-merchant, dispenser of rare and delicious literary gossip; for being one of the very few who cycled alongside for the entire route of the unplanned marathon, handing me sustaining drinks of faith and encouragement.

Pradip Saha, for the friendship, the terraces, the music, the landing paths, and for ensuring I didn't get too sentimental about things Bengali.

Chandrika Grover, for her briskly loving friendship, for the timely kicks in the right places, for providing succour in the most amazing ways.

And Ashish Mahajan, for being the constant pin that stops the grenade of my life from exploding.

In terrible missing of Annie Mathews, loving friend, chief barkeep at the Snorting Guffaw Saloon, without whom the celebrations around this completion will not be the same. Unlike what you believed in, I do hope there is an After in which you have no choice but to read this book.

In London, where more than half my life was lived while writing this novel, my eternally inadequate thanks to:

Salil Tripathi, jigri dost, fellow writer and columnist, the dhokla to my ganthia, for his unquestioning love and support during the darkest days, for letting me take over his house and such a large sector of his life.

Ameya Tripathi, for taking the time to provide me with such a startlingly detailed and incisive reading at a critical juncture.

Bruce Calderwood and Vivienne Bennet, for their life-reviving camaraderie, hospitality, rigorous readings and feedback. Perhaps we can finally move on the flavoured-vodka start-up?

Amanda Austen, for being a friend beyond all normal definitions of friendship, for the huge generosity and constant humour. For holding me together in the darkest moments.

Anita Roy, mate, critic, writer, Earth Mama, language-doctor, spirit-goalie, for inspiring me with her writing and life force.

Kamila Shamsie, comrade, fellow explorer of the story-forest, for quietly setting an example of what a passionately dedicated writer's life looks like, for her patient, good-humoured encouragement over the years.

Pete Chalk and Nyarai Moyo-Chalk, Karen Martinez and Andy Lambert, Rashmi Varma and Subir Sinha, for their heroic friendship.

The Vajifdar-Coopers, Monique and David, for their affection and advice.

Sinead MacInnes, for being her amazing self in such close vicinity; for giving so much to the ones I love most.

In grieving memory of Cassandra Ballchin, for her reading, advice and encouragement at the early stages of the writing and for so much more.

Across the writing of the novel, Berlin, particularly Harun Farocki and Antje Ehmann's home in Lichtenberg, was a sanctuary, not least for working on this book. We lost Harun ten years ago – but with Antje's unwavering generosity, the novel grew and was finally completed in Harun's study, perhaps with his rigorous and mischievous spirit watching with a raised eyebrow. Through some of the toughest moments of my life, Antje provided me with a sheltering and nourishing second home.

There are no words either in English or German that can express my gratitude here to the much-missed Harun, to the ever-present Antje, or indeed to the high-voltage love, energy and intelligence of Elfe Brandenburger, writer, reader, thinker, film-maker, soul-massage specialist, for her close reading and comments on the final version of the book.

Beyond location:

Laurence Hugues, fellow writer, fellow cine-freak, for her continuing love, support and advice on all things French, and on all things Life. And also for the priceless gifts of Paris and Noirétable.

Lynn Innes, for her reading and encouragement.

Sanjiv Shah, Sanjay Baba Kapoor, Paromita Vohra, Srirupa Roy, Tenzing Sonam, Indrajit Hazra, Sonia Jabbar, Sayantoni Palchaudhuri, Debjani Sengupta, Supriya Guha, K. Jayaram, Tridip Suhrud, Mukund Padmanabhan, for their friendship, readings, advice, hand-holding, wisecracks and wisdom.

Varun Andhare, for all the unstinting and attentive input as the clock ticked down.

Tony Cokes, for being there with his love and calm inspiration across my life.

The most special thanks to Sumanta Banerjee, great historian, friend, sage and occasional drinking partner, for everything, but especially the gift of helping me understand our recent turbulent past.

+

Itu Chaudhuri, for once again changing the definition of cover designer, for the deep engagement with the writer, the text and its visual needs.

+

Beyond the category of any simple thanking and gratitude: Gita Sahgal, co-parent through all sorrows and joys, and indefatigable supporter of my work. Thanks also to Nayantara Sahgal for her warmth, wisdom and enormous fortitude. Losing our beloved younger son and grandson remains outside what is imaginable or acceptable; hopefully, the completing of this book will help us all to keep going.

+

This book could not have been written but for the constant contribution of ideas, criticism and energy – from the first draft of the first section to the very last full stop – by Meenakshi Ganguly, best friend, reluctant kid sister, quasi-parent, who managed to keep me on track without losing her temper too often.

+

The greatest thanks of all to Latika Gupta, for taking on the challenge of seeing this book to completion no matter what obstacles life, or I myself, put in the way. There is no way to succinctly describe the enormous emotional commitment and mental effort she put into this task over many years, at close quarters and at long distance, a commitment that goes way beyond what one could reasonably expect from any close friend, partner, editor or supportive critic.

+

Finally, my thanks to Kabir Joshi, for his incredible love, patience and faith in my ability to complete this work, and for ensuring everything continues to hold meaning. I promise to do things differently next time.